DARK INSIDE

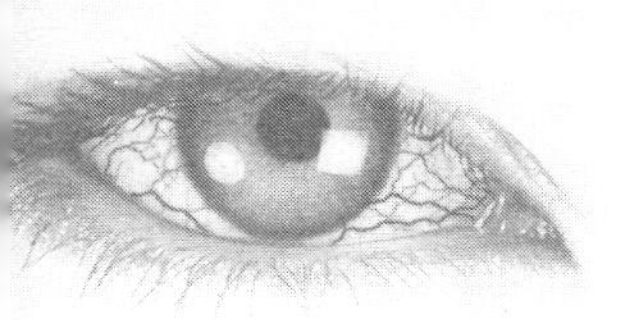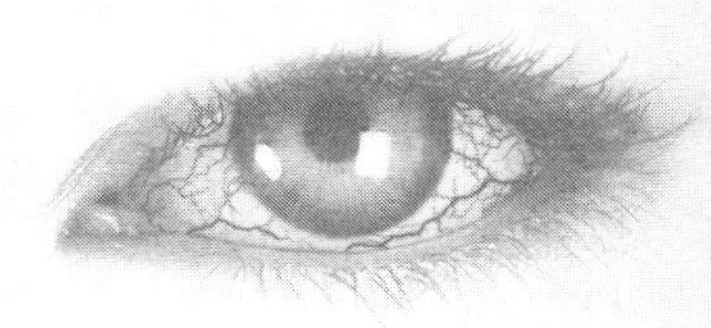

JEYN ROBERTS

DARK INSIDE

SCHOLASTIC INC.

To my parents, Don and Peggy Roberts.
Your love and support know no bounds.

This book is a work of fiction. Any references to historical events, real people, or real locales are used fictitiously. Other names, characters, places, and incidents are products of the author's imagination, and any resemblance to actual events or locales or persons, living or dead, is entirely coincidental.

ISBN 978-0-545-49902-6

12 11 10 9 8 7 6 5 4 3 2 1 12 13 14 15 16 17/0

Printed in the U.S.A. 40

First Scholastic printing, September 2012

Book design by Krista Vossen
The text for this book is set in Bembo Std.

ACKNOWLEDGMENTS

Thanks to:

Alison Acheson for all her support and teaching skills. And to all the wonderful people in my writing for children class at the University of British Columbia.

Mimi Thebo at Bath Spa University for being my mentor and guide.

Kaliya Muntean and Fiona Lee, who are wonderful muses and great friends.

Matthew and Shauna Hooten for being such good support.

Ruth Alltimes at Macmillan for being an outstanding editor and having such patience.

David Gale and Navah Wolfe at Simon & Schuster for more fantastic editing skills.

And I'd like to thank my agents, Julia Churchill and Sarah Davies. Without them, none of this would have been possible.

NOTHING

I'm standing at the edge of existence. Behind me, a thousand monsters descend. Their disguises change with each stride.

When they look in a mirror do they see their true selves?

Arms open wide. In front of me is nothing. No one ever knew how existence would end. Sure, they made assumptions: fire, flood, plague, etc. They studied the skies for locusts and watched for rain. They built their cities, destroyed the forests, and poisoned the water. Warning signs left behind in the ruins of ancient civilizations have been misinterpreted. The sins of mankind are always to blame. But who would have guessed it would be so gray? So empty.

Is there really a way back?

Hello? Is there anyone there?

Sorry, wrong number.

There are too many thoughts to cover in such little time. I knew they would find me. I'm glowing in the moonlight. My darkness was too bright to hide forever. They find all of us eventually. They play the odds, and they're up a thousand to one.

In front of me is nothing. No bright lights, no darkness. No energy. Just nothing.

There is no future because we no longer have a past. Our present is devised of basic survival, and it's about to end.

They have made sure of that.

I am Nothing.

I am existence.

I am pain.

I kneel down in the dirt and write some of my last words. I'd speak them, but there is no one left to listen.

GAME OVER

MASON

"There's been an accident."

No words have ever been so terrifying.

It was a sunny day. Beautiful. Early September. He'd been laughing. School had just started. Someone told a joke. Mason had finished first period and returned to his locker when the principal found him. Pulled him aside and away from his friends and spoke those four words.

There's been an accident.

Twenty minutes later Mason arrived at Royal Hospital. They wouldn't let him drive. His car was back in the parking lot. Mr. Yan, the geology teacher, drove. He'd never even met Mr. Yan before. He'd never thought to study geology. Since when did any of that matter?

It was sunny outside. Bright. Hot. The days were getting shorter and girls were noticeably wearing fewer clothes. Warm light filtered through the Honda's window, warming Mason's jeans. He absently thought about removing his hoodie, but the consideration was too casual. Too normal. How could he think of being warm? How selfish was he?

The teacher offered to come in, but Mason shook his head.

No. His head bounced up and down when asked if he'd be all right. Yes. He'd be sure to call the school if he needed a ride home. Yes. As Mr. Yan drove off, Mason noticed that his white Honda Civic had a dent in the bumper.

Another car drove through a red light and hit her. Side collision. Your mother was the only one in the car. She's at the hospital. We'll take you there. You can't drive—you're in shock.

Shock? Was that what this was?

Somehow he made it inside. A woman in admitting told him where to go. She was eating a bagel. There was a coffee stain on her sleeve. A permanent frown tattooed into her forehead, her mouth drawn taut against her teeth. She pointed toward the main room and told him to wait. There were too many people around. More than the waiting room could hold. It seemed awfully busy for a Wednesday afternoon. He couldn't find a seat. So he squeezed his slender frame into a corner between a vending machine and the wall. From there he could see and hear everything.

Ambulance lights flickered through the windows. Paramedics rushed to bring stretchers through the emergency doors. Doctors shouted in the hallways and nurses ran with clipboards and medical supplies. People crowded the tiny waiting room's chairs. None were smiling. Most stared off into space while others spoke in hushed voices. A woman a few feet away kept opening and closing the clasp on her purse. Her eyes were red and puffy, and when she looked at Mason, tears welled up and rolled down her cheeks. She was holding a pink blanket in her lap; drops of blood stained the fabric.

Mason looked down at his feet. He didn't want to see any more. His shoelace was coming untied.

Eventually a doctor called his name.

"They're taking her into surgery," the doctor told him.

"There's nothing you can do except wait. We can call someone if you'd like. Are there other family members you'd like us to contact?"

There was no one else. Just Mom and him. Mason's father had died five years ago, when he was twelve.

"Will she be okay?"

"We're doing the best we can."

Not an answer. That wasn't a good sign.

A nurse brought him coffee. The paper cup burned his fingers, but he didn't drop it. Instead he raised the liquid to his lips and took a large gulp. Burned his tongue. He barely noticed. He placed the cup on the waiting room table and promptly forgot about it.

His phone began to ring. People glared at him. A mother with two small children looked at him as if he were pure evil. There was a sign on the wall reminding people to turn off their cell phones. No electronics were allowed in the emergency room. Why hadn't he noticed it before? He hit the off button without taking the call. There was nothing to say, anyway.

More ambulances arrived, and stretchers and paramedics piled in through the doors. The waiting room went from being crowded to ridiculously out of control. Where were all these people coming from? They were beginning to overflow into the hallway. No one seemed to know what was going on.

There was a television mounted in a metal frame above the heads of a young Asian family who didn't speak a word of English. The grandmother was lying on a stretcher pushed up against the wall by the nurses' station. The orderlies didn't know what to do with her. Stretchers filled with people were lining the hallways. The hospital seemed to have run out of room.

The television was turned to a local channel and a talk-show host was interviewing someone about an upcoming movie. The volume was low, and very few people paid attention. Mason watched for a bit, a helpful distraction although he couldn't hear the words. He was still pressed up against the vending machine. Glancing at his watch, he discovered it was almost two. He'd been there for four hours and had no idea what was going on. Was his mother still in surgery? He thought about asking the nurse for an update but changed his mind quickly once he saw the line of twenty people screaming for attention. No one else was getting information, why should he be any different?

"Mason Dowell?"

The doctor had stopped in front of him and Mason hadn't even noticed. He was holding the same clipboard from before and his face was stern and unreadable. Blinking several times, he looked down at the paperwork with heavy eyes.

"Is she okay?" The words blurted out. He hated the sound of his voice. High-pitched. Breathy. Panicky.

"For now." The doctor wouldn't look at him. "We've managed to stop the internal bleeding, but she's still unconscious. All we can do is wait. I think it might be best if you go and get some rest. I can try and arrange for someone to take you home."

"Can I see her?"

"There's nothing to see. She's just resting. We're very busy right now. Go home and get something to eat. Make some phone calls. Come back later tonight and you can see her then."

Someone gasped.

Both of them turned to look. The waiting room had grown awfully quiet. Everyone stared at the television. Someone rushed over and turned up the volume.

It took Mason a few seconds to realize what he was looking

at. The talk show had been replaced by a news bulletin, somewhere live on location. Fire trucks and police cars blocked the remains of a building. They were using hoses to control the flames that burst through the destroyed structure. Emergency lights flashed and people rushed about, but it was impossible to recognize them because of the smoke and dust.

"I repeat," the news reporter's voice said in the background. "Tragedy strikes at local Saskatoon High School. Channel Nine doesn't know all the details yet, but we believe that four men and three women entered the school around one thirty, armed with explosives. The bombs were ignited in the gymnasium, cafeteria, and about five classrooms. There is no word on who did this or if it's linked to a terrorist organization. We are not sure of the casualties yet, but estimates are in the hundreds. They're bringing some of the bodies out now."

The camera panned over to the building, where officials were bringing out black bags. The glass entrance was destroyed and half the doorway had caved in. Mason had walked through those doors a few hours ago.

"That's my school," he said.

No one heard him.

"I've never seen anything like this," the reporter said. Her voice was shaking and constrained. She was no longer reading the script; the words leaving her lips were her own. "The whole school has been destroyed. It's all gone. What kind of monsters would do that?" Tears glistened in her eyes.

The camera panned over to the left as a police officer walked into the shot. His forced expression filled the screen. "If you or anyone you know has children attending the school, please do not come down here. I repeat: Do not come down. There is nothing you can do to help, but there is a number you can call." Local numbers came up on the screen. "I repeat: Do not come down. The authorities are busy and cannot help you."

The camera panned across the parking lot and the hundreds of cars that remained empty. Mason spotted his Toyota Corolla next to a smashed Ford truck covered in rubble. Funny, his car looked untouched. There didn't seem to be a single scratch.

"That's my school," he repeated.

"Son?" The doctor put his hand on Mason's shoulder. "You'd better go home."

"Yeah, okay." The weight of the entire hospital crushed down on Mason's back. He needed to get out of there and make some phone calls. Find out what happened.

"Let me get someone to take you." The doctor looked around the waiting room. "Stay here and I'll go see who's getting off duty. Give me twenty minutes."

"No, don't bother. I can go myself." Mason zipped up his hoodie. If he hurried, he could get to the school in less than half an hour.

"I don't think—"

"It's fine." Mason stepped backward. "I'm not that far away. I've got to go. I'll be back in a few hours. I'll—um—eat something like you said. Take a rest. Have a shower."

The doctor smiled. "Do what you've got to do. We'll see you this evening. Your mother is lucky to have you."

It was still bright and warm outside. Sunny. Beautiful. Shouldn't it be darker? Mason stumbled over the curb, nearly falling right into the path of an incoming ambulance. He stepped backward as red lights washed over him and the vehicle sped by. His cell phone bounced out of his hoodie pocket, but he managed to grab it before it hit the ground. Turning it on, he remembered that someone had called earlier. There was one new message.

"Dude!" The voice on the recording was his friend Tom. "I heard about your mom. I'm really sorry. Hope she's all right. I'll call you the second I'm done with class. Let me know if you're still in the hospital. I'll head down. Gotta go. Coach'll have me running laps if I'm late again."

There was a beep and a voice asking him if he wanted to replay the message, save it, or delete it.

Running laps. Gym.

Explosives.

Tom had been in the gym along with all the others. Kids he'd grown up with. They were all the friends who shared his life. He should have been in gym. He would have been if it hadn't been for those four horrible words. Had his mother just saved his life?

He scrolled through his phone until he found Tom's number. Pressed the button and held it against his ear. Waited for it to ring. Nothing happened. It didn't go straight to voice mail. Not even a recorded voice telling him to try again.

Ending the call, he looked though his list of numbers. Dozens of them, all friends, every single one had been at the school. If he called them, would he get nothing but dead air? He wasn't brave enough to try and find out.

Flagging down the first taxi, Mason climbed in and asked the driver to take him to the 7-Eleven a block from the school. He'd walk the rest. He nervously ran his fingers through his tousled brown hair, trying to distract himself; anything to keep him from kicking the backseat and screaming.

He needed to see. To make sure. He wouldn't allow himself to believe it was real until he saw it with his own eyes.

ARIES

The man on the bus had gone insane.

At least it seemed that way. He was rocking back and forth in the seat, muttering to himself in a language that Aries didn't understand. Twice he got up from his chair and wandered down the aisle, stopping every few steps to shake his head and cover his ears. Finally he plopped down in the seat right in front of her and rummaged through the pockets of his coat.

"What's wrong with him?" Sara hissed in her ear. Her eyes were wide and she was pressed back in her own seat as far as her body would allow. She twisted strands of hair between her fingers, something she did only when she was nervous.

"I think he's mentally ill," Aries whispered back. She glanced around, avoiding the stares of other people who were trying hard to pretend the insane man didn't exist. A few rows in front of her, a guy around her age watched her intently. A book was open in his hands, but he didn't appear to be reading. His eyes were dark and almost hidden behind his longish hair. He gave her a tiny smirk and she pulled her gaze away, her cheeks burning.

"They shouldn't allow those sorts of people on the bus in

the first place," Colin said from the seat behind them. He was the drama king of the school, and Sara thought he was the greatest thing in the world. Aries thought he was arrogant and liked himself a little too much. She put up with him because of Sara. Isn't that what friends did? They'd been permanently linked since they were little, and she'd walk across fire for Sara. Putting up with an obnoxious boyfriend like Colin was part of the best friend code. She knew she'd put Sara through worse during their years of friendship.

It was a beautiful Vancouver evening, one of the nice ones where it wasn't raining, and they were on their way back to Clayton Heights High School for rehearsals of *Alice in Wonderland*. Aries had the role of Alice, and Colin was still complaining about Ms. Darcy, the drama teacher's, choice of play. There was no male lead in *Alice in Wonderland* and Colin was determined to let the entire world know he'd been robbed.

"What if he attacks us?" Sara said. She was going to be the Queen of Hearts, a role, she joked, that had been created just for her. Sara didn't understand why little girls wanted to be princesses when they could be queens. Even her cell phone had a tiny dangling jewelled crown attached to it.

"He won't do anything," Colin said, and he wrapped his arms around Sara. "Not while I'm here."

The man suddenly let out a stream of cuss words that made almost everyone on the bus blush. Colin's cheeks reddened, and instantly he didn't look so sure of himself. Letting go of Sara, he leaned back in his own seat and looked up. Reading the bus ads suddenly seemed more important than reassuring Sara.

Aries rolled her eyes and pressed the buzzer. They were getting off at the next stop. Colin would be able to leave without his cowardice being properly revealed. The moment they got to school Colin would probably tell the story about how he'd been preparing to stand up to the crazy guy on the bus. Then Sara would smile and kiss him on the cheek and pretend he was the hero he wanted to be. Aries would politely join in, keeping the secret truth to herself. Boys could be ridiculously stupid sometimes.

She looked back at the strange guy. He was still watching her. He'd put the book away, but he wasn't getting up. One leg rested on the seat, slender fingers tapped absently at his knee. So intense-looking. She tried to place him; did he go to her school? She couldn't tell for sure.

Colin got up out of his seat, clinging to the safety rail. Sara joined him. Aries zipped up her backpack and was about to move when the insane man turned around and looked right at her. She froze, half off the seat, when he reached out and grabbed her arm. His fingers were icy cold.

"Pretty girlie," he said. "Brace yourself. It's about to open."

"Excuse me?"

"Couldn't keep it closed forever. Too much hate. They found a crack. Let it out again. Here we go. Ten, nine, eight." Spittle flung from the man's lips, and his grip tightened on her arm.

"Let go of me," Aries said. She pulled backward but it was useless. She grabbed hold of his filthy hand and tried to pry his fingers off. She didn't want to touch him; his gray skin was clammy. His clothing was filthy and he smelled faintly of spoiled milk. Crumbs were stuck in his beard, and his cheeks were pockmarked and scabbed. Her stomach lurched as she asked him again to let go.

"Hey!" Colin yelled out, but he didn't move to help. He was frozen. Sara stood beside him, her mouth wide-open, but no sounds came out.

"Seven, six, the cities are collapsing around us. Five!" the man said. "Game over! Four! Hear the screams. Feel the power! Three!"

The bus lurched, rising up over the top of something, and then crashed back to the ground. People fell forward in their seats. There were screams as several people slammed about in different directions. Colin staggered against Sara, sending her down the aisle and crashing against an old lady with groceries. Mandarin oranges rolled away, and a bottle of spaghetti sauce exploded. The strong smell of spiced tomatoes filled the air.

But Aries and the insane man didn't move. His eyes were fixed on her. She looked right into them.

She expected his eyes to be bloodshot. Crazy people always had bloodshot eyes in books and movies. It was the standard insanity cliché. But his weren't. They were something else.

The veins in his eyes were black.

"Two."

The bus lurched again, the driver slammed on the brakes, and more people screamed. They came to a sudden stop in the middle of an intersection, and other cars honked their horns in protest. A sophomore girl was thrown forward, her purse dangling from her shoulders. Her back cracked against the metal railings. People surged out of their seats and onto the floor, trying to get free. But the doors weren't opening. Men banged their fists against the glass windows.

Still Aries and the crazy man didn't move.

"One."

The ground exploded.

The bus staggered forward. The road beneath them began to break apart; pieces of concrete vibrated and scattered as if alive. A fire hydrant burst, and water surged upward, raining down into the intersection. Power lines swayed until wires tore and flayed violently. The lights from the businesses and street surged and went dark. Cars hit their brakes and crashed into one another. Through the window, Aries watched people trying to climb out of the wreckages, while others ran for the safety of the parking lot and sidewalks. Beside the intersection a grocery store rocked on its foundations. Glass shattered, sending tiny projectile missiles in all directions. People covered their heads with their hands to avoid being sliced apart. They fell over one another as they tried to keep their balance on the shaking ground.

A moment ago people were frantically trying to get off the bus. Now they turned and started pushing their way back in. The ground kept vibrating, and the bus groaned and heaved; a giant chunk of concrete smashed into it from behind, forcing the back of the bus up into the air several feet.

Aries could hear Sara calling her name, but she couldn't see her through the confusion. People were all around her, crawling along the floor, climbing over the seats, banging against the glass to try to save themselves.

"What's happening? What's happening?" Someone kept repeating the words over and over. Another person was calling for help. Others were screaming. Over the noise, the crazy man began shouting something that sounded foreign. She couldn't tell if he was laughing or crying.

Somewhere in the distance there was a loud explosion. The bus windows shattered, forcing Aries to cover her head and duck down between the seats. Bits of glass rained down on her, catching in her hair and bouncing off the backs of her hands. The crazy man had released his grip. She no longer heard him, but he was close. She could still smell the scent of sour milk.

A delivery truck sped through the intersection and crashed

into the side of the bus. The collision was powerful; it rocked the bus, which tilted over onto its side. Aries grabbed hold of the seat and held on tightly. Bodies crashed against her. For a brief second she saw Colin's face pressed up against her leg, but he disappeared quickly in the sea of struggling bodies.

The ground continued to shake.

Hours? Minutes?

And then it was over.

The bus was deathly quiet. Aries lay there, her back against the metal window frame and the broken cement, unable to think about anything. Her leg hurt but not enough to make her think it was broken. Liquid dribbled down her face, making her forehead itch insanely. She couldn't free her hand to scratch or check if it was blood. Was she bleeding? She wasn't sure. There was too much weight pressed against her chest. Her arms were stuck. Too many people were lying on top of her. Breathing deeply, she inhaled dust and started coughing. The taste of copper was heavy in the air.

Wiggling her fingers, she tried to pull her hand free. She had to yank hard; her arm was stuck underneath someone's back. She pushed against the body weighing her down, almost screaming when the head rolled toward her, showing the insane man's face. A tightness stretched across her chest, cold air filled her lungs, and she was positive she'd stopped breathing. The edge of her vision darkened into a tunnel. She was going to pass out.

What if he woke up? His lips were practically touching her cheek. The sour milk smell invaded her nose. If he moved she was going to have a heart attack on the spot. She looked straight up through the broken windows and at the sky. Pictured how good the fresh air would feel against her skin once she got free.

A hand reached out. "Here," a voice said. Fingers tightened around hers, giving them a soft squeeze. The hand was warm and soft. Firm. Reassuring. The dark-haired guy appeared in front of her. With his free arm, he grabbed hold of the crazy man's jacket, yanking the body backward and off of her.

"Is that better?"

She nodded. Somehow she managed to find her legs somewhere in all that clutter and she brought them up to her chest. The guy continued to hold her hand, helping her maintain balance while she struggled to her knees.

"Sara?" Her voice was loud and strained.

The bus was full of bodies, some of them moving, most of them still. Grabbing hold of a seat's metal railing, she pulled herself up until she was standing. The seats were still bolted to what was now the side of the bus, crowding the small amount of free space. Bits of glass quivered above her head, raining down the occasional shard.

There were so many bodies.

"Let's look for her," the guy said.

He was still holding her hand, and she allowed him to gently lead her toward the front. She stepped through the bodies, stopping to check the faces of everyone she passed. What had Sara been wearing? She couldn't remember. Her jacket? A hoodie? Which one? Other people started to get up, staggering and tripping as they tried to make their way off. Because the bus was lying on its side, they couldn't go through the door, so someone took one of the emergency hammers off the wall and smashed his way through the front window. A woman whose arm was bent awkwardly began to climb over the steering wheel to get outside. Other people searched around, looking for their friends and family members. She saw Colin step over the body of the elderly lady. His foot came down on one of the mandarin oranges, squishing it into a mushy pulp.

"Help me," she called out. "I can't find Sara."

But Colin ignored her. She could see in his eyes that he was set on getting free. Unfocused. Rattled. His hair was sticking up and his cheek was splotchy with grime. She'd never seen him look dirty before. Even his fingernails had been meticulously clean. He moved past her, never giving her a second glance.

She thought about calling after him, but it seemed pointless. Instead she concentrated on methodically moving among the bodies, desperately searching for her friend. Voices called out, pleading, asking for help. Someone screamed for his mother, begging her to come because he couldn't understand where he was. Everywhere was pain and death. A few hands reached out weakly for her, and she helped free a man from underneath an unconscious woman. The man's ankle was broken and beginning to swell but he still managed to crawl toward the front. She continued to look for Sara, but she wasn't there.

"Why don't we check outside?" the guy said. She nodded and allowed him to put his arm around her. It seemed like the right thing to do. His body was warm, and the muscles beneath his jacket pressed against her, drawing her in, comforting her.

Maybe Sara had already managed to get out?

An overly pregnant woman struggled to stand from between two crushed seats. "Please, help me," she said.

The stranger let go of Aries and they both put their arms around the stunned woman. Blood trickled down her forehead from where she'd smashed her face into the window. The three of them stumbled through the front window and onto the broken street. There were benches at the bus stop, and they helped the woman over and sat her down. Another woman came over to lend a hand. Blood seeped from a gash in her forehead, but she crouched down beside the expectant mother and began talking to her calmly.

The first thing that struck Aries was the lack of noise. There were so many people standing around, many of them covered in blood and injured. But they were quiet. They moved about, some helping one another, barely uttering a single word.

The street was destroyed. Most of the concrete was torn apart; it lay in piles, strewn across the ground. There was broken glass everywhere. It crunched beneath her feet. The sun was beginning to set; the sky was filled with pinks and purples. Long shadows spread out across the ground. Normally by now the street lamps would start to switch on, but with the power out, there would be no city glow. Soon everything would be pitch-black. Aries shuddered. The thought of being on the streets once the sun went down was enough to make her feel like she was five years old and terrified of closet monsters or things that hid under the bed.

The building on the corner had imploded. It used to be a grocery store. Now it was nothing but a pile of debris. Shopping carts lay on their sides where the parking lot used to be. Some of the wheels were still spinning. How many people were trapped inside? There were dozens of cars in the lot, many of them rolled over on their sides. The smell of gasoline was strong.

Walking the length of the bus, she studied the faces of everyone around her. She moved between the groups, bending down to check people lying on the ground. There were a lot of dazed and pained expressions, but none of them were familiar. None of them were Sara.

One of the drivers had a first aid kit in his trunk. He

opened it and began handing out supplies. The stranger from the bus came over holding a sterile white bandage. "You're bleeding." He brought the gauze up to Aries's forehead and pressed gently against her skin. "Hold this. Are you all right?"

She put her hand up, fingers touching against his as she took control of the bandage. She pressed carefully against her own skin but there was no pain. When she pulled the cloth away there was dark blood. "I don't think it's mine," she said. "I'm not hurt."

"Good. Did you find your friend?"

She shook her head.

"Well, let's try the bus again. We'll keep looking for her." The guy turned back toward the wreckage, and she followed. She liked his calmness, the way he carried his body when he walked. It made her feel safe. Stronger. She saw Colin standing in the road and thought about calling out to him but then changed her mind. He'd ignored her before; she doubted he'd be much help now.

"What happened?" she asked as they climbed back on the bus.

"Earthquake," the guy said. His eyes flickered in the dying sunlight. "It's like the ground just opened up and swallowed us whole."

Brace yourself. It's about to open.

The crazy man had said that just before he started his countdown.

But how was that possible? No one could predict earthquakes—could they?

"Sara has to be in here," Aries said, her voice sounding heavy and strange in her ears. "She's blond. Wears glasses. I need to find her."

"We'll find her."

"I can't remember what she's wearing."

"I saw her sitting with you. I know what she looks like."

"Isn't that weird that I can't remember? I should know. She's my best friend. Oh, God. What if she's dead? I've got to tell her mom."

The guy turned and placed a hand on her shoulder. She looked into his eyes, wondering how they could be dark and piercing but friendly and soft at the same time. She tried to recall if she knew his face. He seemed familiar in a vague sort of way. Did they go to school together?

"We'll find her," he repeated.

And they did. But by then it was too late.

CLEMENTINE

Outside, the wind pressed against the small town hall, shaking the windows and seeping through the cracks. A major draft blew across the floor, numbing the noses and ears of everyone seated. The room had been built more than a hundred years ago when the town of Glenmore was first established. Wonderful inventions such as insulation didn't exist back then. No wonder the people looked sad and depressed in the black-and-white pictures decorating the walls.

Clementine sat squished between her mother and father, second row from the back and right by the aisle and entrance. The meeting was for seven, but they'd arrived late; Mom had been desperately trying to reach Heath on the phone, but all the lines were down. Heath was in Seattle getting a degree in computer programming.

A lot of people were dead in Seattle. The earthquake had destroyed most of the West Coast, from California to Alaska.

Clementine didn't believe for a second that Heath was dead. Mom had one of those built-in sensor detectors that went off whenever her children were in trouble. She'd known immediately when Clementine fell from the pyramid during cheerleading practice and sprained her ankle. When Heath got into a car accident, she'd called him less than a minute after to make sure he wasn't hurt. Her spider senses tingled when her family was in trouble. If Heath was dead, she'd know.

When Washington got their phone lines working again, they'd receive a phone call or e-mail from Heath, joking about how he was shaking things up in the city and telling them not to worry.

But there was always the possibility that wasn't true. Who knew how these mother/child instincts worked? Maybe there was some sort of time-zone limitation?

"If we don't reach him by tomorrow morning, I'm driving to Seattle myself," Mom said just before they left for the town meeting.

"Come on, honey," Dad said. "I'm sure Heath is fine. They'll get the lines fixed and he'll call. Just give it a few more days. You'll see."

But Dad wasn't confident with his words. As he'd spoken, he'd stared at the ceiling and hadn't taken Mom's hand as he normally did when he was trying to be reassuring. So Clementine knew that tomorrow morning Mom would load up the SUV and take the two-day trip to Seattle. She decided now that she'd go too. She'd miss the big game on Friday, but that wasn't nearly as important as making sure her brother was alive. Part of her was excited about the journey. She'd never taken a road trip west before. The other part of her was terrified and guilt ridden.

Dear Heath, you'd better be okay. You promised me that if I ever made it west to Seattle you'd take me sightseeing. I guess that's out of the question. In all honesty, knowing you're safe is more important than getting the chance to see the rock 'n' roll museum.

The town hall was crowded. Almost everyone was there.

Glenmore was small, just under a thousand people, but nonetheless, the tiny building could barely fit all of them. Craig Strathmore, the linebacker, was five rows up from her. He'd waved to her when they'd walked in, a gesture that warmed her stomach. As far as farm boys went, he was one nice piece of cowboy. Up toward the front, Clementine saw Jan and Imogene, other cheerleaders she hung out with. They were sitting with their parents too. It was obvious that neither of them had come willingly. Jan played with a strand of her hair, lazily scanning the crowd with a bored frown on her face. She turned and spotted Clementine, than made a big show of rolling her eyes and shrugging her shoulders. Clementine grinned back.

She was about to ask Dad if she could go and sit with them when the mayor took the podium.

"Attention. Call to order."

The room immediately went quiet. Eyes forward, people waited for him to speak. It was the first emergency meeting in over thirty years. Although everyone knew what the mayor would talk about, people were still curious to know what the town of Glenmore was going to do. Clementine was already envisioning the multitude of bake sales and potluck dinners in the church parking lot.

"As you know, there's been a plea from the president for all Americans to help out in this time of trouble," the mayor said. Someone must have set the sound system wrong, because there was a sudden screech of feedback. An assistant immediately ran up to play around with the buttons, and the mayor tapped the microphone a few times before he continued. Some of the older folks in the front rows took out their hearing aids. "We've been asked to send supplies to the coast and any people who might be willing to volunteer with cleanup.

They've got a lot of missing people over there, some of whom are from this very town."

Although they weren't rude enough to turn around and stare, Clementine could feel hundreds of pairs of invisible eyes focus on her family. No one else had people on the West Coast.

She caught Craig giving her a sympathy glance before his father whispered angrily in his ear, forcing him to turn around and face the front again. The whole scene struck her as funny, and she found herself struggling not to giggle.

Dear Heath, if you die, then I'd better get your car.

No, it wouldn't do her any good to laugh.

The discussion carried on with a lot of uproar. What about all the violence—those rumors about people killing each other for no reason? How long would it take before that sort of behavior found its way over to Glenmore? How would they protect themselves if half the men left to go help on the coast?

"We need all able bodies here," someone shouted in the crowd. "We don't need them off where God knows what might be happening. That's a death order if I've ever heard one."

"It wouldn't be very Christian of us to not help," another said. "The orders came from the president himself."

"How dare you say I'm not Christian, Hank. Where were you last Sunday? Watching the game on TV?"

"Order! Order!"

Clementine knew the exact moment the door opened, because a gust of wind blew up against her neck, sending icy shivers down her spine. She should have worn her warmer jacket, but it was September. Isn't it still supposed to be relatively warm in September?

She turned her head to look at the latecomers. Henry and James Tills had entered the town hall. They were both smiling, but neither looked happy.

Something was wrong with Henry's eyes. If she hadn't known him as well as she did she might have thought he was wearing contacts. But Henry wasn't the type.

"Evening, boys," the mayor said. A squeal of feedback went through the microphone again, causing several people to cover their ears. "Little early for that kind of protection, don't you think? No need to be arming ourselves just yet."

Murmurs broke out among the people in the hall, and many of them turned in their seats to watch the door. It wasn't until Henry and James passed them in the aisle that Clementine noticed the weapons. Mom immediately reached out and squeezed her hand.

"Clem," she whispered. "You need to leave. Get up."

"What?"

"Leave now," Mom yanked her forward in her seat, pushing her right onto the floor. Clementine's knees scraped against the cement. One of her shoes slipped off her heel, but she didn't get a chance to search for it before Mom shoved her again, forcing her into the aisle.

She was about to open her mouth to protest, but she saw the look on her mother's face. So instead she pulled herself up to her feet and brushed the blond hair back from her face.

The town hall had grown awfully quiet.

She took a few steps backward toward the hall doors. Henry and James Tills had already passed her. They were making their way down toward the center of the room. Neither of them looked back at her as she stood stupidly with her hands at her sides. She glanced over at Mom, but she wasn't looking. She was staring straight ahead as if concerned that any unexpected movement might cause the wrong kind of attention.

Clementine focused again on the only other two people standing in the room.

James held the weapon in his arms, but there was something wrong with the way he was standing. His back was twitching as if he were having a seizure. Muscles rippled against the tightness of his shirt. There was blood on his pants. His leg made a sickening squelching noise every time he placed weight on it. She stared at James's jeans, watching the movement of his ankle. She couldn't stop looking at the way his foot dragged against the ground when he stepped forward.

Mom reached out and grabbed her arm, breaking her paralysis. She looked into her mother's eyes and saw something she'd never seen in sixteen years. Her strong, confident, stubborn mom was freaked. That wasn't right. Mom was the one who always kept everyone together. She never fell apart. She was too solid that way. Strong. Clementine opened her mouth to speak, but Mom brought a finger to her lips. Her hands were trembling.

"Go," she mouthed silently. Beside her, Dad motioned with his hands. Shooing her away like an annoying fly. His eyes never met hers; they were focused on the backs of Henry and James. There was no mistaking the concern on his face either.

Clementine shook her head. "Come with me," she mouthed back.

Mom grabbed her arm a second time, pushing her away from the chairs. Clementine began slowly moving toward the entrance, walking backward, afraid to take her eyes off the two men. She'd known both Henry and James since she was a toddler. These men were liked. They were served coffee and pie at the diner and helped out with the town festivals. Henry played Santa every year for the church Christmas party.

But panic filled the room like an electric charge. Everyone was frozen in their seats, waiting for the proverbial pin to drop. Even the few people in the back row who could see Clementine silently sneaking away seemed to ignore her completely. What would happen once Henry and James reached the front of the room?

She didn't find out. Her shoulders brushed against the doorframe and her fingers found the handle. Looking back at her parents, she saw that her father had risen from his seat along with a few of the other men. Her mother was staring at her hands. Clementine pushed down on the latch, letting the door open a few inches, worried that the sound might draw attention to her actions. What if the wind knocked the door right out of her hands? Another foot and soon there was enough space to squeeze her body through. There was a second of panic when she turned her back to the men to make her escape.

Once outside, the wind whipped ferociously at her neck. She closed the door as quietly as she could. What if the noise made everyone turn and look? Even worse, what if it locked and her parents couldn't get free? It felt like a betrayal, turning the handle till the latch clicked. She was leaving them all behind. Her mother and father. Her friends. She didn't know what fate she was giving them. So far nothing had happened. This was a small town. Things didn't happen. Her mother was probably overreacting, but something inside her was also telling her to run.

To leave everyone behind, though? That seemed cowardly.

She decided to wait on the steps until everyone came back out. They'd laugh about it later on the ride home. Tomorrow they'd pack their bags and drive west to Seattle to check on Heath. It would be a good story to tell him.

A car's engine roared to life and headlights switched on, bathing her in blinding white light.

"Well, well, well, we've got ourselves an escapee."

She knew that voice. It belonged to her neighbor Sam Anselm. She took a few steps forward until she could see through the headlights' glare.

The town hall was surrounded.

There were at least twenty men and women, armed and ready to ambush. They had positioned their cars around the building so that no one would be getting out. Clementine took another step, painfully aware that Sam had his gun tracking her movements.

"What's going on, Sam?" Her voice sounded taut and strange in her throat. She swallowed hard but it didn't help.

"I think you need to go back inside, young missy," Sam said. "That is, if you really want to know."

"And if I don't?"

"Then we'll have a little party out here. Just the two of us."

Sam was on her before she had time to react. Grabbing hold of her arm, he dragged her away from the town hall and toward his truck. She yanked hard, trying to break free, but his grip was too strong.

"Sam. Sam, stop it, please," she said. The others were beginning to descend on the town hall with their weapons raised. "Don't do this."

"But I enjoy it," he said.

She stumbled over the walkway and almost fell, eyes filling with tears from the pain of him dragging her along. The muscles in her arm flared, and she was afraid he might tear the ligaments if she continued to fight. So she allowed him to pull her a few more feet, until he stopped at the edge of the parking lot.

His hand abruptly let go of her arm, and he stared at her as if he didn't know who she was. His eyes grew wide and confused.

"Clem?"

"Sam?"

"I didn't hurt you, did I? Please say I didn't hurt you." His hands reached out and grabbed her shoulders.

"No, I'm fine. I—"

"You've got to get out of here. Now! Before I go back. I go in and out. My brain. The voices. White noise. They're so loud. I can't stop them. They're telling me to do things."

"What are you talking about, Sam? I can't go. My parents are inside."

"Leave. You have to go or they'll kill you. I'll kill you. Once it takes over I can't stop it."

"What? What takes over?"

"I don't know. The voices. The things inside my head. They're real. Curled up against my brain. Fighting me."

He gave her a shove backward and she thought about how her mother had done the same thing moments ago. Everyone kept telling her to run, but no one was saying where they wanted her to go.

Gunshots fired against the night. They came from inside the town hall. Someone screamed.

Everyone she knew was inside that building.

"Run," Sam said, reading her mind. "You can't save them. Don't go home. That's the first place they'll look for you."

"But where will I go?"

Sam dropped to his knees, clutching at his ears and screaming. His gun dropped to the earth beside him, and she thought about trying to grab it. But she didn't know anything about weapons; it would be useless in her hands.

When Sam raised his head, his eyes were clouded and there was no recognition when he looked right at her. He'd bitten his lip or cheek when he fell. He smiled; she could see the blood on his teeth. Her heart pounded and skipped a beat.

Sam no longer appeared to be home.

She decided to do what she was told. She turned and ran.

MICHAEL

"I can't take this anymore. Toss in some music or something; I'm sick of the news."

They were driving in Joe's truck. Not anywhere in particular, just wasting time. Something they did every afternoon after school let out. They'd been doing this ritual since they both got their driver's licenses last year. Michael rolled the window down, enjoying the way the wind caught his long brown hair.

"What do you want to hear?"

"I don't care. Anything except this crap. Who cares about an earthquake?"

Michael cared, but he didn't bother admitting it. Besides, Joe was right, the news hadn't broadcast anything original in hours. Just the same old stuff since the initial reports started coming in last night. Most of the information played on a loop. No one seemed to know anything. Searching through the music, he settled on Green Day, the only CD that wasn't scratched beyond recognition. Joe didn't take good care of his things.

"So you heard about Sasquatch?" That was Joe's pet name

for Mr. Petrov, the crazy old Vietnam veteran who lived down the street from the school. He was known for screaming at teenagers who came too close to his front lawn. He also had one of the only houses that was toilet papered on a regular basis.

"Yeah, he attacked the mailman or something yesterday."

"Bit his earlobe off," Joe said. "Clear right off. Chewed on it for a while too before the police hit him with a Taser. I mean, how messed up is that?"

"What did they do with him?"

"Heard they hauled him off to the nuthouse. About time, too. It's not like it's news. He's been loopy for years."

Michael tapped his fingers gently on the car door in time to the music. It was strange to think of Mr. Petrov's house as being empty. He'd been a bit of a shut-in, rarely leaving his yard except to buy groceries every single Monday at the Safeway. He was a local attraction. There wasn't much else going on in Whitefish.

"Do you think they'll put his house up for sale?" he asked. "He doesn't have any family, right? I wonder what will happen to his stuff?"

Joe didn't answer. Tapping the brakes, he slowed the truck and swerved slightly to the right. "What the hell is that guy doing?"

Michael looked. Ahead of them, the drivers of a motorcycle and a car appeared to be in an argument. The car driver, with his head clear out the window, was screaming obscenities at the guy on the bike. Honking his horn several times, he hit the gas pedal as the biker tried to speed away. His license plates were out-of-state—Idaho.

"That's some serious road rage," Michael said.

Joe leaned his head out the window. "Just say no, dude," he screamed. "It's all about the love."

"I don't think you're helping."

The car honked its horn again, the red brake lights glowing as the driver slowed down to keep the same speed as the motorcycle.

The biker decided he'd had enough. He revved the engine, and the motorcycle gained speed, edging ahead until he'd almost passed the car.

"Oh my God."

The driver swerved his car straight into the motorcycle's path, front fender meeting with back tire. The biker lost control; the machine spun sideways and into the path of a Mack truck. Both rider and bike were propelled toward Joe's car. The guy's body twisted and turned, doing airborne cartwheels, a rag doll tossed through the air. Joe slammed the brakes while spinning the steering wheel, sending them into the ditch.

Over the sound of Green Day, Michael heard the body as it smashed against the pavement. There was a squelching noise, like a water balloon exploding upon impact.

The truck came to a stop right at the base of the tree line. Michael's body jerked against the seat belt, shooting pain along his chest and up into his shoulder.

"Oh my God, did you see that? Did you see that?" Joe's voice raised several octaves. "I'm gonna hurl." He barely managed to get the door open before the contents of his lunch forced their way up.

There had to be something wrong with his eyes. Michael knew he couldn't have just witnessed that. Had the driver done it on purpose? It sure looked that way. What kind of person would do such a thing? He had to be wrong. People don't do things like that.

Michael opened his own door and jumped out before Joe's vomit smell overpowered him enough to attack his own churning stomach. Scrambling up the ditch, he joined the group of onlookers surrounding the crash scene.

Several cars had stopped in the middle of the highway, including the Mack truck and the enraged driver. People got out of their vehicles, but they didn't know what to do. Most of them stood around with bewildered expressions on their faces. Someone brought out a camera and started taking pictures.

The biker was dead. His body was sprawled in the road, leaving a thick trail of blood from where he'd skidded across the pavement. His helmet was still protecting his face, and Michael was glad he didn't have to look at the guy's eyes. Turning his gaze away, he searched for the driver of the car. If Michael had been the one to do something like this, he'd be a complete mess. Probably ready to go toss himself off the nearest overpass. A few months ago he'd hit a deer by accident and he still had nightmares about it. Hitting an animal was one thing; he couldn't imagine the guilt of hurting a human.

The road-raged driver had parked his car a ways down the road. He moved back toward the crowd, his face bright red and breathing heavily. Talking to himself, he paused once to scream at an elderly couple cowering by their car.

The guy walked past the crowd of stunned onlookers, sidestepping the ruined motorcycle, and stopped in front of the body. He began to scream at the dead man, hurling a wrath of insults, while kicking at the motorcycle helmet.

The crowd froze. No one knew what to do. Someone started to cry, whimpering sounds mixing in with thudding sneaker kicks. Finally the trucker stepped forward, grabbing the guy by the back of his jacket and pulling him away. He spoke calmly considering the situation, but his words had little results. The enraged man turned his focus on the Mack guy and began attacking, scratching at the trucker's face as if he wanted to rip the poor guy's eyes right out of their sockets.

It was enough to make Michael jump into action. He caught the attention of another man several feet away. The older guy, with a receding hairline, nodded at him. Both of them stepped forward. Michael pushed the insane man backward while the other grabbed him by the arms to try and stop his advances.

But the guy wasn't going down without a fight. In the end, it took six of them to get him on his stomach, with both the trucker and a burly guy sitting on top of him. The enraged guy continued to scream, spittle flying from his lips as he cursed at anyone who got too close.

"Don't move," the balding man said. "I've got a phone in my car. I'll call the police."

Michael glanced over at Joe, who was sitting on a rock by the side of his truck, his face pasty. A few other people had joined him, mostly women and the elderly couple. Everyone was making an effort to stay as far away from the insane man as possible. Although he was momentarily subdued, Michael didn't blame them.

"Phone's out," the guy said, returning to the scene. He was holding an iPhone. "I'm getting a signal, but I can't get through. Anyone else have one that works?"

"It doesn't matter," the trucker said. He nodded back in the direction behind them. "Cops are coming. I can see the flashers."

In the distance, Michael could see the red and blue lights as the police car tried to make its way through the group of onlookers. It seemed a little strange; the accident covered all four lanes of traffic, but there were fewer than a dozen cars stopped along the road. Shouldn't there be more? Where was everyone? Had the police already diverted traffic?

Someone pulled a blanket from their car and covered the dead man. Only, his body was too long, leaving the bottom part of his calves and his feet sticking out from under the plaid fabric. It couldn't cover all the blood, either.

The police finally worked their way through the small crowd. Michael knew one of them, Clive Templeton, who had graduated from his high school only a few years earlier. Clive was the first to reach the scene. The other, Officer Burke, stopped to talk to the hyperventilating elderly couple.

"Everyone stand back," Clive said. He talked with the balding guy and the trucker for a while. Michael didn't get involved; he hadn't seen anything different from the others. After a few minutes, Clive and Burke handcuffed the still-screaming man, grabbed him by the arms, and brought him up to his feet.

"Everyone can return to their cars," Burke said. "There's nothing more to see here."

That didn't seem right. Shouldn't they be gathering information from the other bystanders? Michael was no criminal expert, but shouldn't they have witness accounts for when this went to court? What if the guy pleaded not guilty? Stepping forward, he decided to offer up his phone number or something in case they needed him.

But the cops were ignoring him, pushing people back and away from the scene. The trucker got back in his cab and started up his engine. The balding guy came over to stand next to him.

"This is wrong," Michael said.

"It's strange all right," the guy said.

"Shouldn't they be doing more? I mean, there's not even an ambulance here yet. What are they supposed to do with the body? Put it by the side of the road and hope the wild animals don't eat it?"

The guy snorted. "Maybe they've got one on the way."

"I hope so." He turned to hold out his hand to the balding man. "I'm Michael."

"Evans." They shook hands. Evans handed him a business card with his name on it. "Just in case. You never know if you might need it."

Clive wandered over to where they stood. "I said back to your car," he snapped. He was wearing sunglasses, the mirrored kind; it was impossible to read his expression. "Don't make me kick your ass, Mikey boy. School's out."

Michael put the card in his back pocket, nodded at Clive, and backed away. There was something creepy about not being able to see the man's eyes. Evans appeared to be thinking the same thing; he turned and headed back to his car without so much as a wave of his hand.

Back at the truck, Joe was inside, twisting the key, but the engine wasn't roaring to life.

"I don't know what happened," he said. "Musta broke something when we hit the ditch. It ain't starting."

"Great." Michael looked back at the officers. What would their reactions be? Most of the crowd had dispersed; a few people were putting their cars in gear and pulling back onto the highway. The trucker was gone, the tail end of his cargo disappearing around the bend. Evans waited at the side of the road, sitting behind the wheel, watching the officers. They were holding on to the enraged man, speaking to him in low voices. The guy didn't look so angry anymore. His complexion was pale, eyes wide. He was trembling.

"I said, get back in your vehicles," Burke said, walking over to the truck. He swung his weapon around until it was aimed right at Michael's head. "Don't think I won't shoot you, kid."

Michael's legs quivered as his body temperature dropped. He didn't know how to respond. What words could he use to get that gun away from his face? He opened his mouth twice, but nothing came out. "Our truck's not working," he finally muttered, pointing a hand over in Joe's direction. He didn't dare take his eyes off the gun.

"That's not my problem," Burke said.

Evans's car pulled up beside them. "Come with me," the balding man said. "I'll give you both a ride home."

Burke nodded toward Evans, signaling that they should take the offer. Lowering his weapon, he turned his back and returned to where Clive held the handcuffed man. Michael glanced at Joe, who wasn't waiting to be asked twice. They both climbed into the car, Joe stuffing his lanky body into the backseat.

"Thanks." Michael rolled down his window as Evans started to pull away from the scene. As they distanced themselves, he watched the scene gradually growing smaller in the side mirror. They got only about fifty feet away when it happened.

Officer Burke was holding on to the driver one moment; the next he simply let go. The handcuffed man stood there for a few seconds, looking between the cops and the woods. Michael saw Clive give him a hard push.

"What the hell?" Michael turned in his seat. Evans slammed on the brakes as the motorcycle killer ran, hands still cuffed behind his back, straight for the tree line.

He never got a chance. Burke raised his gun, aimed, and shot the man before his feet left the pavement. The guy flew forward, hitting the ground and rolling several times before coming to a stop at the bottom of the ditch.

"He just shot that guy," Joe blurted.

"Get us out of here, now," Michael said to Evans, surprised

at how calm his voice sounded. Inside, his thoughts were screaming. From behind them, Clive turned his gun toward them and pulled the trigger.

"Get down," Evans shouted as he slammed his foot on the gas.

The rear window shattered, spraying Joe with glass. He ducked, even as Evans pulled away, spinning tires and leaving smoking black marks on the pavement.

They spent the next five minutes driving at top speed, but it didn't look like the police officers were going to give chase. Eventually Evans slowed the car down to a reasonable pace.

Michael found his phone in his pocket but paused when he realized he had no idea who he should call. If he dialed 911 would anyone believe them? He'd just witnessed the entire thing and he couldn't quite understand what happened. He punched the numbers into the phone anyway, but all he got was a busy signal. He tried a second time. Then a third. This time he got a recording: There are too many people trying to get through—please dial again. What the hell was going on? He'd never heard of 911 being busy before. Who else was there? Dad was in Denver on business, and he couldn't think of any reason for actually calling him except he was terrified. Finally he dialed Dad's number regardless, but the call didn't go through. He didn't even get an out-of-service message.

"Phone's not working," he said.

"Radio's out too," Evans said. "I can't get any of the stations. I can't even get dead air. It's weird. Maybe the trees?"

"We always get radio here," Joe said. "There's a broadcasting tower not too far away."

"Then it's something else," Evans said.

They drove along in silence for a bit. Joe kept busy picking bits of glass off the backseat and tossing them out the window. Finally he raised his head and looked around bewilderedly. "I need to get home," he said. "Mom's gonna pitch a fit when she finds out I left the truck behind."

"We're sure as hell not going back to get it," Michael said.

"It's our only car, too," Joe said. "The Jeep's in the shop. Dad took it in this morning for a brake job. I'm supposed to drive him back there tonight to pick it up."

"They'll understand."

"I don't know. Dad was in a real pissy mood this morning. He was acting weird."

"Let's just worry about getting home in one piece."

"I can drop you off," Evans said. "Where are you from?"

"Whitefish," Michael said.

"I know where that is. I'm staying at the hotel there."

"Thanks."

It didn't take long to get back to town. Michael gave Evans directions, and they pulled up to Joe's house first. He got out without saying a word and headed up the steps to his front porch. He was in shock. Michael didn't blame him. Had they really just witnessed both a murder and an execution?

When Evans pulled into the driveway in front of Michael's apartment, the building was quiet. What had he been expecting? Flashing blue and red lights? Would Clive and Burke come back for him? He didn't want to think about it. He didn't think they knew where he lived, but that didn't really mean much. They were cops, after all. They'd find him if they wanted to.

Evans must have read his mind. "If they come back for you, I'm staying at the Super Eight. Room six-fourteen. Come and find me if you need help."

Michael nodded and got out of the car. As he watched the balding man drive off, his hand closed around the business card in his back pocket.

ARIES

The stranger was less squeamish about moving among the dead. As he worked his way across the bus, he stopped every few feet to reposition the bodies in order to see their faces. Aries struggled along behind him, trying to keep her balance. There weren't many free spots to put her feet. She didn't want to accidentally step on anyone's arm or fingers—or, even worse, someone's face—and the thought that one wrong movement might send her tumbling down onto the pile of bodies terrified her. So she followed the stranger carefully, stepping where he stepped, and held on to the seat frames as tightly as possible.

He picked up someone by his jacket and shoved him aside. Underneath were more bodies. They were piled on top of one another like a collapsed cheerleading pyramid. He reached out his hand and checked the pulse on someone's wrist. "This one's still alive."

Aries strained to see who the hand belonged to, but she couldn't tell in the mass of clothing and bodies. Her hopes were dashed when the stranger moved aside someone's backpack and revealed the face of a middle-aged woman.

"Should we carry her outside?" She'd taken first aid years ago in school but couldn't remember the proper steps. You weren't supposed to move people in case they had neck injuries, but wasn't staying there worse? It was dangerous leaving them in the middle of the road where another car might hit them. What if a gas leak happened and the bus exploded? Aren't you supposed to get them out of harm's way?

"No," he said. "We'll leave her here."

"When do you think the ambulance will come?"

The stranger climbed to his feet and brushed his hands against his jeans, leaving behind a smear of blood. Continuing forward, he avoided looking at her. "There won't be an ambulance."

Aries froze. "What do you mean?"

"The entire city was just destroyed. The roads are torn apart. Thousands of people are dead or dying. Do you really believe help will come?"

"But they've got to come."

"*They* don't have to do anything."

"These people will die."

The stranger glanced back at her over his shoulder. "And so will millions of others. What's a few more?"

"What do you mean millions?"

"This went farther than just Vancouver. Seattle, Los Angeles, Mexico. Even Alaska if we look in the other direction. A lot of people live on the West Coast. But it's not just North America. An earthquake of this magnitude probably reached Asia."

"Oh."

The stranger continued on, shuffling bodies aside, checking the occasional pulse. He was several feet away, almost to the back of the bus.

Aries knelt at the feet of the middle-aged woman, who

was barely alive. She placed her hand against the lady's forehead, trying to think about what she could do to save her life. The small amount of training she'd received years ago was not enough to help her in such a situation. She knew how to do mouth-to-mouth resuscitation, and that was it. She picked up the woman's limp hand and squeezed it gently, seeking something comforting to say. Even in her unconscious state, the lady still might be able to hear.

"I think I found your friend."

He was standing at the back of the bus and she couldn't see where he was looking. Getting to her feet, she loosened her fingers, allowing the hand of the dying woman to drop to the ground, and went for Sara instead.

"Is she dead?"

The stranger looked away too quickly. That was all the answer she needed. Her bottom lip began to quiver and she breathed in deeply to try and hold back the sobs. Holding tightly to the mangled seat, she focused on maintaining balance and blinked several times to keep the tears from blurring her vision. She was determined to remain calm. She would not fall apart on the bus in front of this stranger. There would be plenty of time later once she was alone. She would be brave.

"You don't have to look," he said, seeing through her facade. His eyes softened. "If you've got a picture, I can identify her for you."

She almost accepted, but she knew if she didn't look she'd regret it. "No, I'm fine." She took another deep breath, closed her eyes, and counted to three inside her head. Opening her eyes, she focused on the image before her.

The person lying on the ground, her neck shoved awkwardly against the mangled seats, was Sara. Her eyes were open, staring at the ads for résumé building and continuing education. One hand rested gently on her chest, the other disappeared beneath her body. Legs splayed in different directions. Blood dribbled from her mouth, already starting to cake and dry. Her neck twisted and unnatural, bits of blond hair stuck against her bloodied face.

Why did her eyes have to be open?

"That's her," she whispered.

"I'm sorry," the stranger said.

How long would it be before someone could take Sara away? She would have to call Sara's parents. Maybe they could find a way to come and get her if they were okay. They didn't live that far away. She took her cell phone from her pocket, but there was no service. That didn't really surprise her; the earthquake would have temporarily destroyed all means of communication.

She'd have to walk, then. If she left now she could get there in a few hours. But was it safe to leave Sara alone? What if someone did something to her body? She caught the dead glaze of her friend's eyes, accusing her, begging her not to leave.

"Can you close her eyes?"

She was thankful that he didn't smirk or give her a look. Instead he reached over and ran the tips of his fingers against Sara's skin, closing those beautiful gray eyes forever.

"Thank you."

"We should go. It's not safe to stay here."

"Can we cover her up with something?" She felt stupid the moment the words left her lips. "I mean, it just seems wrong leaving her like that."

The stranger unzipped his jacket. Carefully he placed the clothing over her deceased friend. It covered only her face and shoulders, but it made Aries feel better. At the same time she worried about the guy. He had on only a shirt now, and although it was still September it was starting to get chilly. She could see his muscles against the tight fabric. His arms were pale and bare; she wanted to feel them around her again. Comforting. The thought warmed her cheeks and she looked away in embarrassment.

"You don't have to do that," she said.

"I know."

"You'll be cold."

"I'll be fine."

There were a few more bodies to check, but in the end, Aries and the stranger got off the bus by themselves. Everyone there was dead, dying, or unable to move. There was nothing they could do to help, so they left. It seemed wrong, but there weren't any right answers to hand in.

The first thing she noticed when they got back outside was how different the air smelled. There was no brisk night air smelling faintly like leaves and car exhaust. There was a sickening acrid flavor that stuck to the insides of her nostrils, threatening to make her gag. In the distance, the skyline was orange and red from where a fire raged. Monstrous black clouds of smoke rapidly spread through the night, pushed by the wind. Bits of ash fell from above and stuck to their hair. Gray snowflakes.

"Can you hear it?" the stranger asked. He stood, arms at his side, eyes closed, face pointed up toward the sky.

"Hear what?" She strained her ears but there was no unusual noise.

"The nothingness. No fire trucks, ambulances, police cars. No people, cars, stereos, televisions, computers. All the things we use to replace the silence of loneliness. All the distractions we buy that fill up the empty voids inside our souls. It's all gone."

"Are you saying our souls are empty?"

"No, I'm saying they've been filled."

"With what?"

The stranger smiled at her. "Humanity has found a cure to a disease they never knew existed."

"You sound just like the crazy man on the bus."

The smile faltered. "Sorry. I was just thinking out loud."

She gave him a long look but couldn't really see anything wrong with him. He didn't look like he was crazy, not in the way the guy on the bus was. He was clean and dressed nicely. His black hair was freshly washed and shiny. There was a seriousness about him and he moved gracefully. He reminded her of some of the others she knew from drama class. He probably read a lot of literary fiction, maybe wrote stories while reciting Dylan Thomas poetry from heart.

"I don't know your name," she finally said. It was lame, but she couldn't think of anything else to ask.

"Daniel."

She wasn't surprised. He looked just like she'd expect a Daniel to look.

"I'm Aries. You know, like the horoscope. But I'm actually a Gemini." It was the standard speech she gave people when introducing herself. Normally she thought it was rather witty, but tonight it sounded stupid. It wasn't the right time to try and make little jokes.

"How ironic."

She couldn't tell if he was mocking her or being clever himself. It was hard to read his expression. His face was unmoving; he didn't seem to have any emotions at all.

A thought occurred to her. There was no one else around. Alive at least. Who knew where Colin ran off to? Probably cowering somewhere, he'd be useless if she needed him anyway. Suddenly she was aware of just how unsafe the situation was. Though she wasn't scared. For some reason her body remained strangely calm. Somehow Daniel made her feel safe even though she knew he could be a threat himself. Maybe it was because he'd already pulled her out from the mountain of bodies. He'd been there for her when she needed it. He seemed truly concerned for her.

The thought made her realize there were others probably worrying about her. Her parents. She reached inside her jacket and clenched her fingers around her useless phone. Were they frantically trying to call her right now? Were they hurt? What if the house hadn't survived the earthquake?

"I should get home and check on my parents," she said. "I need to contact Sara's mom too."

"Do you live far from here?"

"About five miles. But I can walk."

"You'll never make it."

She involuntarily took a step backward.

Daniel was fast. He reached out and grabbed her before she could defend herself. She didn't even get a chance to scream.

"Listen to me, Aries. Something bad is about to happen. Worse than this." He waved his arm around at all the destruction. "It'll make this look like a walk in the park. Don't ask me how I know, I just do. If you don't take cover now, you won't live to see morning. Hell, you probably won't live to see midnight."

"How do you know—"

"Didn't I just tell you not to ask?" He shook his head slightly. "A lot of people are going to die, and it's only the beginning."

Somewhere off in the distance there were screams. Daniel

stiffened and Aries turned around to try and see where the sound was coming from. The sun had almost completely disappeared into the west. The roads were dark; there were no streetlights. Through the twilight she could make out the shapes of people running. They were several blocks away. There were more screams, the sounds of people in agony. One of the shadows stumbled and hit the cement. Others descended on it in a frenzy.

"They're attacking that person."

"They'll come after you, too."

"What? Can't we do something? Call the police?"

"The police can't stop it. No one can. It's too late for that."

"But—"

"Enough. I need you to trust me. I know that's asking for a lot, but you'll have to take a leap of faith. Let me help you."

"Why?"

"Why not?"

"That's not enough of a reason."

"We're beyond reasoning."

"That's not an answer."

Daniel frowned at her. Turning on his heels, he walked a few feet away and then promptly came back. "You're infuriating. Did you know that? Can't you just stop thinking for one second and let me help?"

"Why are you telling me all this?"

"Because I have to tell someone. I can't keep it inside of me. I may not get a second chance."

She almost made a sharp retort but paused. He was scared. Why didn't she see that before? The wideness of his eyes frightened her too, at least enough to stop talking. Behind her, another scream rang out, loud and angry, almost a weird victory shriek. The group of attackers was getting closer. How long before they reached her? She nodded at him, dumbly. She would go along with him for now, while it was still dark and unsafe. She could give him the slip later if she needed to. It might take a few extra hours to get home, but it wasn't like anyone was going anywhere. Hopefully her parents were at home and waiting for her. Mom had told her they had nothing planned. When she didn't show up, surely they'd assume she'd contact them as soon as she could, and at least wait for a while before going out to search for her. If only she could call them. Maybe the landlines were still working. She'd have to find a phone and try.

"Okay." He reached out and took her hand. "Let's find you someplace to hide."

They checked the grocery store first but quickly agreed that it wasn't viable. The front doors were caved in, leaving splinters of glass and rubble. Anyone inside was probably dead or trapped. Even if she did manage to crawl in, she might not be able to get back out. The thought was enough to drive her into a panic.

"There's not much else here," he said. "You need someplace with shelter and food. You might be there for a while."

"We could try the school," she offered.

"Where?"

"A block away," she said. "We were headed there. We had rehearsal. *Alice in Wonderland*. Sara was the Queen of Hearts. She was so excited about it."

A loud bang made her yelp. Gunshots. The group of attackers had reached the accident. They had circled the bus, outnumbering those too injured to run. Through the dimming light, Aries could see the remaining victims trying to get free. One of the men—the bus driver, she thought but wasn't too sure—had a gun. He waved it blindly, sending shots into the air. Two men came at him from behind, bringing him to the ground. Even at a distance she could hear the sound as his head smashed into the pavement. Beyond that, the pregnant woman tried to crawl away until she was dragged back by her hair.

"They're killing them."

Daniel ignored her. "It's time to go." He grabbed her arm. "Show me where the school is."

"It's a block over. That way." She pointed toward the alley behind the grocery store. "But those people need help."

"If you try to help them, you'll die too."

The path before them was pitch-black. Reaching into her bag, she pulled out the miniature flashlight Dad gave her to put on her key chain.

"Here." She removed it and handed it over. "Maybe this will help."

He accepted the tiny metal object, turning it over in his hands before testing the light on the ground between them. "Thanks, but we'd still better stick to the shadows."

Easy enough directions.

The school was dark. She'd never seen it without any lights before. The building rose before them, three stories of eerie silence. She could smell the freshly cut grass; earlier that day she'd seen the gardener riding the mower.

It remained miraculously intact—a bit surprising considering the store beside it was a pile of rubble and the road looked like a construction crew had taken several jackhammers to it. There were five cars in the parking lot, all of them with shattered windows. Whoever owned them wouldn't be driving away anytime soon.

"Why didn't it get destroyed?" she wondered out loud.

"Is it new?" Daniel's voice was calmer than before. Even the tenseness in his shoulders had eased up a bit.

"The school? Yeah, about ten years, I think."

"Earthquake regulations. It's probably reinforced."

"Still. It's creepy."

"But it'll keep you safe. Come on."

They crossed the lawn and headed over to the side where Aries knew the entrance would be unlocked. Just around the corner were the doors that led to the theater. They were supposed to be having rehearsals. There was a good chance that some of her friends would be there. Right about now she could use a familiar face.

As they moved closer she could see that some of the windows were shattered. Bits of grass lay in the flower beds below. Still, there was very little damage considering the quake was so massive.

"Maybe we'll find Colin," she said. "I wouldn't be surprised if the coward came here. I hope he did. I really want to have a word with him."

"You'd be better off if it's empty," Daniel said. "Groups are bad. People do stupid things when they're together."

"But you're here," she said.

"Not for long."

She paused, her hand on the door. "What do you mean? Are you taking off?"

"You'll be safer without me."

Her stomach lurched and ice shot up along her spine. The thought of being alone in the school was enough to bring tears to her eyes. She didn't want to be on her own. She'd freak out. She grabbed hold of his arm, holding on tightly.

"You can't leave me. I need you."

She peered into his eyes, but it was impossible to read his expression in the darkness. Did he really think his being there was going to be dangerous? She couldn't imagine why he believed this. People worked better in pairs, didn't they? Two sets of eyes were better than one. She thought of being alone in the school, in the darkness where anyone would be able to effortlessly sneak up on her. The same panic she'd felt outside the grocery store coated her body, forcing her to shudder involuntarily.

"Please don't leave me," she finally said.

"Fine," he said.

"Promise?"

"Sure."

The school was dark and the silence was heavy in the air. Up ahead she could see that the emergency lights were on in the hallways, so at least there would be a small amount of light. It would help; at least they wouldn't be groping at the walls blindly to try and find the theater.

"It's so quiet," she said.

"That's a good sign," Daniel said.

"We should check the theater first," she said. "There might be people there."

"Where is it?"

"Just down the hall on the right. Follow me."

As they walked, Aries continued to talk. She'd never experienced the school so quiet before, and it creeped her out. At least by talking she could almost block out the eerie silence that was louder than any of the words that escaped her lips.

"Maybe Ms. Darcy will be there," she said. "She's really cool for a teacher. I get good marks in her class. She's the one who's directing *Alice in Wonderland*. Colin was against it, but that's only because there's no male lead. He always wants to be the center of attention. You'll like her. She'll probably know what to do. Not because she's an adult but because she's pretty smart."

She paused when she realized she could hear her own footsteps on the tiled floor but nothing else.

Turning around quickly, she saw nothing but empty hallway.

Daniel was gone.

NOTHING

They know we're here. They're coming for us. What lies beneath has pushed its way to the surface once again. Time to get away while there is still air left in our lungs.

But they will still come.

No matter how much we run and jump and hide.

They've known all along.

It's a game, you see. A simple ploy. If they were to get rid of all of us, then it would be Game Over for all eternity. What fun would that be?

So they will keep some of us alive. Let us breathe and eat and hide. Every now and then they will even let us breed. Then they hunt us anyway. But make no mistake, this is a calculated plot. They will take the ones they need for their future and destroy those they see as worthless.

They have plans for us.

They've already won.

They will remain smart during the annihilation their rage brings.

They walk the riverbed in their fancy clothes and diamond rings. They slouch through the streets with their shopping carts and mismatched shoes. They walk among us, which makes them especially hard to find. A family member perhaps. A lover. A child. This is how they survive and we die out. They are much cleverer than us.

They've been here for a very long time.

Just like animals can sense an earthquake, they felt it coming. They could taste the fear on their lips. It ignited a spark inside of them. Chaos. Perfect, lovable, candy-coated, goes-down-oh-so-sweet anarchy. A time to surge forth. Arrange their massacre. Send out their messengers. Plenty of time for preparation. They gathered their numbers and organized their attack. They didn't even need to RSVP.

It was the perfect plan, and they are the weapons that our leaders keep warning us about. They are the things that hide in your closet and fuel your fear. They lurk in both alleyways and living rooms. They sit across from you at restaurants and push past you to ride the bus.

They are the dark thoughts inside of us we pretend we don't hear. We ignored them but they didn't go away. They grew stronger. Louder. They began to make sense.

I can feel them inside me. The voices are tonguing secrets in my ears that travel down my vertebrae. A thousand squirming insects are chewing on my stomach lining. Mice crawl around inside my intestines. Cockroaches pick at the veins behind my eyes. The voices scream inside my head, but yet they never say more than a whisper. I can't breathe. I can't think.

I'm being eaten alive.

I look forward to death. It will be peaceful compared to this.

MASON

Sometime after two in the morning, Mason's mother drew her last breath. No one noticed or bothered to come. They probably wouldn't know what to do anyway; the morgue was filled to maximum capacity. He hadn't seen a doctor or even an orderly in over six hours. The hospital was in chaos.

Mason was holding her hand when she went. He'd been sitting by her bedside all night, unable to do anything except watch the rise and fall of her chest as the machines helped her breathe.

Thousands of people had died in the past twenty-four hours. Maybe even more—he'd heard nurses talking in the halls about the earthquakes. But he didn't know anyone on the West Coast. Besides, there were more important things on his mind. Hearing about the deaths of strangers didn't fill him with a lot of sadness.

But the bottom dropped out of his world when his mother joined them.

Earlier he'd had the television on to try to gain some understanding. The media was reporting that 123 schools had been bombed. People were screaming words like "terrorism," "mass suicide," and "organized plots," but so far there was nothing to show that the attacks were anything but random.

Then there were the earthquakes, six of them all over the world. Each of them measured at least 9.5 on the Richter scale. The West Coast was utterly destroyed. The quakes caused tsunamis. Rumor had it that most of Hawaii was gone and the casualties in Asia were in the millions.

The television networks were no longer scheduling regular programming. A thousand channels around the world were broadcasting nothing but news.

None of that mattered to Mason as he clung tightly to the cooling hand of his mother.

His friends were all dead. Only a handful had made it out of the school alive. His teachers were dead, even Mr. Yan with his dented Honda Civic.

Something horrible was happening, but Mason was too numb to truly care.

Earlier the taxi dropped him off by the 7-Eleven and he walked over to the school. The situation was surreal; he spent a bit of time wondering if he'd stumbled into someone else's dream. The sky overhead was thick and dark. Above his school was a continuous murky mountain of ash and smoke that sucked up all the scenery. The air burned his throat when he inhaled. It made him light-headed and he tripped over the sidewalk twice until his lungs and brain grew accustomed to the lack of oxygen.

The remains of his high school lay out before him, a pile of rubble and fire. No one even noticed as he crossed over the barriers set out for crowd control and moved toward the gymnasium. The firemen were busy and the police officers were over by the growing crowd of panicky parents and curious onlookers. Ambulances and paramedics rushed about, but there didn't seem to be many survivors left to take to the overcrowded hospital.

Chaos.

There was already a memorial section, and he moved among the lit candles, flowers, and pictures of his former fellow students and friends. He saw Tom's dad talking to another parent while his mother sobbed uncontrollably. Quickly, he moved on before anyone noticed him. He didn't want to have to explain why he was still alive.

The gymnasium was at the rear of the building, and Mason slipped away from the noise, ignoring the heat waves cascading from the destruction. What was he looking for? He couldn't answer that. Maybe there was some tiny bit of hope that a few of his friends might have escaped. But was he really expecting to see them being pulled, miraculously alive, from the rubble?

"I just need to see," he spoke out loud.

The parking lot at the back of the building was eerily empty of people. Hundreds of cars, his own somewhere in that sea of metal and concrete. If someone stopped him he'd say he was there to pick it up. Holding his car keys in the open for evidence, he moved as close to the school as possible, searching for any signs of life.

There were no bloodstains on the sidewalks. No bodies piled on one another for morgue removal. No half-burned books or personal items that might have been thrown through the air during the explosion. Had he been expecting that?

There was nothing to suggest that beneath the debris, hundreds of bodies waited. No proof at all that his school had become a tomb.

He methodically checked around the gymnasium doors to see if there might be a way to slip inside and take a look. But the entire back wall had collapsed, and the only way in were a few cracks big enough for a small animal. Heat poured off the building, burning his face, and the back of his neck grew wet with sweat. Getting down on his knees, he poked through the remains, hoping to find something that might have belonged to one of his friends. Eventually he found a pencil case, bright blue with pink flowers, that looked familiar. Inside were a few pens, an eraser, and a folded note. He opened it.

SEE YOU AT THE MALL
AT FIVE.

Yeah, nope.

No one was meeting anyone at five.

He held the note tightly and reread it several times. *I must be in shock,* he thought. *I've lost all feeling in my body. This is what they mean when they say we go numb inside. Everyone's dead and I don't feel a thing. Mom's dying and all I can do is come down to the school and pick up a pencil case? What the hell's wrong with me? It's like they never existed.*

There it was again, that feeling as if he were in someone else's dream.

"Hey, you." A voice broke through his daze. Off in the distance a fireman was moving steadily toward him. "This is a restricted area. Get the hell away from here."

Mason turned and sprinted toward the parking lot. He found his car exactly where he left it that morning, right beside the blue truck with the broken window. Less than a day had passed, but it felt more like weeks. He'd been happy this morning. Hadn't Tom told him that great joke and made him laugh? They'd been planning a camping trip to Chestnut Lake for the weekend. Swimming, camp fires, some hiking—the kind of stuff he and his friends loved doing.

How did the world change so quickly?

He knew he probably shouldn't be driving in such a weird condition, but it didn't stop him from starting the ignition and pulling the car into reverse. Wheels squealing, he tore out of the parking lot, putting on the sunglasses he'd left on the passenger seat a few hours ago.

He didn't go home. Instead he drove around until his gas tank was nothing but fumes. Stopping to refill, he grabbed a bag of chips that he ate but didn't taste. Glancing at the clock, he decided he'd spent enough time away as the doctor ordered. He headed back to the hospital because there was nothing else he could do.

His mother's hand was so cold. Her body was relaxed; most of the wrinkles she fussed about had disappeared from her motionless face. Her hair fanned the pillow, dark brown like his own, thick and shiny, only a few gray hairs showing her age. She was beautiful, his mother, the woman who'd always been there for him. Two weeks ago he'd given her roses for her birthday and she'd been so happy. They'd gone out for dinner together, but she'd paid the bill. She wouldn't let him treat her when she knew he was saving his money for college.

Gently he touched her cheek and pulled the covers up to her shoulders before he turned off the light and left the hospital.

It was quiet outside. The night air was cool on his face and the moon was half a sliver in the sky. He got into his car and was surprised to see the cashier booth unmanned, with the barrier open. He'd been at the hospital for several hours and probably owed at least twenty bucks for parking. But since no one was there, he left without paying a dime.

There were very few cars on the streets. Everyone was inside, glued to their television or on the phone, desperately trying to reach foreign relatives in faraway places. Hadn't he heard something on television about the phone lines being down in several countries? Could the earthquakes really have caused all that? How many people were out there dialing and getting nothing but dead air? Hundreds or thousands must be desperate for news on their loved ones. Lucky them, at least they still had hope.

Diefenbaker Park was dark and silent. Normally there would be dozens of cars filled with teenagers drinking beers and having a good time. There would be couples parked in the lot that overlooked the river, sharing intimate moments before curfews called them home. Mason came here often with his friends; it seemed natural to him to be there now, and that's why he'd pointed the car in its direction. He hadn't even realized it until he pulled through the gates. Good thing his subconscious was paying attention to the roads. At least he'd put on his seat belt. His life might be over, and everyone he knew might be dead, but at least he didn't seem to have a desire to join them yet.

That had to be a good sign. Right?

He parked the car over by the train bridge and turned the key. The silence filled the car. He had to roll down the window to let some of it out. Is this what going insane felt like?

Eventually his eyes adjusted to the darkness, and the outlines of the trees became less blurry. He wished he had something to drink; something strong that would burn a hole in his stomach and shut down his brain. Back at the house he knew where his mother kept a bottle of whiskey. Why hadn't he thought to bring it with him? It's not like he had to worry about her catching him anymore.

Freeing himself from the seat belt, he got out of the car, slamming the door behind him as hard as he could. The noise echoed across the park, and in the distance an owl hooted.

A few feet away from the car was a garbage can. Mason approached it and kicked it hard. It toppled over, lid rolling away, trash flying. He kicked it again, sending it pivoting, lop-sided, into the middle of the parking lot. Again and again his foot met with plastic, leaving scuff marks and dents against the smooth surface. It emptied quickly, and cans, chocolate wrappers, and bags of dog crap scattered across the ground. He stomped on the cans, crushing them underneath his shoes, spreading bits of gravel, and creating dust clouds.

When he was finished he looked around at the clutter and destruction he'd created but it didn't make him feel better. His car was a few feet away, silent and dark against the night. He moved over toward it and kicked a tire several times in rapid succession. White heat flared through his leg and into his brain. But the pain didn't work the way he wanted it to.

The numbness was still there.

He wanted to feel. Something. Anything. The emptiness inside was worse than anything he'd ever experienced.

He could almost hear Tom's voice taunting him about turning emo. How he wished his friend were there to share his grief, but he was also thankful he was alone. Telling people his mother was dead would make it real. He could almost pretend it wasn't so if he didn't say it out loud.

Gravel crunched behind him and he spun around, half expecting to see a police car. Would they arrest him for destroying the trash can? He'd never vandalized anything before. Sorry, Officer—didn't mean for all that destruction, but my mother and all my friends died today. Isn't that worth a Get Out of Jail Free card?

But it wasn't a cop, just some guy walking across the parking lot toward him. Normally Mason would have turned back to his car without giving the guy a second glance. A lot of people walked throughout Diefenbaker Park late at night, and even the homeless people sometimes curled up on the benches.

But the guy was carrying a baseball bat, and that made Mason take notice.

And he was coming straight for him.

He didn't have time to react properly. The guy crossed the remaining few feet in three strides, raised the bat, and brought it down toward Mason's head. Luckily, Mason instinctively stepped backward, the weapon missing him by inches.

"What the hell?"

The stranger didn't answer. His response was to raise the bat again. Mason took a good look at his face. His lips curled and his eyes burned with hatred, although Mason was positive he'd never seen this person before. Why on earth was he trying to bash in his brains?

Mason moved again but not as quickly. The bat met with his shoulder, the impact vibrating through his entire body. Endorphins flooded to his brain, sending waves of nausea straight to his stomach. All rational thought died. The edge of his vision went blurry and then dark. His arm went instantly limp, dangling uselessly at his side as he swallowed twice, trying to keep the bile from rising in his throat and pouring from his lips.

Mason's knees hit the ground and the stranger raised the bat again. Thoughts jumped through his brain, popping out at him between the pain and dizziness. He was going to die. The nut job with the baseball bat was going to take him down in a matter of seconds and it would be over.

The thought sobered him enough to make him push forward on his legs and slam his body into his opponent. The baseball guy grunted, the first sound he'd made since the attack started, and he took a few steps backward before the weight of Mason's body brought him down. He didn't let go of the weapon, though, and he brought it back up in the air as the two of them struggled.

Mason picked up a handful of dirt and threw it in the guy's eyes. It didn't even make him blink. Using his good hand, Mason reached out and grabbed hold of the baseball bat, desperately trying to keep the guy from using it. A second blow and he'd be done, especially if he took a shot to the head. Shoving forward, he tried to get the upper hand by pressing all his body weight on top of the guy's arm. If he could get him to drop the bat, he'd have a better chance. His car was just five feet away. All he needed to do was get inside and lock the doors. A tiny bit of hope quelled the queasiness in his stomach. He might just get through this.

He didn't want to die.

He was a little surprised to realize this.

But the guy wasn't letting go of the bat without a fight. Mason shifted his leg over until his foot pressed up against the guy's wrist. He managed to bring himself up to his knees and press all his body weight against it, but the weapon stayed firm in the stranger's hand. It was an awkward position, and in a matter of seconds the guy bucked Mason off himself. Falling backward, Mason hit his shoulder against the pavement and white stars filled his vision, bringing with them a wave of dizziness. Rolling over onto his back, he gazed at the guy as he straightened, bat in hand, and situated himself right beside Mason's head.

"What do you want?" Mason mumbled.

The guy didn't say a word. Instead he brought the bat down.

Mason rolled to the left, grabbing the guy's ankle and dragging him down a second time. This time the guy dropped the bat and it bounced against the pavement, making a hollow sound as the aluminum hit the rocky surface. It didn't roll far enough away, though; it was still within reach. Mason managed to bring up his leg and kick out wildly. His foot met with the stranger's nose, and he could actually feel the cartilage breaking beneath his shoe.

Grabbing hold of the guy's jean jacket, Mason pulled himself up against him, like climbing a sideways ladder. His hands caught hair and he didn't stop to think.

He reacted.

The vibration spread up his fingers and into his arms as the head met with concrete. The guy immediately stopped moving.

Mason shoved himself off the body and crab walked backward, stumbling and falling when he tried to put weight on his bad arm. He shuffled along the ground until his head met with his car. Leaning against the smooth metal, he waited apprehensively for the man's body to move.

It didn't.

He lasted about ten seconds before the bile in his stomach pushed its way to the surface. Crawling to his knees, Mason heaved into the dirt. As he puked helplessly, his body tensed, waiting for the moment when the baseball bat would crack against his skull.

Nothing happened.

When it was over and his head had cleared enough to look, he saw that the man was still lying on the ground. Even through the darkness Mason could see the pool of blood spreading from underneath his head.

Had he killed him? Using the car as a crutch, Mason

managed to climb to his feet and stumble the few feet back until he was standing over the stranger. The man faced the sky and his eyes were closed. Mason couldn't tell if he was breathing or not, and he didn't want to lean in closer to get a better look. Picking up the baseball bat, he tossed it as hard as he could. It cleared the parking lot and landed a few feet away in the bushes.

He staggered back to his car and got in. Starting the engine, he winced as he placed his injured arm on the steering wheel. He backed out carefully. Even if the guy was dead, he didn't want to drive over him.

He made it only to the edge of the park before he had to pull over. His hands were shaking so badly he could barely hold on to the wheel. Turning off the car, he waited for the panic to subside.

Had he really just killed a man? Was he a murderer? No, it was done in self-defense. There's no way any court would convict him. But he'd left the scene of the crime. Should he have kept the baseball bat as proof that the guy had a weapon? What if someone came along and took it? A small cry escaped his lips. A man might be dead and the only thing that worried him was whether or not he was going to be arrested?

Shouldn't he be worried about the stranger's family? Should he try and find them? Wouldn't they be worried?

He realized he didn't care. There was no empathy in his brain.

Was he that dead inside?

He knew he should go to the police, but it was the last thing in the world he wanted to do. He made sure the doors were locked before he closed his eyes and leaned his head back.

He'd be better once he slept for a bit.

CLEMENTINE

There had been screams.

Begging. Pleading.

Agony.

Then silence.

Around four in the morning the gunshots finally ended. Shortly after that the screaming winded down and soon there was silence. No more voices. The only sounds were the crickets and wind echoing through the rafters.

Clementine was hiding in the barn. She had run the mile to her house, but when she'd arrived, she'd known immediately it wasn't safe. Whatever had happened to her parents and the folks at the town hall was happening to all the citizens of Glenmore. And Sam let her go free. He warned her specifically not to go home. Her house would be the first place they'd search if they came for her.

Scratch that. *When* they came for her.

It was just a matter of time.

Dear Heath, I promised myself I wouldn't think about them until I'm safe. Help me find a way out of this and then I'll allow myself to fall apart.

She had stood outside her house wondering what to do. It didn't take long to decide to hide in the barn. She had plenty of time afterward to regret that decision. She could have grabbed her cell phone and called someone. She should have taken the keys to the truck. If she had done that she'd be on the road and halfway to Des Moines by now. She could have gotten help. She could have run into the fields and taken cover in the corn. It would have provided better shelter in the long run.

Because she knew that the second they finished searching the house they'd come and check the barn.

Stupid! Stupid! Stupid!

She was trapped. The time to run had been hours ago while they were still busy at the town hall. Her parents' farm was right on the edge of town. They'd be getting close by now.

How many of them were there? She'd been too panicky to count. There had to be at least a dozen, maybe more. These were people she'd grown up with. Sam. He'd helped her dad repair a fence less than a week ago. He'd been in a good mood and she'd given him lemonade and some of her mother's cookies.

All these people she thought she knew. There were memories attached to all of them. Good memories. What happened to change them into killers?

She needed to get into the house. She didn't even have to go that far. The keys were in the fruit basket on the kitchen table, ten feet from the back door. She could be in and out in less than thirty seconds.

But every time she tried to convince her brain of the logic of moving, her legs refused to participate.

Dear Heath, remember last summer, before you went off to college? You told me if there was ever an issue with guys I could call you and you'd come instantly and rough them up. Well, I've got some problems and could use a bodyguard right about now. Your tough baby sister isn't as strong as she thought she was. In fact, she's turning out to be quite the marshmallow. People keep telling her to run and she goes the distance. Should have signed up for cross-country this year. I'd be heading for the Olympics in no time. Do they have a gold medal for being cowardly?

If only telepathy worked.

What was that stupid mantra that Imogene was always chanting? *I'm a strong and beautiful woman. Everything I touch will turn to gold.*

Yeah, and *I must, I must, I must increase my bust.*

A cracking noise outside the barn, and her heart instantly doubled up. Someone was standing outside the doors. They'd found her.

No, they hadn't found her. *Stop overreacting*. She needed to get control of herself; otherwise she'd jump up the minute they walked through. Hey! Here I am! Over here!

Remain calm. Count backward from twenty to try to slow her breathing. Push her heart back down her throat and force it into submission. She could do this. Her hiding spot in the corner was good. She'd managed to cover herself adequately with hay and an old horse blanket. On first glance she probably looked like a big lump of nothing. Didn't the heroine always go up into the rafters in the horror movies? Staying on the ground would give her leverage. When the killer went up to search the dead end, she would slip quietly out the door. She would run into the house and grab the keys and be on her way before the killer even knew she was gone. She'd go to the police in Des Moines and they'd send out the army or the FBI, and Sam, Henry, James, and the rest of the not-so-God-fearing nutcases of Glenmore would be arrested.

And for Christmas she'd get a pony and a Porsche.

They had guns. She may be fast, but there was no way she could outrun a bullet.

The noise came again. She'd been so busy fantasizing that she barely heard it. But it was there, a tiny scratching sound. Footsteps crunching in the dirt. A small cough. She covered her mouth with her hands.

There was a loud noise as someone grabbed hold of the doors and slid them open. More footsteps. She couldn't tell if it was one person or two and she wasn't stupid enough to pop her head up and check. It had to be just one. If there were two they'd be talking to each other. But who was it?

From her hiding spot under the blanket, she could just make out the five feet of flooring in front of her. Why hadn't she thought to try to reposition herself where she could get a better view of the door? She waited, her ears perked for what might be coming.

The person began moving toward the middle of the barn. They were taking their time, small unrushed steps, obviously in no hurry to kill her. They had to know she was there. Maybe they could smell her fear?

The person began to whistle. *Oh my darling, oh my darling, oh my darling, Clementine.* How she hated that song. Heath used to sing it to her whenever he wanted to annoy her.

She should have grabbed a weapon. Anything. There were so many other courses of action she could have taken. Instead she'd managed to pretty much serve herself up on a platter. She sure was living up to that blond-cheerleader stereotype.

A few weeks ago someone e-mailed a joke questionnaire on how to survive a zombie attack. She'd scored pretty high. Of course she'd stated she'd head down to the local weapons store and arm herself before holing up in an isolated cabin in the north. Okay, so it wasn't the best thing to use as a comparison to how well she could do in a real-life emergency situation, but the whole concept kept creeping into her mind. What a joke. She couldn't even survive a few hours up against psychotic humans.

The whistler moved slowly and steadily across the barn. At least she'd been smart enough to hide in a corner close to the door. As he passed her she fought the urge to move. She was like a mouse being hunted by an eagle. She needed to stay still and not jump and flee. Running blind never served the mouse justice, and it probably wouldn't work for her.

Funny how her legs had refused to work earlier, and now they were itching to kick.

Dear Heath, you were right. If I get out of this alive I'll take those tae kwon do lessons you said I needed. Just promise me you'll be here to help me get those punches right. Give me a sign to let me know you're not just a figment of my imagination and are still alive and well in Seattle. It'll give me the courage to kick ass. I promise.

She needed to stop this. Talking to her maybe/more-than-likely dead brother wasn't going to help the situation.

Meanwhile the whistler had grown quiet. She strained her ears, listening. Was he gone? Had he slipped back out the door while she was making all her imaginary resolutions?

No, there it was again—the sound of a boot scraping against wood from across the barn. Her assailant was climbing the ladder to the rafters. All she had to do was wait until he reached the top and she could get out. Moving as slowly as she could, she pushed the blanket off her head to get a better view. The doors to the barn were wide-open. She could slip out without making a sound.

Her assailant swung his foot up onto the beams. The creaking noise above was the signal she was waiting for. It was now or never. Carefully she pulled back the blanket and scanned the area. The barn floor was empty. She didn't even look at the rafters. She forced herself to walk quietly instead of run, fully aware that her back was like one giant target. There were no shouts or sudden footfalls. No one rushed toward her. She moved quickly but cautiously. One misplaced step, one creaky board, could end it.

Outside the air was cool on her face. She had forgotten to breathe. She inhaled heavily, and her wobbly legs continued to hold her weight. Avoiding the urge to lean against the barn and rest, she forced herself to keep moving. She would get the keys. The truck was hidden on the other side of the house. Whoever was in the barn would probably be there for at least ten more minutes. With a little luck she'd be able to start the car and be halfway down the lane before he got out of the rafters.

It was one hundred feet from the barn to the house. She could see the porch light burning. Turning it on was the last thing her mother had done before they left for the town hall. She always left it on no matter how much her father grumbled over the electric bill. They would never wait up for her again.

Dear Heath, I've really gone and messed things up. It's not like an exam where I can take notes. I don't get a chance to repeat this if I fail. Help me reach the truck. Give me strength, brother.

One hundred feet. Not far at all. But it was similar to crossing the open sea, and she didn't have any shark repellent.

It was time to go. No time like the present. If she waited too long it would be game over. She began to run, silently cursing herself every time her foot hit the grass. She couldn't be making that much noise. She was light enough to always be on the top of the cheerleading pyramid, and her mother was constantly complaining that she needed to gain a few pounds to fill out properly.

When she reached the safety of the house, she was overcome with such relief that she almost broke down in tears. Instead she forced herself onward, making her way around the side to the back.

Her hands were shaking as she unlocked the back door. The interior of the house was dark. Mom may have left the porch light on, but Dad had the sense to make sure the house wasn't burning any extra electricity. Leaving the key in the lock, she crossed the kitchen in three strides. She reached blindly into the fruit basket until she felt the leather key chain. Mom's address book was open on the table. She ripped Heath's address out as quietly as possible, folded the piece of paper, and stuck it in her pocket. Now all she had to do was get back out to the truck.

"Clem?"

She nearly peed herself.

Craig Strathmore stepped out from the shadows beside the fridge. His eyes were wide and unsure. His hands were clasped together and pressed against his stomach, white-knuckled in an awkward prayer. There was a small gash under his right eye; blood was smeared across his cheek from where he'd wiped it.

"Thank God it's you," he said. "I was looking for you."

"Craig? What happened? Why are you here?"

He looked down at his feet before taking another step forward. "Town hall. They're all dead. I don't understand. Henry Tills killed my parents. Shot them down. I mean, I've known him my entire life. My dad bowled with him. How could he do that?"

"I don't know."

"I slipped. Henry raised the gun at me and I slipped. Wet floor. Fell. The shot missed me by inches. He would have gotten a second chance, too, but he got distracted by my mother. Killed her. Right in front of my eyes."

"I'm sorry."

"I saw you sneak out the doors. I didn't know where else to go. I hoped maybe I could find you. I don't understand. Why are they doing this?"

"I don't know. But we've got to get out of here."

"Okay. Where are we gonna go?"

"Des Moines. The police will know what to do. We have to hurry. Someone's in the barn looking for me. You're lucky they didn't find you first."

"I'm scared," he whispered. His voice shuddered, and he closed his eyes tightly, his forehead crinkling into tiny lines. He'd aged twenty years in the course of a single evening. He opened his arms and waited, looking like a small child awakened from a bad dream.

There were dark stains on his letterman jacket, and it took her a few moments to realize it was blood. He was covered in it.

She didn't know what to do. How much time did they have?

Holding out her arms, she embraced him. She couldn't do anything else. She was helpless. His hands wrapped around her, resting on the small of her back, fingers cold and stiff on top of her jacket.

They rocked back and forth on the linoleum floor. He held her tight, desperately; she could feel the tautness of his chest pressing against her. Muscular arms gripping, pressing weight against her body. His head dropped down to rest against the curve of her neck. He exhaled into her hair; lips puckered and tasted her skin.

"Craig?"

"Yes?"

"You need to let go now."

"And if I don't?"

She tried to pull back. Fingernails dug into her jacket, gouging her back. He drew her in closer than she would have believed possible, lips pressed against her ear. He began to whistle.

Oh my darling, oh my darling, oh my darling Clementine.

She would have liked to scream but her throat closed. All the air inside her lungs was vacuumed out of her body.

"What's the matter, darling Clementine?"

She twisted her body, let her legs go slack, tried to worm her way out from his grasp. But he wasn't letting go. She clawed at the back of his jacket, his arms; she couldn't reach high enough to scratch at his face. He had made her his prisoner and she'd welcomed the embrace.

Stupid! Stupid! Stupid!

"You should have heard your mother's screams," Craig whispered in her ear. "They were exquisite. How she cried."

This was not Craig. This person holding her was not the guy she knew. Two months ago they'd been driving and hit a raccoon. The Craig she'd grown up with had pulled over to the side of the road and gotten misty-eyed. He may have been a football star, but he loved animals and was a vegetarian. The boy she knew would never get off on trying to scare her like this.

"Who are you?" she asked. There was something odd about his eyes. They were darker. At first she thought the shadows were playing tricks on her. But that wasn't it. The veins were black.

"I'm Craig."

"No, you're not."

"I'm the darkest corner of his soul. I'm all the things he

wanted to be, everything he dared to think when no one else was around. I'm the real Craig Strathmore. I'm his evolution. His true self."

"No. You're. Not." Raising her foot, she slammed her heel down onto the side of his leg. Craig grunted and loosened his grip just enough for her to slide out of his grasp. She dropped to the floor, reached out, and grabbed the first thing she found, which happened to be the paperweight her mother used to keep the kitchen door open. She brought it up and drove it straight into his knee.

Craig grunted both in surprise and pain. She climbed to her feet and started for the door, but he grabbed her ankle, bringing her back to the floor and cracking her knee on the linoleum. Her cartilage made an awful thunking noise, but she stumbled on, ignoring the pain and kicking out at him with her uninjured leg. He brought his arms up to defend his face, freeing her for one quick moment.

It took her a total of three seconds to get outside. Pressing the unlock button on the key chain, she threw open the car door and climbed into the cab. The engine came to life on the first try, and she turned on the headlights before putting the truck into gear.

The driveway to her parents' house was filled with people. There were at least a dozen of them, standing completely still and staring back at her. She recognized Henry and James Tills, Sam Anselm, and some of the others she'd seen earlier at the parking lot. Their clothing was wet with blood, black and shiny in the moonlight.

They were blocking the road.

Craig Strathmore, or whoever he was now, came out onto the front porch, limping, his eyes blazing, and heading directly toward her.

She didn't need a road. She hadn't been raised on a farm for nothing. Putting the car into first gear, she pressed hard on the gas, spun the wheel, and drove directly into the cornfields. It was a bumpy ride but the truck had four-wheel drive for a reason.

She didn't look in the rearview mirror to see if they were following her.

It was two miles to the road through the fields. She made it in record time. Her tires crunched as they spun up onto the highway. She pointed the car in the direction leading away from Glenmore.

She drove for an hour before finally pulling over to the side. There was no other traffic. She hadn't seen a single vehicle.

Dear Heath, there's something weird going on. The earthquakes were scary enough, but then the news started reporting all this violence. I didn't really believe it until tonight. It's everywhere, isn't it? Whatever it is, once I'm done in Des Moines I'm coming to find you. It was what Mom wanted, and I'll grant her that last wish. So you'd better not be dead. I'll be there as soon as I can. I'll be mad if you go on without me. Don't leave me alone like this.

She turned on the radio but couldn't find a station. Nothing but static. She played with the dials for about ten minutes, even climbed out of the truck to check the antenna.

It was as if she were the last person on earth.

MICHAEL

He awoke to the last rays of the western sun warming his pillow. Sweat covered his body, enough to soak the hairs behind his ears, and his upper body felt slightly damp. He hadn't meant to fall asleep; in fact he was shocked he'd done it. A few hours ago he didn't think he'd ever close his eyes again. After Evans dropped him off, he couldn't stop pacing. Every few minutes he'd look out the window, heart pounding, muscles stiff enough to shatter. After an hour or so, he didn't know what else to do so he lay down for a bit to try and clear his head.

Getting up off the bed, he stumbled into the living room, tripping over the bag of garbage he'd placed by the door but forgot to take out that morning.

The television still wasn't broadcasting, and he didn't even bother to check the Internet. In the kitchen he turned on the coffeepot and then went over to the window to take a look. A part of him still believed that the two officers were going to show up at his doorstep any minute, ready to finish him off because of the crimes he'd witnessed.

But the street was empty. Whitefish seemed to have shut down early.

They hadn't gone straight home after dropping Joe off. Instead, he and Evans had driven to the police department and found it empty. No cars in the parking lot. The front doors were locked. They'd banged on the glass, but no one came.

Since when was a police department allowed to shut down?

Michael had tried his phone again, but still nothing. Evans said he'd talked to several people and they all repeated the same thing. Nothing electronic had been working properly since the earthquakes. Phones, Internet, television, and even the radio. All forms of communication were erratic or on the blink.

"It's like something's making things and people go crazy," Evans said. "I was out by Great Falls yesterday. It's happening there, too. A bunch of idiots killed each other during a bar brawl."

"You think so? Is that even possible?"

"Dunno," Evans said. He smacked his fist against the car radio, but there was nothing but static. "We need information. Didn't you notice? There weren't any updates today. Just the same prerecorded crap on a constant loop. You know it's scary when the reporters stop broadcasting."

Michael was surprised.

"How can there be no news?" he asked.

"I don't know," Evans said. "But it's bad. We're being kept in the dark. My guess is what happened back there on the road isn't isolated. I think a hell of a lot more people are going to die."

Michael played the conversation over in his mind as he looked out the window. At the time he'd thought it was a bit overdramatic. Now he wasn't so sure. Normally, this time of evening there would be people walking around on the street. But he couldn't see anyone.

Definitely odd.

From the apartment below him, he heard the muffled sound of their door buzzer. No accompanying footsteps followed it. He poured some coffee and added a lot of sugar. There was no milk in the fridge. He would have to remember to buy some tomorrow.

Heading back to his bedroom, he paused at the front door when he heard another door buzzer, this time from his neighbor's apartment. He checked through the peephole to make sure no one was there before unlocking the door and stepping out into the hallway. His apartment faced the back, so there was no way to know who was at the front door unless he checked the window at the end of the hallway. Another buzzer went off; this time the muffled noise came from his neighbor in 415. Still no one answered. He began to think he was the only one left in the building.

He wasn't so sure he wanted to know who was out there. Stepping back inside his apartment, he double locked the door. Crossing the floor, he put his coffee mug down on the table. He turned and stared at his own intercom.

BBBUUUUZZZZZZ

He almost screamed like a girl. Recoiling back from the door, he tripped over the garbage a second time, falling backward and landing on his backside. The sheer terror of the situation caused him to bray loudly, like some sort of deranged donkey.

"Ohcrapohcrapohcrapohcrap."

Pulling himself up to his feet, he moved over toward the intercom, part of him desperately wanting to push the button. But the other half of him screamed, because wasn't it better to let them think he wasn't home? The receiver stuck out at him like it had a great big Don't Touch sign on it.

BBBUUUUZZZZZ

He couldn't help himself. He had to know.

Fingers pressing, he could hear the sound of outside air come through the tiny speakers. He didn't say anything; he didn't know how to respond.

"Hello?" The voice was slightly gargled. "I'm looking for someone. Michael. He lives in this building."

Evans.

"Hey," Michael said. "It's me. I'll let you in. Four-twelve."

He could hear the weird vibrating sound as the door unlocked. Evans muttered something, but he didn't catch it. A few minutes later when the knock came at his door, he peeked through the eyehole to make sure Evans was alone.

He was.

"What's wrong?" Michael opened the door, and Evans brushed past him as if he couldn't get inside fast enough. Michael closed the door and locked it. Whatever was chasing him might not be that far behind.

"Have you been outside?" Evans asked.

Michael shook his head. "I've been home since you dropped me off. Why? What's going on?"

"The entire town's gone crazy. They've blocked the roads. People in cars. They're not letting anyone in or out of town. They're shooting anyone who tries. Those cops we saw earlier. They're dead. Someone lynched them."

"What?"

"They're all dead," Evans continued. "They're pulling people out of their homes. Chasing them down in the streets. A group of them torched the supermarket. It started about an hour ago. I was at the gas station trying to call my wife from a pay phone. Some guy came after me with a crowbar."

"But . . ."

"I think I killed him. Don't look at me like that. What was I supposed to do? Gray-haired or not, he had a crowbar. Tried to splatter my brains across the walls. I had no other choice."

"Okay." Michael kept his mouth open, but nothing else came out. Instead he went back over to the door and double-checked the lock.

"Look." Evans started pacing around the cramped living room. "I've been driving around. I didn't know where else to go. My wife. I can't get ahold of her. I've got a little girl, too. You've gotta help me. I need to get home to them. I don't know what to do. They've barricaded the roads. I can't get out."

"Okay. Where's your wife?"

"Somers. Right on the lake."

Michael nodded. "I've been there. That's not very far."

"How are we supposed to get there? We can't go by car."

"There's got to be a way," Michael said. "There are other roads. They can't have barricaded them all."

"You don't get it, kid." Evans stomped over to the window and pointed out at the street. "It's psycho out there. They're killing everyone. It's only a matter of time till they find us.

"It's the earthquakes," Evans said. "Something happened that's . . ." He paused. "Something's turned people."

"But we're both fine," Michael said.

"For how long?"

Michael went over to the phone and picked it up. Tried calling his mother's number. Nothing. Suddenly, more than anything else in the world he wanted to hear her voice. He'd be satisfied with a recorded message saying she wasn't home. But he couldn't even get that.

What about Dad? Was he okay? He was supposed to get back from Denver in a few days. They were going to the football game this weekend. The tickets were on his dresser.

"I need to get home," Evans said. "My wife. My daughter. She's only two."

"Maybe I can help you," he said. He looked over at the fishing rods leaning against the couch.

He didn't want to go outside. More than anything he wanted to crawl into bed, pull up the covers, and wait for this whole thing to blow over. The lock on their door was strong and there was more than enough food to keep him alive for several weeks. But he knew Dad would be disappointed in him if he took the cowardly way out. Especially when there were children involved who needed help.

He took a deep breath. "I know a way out of here. We can walk." Michael went over to the window and saw that the street below was still empty. "There are trails not too far from here. I know of a few that loop around back to the highway. They'll take us about five miles from town. There are ski resorts out that way. We might be able to find a working phone or even someone who can give us a ride."

Evans nodded.

"Just let me get some stuff. I think we've got a flashlight kicking around. Not sure about batteries. There's water in the fridge. Why don't you grab it and whatever else you can find in the cupboard?"

Michael was surprised at how calm he felt. He went into the den, where he was pretty sure he'd last seen the flashlights. Sure enough, he found two of them in the back of the closet. Both of them worked.

Evans had reached out for him and Michael had found the solution. The fact that the older man needed help was the very thing that was keeping Michael from falling apart. His mother was like that, always the one to take control in serious situations. Although he hadn't seen her in years, he couldn't help but think she'd be proud of him for helping this man in his time of need.

Back in the living room, Evans seemed much better. He'd grabbed the water and shoved it into the backpack Michael gave him.

"We don't need much," he said. "There's tons of gas stations along the road. We'll be able to find what we need. It shouldn't take us more than a few days tops, even less if we can catch a ride with someone."

"You sure you won't get us lost?" Evans asked.

"I grew up here," Michael said. "I know the woods." He grabbed his jacket and put it on. "I need to go check on Joe first. Do you just want to hang out here? It won't take long. I know a good shortcut."

"Don't," the older man said. "I went there first."

Michael noticed that Evans's hands were shaking. There was dried blood on his fingers from when he got attacked by the guy with a crowbar. "Was it bad?" he finally asked.

Evans nodded.

Joe had three younger sisters. His parents were cool. Michael turned away from Evans, not wanting the man to see the tears burning in his eyes.

"What about your family?" Evans asked. "Any idea where they are? Should you leave a note? I mean, how old are you anyway?"

"My dad's in Denver," he said, trying to keep his voice from trembling. "At this point there isn't much I can do about him. I can't reach him on the phone and he's not due back for a few more days. I haven't seen my mom or sister in years. Mom's remarried. They're out east. And I'm seventeen."

"Good God, you're just a kid."

"Hey, you asked me for help."

Evans put his hands up. "I didn't mean it that way. You just seem a lot older. At seventeen, I'd probably have been hiding in the closet and sucking my thumb through something like this."

The comment made Michael feel oddly proud. He put his hand on Evans's shoulder. "We'll get through this. We'll find your wife and child."

MASON

Mason couldn't sleep. He moved across the house in the dead of night, the almost empty whiskey bottle firm in his fingers. He was drunk but it wasn't a good time. Happy hour was over.

There were pictures on the walls, chronicles of his life:

—Disneyland when he was seven. He cried because he wasn't tall enough to ride Space Mountain.

—A five-year-old Mason wearing his dress shirt and tie for his cousin's wedding. He'd been the ring bearer. Someone had spilled red wine on him just before he walked down the aisle. He'd cried.

—A baby with a bright red nose, laughing while playing in the bathtub. One of the rare times he hadn't cried.

—A picture of him and a bunch of his friends on the first day of high school. Tom had his arm around him. They'd dropped by the house after class and Mom had made the whole group sandwiches without complaining. A bunch of happy, hungry teenagers.

—Seventeen and standing in front of his new car. Okay, it wasn't new but he had been thrilled just the same. He'd saved up for it for a year by working part-time at the mall. Mom had come through at the last minute and chipped in a few grand so he'd buy something safe and not a relic from the eighties.

—Mason at four. Back when Dad was still alive. In the picture, his mother was holding him, they were both wearing sunglasses, and he had on Dad's baseball cap, which was several sizes too big. Mom looked so happy; her hair was loose and blowing in the breeze. Dad had taken the picture, and afterward they walked along the beach holding hands. The tide was out and Dad picked up some of the heavier rocks so that Mason could watch the baby crabs scuttle away. Afterward they had fried shrimp, and Mom laughed because Mason thought the marinara sauce was ketchup and poured it over his fries.

The picture slipped from his hands. He watched it drop in slow motion and hit the ground, the glass cracking across his mother's face. Dropping to his knees, he picked up the broken frame and shook away the glass, fingers trembling; he removed the picture from its casing and turned it over so he could read the inscription.

STANLEY PARK. SECOND BEACH.
VANCOUVER, BC, MASON AND MOM—
ENJOYING THE SUN.

He couldn't stand to look at it anymore. His eyes scanned the room, desperately seeking something else to grab his attention. Immediately he found his reflection in the darkened flat screen.

The television was no longer broadcasting.

Sometime around two the stations went off the air. There

was no warning. No emergency broadcast system. No lecture on how this was a test, only a test. Everything went dead, and black filled the screen.

The Internet was down too.

He didn't even bother to check his cell phone.

Before it went off the air the television was full of questions. News announcers told people to remain calm while glancing agitatedly offscreen. Stay inside. Lock your doors. If you feel you can't be alone or that you're in danger, call the local police for a listing of safe areas to relocate.

Remain calm.

Helicopter reporters circled the skies, their cameras shooting footage of riots in the bigger cities like New York and Chicago. People were behaving erratically all over the world, even in places where the earthquakes hadn't hit. Don't panic. Los Angeles was gone. All electronic communication was halted. No one knew the exact extent of the damage. A few reports came in from Seattle and Portland. The cities were in ruins. The death count was immeasurable.

Don't panic.

Something was happening to the citizens of the United States and the rest of the world. People were going crazy. Hurting each other. They were bombing schools and government centers. Strangers were setting things on fire. Reports of shooting sprees at restaurants and hospitals were popping up. Children were being hunted down in playgrounds and preschools. People were attacking randomly at both loved ones and complete strangers. The melted bag of frozen peas on the couch was testament to the last one. No matter how much Mason drank, his shoulder still hurt. Several times during the evening he stood in front of the bathroom mirror and moved his arm as much as he dared. He flexed his fingers and worried about the swelling and bruising when he took off his shirt. He'd toyed with the idea of going back to the ER but didn't think he'd even get through the doors. He wondered if his mother was still in the intensive care ward, dead and forgotten. Was her body stiff by now? Rigor mortis lasted only so long, didn't it? Maybe her body was soft again, slowly decaying, cellular structures breaking apart, and there was no one there to put her in cold storage down in the morgue. She might never get a burial; instead the hospital bed would become her tomb. Would she mummify? Or would she simply rot away?

He should go back and get her. There was a shovel in the garage; he could bury her in the garden. It might not be as glamorous or sacred as a cemetery, but his options were slim. He couldn't bear to see her body again, though. What if it was already bloated? What if he'd been wrong and she'd still been alive? What if she was dying right now and calling out his name and he was selfishly pissing away her only bottle of whiskey? No, he couldn't go back. He just wanted to stop thinking. It was easier that way. The numbness hadn't left him; if anything it was spreading. When he looked at the pictures, there was no emotion, even though he knew there should be. He should be sad.

But he wasn't.

He felt nothing.

The drinking didn't help.

Somewhere in the darkest recess of his brain, a button was pushed. Everything he cared about simply vanished. He'd malfunctioned.

It was better this way, or at least that's what he told himself. Caring only led to heartbreak. He'd probably be curled up on the floor in his bedroom, crying like a baby, if it weren't for the numbness. This way he was able to still function, or he would tomorrow morning once he sobered up.

He was done mourning.

It was time to act. Whatever was happening was going to continue. He needed to find someplace safe if he was going to survive, a nice rustic cabin in the mountains where he could silently wait the whole thing out. Maybe he could find a beach, become a castaway where the sun could warm his body. He'd do it alone; he didn't want people around. They'd only hold him back. He didn't need anyone.

All he had to do was burn his bridges.

There was a gasoline can in the garage for the lawn mower. Drunkenly, he stumbled out to find it in the corner underneath some tarps. Back in the house he started with his bedroom. A clean start would make everything better. There was nothing he wanted. He sprinkled his bed with a healthy dose of the flammable liquid and then moved on. Next were the guest room and the bathroom. He passed his mother's bedroom—no need to go in there. He briefly considered taking her jewelry but then decided against it. It's not like he'd be able to sell it. The odds that the pawn shops might be open during this crisis were laughable. Downstairs he soaked the television and the couch. In the kitchen he baptized the microwave, table, and curtains. Methodically he moved from room to room until he finally ran out of gasoline. It was enough; he'd managed to do sufficient damage. When he lit the match the entire house would burn. Maybe he could roast marshmallows.

Back in the living room, he dropped the canister on the floor and looked around for the whiskey bottle. He found it, but somehow he'd tipped it over and the last remaining liquid had spilled out and stained the carpet. His brain became assaulted with white noise. Darkness clouded his vision. He couldn't even think straight enough to try and step back and figure out where the rage came from. Picking the bottle up off the floor, he blindly hurled it at the wall. It smashed against the television, cracking the screen and sending bits of glass across the floor.

It wasn't enough. Over at the wall he tore down the pictures. One by one, he slammed them to the floor, stomping on the frames and grinding the glass into dust beneath his heel. The bookshelves were next: Mom's paperback collection. He pulled them down, tearing the covers off and crushing the contents inside. The vase he'd given her was thrown at the fireplace, her plate collection used like Frisbees. In the kitchen he toppled the refrigerator, hurled the chairs out the window, uprooted the plants, and used the silverware for target practice.

He began to cry. Big whooping sobs that consumed him, blinded him, but still he carried on. He almost made it to the bedrooms but collapsed on the stairs when his legs refused to keep moving. Closing his eyes, he felt the rage disappear as quickly as it had come, and he was left there sobbing on the carpet, his back against the railing, completely unsure of what he'd just done.

When there was nothing left inside, he laid his head down on the carpet and stared at the wooden railing. He was even emptier than before. How was it possible that hollowness could dig so deep?

Breathing heavily, he wiped his nose with the back of his sleeve.

It was late and he was tired. He couldn't remember what he was going to do. The smell of gasoline was strong, but there was no memory of why.

Eyes closed, his body gained a few hundred pounds. It was too much effort to do anything except lie there awkwardly. All he needed was a few minutes, and then he'd get back up and do whatever he was supposed to do.

He slept. There were no dreams.

When he woke the next morning, his head was pulsating from the whiskey and the fumes. Picking himself up off the stairs, he couldn't remember how he got there. All he could remember was taking the whiskey bottle from its hiding spot and the first few swigs. His back was all messed up from sleeping crooked; he must have pinched a nerve. His shoulder throbbed; he could barely move his arm. Stumbling, wincing, grabbing his head with his good hand, he made his way into the bathroom to find some medicine.

In the mirror a worn-out person stared back at him. There were black circles under his eyes and his hair was tangled. Taking off his shirt, he winced when he saw the black-and-purple pattern across his shoulder. He splashed some water on his face, and the coolness quenched his skin. He chewed down two Tylenol without taking a drink.

The living room was a disaster. Everything was destroyed or lying on the ground. He was pretty sure he'd done it. But he couldn't remember exactly.

Did he pour the gasoline?

The Stanley Park picture was on the ground, and he picked it up, turning it over in his hands so he didn't have to see the smiling faces. Folding it carefully, he tucked it into his back pocket.

Mom and Mason in Stanley Park.

He'd felt safe there.

It would be nice to see Vancouver again.

The kitchen was worse. He wandered from room to room trying to retrace the steps he'd taken, but his mind was a blank slate. In his bedroom he tried turning on the television, but none of the channels were working. His cell phone said there was no signal.

The world was in chaos. He remembered that much. In the hospital his mother was rotting on a bed. Had anyone come to take her away?

He grabbed his jacket and car keys. If he was going to survive this, he needed to be where he could get news. The whole world couldn't be cut off. There had to be other normal people out there. He'd find them.

But he wouldn't care. Never again would he get close to someone. They'd only leave him, and he was going to do whatever it took to outlive this war. This sickness. Apocalypse? Who cared what it was. Out of sheer defiance he'd beat it.

He paused at the front steps before he left. The match lit on the first strike. The flame hurt his eyes, made his heartbeat throb at the back of his brain. He set the packet ablaze and dropped it in the closest gasoline puddle.

From the safety of the car he watched the flames eat away at the living room blinds. The street was completely empty; no one witnessed his crime. He didn't know if his neighbors were hiding away behind closed doors or if they'd fled like he was about to do. He didn't really care.

Something was happening to him. Mason didn't know what it was, but deep down inside his soul, he was changing. A tiny voice in the farthest corners of his mind was whispering things he wanted to hear, forcing him to behave in a way that was foreign to him. A new Mason.

"I'm going crazy," he said. The words echoed through the car.

He floored the gas pedal and, tires peeling, backed out into the street. As he drove off he didn't bother to take one last look at his house going up in flames.

ARIES

She stood in the hallway and wondered what to do next. Now that Daniel was gone, bravery leaked right out of her body and onto the cold tiled floor. The theater was only a few steps away, but her feet no longer wanted to move. They were stuck to the floor by all the panicky substances discharging from her pores.

He'd promised he wouldn't leave her.

What else did he lie about?

How long had she continued talking once he sneaked off? She'd been babbling away for a while, trying to avoid a horrendous panic attack. It took all the self-control she had to keep from screaming or bursting into tears. But it was better than the alternative. There was something terrifying about all the silence, and filling it with sound was her way of keeping sane. Now that she had no one to talk with, she could hear the stillness creeping in at her from all directions. Taking a deep breath, she continued on toward the theater. If there were people there, she'd become calmer. Daniel had lectured on the dangers of groups, but he'd forgotten about the comfort level of friends. It cut down on the silence. Someone would know what to do.

Right?

But somehow, deep down inside she knew Daniel was correct. Bad things were happening. They were going to get worse.

There were six people in the theater. They were huddled together in the first two rows. All eyes turned to Aries as she descended the steps. At least the emergency lighting was still working. The theater was dim and heavily coated with shadows, but she could make out the faces of her classmates.

"Aries?" Jack King stood up from his chair to get a better view, his sandy brown hair illuminated by the emergency lighting above him. He had the role of the White Rabbit.

"Thank God you're here." That was Becka Philips. She was the Mad Hatter. Colin had pitched a fit when she was given the part. It was the role he wanted, and he couldn't handle the idea that a girl was taking the other lead. He'd spent the whole week mumbling about sexism.

Speaking of Colin, he was sitting in the first row, being comforted by Amanda Steeves, the lighting technician. Aries's first reaction was to do something dramatic: walk up to him and slap him for leaving her to find Sara. But she managed to retain her calm. It wouldn't bring Sara back, and all she'd do was make a scene. She knew his character; it was exactly what she'd have expected of him. Sara may have overlooked his obvious flaws, but Aries wasn't fooled. Colin was not someone she could trust.

"Are you hurt?" That was Ms. Darcy, the drama teacher.

"I'm fine," she said.

"Were you in it?" Becka asked as she came over to give Aries a hug. "We were in here when it happened. The whole building shook. Ms. Darcy wouldn't let us go outside to check. Did you see the cars in the parking lot? They're all trashed. And no one's phones are working."

"I was on the bus. It's a mess out there. Lots of people are hurt. There's no power and the roads are wrecked. The ambulances can't get through."

"You were with Colin?" Becka looked back at Colin incredulously. "Why didn't you tell us you were with Aries? Where's Sara?"

Aries glared at Colin. He refused to look back at her. Instead he conveniently found something fascinating with the stage lights.

"Sara's dead," Aries said. "A lot of people died. I would have been here sooner, but I stayed behind to help. Well, sort of."

"Oh." Joy Woo, the Caterpillar, put her hands up to her mouth.

Colin stayed in his seat as he listened, an unreadable expression on his face.

No, there was pain in his eyes. He was trying to hide it, but she caught a glimpse. It was good to see he did care, even if he'd been all about saving his own skin at the time.

Ms. Darcy approached Aries, a pained expression on her face. Reaching out, she took Aries's hand and squeezed it gently. "Are you all right?" she asked quietly. "You're sure you're not hurt?"

"I'm fine. I was lucky."

Becka started to cry. She'd been as close to Sara as Aries was. They'd grown up next door to each other. Joy immediately put her arms around her. The others sat numbly, unable to respond. There was a long silence that followed, broken up by the occasional sniffle as Becka buried her face in her jacket.

"What do we do now?" Amanda muttered.

Colin stood up from his chair. "I'm going home."

"We should stay here," Aries said. "It's not safe outside."

"We're sitting ducks," Colin snapped. "What about after-shocks? This whole building could go down."

"I don't want to get crushed," Joy said.

"No one's going to get crushed," Aries said. "On the way over here I met this guy. He told me the safest place to be is the school, and I agree. Our parents know we're here. They'll come for us when this is over. We just need to be patient and stay put."

A lot of people are going to die, and it's only the beginning.

Daniel's words. She couldn't tell them he said that. It sounded crazy. But she'd seen it; the mob of darkened shadows tearing people apart on the street. She knew she should warn everyone, but Becka looked like she might fall apart. She didn't see the point in terrorizing her more. Besides, they were safe in the school. It was very unlikely that anyone would come searching for them as long as they kept hidden in the theater.

"I agree," Ms. Darcy said. "I think we should wait for your parents to come pick you up. It shouldn't take long once the roads are cleared."

"If they're okay," Becka said. "How do we know they're not dead?"

"I think right now we need to be more positive," Ms. Darcy said. "Until we're given a reason to believe otherwise."

The decision was made. No one dared question the teacher. She was the only adult and technically in charge. She was supposed to know what to do in these situations. But there was an anxious expression on her face and something odd with the way she tilted her head when she spoke. She was trying hard to hide it, and none of the other students noticed, but Aries saw through her fake demeanor. There was no mistaking it. Ms. Darcy didn't believe her own words. She knew.

"So where is this guy, then?" Colin said. "If he thought it was so safe here, then where is he?"

"There were others to save," Aries said. "It was more important to him than running like a coward with his tail between his legs."

Colin gave her a hard smile.

"Good for him," Ms. Darcy said. "Now maybe we should go down to the prop room. I saw an old boom box there a few weeks ago. If we can get it working we might be able to get the news on the radio."

"I have to leave."

Aries and Ms. Darcy were downstairs in the prop room. They found the boom box in the corner, half hidden under some stage wigs. It was monstrously huge, a forgotten relic from the eighties. Aries was doubtful it would work, but they wouldn't know until they managed to find some batteries.

"What do you mean?" Aries asked. "You agreed with me."

Ms. Darcy stared at her, her chin quivering. "I have two small children at home with a babysitter. I can't wait for a rescue party. I have to go and make sure they're safe."

"I understand."

"The others will, too. I'll make it simple. I'll slip out when no one's looking."

"But I don't know what to do."

Ms. Darcy grabbed her by the shoulders and pulled her close. "Just keep doing what you're doing. I wouldn't have put this on you if I didn't think you could handle it. You're one of my smartest students. The kids look up to you. They'll listen. Keep them at the school. Whatever you do, don't let them go outside."

"But what if they don't listen?"

"They will."

"Not Colin."

"Then let him go. You can't save them all."

"People are dying," Aries said. "I've seen it. Sara's dead. Maybe you can wait till morning. We can organize something. We can help you get back home."

"It might be too late by then."

"You know what's happening out there, don't you," Aries said.

"I do. That's why it's so important you keep them inside. Listen to me, Aries." Ms. Darcy pulled her closer and spoke directly in her ear, although there was no one else around. "Something bad is about to happen. It's already started. I know you're feeling it too." Ms. Darcy shuddered. "It's like an electric charge. I can't explain it. I've been sensing it for weeks. It's bigger than any earthquake, and in the end it'll be far worse than a few buildings collapsing."

"I feel it."

"The others don't."

"They're lucky."

"Be careful. But understand when I say I don't want you coming with me. Stay here while you can. Wait out the worst of it. If we're lucky it'll end soon and your parents will come and find you."

"It's not going to end." Once the words were out of her mouth, she realized they were true.

"I can't believe that."

Aries took a deep breath. "I hope your children are safe and that you make it home to them."

"Thank you." She took her keys out of her pocket and passed them over. "If no one comes by morning, try using the phone in the office. It might be working then."

"Okay."

The boom box didn't work even though they tried both sets of batteries. Leaving it behind, they went back upstairs to wait with the others for morning to come. Aries took a seat next to Jack and wrapped her jacket over her body to use as a blanket. It was done more out of need than comfort. There was no way she'd be sleeping anytime soon.

Ms. Darcy slipped out the door somewhere close to two in the morning when most of the students were dozing in their chairs. She made it look like she was going to the bathroom; she didn't even take her purse or jacket. Aries watched her go, swallowing the voice inside her begging silently for her to stay.

Ten minutes or so passed before Jack whispered in her ear. "She's not coming back, is she?"

"No."

Aries imagined her parents sitting in the living room, holding hands while watching the news. They were probably worried sick. Every ten minutes or so her father would get up and pace the room while her mother rushed off to make him coffee and check the phone lines. She tried to keep the image in her head, because the alternatives were worse. She didn't want to picture them dead just yet. She would continue to believe she'd see them again.

Not like Sara.

"If they don't come for us by morning, we'll figure something out," she said.

She woke to Joy gently shaking her. The last thing she remembered was checking her watch sometime after five a.m.

"What time is it?" Rubbing her eyes, she stretched in her

seat, her jacket sliding to the floor. The coolness of the theater bit against her skin, forcing her to shiver violently.

"Just after seven," Joy said. "Ms. Darcy's gone. Colin's pitching a fit in the lobby. You'd better come."

She was instantly wide-awake. The lobby had windows facing the street. He was right out in the open where anyone could see. The group of killers she'd seen last night might still be out there. If the wrong person happened to walk past, they'd all be dead.

Brace yourself. It's about to open.

Humanity has found a cure to a disease they never knew existed.

There was a connection between what the crazy man and Daniel had said. Something had been triggered with the earthquake. Something awful.

And more people were going to die.

They were all waiting in the lobby. The morning sunlight filtered through the glass, warming Aries instantly. She scanned the outside area, but it appeared empty. For now.

"Get away from the windows," she said. "We need to go back in the theater. We're too in the open here."

"Isn't that the point?" Becka said. "Don't we want people to find us?"

"Not if it's the wrong kind," Aries said.

"And what exactly do you mean by that?" Amanda's voice raised a few octaves.

She had to choose her words carefully. She knew how crazy it sounded. The others were still clueless about the dangers outside. For all they knew, last night was nothing but an earthquake. They hadn't seen those people being beaten to death.

"There are rioters out there," she finally said, completely aware of how lame the excuse was. "They might hurt us."

"You're joking, right?" Colin laughed loudly. "Rioters? That's your big fear? Who cares? You're such a girl, Aries. Go back inside and let the men talk."

"I did go back inside," she said. "I went back inside the bus and found Sara dead. What did you do? You ran like a coward. You left her."

"You take that back."

"No."

Jack stepped between them, putting his hands out as if he was afraid they might start tearing at each other's eyes. "Come on, guys," he said. "We're all tired here, and this isn't helping. Let's go sit down and talk about it. We'll figure it all out."

"I want to go home," Becka said.

"Yeah, well, we all want to go home," Colin said. His eyes never moved from Aries's face. "But the bitch here keeps going on about how we have to wait things out." He glared in her direction. "Why is that again? Really? Oh right, some stranger told you it's not safe and you believed him. And where is this mystery guy? He split—the exact opposite of what he told you to do."

"There's no need for that, man," Jack said.

"It's not just Aries," Joy said. "We took a vote and the rest of us agreed. We promised Ms. Darcy. We're safe here. It's something our parents would want."

"Don't you ever think for yourself?" Colin snapped back.

"Don't talk to her like that," Aries said. "You're really something, Colin. Left your girlfriend to die and now you're shouting at Joy?"

Colin pushed past Jack until he was inches away from Aries. "You'd better stop talking like that. I swear, I will hit you. I don't give a damn if you're a girl."

Jack grabbed his arms from behind, pulling Colin away.

Becka and a few of the other students got between them, making a wall of bodies. They all began yelling at one another, taking sides although none of them really knew what they were arguing about.

They were still in the lobby. Out in the open. Vulnerable. Loud. People would hear them through the glass.

She needed to get them back in the theater. Fortunately, Jack seemed to be thinking the same thing.

"Enough of this," he said. "Let's go back inside and sit down. We can discuss this like adults, right? Right?"

Jack's words worked. Colin stared him down for a few seconds before he finally nodded and turned and went into the theater without saying a word. The others followed.

The cold chill running through her subsided a bit once everyone was back inside. Jack waited in the lobby with her as she glanced out one last time to make sure the street was empty.

"He's being a real ass," Jack said. "I'm sorry."

"I'm not," she said. "I expected it."

They returned to the theater to find Colin putting on his shoes.

"Let's just wait a little longer," Aries said. "It's still early. There's no need to rush. People might be on their way as we speak. I'm sure it's just a matter of time."

"We don't want to do anything foolish," Jack agreed. "I saw some power lines on the street. They could still be active."

"And what are we going to do for food?" Colin snapped. "We could be stuck here waiting for days. I don't plan on going hungry."

"There's always the cafeteria," Joy said. "The main keys are in the office. I was a teacher's aid last semester. I know where they are. All we have to do is get them. I'm sure we can find plenty to eat there."

"Maybe we should do that now," Aries suggested. "I'll go. Anyone want to come with?"

"I'll come," Jack said.

"Me too," Colin said. He'd calmed down a bit. "I need to get out of here. I'm going crazy just sitting." He looked directly at Aries when he spoke, obviously implying that it was all her fault. Give him a few more hours and he'd probably find a way to pin the entire earthquake on her too.

It didn't help that he was trying to lead the group in a direction that Aries knew was dangerous.

"Try to find a radio or something," Becka said. "Maybe we can get some news. And check to see if the phones are working."

"I'd kill for some coffee," Joy said with a grin. "And maybe some pancakes? Bacon and eggs? Sausage? Do you think they'll have cake?"

"Stale crackers it is," Jack said with a grin.

Jack found a duffel bag behind the stage and emptied it of someone's gym clothes. Swinging it around his shoulders, he climbed the steps and headed back out into the lobby. They would all go except for Amanda and Becka, who stuck behind just in case someone happened to wander by and rescue them.

The cafeteria was on the other side of the school. It would take about five minutes to walk. The office was in the middle by the main doors. They would stop there first.

"I never realized how creepy the school is," Joy said. "It's so empty. I keep expecting something to jump out at us. Did it always echo like this?"

Everyone laughed except Aries.

"Would make a great horror movie idea," Jack said. "Student by day, killer by night, and the halls will run red with blood."

"Okay, enough already," Aries snapped.

"Sorry, just a joke," Jack said.

They walked the rest of the way in silence. The main office doors were locked, and Aries pulled the keys from her pocket.

"Where'd you get those?" Colin instantly wanted to know.

She ignored him and opened the door. They stepped inside. The office was dark, the blinds were closed, and Jack immediately went over to open them. Aries almost shouted out to him but stopped. What could she say? They needed the light to find the keys and she still wasn't ready to announce to the group about how unsafe the outside world really was. Plus, how could she explain when she didn't fully understand herself?

"I'll get the keys." Joy walked over to the administration desk and started rifling through the drawers. "It's really something. The master key opens every lock in the school. Maybe we should take a peek at our permanent records while we're at it. Do you think those really exist, or is it a myth?"

"I sure hope not," Jack said. "I peed my pants in the first grade. If that comes out I might never make it into university."

A black office phone sat on the desk next to a pile of papers. Aries picked up the receiver and pressed the line button. There was no dial tone. She checked the box to make sure it was plugged in and tried again. Still nothing.

"Oh, God." Jack's voice was stilted. His fingers gripped the last blind sash tightly, frozen in midtwist.

Aries made it to the window first. Her eyes followed Jack's gaze. Fifty feet away from the window, a body lay in the grass. The person was facing the ground, covered in blood, impossible to recognize.

Almost.

The bright green blouse gave her away.

"That's Ms. Darcy," Colin said.

Joy turned and promptly threw up all over the closest desk.

"Oh God, oh God, oh God," Colin chanted, putting his hands up against his ears as if he wanted to block out the sound of his own voice.

"What happened to her?" Jack said. "Why would someone do that? That's gotta be more than just rioters."

"It's evil," Aries said, and she finally understood fully what the crazy man on the bus meant when he said "game over."

There would be no bonus lives to help them get a higher score.

"Someone's out there," Jack said.

Just beyond the grass, closer to the main road, stood three people. They were staring at the school. No, change that. They were staring straight at them.

Aries pulled Jack away from the window.

"We need to get out of here now," she said.

No one seemed to listen to her. Time was moving too slowly. They weren't going to be fast enough. Her heart thumped loudly in her ears. Jack moved away from her in slow motion, his eyes focusing back on the outside world.

"We have to leave," she said again, louder, trying to block out her heartbeat. "We have to get Becka and Amanda."

Jack finally looked at her. "Okay."

But he still wasn't moving. None of them were.

"Come on," she screamed, pulling both him and Joy at the same time. "If we don't go now we're going to die."

"What's happening?" Joy said. "Who did that to Ms. Darcy?"

"They'll kill us next." That seemed to get everyone's attention. "Let's go." Thankfully Colin didn't argue.

They ran down the halls, almost making it to the theater before the screams started.

"That's Becka," Joy cried.

They all stopped and waited, frozen and unsure of what to do. The screams continued for what seemed like an eternity before abruptly stopping. Silence filled the halls, pressing down on Aries's skull. She couldn't speak; her tongue was glued against her teeth. She could feel Jack's body pushed up against her from behind, tense.

"What do we do?" he said.

"We have to leave now," Aries said.

"What about Becka and Amanda?" Joy whispered. She may have spoken the words, but she was already walking backward, away from the theater.

"We can't help them anymore," Aries said.

They heard the grinding noise of the theater doors opening. Footsteps echoed across the tiled flooring.

"Run," Jack said.

They did.

NOTHING

I can feel them. All of them. Their thoughts. Their voices whisper in my ears. I hear their prayers, and their pain passes through my body like a million electric volts.

I know their crimes.

They will make sure I witness every last one of them.

In New York City, a janitor blocks all the exits and dismantles the power supply before setting fire to the building. He spends his morning going from building to building, committing several acts of deadly arson before he finally traps himself in his own explosion and dies instantly.

In Houston, hundreds of inmates escape a local prison and go on a bloody rampage through the streets. The police force isn't capable of protecting the people, especially since many of the officers turn their weapons on the innocent crowds instead.

In Barcelona, a priest walks into a church with a gun and kills everyone during morning mass.

Riots in London stain the cobblestone redder than anything Jack the Ripper ever dreamed of.

A young preschool teacher in Toronto gives her students a

deadly mixture of arsenic and fruit punch. When she comes back long enough to realize what she's done, she downs the last remaining drops in two swallows.

Game over.

People are killing each other all over the world. Brothers attack sisters. Husbands and wives destroy their children. There is no explanation for the average person to understand. In the last remaining places where the media is able to reach the public, they have no answers.

But I know.

I can't block it out. They have dug their claws into my skull. There is no place in the world where I can hide, because they know where to find me. They don't even have to try. They've got the keys to my brain and they're emptying my thoughts and refilling it with theirs.

Not too long ago I think I was normal. I had a mother.

She'd need to light a lot of candles to save my soul now.

Somewhere through the darkness I catch a thought. A small memory. There is a lot of white sand; it stretches in all directions, farther than I can see. In front of me is a blue ocean. It's gigantic. But I'm very small. A child, perhaps, no older than three or four. I hold on to my bucket and shovel while my parents spread out a blanket over the white, pure sand. It's hot on my feet.

My father calls out to me.

My mother is smiling.

She looks so happy.

And then it's gone.

I want to grab these memories and hold tightly. I'm afraid that if they disappear, I'll never experience them again.

There must be a way to fight this. To block out the black thoughts and make the voices go away. But with each memory fading, their hold on me strengthens. Soon the person I was, still am, will be gone. I'll be hollow.

I am not the first and I will not be the last.

There are so many empty people walking around on this little planet. Lonely people. Angry people. Bitter. Forgotten.

They were easy to fill.

Three Weeks Later

MICHAEL

"What do you think?"

The binoculars were cracked, and Michael saw the world in two halves, both of which were colorless and slightly out of focus. It hurt his eyes and he blinked several times to try and make the world look normal again.

What did he think? They had stumbled across the ranch house just before noon. They almost hadn't seen it; most of the building was hidden behind an overgrown acre of evergreens.

"Well?" Evans tapped his finger on the side of Michael's head. Hard. To get his attention.

"Empty." Michael scratched his head and raised the binoculars again. They'd been watching from the bushes for a few hours now. There had been no movement from inside, but that didn't mean anything. Nothing was ever empty or free. But they were farther away from the city; there was always the possibility that they weren't bothering to come this far out. They hadn't seen anything for several days. This could be a free zone. "Maybe," he finally said. "It's worth looking at."

"Maybe not."

"We can't take that chance." They were out of food, having

divvied up the remaining package of saltines for supper two days ago. They'd discussed hunting. There were plenty of wild animals, but lighting a fire to cook was too risky. They couldn't take the chance knowing that others would be drawn to the smoke. They were stuck. Who knew when the next meal might come? The last pizza had been delivered weeks ago. There would never be another. And they had a child with them. They'd found a mother with her four-year-old son a few days ago while searching through an abandoned lumberjack camp. It was a miracle they'd survived. But the kid was sickly, and Michael didn't think he'd last much longer without food, maybe some medical supplies, too, if they were lucky.

"There's no such thing as chance anymore."

Michael didn't answer him. They all had their ghosts. Three weeks ago they'd arrived at Evans's house to find his wife and baby daughter missing. His front door was kicked in and there was blood on the carpet. They never found out what happened.

"I think we should take a chance." Billy, one of the other group members, jumped in on them from behind. Landing on the soft dirt beside Michael, he grabbed the binoculars from him in one swift move and raised them to his eyes. "These things are useless, man. How on earth have you been staring through them for the past two hours? I would have shot myself." Tossing them back, he scratched his goatee. "Seriously, that kid don't look so good. We've got to do something and do it fast, or he ain't gonna make it till nightfall."

"I know," Michael said. "But we can't go in until we're absolutely sure it's safe."

"We've been here for hours," Billy said. "If they were in there, we'd have seen something by now. Them Baggers ain't gonna sit in there and wait for us to bore ourselves to death. They would have attacked by now if they's here."

Baggers. A hunter's term. As in "I'm gonna go out and 'bag' myself a deer." Only the Baggers were hunting something completely different. Billy introduced the word several days ago. He'd heard some poor guy mention it before one of the monsters tore him to pieces.

"Maybe."

"How far are we till the next town?" Billy scratched himself again. They were all itchy. Showers were a luxury that none of them could afford or find these days.

Evans pulled out the crinkled map for the tenth time that hour. "Hard to say. We still don't quite know where we are. Could be a few miles, could be a few hundred."

"No ways." Billy grabbed the map. "There ain't a single place here that's more than a few miles away. We ain't that far up north. This here's still civilization. You ain't able to spit without hitting a Taco Bell or Jack 'n' Box."

Michael glanced back at the mother, stretched out on the ground, her child's head resting on her thigh. The boy—Michael couldn't remember his name—hadn't opened his eyes in a long time. Shallow gasps escaped bluish lips, his chest barely rising against his shirt. His face was deathly white, eyes sunken deep into the recesses of his skull. The poor kid probably weighed as much as a small animal. Sure, they'd all lost weight, and most of them would probably run one another over for a hamburger, but this was different. This was a kid. They weren't supposed to go hungry.

Children weren't supposed to know that monsters existed either.

The mother didn't look so good. Blond, matted hair that probably hadn't been brushed since this whole ordeal started. She looked washed-out. Faded. There may still have been a sun in the sky, but its rays weren't warming her skin. She was singing softly to her son, a song that Michael hadn't heard since he was really young. He could barely make out the words.

She shouldn't really be singing. The noise might attract the wrong kind of attention. But Michael wasn't about to tell her to stop. It might be the last time the child ever heard her voice.

No one wants to go off into the darkness alone.

"Screw it." He turned his attention back to Evans and Billy. "Let's do it. Get the others."

There were twelve of them in the group. Michael and Evans joined them two weeks ago, back when they were five. Since then they'd picked up a few more as they traveled the road. The mother and son were the latest find. It was getting difficult now that the group was so big. There was no safety in numbers, just more and more people to try to keep an eye on. Bigger meant more food was needed. It also meant louder.

But Michael liked being in a group. It made him feel wanted. He liked being a part of something. It was the type of person he was. Right in the center of things he was confident and strong. Dad said he was a natural-born leader, and if he were around he'd be proud to know Michael was coping. Michael knew there was still the possibility Dad was holed up somewhere in Denver. He knew a lot about survival. He clung to the idea that they'd cross paths again one day, and he looked forward to telling his father about how well he'd done. He was, after all, leading this group and he was younger than almost all of them. Evans had to be at least forty. Billy was thirty, but he looked older because of his missing teeth.

At seventeen, Michael was the one they looked to when they wanted answers. He'd never planned it that way. It just happened.

He got up, wincing as his knees popped. He'd been sitting for too long. Wandering over to where the mother sat, he knelt down beside her. Why couldn't he remember the name of the child? He should ask her, but he didn't want to look stupid. It was embarrassing that the leader couldn't remember all the names of his flock.

"Hey." He spoke quietly.

She stopped singing and looked at him. Her eyes were unfocused, staring right past him. Blinking several times, she finally managed to look at his face. Her eyes were bright blue but clouded.

"We're going to go check out the house," he said. "Do you want to come? You can stay here, but I think it's better if we stick together. I can help you. Do you want help? I can carry him."

He reached out his arms, but she pulled away, clinging tightly to her child. "No," she muttered. "I've got him. Do you think there'll be a bed? It would be nice to lie down for a bit."

"We won't be able to stay long," he admitted. "We're just going in to see if there's food. It's not safe to stick around."

"Just for a bit," she repeated. "He needs to rest. He's not well."

Michael nodded. "We'll see what we can do."

She stood up by herself, still holding the child, and started walking toward Evans. Her legs were shaking but she managed to keep it together.

There was something oddly comforting about her strength. Michael wondered, if he ever had a child, would he have the same determination to keep him safe? No matter how weak she became, she'd never give up.

He planned on being that strong. Who knew how long this war would continue. The Baggers had the upper hand, but if enough people banded together, they might be strong enough to regain power. Even if they managed to take down one Bagger at a time, well, that would be considered a good start.

Michael wanted to believe that. He had to believe that. Even with the entire population on the brink of extinction, he preferred to remain an optimist. It was impossible to tell how many people had died, since there was no more communication. It would be nice to find a short-wave radio or something. There might be other survivors using such devices. But so far the group had found nothing in the houses they'd searched except cell phones, computers, televisions, and all the other sorts of now-useless communication gadgets he'd grown up with.

Once upon a time he'd thought his cell phone was the one thing he couldn't live without. Amazing how quickly the tides can turn.

The Baggers were definitely being smart. Rumors were, they were the ones who managed to shut down the networks so quickly. They were the ones who blocked the cell phone towers and destroyed the Internet. Without communication, the world was thrown into black panic. There was no one to tell them what was happening. No information on safe places to go or what sorts of steps to take to protect themselves. The only way to find out if your loved ones were alive was to get in a car and travel. That's how the Baggers managed to kill so quickly. People put themselves out in the open and became sitting ducks.

Or at least that's what the group speculated about late at night while waiting for sleep. They also talked about why some people had become Baggers and others hadn't. Why and how had the change happened? What would the Baggers do with the world they'd destroyed? And left unspoken was the fear. They weren't Baggers. Yet. Evans figured if they hadn't turned by now, they weren't going to. Michael agreed with him. But the fear always crept in. Was it just a matter of time? Would he wake up one night with one of his peers about to rip out his throat?

No, he wouldn't think like that. And whatever it was, it didn't appear to be catching. He had to believe that. They all did.

But for now there were plenty of other people out there. Still normal, hiding inside their houses, taking refuge in whatever safe places still existed. Michael planned on finding them.

"We ready?" Evans appeared, folding up the map carefully and putting it in his pocket.

"Yeah." Michael's stomach growled, reminding him of the important things. "Let's do it."

They both made fists with their hands and lightly punched each other. It had become their mantra, their good-luck charm.

Billy and he took the lead, with Evans following at the rear. They were the three strongest and the least affected by hunger. At least that's what they led the others to believe. In reality they were just better at pretending the grumbles in their guts didn't bother them.

It wasn't much of an army, but they'd managed to survive. They were tough enough. But they'd never gone this long without eating before. How much longer would their strength last?

They moved along the tree line, sticking closely to the woods in case they needed to run. Vigilance would get them only so far. Realistically, if they were spotted now, they wouldn't all get away. They knew this—survival came at a price. Over the past few weeks they'd all survived a Bagger attack. Or two. Or three. They knew the consequences. Not everyone got out alive. They'd seen loved ones die. Even worse, some had watched the people they cared about turn on them. But as long as they stuck together in a group, they were still human. As long as they were human they were still alive. Michael watched the house carefully for movement. A tiny flicker, parting of a curtain—anything he might have missed before. A bubble of icy liquid churned away in his stomach. He was getting so used to being afraid, he barely noticed anymore. Goose bumps on his skin were as common as breathing. It was smart to be scared; it was the one thing that was keeping them alive. "Caution" was the new secret word.

Wait.

Did something move in the window?

No. He was imagining things. The hunger was playing tricks on his mind.

But still . . . he couldn't afford to be wrong.

He paused to listen. Nothing seemed to be out of place. Squirrels chattered away in the trees above them, and in the distance he could see a thin V in the sky as a flock of Canadian geese chased the sun. The ranch house remained silent in front of them, a sentinel abandoned, just waiting to protect hungry strays. The back door was within their vision, closed and probably locked. They might find a key in the mailbox or hidden under a mat; if not they would break a window.

The yard was unkempt; the grass was growing wild and didn't look like it had recently been disturbed.

Everything appeared normal.

So why was his body temperature dropping at an alarming rate?

"I got a bad feeling about this," he said.

"You say that every time." Billy snorted and spat on a charcoaled evergreen.

"This is different."

"There's nothing here. You said so yourself. We've been watching the building for hours. I'm hungry, man. There's food inside that there house. I can smell it. Maybe they'll have canned ham. I could really go for some of that. Maybe some relish that hasn't gone bad and some potata chips to go with it."

Billy, deep into food fantasy, continued to discuss his dreams openly as he passed Michael and moved toward the ranch house.

"Hey!" Michael jogged a few steps to get back in the lead. Keeping his eye on the upstairs window, he led the group up to the backdoor. Nothing moved.

It was easy to exaggerate things when your body was fueled by adrenaline.

Michael and Billy climbed the porch steps while the others waited at the bottom. The mother held her boy in her arms, her fingers tangled in the child's white-blond hair. Her legs were obviously unstable, and even from a distance Michael could see them shaking under the extra weight. Evans stood close to her side, watching her carefully in case she might stumble.

The porch was empty except for a few folding chairs leaning against the side of the house. Brass window chimes hung from the corner, unmoving and silent. Piles of dead and burned leaves had collected in the corners. Off to the side were an old-fashioned push lawn mower and a slightly rusted barbecue grill. Nothing looked disturbed or out of place. The chimes were covered in cobwebs. No recent footprints in the dust either.

The door was shut, and when Michael tried the handle, it didn't budge. Locked. A good sign. There was always the chance that survivors might be inside, barricaded and waiting for help. Even better if they had weapons. Finding healthy people en masse would be proof enough that the Baggers hadn't reached this far north and they could let their guard down, even if only for a little while. It would be nice to sleep without keeping both eyes open.

No key in the mailbox. He ran his fingers along the top edge of the door. Then, bending down, Michael stepped off the welcome mat and turned it over. Nothing but a bit of dirt and a few pebbles.

Billy joined him, turning over the flower pots in the window. Dirt spilled onto the wooden floorboards.

"No key," Michael said.

"Let's break a window, then," Billy said. "No pain, no gain."

"No noise."

"Less is best."

Billy took off his jacket and wrapped it around his arm. Leaning against the door, he pressed hard and quickly, shattering the pane. The sound of glass breaking and hitting the floor caused them all to inhale deeply.

They waited.

The wind shook the dead evergreen branches, and the brass wind chimes crashed together. The icy-cold sensation was back again, and the hair on Michael's neck pulled away from his scalp.

Picking bits of glass from the frame, Billy cleared enough of a hole to reach his arm through and turn the lock. Metal scraped behind the wood, and the door creaked open a few inches.

"In," Billy said. "We'll be eating like royalty soon enough."

"Quickly," Michael said. "In and out. We're too open here."

"You're doing that paranoid thing again. You've got to chills out, bro. There ain't no Baggers here. We're safe."

They were never safe.

Michael knew this. But a lecture at this point wasn't going to work when Billy's mind was set solely on the purpose of fueling his belly.

The back door led into a small mudroom. Jackets for all seasons hung on wooden pegs, and shelves were filled with shoes and boots. One of the coats closest to the door was bright pink with a fake-fur hood. Mittens with strings hung on the peg beside it. On the floor was a school bag, unzipped, loose-leaf pages of children's handwriting poking through the opening.

Michael immediately glanced back at Evans to try and gauge his reaction. The older man stared at the pink jacket, a stony expression on his face. It would be hardest on Evans; he would never fully know what happened to his family. And there would always be reminders around to guarantee he never stopped thinking about it.

Evans reached out and touched the jacket gently. Michael stopped himself from asking if he was all right. No one else noticed the gesture, and it was too private to bring to everyone's attention. Michael found the light switch on the wall and flicked it a few times. Nothing happened, but he'd been expecting that. The last of the power went out weeks ago. He did it out of routine, and not because habits were hard to break but because it gave him hope. Maybe one day they'd have the luxury of pressing buttons again and getting everything they wanted. But right now there were more important issues at hand than dreaming—namely Billy, who'd pushed ahead of the group and entered the kitchen without double-checking for danger.

Michael chased after him and into one of the nicest kitchens he'd ever seen. It was enormous, bigger than the whole of the one-bedroom apartment he used to share with his father.

Billy was throwing open cupboards at an alarming speed. So far he'd found nothing but row upon row of dishes, coffee mugs, and Tupperware. The counters were filled with all sorts of fancy appliances. Toaster oven, espresso maker, blender, mixer—everything strategically placed, as if Martha Stewart did the decorating. A gigantic kitchen island had rows of copper pots hanging above it and a large silver fruit basket with moldy apples and pears. The rotten fruit was the only proof that someone had actually once used the kitchen.

"We should check out the rest of the house first," Evans said. He'd approached Michael and was standing beside him, watching Billy search. One of the other group members opened the stainless-steel fridge, and the smell of sour milk and rotten vegetables wafted through the room. Michael covered his nose. It was enough to make his stomach stop grumbling.

Evans moved across the room to help the mother, still clinging tightly to her son, sit down at the table. Michael went over to the fridge, suppressing the urge to gag from the smell, and sifted through the shelves until he found a small can of fruit cocktail. He pulled a spoon from the drawer and brought it over to the mother.

"Here," he said as he opened the top, sugar syrup dripping on his fingers. "See if he'll eat this."

"Thank you," she whispered.

"Jackpot!" Billy shouted from across the kitchen. Too loud. What the hell was he thinking? He knew better.

But Billy had found the pantry. All he could think about was the row upon row of groceries facing him. There was so much there. It really was a bonanza. Dozens of cans of food: soups, corn, peas, chili, tuna, salmon, pears and other assorted fruits. There were even some tiny cans of ham, just the thing Billy was dreaming about. Bags of chips and pretzels, boxes of cereal, granola bars, all sorts of things that didn't go bad—they would have enough food to last them a few weeks once they sorted through everything.

Billy tore open a package of granola bars and threw one at Michael. He fumbled the catch and picked it up from underneath a chair.

"I'm gonna go take a look around," he said to no one in particular. "Don't get too comfortable. We still don't know if we're alone."

The mother looked slightly alarmed at the thought. She perked up in her chair, spilling fruit cocktail all over her child's shirt.

"I'll come with you," Evans said. At least two of them still had their priorities straight. Michael understood that they were hungry and all that food clouded their judgments, but this was exactly the sort of thing the Baggers would expect. However, the group was spread out across the kitchen, many sitting on the floor, stuffing their mouths with anything they could grab. Going on about safety at this point would only make Michael appear whiny. That was one of the downfalls of being young.

Michael and Evans moved through the doors and into the living room. A leather couch, covered in a thin layer of dust, dominated the area. On the wall was a fifty-inch flat screen, complete with a bookcase filled with hundreds of movies, many of which were Disney cartoons. On the floor in front of the entertainment system was a doll, half undressed.

They found suitcases by the front door. Michael lifted one.

It was heavy. "Looks like someone left in a hurry," he said.

"Let's hope so," Evans said. They still hadn't checked out the upstairs.

Back in the kitchen they heard Billy whoop.

"That idiot's gonna get us killed," Evans said.

They walked up the stairs together and checked out all the rooms. There were five bedrooms and two bathrooms, all of which were empty, to Michael's relief.

"Water's still running here," Evans said as he came out from one of the bathrooms. "There's a barbecue out back with some working propane too. I can boil us up some heat. We're looking at showers tonight as long as we're quiet."

"Can't remember what clean feels like," Michael replied. When was the last time he showered? He reached up and scratched at his scalp. His long hair was greasy and the ends were beginning to dread.

"I'm looking forward to it. After living with you for three weeks, I can honestly say you need it."

"This coming from a guy who farts *and* snores."

"You've got to stop using that hair gel, kid. It's starting to rot your brain."

They grinned at each other.

Back in the kitchen, the group was looking slightly bloated from stuffing their faces. Only the mother didn't seem to have eaten, mostly because her son hadn't been able to swallow the fruit cocktail.

"Come on," Evans said to her. "There's a room upstairs. Let's get the boy rested for a little bit. I think it's safe for us to spend the night. But only one. We need to move on by sunrise. The rest of you better not get too comfortable. I'll be expecting us to work for our dinner. I want lookouts at both doors and even outside."

Michael nodded. He couldn't have said it better himself. He helped the mother to her feet. She refused his offer to take the boy but allowed him to lead her upstairs to one of the empty bedrooms.

They were safe. Miracles still did happen.

MASON

In the middle of downtown Calgary, his car finally gave out. There was a loud noise like a gunshot, and he instinctively ducked and hit the brakes at the same time. The steering wheel jerked in his hands as he ground to a halt. The engine sputtered, then stalled completely. The blacked-out traffic light swayed in the wind above his head. The only movement on an otherwise empty street.

Cursing, he pulled the keys from the ignition and flung them against the dashboard. What was left of the city seemed to be taking the destruction and death seriously and barricading themselves in their homes. How many people were still alive? How many of them weren't insane? Or infected? Or whatever the hell this was? Several weeks later and Mason (and probably everyone else in the world) had no clue what was happening. Communication was still down, anyway. If anyone out there did know what was going on, they couldn't share.

All he knew was that people were dead. Lots. If the televisions were still broadcasting they would call this an epic pandemic.

He was parked in the middle of the intersection. The traffic lights above his head stayed dark. The city was a graveyard of electric wires and appliances. He'd driven most of the night and hadn't seen a single light, because most of the rural communities were blacked out too, with the exception of the occasional farmhouse that was probably using a generator. Mason wasn't about to pop his head in the door to ask. The last thing he wanted or even deserved was company.

He would never feel anything again. Somehow he wasn't the same Mason he'd once been. His mother died so he could live. As far as Mason was concerned, she'd left him with a curse.

Several buildings off Deerfoot Trail were on fire. He could see the black smoke in his rearview mirror. Half an hour ago, he'd been right in the middle of it, holding his shirt over his nose with the windows rolled up tightly. It was slow moving, too many cars in the street, doors open and abandoned. There were dead bodies alongside the road. Burned. Mouths open in silent agony. The crazy monsters roaming the city must have chased them into the fire. Which was worse? Dying at the hands of insane people or burning alive? He wasn't sure.

When he'd driven past, he'd kept his eyes focused in front of him, pretending the bodies didn't exist, trying to convince himself that the smell in the air wasn't that of roasting flesh.

He decided he'd never drive through smoke again. The next time he found fire, he'd bypass the city entirely. It wasn't worth the memories. Or the smell. He'd have to ditch his clothing the first chance he got.

You forget the good and remember the bad. His mom used to say that. Bits of her still wormed their way into his memory when he least expected. The smell of her perfume. The way she smiled. He was trying so hard to forget. He'd traveled many miles over the past few weeks, but she continued to give chase. When he fell asleep she was there. When he stopped to take a break or let down his guard she was the only thing he thought of. Eyes closed, hooked up to machines, taking her last breath before giving up the fight. She never even got to say good-bye.

No. He wasn't going to remember this.

Leaving the keys in the ignition, he climbed out cautiously and wandered around to the front of the car to take a look.

Both front tires were blown.

Glancing back at the road behind him, he could see bits of glass reflecting the morning sun. How on earth had he missed that? Cursing again, he slammed his fist down on the hood.

Now he'd have to find another car. That shouldn't be too hard. There were probably a dozen dealerships within walking distance. He could have the pick of the lot. No Hummer or Porsche was beyond his reach. But he'd never cared about flashy cars in the past. He didn't know the difference between six cylinders and sixty, so now wasn't really any different. Besides, a fancy car would burn gas faster, and that meant stopping more. He didn't trust the gas stations. They were out in the open, and who knew what might be lurking around. No, the only car he wanted was one that worked—tires and all.

It wasn't safe being in the middle of the intersection.

How long till he was discovered?

"Need some help?"

Mason turned quickly, hands up in defense, but one look at the man behind him and he instantly relaxed. The guy had to be at least seventy. His white hair was neatly combed and slicked back. He was wearing one of those suits that hadn't been in style since the fifties, along with a tie and a red polka-dot handkerchief in the pocket. And he was missing a leg. Under his arms, his weight rested on a pair of crutches.

"Didn't mean to scare you," the old man said. "But I don't think there's any non-terrifying way to greet someone these days."

"Yeah, I guess," Mason said.

"I'm sure you can deduce I'm harmless," the man said, tapping his crutches on the ground to prove it. "I'm hoping the same of you. Never heard one of 'em making a fuss over such a little thing before. Not when there are thousands of available cars sitting about. So I think that makes you pretty human."

"I'm normal," Mason said. He wanted to do something too, so he turned around in a slow circle to show there was nothing behind his back or up his sleeves.

"Normal, huh?" The man laughed. "Is there such a thing as normal anymore?"

"Probably not."

The old man twisted around on his crutches and scanned the road. "I don't know about you, but I'm not overly fond of staying in the open for too long. I live just down the street. Why don't you come back to my place and I'll fix us up some tea and breakfast while we try and figure out how to get you on the road again. What do you say?"

Mason glanced back at the blown tires attached to the car he'd found just outside of Drumheller. His own car was abandoned at the side of the road outside of Rosetown. He'd had a terrible time leaving it behind. It seemed silly now, loving a car. It was just a piece of metal with some fancy bits that moved when he used a key. He couldn't remember why he'd been so attached to it. That seemed like a million dreams ago. Reaching through the window, he grabbed the bag he'd packed the morning he'd burned down his house. From the sun visor he grabbed the picture he'd carried in his pocket. *Mom and Mason—enjoying the sun.* Happy, cheerful Mason—when did he grow up?

"Let's go," he said.

"I'm Winston Twilling," the man said. "But everyone calls me Twiggy. At least, they used to call me Twiggy. No one calls me much of anything these days, I guess."

"I'm Mason Dowell."

"Pleased to meet you. Wish the circumstances were better. But we can't all be eating cake and crumpets these days. But I've got some good tea. Swiped it from the fancy market down the street. They have an entire aisle dedicated to the fine world of teas and coffee. Wouldn't shop there before—they used to just gouge people on their prices. But a free lunch is a free lunch. At least these days it is. Who's gonna complain?"

Twenty minutes later Mason sat in the only chair in Twiggy's bachelor apartment and waited while the man fiddled with the buttons on an old propane stove that now ran on gasoline. Mason stifled a yawn with the back of his hand. It was getting harder and harder to get a full night's sleep these days. Twiggy, however, looked like he'd had ten hours the night before. The old man's eyes were bright and energetic.

Twiggy's apartment was more like a museum than a home. There were shelves overflowing with everything imaginable. Thousands of books, notebooks, statues, loose articles, and knickknacks, piled and tossed until every corner was filled. On the walls were a collection of maps of the world. Maps of the solar system. Maps of subway routes and what looked like small towns. There were drawings and pictures, mostly of places—waterfalls, beaches, jungles, canyons, ruins of ancient civilizations, and even a few smiling people—stuck in place with thumbtacks and pushpins, several of which overlapped into one gigantic collage.

Binders and newspaper clippings were stacked in corners. Even the kitchen had boxes of books pushed up against the refrigerator and cupboard doors.

The place made Mason feel slightly claustrophobic, but it didn't seem to bother Twiggy in the slightest.

"It was a push-button generation," Twiggy said. "We never needed to work for anything. Anything you wanted was within your reach. If you were hungry you popped something in the microwave and pressed a button. If you wanted to drink you turned on the coffeemaker. We used buttons for elevators, cars, televisions, alarms—hell, if you could think it up, someone would invent a button for you to press in order to have it. Now, I'm not one of those old farts who goes around talking about how much better the world was when I was a boy. It wasn't. At least, it wasn't a few weeks ago. Can't really compare it to today, can I? Nothing is worse than this."

Mason nodded. He stared at a stack of books that looked dangerously ready to topple at the slightest breeze. Twiggy's apartment wasn't dirty, but it wasn't exactly clean, either. The dishes were done and neatly stacked in the cupboards, and the bedding looked freshly washed. But everything was worn—old and faded. Mason couldn't help but think it must be a depressing place to live.

Twiggy caught him looking around. "Yeah, it's not much, but its home. I've lived here a long time. I guess if I really wanted to, I could find myself a nice condo in the downtown core. I'm sure there's plenty of good real estate waiting around these days for someone to grab it. Might get a real steal of a deal."

Mason nodded, distracted by a smushed bug on the ceiling.

"But this is mine. It's not the building but what's inside that counts. Been here thirty-some years. Could have left it behind a long time ago, but never felt like I needed anything else. Aside from books and knowledge, I've always believed in a simple life. Never married, no kids, nothing but my job and that was enough. Even after I retired I still didn't feel like moving down to Florida or whatever it is old people do these days. Besides, can you imagine how much it would cost to move all this junk?"

"What did you do?"

The kettle began to whistle and Twiggy switched off the burner. He poured the water into mugs containing fancy-looking tea bags. For a one-legged man, movement was not a problem for him. Balancing on one crutch, he picked up a mug and brought it over to Mason without spilling a single drop.

"I was a sociology professor at the university," Twiggy said as he went back to the kitchen. He picked up a bag of cookies and tossed them at the bed before retrieving his own mug. "Don't look so surprised, us nutty professors always look like twenty miles of bad road. I think unmanageable hair and tweed suits are part of our chemical makeup."

"Cool."

"Extremely," Twiggy said. "I specialized in downfall, the destruction of societies. As you can imagine, this whole event has caused quite a stir in my attention span."

A scream sounded from outside the window, and Mason jerked his hands up, spilling hot tea across the front of his shirt. Swearing, he jumped to his feet, pulling at the cloth to try and prevent the scalding liquid from burning his chest.

Twiggy hopped over to the window and pulled aside the curtain to get a better look. "Can't tell if that was one of them or someone in trouble. Not that we'd be able to do much."

"Should we go take a look?" Shirt cooling, he joined Twiggy at the window, which faced an alley. There was no one in sight.

"Not a chance. I may be old, but I'm not looking to die just yet. I saw them tear apart a looter a few days ago. Dumb idiot was trying to carry one of those seventy-two-inch televisions. Don't know what he thought he was gonna watch it with? Maybe he thought it runs on pixie dust? Who knows? They did him in just the same. Never heard a man scream that way. You'd best keep low if you want mankind to survive."

Mason turned from the window. He knew Twiggy was right. It seemed irrelevant anyway—the screamer was gone. Or silenced.

Twiggy closed the window and pulled the curtain. Moving back toward the bed, he sat down. "You don't talk much, do you?"

"Not really."

"I doubt it's because you don't have much to say."

Mason shrugged.

"I'm not going to ask you who you lost," Twiggy said. "It's all over your face. But I'll tell you this. Going off into the wild and being a hero isn't going to bring them back. Now isn't the time to be getting survivor's guilt."

"It's not that," Mason said.

"You want answers? There aren't any."

"Why?"

"Good question." Twiggy scratched at his leg. "But I don't have that answer. Why does anything happen? I think the disease just got too deep."

"Disease?"

"Humanity."

Mason shrugged again, mostly because he didn't have a clue how to respond. Twiggy was staring at him intently, and he was getting uncomfortable. His algebra teacher used to do the same thing all the time, especially when he knew Mason didn't have the right answer. Maybe it was a teacher thing?

"Born into blood, raised by blood," Twiggy said. He hobbled over to the bookcase and took down a scrapbook, passing it to Mason. The first page had a black-and-white photograph of a wasted world. Broken buildings loomed in the background while hundreds of dead bodies littered the streets. "Humans are the most violent species on the planet. We have a brilliant history of all the ugly deeds we've done. We're rotted straight to the core. The disease finally won the battle. We've never had a cure, and the symptoms are out of control. We're finally doing something right by wiping ourselves off the face of this planet."

"So you're saying we're responsible? We created this?"

"Not directly," Twiggy said. He turned over a few pages for Mason until he found what he was looking for. Ancient ruins. A temple covered in vines and overgrown bushes. Mummified skeletons with their jaws forever open in agony. "It's the end of days, Mr. Dowell. Like all great societies before us, ours has begun to eat itself—cannibalize, if you will—from the inside. Think of all the great societies in the past. Mayans. Aztecs. Romans. All advanced for their time. All destroyed and gone today. They've left behind nothing but a few hints for people like me to come and dig up."

Twiggy pointed to a picture on the wall. Hundreds of dead bodies piled together. "Murambi Technical School in Rwanda," he said. "The genocide of an entire culture. Hundreds of thousands killed. Hacked into pieces with machetes. Slaughtered. Not pretty, is it?"

"That's messed up."

"It's our turn to eat ourselves from within. Something happened that roused the destruction on a universal scale. We are no longer a cluster of societies living off the land. We've globalized and grown too big. Now something's made us go strange in the head. Took away our free will. Humans are dogs, you realize. There is a pack leader that starts us off down the path to destruction. But someone or something always comes along to throw us a bone first. Philosophers like to argue that we have free will, but I think the majority of people can't stop themselves from following. Whatever is controlling this, it picked the perfect time to plan its attack. I think it was the earthquakes. Animals can sense them, did you know that? Fact. But something caused the ground to split, and it's angry. It's come for us, you see. And we've invited it in with open arms."

"I don't believe in that sort of crap."

"Doesn't matter what you believe in. Do you think things will stop or change because you've forgotten what the bogeyman looks like? Maybe that's what pissed it off, so to speak. It doesn't like being forgotten. So it decided to shake things up a little."

Twiggy took back the scrapbook and turned a few more pages until he came to a picture of total devastation. A woman held her dead child in her arms, her face taut as she tried to keep from falling apart. Dead bodies were lined in a row behind her. People stumbled around the debris, desperately searching out their loved ones. Another picture—the bodies of two young girls, side by side, rotting in the streets because there was no one around to bury them.

"There have been earthquakes before," Mason said.

"True. And maybe there were bad things lurking about during those disasters too," Twiggy said. "Maybe some were misdiagnosed. We'd have to go back and look to see if there's a connection. But that's a moot point right about now. I doubt I'd be able to get my hands on any research material these days. Just think, maybe millions of years from now they will find our cities buried under the dirt and try to understand what brought on our demise. Imagine what they'll think of our laptops and microwave ovens."

"I don't believe in evil."

"Once again, we're only tiny pawns in this game. Belief has nothing to do with it. For all we know, this evil could have killed off the dinosaurs. Or maybe it really was a meteor. Or maybe history was just created from God's hands to give us something to argue about over dinner parties."

From beyond the closed window, the muffled sound of glass breaking reached their ears. Mason's body stiffened, and it annoyed him that such things were still affecting him. Twiggy didn't even twitch. How long would it take before screams and breaking glass wouldn't even have Mason blinking his eyes? Would he ever become as calm as the old man in front of him? Maybe if he wasn't this highly strung he might be able to get some sleep at night.

"It'll be dark soon," Twiggy said. "I'd invite you to stay, but as you can see, I'm not exactly set up for company." He pointed at the single bed.

"I should get going anyway," Mason said, standing. "You wouldn't happen to know where a car dealership is, would you?"

"Hold on." Twiggy hobbled over to the dresser and opened it. Reaching inside, he pulled out some keys and tossed them at Mason. "Downstairs in the garage. Not much, I'm afraid. Just an old, beat-up Honda. I don't drive it a lot, but it'll do you well enough. There's a full tank of gas."

Mason squeezed the keys tightly in his fist. "Are you sure? Do you want to come with me? I'm not sure where I'm going yet, but you're welcome to—"

"Let me stop you right there," Twiggy said. "I'm not going anywhere, Mr. Dowell. It's not my world out there. I'm safe here. I have everything I need and the fancy grocery store down the street from which to steal. I'm not a man who deals well with change. I have no desire to join you in your adventure."

"Okay," Mason said. "I had to ask."

"Yes, of course you did." Twiggy laughed. "And now that you've asked, you can move on with a clean conscience. It's good for the soul. Now thank me kindly and start moving on."

"Thank you."

"You're welcome."

Twiggy saw him to the door. "Just follow the stairs to the basement. It'll be parked in the back corner. I doubt there'll be anyone down there. The door's automatic; you'll have to do it manually. Try not to let anyone in when you leave."

"Thanks for all your help." Mason turned to go.

"Oh, Mr. Dowell? One last thing."

Mason turned back to face Twiggy. "Yeah?"

The coffee mug sailed through the air, smashing into the side of Mason's face. White stars exploded in all directions, and the edges of his vision instantly distorted. He couldn't control his body—knees buckled, arms became dead weights, and his legs fell out from underneath him like some slow-motion dream. He cracked his head on the doorframe on the way down.

He couldn't move. Through blurry eyes he watched Twiggy hobbling toward him, his crutches stopping dangerously close to Mason's face. He wanted to do something, but his eyes weren't focusing. He couldn't breathe.

The last thing he saw before the darkness took him was Twiggy leaning over him, a crooked smile showing yellow teeth. His eyes were funny. Bloodshot. But the veins weren't red. They were black.

"Trust no one," Twiggy said.

Then nothing.

NOTHING

I don't feel like talking today. Go find someone else to bother.

I mean it. Stay away.

Don't make me hate you.

ARIES

She was cold. Freezing. Her fingers were white and stiff. Something was wrong. October never used to be this cold. And wet. The tiny Gastown apartment was waterlogged. Vancouver may be known for its precipitation, but this was overdoing it. It'd been raining for a week and there was still no sign of it giving up. The clouds were fat and gray, the land pregnant with swollen tears.

Funny how a gray sky made her want to curl up in a ball and start crying, especially after everything else that had happened in the past few weeks.

Depressing.

She pulled the blanket tighter around her shoulders. It was itchy and stained and smelled faintly of mold, but at least it kept her somewhat warm. There was no such thing as luxuries anymore. Besides, she hadn't showered in days; she probably didn't smell like roses either. When was the last time she saw her own reflection in a mirror?

Through the window she watched the solitary person walking in the rain, pushing a squeaky shopping cart. The person had no face, at least not one that was visible, and was covered in a makeshift raincoat; the eyes were blurry through the clear plastic.

"It's one of them."

She turned toward the voice. "How can you tell from this distance?"

"No one sane would be outside in this weather."

"Har-har. Very unfunny."

Jack shrugged. "I'm still not going to take any chances and invite him up here for a cup of tea."

Aries nodded. "Yeah, I hear you. Better safe than dead."

"The saying is 'better safe than sorry.'"

"I wouldn't be sorry. I'd be dead." Aries closed her eyes and leaned back from the window. She was tired. They all were. No one got much sleep these days. Who has time for napping when staying alive requires so much effort?

They'd done well so far. They were still alive. At least some of them were. That had to count for something. How many people were left? Ten percent of the city? Five? It was hard to tell when so many were in hiding. There weren't as many screams these days, and that was a blessing in disguise. But less meant less—not more. Should she include the monsters in her head count? Could you consider them human anymore?

"You should take a break and get some sleep." Jack leaned over and grabbed the water bottle from the window ledge.

"I'm fine," she said.

"You've been here for at least six hours. We're supposed to be doing this in shifts, remember? It's okay to give someone else a chance. They aren't going to come breaking down the doors if you close your eyes. I'm here. I'll watch over you."

"It's not that."

"You don't trust me?" He brought the bottle to his lips, but she could still see the smile concealed behind it.

"I trust you." She grabbed the bottle back before he got a sip. Water sloshed out, soaking his nose and forcing her to grin like an idiot.

It was nice having these moments when they could forget what was going on outside and share a silly laugh. The problem was, it didn't happen often enough. Aries placed the bottle back on the ledge and scanned the street below her. The shopping cart person was still moving steadily toward them. In a few minutes they'd be within earshot. That was enough to sober her up.

Whatever humanity had become, it still had good hearing.

They waited silently while the figure moved past the building. It moved slowly, pausing once to sniff the air and glance back down the road from which it came. It kicked an old soda can into the gutter and picked up something off the street: a bicycle helmet with a long crack down the side. It rustled around in the shopping cart for a few moments before pulling out a human head. Jack gripped Aries's shoulder. They both watched silently as the plastic-clad person placed the helmet on top of the severed head before stuffing it back under the tarp. Eventually the person started moving again, heading back down the street in a continuous shuffle. It wasn't until the monster turned the corner that Aries realized she'd been holding her breath.

"I think we're safe," she muttered. Her heart was thumping hard, and she was angry that she was still scared after three weeks. She wanted to be stronger. She had to be stronger if she was going to run this group. They all looked toward her, except Colin, but he still grudgingly went along with whatever she suggested. Well, most of the time.

Movement on the street caught her attention. A stray German shepherd stuck its head out from behind a parked car.

A smaller dog, maybe a shih tzu, crouched behind it. They'd obviously been waiting for the monster to leave too. The shepherd sniffed the air before cautiously moving out toward the middle of the road, where it stuck its nose into a pile of newspaper. When it raised its head, it was chewing something. Plenty of garbage for the animals these days.

"There are other survivors out there," she said suddenly. "There have to be. We can't be the only sane people left in the world. It would be nice to find them. We'd be stronger. We don't even have any weapons."

"We'll find others eventually."

She took a sip of water. Her throat was always dry these days. "We should be looking for them. Sending out search parties. It wouldn't be too hard to do."

"It would be suicidal. You said it yourself, we don't have weapons."

"Then we'll get some."

She yawned, and tried to cover it up by coughing.

"You're tired," Jack pressed.

"I just don't feel like sleeping right now."

"Who do you see when you close your eyes?"

Aries shot him a look. "That's personal."

"I see Ms. Darcy."

She nodded. "Me too."

And a million others.

It wasn't sleep that she feared. It was the time before sleep when she rested her head down on the pillow. She couldn't turn off her brain; it became an open invitation for all the events she'd witnessed over the past weeks. There were too many thoughts, and this was the prime time for them to creep their way into her head. Closing her eyes meant seeing and imagining the bodies of both strangers and the people she loved. Their screams echoed like a scratched record on an endless loop. She wanted sleep. She wished desperately for it to come to her. But she couldn't clear her head. She didn't know what tricks to use to make it all go away.

She blinked several times to try to ease the soreness from her eyes. Clutching the blanket, she pulled it back over her shoulders. "Where are the others?"

"Second floor. They're trying the laptop again, but I think the battery's about to die. Personally I would have given up on it a long time ago. It's broke, can't be fixed. Thing's useless anyway without the Internet. Colin's on the roof. He said something about needing fresh air, but I think he's just tired of the smell. Can't say I disagree with him. I wish we had drugs. If my head gets any stuffier it's gonna explode."

The building in which they were hiding had a foul odor of mold and fried eggs. It had been the brunt of bad jokes over several sleepless nights. What smells worse than ten-day-old maggot breath? This place. What smells worse than Colin's feet? This place.

They laughed silently in the darkness. You had to laugh if you wanted to live. But you did it quietly. Who knew what lurked in the shadows outside?

Six of them lived. Colin, Joy, Jack, and Aries were the only ones lucky enough to make it out of the school alive. They'd met up with Eve and Nathan a week later. They were a brother-and-sister team that managed to survive inside a 7-Eleven by hiding behind a bunch of boxes in the store room. Together they were six. Alone they were, well, alone. She remembered what Daniel said to her before he disappeared. Groups were a bad thing. People do stupid things when they're together. She disagreed. Being part of a group gave her strength. She'd never have made it out alive if it hadn't been for her friends.

Daniel. Was he out there somewhere, hiding in an abandoned grocery store or holed up in some earthquake-ravaged building like hers? She thought about him often, more than she'd ever admit. She wondered if he was still alive or one of the numerous corpses that littered the streets like the aftermath of some bizarre death parade.

When they'd escaped the school and ran blindly into the street, she'd been surprised that the group automatically headed toward the bus stop and the grocery store. Her heart exploded in her chest when she recognized the overturned bus, knowing that her best friend was still trapped inside with Daniel's jacket thrown over her. It would be her final resting place; no one was coming to give her a proper burial. Thankfully they ran straight past. No one thought of taking cover there.

Luck was on their side and they found shelter in someone's garage. They huddled in the darkness, listening to the screams, waiting for someone or something to open the door and find them. It was a miracle they made it through without detection.

"They're going from house to house," Jack informed her during the first night. It was three a.m. and everyone was dozing except the two of them. Jack was peering out through the window, cautiously.

"Who?" she asked. A waterfall of cold ice ran its way down her spine.

"Six or seven of them," he said. "They just dragged someone out into the street. She's in a bathrobe. Oh God, there's a child, too."

Aries joined him at the window. She couldn't help herself.

"Are you sure you want to see this?" he whispered.

She nodded and he pointed farther down the street where she could see the group of people circled around and tearing apart their victims. A soft cry involuntarily left her lips, and she covered her mouth with both hands.

Jack put his arm around her and pulled her close. She buried her face in his chest for a few moments before anger overcame her. No. She wasn't going to cower. She'd have to be stronger if she wanted to get out of this alive. Pushing away from him, she forced herself to watch the group finish up their job before moving on to the next house.

"They'll get here eventually," she finally said.

"There's a car cover in the back," Jack said. "We can hide under it."

"We need weapons," she said.

Luckily for them, the murderous mob never checked the garage. By the time they reached that house, dawn was breaking in the sky and the killers must have been exhausted. They broke down the door of the house across the street. Aries clung to Jack when one of the monsters threw a helpless woman through the living room window. After checking to make sure she was dead, the killer casually wandered back inside and closed the door. They must have decided to rest, because the house grew quiet.

Aries spent the entire day believing she'd be dead by nightfall. But when the mob resumed their killing spree that evening, they miraculously skipped their hideout.

The rest of the block wasn't so lucky.

Three days later Aries and her friends moved on. Mostly because they were hungry and if they stayed any longer they'd be too weak. They slipped out under the cover of night.

There were dead bodies everywhere. It was almost impossible to move without hitting a hand or stomach. Joy stepped on someone's fingers, accidentally breaking them beneath her boot. She threw up on a discarded book bag. Everyone huddled around her, but not out of concern. They were terrified that the noise might draw attention. Although Joy was on the verge of hysterics, she managed to keep it together. But she was more cautious where she stepped from that point on. They all were.

There was blood. It may have been dark outside, but Aries could see the endless splashes of dried liquid on the cement.

It was the longest walk she'd ever endured. Every time they heard a noise they jumped in the bushes or took cover behind a car. When people screamed or called out for help they turned and walked in the opposite direction. A body still oozing fresh blood put them into a full-blown panic, but only because it meant one of the psychotic humans was close.

Eventually they made it to the downtown core, where they found Eve and Nathan. They spent the night under the Granville Bridge, where they crawled up onto a cement pillar. It was cold and miserable, and Aries spent the entire night afraid to close her eyes. She couldn't get past the fear of falling asleep, rolling off the bridge, and hitting the dark waters below.

The next evening they found the apartment block. Set above a restaurant, it had no way inside on the first floor except for two giant iron doors with heavy-duty locks. The windows on the second and third levels were broken, and a corner of the roof had caved in during the earthquake, but it was secure. A dropped key by the steps gained them access. No one else was inside.

It became their haven.

The building wasn't exactly livable. Many of the apartments were empty; it seemed the place was undergoing renovations when the earthquake happened. The few places that had been inhabited were sparsely furnished. They found a bit of food in the cupboards and the rest they managed to scrounge by sneaking out in the dead of night to the convenience store down the street. After a few weeks of living on chocolate bars and bags of chips, they were starting to get jittery. The sugar rushes were wearing down their bodies and tripping out their minds. Aries was tired all the time, and she was positive the others felt the same way. She knew there were other shops farther into the city, some maybe as close as a few blocks away. But getting to them would be risky. They were all running short on bravery these days. Maybe after a few days of starving, they'd change their minds. But it hadn't happened yet.

All they did was sit around and wait. The building was damp because of its age and all the rain. The lack of windows meant a constant draft they couldn't escape. Her body constantly felt soggy.

If they found other survivors, they'd be stronger. They could form a community. They'd be able to divide the responsibilities better and get more organized. It would be good to find a doctor. Even a police officer. They could learn more about self-defense. They could learn to protect themselves. The bigger the group, the tougher they'd be. Maybe eventually they could find a way to communicate with other cities.

If they could find a way to share their stories they might be able to find a way to defeat the monsters.

"Maybe I will take a break," she said. Forcing herself to stand, she ignored the strained ligaments and pulled the blanket off her body and draped it over Jack's shoulders.

"Good," he said. Sniffing at the scratchy wool, he made a face. "This is disgusting."

"Better than nothing," she said. "I'm gonna go make some coffee. Do you want?"

"Caramel macchiato with extra foam. Double shot of vanilla, too."

"Black it is, and if you're lucky I'll stir it with a Twix bar."

Jack laughed. "You're on."

She paused at the door, keeping her face hidden from his. "Sometimes when I close my eyes, I'm afraid of my mind going dark. Like I'll wake up changed into one of those things."

"If you were one of them, I think you'd know it by now."

"We don't know that. We don't know how any of this works. Why'd they change in the first place?" She turned to face him, and her eyes found his.

"You're right," he said. "We don't know. But I'm going to continue believing that no one else is going to change. Otherwise I'll just drive myself crazy wondering. I can't live that way."

She nodded. "You make sense. I don't remember you being this sensible back in school."

"I'm shockingly intelligent sometimes."

"I see that. One Twix bar coffee coming up for you." She left him by the window and headed down toward the kitchen they were using. No one was there, and she poured some bottled water into a pot. Placing it on the Coleman stove, she turned on the gas. They were running out of propane. Soon this luxury would be over too.

While she waited for the water to boil, she leaned against the counter and stared absently out onto the street. It was empty, but she couldn't help but think of all the people she hoped were still alive. She often thought about her parents. Were they safe? More than anything else in the world she wished she could stop by her house and see if her Mom and Dad were waiting. Their faces were strong in her memory.

She imagined the reunion several times a day, the surprised, relieved looks she'd get when she walked through the door. She'd give anything to curl up in her bed with her warm blankets. Her bed was the unreachable dream.

But her house was all the way on the other side of the city. Even if she managed to find a car, it would take hours just to try and navigate around all the stalls and accidents. All the bridges were jammed with abandoned cars. There wasn't a way in or out of the downtown core. Walking would be impossible. There were too many of those monsters just waiting to snatch up the last of humanity.

It was farther away than the moon.

CLEMENTINE

Dear Heath, I'm such an idiot and now I'm going to die. If there is a heaven, I hope you're waiting for me.

Lying on her back in the baseball dugout, Clementine held a shaking hand over her mouth. Less than two feet above her, strange voices held a discussion about what they'd like to do if they found a nice young girl.

"Getting harder and harder to find a chick," one of them grunted.

"That's cuz you keep killing 'em," said the other. "I dunno why you had to go and off that pretty brunette. I would have liked to spend some more time with her. Gotta appreciate it: soon good women gonna be a thing of the past. You know I only like the ones who scream, and they're gonna be extinct like the dinosaur."

"Better enjoy 'em while we can, then."

Thankfully it was dark, but if one of them had happened to glance down they might have seen the moonlight reflecting off her eyes.

It seemed like a good idea at the time. Hide in plain sight, where they'd never think to look—it was ingenious. She'd exhausted all other forms of safety. The first few nights she'd pulled off the highway and tried sleeping in the truck. But that never felt right. Every time she closed her eyes she'd visualize a hand smashing through the windshield, bits of glass pelting her body as thick arms reached out to grab her hair. Even if she drove down old service roads where the odds of anyone finding her were almost zero, she still heard imaginary noises every time she tried to relax. Saw shadows moving through the darkness. She started looking for abandoned buildings, farmhouses or gas stations where she might be able to lock herself in an upstairs room for a few hours' sleep.

She ended up bypassing Des Moines completely. It was obvious there'd be no police there to help. She'd seen the squad car half an hour before reaching the city limits. It was flipped over on its back, and the officers inside had been beaten to death, their weapons gone. They weren't the only victims on the side of the road. The highway leading away from the city was filled with cars, some abandoned, others filled with dead bodies. What happened in Glenmore was happening across the rest of America. On the other side of Des Moines, she ran into a couple of adults who told her that the crazy people were going from home to home, dragging out the hidden and killing them in the streets. After that, houses became a threat too. She couldn't even look at one without involuntarily shuddering.

No place was safe.

"They're barricading the main highways too," the older woman told her before they parted. "Disguising themselves as military. Pulling people out of their cars and shooting them. Up north they were everywhere. Dead zones. Miles of cars filled with bodies. Be careful. Avoid the main roads."

She continued on, refusing the offer from the couple to

join them. They were heading south and she wasn't about to abandon her goal of reaching Seattle. Her parents were gone, their bodies abandoned with the only town she'd ever lived in. She owed it to them, especially her mother with her eerie premonitions, to try to let her brother know what happened.

But it was slow moving. Getting gasoline could end up being an entire day's ordeal. Luckily for her, she'd spent the past two summers working at the Gas N Go and knew how to get gasoline out of the underground reservoir. It wasn't an easy job and often took her hours of surveillance before she even attempted to go near the station.

Avoiding the vulnerable highways was the other major distraction. Many of the service roads weren't mapped, and often she'd reach dead ends after driving for hours.

She was on her third vehicle since she'd left her parents' house three weeks ago. Her original truck she abandoned after she swerved into a ditch while trying to avoid hitting a couple of cows that had wandered into the middle of the road. She took the second car off a lot but lost it in the first major barricade outside of Sioux City. She spent several days hiding in the back of someone's van, trying to gather enough courage to move on. Eventually hunger and the smell of her unwashed body was enough for her to sneak along the road until she reached what remained of civilization. Luckily for her, most of the area was already abandoned or dead, so she picked up some supplies and a new ride from a grocery store parking lot.

She kept telling herself it wasn't theft, that the cars and trucks she took weren't being used and it's not like the real world existed anymore.

I'm coming, Heath.

She refused to believe he was dead. Naive or not, the hope kept her strong.

Sleeping in the baseball dugout was a good idea. Who on earth was going to come searching for her there? It wasn't like anyone was going to try to get a team together for a friendly competition. The field was beside a burned-down high school, so she didn't have to worry about people being attracted to the building. There was no one left alive to hide in it, anyway.

She had a sleeping bag. It was unzipped in case she had to make a hasty retreat. But she'd fallen asleep at the wrong time and been awakened by the sound of the two men walking across the dirt. The chance to escape had been twenty minutes ago.

Now her brilliant idea lay thrown in the mud, and the hope of surviving the night diminished with every second.

They must have heard her heartbeat. How could they not? It was hammering against her rib cage, threatening to tear its way right out of her chest.

"Town's dead," one of the voices said above her. Clearing his throat, he spat in the dust, inches from Clementine's face. Spit bubbles popped in the moonlight.

"Was fun, wasn't it?"

A throaty chuckle drifted downward.

Remaining calm was impossible. Every vein in her body ached to run. Dendrites exploded, sending false information to her brain. A million insects crawled around on her skin; spiders scratched their legs through her hair. Knees ached, longing to expose her through involuntary kicks. A tickle in the back of her nose threatened a full-blown sneeze. Even her eyes begged to be blinked.

"We should call it a night, then."

"Sounds good."

Footsteps crunched and she almost cried out in relief. But then one of them paused.

"Hold up, gotta take a leak."

The sound of the zipper almost brought her to tears. Even though she knew it was coming, she still jerked when the stream of urine hit her opened sleeping bag, sending a stream of liquid across the waterproof fabric and straight onto her shirt. Why hadn't she thought to cover herself properly? She bit down hard on her lip to try to prevent the fumes from reaching her lungs.

It went on forever, the liquid soaking through her clothes, touching her skin, staining her body.

"That's better." The zipper went back up, and the man moved away from the dugout.

She continued to lie there, soaked and frozen, long after the footsteps faded away. Part of her kept thinking they were waiting for her. She hadn't fooled them one little bit. The second she stood up they'd be on her, tearing her apart, doing deeds a million times worse than anything her mother ever warned her about.

It was the smell that finally jerked her into action. She couldn't take it anymore. Carefully she rolled the sleeping bag aside, trying to avoid any more urine reaching her clothing. Waiting on her knees, she listened to the night, ignored the chirping crickets and swaying prairie grasses, until she was satisfied she was truly alone. She'd have to take the chance. Otherwise she might fall apart and start crying.

Standing up quickly, she scanned the surrounding field, and it was empty. The urge to cry again struck her, but she kept busy by examining her shirt. Her first instinct was to rip it off, but she didn't have anything else to wear. Removing it would leave her even more exposed, and she didn't think she was strong enough for that.

No, she'd have to find something else. The main area of town was just two blocks away. Surely she'd find a clothing store or gas station that sold souvenir shirts. Urine-covered girls like herself couldn't be choosy. Glancing down at her sleeping bag, she decided to leave it behind. It would only stink up the truck, and there was no way she'd ever sleep in it again now.

The truck was parked out past the burned high school, down a side street where other parked cars added camouflage. She'd leave it where it was for now. The two men (and lord knows who else) were still close enough that they'd hear if she tried to drive. But if she hurried, she could find a store, grab some clothes, and be ready to head out within the hour. There would be no more sleeping tonight. Hopefully tomorrow she'd have better luck.

She moved slowly across the baseball field and back toward town. The silence was good but also unnerving. There were no alleys here to sneak down, so she kept to the sidewalks, shadowing the houses, prepared to run and hide at the slightest breaking branch.

The main street was actually Fourth Avenue. There were no working street lamps, and she was happy about that. A quick glance showed row upon row of empty parking spaces. Not even a single abandoned truck. The street was lined with glass-windowed shops, a hardware store, a pharmacy, three bars, a grocery store, and an insurance and travel place combined. Two motels offered satellite television and air-conditioning. At the end of the block she found what she was looking for. A small thrift store with a rack of secondhand shoes still left out on the sidewalk. The door was shut, but when she tugged at the handle, it opened.

Bells immediately chimed above her head.

It took every ounce of willpower to keep from turning and running off into the night.

Nothing happened. The bells stopped rattling, and the sounds of empty street filled her ears. She couldn't even hear the crickets anymore.

Why hadn't she thought to check the door for bells? She was getting careless. She'd never have done that a few days ago. She'd have waited about half an hour to make sure the store was empty, gone around and checked the back for exits, made sure she really was alone—and then she would have cautiously checked the door for bells and whistles before she opened it.

But she was tired. People make mistakes when they're tired.

Fools and their lives are soon parted.

Glancing down the street, she shrugged and entered the shop. Might as well go ahead now that the whole town knew she was there, but she'd check for an exit before she allowed herself to go on a shopping spree.

She found it in the back, a locked door with a darkened exit sign. Unlatching the lock, she pushed the door open and found herself practically in someone's backyard. It would provide a good escape if she needed one. Satisfied, she closed the door, latched it up again, and proceeded to the front, already dreaming of how good it would feel to remove her shirt and put on something fresh. There was a small bathroom and half a bar of green soap and an orange towel. She returned to the front, where she found a bottle of water behind the counter—that would help rinse off some of the grossness.

Picking through the rack, she discarded the first few items because they were either too large or too bright. Darker colors were safer. Pushing aside a worn pink cardigan, she found a blue-and-green plaid shirt that looked to be about her size. She glanced back at the front door to ensure she was alone before yanking off her top and dumping the stinking garment on the floor.

She soaked the towel with water and ran it along her body, trying to remove all traces of urine. Using the soap, she cleaned quickly, her eyes constantly keeping watch on the door. She moved quietly, a tiny mouse removing all traces of scent so that the snakes wouldn't find her.

She almost cried out in relief when she pulled the shirt over her body and did up the buttons. It fit perfectly, and there was such a wonderful feeling to be free from that rank odor. Turning to leave, she paused, thinking that it might be a good idea to grab an extra change of clothing in case something like this happened again. Who knew when she might come across another clothing store? She should grab a coat, too.

She found a jean jacket a size too big and slipped it on. It would do. Back at the rack, she pulled out a black sweater and a shirt that said Michigan State. She found a bag behind the counter and shoved her new items inside.

Dear Heath, that's quite possibly the quickest shopping spree I've ever been on. You'd be proud. You always said I had too many shoes. Now I'm down to one pair. They're made for walking, and I'll be heading out soon enough to find you.

She came from behind the counter but froze when she looked out the window and saw the men from the ball park on the sidewalk. Quickly she dropped to the ground, her heart thumping against her chest and pounding in her ears. Icy saliva filled her mouth; she couldn't swallow it.

The bells chimed as the door opened.

"Come on, sweetie," the first guy said. "We know you're here. We saw you from the window."

Her eyes darted across the counter shelves. She needed a weapon. Anything. Behind the assorted bags she saw a letter opener. Fingers closed around the metal. It would have to do.

"We ain't got all day, girlie."

She raised her head and stood her ground. She didn't want them coming around the counter to grab her. At least this way there would be space between them. Maybe she still had time to run. But could she get to the back room and unlatch the door before they caught her? She couldn't tell.

Dear Heath, give me strength.

"Well, ain't you a pretty one."

They knew what they were doing. As the first one talked, the second started leisurely moving his way toward her, trying to get around the counter so they'd have her cornered.

"Stay back." She raised the letter opener in defense.

"And what are you going to do with that, sweet pea? Stab me?"

Number Two was almost on top of her. She had to act. Hurling the shopping bag with all her might, she turned and darted toward the back room.

She made it to the door, but a hand clamped down on her shoulder before she could unlatch the lock.

"Bitch, I'm gonna—"

She didn't think. The letter opener moved through the air of its own accord; she was positive it wasn't her using it. Silver metal sliced the stomach flesh of its victim. How could something travel through tissue and muscle so easily?

The man grunted. She couldn't tell which one—it was too dark to see much of anything. He slouched against her, pressing her body up against the door, his breath heavy on her face. She could smell beer and potato chips. Onions. Shoving him with all her strength, she managed to twist around until she could reach and turn the lock. The door swung outward, sending both her and the man sprawling into the street.

She didn't pause. Kicking at the dropped man, she squeezed her body from underneath him, crawling away until she managed to get her legs up, and tore into a run. From behind she could hear the other man screaming at her, but if he gave chase, he wasn't fast enough to catch her.

Six blocks later, she unlocked her truck and started the engine before she even got the door closed. Slamming her foot on the gas, she tore off into the night, leaving behind the town and everything in it.

It wasn't until she got several miles away that she pulled over, letting the engine idle, and finally scrubbed at the tears that threatened her vision.

There was fresh blood all over her shirt. Her body was sticky again.

And after all that trouble, too.

MICHAEL

"Hey!"

A voice reached through the darkness.

"Hey! Idiot. Wake up. We've got to get out of here now."

Michael forced his mind away from the haziness that wasn't his dreams. When did he fall asleep? Wasn't he supposed to be on watch?

"Whatisit?" His mouth tasted like raunchy cotton balls. His neck was against the window frame, bent at an unusual angle. Already he could feel the knot worked into his muscles. There would be pain once he stretched out.

"There are bodies in the basement."

He was off the floor in an instant. "What? What do you mean, bodies? Who?"

"People. I dunno. Maybe the ones who own this house. Who the hell cares. We've got to get outta here. It's a bloody trap is what it is."

Evans's face was pale, his eyes wide and looking in every direction except at Michael. He rushed over to the window and stared out into the night. Michael joined him, but there wasn't anything to see. It wasn't a clear night, even the stars were invisible. When did it get dark? The sun was still in the sky last he looked. How could he do this—falling asleep while on duty? These people depended on him. He'd told Evans and Billy he would search the upstairs for useful things: weapons, clothing, that sort of stuff. He hadn't even made it past the first bedroom. What kind of leader was he if he couldn't do a simple thing like stay awake?

If this was a trap, then the Baggers would be coming. They might already be here; it was too dark to tell. The surrounding acres of forest made the ranch house the perfect hideout, but it was also a great location for an ambush.

Why hadn't he thought about that earlier?

"Who else knows about this?"

"No one." Evans pulled away from the glass. "I was checking the basement for the hot-water heater. Wanted to try and get some heat. I found them way in the back by the utility room. Stacked in the corner like wild meat. Something put them there. They didn't just die like that."

"That's screwed. Where are the others?"

"Billy and the rest are sleeping in the living room. Idiots ate too much and they all crashed. I think the mother's still in the bedroom with her sick kid."

"Get her up first," Michael said. "She'll take longer than the others. Make sure all the doors and windows are locked. Then tell Billy to try and gather up as much food as possible. But not too heavy. It'll just slow us down if we have to run."

"What are you gonna do?"

"Find some weapons."

Evans rushed off, leaving Michael alone in the master bedroom. He set to work, going through the closets, pulling boxes off the shelves and emptying the contents over the hardwood floors. What kind of people lived this far out in the middle of nowhere and didn't keep weapons? There had to be something. He tried to remember if he'd seen a shed in the garden, but he couldn't think hard enough. His mind was still hazy from being asleep for so long.

Maybe they were overreacting. Just because the bodies were hidden in the basement didn't mean the Baggers were watching the house. These killers were all sorts; it was possible that these ones just happened to be the neat-and-tidy kind after a kill. Maybe they spent the night and didn't want to deal with the smell? Or maybe they found the family hiding in the basement and finished them there. If they'd killed them elsewhere in the house, wouldn't there be some sign of a struggle? Pooled blood on the floors or streaks on the walls—there'd be evidence somewhere, right?

The bed.

Michael turned around and looked at the duvet. It was burgundy with a black-and-silver design. On top were half a dozen pillows arranged against the post. The bedroom was neat and orderly; even the clothing in the closet was arranged according to color and style. He'd gone through the contents of the bathroom earlier, and all the toiletries were neatly stacked and freshly dusted.

So why were the pillows crooked?

Michael reached out and picked up the closest, pulling them off two at a time until pillows littered the floor. Grabbed the side of the duvet and yanked the entire thing back in one dramatic heave.

The sheets were stained with blood. No, that wasn't the right word. They were swimming in the stuff.

"Oh, God."

He had to get Evans. Crossing the room, he put his hand on the doorknob, twisted, and started to open the door.

From downstairs came the sound of breaking glass. Wood splintered as the back door was kicked in. Billy shouted something, but the words were lost in the distance. Someone screamed.

Too late.

Slamming the door, he instinctively turned the lock. As he moved toward the bed, his heart jolted its way into his throat. Screams echoed up the stairs, voices he recognized. Something or someone thumped against the wall. More glass shattered.

He should move. Do something. But he couldn't. His legs were stuck to the floor. Blood rushed to his head, pounding in his ears, blurring out the screams and crashes. They were being slaughtered down there and he couldn't do a thing to stop it.

"Michael."

A fist slamming against the door broke his paralysis. Jumping, he stepped backward, tripping over the side of the bed, where he fell and cracked his back against a wooden hope chest. He sat down hard, chomping down on his tongue. He tasted blood; it filled his mouth, forcing him to gag. Stomach clenched, he crawled toward the bathroom and shoved his head in the toilet.

"Michael, open the damn door. We need help."

He could hear Evans screaming at him, but he was too far away. The voice was distant and blurry, like something out of a bad dream. He banged a few more times, his fist rattling the frame.

Then nothing.

Michael stood up on shaky knees and turned on the faucet, splashing water on his face. His sense of reality had gone out the window. He needed to think, get his brain working.

If he didn't act soon, they'd finish up downstairs and come for him next. But something turned off inside of him. All he could do was stand in front of the mirror and stare at his wet face. Brown eyes stared back at him. He brought his fingers up and pulled at a few of the long strands of greasy hair.

Is this what a coward looked like?

"What the hell are you doing?"

He started to scream, and Evans covered his mouth with lightning speed. How could he not have noticed there was an adjoining door to the bathroom?

"I. I can't. Don't touch me. I'm okay, man, I'm okay." The words regurgitated from his lips, no rhyme or rhythm. Babbling.

Evans slapped him hard. "Snap out of it."

It worked. The pain burned across his cheek, kicking his body back into action.

"You didn't have to do that," he lied.

Evans didn't respond. He turned and headed back to the other bedroom, where the mother sat on the edge of the bed, rocking her half-dead child and whispering to him that everything was going to be all right.

"We've got to get out of here," Evans said. He moved past the mother and looked out the window. "We'll have to climb out on the ledge."

"I can't do that," the mother said. "We can't. We're not strong enough."

"I'll carry him," Evans responded.

Michael looked at him with resentment. Evans was taking charge. Just like that. He didn't throw up or lose all control of his body. He kept cool.

"We could try hiding," he said. "They may not know we're up here."

"Don't be daft," Evans snapped.

Michael's eyes hardened.

Something slammed against the door. The mother let out a yelp, pulling her child closer, nearly to the point of suffocation. There was a low, guttural hiss from the landing outside the room, and someone tested the lock.

A second bang.

A third.

The door cracked and groaned under the weight. They were coming.

Evans couldn't get the window open. He pulled at it with all his strength. "Help me," he snapped at Michael.

The wood of the door splintered.

He didn't want to die. Not here. Not like this.

The door gave way. The Baggers filled the room. Four of them in total: three males and one female. Two of them were holding hands as if they were on some sort of psychotic honeymoon. Clothing soaked and stained, they dripped blood all over the floor, grinning like wild hyenas closing in on the kill.

I now pronounce you husband and wife. You may kill the congregation.

The ridiculousness of the thought almost reduced him to hysteria.

The choice was easy. It wasn't actually an option, just picking life over death. Michael stepped back into the bathroom, slamming the door and locking it.

The last thing he saw was the look on Evans's face. They locked eyes, Evans's narrowed until almost completely closed. Hands curled into tight fists. Disgust. Pity. Not because of the Baggers.

Because of him.

Betrayer.

No time to change his mind. Already one of the Baggers was working on the bathroom door, slamming his body against it. Michael had only seconds to act. Turning, he fled over to the bedroom window. It wouldn't open either; there must have been some sort of locking mechanism he wasn't seeing. Figuring it out would take too much time. On the bedside table was an alarm clock. Michael picked it up and threw it straight through the glass. He grabbed one of the pillows off the floor and used it to clear the frame of the remaining shards.

Evans shouted. The child was crying. Loud wails abruptly cut off. Evans screamed again, but he couldn't hear the words. Something slammed against the wall, shaking the foundation. A painting over the bed fell, raining glass over the bloody mattress.

He stepped out onto the roof. Scrambled to the edge and jumped without looking. He hit the ground and rolled; his ankles and knees screaming in protest. White-hot heat shot through his side, knocking the wind out of his lungs. His face took a dive in the dirt; twigs and pebbles grinded against his tongue. Lying on the ground, he gasped, unable to move, unable to breathe.

For half a minute he lay helpless, tears leaking out of the corners of his eyes and soaking the ground where his cheek rested. His body slowly came back to life as the air started to reach his lungs. Pressing his hands into the ground, he got onto his knees, puffing as if he'd just run a marathon. Dirt-colored drool escaped his lips.

He needed to move. They would be on top of him in seconds.

Finally his legs had enough strength and he managed to

start running, wobbly at first, swaying back and forth with drunken steps. He headed straight for the trees without looking back. He knew if he saw them coming after him, he'd freeze again, useless, and they'd be all over him, too.

MASON

Pop.

Pop.

Bang!

The world returned in an instant. His brain struggled to place mental imagery to the sounds. Not a car backfiring. Not gunshots. He knew that sound. He'd heard it enough times in the past. Someone was shooting off firecrackers just outside the window.

He couldn't have been unconscious for long. A few minutes, maybe—not enough time for Twiggy to do anything. Mason was still lying on the floor, head throbbing, hair soaked in tea. At least he hoped it was tea. The broken mug lay inches from his nose.

Twiggy was over at the window, head sticking out, leg bopping up and down as he screamed at the intruders.

"Heathens. Leave. You're not welcome here. Don't make me come down there and get you."

Mason sat up too quickly. Stars exploded across his vision, forcing the room into a spin faster than any amusement-park ride he'd ever encountered. He raised a hand to the side of his head; the fingertips came back bloody. Struggling onto his knees, he managed to stand by leaning against the wall for support. The door was still open; Twiggy hadn't bothered to close it after the attack.

"You." Twiggy turned his attention away from the window. He'd left his crutches by the bed. Bouncing up and down on his leg, he seemed to be deciding if he could cross the room before his prey got out the door.

Mason was closer. Reaching out, he picked up the crutches and threw them into the hall. His legs continued to sway, but the stars were gradually beginning to fade. Vision growing stronger, he found his bag on the floor and picked it up.

"You woke up sooner than I expected," Twiggy said. "What a shame." His face showed visible disappointment.

"Why?" Mason asked. "You could have killed me back on the street. Why all the acting?"

"Had you fooled, didn't I?" Twiggy said. "I always liked a show. Better than simply putting a bullet in your brain. I needed to see if I could convince you first."

"What the hell did I ever do to you? What did any of us do?"

Twiggy's face erupted in various shades of red. "Are you that stupid? Wait, don't say a word. You kids today think you know all the answers. You're nothing but a bunch of lazy bums. You're the reason society is faltering. It's because of you that the world needs to be cleansed. Because of you the voices come to us, turning some of us into mindless pack dogs. The rest of us receive clarity. I see everything that needs to be seen."

"That's an excuse."

"No excuse," Twiggy snapped. Spittle flew from his mouth. "We've been around for a long time, Mr. Dowell.

Longer than you or any of your stupid little friends could ever conceive. Sleeping in the shadows and waiting for the right moment. A disease you might call us. A plague. Evil. From beneath the ground, it rises as it has done many times in the past. It's given us our mission. We're cleansing. Removing the world of the filth it created. Rewriting, erasing the slate. How lucky we are to be a part of it. It chose me for a reason, and I am happy to serve. I'm one of the special ones, still able to keep my intelligence. My orders will be more complex and fulfilling than those of the insane heathens outside."

"So you're nothing but a dog, then," Mason sneered.

Twiggy laughed. "Do you know why some of you are allowed to stay alive? It's the fear. The pain. The enjoyment we get as we tear your skin to shreds. We feed on it."

"Maybe I'm just smarter than you," Mason replied. "Isn't that what you said? Free will? Maybe I'm able to fight it. But you're just weak. A sucker."

"You won't be singing that song when I tear the tongue from your throat."

Mason's legs were stronger. He calmly turned and stepped through the door. "Good luck with that, hoppy."

"You're all alone now," Twiggy screamed behind him. "We'll find you. You'll never hide long enough. We'll find you and kill each and every last one of you. All alone. Run, Mr. Dowell. You won't get far. Don't sleep! Don't sleep!"

He was fine with the hallway. The stairs required a bit more navigation. His balance was off, but he managed to get down by holding on to the banister and taking the steps one at a time. Twiggy continued to scream, and every time Mason glanced back, he half expected to see the old man hobbling toward him at full speed. But the staircase stayed empty.

Whatever world savior Twiggy thought he was, he knew his limitations. Next time he'd just have to hit his victim harder and make sure he stayed down.

Outside, the light burned straight into his brain, making him cringe. He paused at the door, unsure of what to do next.

First things first—he needed to get as far away from the building as possible. Then maybe he could find someplace to crawl into for a while until his brain stopped punishing him. What was the deal with concussions again? No sleeping. He'd have to stay awake. Maybe he could find a hotel with a swimming pool. Cold water would be a blessing and it would keep him clearheaded. It was a good idea. Up ahead he could see some signs for a Travelodge. Only a few blocks away; he could manage that. Close enough to walk to without dying, and far enough that Twiggy wouldn't follow.

It was hard moving. The sun pounded down on his back, making him sweat through his shirt. Squinting made his head want to explode, but the bright light made it throb worse. He kept his eyes on the ground, concentrating on moving each foot forward without tripping. His backpack weighed heavily on his shoulders, digging into his back, pushing him down.

He saw the couple cautiously coming toward him when he finally looked up. They were both wearing hiking clothes, with backpacks and sleeping bags. He froze, trying hard not to sway back and forth.

Keep cool, Dowell. Stand your ground.

"Hey," the guy said. "Need help?"

Mason didn't say anything. His knees shuddered. He was 100 percent positive he couldn't move another step. Something happened when Twiggy hit him: damage to his central nervous system or something.

"Hey," the girl said. They were closer now, almost on top of him. "You're really hurt."

"Stay away," he muttered.

"You're bleeding." She reached out to touch him, and he jerked back, almost toppling in the process.

"Watch out, Chee," the guy said. "He's scared."

"Screw you," Mason said.

"It's okay, man, we're cool."

"How do I know you're not one of them?"

The girl snorted, her hair flipping up behind her. "How do we know *you're* not one of them?"

"If I was, you'd be dead by now."

The girl stepped backward. "Well, if you're going to be a jerk about it . . . Come on, Paul. We don't need this."

But the guy didn't move. "We can't leave him. He'll be hunted down."

"He is pretty messed up."

Mason didn't know what to do. They seemed normal, but so had Twiggy. Who was he supposed to trust in this new world? More than that, who could trust him? Maybe that's why he was still alive and Twiggy hadn't killed him.

There was too much darkness inside his brain.

Until he knew for sure, he was better off alone. He knew this.

The guy sensed his wariness. "Look," he said. "We're cool. We're not gonna hurt you or try and rob you. We're in the same boat, man."

Mason decided to take the chance. "I'm sorry," he said. "Some crazy guy with one leg just invited me up to his place for tea and then tried to bash my head in with a mug. I'm a little short on trust right now."

"One leg?" The girl snorted again. "And he still managed to do that?"

"He seemed pretty normal at the start," Mason snapped, but a grin started to appear on his face. "I mean, how much trouble can a one-legged person be?"

"Is that some sort of bad joke, or are you really asking?" The girl grinned back.

"Little bit of both."

There was a short, awkward minute, while the girl visibly grew impatient. She glanced back and forth between them, shuffled her feet, and finally decided she'd had enough of the silence.

"I'm Barbara Flying Eagle, but everyone calls me Chickadee or Chee 'cause I'm so tiny. I hate Barbara, so don't ever call me that. Yuck. And this here is Paul Still Waters. We just call him Paul. But he's so tall, he won't hear you unless you shout."

Mason grinned again. The girl was definitely small. She had to be a little less than five feet tall. Her hair was long, almost down past her bum, making her appear even tinier, if it were possible. The guy beside her, Paul, was the complete opposite. He towered over her, gawky and serious; Mason instantly knew they were one of those couples that people always joked about in a friendly way. Night and day. Fire and ice.

"I'm Mason Dowell," he said.

"It's good to meet you," she said. "Now that we've got all that out of the way, I suggest we get the hell outta here. Didn't you hear the shots earlier?"

"I thought they were fireworks."

"Sure, the kind that come flying out the barrel of a gun."

They started walking, moving slower for Mason's sake. His legs were working again, but his head still felt fuzzy. Pain clawed at the insides of his skull. Chickadee and Paul stayed in the lead, walking about five feet ahead. They may have exchanged names, but neither side was taking any chances.

They were still strangers.

"Where are you headed, Mason?" Chickadee asked, keeping her voice low. She nodded toward his backpack.

"West," he said. Absently he reached his fingers into the back pocket of his jeans to make sure the Stanley Park picture was still there. "Vancouver."

"Cool," she said. "We're going north. Paul's got an uncle in the Yukon and we figure we'll head up there. Not a lot of people. Can't imagine it's been affected like it is here. His closest neighbor's about an hour away."

"Sounds like a good idea."

"It will be if we can last that long," Chickadee said. "It's pretty scary. We had some trouble this morning coming through the city. Did you see the fire? Couple of the crazies chased us, but we lost them in the smoke. They're bloody everywhere."

"I drove through some of it," Mason said. "But my car broke down a few blocks away. That's how I met Twiggy."

"We drove for a bit. Got stuck in one of those roadblocks a few weeks ago. They came at us with shotguns. I've never been so scared in my life. Luckily it was nighttime and we managed to hide in a wheat field. But we lost Trevor. He was my sister's boyfriend. My sister, she died a few weeks ago when this all started. I still dream about her every night. Paul lost his entire family because his older sister went crazy. Attacked everyone in the middle of the afternoon. I still don't know where my mom is. I'm hoping she's all right, but I doubt it. She didn't deal well, if you know what I mean."

Mason nodded. Chickadee waited a few minutes to see if he'd talk, but Mason wasn't ready to share. They'd just have to wonder. When he didn't speak, she continued to prattle on in a half whisper, filling the dead air with endless banter as they walked. He only listened halfheartedly, though. It was hard concentrating when his head throbbed the way it did.

"I need to stop," he said after a while. They were at the hotel he'd spotted earlier. "My head hurts," he added when they both looked at him. "But you can go on. I'm fine by myself."

Chickadee and Paul glanced at each other before she spoke. "No, it's cool. This place is as good as any, and I'm pretty tired myself. We can get separate rooms and lock each other out if you're still scared."

"I'm not scared of you," he said.

"Okay, just wary, then." She giggled. "But it's a good idea. It'll be dark soon. I don't like being out at night. Too hard to spot them coming."

The hotel had an indoor pool, but it would be a long time before people were able to enjoy the chlorine water again. They took adjoining rooms on the twelfth floor, figuring they'd be safest at the top. It was a long hike up, and by the time they got to their rooms Mason was ready to collapse. Normally he was in excellent shape. If Tom and his friends were watching him from heaven they were probably laughing their asses off.

They came to Mason's room first. Chickadee opened the lock and passed over the key. "Remember," she said. "We're right next door if you need anything."

"I'll be fine," he assured her. "Just need to lie down for a bit."

"You sure you don't have a concussion?" She eyed him cautiously.

"No," he said. "I don't think so. Just a headache. Wish I had some Tylenol, but I'll make do."

"I'll go get you some," she said. "Just let me drop my stuff. I saw a gift shop downstairs. I'll probably find a bottle there."

He didn't want her going back down all those stairs just for him. "I'll be fine," he said. "Honest."

"Okay."

"See ya," Paul added. It was the most he'd said in the past half hour. From what Mason could tell, Chickadee did all the talking for both of them.

He closed the door and tossed his backpack on the floor. The room was dark—no electricity of course—so he moved to the window and opened the curtains a little bit. He didn't think anyone would notice him that far up, but it was better to be safe than sorry. Glancing down onto the street below, he could see some people trashing a car with what might have been a baseball bat or a crowbar. A few blocks over to the right, a group of people had cornered someone. They were closing in on the kill. Even farther away, a group of people were stacking bodies into what looked like a gigantic bonfire.

Mason didn't watch after that. He lay down and tried not to think about it. Next door he could hear Chickadee jumping on the bed. Her muffled voice was cheery.

He wanted to be alone. Yes, he knew that. But at the same time, he was thankful he'd run into them. Chickadee's cheerfulness was contagious, and Paul looked like the kind of guy he'd want on his side if he was backed into a corner.

Closing his eyes, he fell asleep.

He awoke to a small tapping on his door. It took him a moment to remember where he was. The darkness was disorientating, and he couldn't understand why he was sleeping in a strange bed. Twiggy must have hit him harder than he first thought.

"Mason?" Chickadee's voice was soft through the wooden frame.

"Yeah, hold on a sec." Rolling over, he pulled himself up into a sitting position and immediately checked his head. There was a lot of dried blood, and it hurt when he pressed his fingers at the spot, but his headache was gone, along with the dizzy sensation.

His knees didn't buckle when he stood, and he took that as a good sign. Stumbling over his shoes, he maneuverd through the darkened room and tried to find the door. Chickadee waited with a candle in one hand, a gift shop bag in the other. Paul stood behind her munching on a bag of tortilla chips.

"I brought you some stuff," she said. "Don't bother to pay me back. I'm loaded these days. Money to burn."

Mason grinned. "Hold on," he said. "I've got the curtains slightly open. Let me close them before you come in with that light."

They waited at the door while he checked the window. The streets looked so tiny below him; he couldn't see much of anything. If the monsters were out there, they were camouflaged by the night.

"I brought you some Advil," she said. She pulled a tiny bottle out of the bag and tossed it at him. "Couldn't find any Tylenol."

"Thanks." He turned the bottle over in his hand but didn't open it. "My head feels better. I'm not sure I need this."

"That's good." Reaching back into the bag, she pulled out a six-pack of root beer. "I didn't get any booze," she said. "I had a feeling you probably wouldn't want any and Paul doesn't drink."

"That's fine," he said. "Yeah, I think I've had enough head pain to last me a while. I'll stick to sugar." He cracked the can and took a long drink. The root beer was warm, but he didn't mind.

"Most of the food's gone bad in the kitchen," she said. "But I managed to find some peanut butter and crackers." She turned the bag over and dumped it on the bed. It was mostly junk—potato chips and chocolate bars—but there were also a few wrinkled apples, along with the aforementioned peanut butter and box of saltines.

"Wow," he said.

He didn't touch the food. His stomach was too jumpy, so he stuck with the root beer and ended up swallowing a few of the Advil just to play it safe.

Paul and Chickadee divvied up the crackers, sticking their fingers in the peanut butter since she'd forgotten to grab a knife. They ate in silence for a while, the candle flickering softly on the bedside table.

"We'd like to come with you," Paul said eventually.

"Huh?" He'd been absorbed in his own thoughts.

"We want to go west," Paul said.

Mason stared at him blankly.

"We're not really heading north," Chickadee said. "I mean, we want to, but we don't really know where Paul's uncle lives. We don't even have an address. I guess it's just kinda a pipe dream?"

"Oh." Mason shrugged. "I guess that doesn't help."

"But if we go with you, at least we'd be together," Chickadee said. "We like you. Paul and I. We'd be safer as a group."

Mason shrugged.

"We don't take up much space," Chickadee said, sensing his reluctance. "Really, Paul may be a giant, but he's quite quiet. You won't even notice he's here. I'm a different story. I have this habit of talking endlessly, but most people find it charming. Why else would I be named after the cutest bird in history?"

"It's not that," he said. "I'm just not sure it's a good idea." How could he tell them the truth? That he didn't want them to come because of his darkness. He didn't deserve company. He wanted to be left alone so he didn't have to watch out for others and take care of anyone else too. He could be tougher by himself.

"Three pairs of eyes are better than one."

Mason swallowed.

Chickadee leaned in close. She continued to stare at him, refusing to blink. He couldn't help it; he broke into a smile.

"See," she said, leaning back and grinning, too. "You can't resist me."

He glanced over at Paul, but the taller guy didn't seem to be paying him any attention. Looking out the window, Mason figured he was obviously happy enough letting her do the negotiating. Paul knew what Mason was just learning for himself. Chickadee was good at getting her own way.

"So you want to go west, then?" he asked.

"West is warmer than north," Paul said. "Hell, it's warmer than here, even with the Chinooks. It's gonna be cold soon. Polar bear cold. I think we should head for the coast. Vancouver's really the best place to be. It doesn't get cold there. Mostly just a lot of rain. It'll get us through the winter alive."

Chickadee nodded. Her mouth was full of peanut butter. She chewed several times and swallowed. "I love Vancouver. I haven't been there in about two years. I'd love a chance to swim in the ocean again."

"Okay," Mason said. "Let's do it."

He'd worry about everything else later. It's not like he couldn't leave them if things went downhill.

"I'm so excited," Chickadee said. "This is the first time in a long while I've felt happy about something."

"Me too," Mason said, and he was surprised because it was true.

The next morning they gathered in the lobby, where Mason grabbed a map book from the gift shop. There were only a few roads between Calgary and the coast. They'd have to be careful.

NOTHING

I'm back.

I think I missed me.

There's blood under my fingernails. Dried on my clothing; matted in my hair; stained on my shoes. It's seeped through my skin, mixed with my own DNA, and I've absorbed all of its power.

I'm pretty sure it's not mine.

Life is a blur. I go in and out of time. The gray light takes over my body, eats my mind, and leaves me with the voices. I hear them. They curl up inside my frontal cortex and force all the warmth from my blood. Existence. Am I existing?

Why am I conscious when so many others are not? Are they doing this on purpose, and if so, why? Or is my brain wired differently from the average person's? What makes me stronger? Sometimes I wake up, and even if just for a moment, I'm aware of the things I've done. I'm pretty sure there aren't a lot who go back and forth the way I do. If all of them are having the same moments of clarity, I think there would be less killing. Less destruction. I can barely live with myself.

I wish I could stop remembering. I don't want to remember.

If they're going to steal my mind and control my body, why do they insist on giving me occasional freedom? If I must kill, then why do they torture me with blow-by-blow replays?

The girl. I remember her. So young. So pretty. I wanted to help her, but I can't be trusted. She was confused and I understand that. She wanted to be a part of something good. But I could see her darkness. The potential to kill was already inside her soul. She was no different from the others, only she didn't see it yet.

Eventually they will come to all of us. The chaos they've created will transform to a new world order.

Death will be a dream.

ARIES

"I'm not doing it."

"You agreed. Just like the rest of us."

"I changed my mind."

They sat in a half circle in a tiny one-bedroom apartment on the second floor. Jack was in the middle, holding a cardboard box with all their names thrown in. The rules were simple, and everyone agreed to it. Three names would be drawn, whoever got picked would take the trip. They were running out of food. This needed to be done.

Joy's name was the first drawn. She didn't say a word.

Aries's name came next. She'd planned it that way with Jack when she first approached him about the idea.

"Make sure you put my name somewhere you can easily pull it," she said. "I'm not sending them off without me. Consider me a silent volunteer."

"Let me come too, then." Jack brushed a strand of sandy brown hair from his eyes. "You're not going without me."

"No," she said. "You need to stay here in case I don't come back. So make sure you don't pick yourself."

Anyway, that was the plan. They all agreed. With Joy and

Aries on the list, they needed only one more. But Colin wasn't so eager when his name was chosen last.

"I'm not doing it," he said.

"Christ, I'll go," Nathan said. He took the box from Jack and started searching for his name. "I don't mind. I want to go."

"No," Aries said. "We all agreed. He can't go back on his word."

"I've got a cold," Colin said. "I'm not leaving this building unless I'm in perfect health. It's too risky."

"It's one excuse after the other with you," Eve said. She lowered her voice to try to match Colin's tone. "I'm too tired. I can't cook. I don't wanna!"

"Eve, stop it," Nathan said.

"I'm just tired of it," Eve said. "He's not very useful. And now he's going to screw everyone else because he's a coward."

Colin jumped to his feet. "You take that back."

"Make me."

"Children!" Jack jumped in between them. "Play nice. I'll go. I'll take Colin's place."

"No," Aries said.

"Okay, this needs to end," Nathan said calmly. "It's not worth the argument. I'm going and that's final."

Aries nodded at him. Nathan was right. Lately Colin picked a fight over every suggestion. He never wanted to do anything or be helpful. He wouldn't take a guard shift at night; instead he made excuses about how tired he was. He wouldn't help search the rooms for useful items; it was Joy who found the bicycles in the storage room. The world may have changed, but Colin hadn't. He was arrogant as always; being difficult was just another day for him. Of course, he wasn't the only one. They were all at each other's throats these days. Blame it on the lack of food, lack of space, lack of comfort, the inability to remain calm and collected. But Colin seemed to go out of his way to work the others into a pissing frenzy.

Nathan was right. It wasn't worth the argument.

"Fine," she said. "Nathan, Joy, and I will make the trip."

Jack slammed the box down on the table and left the room.

Aries started to chase after him and then stopped herself. She couldn't make everyone happy and she was tired of having the peace-keeping job. Jack would cool off on his own. There were more important matters to deal with.

"Let's plan this, then," she said.

"I'm going to go make some tea," Eve said. "Anyone want?"

Eve left with her orders. Aries stared at Colin, who sat back down on the floor and started leafing through an old magazine. He acted as if the argument never happened, as if he hadn't just forced Nathan to make a trip that he'd agreed to when he put his name in the box. It was *Alice in Wonderland* all over again, with Colin making a scene because everything wasn't going according to *his* plan.

Finally she turned her back on Colin and sat down with Joy and Nathan. She would be the bigger person. She'd get over it. Being this annoyed was terrible. It was a side of herself she didn't like seeing. Plus it was too exhausting, and she needed to save her strength.

"I'm thinking we should take the bikes," she said. "They're in good shape, Jack looked them over. We'll be faster that way—but more in the open."

"What happens if we find other normal people?" Nathan said. "I think you're right. There's got to be lots out there."

"That's why I want to pick up some handheld receivers. If we're going to start searching the city, we need to keep in touch."

"Agreed," Joy said. "Let's make a list of the important things besides food. Less stinky blankets for one. I need a coat, too. And let's not forget weapons. We need to arm ourselves."

"We all need coats," Nathan said. "This could get heavy. Are you sure we can manage with bikes? We could steal a car. Anyone know how to hot-wire?"

Colin snickered.

Aries ignored him. "Cars are loud. Might as well slap a Here I Am sticker on our foreheads. They'll follow the sound. If we can make it in without them knowing, we'll have more time to shop. I don't want us getting trapped inside."

"And we don't want to drag them back here either," Joy agreed. "So far they haven't found us. I'd like to keep it that way."

"Me too," Aries said.

"Okay," Nathan said. "Bikes it is. Maybe we can get some of those large camping backpacks. That way we can take more stuff."

Colin snickered again.

"Do you have something you'd like to say?" Aries asked.

"Nope," Colin said, never taking his eyes off the magazine. "You're doing just fine. Keep on planning. If you find any hot female survivors, send them my way. I could use a change of scenery."

"Why are you even here?" Joy asked. "You've made it clear you don't want to be a part of this. So why don't you just take off? Go read somewhere else. I don't want to look at you."

Colin threw the magazine aside and jumped to his feet. "Wish granted," he said before disappearing into the hallway.

"He's horrible," Joy whispered after he stormed off. "He complains about everything and everyone. Yesterday he screamed at me because the coffee's gone. I don't even drink coffee."

"He's having trouble adjusting," Aries said. "I think he . . . misses Sara too."

"If he's so miserable he should just leave."

"Where would he go?"

"Right now I don't care."

Aries didn't either, but she kept her comments to herself.

Part of her wished that she'd never gone to the school. She should have ignored Daniel's warnings and tried finding her parents. She might have reached them or ended up someplace completely different, with people she'd never met before. People who didn't constantly remind her of everything she'd lost. She still couldn't look at Colin and not see Sara. No, that wasn't fair. Both Joy and Jack were good people; together they'd helped one another. She couldn't have come this far without them.

She had to take the good with the bad. She'd put up with Colin because no one else would. She'd continue to defend him because they were a group and they had to stay a group in order to survive. If things got to the point where they started turning their backs on each other and kicking people onto the street, well, then they weren't any better than the monsters.

"Let's go take a look at the bikes," Nathan said, trying his best to change the subject.

"Okay," Joy said. "I get the blue one."

Night came quickly.

Aries had a list. It was tucked away in her jeans pocket. Nathan and Joy each had one too. They discussed it for hours, trying to reduce the necessary items to the bare essentials. No point in carrying what they didn't absolutely need. If they pulled this off successfully, then they'd try again. Her job was to find clothing and sleeping bags. Nathan and Joy were on food duty.

The store was roughly eighteen blocks away. One of those big all-in-one, shop-till-you-drop, everything-under-one-gigantic-roof places. They weren't even sure they'd be able to get inside. They didn't know who might be there waiting or if it was still standing. The earthquake destroyed so much, and lately there'd been lots of fires. The city was covered in a smoky haze. So many what-ifs. But they had to try.

They waited behind the locked door while Jack and Eve checked to make sure the streets were empty. Aries absently squeezed the brakes on her handlebars. It was like psyching themselves up for war, bicycle messengers heading out to acquire foodstuffs to save their troops.

"I feel like I'm getting ready for a journey into hell," Joy said. "I used to love shopping."

"Me too," Aries said. "But I don't remember it being such a violent sport. Except maybe on Black Friday."

Nathan gave them a forced grin through the murky room.

"All clear!" Eve poked her head out from the top of the stairs. "Don't go right. A group of them just headed off in that direction. Straight ahead is clear, but there's a lot of smoke two blocks over by the Irish Pub. Low Road's clear. I'd head that way."

Nathan waited while Eve raced down the stairs. It would be their first time apart since this whole ordeal began. Although she was trying hard to be strong, Aries could see the worry in her eyes. She threw her arms around him and held on tightly.

"I'll be back," Nathan told her when it became apparent she was having trouble releasing him.

"You'd better," she whispered, reluctantly letting go. "I still need you."

Nathan nodded and turned back to the group. "Let's do it." Reaching out, he unlocked the deadbolt and gave the iron doors a hard shove. Fresh night air swept over Aries's face. For the first time in weeks she found herself wishing it was raining. The pelting drops would have helped cover the noise they were about to make.

"Remember," Aries said, "if we get in trouble, split up. We'll meet again at the back of the store. The loading docks. It'll be darker than the parking lot. And if there's trouble, go inside and get what you can."

"Sounds good," Nathan said.

Joy nodded.

Pushing her bike out into the street, Aries placed her foot on the pedal and lifted her leg over the saddle. The bike was small and Jack had raised the seat so that her knees wouldn't be hitting the handlebars. He'd found a small bottle of oil in the maintenance room and spent most of the day oiling the chains to guarantee less friction.

They pushed off silently into the night. Tires crunched against the cement, but the noise was minimal. Unless they directly crossed paths with one of the killers, they'd be able to make it to the shop without being discovered. Although her heart jumped around in her chest, the muscles in her arms relaxed a little. The air cooled her face, and she inhaled deeply, such a wonderful change from the moldy apartment.

It was hard.

The earthquake destroyed a lot of the city. Most of the buildings were still somewhat attached, but glass littered the streets, and pieces of concrete and brick made everything more challenging. There were holes in the roads too, some of which sank deep into the earth.

Abandoned cars filled the streets, making it impossible to

bike in a straight line. The roads became a maze in which they were forced to crawl along, weaving in and out between the silent machines. Many of the car doors were left open, adding to the obstacle course. Aries turned left to bypass a van and swerved to avoid riding straight into a mailbox.

There were bodies on the roads, on the sidewalks, in cars, on benches, everywhere. Some of them were seriously starting to decompose. The fresh air that felt so wonderful on her face began to change. The smell of rotting flesh reached her lungs and was absorbed into her clothing.

She began to breathe heavier. The ride got even harder; she was out of shape after hiding out in the apartment for the past three weeks. Her calves ached and sweat poured down her forehead and into her eyes. She kept rubbing her face, and soon her hands were slippery with perspiration. Her handlebars grew sticky. She glanced over at Nathan, who barely looked winded at all. Joy, however, lagged behind them, and Aries felt better knowing she wasn't the only one having trouble.

When they got through this, she would start exercising on a daily basis. Running up and down the stairs or doing push-ups—whatever she could do to keep healthy.

She almost didn't notice when Nathan hit the brakes. Pulling on the hand gears, she stopped hard, almost flipping herself right over the front tire.

"What's going on?" Joy whispered.

"Over there," Nathan said.

They all looked at once.

A block ahead, a group of people moved down the street. The darkness made it impossible to see any faces, but there were too many of them to take a chance on finding out.

"This way," Nathan said. Turning his bike to the left, he

jumped the sidewalk and headed straight into a courtyard. Aries and Joy followed.

"Do you think they saw us?" Joy asked. They were moving slower now. The cobblestone was slippery and the tires wobbled side to side on the uneven surface.

"Not sure," Nathan said.

They passed through the courtyard and into the next street over. They continued in the direction of the store, but Aries knew something was wrong. It was too quiet.

They were waiting for them at the intersection. Two dozen people or so emerged from the shadows. They came from all directions at once, running, closing the gap.

"Split up!" Nathan screamed.

Aries turned her bike left, toward the closest group. She took the direct approach, straight through the crowd. Someone grabbed hold of her shirt, almost yanking her backward. She managed to stay on her bike by delivering a blind kick. She heard a loud grunt as her foot struck home, and the hand on her shirt loosened.

She didn't look back to see how the others were doing. There wasn't enough time. Hitting her brakes, she swerved to avoid a greasy-haired attacker, turned sharp toward the right again, and pushed all her weight onto the pedals, picking up speed but going in the wrong direction.

The street ahead was clear. Behind her, shoes slapped the pavement, and people screamed and swore, but the sounds began to decrease as she gained speed. She kept up the pace for a few blocks and then turned again. There was a path she knew would take her back in the right direction. There were no more sounds behind her, but she was too spooked to turn around and look. Up ahead she could see the road she needed to take. Increasing her speed, she pumped her legs with everything she had.

She hit the corner too sharp and felt the tires slide out from underneath her. Her jaw clamped down as she hit the pavement, cutting off the scream that should have come from her lips. Her jeans tore as she sailed across the ground; gravel and dirt bit through her skin, blazing a trail of white-hot fire against her leg.

When she opened her eyes, she expected to see a group of people staring down at her. But the streets were empty. She listened, but there were no more footfalls. No screams. Nothing. All she could see was the night sky glaring down at her. Pulling herself up, her entire body resisted, screaming at her. Everything hurt—even her eyelids complained.

But she couldn't afford to listen.

Legs shaky, she picked up her bicycle from where it lay spread out beside an abandoned car. The forks were a little bent and the handlebars were scuffed, but the chain was still on and the tires looked like they'd turn. Limping, she pushed the bike a few feet to make sure it wasn't broken. Climbing back on, she ignored the pain and started pedaling. When she got to the store, she'd take the time to check out her damage. Until then she'd grit her teeth and fight the throbbing mess that used to be her body.

It took her a few blocks before she got back on track. She wasn't overly familiar with the area, and it was even harder at night with the shadows mixing up her sense of direction. But eventually she found the path that led along the inlet and farther into the city. She moved silently, aching, her heart beating rapidly against her chest.

She almost cried out in relief when she saw the store. It stood out against the night, the bright white building with miles of empty parking spots. It didn't appear damaged. Even the windows were intact as she pedaled up to the front. She tried the doors, but they were locked. Cupping her hands against the glass, she peered inside but couldn't see much. The store was dark, the aisles empty. Nothing seemed out of order.

It was a miracle that it had lasted this long without being looted. But they chose it because it was farther out in the industrial area and hopefully there'd be fewer people. Maybe this had saved it. The Costco was much closer, but it was in the middle of downtown, and they'd all agreed it was more of a risk.

She decided to head around to the back and see if the others were there. A small voice in her head spoke to her, asking her what she'd do if Nathan and Joy didn't show up. She tried to ignore it, but it was strong.

She'd have to be stronger.

Behind the building, she climbed off her bicycle and pushed it as she walked the length of the store. The loading docks were at the other end. The big double doors were pulled down and locked tightly. She stepped up to the side entrance and tried the handle. If it was locked she'd have to try and find another way in. She didn't know the first thing about breaking into buildings.

It opened.

Stale air hit her face. It was pitch-black inside. She stood at the door for a few minutes, listening to the emptiness of the building. If someone was inside they might not have heard her open the door. But if someone was inside hiding, wouldn't they have locked the door to begin with? It would have been the first thing she'd do. She pulled out the flashlight Jack found back at the apartment block and turned it on, shining it inside the massive room. There wasn't much there, lots of boxes, a receiving desk, and two hallways that led off in different directions.

There was no indication that anything had been disturbed recently. None of the boxes were opened, and the receiving desk had a thin layer of dust on it. She tried shining the flashlight on the floor, looking for fresh footprints in the dust. She couldn't see anything.

Pushing her way through the back doors, she moved onto the sales floor, carefully scanning the area to make sure it was clear.

She stopped in electronics first to grab some batteries. They were a much-needed asset for the flashlights. At the Duracell section something caught her attention and she moved farther down the aisle. In front of her were dozens of handheld receivers. Walkie-talkies, her father used to call them. He had given her a pair when she was younger. They used to take them camping and talk to each other, pretending they were survivors in the wilderness. She pulled down two of the most expensive packages she could find.

She was about to move on when someone coughed.

She ignored the pain in her leg and spun around. The aisle was empty. Cold shivers ran along her spine. She'd definitely heard something. But from where? And who? It couldn't be Nathan and Joy. They would have said something.

Cautiously she moved along the row, stepping quietly, preparing herself for the moment when something jumped out at her. But nothing happened. She turned the corner, holding the flashlight ahead of her body, ready to use it as a weapon if need be. But the main aisle was empty too.

Maybe she was hearing things. But then something caught her eye over by the bedding displays, a pink futon with purple pillows.

A shadow moved. She heard the click of another flashlight as the bright light shone straight into her eyes, blinding her. She squinted, trying to see.

The light fell away from her face as the person in front of her dropped to their knees. A man wearing a black hoodie and torn jeans rocked back and forth several times before toppling over on his side, the flashlight falling from his fingers. He didn't make a sound as he landed on his stomach, his face away from her. Black hair spread out across his cheeks. She moved toward him, wondering if she should say something. She wished she had a proper weapon. She should have gone into the sporting-goods section and grabbed a baseball bat. Why didn't she think of that before?

Aries moved closer until she could see the man's face.

The breath caught in her throat.

It was Daniel.

CLEMENTINE

Her sneakers had a hole in them. She couldn't remember ever wearing a hole through a pair of shoes before. Not like this. Not from walking.

She was tired. Her legs ached in a way they'd never hurt before. Her feet were on constant fire. There was a permanent knot in her lower back, and her shoulders hurt from carrying the backpack. She knew she should be taking breaks but was afraid she'd be unable to get up again once she sat down. For two days she'd continued down the road. Two days without seeing a single person. The latter she wasn't complaining about, although in this new world she missed having people to talk to.

Dear Heath, I talk to you a lot these days. It's kinda nice, although I wish you could actually talk back. I miss you. I don't think I ever thought about it before. You were always there, even if it was just a phone call. But did we ever have full conversations? You're my brother. Shouldn't we have said more?

I really hope you're alive and waiting for me. It'll justify all this talking in my head. I'll know that I really am reaching you and not a ghost.

She thought about the last sentence and repeated it a few times over in her mind. She didn't want to believe but secretly accepted that there was a good possibility her brother no longer existed in this world. She tried not to think about it. She wanted to continue being the optimist. She needed that destination; if Heath was dead, then her journey was pointless. Where else would she go?

If you are dead and in heaven or whatever sort of afterlife you've discovered, tell Mom and Dad I'm doing fine and that they don't need to worry about me. They raised one tough cheerleader daughter. Go team!

She stopped, reached back, and grabbed her water bottle, which had been filled at the last stream she'd passed. Taking a long drink, she barely even noticed the cool liquid slide across her tongue. Nothing tasted right anymore. Even her taste buds were exhausted. When was the last time she ate? She couldn't remember. Food no longer held any interest.

Night came, but she barely noticed. Her feet continued to slap the pavement, one step at a time. Right, left, right, and again left. One and two and three and four, one and two and three and four, two-four-six-eight who do we appreciate? Yay, Glenmore Goblins! Football seasons and forgotten cheers haunted her mind. A repetition of rhymes echoed with each step. A few times she almost walked right off the road, only noticing when her shoes stumbled over grassy hills instead of pavement.

When she finally fell, it didn't register in her brain until she was tumbling through the air. Surprised, she didn't even have time to put out her arms to brace herself. She hit the grass sideways and rolled down the embankment and into the ditch. Landing on her back, she blinked several times before realizing she was staring up at the night sky.

It was glorious. Millions of stars glittered down at her, the moon full and bright, a perfect circle. She could see the craters etched on its surface. She reached out her hand and tried to touch it, but it was just beyond her reach.

"The Big Dipper," she spoke out loud. "Cassiopeia. Orion's Belt."

These stars would always be here. Hundreds of millions of years in the future, when mankind was gone from this earth, they'd still exist.

How long till she was gone?

I'm going crazy, Heath. I've heard of that happening before. Lack of sleep can do strange things to people. I just need to rest, but I can't sleep. I'm so afraid. I don't know what to do. Help me.

There were no answers. Heath wasn't taking her calls.

It was peaceful lying there in the ditch. She knew she should get up and continue on. But she couldn't. Her legs finally decided they'd had enough.

I'm paralyzed.

The fear left her. Nothing she could do. Nothing except close her eyes. It would be so wonderful to do that.

So she did.

She woke with a start. Confused, she sat up abruptly, immediately scanning the area for clues. Her clothing was damp and covered in evening dew. She couldn't remember why she was there.

As she pulled herself up, her knees popped, and her legs were stiff. Stretching, she walked back up to the road and looked around. She was in the middle of nowhere, on a road she couldn't remember. Bits and pieces came back to her: tripping and falling into the ditch, staring up at the stars.

The sun was in the west. She looked down at her watch

and saw it was a little past four. That meant she'd been asleep for over sixteen hours. She didn't remember a single thing. There were no dreams, just blissful, obviously well-needed, deep sleep.

So that was the big secret, huh, Heath. All I had to do was walk myself to the brink of death before I finally managed to get some shut-eye. I guess in a way it was a good thing. I didn't die. They didn't find me. Maybe now my brain won't start to freak out every time I try to sleep.

She took a long drink of water and started walking.

She found the main highway around six. She followed the sun and turned right. The road was completely empty, not even a single parked car that she could borrow. By seven the sun was beginning to set, turning the sky a brilliant reddish pink.

She didn't exactly know where she was anymore. Maybe Montana. The countryside was changing. No mountains yet, but they were coming. She could see them just beyond the horizon, small, bumpy breasts on the landscape. Soon she'd be right in the middle of the Rockies. Hopefully she'd have a car again by then.

Dusk was completely upon her when she turned the corner of the road and saw the beginning of a town. Stretched out in between the trees was a gas station with a large parking lot filled with empty cars. She could see a sign up ahead but couldn't read it from where she stood.

"Finally," she muttered.

She would tread carefully. She stepped off the road and into the woods, determined to walk around to the back of the building first to make sure it was empty. But it was easier said than done. She was a prairie girl, used to wheat fields and flat open skies; going through the underbrush was alien territory. Branches snagged at her hair. Her arms collected scratches, and twice her feet got stuck in the millions of roots that seemed to have no purpose except to trip her up.

Ahead she could see a clearing in the fading twilight. Excited, she pushed herself along, climbing over some rocks and navigating a monstrous tree stump. The terrain spread out before her, a strange puzzle that required full concentration. Her focus was so intense, she almost walked face-first into the legs. A small yelp poured from her throat when she looked up and saw the body attached to them.

Scrambling sideways, she hit another one. The body jolted, spinning around lazily from her touch.

They were everywhere. Dozens of bodies hung from the trees. Some of them had their hands tied behind their backs. They swayed in the breeze. The ropes around their necks continued up into the high branches above. She moved forward into the clearing until she was surrounded. The smell hit her, assaulting her stomach, forcing the water she'd drunk earlier to rise into her throat. Pulling her shirt up over her nose and mouth, she held her breath.

She studied the clearing until she found a path that led her from the death site without her having to touch any more of the bodies. Running along the trail, she couldn't get away fast enough. She didn't stop until she came out at the side of the gas station.

She would go in and get what she needed. Find the keys to one of the parked cars and get the hell out. She didn't want to linger. Not while all those bodies were so close.

The front doors of the gas station were busted. Glass covered the ground, and she carefully stepped over it, trying to make as little noise as possible. Inside, the place was trashed. The aisles were littered with chocolate bars, chips, and all other sorts of roadside goodies. Motor oil bottles had been opened and thrown against the walls, leaving a slippery pattern on the floor. Footprints led behind the counter, where the cash register lay opened and emptied. Cigarette packages were strewed across the surface.

The glass doors to the cooler were shattered. Most of the items were gone, but she managed to grab a few bottles of water and a can of Pepsi that had a big dent in it.

Just beyond the counter were doors that led into the truck-stop restaurant. She decided to try her luck over there. More than anything else in the world she wanted to find food that didn't come from a can. Stepping past a toppled gum machine, she carefully avoided the colorful marble-sized balls. The last thing in the world she needed was a broken ankle.

The restaurant was gloomy. The sun was almost completely set, nothing left but a bit of reddish glow. The blinds had been pulled down, the coffeepots smashed; the remains of month-old key lime pie stuck to the walls.

She wouldn't have even seen the guy in the corner except he moved. Instantly she froze, debating how many steps to the door and whether or not she could get there before he grabbed her.

"You can relax," he said. "I'm cool."

He sat in the back booth, his hand cupping a mug, spinning it around casually as if he was simply waiting for the waitress to bring him a refill. He was young, around her age, his long brown hair combed back from his face and tucked behind his ears. She couldn't make out his eyes in the fading light, but the look on his face was gentle. Sad. But everyone looked sad these days.

"Are you?" she asked. "Why are you sitting there in the dark?"

"No place else to go."

She nodded. She completely understood that.

"But you can get what you want. I won't move." The guy held up his hands and placed them on the table. "I'd leave, but I just don't think I have the energy."

She moved closer to him. The voices inside her head didn't scream to run. There was so much sorrow in his voice. If he was tricking her, then he was the best actor she'd ever met.

"You're not going to run?" He sounded surprised.

She shrugged. "Should I?"

The guy chuckled. "I said I was safe, didn't I? Maybe I need to be more cautious of you. But you strike me as normal. Though, what is normal these days? I don't think I know anymore."

His fingers were long and graceful. She'd always been attracted to hands, something about them, the way they moved. His looked like a musician's; they tapped against the table to a silent tune.

"Do you live here?" she asked. "I mean this town. Not this diner."

He shook his head. "Just passing through. You came from around the back. I watched you walk past. You saw the bodies, didn't you."

"Yeah."

"I think they rounded up the entire town. There are more in the streets. They've hung them from the lampposts. I think they gathered them up and hung them like some old-fashioned vigilante thing. Only I don't think the Baggers are extracting justice."

"Baggers?" She sat down across from him at the table. "Why do you call them Baggers?"

"I dunno. Got it from Billy. Said he overheard it from this

guy down South. It's 'cause when they catch you, they bag the hell outta you. Like when someone says 'I'm gonna go bag me a deer.' But they're killing more than deer, aren't they."

"Makes sense." She wanted to ask him who Billy was, but the look in his eyes when he mentioned the name was enough to make her not do it. Instead she offered up her hand to shake. "I'm Clementine."

"Michael." He took her hand and gave it a quick pump before going back to twisting his cup. There was a bit of liquid at the bottom, and she could smell the alcohol on his breath. Not like it mattered out here—no one was going to card him.

She pulled out her dented Pepsi and opened it. Took a long drink. The carbonated sugar water felt wonderful on her tongue. She put the can down and waited for him to speak. It was awkward; she didn't really know what to say. It had been too long since she'd talked to someone.

The last of the sun was gone and they were sitting in the shadows now. Soon it would be too dark and they'd have to use a candle. She had some in her backpack but didn't bring them out. They'd have to go into the back room. From where they sat, a little light might attract someone.

"Where are you headed?" he finally asked.

Relief washed over her. She could answer this one. "Seattle. My brother, Heath, is there. At least I hope he's there, I don't really know for sure. We couldn't get ahold of him after the earthquake, and my mom and I were going to head out together. But that didn't work out so well. My . . . my parents were shot down along with the rest of my town. I think, well, I'm pretty sure I was the only one who got out."

"Does that make you lucky?"

She shrugged. "I guess you could say that. What about you?"

Anger flashed in his eyes. His fingers froze on the mug, gripping it until his knuckles turned white. "My family is dead," he finally said through gritted teeth. "At least I think so. I haven't seen them since this started. And so is the group I was traveling with. The Baggers found us, and if it's all right with you, I'd rather not talk about it."

"I'm sorry."

"It's not your fault." Reaching down onto the seat, he pulled out the bottle of whiskey and poured himself another. "Want some?"

She shook her head. She wasn't much of a drinker; she tended to get physically sick once the room started to spin. It made even less sense to drink these days, but she wasn't about to tell him that. It wasn't her business.

"I'm done anyway after this," he said. "I can tell you're not impressed. But I'm not drinking to get drunk. Just needed one. It's been one of those days."

"It's okay," she said. "I understand that."

"Besides, it's not safe to get too whacked out. Never know if they're watching."

She nodded again. "Do you think they're still around?"

"The ones who did all the hanging? No, they're long gone. I spent the afternoon searching the town. If they were here, they would have found me by now. I've been sitting in this spot for a few hours. Made it real easy for them to come get me."

She didn't know what to say. It almost sounded like he had a death wish, waiting in the dark for the monsters to come.

"Why don't we make some dinner," he said, as if reading her mind and wanting to change the subject. "Are you hungry? I found a little Coleman stove and some propane back at the hardware store. There's not much to work with, but I'll bet I can throw something together. I'm pretty decent. Used to do all the cooking for my dad."

"Sure."

They moved into the kitchen, where she was able to bring out her candles and get them some light. The only windows into the room were on the door, and she covered them up with newspaper and taped it in place. Anyone passing by wouldn't see a thing.

She found some potatoes that looked pretty decent and started boiling water on the stove while Michael went through the cans looking for something decent to work with. To their surprise the big walk-in freezer was still cool, and they found some semi-defrosted hamburger meat and decided to take a chance. They ended up with chili burgers, mashed potatoes, and some half-melted ice cream for dessert.

"Enjoy," he said. "This is probably the last time you'll ever get ice cream and hamburgers. It'll be a long time before anyone makes anything that doesn't come out of a can. It's not like we can start planting gardens anytime soon. And I don't know about you, but I'm not really the type to go out and kill a cow."

"As long as I'm not forced to eat Spam and canned turnips, I'll survive," she said. "I don't get Spam. What exactly is it? Ham? Lunch meat? It's creepy."

"Maybe a bit of both?" He bit into his second burger, leaving chili sauce at the corner of his mouth. "I agree, it's nasty."

"I guess I can't complain," she said. "I've been living off Oreos and Goldfish crackers since this whole thing started. I think I've drank enough Red Bull to last a lifetime. And I don't even like Red Bull. It tastes like cow pee."

Michael laughed. "You're a connoisseur of fine tastes. However will you survive this apocalypse?"

"I don't know. Maybe I can find a sushi place that still delivers."

It was nice. The food tasted amazing and the conversation was fun. It reminded her of happier days. For the first time in weeks she was enjoying herself. She let down her guard and forgot about all the dangers outside. She hadn't realized how much she needed it. Michael seemed to be doing better, too. The pained expression on his face softened, and when he laughed, she saw some sparkle in his eyes.

"I never asked you where you're going?" she said after they'd finished their meals. She sipped on a bottle of orange juice while he drank one of her water bottles.

"Haven't really been going anywhere," he replied. "I was with a group of people and we were pretty much just going around looking for food. Never had any destination in mind, just wanted to be somewhere safe. That didn't work out so well."

"You're welcome to come with me."

He looked away from her and studied the kitchen for the longest time. She became embarrassed. Had she done something wrong? Asked too soon? Was there some sort of grace period in this new world? Maybe he thought she was coming on to him. He probably thought she looked terrible or maybe she smelled. She hadn't had a chance to clean herself up in days. She must look awful.

"Yeah, maybe," he finally said.

Her cheeks flushed.

"I don't mean to sound like a jerk," he said, reading her mind once again. "It's not you. It's me. I'm terrible at this stuff. The last group of people I was with are dead. Maybe I'm unlucky. Are you sure you want me tagging along?"

"I'm willing to take my chances."

"Okay, then."

She looked down at her dishes, the remains of the ice cream sticking to the bowl. "I guess we don't have to clean up. It's not like anyone's going to complain."

"One of the benefits," he said. "Look, there's a motel just down the road and I'll bet we can spend the night there. Or if you want we can head out. I'm not really tired anymore. Might be better to set off in the daylight, though. It gets pretty dark around here, and we can't exactly use flashlights. We'd be spotted a mile away."

"Yeah," she said. For the first time in weeks she wasn't tired in the slightest, but it probably wasn't logical to go back on the road now. He was right. They'd be better off waiting till morning. "We can check out the motel. Would be nice to clean up a bit."

"There's a clothing shop in town too," he said.

She looked down at the plaid shirt she was wearing. She'd forgotten it was covered in dried blood. It seemed like ages ago that she'd stabbed that guy, that Bagger, who tried to hurt her.

"Yeah, that's a good idea also."

"Then let's go find your brother," he said.

She smiled. Having him around was going to be nice. Safe. He made her feel safe for the time being.

MASON

"I don't think it's such a good idea." Paul stroked his chin, which was now covered with several days' worth of stubble.

"You said the same thing about Canmore. We need supplies. We've got no more food. And I for one am starving. You've got a hungry bird here, and my tail feathers are starting to get heated up. I need sugar."

Mason snorted. "What exactly does that mean?"

Chickadee laughed. "It means I'm getting bitchy."

They were crouched in the woods at the turnoff to the town of Banff, once a major tourist resort. Now the roads were lined with forgotten cars and camper vans. And bodies. It wasn't pretty, and Mason spent a lot of time averting his gaze toward the gravel. A few weeks ago he'd told himself that he no longer cared. The numbing effect still hadn't worn off; the anger inside him lay dormant, wrapped around the darkest corners of his brain. But as time went on, little bits pushed their way forward. Certain memories refused to be forgotten. He thought about his mother a lot, wondering if she was still in the hospital and what her body might look like. He thought about Tom and wondered if his friends experienced terror as their bodies crushed and snapped. Or had it been over quickly and painlessly? Did they even have a chance to run as the school tumbled down around them?

Too many thoughts whispered inside his head.

Despite this, he found it was hard not to be cheerful at times when Chickadee was around.

"You must have been a Buddhist monk or something in a past life," she had proclaimed a few days after she met him. "I swear, people who have taken vows of silence say more than you."

Mason had shrugged and turned his head, but he knew full well she'd seen the smile on his face. At first he resented it, hated the fact that he was enjoying the company of his new friends. A good part of him still didn't believe he deserved it. But as the days went by, a little bit of company went a long way. He was lonely. He hadn't realized it. Having some new friends made the nights a little easier.

"I think it's too big," Paul said again. He was by far the most cautious of the group. Mason figured he was the reason Chickadee was still alive. She was spontaneous, always ready to jump in without checking things out. It was almost as if she didn't realize the danger actually applied to her. Or she didn't care. Paul was the opposite; he took time to assess the situation, carefully thinking through his actions, constantly aware of the consequences.

"It's not really a big town at all," Chickadee said. "I've been here. Nothing but hotels and bars. I think we'll be safe."

"We should go on."

"The next town is days away," she said. "I can't wait that long. There's a Safeway there. I need a pharmacy." She gave Paul a long look, and Mason saw the way he turned and avoided her gaze.

"Why do you need a pharmacy?" Mason asked, alarm bells going off inside his head. "Are you okay?"

"I think I'm coming down with a cold," she said a little too quickly. "Nothing serious."

She didn't look sick, but she did look tired. There were bags under her eyes, but all three of them looked like they were dying for a good night of uninterrupted sleep.

"You sure?" Mason put his hand up to her forehead, and she quickly knocked it away.

"Just a cold, nothing else." She bit her lip and frowned, a look he knew meant she wasn't planning on saying anything else.

"Then we go in," he said.

"Two against one," Chickadee said.

"Fine." Paul stood up and headed off. When he was in the middle of the road, he paused without looking back. "Well, are you coming?"

Mason and Chickadee shrugged at each other and started to follow.

They headed down the center of the road. There weren't as many abandoned cars there, but lots of garbage lined the concrete. Opened suitcases—stripped and rummaged through—candy wrappers, even a smashed laptop.

"Looks like there was one hell of a party," Chickadee said as she stepped around a broken gin bottle. "Can we stop for a second? I've got to pee."

"Sure," Mason said.

Paul didn't say anything, but he turned around and knelt down on the road to study something. Chickadee pulled some tissue from her pocket and dashed into the woods. Mason watched her go, making a mental note of where she was before turning his attention to an abandoned iPod.

Picking it up, he tried to make it work, but the battery was dead.

"She's not my girlfriend," Paul said.

"Huh?"

"We're not dating. I kinda get the impression you think we're a couple. But we're not. Chee and I have known each other since we were babies. I think of her like a sister. She's tough as nails. Had a really rough life. Both parents were drunks. They beat her too. She'd come over to my place in the middle of the night with bruises all over her body. I used to wish I could help her, stop her pain, make it go away. But I was too little then, and now it's too late. You need to know this."

"Why?"

"I won't stand by and watch her suffer."

Mason shrugged. "I won't either. That's why it's cool that there are two of us. We can protect her."

"We can't save her from everything."

"What are you saying?"

Paul didn't answer. Chickadee emerged from the woods, her braids bouncing against her chest.

"Much better," she said. "Now let's go rock this place!"

At the edge of town was a plaque that gave a brief history of Banff. Someone had spray painted the words "Baggers Rule" in bright red letters over it. But Chickadee strode by as if it wasn't even there.

Five dead bodies lay at the entrance to the Safeway. Stacked on top of one another like some sort of bizarre card house. Blood still drained from the cuts on two of them. It was enough to make Mason want to turn around and head back to the highway. But Chickadee calmly walked past them, too, and headed into the store. Mason and Paul had no choice but to follow.

He liked her bravery. In fact, the more time Mason spent with her, the more he grew to adore Chickadee. Now that he knew Paul and her weren't a couple, he began to look at her in a different light. She wasn't what someone might consider beautiful; her nose was crooked and she was too short. She was also about twenty pounds overweight, but none of that really bothered him. Her personality trumped everything. The more she talked, the more beautiful she grew. She probably never had trouble getting dates.

But this wasn't the time or place for falling for a girl, Mason reminded himself as they walked past the doors and into the grocery store. It wouldn't do any good to start complicating things. It could be dangerous to have a crush. Better to concentrate on other stuff.

They walked through the aisles, checking to make sure the place was empty first. Aside from a few dead bodies, the store was clear.

"I'm so sick of canned food," Chickadee said. "If we were back at home I could have cooked you up a great meal. I'm a totally fantastic chef. You'd fall in love with me instantly. I'm that good."

"Really?"

"Yup." She picked up a box of Kraft dinner and frowned at it. "My grandmother taught me how. She used to tell me stories too about how enchanted Indian maidens would cook special foods in order to snag fancy warrior braves. I think she was hinting at something, but at that age I mostly found boys icky."

"And now?"

Chee laughed. "It made me a great cook. But I still scare the boys away. I think it's my dynamic personality. Mom always said my name should have been Barbara Talks Too Much."

Mason snickered.

"And if you ever call me that, I'll torture you for all existence. Even after I'm dead . . ." She paused as Paul reached out and took her hand. They stared at each other for several seconds before Chickadee pulled away.

"Not so loud," Paul said. "We don't know who is listening."

Chickadee lowered her voice to a whisper. "I'm gonna go get some cough syrup. Why don't the two of you finish grabbing the food?"

"Are you sure that's a good idea?" Paul asked. "Maybe I should go with you. I don't like you being alone."

"I'll be fine," she said. "Only fifty feet away. You'll hear me if I start screaming." She turned and scooted off down the aisle before either Mason or Paul could respond.

"I don't like this," Paul said. "We'll just grab whatever and get the hell outta here."

"Sounds good," Mason said. He immediately opened up his backpack and started shoving canned food inside, barely even taking the time to read the labels. They split up, him heading off toward the granola bars and trail mix, while Paul headed toward the produce to see if he could find anything worth scavenging.

The store was thoroughly looted, almost empty, but Mason still managed to find some granola bars lying on the shelves. He opened the packages and tossed the individually wrapped bars into his backpack. The secret was to get rid of as much packaging as possible. That way he'd have more room for extras. Reaching down on the floor, he scooped up a few bags of fruit snacks and shoved them in too.

It didn't take long to fill his bag, and he wandered over to the produce section, where the smell of rotting fruits and vegetables assaulted his nose. Everything was covered in green mold. Covering his mouth and nose with his shirt, he looked around but couldn't find Paul. Heading over to the pharmacy, he decided to see how Chickadee was doing. He didn't see her at first, but then he heard the sounds of jars being pulled off the shelves behind the pharmacy counter.

He rounded the corner and saw Paul and her tossing bottles on the floor.

"There's nothing here," she said. "They've looted everything."

"That's it, then," Paul said.

"That's not it," Chickadee said. "We'll find something. There's got to be something here. Check the fridge again."

"It's empty. Everything's on the floor."

"What about this one?"

"Expired. It's useless."

She tossed a few bottles aside, breaking one. The sound of glass cracking filled the store.

"What are you guys doing?" Mason asked.

Chickadee jumped. "Don't do that. You scared the crap outta me."

"If you're into hard-core stuff, that's just not cool. I'm not into that." Mason stood his ground and glared at Paul, who simply stood up and walked away from the mess.

"We're not looking for drugs," Chickadee said. "And I'm really insulted that you'd think that, Mason. Haven't you listened to anything I've said? I don't swing that way. I don't even drink. I was just looking for some penicillin. I'm worried that this cold could turn to strep throat. It happens to me a lot. That's all. Honest."

"And there's nothing here," Paul said. He calmly walked over to where Mason stood and grabbed a red-and-white bottle of cough syrup off the shelf. "You'll just have to make do, Chee. If you get worse, we'll deal."

Mason didn't know what to do. He wanted to believe them, he really did. But it was awfully suspicious. Neither of them seemed to be the types to do drugs, and he hadn't caught them behaving oddly or spaced-out since he'd met them. But something was definitely up. He just couldn't figure out what.

"Don't be mad, okay?" Chickadee said. She came around the counter, and Mason could see she wasn't holding anything. She opened her bag and showed him the contents. Nothing but protein bars. "I'm not into drugs. In fact, I'm hurt that you'd think otherwise. Please believe me."

Mason nodded. "Yeah, okay. I believe you."

From outside a gunshot sounded. Footsteps pounded on the cement, and one of the store windows shattered.

"Time to go," Paul said.

They headed around back to the storage area and exited through the loading bay. Outside, the sky glowed red and pink.

"Let's find a place to spend the night," Paul said. "There are enough hotels here that we should be able to grab one without being found."

"Let's do it," Chickadee said. She gave Mason a big grin.

They ended up in one of the cabins on the outskirts of town. Mason went into the lobby and found some keys while Paul walked around the perimeter to make sure no one was lurking in the bushes.

The room was small with bunk beds and a couch that folded out.

"I get top bunk," Chickadee said. She ran over and climbed the ladder to settle in. She bounced up and down on the mattress, her head nearly hitting the ceiling.

Mason sat down on one of the chairs and watched while Paul checked the windows. Pulling the curtains closed, he double-checked the lock on the door before heading into the bathroom to make sure they had an exit strategy.

"I'm exhausted," Chickadee said. She yawned three times in rapid succession. "It's been forever since we've had a bed. How long has it been since we left Calgary?"

"Four days," Mason said.

"That's crazy. I used to make the drive all the time and it only took about an hour and a half. We could make it to Vancouver in two days if we drove fast. Never dawned on me that walking would take so long. No wonder my poor feet hurt. I need a pedicure. I'll have crusty granny feet if this keeps up."

"If it weren't for all the roadblocks we'd be able to drive," Mason said. "It might get better outside of Banff, but it'll probably be worse once we hit the Fraser Valley."

"You know a lot about the area, then?"

Mason shrugged. "A bit. We did go camping there almost every summer. It was Mom's favorite place."

"I'm sorry."

"Why? You didn't kill her."

"I'm just sorry. Sorry that there won't be any more camping trips for kids or rock bands or even new books to read. No more movies or fresh bags of popcorn. It really sucks when you think about it. Of course, there is the possibility that we might be able to win this war, but not for a very long time. Probably longer than you and I will ever exist in this world."

"I try not to think about it."

"Sometimes it's all I ever think about."

"Why? It'll only bring up bad memories."

Chickadee jumped off the bed and walked over to where

Mason stood. She paused less than a foot away from him. "There are different types of people in this world. There are people who accept what's in front of them unquestioningly. They live in the dark. In defeat. Ignoring what the future might bring or how they might help to make things happen. Then there are people like me. Optimists. They too live in the dark, in times like these, but dream of the light. I trust in the possibilities of betterness. I believe there is more to life than this. I have to. There's no other choice for me."

She leaned toward him and he could smell her hair. Coconut. One of her braids brushed against his arm and she looked up into his eyes. He realized he wanted her to look up at him like that forever. Her beautiful face, bright and shiny and full of life—there was no one else as truly amazing as her left on the planet. Mom would have loved her.

"Bathroom's clear," Paul said as he came back into the room. "There's a window there, big enough for us to squeeze through if we have to make a quick exit."

"Excellent." Chickadee bent down to retrieve her backpack. "So what's for dinner, then?"

They tossed their findings on the floor and ate a meal of canned beans and granola bars, and split between them two apples that somehow managed to avoid growing moldy. They washed it down with cans of warm root beer and orange Crush. Afterward they sat and listened to the silence while the room steadily grew darker. They were too close to the main road to risk having candles.

"Tell us a story, Paul," Chickadee said after a while. She turned to Mason. "Paul's great-grandpa used to be a real storyteller back in the old days. Paul knows all the old legends. They're really good."

"Cool."

"You've heard all my stories," Paul said.

"Yeah, but Mason hasn't. You've got to tell one to him. Tell him about the coyote stealing fire."

Although the room was dark, there was no mistaking the look Paul gave Chickadee. Mason didn't know what to make of it. Maybe they had a fight earlier and he missed it. But Paul didn't really seem angry. He looked hurt, not physically, but mentally. His eyebrows were tight together, and there was a deep longing behind his eyes. Maybe he was in love with Chickadee—that might explain it—but he'd said himself that he thought of her as a sister.

Whatever it was, Mason's chest tightened when he saw the way Paul looked at her. There was such deep sadness in his eyes.

"I'm going to tell a different story," Paul began. "Once, thousands of years ago, there was a tribe that lived along the banks of the Pacific Ocean where Vancouver stands today. They were hunters and gatherers. The men would travel the forests and the wives would collect the oysters and clams from the shore. This was before the arrival of the white man, and the people lived somewhat peacefully with their neighboring tribes.

Most of the people in the village were happy, but there was one warrior brave who always wanted more. He wanted to travel and visit the world beyond his borders and fight in wars he knew he'd win, but he came home disillusioned. There was no place impressive enough to claim his heart. He wanted love, but no woman was beautiful enough for him; he wanted to eat great foods, but the oysters tasted like sand and the deer were never tender enough to his tongue. Because of this he became cold and bitter, and he'd spend his days away from his family and tribe, refusing to help or contribute anything at all to the community.

One day he decided to go for a walk. While down by the ocean shore, he came across a canoe with a strange man. Unbeknownst to him, this stranger was Khaals, the great transformer, a spirit of legend and fear. Khaals had the ability to change people into animals or even trees and rocks. He often punished people for their wrongdoings and was known for not being sympathetic. If a warrior boasted about his kills, Khaals might show up and turn him into a deer so that he'd know what it's like to flee in fear. If a man chased women other than his wife, Khaals would turn him into a tree so he'd never be able to run again.

"Why do you walk along the sand?" Khaals asked. "I hear your people celebrating in the distance. Why are you not with them?"

"There is nothing worth embracing," the brave said. "What is the point of living when I know I will just die? What is the point of loving when all the women are shallow and ugly? I have seen all there is to see, and there are no wonders for me to behold. I've done everything worth doing. Life is no longer a challenge. I'm bored."

Now, Khaals was not the type of spirit to anger, and the brave's words displeased him. He looked down on the warrior and read deeply into his mind.

"You think life is boring? I'll show you what it's really about," Khaals said, and he turned the brave into a wide, polished rock.

"I'll be back when you find something worth living for," Khaals said.

The brave lay trapped in his rock prison for thousands of years. The world grew up around him. He watched his people fall to the white man, watched the city grow and surround him, and saw the horrors that mankind was capable of doing. His mind never softened and his desire never grew.

Then one day a woman appeared. She was an ordinary woman—nothing special about her. But she carried herself on the wind, and the scent of wildflowers blossomed in her hair. She sat down on the rock and brought out a book to read. The softness of her touch moved the warrior, and he found himself missing her when she left a few hours later.

To his delight she returned the next day with book in hand, and the next day after that. Soon he found himself waiting only for her arrival and devastated with each passing. He longed to talk to this ordinary woman, touch her hair, and tell her how important she was to him.

One morning, after several months, the warrior was surprised to see the shape of Khaals's boat on the water. The transformer had returned for him as promised.

"Do you know why I've come back?"

"I've found something worth living for," the brave replied.

"But she is not a great beauty," Khaals said. "She will not bring the world to you. She will not make the food taste any better. She is nothing but ordinary."

"Her hair holds the wind and her eyes will see my soul," the brave said. "The oysters will taste of the ocean instead of sand because she will help me see their true flavor. She is beautiful enough for me."

With that, Khaals transformed the rock back into his true self. When the woman returned she found the warrior in its place. They instantly fell in love.

For many moons they shared all their time together. And the food did taste better and the rain that fell from the clouds was soft and warm on their skin. The warrior reached up into the skies and plucked the stars from their cushions and placed them in her hands.

But the woman was sick. She was dying.

When the warrior found out, he was beyond angry at Khaals. What was the point of bringing this beautiful woman to him if he would only lose her? Khaals had given him a taste of life, and now he would take that away.

The woman grew weaker. His fury grew, and realizing he couldn't stand to watch her wither, he did the only thing possible. He told her he no longer loved her. He looked deep into the pain in her eyes, but he couldn't take back the words.

He left.

He walked back to the ocean shore and called for Khaals.

"Why did you do this?" he asked when the transformer appeared. "You gave me life and then took it away. I was better off as a rock. At least then I didn't have to feel. You tricked me, and for that I left her."

"You left her because you couldn't face the pain," Khaals said. "You had true love, but you were selfish and turned your back. You are not strong. And because of that I shall leave you as you are. An empty husk to walk for all eternity."

And the warrior became a rock again, only this time he could move and speak. But he never tasted the ocean or smelled the wildflowers on the wind. He never felt the rain on his face or knew the joy of living.

He was never strong again.

Chickadee was crying. She tried not to let anyone hear, but a few sniffles filled the room. When Mason looked back at her, the tears on her face were as big as crystals.

"I'm such a girl," she said.

"That's okay," he said.

"It was just a really sad story," she said. "I can't imagine what it would be like going through life without feeling. Or feeling so much that you couldn't stand to watch someone you love die."

"Maybe he couldn't bear to bury her," Mason said, thinking of his own mother. "So that's why he left."

"Either way it's just a story." Paul yawned and went over to the couch and picked up a blanket. "I'm tired," he said. "It's time for bed."

Mason wanted to ask him why he told that particular story, but Paul rolled over on his side, facing the wall, making it clear he had nothing more to say. Chickadee reached out and touched Mason's arm, getting his attention.

"I'm tired too," she said. "Can I still have top bunk?"

Mason gave her half a smile. "Sure. I'll take first watch."

"I'll take second," Paul said. "Wake me in a few."

Mason went and used the bathroom and tried washing off some of the dirt and sweat on his face with a water bottle and one of the towels on the rack. It helped a bit. He rubbed his tongue along his teeth, deciding they'd have to remember to grab some toothbrushes soon. The face in the mirror was unfamiliar; it felt like years had passed since he last saw his own reflection.

Yawning, he returned to the room and sat down in the chair by the window. The air around him was quiet, but he knew no one was sleeping yet. When he roused Paul several hours later, he had the feeling Paul still hadn't slept at all. They silently traded places and Mason crawled into the bottom bunk, pulling the covers up to his chin.

He lay in the dark, staring at the wood above him until his eyes grew heavy enough to close.

At the moment before he fell asleep, he heard Paul's voice reach out through the blackness.

"I'm not strong enough."

But he was too tired to respond.

When he woke the next morning, Chickadee was sitting in the chair by the window. Her body was stiff and she held her head in her hands as if she couldn't keep her neck upright without the help. Her entire body trembled. How long had she been sitting there? Why didn't she wake him up?

"What's wrong?" he asked.

"He's gone."

"Huh? Who, Paul? Where'd he go?"

"Just gone. He left me. Us."

Mason pulled at the blankets wrapped around his legs. They clung to his body, refusing to let go. Eventually he freed himself and moved over to the window where Chickadee waited, tears streaming down her face.

"He can't be gone," he said. "Maybe he just went for food."

"We have food."

"Did you look outside?"

"He's not there."

"Why would he do such a thing? I don't know Paul as well as you, but I can't imagine he'd wander off like that. He cares about you."

"That's the problem." Chickadee finally looked away from the window. She reached over and took Mason's hand. "He cared too much to watch me die. Just like the story."

Her fingers were soft and slightly damp from the tears. Mason didn't know what she wanted him to do. She was seeking comfort, but there were no words he could use to make things better. There was something visible just behind her eyes, an answer to a question he didn't want to ask.

"Are you dying?" The words hung in the air like a bad smell.

"We're all going to die."

"But are you sick? Is there something you're not telling me?"

"I'm not sick."

"Okay."

A can of lukewarm Pepsi rested on the table. Chickadee reached for it and took a long drink. "I'm so thirsty," she said. "I think I've cried all the liquid out of my body over the past few days. How much more before I shrivel up into a husk?" She squeezed his hand and pulled him closer to her, so their noses were almost touching. "Please don't leave me, Mason. I don't think I could stand it if you go."

"I'm not going anywhere."

"Promise me."

"I promise."

Her lips brushed his, a small kiss. It happened so quickly he couldn't fully decide if it was actually real or his imagination. Opening his arms, he pulled her into him, wrapping himself around her and trying to keep her safe.

They stayed that way as the minutes passed and his arms cramped, but he didn't let go. The front of his shirt grew wet and uncomfortable, but he barely noticed. Finally she pulled back, and he released her reluctantly.

"Do you want me to go look for him?"

She sniffled and shook her head.

"What do we do now?"

"We move on."

Mason nodded. It sounded like the right thing to do.

ARIES

"Daniel?"

The figure on the floor rocked back and forth, but his eyes remained closed. Aries moved around to the side, trying to get a better look at his face. Daniel's eyelashes were fluttering, but he didn't wake up.

From behind her she heard the sounds of people. Nathan hissed her name. She could see their flashlights from across the store.

"I'm over here," she half whispered, half shouted.

Aries turned her attention back to Daniel, still sprawled out across the ground beside her. She couldn't believe it was him. She'd spent countless hours remembering their brief conversations, playing his words over and over in her head like a broken record. She never thought she'd see him again.

But here he was.

Serendipity?

There was a deep cut on his forehead. He was no longer bleeding, but his hair was matted from where the blood had drained out while he slept. A small red stain spread out like an inkblot on the yellow tiling. His face was pale with the exception of a bruise on his cheekbone.

She picked up the flashlight he'd been holding. It was small and blue. The same one she'd given him. He'd kept it. Not just kept it; he'd been holding it. Did that mean he thought about her, too? This was an entire store filled with better flashlights—why did he still have this one?

She smiled, even though she knew it probably wasn't anything worth getting excited over. But still, it might be a sign. A good one.

The black jacket covering his body didn't look very warm. The corner of the sleeve was torn. Something shiny stuck halfway out of the pocket. Without thinking, she reached over to touch it. The object was metal and cold to the touch. She pulled it out, a small switchblade with blood on the blade. Shuddering, she dropped the knife on the floor.

He moaned and his eyes fluttered again. She was worried that he might be sick, so she placed her palm against his forehead. His skin was boiling.

"Aries?"

She jerked back in surprise. Daniel's eyes stared up at her, dark brown and piercing but still rather dazed. He looked past her as if she wasn't really there.

"You remember me," she said. Her stomach gave a little leap, as if she'd just gotten on the roller coaster at Playland.

"Aries, but you're a Gemini."

She nodded.

"I'm happy you're alive. I thought you might be dead." He tried to hoist himself up on his elbows but winced instead, his head resting back on the cold ground. All his strength seemed to drain out over the tiles.

Yes, she was alive. Anger flared through her, if for only a

moment. He'd left her after making a promise. For the past several weeks she'd thought about all the things she'd say to him if they crossed paths. Why did he help her and then disappear? How come he knew so much? He'd told her this would happen—he knew people were attacking and that the world was ending. How did he know? How come she knew? She remembered her conversation with Ms. Darcy before she left.

Something bad is about to happen. It's already started. I know you're feeling it too. It's like an electric charge. I can't explain it. I've been sensing it for weeks.

She *had* been feeling it. At the time she didn't know what it was. It started small, a strange sensation in the back of her brain that swept across her nervous system, like receiving dozens of small static shocks. She'd thought she was coming down with something. When the earthquake happened, she'd been too distracted with Sara to fully understand it. But afterward, trapped in the abandoned apartment, she'd had plenty of time to work through the details. Her thoughts always returned to Daniel. He was the key. He knew something that she didn't.

But now, with him lying on the floor, looking so wilted, she couldn't bring herself to verbally attack him. Her concerns and fears changed to whether or not he was dangerously ill.

"Looks like I'm doing better than you," she said, reaching out to touch his forehead again. "You've got a fever. How long have you been sick?"

He shrugged. "It's nothing. Comes and goes."

"Do you think you can be alone for a few minutes? I'm going to get you some Tylenol from the pharmacy section. I should get you up on one of the bed displays. It'll be warmer."

He smirked and started coughing violently. She waited for him to finish.

"I've been alone for a long time. I can handle a few more minutes."

"That's right. You don't care much for company."

"Aries?" Joy appeared with Nathan by her side, staring down at the unconscious boy in surprise.

"This is Daniel," Aries said. "Remember? I told you about him."

"The guy who helped you after the bus crash," Joy said. Her eyes lit up immediately. "I'm Joy. This is Nathan."

Daniel blinked a few times, trying to hold back the pain. "I'd shake your hand but I'm not sure I have the strength."

"Are you okay?" Nathan asked.

"He's got a fever. Maybe you can help me get him onto one of the beds."

Ignoring Daniel's protests, the three of them managed to get him over to one of the displays, where Aries helped him lie back on a bright pink bedspread. She grabbed a blanket off the shelf and covered him.

"We should check the pharmacy," Aries said. "Maybe we can find something that'll help."

Joy nodded. Nathan looked a little uncertain. Aries grabbed his sleeve, pulling him along whether he liked it or not. "We'll be right back."

Daniel didn't say anything. Closing his eyes, he relaxed into the pillow. It wasn't like he'd be going anywhere soon.

"Sorry we're late," Nathan said once they were out of earshot. "Had a little bit of trouble. Took us a while to shake them. Man, those psychos can run."

"I lost my bike," Joy said. She was bleeding from a cut on her arm, but aside from that they seemed fine. "Nathan had to double with me. Not fun."

"Good thing you're light as a feather," Nathan said. "Otherwise we might not have gotten out."

"They brought me down," Joy said. "Pulled me right off my bike. One of them tried to bite me. Can you believe it? Just like a bloody zombie movie. I would have been toast if it hadn't been for Nathan. He's my new hero."

"We were lucky," he said. "I managed to knock one of them out. It felt amazing. I haven't been in a fight since I was a little kid. What happened to you?" He'd noticed Aries's torn jeans leg.

"Took a spill," she said. "Cornered too fast. My own fault. Luckily I'd already lost them."

"We'd better find something for you, too," Joy said. "That might get infected. Does it hurt?"

"Yeah, it stings but I'll live."

"We'd still better be careful," Nathan said. "Do you think you can trust that guy? I mean, how well do you really know him?"

"I can't believe you found him," Joy said. "What are the odds?"

"It's weird," Nathan said. "Why is this guy here of all places? And he's just sleeping in the store when the back door was unlocked? Does he have a death wish?"

"He's sick. Maybe he just got desperate. And he doesn't like groups," Aries said. "He's got this idea that people are safer being alone."

"Not me," Joy said. "I don't think I ever could have gotten this far by myself. But aren't you mad at him? He left you, right?"

"It's not important," she said. "He's here now, and he needs help."

In the pharmacy department, they found the fever medications, but there were a lot to pick from and she was momentarily overwhelmed.

"This one's good." Nathan handed her a bottle filled with burgundy liquid.

"How do you know?"

"My mother was a nurse. She always kept this stuff on hand. It tastes disgusting. But it works."

"Okay." She opened the box and slipped the small bottle into her pocket. "Anything else? I mean, what if he needs more?"

"Give him some Tylenol."

Joy grabbed the closest red-and-white bottle from the shelf. "Got it."

"And you're going to need this," Nathan said, pressing a bottle of saline solution and some gauze bandages into her hand. "For your leg. You're bleeding."

She'd forgotten about her own problems. They seemed so unimportant compared to everything else. But Nathan was right. She'd have to clean herself up or she might find herself with a nasty infection. Such things could be fatal in this new world. A clean pair of jeans would help too.

"Look." Aries glanced back toward the housewares section, but of course she couldn't see anything from where they were. "We've got to change our plans. I can't leave him, and I doubt he's strong enough to travel. I think you guys should get the stuff we need and head back without me for now."

Nathan looked at her in disbelief. "I don't think that's a good idea."

"I'm not leaving him. He saved my life."

"It's not safe."

"It's as safe as anywhere else," Aries said.

"But we need you," Joy said. "Who's going to carry your stuff? We promised the others."

"Look," Aries said, taking both Joy and Nathan by the arms

and leading them away from the pharmacy. "You can take my bicycle. There's a whole bunch of them in the sporting-goods section. I can always grab another. We can get one of those baby carriages that attaches to the back of the bike. You guys can carry more stuff that way without being slowed down. And I got some handheld receivers from electronics. We can keep in touch now. You'll be able to reach me whenever you want. I'll be back as soon as he's well enough to travel. One day, two tops."

"I don't like it," Nathan said. "And I don't think the others will either."

"I owe him my life," she said. "I have to return the favor."

An hour later they were ready to go. Both Joy and Nathan were loaded up with the goods, but not enough to slow them down if they got in trouble. Aries made sure of that. It was still dark outside, but in the east, the sky was beginning to lighten. If they were going to leave, it had to be now.

"We'll call you when we get back," Joy said. The handheld receiver was strapped to her backpack, making her look like an overburdened bicycle courier.

"Be careful," she said.

"You too."

Joy turned and unlocked the door. She pushed her bicycle through the opening, a tough job considering she now had a baby trailer attached to the back. Aries helped her navigate the stairs. Outside the air was cool and fresh. She could smell the salty scent of the ocean, along with faint traces of smoke. Because of the earthquake, then the looting and killing, a lot of buildings were still on fire. She couldn't remember the last time the sky didn't look like a giant smoke screen. Everyone's clothes constantly smelled acrid.

"Lock the door behind us," Nathan said. "If they break the window, go into the office. You'll be safe there."

While searching the store, they'd found a small office with no windows and a nice lock on the inside. If something were to happen, she'd be able to get Daniel in there without much effort. They'd be trapped, but at least they would be out of harm's way.

"Will do," she said.

Joy gave her a quick hug before climbing on her bike. Aries watched them ride off, wondering if she was doing the right thing.

Sighing, she turned and headed back into the building to wait for Daniel's fever to break.

He hadn't moved since she'd last seen him. She sat at the edge of the bed for a bit and watched his chest as he breathed. People always looked beautiful when they slept, vulnerable and innocent. She wanted to gather him in her arms and hold him tightly until he woke up. Reaching out carefully, she brushed a bit of hair away from his eyes. He didn't move. Running her finger along his face, she was amazed at how soft his skin was. Her heart began to beat faster; she could feel it pounding in her chest. His mouth was parted slightly, straight white teeth barely showing. She touched his lips and then drew her hand away quickly.

In his sleep, he mumbled something she couldn't understand. His lips curved into a slight smile. But at least he didn't wake up. She wasn't sure how she could have explained her sudden desire to touch him.

Embarrassed, she got up off the bed and pulled the covers over his chest, tucking him in gently to make sure he stayed comfortable.

Sitting down on the floor next to the bed, she removed her jeans and rubbed the saline solution over her wounds. It stung but not unbearably so. Gravel was stuck to her skin, and she picked out the pieces she couldn't wash away. The process was painful, and it didn't help that her muscles ached and trembled every time she jerked back in agony. Eventually she managed to clean herself enough to be satisfied, and she wrapped the gauze around her leg.

She threw her ruined pants aside and picked up the pair of sweatpants she'd found in the clothing aisle and put them on. At least they'd be more comfortable and less clingy than the jeans.

Yawning, she grabbed some pillows and a blanket from the shelf and made herself a little bed on the floor beside Daniel.

What would happen if the medication didn't work and he got worse? It's not like she could take him to the hospital. It was such a strange thought. There would be no help in this new world. Even simple things like fevers could kill.

"You're not going to die," she whispered in the dark. "I won't let you."

Covering herself up, she lay on her back, eyes opened, and waited for morning to come. It took a long time before her brain stopping working overtime with all the what-ifs and her eyelids grew heavy.

She didn't mean to fall asleep.

She woke, disorientated, not understanding the sharp discomfort in her lower back and why she was lying on the hard floor. Sitting up quickly, heart pounding in her chest, she looked around wildly.

"Good morning."

"Daniel?"

"Were you expecting someone else?"

Pushing her hair back from her face, she winced. Sleeping on a frozen floor was never a good choice.

"Bad dreams?"

She shook her head. "Nope, just forgot where I was for a second."

"That happens to me sometimes too."

"You sound a lot better." She pulled the blanket aside and climbed to her feet. Stretched. Felt her joints pop in her legs and back.

"I am, thanks to you. I think the fever's gone."

"Really? Excellent."

He did look better. Although his face was still pale, it didn't look as pasty or sweaty. Last night she'd taken some baby wipes to his forehead and gotten rid of most of the blood. She'd covered the cut with white gauze and used nonstick tape to keep it in place. He looked like a wounded soldier straight off the battlefield. At least his eyes were no longer glassy and he focused on her without difficulty. Such an intense stare, as if he was drilling straight into her brain.

"You still have my flashlight," she said.

He reached into his pocket and pulled it out. "Of course. I knew if I kept it, you'd find a way to come back to me."

"Um . . . I . . . ah." Brilliant conversation at its best.

"But now that you know I'm healthy, you need to leave."

"What?" She glared at him in disbelief. "No. It doesn't work that way."

"Yes, it does. I haven't changed, Aries. I still don't want to be in a crowd. You're a nice girl and I like you a lot, but it's not safe for you to be around me."

"You said that before. I don't believe you."

"You're still alive, aren't you? Because of me. Because I took you to the school, even if I did leave you there."

She couldn't argue that. It was true. She decided to take a different approach. "Why are you against people? It's worked for me. We need to stick together if we're ever going to stand up for ourselves. You're acting as if you're one of those monsters."

"Maybe I am."

"You're not. I'd know if you were."

"Would you?"

"They're crazy."

"Not all of them."

"They kill for no reason. That makes them crazy."

A water bottle sat on its side where Aries left it last night. Daniel picked it up and took a long drink. "Some of them are crazy. I watched one of them break its own neck the other day. Got its head between two metal railings of all things. It tugged and yanked until the bones cracked. Took a long time to die. So yeah, some of them really are stupid. But not all. That same day, a group of them got together and burned a library to the ground because they knew people were hiding inside. They waited at the exits and pegged their victims off one by one as they tried to run. It was a calculated plan."

"That doesn't mean they're not crazy."

"Some of them could fool you," he continued. "Some of them can talk normally. They can trick you into believing they're innocent. That's why you can't trust anyone. Do you really know these friends of yours? Would you trust them fully with your life?"

"Yes." She didn't even have to think about the answer. Colin's face, however, did flash into her thoughts, but only for a moment. He was too much of a coward to be a killer.

"You're stupid, then."

"And you're nothing but an ass."

"Because I'm trying to help keep you alive?"

"I don't need your help."

Daniel chuckled. "You know, I believe you're right on that one. You've managed to do quite well. Very few people have made it this far. I'd ask you where you're holing up, but I don't want to know."

"I want you to come back with me." There. She said it. She had a million questions to ask him, especially how come he knew so much? But they'd have to wait until she got him somewhere safe.

"No."

She wanted to grab him by the shirt and slap some sense into him. He infuriated her. What made him this stubborn? "Fine. Have it your way. But don't expect me to come running the next time you can't get off the bed."

"Then you'll leave?"

"Not until nightfall. It's not safe to go anywhere during the daytime."

She was surprised to see him nod. "You're right. I guess we'll just have to put up with each other until then." Getting off the bed, he peeled the dirty shirt off his body and dropped it to the floor.

She blushed and looked away. But not before she caught a glimpse of toned muscles and yellowish bruises on his abdomen.

"I'm going to find a new shirt," he said, and she could hear the amusement in his voice. "Then I'm going to get something to eat." He began to walk away, his bare feet slapping on the tiled flooring. "You're welcome to join me. I promise I'll wear something a little less revealing."

A dozen retorts came to her mind, but every single one was too lame to repeat. After he turned the corner, she picked up her pillow and threw it in his direction. Not exactly the world's greatest comeback, but it made her feel a little better.

She took the handheld receiver from her bag and turned it on. She put her mouth up to the speaker and then paused. What was she supposed to say? She'd talked to Joy briefly last night once they made it home safe and she'd promised she'd call again in the morning to give an update. Sure, Daniel was feeling better and that was something to report, but she didn't know where to go from there. It was her responsibility to bring him back, but he seemed intent on staying behind. It was odd.

"Anyone there?" she said into the tiny receiver. She felt stupid. Wasn't there something else she was supposed to say, like "over" or "ten-four" when talking into these things?

There was a pause and then a click. "Aries?"

"Hey, Jack."

"Wow, the reception is amazing. No background noise or anything. Are you still at the store?"

"Yep. I'm pretty much here till nightfall. How's everyone doing? Nothing bad happen?"

"No, things are great here. Everyone changed their clothes and ate some food. They're all in good spirits. Even Colin. How's the guy? Better?"

"Yeah. His fever's gone."

"Brilliant. I'm looking forward to meeting him. We'll see you later tonight, right?"

"Yep." She didn't exactly know why she lied, mostly because the truth was too complicated to discuss through a little plastic box. They'd just have to get the whole story once she got back.

And who knew? Maybe Daniel would change his mind. It was a long ways till the sun went down.

She went looking for him and found him in the toy department. He'd put on a fresh shirt, a black top that fit snugly. He'd also changed his jeans. His feet were still bare. The makeshift bandage on his head was gone and his hair was wet. He'd taken the time to clean himself up.

"You look good," she said, immediately regretting the words when he gave her a sideways glance, one eyebrow raised, and a crooked grin. "I mean, even less sick. Better than last night."

He laughed.

That's it. She'd had enough. She was done talking. If she kept her mouth shut, she'd stop putting her foot in it.

"You're looking a little stiff yourself," he said. "What did you do to your leg? You're moving as if you've forgotten how to use your knees."

"Just a scrape," she said. "Nothing I can't handle."

Actually her leg hurt even more than it had last night. When she took the tumble she'd somehow managed to pull all the muscles in her inner thigh, and the long wound was making it difficult to walk. Every time her skin stretched she wanted to scream, but there was no way she'd ever admit it. Especially to him.

"You don't strike me as the princess type."

"What's that supposed to mean?"

Daniel smiled. "It means that I'd still go out of my way to rescue you, but you'd probably smack me across the head and try to slay the dragon yourself."

"Let's not forget who rescued who last night."

"If you want to call it that, sure. So as a reward, I've got a gift for you," Daniel said. She realized he was holding something behind his back.

"What?"

"Something that'll make our day a little more bearable," he said, bringing the item out for her inspection. Monopoly. World Edition.

She laughed. "I'm gonna kick your ass."

"You're on. But I get to be the car."

Unwrapping the plastic, they spread the game out over one of the display tables back in the housewares department. They played three games, two of which she won. They raided the junk-food aisle and brought back bags of potato chips, cheese-flavored popcorn, and cans of iced tea.

Several times she tried questioning him about whether he knew more about what was happening. He seemed to know so much, but he refused to answer or he quickly changed the topic. Eventually she stopped asking.

"I think I've officially had enough Monopoly to last a lifetime," she said after the last game. She checked her watch. Six thirty. She stood up and walked to the edge of the main aisle. From across the store she could see the large entrance doors. Outside the sky was beginning to darken.

"Days are getting shorter," Daniel said.

"It's gonna be a cold winter," she agreed. "Especially with no heat or power. We should have gone south."

She was joking, but as usual he didn't get it.

"You never would have made it."

"Aren't you ever optimistic about anything?" She crossed her arms over her chest. Funny how just talking about the weather could make one cooler.

"Nope."

Earlier she'd taken a cardigan off the rack that she liked, dark forest green with brown wooden buttons and a hood. Daniel picked it up off her chair and handed it to her. She pulled it around her back, but her arm got tangled up in the sleeve. Reaching over, he touched her arm as he helped. Continued to hold her as he looked down into her eyes.

"You've got to go soon," he said.

"Come with me."

"No."

She yanked her arm away from him. "What is wrong with you?"

But he wasn't paying any attention. Instead, he stared over her head, his eyes focused on the main entrance, a taut look on his face.

"Did you hear that?"

She instantly stiffened. "What?"

Ignoring her, he brushed past her and into the main aisle. She followed just behind him, moving closer to the front of the store. Daniel knelt down behind a laundry-detergent display and she joined him.

Outside, the parking lot looked empty. But it was dark and there were a lot of shadows. She couldn't really see anything.

"They're out there," he whispered.

"What? Where? I can't see them."

"I feel them."

Glass shattered. Something bounced across the floor, coming to a full stop twenty feet away from them. A rock.

Daniel turned and grabbed her arm. He began walking quickly toward the back of the store and the loading docks. Earlier she'd packed up her backpack and left it in the bay along with her new bicycle.

"Aries," he said as he dragged her along. "Listen to me. You've got to listen. I need you to leave. Get out while you can."

"I can't leave you. Come with me."

He shook his head. "You don't understand. They're here for me. Not you. Just me."

"You're right. I don't understand." She tried to yank her arm away from him, but he was too strong. "Stop it. You're hurting me."

He ignored her protests all the way to the loading docks. Pushing a flashlight into her hands, he checked through the peephole in the door before unlocking it. She waited stupidly while he pushed her bike out into the back lane. She tried to listen for sounds coming from the store, signs that the insane people had made their way in, but she couldn't hear anything.

Once Daniel finished checking outside, he came back for her. Grabbing her arm again, he literally dragged her out into the lane.

"I'm not leaving you here," she said. Tears formed in her eyes. She couldn't do it. There was nothing he could say that would make her go away. She wouldn't leave him to die. Enough people had died already. She wouldn't allow another.

"It's okay," he said. Pulling her toward him, he drew his arms around her, hugging her tightly. Whispered in her ear. "I'll be fine. You're going to have to trust me on this."

"No." She tried to untangle herself from his grasp. He was just too strong.

"Aries." When she didn't respond, he grabbed hold of her chin and forced her to look at him. "I'm going to tell you something important and I don't want you to forget, okay?"

She nodded, choking back a sob.

"They're not all bad. Remember this. Some of them still feel the light. I'll be fine. I promise. And I'm not going to break that promise either. When this is over I'll find you."

"We're on Alexander Street. It's the only building with the roof caved in. You can't miss it."

He sighed. "I told you not to tell me."

"I'm sorry."

"I have to leave now. Let me go."

She did.

He didn't say another word. Instead he ran up the stairs toward the store and disappeared into the darkness of the receiving bay. The door closed behind him and she was alone.

When her paralysis broke, she took the stairs two at a time and grabbed the handle. But the door was locked.

She didn't know what to do. Everything had happened too quickly. Sitting down on the steps, she tried to weigh her options. She couldn't get in from the back. It would be suicidal to go around to the front.

He'd won. He'd gotten his way. Now she had no choice but to leave. She'd have to believe him.

Red-hot anger pulsated through her body. Jumping to her feet, she grabbed her backpack and pulled it over her shoulders. Fine. If that's the way he wanted it, then let him go. She was through playing his game. If he'd rather get himself killed than be with her, well, she wasn't going to fight him.

By the time she reached the apartment, the butterflies were still rioting inside her stomach. The fear of the unknown. Daniel. The monsters disguised as people.

How could she prepare for a war she knew she couldn't win?

NOTHING

We forget how truly fragile we are.

Skin. We do so much to it. Burn it. Tattoo it. Rub chemicals into its surface. Sometimes we scrape it, pierce it, poke holes through its softness.

Skin holds us together. It keeps the blood inside. Without it, we die.

When the knife slashed through her skin, she gave a look to suggest she couldn't believe I'd hurt her. Such surprise. Shock. She would die. The blood rushed past her skin, no longer trapped inside her flesh, and pooled onto the floor beneath her toes.

She thought she'd live forever.

"You need to have thicker skin," I told her. Famous last words. Spoken to me in my former life by someone I once loved.

Thicker skin.

But in reality I needed a stronger brain.

I have three scars aligning my body. They are a diary of sorts, chronicling my life according to the things I've done. The things that have been done to me.

1. A round scar the size of a quarter on the middle of my right palm. At the age of five my father punished me by pouring boiling water onto my skin. Forced me to hold out my hand and poured the water straight from the kettle once it boiled. It was for my own good. I'd been bad.

2. A large scar on my knee from falling off my bicycle. I was seven. I had stolen something trivial and the grocer came after me. Of course I got caught. I had my finger broken as punishment, and he refused to take me to the hospital. My skin still wasn't thick enough.

3. A thin line along my wrist from where I tried to let the blood come out.

I'm not proud of the things I've done. Or of the things I know I will do in the future. We became evil because we deserved it, not because we lived our lives as saints. The darkness cannot go where the light holds warmth. Sometimes it is easier to embrace the pain than fight against the fire. Free will isn't always about choice; often weakness plays the game.

If you heard all about my childhood, you'd refuse to lay the blame on my side. You'd say I was a victim. Not guilty. But the voices know better. They still saw fit to judge me. To claim my soul.

I want to stop. I want someone to help me.

Help me, before I kill her.

MICHAEL

"It's cold," Clementine said.

They'd stopped for a lunch of canned spaghetti and dried fruit, stuff they found in an outlet store a few days earlier. A rest stop next to a lake, one of the many dozen tourist attractions spread across the Rocky Mountains.

"It's going to snow," he said.

"How do you know?"

"It smells like snow."

Clementine sniffed the air and gave him a confused look.

He'd forgotten that she'd never traveled through the mountains before. She was from the prairies, a place where everything was wide-open. So different from his upbringing in the valley, where lakes and trees were just another part of the boring scenery and the winters were cold and uncomfortable.

"I guess it's one of those things you get good at noticing," he said. "I can't explain it, but you can always tell the way snow smells out here. I dunno."

"We're not dressed for snow," she said, and he realized she was right.

They wore jean jackets and hoodies. No winter coats or

gloves or scarves or even boots. Why didn't he think about it when they passed their last outlet store?

Because other things were on his mind. The thought that haunted him the most was of the mother and her small son. Had it hurt? He hoped the Baggers had shown mercy and killed the child quickly. Why hadn't he done something to try to save them?

Besides, September had been hotter than hot. Yeah, sure, it was October now, but it was still warm. Or it had been. Yet he should have thought about how unpredictable mountain weather could be.

"Let's get going," he said. Jumping down off the table, he picked up his backpack and slung it over his shoulder. "If we keep at it, we should be able to find a cabin or something to spend the night. There's lots of places around here. We just have to find them."

"Okay."

"Having a bit of snow might be a good thing, too. If we're lucky it'll send the Baggers south. It's gonna be a cold one without electricity."

"Seattle will be warmer," she said. "Heath said it just rains there."

The first flakes hit them as they stepped out onto the road. Just a few tumbling lazily down from the darkened clouds above.

"See," he said. "Can I call them or what?"

"It's beautiful," she said, her head tilted upward. "I love the first snowfall of the season. I always liked to take a walk in the fields and just stare up at the clouds. It's almost as if the entire sky is dancing just for me."

Michael hated snow, but he didn't tell her that. It meant shoveling and frozen faces, hibernating in the basement and playing video games until he grew bored to death. Winter always made him want to curl up and sleep. Mom used to joke that he was part bear. He'd been planning on going to university in California or Arizona, someplace he knew would be hot all year long.

The snow melted at first when it hit the pavement, but after thirty minutes or so, a fine film of white began to cover the surface. Large flakes dominated the sky, falling faster and harder with each new footstep. Michael grew worried but tried not to show it. He didn't want to frighten her, but the world around them appeared to be getting ready for an all-out blizzard. A strong wind blew up behind them, pressing against their clothes, trying to rip the hair right off their heads. The sun was fully gone. Not even three in the afternoon, but the woods were dark. The snow blocked everything else out.

They needed to find shelter.

"How is this even possible?" she yelled over the howling wind. He could hear her teeth chattering in between words. "It was sunny and warm this morning."

"I've seen worse," he shouted back.

"Really? You could actually see it? I can't even see the road in front of us."

It was true. Visibility had completely gone down the toilet.

"Just keep your eyes peeled for turnoffs," he said. "There's gotta be something around here. I grew up in this area. There are hundreds of cabins nearby."

All right, it was a bit of a lie. He'd lived farther south where dozens of ski hills dominated the terrain. Right now he didn't have the foggiest idea where they really were. For all he knew they could have gone too far north and crossed the border into Canada. He'd been going around in circles a lot lately, not paying attention to where the road led. With the group, their main priority had been to find food. But alone, well, no matter how much he traveled, he couldn't seem to get far enough away.

But he didn't mention a word of this to her. The last thing in the world he wanted to do was scare her more than she already was.

He hadn't wanted to scare the others, either. Look where that got them.

The blizzard continued, and it wasn't long before they were up to their ankles in the white powder. The sun disappeared completely and nightfall took over. The wind howled at their backs. Michael's face started to hurt and his toes grew alarmingly numb. Clementine didn't complain, but he could tell she was suffering as much as him. She pulled her jacket tightly around her neck with both hands, trying to keep the snow from falling down her shirt. Her cheeks and forehead were bright red and her blond hair whipped uncontrollably around her head.

They trudged along.

If they didn't find shelter soon they would freeze to death. It struck Michael as ironic. This seemed like the wrong way to die considering the circumstances.

But he wasn't ready to die. Not when he still wanted to live.

"What's that?" Clementine shouted over the wind.

Michael looked and didn't see much at first. But then he spotted a shadow through the storm. Thin and long, stretched out along the road. It took him several minutes before he finally realized what it was.

"Mailboxes," he said. "Those are mailboxes."

A big rectangular row of metal boxes, stacked on top of one another, the kind in rural communities. Three rows of four. Often people lived too far out for the post office to travel to, so they grouped them together in one area.

"There must be houses close by," he said. "We're saved."

But Clementine wasn't rejoicing the way he thought she would. Instead she peered back the way they'd come, staring into the white nothingness.

"What do you see?"

"Something's moving back there."

Michael turned his attention back toward the road behind them. At first he couldn't see anything except snow, but then it was there for a quick instant: someone darted across the path and stepped into the bushes. Another figure followed a moment after.

"Oh, God," he said. "They've found us."

Grabbing her hand, he began to run. He didn't have to drag her along—she came willingly. "Hold on tight," he said. "If I lose you in this I might never find you."

She clenched his hand tighter.

He didn't see the first Bagger until he was inches from his face, the black veins in his eyes burning. The monster stepped out in front of him; Michael was moving too fast to stop. He slammed into it, knocking their foreheads together and falling down into a heap, dragging Clementine along with him. His face ended up right against the Bagger's mouth, and he could smell the stench of tooth decay. Letting go of Clementine's hand, he shoved upward, trying to get far away from the crazy man.

The Bagger grabbed his arm. "What's your hurry?" he snapped.

Clementine darted in from the right, kicking the man hard, and he fell, loosening his grip on Michael enough for him to pull free. Too much time was wasted. The other Baggers emerged from the woods. There were at least five of them, each as poorly dressed and unprepared for the cold as them.

"Come on," Michael said. Reaching out for Clementine, he realized he couldn't see her anymore. She'd simply disappeared into the whirling snow. He backed up several feet, losing track of the Baggers and stepping unexpectedly off the road. Falling, he stumbled into the bushes and tripped over a root, his already numb hands plunging into half a foot of icy snow.

He wanted to scream out for her, but he knew it would only alert the Baggers to his location.

From a distance he could make out the shapes of people moving in more than one direction. But which one was Clementine? It reminded him of one of those game shows where you had to pick the right box in order to win the million dollars. Moving toward the closest shadow, he hesitated.

Even if he found her now they couldn't run. There was nowhere left to run to. One couldn't outrun a blizzard. They'd only get lost in the woods and freeze to death.

Changing his mind, he started walking in one direction, hoping that might work, but he was all turned around and pretty sure he was only going in circles no matter how straight he tried to travel. He came across footprints in the snow, quickly being filled by the falling flakes. He couldn't tell if they were his own or someone else's.

He didn't even see the cabin until he stepped right into the stairs, smashing his leg on the wooden railing.

Scrambling up on all fours, he yanked open the screen door and checked the dead bolt. Locked. Without even pausing, he glanced around until he spotted the woodpile in the corner. Picking up the biggest log, he hurled it into the door's small window. Reaching his hand through the hole, he unlocked the door and stepped into the living room.

She's still out there.

He didn't care if the house was empty or not—he'd worry about that later. Running straight through to the kitchen, he pulled the drawers out, scattering kitchen supplies until his numb fingers closed over a sharp paring knife. His knuckles were bleeding; he must have cut them on the glass, but it didn't matter.

He returned to the front door and paused. If he went back out into the blizzard, he might not be able to find the house again. It was sheer dumb luck he'd found it in the first place.

He needed help.

Back in the kitchen, he tore through the cupboards again, fully aware that every single second counted. The longer he waited, the farther away Clementine could be. Had the Baggers found her yet? He didn't want to think about it. Finally he came across the ball of twine. This would work. Grabbing it, he didn't even hesitate. Ran straight back out into the cold.

If he could get this one thing right, he might be able to put his guilt behind him.

The storm seemed to have worsened in the few precious minutes wasted indoors. He took the twine and fastened one end to the stairwell. Clenching the rest of the ball tightly, he ventured back out into the whiteness.

He unraveled the string as he moved along, his fingers progressively freezing with each step. Twice he dropped the roll in the snow, and the second time he was forced down on knees to search the growing drifts.

The wind whipped his hair around, catching it on branches and in his mouth. His eyes watered, teardrops crawling and freezing on his cheeks. He thought he spotted a moving shadow but it turned out to be nothing but a tree.

Running out of time. If he didn't find her soon he'd have to retreat back to the house.

Run away all over again.

Run, you coward.

Something reached out and pulled on his jacket.

Screaming, he spun around, numb fingers clutching the knife, ready to stab the Bagger.

"Michael."

He threw his arms around her, dropping both the knife and the string, and pulled her into an awkward hug. She returned the favor, crying and laughing at the same time.

"Come on," he said. "I've found shelter."

Grabbing the twine once more, he got her to take hold of his arm and he began the daunting task of reeling them both back to the cabin.

"I thought I lost you," she said.

"You found me."

"I was so scared. I didn't want to die that way. One of the Baggers attacked me. Tried to claw my eyes out. I hit her in the head with a rock. I think I killed her."

"Good for you."

"She wasn't the first."

They found the steps and he led her up into the cabin. Once inside, he locked the door, but that wouldn't be enough.

In the living room, thankfully only about five feet from the entrance, was an antique china cabinet filled with wineglasses and fancy-looking dinnerware.

"Come on, help me," he said.

They pushed the heavy furniture, dishes and glasses spilling out and breaking on the floor. It took several minutes, but eventually they got it into place. No one would be coming through the door anytime soon. Together they went around to the kitchen and checked the back door. It was locked.

"Should we put something in front of it?" Clementine asked.

"No, we might need it for a quick exit."

"Good point."

Back to the living room they went, and Michael saw the fireplace. Beside it was a neat stack of logs and kindling. Kneeling down in front of the hearth, he began to stack the wood to make a fire. He'd had a lot of experience from camping with his dad, and it didn't take long before the flames caught and a little bit of heat spread throughout the room.

Clementine peeled off her wet jacket and sat in the middle of the floor, shivering while she tried to untie the laces on her shoes.

"I can't feel my toes," she said.

Michael went over to join her. He removed her socks and examined her feet. They were solid white, but at least there were no signs of frostbite. Taking hold of her left foot, he placed a hand on each side and started rubbing it furiously.

"My father used to do this to me after hockey practice," he said. "It works really well. You'll be warm in no time." When he finished with her first foot, he started in on the second. The color began to return to her chilled skin.

"What if they see the fire?" she asked. "Shouldn't we draw the blinds?"

"Yeah, probably a good idea."

They got up and went over to the windows. Peering out into the blizzard, Michael could see only snow. Even the trees were hard to spot. He shut the blinds just in case.

"Will they notice the smoke from the chimney?"

He shook his head. "I doubt it. Not in this storm. We'll have to be more careful once it lets up."

She moved back over toward the fireplace and he noticed she was limping. He wasn't surprised. Her sneakers were of the summer variety, and her wet socks were as thin as nylons. Ignoring his own pain, he headed to the closet by the front door. Inside he found a big woolly scarf and matching hat.

"Here," he said. Taking the hat, he pulled it down over her head. It was too big, but it would keep her warm. Next he wrapped the scarf around her neck.

"I'm gonna go upstairs and take a look," he said. "Maybe I can find some sweaters."

"Okay."

Trying to ignore the feeling of déjà vu, he wandered off, fully aware of what happened the last time he went upstairs to take a look. The last thing he wanted to find again was death.

In the second bedroom he found some winter sweaters and socks. Piling them in his arms, he hurried back to find her wrapped up in a thick blanket.

"It was behind the couch," she said.

They changed into the warmer clothes and sat down next to the fire. There was nothing to do now but wait.

"Are you hungry?" he asked.

She shook her head. "My stomach's too freaked out to eat. You?"

"Yeah, me too."

They sat together for a while, the fire crackling and spitting sparks.

"Last time I had a fire was Christmas," she said. "It was our first holiday without Heath."

Michael went over to the fire and threw another log onto the pile. "You're very close with your brother. You're lucky. I have a sister somewhere, but I never see her. She's with my mom, or she used to be with her."

"Don't talk like that. You don't know for sure."

"You're right."

"Yeah, Heath and I are close," Clementine said. "We used to hang out lots. It sucked when he went to Seattle. I wanted to go and visit, but you get busy with things? School. Cheerleading practice. Craig Strathmore. Now all those things seem unimportant. I can't remember why I cared so much about them."

"I played football and I was also in a band," Michael said. "We were terrible. Our singer always sang off-key. But I agree with you. It seemed so important. Now I don't really care if I never pick up a guitar again."

Clementine shook her head. "Don't say that. We should find you a guitar. Music is one of those things we're going to need. I think that's wonderful."

There was a lag in the conversation while the two of them stared distractedly into the fire. Finally Clementine laughed. "This is so weird."

"What? The conversation?"

"Yeah. We're trapped in this house and those monsters might break down the door any second, but we're talking about cheerleading and guitars."

Michael nodded. "Maybe it's good for us, though. Helps get our minds off stuff."

"I wish I could shut my brain down for a bit. Some days I'd give anything to stop thinking."

"Yeah, me too."

"Why?" Clementine asked after another long silence.

"I don't know."

"Do you think we deserved it? Humans aren't exactly the best things for the planet. Maybe we went too far. Did too much damage."

"I don't believe that."

"Do you believe in God?"

"No. You?"

She paused. "I'm not sure. Maybe. If there is a God, I don't think He's the one doing this."

"Could be a disease."

"Maybe."

"Which means anyone could catch it."

"That would make us immune," she said. "If we were infected, we'd surely be Baggers by now."

"Thinking about it makes my head hurt," he said. "Some things you're just better off accepting. I don't understand, but I know I want to survive. That's all I need, I guess."

She nodded, dropping back into silence.

It was the longest night of his life. Every time the house creaked, his heart pounded at his rib cage. When the wind slammed against the windows, it took all his strength not to jump up and run. He imagined he could hear the Baggers climbing up the steps to the door. He visualized them breaking the windows and climbing in to get them, their eyes distorted in rage.

But nothing happened.

Around two, Clementine drifted off, curled up on the couch closest to the fireplace. Michael grew tired, but he forced himself to stay awake. He kept busy stirring the fire around with a poker for a while. He tried reading one of the books he found on the shelf, but he couldn't concentrate. After reading the same paragraph five times he gave up and put it back. He looked through the DVD collection by the flat screen and decided the owner had terrible taste in movies.

Eventually he sat down in one of the chairs and closed his eyes.

It didn't take long till he fell asleep.

He awoke with a start several hours later. The fire was nothing but a mess of burning embers. Clementine was still on the couch, curled up into a tiny ball, only half her face showing under the winter hat.

He got up and threw a few logs on the fire, coaxing it back to life. The living room was toasty. Once the flames were active again, he looked out the window. The blizzard had ended during the night and the morning sun was beginning to rise over the treetops. The ground was a blanket of rich snow.

He couldn't see any footprints. A good sign.

He'd give the fire ten minutes or so before extinguishing it. The smoke was still too risky, even more so now.

Leaving Clementine to sleep, he wandered over to the kitchen and poked through the cupboards and studied the fancy espresso machine. He missed coffee. The way it used to be so convenient. All he had to do was go into a shop and order up a large or venti or jumbo or whatever fancy word was being used and receive a steaming hot beverage of his choice. Latte. Mocha. Caramel macchiato.

Now coffee was pretty much impossible unless they had the option of fire. Luckily for him that morning, they did. In the bottom cupboard he found a big pot, and he filled it with bottled water found in the pantry. Using the fireplace poker, he held the water over the fire until it boiled. Pouring a generous amount of coffee into the water, he stirred it around with a spoon until it looked good enough to drink.

The coffee was bitter, and the grounds got in his mouth when he reached the bottom of the cup, but it still tasted wonderful. He poured a second and then a third. By then Clementine had started to stir.

"Is it over?" she asked, stretching out on the couch and knocking half the blanket onto the floor. "Has it stopped snowing?"

"Yep." He handed her a mug. "It kinda tastes like sludge, but it's better than nothing."

She took a sip. "It's wonderful."

"We shouldn't stay long. Maybe just take a look around and see if we can get any clothing. They might still be out there, and it'll be easier to find without the storm."

"I was thinking the same thing," she said. "At least now I can feel my toes again."

One hour later they were ready to go. In the garage they found the ultimate item. A monster-sized SUV with four-wheel drive and a full tank of gas.

"We won't get far if we come across a traffic jam," he said. "But at least it'll get us a little farther down the road at a much faster speed. And we can bring some blankets this way. Might not use them, but at least we'll be better prepared."

"Okay, but I drive," she said.

"I'd better wear my seat belt."

She laughed and swatted at him. Ducking, he went around to the front of the car and manually opened the garage door.

They both saw the body at the same time.

Lying facedown, half buried in the snow, it was inches from the garage, one hand reaching out as if trying to grab the air.

"Is it one of them?" she asked.

Michael moved in closer. "I think so," he said.

"Don't touch it!"

He ignored her, pushing the body with his boot, wanting to make sure the person was dead. He'd have to move it out of the way in order to get the SUV out of the garage. He grabbed the body by the shoulders and started dragging it to the side. Clementine came to help.

The frozen body was female. Her mouth was open and filled with ice. "That's the women who tried to claw out my eyes," Clementine said. "She almost found us."

Michael shivered. What would have happened if she'd managed to make it a few more steps before collapsing? Both of them had fallen asleep. They would have been sitting ducks. Mice in a cage. Game over.

"There's another one," she said, and she pointed. Fifty feet away, a body was slouched against a tree wearing a bright red jacket.

"I think we need to leave," he said.

She nodded.

The SUV roared to life on the first try. If they were lucky the vehicle might take them all the way into Seattle.

If they were lucky.

MASON

In Revelstoke they found a working moped. There was only one helmet, which Mason insisted Chickadee wear the entire time, and she put it on without complaint.

She wasn't looking good. Paul's departure hit her hard and she'd lost a lot of the light that seemed to follow her around. She still talked lots, but the cheerful banter was gone. Now her voice had a certain sorrow to it. Sometimes she grew irritated and would snap at him, only to completely break down and apologize. It made Mason uncomfortable. He didn't know what to do to make things better.

"Are you sure you're okay?" he asked for the hundredth time.

"Just tired," she replied.

"Exhausted" was the better word choice. There were black bags under her eyes, and sometimes she seemed to have trouble focusing. Whenever they stopped, she fell asleep, sometimes even sitting up. Her head would nod and soon she'd be breathing softly, her chin resting on her chest.

Mason grew scared. He knew something was happening, and he was completely at a loss over what to do. Every time he tried to bring anything up in conversation, she'd insist she was all right and then change the subject.

He asked her if she wanted to stop in Kamloops. She said no. He asked her again in Merritt. She said no.

"I want to make it to Vancouver," she said. "I want to see the ocean. It's been forever since I last saw it. I'll bet it's beautiful. I want to walk out into the waves and feel the sand squish beneath my toes. It's the greatest feeling in the world, don't you think?"

"I don't remember," Mason said. "I was really young."

"Really? Then we've got another reason to get there fast. It'll be like you're seeing it again for the first time. I want to be the person you're with when that happens. You're gonna just die of happiness."

They made it as far as Hope.

Both of them were on the moped. Mason steered while Chickadee wrapped her arms around his waist. One second her grip was fine; the next moment her fingers loosened and she slipped away, crashing onto the pavement.

"Chee!"

He slammed the brakes. It had been raining earlier, and the back tires fishtailed behind him, forcing him into a half turn, half skid. The bike slid out from underneath him, bringing him down.

Thankfully they weren't going very fast. His leg got caught under the moped, but it didn't do much damage aside from tearing his jeans. As soon as he came to a stop he pulled himself up off the ground and ran to where Chickadee lay in the middle of the open road. She was on her back, her brown eyes staring up at the sky without blinking.

"That was really stupid of me," she whispered.

"Are you okay?" he asked. "Can you move?"

"Yeah, help me up, will you?" She reached out her hand to him and he took it. Gently, he guided her into a sitting position and helped her with the helmet. Her face was pale; she was obviously as shaken as him. "I don't know what happened. One minute I was fine, and then the world went all blurry."

"We've got to . . ." He paused, the words "take you to a doctor" froze on his tongue. The idea seemed so ridiculous; he was annoyed that he'd even thought about it for a second.

"Not really an option anymore," she said, second-guessing him. "I wish there still were doctors. Or artists. Even teachers. They're all gone, aren't they? But you're still here. I'm glad you care about me, Mason."

He picked her up. She'd lost a lot of weight since he first met her; now she was light in his arms. Without saying a word, he started back in the direction of town. If he couldn't take her to a doctor, at least he could find a motel where she could rest for a bit. He wasn't sure if it would help her, but it certainly couldn't hurt.

She wrapped her arms around him as they moved down the hill and under the overpass. Her body pressed tightly against him, she felt both cold and hot at the same time. She leaned her head into his chest and he looked down at her, inhaling the scent of her hair and kissing the top of her head.

"I must smell so bad," she said. "I can't actually remember the last time I showered."

"No," he said. "You don't."

She laughed. "Liar."

"No worse than me," he admitted.

"Then I really stink," she said.

When this whole thing started, after his mother and his friends died, he told himself he was done caring. For weeks he'd kept the numbness inside, a hollow feeling that constantly gnawed at the corner of his mind. He focused instead on being angry, growing to embrace his thoughts of rage. It kept him strong. But Chickadee had somehow managed to get through his barriers and chase the emptiness away. She'd helped him move on. He hadn't even realized how much.

Now the numbness started to creep back into his mind.

There was a group of people on the edge of town fighting over something too small to see. Mason ducked behind a car, pulling Chickadee down to the ground beside him. He had no idea who the people were, but history had taught him that no one was safe, especially those making that much noise in the middle of the afternoon. If they were to spot him now, he wouldn't be able to protect Chickadee. Instead they had to wait till the group moved farther down toward the river before attempting to sneak into a motel that offered free wireless to all its customers. Mason carried her into the main office, where he snagged a set of keys for a room that faced the back.

"Will they come back?" Chickadee asked.

"I don't know."

"What if they're staying in the motel? What will we do then?"

"I don't know."

"Why are you so upset with me?"

"I'm not."

"You sound like you are."

He ignored her. What could he say? He didn't have any answers.

Once in the room, he helped her down on the bed, double locked the door, and drew the blinds. Chickadee started coughing, and he opened up her backpack and pulled out a bottle of water.

"Please don't be mad at me," she said.

"I'm not." He reached out and brushed a few strands of hair off her face. Her skin was warm to the touch, but she didn't seem feverish. Her eyes were bright and wide, and she stared at him like he was the only person left in the world.

"I think I need to rest," she said.

Pulling the blankets off the spare bed, he drew them over her and fluffed up the pillows in a dramatic fashion to try and get her to laugh. Afterward, he sat down in a chair by the window and waited. He couldn't admit this to Chickadee, but he was terrified. He knew she wasn't feeling well—he'd known for several days. She kept insisting she was fine, and he tried to believe she really was just tired. But it was more than that and both of them knew it. The problem was he didn't know what to do. If Chickadee knew the cause of her sickness, she wasn't sharing. He listened to her breathing. It was slow and steady; she had fallen asleep. Good. Hopefully the rest would help her.

Night fell and he continued to wait by the window. Every now and then he'd take a peek to make sure they were still alone. Everything was quiet. Aside from the people they'd seen earlier, the town seemed deserted. A good sign.

They were so close to Vancouver. They could have made it in a few hours if Chickadee hadn't fallen off the bike. Vancouver was a large city—there had to be a lot of people still alive. If he could just get her there, well, maybe there was the possibility he could find a doctor.

He remembered the last night at his house several weeks ago when he destroyed everything in sight. Right now he wanted to go on a rampage against the room. Pull the paintings down off the wall, punch holes in things, smash the television, and break everything in sight. So much rage was building up inside, and he had no way to relieve the tension. When did he get this angry? He never used to be this way. Once upon a time he was a nice guy. He played soccer and hung out with his friends. He'd never been the type to get into fights or do random acts of vandalism. But yet, several weeks ago he'd murdered someone in a park.

Where was this anger coming from? Worse, deep down, why did he enjoy it?

"Mason?"

He was up off the chair in seconds and over by the bed. "I'm here," he said, sitting down beside her. She held out her hand and he took it. Her eyes were wide. Scared.

"I have diabetes."

"What?"

"I'm sorry, I should have told you sooner, but I didn't want to scare you away." She started crying. Big tears fell down her cheeks. "I'm so sorry."

"It's not your fault," he said. Pulling her close, he hugged her and stroked her hair, ignoring the tightness building up inside his chest.

"I should have told you. I should have said something. I just didn't want you to leave. I was so afraid you'd leave me."

"I'm here. I'm not leaving."

"Really?"

"Promise."

He held her. Was it enough? Shouldn't he be doing more? Chickadee continued to cry herself out, and he kept his arms wrapped tightly around her body. There were so many questions he wanted to ask, but he didn't know how to start. He knew nothing about diabetes, except maybe that she needed insulin to survive. When he was in grade school there was a kid who had to inject himself with a needle every day. Did this mean she was going to die? People survived with diabetes all the time. They had normal, long lives. Didn't they?

"There's a drugstore in town," he finally said. "Can I go get something to help?"

She shook her head against his chest. "It's too late. I've been checking the pharmacies all this time, and most of them have been looted. Remember? You caught me looking and thought I was a druggie." She tried to laugh, but it came out more like a choked sob. "It wasn't too hard the first few weeks, but then the electricity went out. Insulin has a shelf date and has to be kept cold. Even if I manage to find some, it will have expired. I've been really careful up until now. Trying to monitor my sugar intake. But it's not helping anymore."

"You told me you weren't sick."

"I'm not. I have a disease. That's a whole lot different than a cold."

"So you kept it from me? I thought we were friends. I thought we were . . ." He couldn't bring himself to suggest something different. What if he was wrong and she laughed? "You should have told me. I would have tried to help."

"I screwed up," she said. "You're right. I should have said something. But I was afraid. Look at what Paul did. He's known me his entire life. But he still left me. I was so scared you'd leave too."

"I'm not Paul."

"No, you're not."

They sat together on the bed for a while in silence. Neither of them knew what to say. Finally Mason couldn't hold back the one question he needed to ask.

"So what does this mean?"

He didn't want to know the answer. He didn't want to know the answer. He didn't want to know the answer.

"Mason?"

"Yeah?"

"Whatever happens, I want you to promise me something. Promise me you'll continue on to Vancouver and feel the ocean. Don't just stand there and look at it. Feel it."

"I don't care about the ocean."

"I do. Consider it my dying wish."

"Stop talking like that. You're not going to die. You'll be fine after some more rest. Maybe I should go check out the pharmacy, just in case."

"Can you stay with me instead? I don't want you to leave."

He hugged her tightly to his chest. "Okay."

"But promise me you'll go."

"Why? That doesn't matter anymore." How could she even think about such trivial things when she didn't even have the strength to sit up?

"It matters to me."

He decided to humor her. "Okay. I promise."

"Mean it."

He should have known she'd see through his empty promise. Nothing ever got past her. She'd known Paul was leaving the night he told his story. That's why she'd been so upset. She wasn't going to give up on this, either. He could tell by the look on her face that she desperately wanted him to go, and he knew her well enough by now to know that she always got what she wanted when she was determined enough.

"I give you my word." And this time he meant it.

She nodded slightly. They sat together in the darkness for a while. In the distance, he heard the haunting, lonely sound of a loon.

"Look on the bright side," Chickadee said after a while.

"What's that?"

"It's not the end of the world."

"Been there, done that," he said with a forced chuckle.

"You know, I'm really glad I met you, Mason Dowell," she said. "Maybe if things had been different, you could have been my boyfriend. There's something special about you. It wouldn't have taken me long to fall in love with you. I would have liked that."

"Me too."

Around two, she slipped into a coma. He pressed his fingers against her wrist and felt the rapid pulsations of her heartbeat. Her body broke out into a sweat, and several times he held her carefully as she twitched and convulsed. He continued to rock her in his arms, whispering softly into her ear, hoping she could still hear.

Sometime in the morning, just as the sun was beginning to peek over the treetops, Chickadee took her last breath.

He didn't try to revive her. All he could think about was his promise. The ocean would be nothing but salt water without her by his side.

The hardest part was letting go of her hand.

Carefully he worked his way out from underneath her body and went to the window. Opening the blinds, he blinked a few times as the sunlight hit his face.

What a beautiful day. The sun was shining and there wasn't a single cloud to be found. On the mountains the pine trees were bright and green. Their branches sparkled with morning dew. Birds chirped happily in the bushes, and a squirrel ran across the motel garden searching for breakfast.

A good day to die.

He went outside and walked around the complex without thinking. He watched a deer grazing before his presence spooked it back into the bushes. A spider spun a web from the top of a rusty swing set. A forgotten shirt hung lazily on a clothesline. He paused to look at everything that caught his interest, but afterward he couldn't remember a thing. Finally he stopped in front of a garden shed, where he found a shovel. At the tree line out the back of the motel, he began to dig.

The sun beat down and his shirt became soaked with perspiration. His lower back ached as the mound of dirt beside him grew and his hole deepened. Blisters formed on the palms of his hands, brutally stinging when they broke and mixed with his body sweat. Twice in frustration and anger he flung the shovel into the woods, listening for the satisfying sound as metal hit tree trunk.

It was hard work. Mechanical. He didn't have to think while he did it. Good. He didn't want to remember. He'd bury his pain along with her body.

Eventually he realized he wasn't alone.

A short, skinny man with a terrible overbite and a dirty baseball cap had come over to watch. When Mason glanced at him, he gave him the thumbs-up gesture.

"What do you want?" Mason asked, pressing his foot down hard on the shovel, cutting deeper into the earth. He wasn't scared of this little man in the slightest. Fear was a feeling, and the angry numbness trumped everything.

"Don't want nothing," the man said. "Just came to see whatchoo doing."

"Go away."

"Not very friendly, are you?"

Scooping some dirt up from the hole, he tossed it in the direction of the man. "Nope."

"You need to learn your manners."

"I'm not looking for a fight." He figured the man wouldn't

want to attack him either. Mason had a weapon, and shovels could really hurt if used properly.

"Why do you think I'd be wanting to fight you?"

"Isn't that what your kind does? Kill anything that moves?" How had Twiggy once put it? Destroy humanity?

"Some of us, yah. But I ain't one of those kind. I ain't looking to kill anything without purpose. I prefer to show the truth."

Mason tossed the shovel into the hole and stood straight. "You know. I keep hearing about these monsters who attack without saying a word. Psychotic nut jobs and all that. But I'm always meeting ones like you who just won't shut up. At this point I'm beginning to wish for one of the crazy ones so I can get some quiet."

The man chuckled and spat on the ground. "So it's peace ya wanting?"

"Yes. So please shut up and go away." Turning his back, he reached for the shovel and started digging again.

But the man didn't go away.

"Aren'tcha wasting your time with this hole?" he said. "I'm assuming it's for that little girl you brought down wit'cha last night. I ain't surprised. I suppose I would have killed her too if I had the chance. But why bother burying her? Leave her in the woods. I'm sure the wolves would like a feast."

Mason froze. "You'd better stop talking right now. You don't have a clue what you're saying."

"What's that? You got her, right? That is why you're digging, right?"

"If you're pushing for a fight, you're gonna get one." His fingers clenched the shovel tightly, ignoring the screams from his palms as his blisters popped and bled.

"Why would I want to do that? I don't fight my kind."

Mason paused. "What the hell are you talking about?"

The man brayed in laughter, doubling over for a few seconds. When he regained his composure, he still continued to chuckle. Mason's temper was on the verge of exploding. He began to picture what it would look like when he smashed the shovel into the monster's smiling face. Imagined him crumpling to the ground the way the man at Diefenbaker Park had.

"You really don't know, do you?" the man finally said. "You ain't figured it out yet."

"What?"

"You belong on our side, boy. You're just the kind of human they like."

In a matter of seconds, Mason closed the distance between them. Grabbing the man by the front of his shirt, he shoved him backward. He stared straight into his black-veined eyes. "You're lying." Pushed him again. "Take it back." Once more.

The look of amusement disappeared, and anger flashed through the strange man's eyes. "You watch yourself, boy. Alls I have to do is scream and they'll come a running. You ain't gonna be so tough against all of us."

"Take it back."

"Take what back? You look in a mirror lately? 'Cause you've got the face." The man wrestled himself free and out of Mason's reach. When he was far enough away, he turned and started walking back toward the main road. "But maybe I am lying. There's a very good chance. Or maybe not. If you're desirable, they'll come for you."

Mason turned and hurled the shovel as hard as he could. It bounced off a tree and fell to the ground several feet away. The hole was deep enough.

Back in the room he went straight for the bathroom. He didn't want to touch Chickadee when he was this filthy.

Stripping off all his clothes, he poured some bottled water into the sink and unwrapped one of the mini soaps. Grabbing a white cloth, he began to wash away the sweat and dirt.

Halfway through it dawned on him that he hadn't looked at himself in the mirror. He paused, the soapy cloth against his chest, and stared blankly at the sink.

What's wrong, Mason? Why won't you look at yourself?

He was just spooked, he told himself. The guy outside tried to freak him out because he was too tiny to take Mason on. It was his only form of action, his way of hurting Mason, because he was too cowardly to do anything else. The guy was probably collecting his friends now, aiming to bring them back to the motel to finish Mason off. And to guarantee Mason would stick around, the monster had tried to scare him into going back to the room and spending a bunch of time in the mirror.

So if that was the case, then why couldn't he bring his face up to look in the glass?

This was stupid. There was no logical reason for him to be scared. He hadn't done anything wrong and he certainly wasn't about to go on a killing rampage. Sure, he was angry, but it was justifiable. Who wouldn't harbor a lot of hate when everyone and everything he cared for was taken away?

"One." He began his countdown. "Two." Grabbing hold of the sink with both hands, he clung tightly until his knuckles were as white as the ceramic.

"Three."

He brought his eyes upward and straight into the mirror. His own face glared back at him, looking both surprised and frustrated at the same time. Sweaty brown hair stuck wetly to his forehead. Blue eyes were tired and bloodshot. What was he supposed to be looking for? Horns? Bloody tears gushing down his hollow cheeks? How about fangs? Nope. The answer was (D) None of the above.

His expression gave him a relieved grin. Suddenly the entire thing seemed ridiculous. Rolling his eyes, he returned to trying to clean the blisters on his hands. He'd have to put some bandages on them before he went back to bury Chickadee. The last thing he needed was an infection.

Grabbing the towel off the rack, he began to dry his body. Caught his full reflection in the mirror. He should be eating more. He'd obviously lost some weight over the past few weeks. Kinda hard to be healthy when the only edible food came in cans or packages.

Pulling a fresh shirt out of his backpack, he dressed quickly. There was a good chance that the lying guy was still out there waiting for him or was on his way over. He needed to get out of here. Get some fresh air. Calm down. Once he cooled off he'd be able to think more clearly.

But he wouldn't leave Chickadee. He'd take care of her first.

He carried her outside and tenderly lowered her body into the grave. Even though he'd wrapped her in the sheets, he could still see how small and fragile her body was. When he tossed the first shovelful of dirt over the clean white cotton, the tears began to flow freely. He ignored them, concentrating on the job instead. He kept thinking he should say something out loud, anything, to celebrate her life and the time they'd shared. But his mind remained blank. There were no words good enough to describe her, anyway.

When it was over, he turned and walked away. He didn't go back into the room to grab his backpack. He no longer wanted it. The road was the only important item he needed.

He'd allow himself to worry about all the other details later while he headed to Vancouver. He had a long road ahead of him and plenty of time to consider his options.

He still had an ocean to feel.

CLEMENTINE

They walked into Seattle. There were no more roads to lead the way. The intricate spiderweb of highways, overpasses, and tunnels were gone, leaving nothing but piles of asphalt and abandoned vehicles where they once were. Glass was everywhere. The city was covered in it. The buildings above were nothing but hollowed-out rebar and ghostly shells. The smell of smoke was strong. Several buildings were still on fire, presumably from where looters had been at work.

Dear Heath, I'm almost there. Have you waited for me? I hope you were somewhere safe when all this happened. Did they teach you earthquake safety when you got here? Remember how Mom used to warn us about what to do if a tornado ever came? I'd be both terrified and excited at the idea of one actually happening. I'm babbling now. Remember how you used to tease me and call me Empty-Head Barbie? Seattle really looks trashed. I've never seen such a mess. I'll be there in a few hours. I hope you get this message somehow. I'll send all the good vibes I have your way. Maybe you'll feel them the way Mom felt us. Either way, hang on tight. I'm coming.

Everything was quiet. Eerily quiet. Dead bodies were everywhere. Some were obviously victims of the earthquake, rotting and stinking from weeks of decomposition. Others were more recent, Bagger prey, still bloody and fresh. In places, they'd been tossed into piles, some of which had been burned. Clementine looked away when they came across the first bonfire. By the time they reached the eighth or ninth she stopped counting, and sometime after that it stopped making her nauseous.

What a strange thing to grow accustomed to.

"Smart," Michael whispered. The smell of decay was strong, almost overpowering, and both of them had their shirts pulled up over their faces. "They're cleaning the place up. They may be crazy, but I guess even Baggers worry about hygiene."

"Why would they do that?" she asked.

"Lots of reasons," he said. "If they plan on sticking around, they'll want to fix things. Get rid of the smell. I've heard that some of them are still pretty smart. They're not all random killing nut jobs."

"I guess that makes sense," she said.

Michael shrugged. "Maybe they're planning on rebuilding civilization. I'm not complaining about a little maid service. I've seen enough dead bodies to last a lifetime. If they want to clean them up, that's fine by me. Maybe they'll fix the roads next. Start up the power. Would be nice to have electricity again. Heat too. It'll be cold soon."

"You make them sound human."

"Aren't they? A lot of monsters are human."

She couldn't argue with that.

They turned the corner cautiously and came across an entire city block demolished by the earthquake. It reminded her of pictures they showed in history class of war-torn Europe after World War II. Such destruction. Hard to believe Mother Nature did that.

"I wonder how many died during the earthquakes," she said. Strange, she'd almost forgotten about the natural disaster. But in a way, the quakes started it all. That's when the killings began.

"Probably a lot here," he said. "I've never seen a city so shattered before. Look at all that glass. I wouldn't want to be underneath it when it fell from the buildings."

She shuddered. People would have been cut in half. Fortunately the Baggers had tidied up this area.

"Any idea how far the university is from here?" he asked.

She pulled out the map she'd taken from a gas station a few hours back. Opening it, they spread it out against the hood of a car, and Clementine tried to figure out where they were while Michael kept watch. They ended up having to walk several blocks until they discovered a street sign. Most of them had been destroyed or had gone missing. Once they established their location, they found the University of Washington on the map.

"Not bad at all," Michael said. "We should be able to get there in a few hours as long as we remain Baggerless."

They didn't reach the campus until nightfall. Not because of the Baggers but because many of the roads were no longer passable. Several times they had to backtrack and find new routes when they came across entire skyscrapers brought down by the quake. The city was now mountains of rubble.

Things got a little better once they reached I-5. There weren't as many buildings and they were able to pick up the pace.

When they finally reached the university, they stopped to look at the gigantic campus map.

"What dorm is he staying in again?" Michael asked.

"Mercer Hall," she said. In the corner of her pocket she still had his address written on a piece of paper. She'd looked at it so many times over the course of the past few weeks; the paper was worn thin from being constantly refolded. She'd ripped the page from Mom's address book, and she often pulled it out when she was depressed and lonely. It was the last thing she had of her mother's. Her only family heirloom.

"There it is," he said, pointing to the northwest corner of the map. "We can either go straight through, or be more careful and stick to the edge and go around."

"Let's go straight," she said. "It's dark enough and I'm tired of walking."

"Your call," Michael said.

As they moved into the campus, Clementine noticed that the damage wasn't nearly as bad as earlier in the streets. Hope rose in her thoughts, and she tried to shove it back into the corner of her mind.

Dear Heath, I'm trying hard not to get too excited. You may not be here. You may be dead. I'm almost at the end of my journey. I'm not sure what I'm going to do if you're gone. I haven't given things any thought past finding you. Where will I go from here? What will happen if I no longer have you to talk with? You've been so helpful to me along the way, even if you don't know it. Please don't be dead.

When they arrived at Mercer Hall she almost turned and ran back in the other direction. Her heartbeat was off the charts, and her palms were sweaty. She hadn't felt this way since a year ago when she waited for Craig Strathmore to pick her up for their first school dance.

"You look like you're going to throw up," Michael said. "Do you want to wait for a bit? We don't have to go in right away. Probably smarter if we sit back for a few hours and scope the place out. Anyone could be in there."

"No," she said. "I have to go now or I'll lose my courage. You're welcome to stay out here if you think it's unsafe."

"I never said I wasn't game," he said, giving her a reassuring grin.

The walkway was surrounded by trees and bushes. Mercer Hall was old and made of brick; it stood against the night, quiet and foreboding. Together they made their way up to the front. The wood-and-glass door was smashed and held open by a battered chair. Not a good sign.

Clementine gently stepped around the seat, wincing as the door squeaked and a piece of glass fell from the frame. Nothing came running around the corner to attack. No voices shouted out at them. She turned on her flashlight, and a circle of pale light struck the floor.

Inside, the vending machines were pried open by crowbars. Change littered the floor along with dented cans of pop. A few candy bars, stepped on and squished, and some empty wrappers. Michael picked up a can of Coke and opened it, taking a drink.

The elevator was jammed open, and she could see the wires leading down into the darkened shaft. They found the stairs and headed up to the third floor. Dried bloody palm prints covered the fire door as if someone had attempted some abstract art.

They could hear music when they reached the top, faint, coming from one of the far back rooms on the right side of the hall. It wasn't a good sign. Michael put one of his fingers up to his lips, and she nodded, almost offended that he thought she might start calling out her brother's name. She wasn't *that* stupid.

There were a lot of overturned chairs in the hallway. Piles of clothing and other sorts of personal items were tossed haphazardly in piles on the floor. Some of the doors were open. They walked farther inside, turning left and away from the music, Clementine counting the door numbers until they came across Heath's room.

The door was wide-open.

Her heart instantly dropped into her stomach. But she'd come this far. She would check out his room, even if it meant finding his body.

Michael reached out and took her hand. His fingers were warm and soft and she instantly felt a little stronger. Holding her breath, she closed her eyes tightly and stepped into the room.

When she found the courage to take a peek, she saw the room was empty. She immediately spotted the Glenmore High sweatshirt lying on the bed. Next to it was the brown sweater that Mom had bought Heath last Christmas.

Picking up the sweatshirt, she touched the fabric with her fingers. Her vision grew blurry as she fought back the tears. It wouldn't do her any good to cry. She still didn't know anything.

You're not dead yet. Not a memory while there's still hope. I won't believe it until I see your dead body.

She scanned the room; it was hard to take everything in at once, especially since the place had been obviously ransacked. The drawers were open on all the cupboards, and clothing was strewn across the floor and bunk beds. A computer monitor had been smashed against the wall. Something green and extremely moldy sat under the desk. There were socks everywhere. She looked for anything of value. A clue.

A note.

Someone walked right past the door, a guy with a towel wrapped around his head. He froze the moment he realized he wasn't alone. Turning carefully, he stared at them apprehensively. Wearing a pair of boxer shorts and a Batman shirt, he hardly looked threatening.

Clementine immediately knew he wasn't a Bagger. There was no way he could be faking that kind of fear. She held up her hands carefully, reassuringly—letting him know they weren't a threat either.

"Um . . . can I help you?"

"The guy who lives here," she said. "Heath White. Have you seen him?"

The towel dropped to the floor. "Heath? Yeah, he's gone, man. He split."

"Do you know where he went?"

"Him and his roommate took off somewhere. No idea. They asked me along, but I wouldn't go. I ain't leaving this place. It's much safer than being out there."

"You keep playing music like that and it won't be," Michael said.

"Nah," the guy said. "They've come and gone. Cleaned out the building. And I've got a good hiding spot."

"What if we were Baggers?" Michael said. "You'd be dead."

The guy looked puzzled. "Baggers? Is that what you're calling them, or is that what they call themselves?"

"What does it matter?" Michael said. "Their name or ours, you'd still be dead."

The guy shook his head and shrugged. "They said I wasn't worth it. They came and left and said I wasn't good enough to die. They took Stebbins and killed a bunch of others, but they left me alone. I doubt they'll come back."

"Why would they do that?" Clementine asked. "Why not kill everyone?"

"I dunno. Maybe they thought they were useful? They went after the tech students. Computer programming. Could be they want to get all the computers working again. How the hell should I know? I think there were some chemistry and premed guys, too."

"Rebuilding," Michael said softly. "By force."

"Who did they kill?" she asked.

The guy ignored the question. He was too busy studying Clementine. "Are you Heath's little sister? He talked about you sometimes."

She nodded. "Did he leave a message? Did he give you anything for me?"

"Nope." The guy picked his towel up off the floor. "Hey, do you want to go out with me sometime? You're seventeen, right?"

"You do realize you're not wearing any pants, *right*?"

"Whatever." The guy scratched at a pimple on his neck. "But I think he left a note somewhere. Maybe. I can't remember. If it's okay with you, I'm gonna go back to my room and check out my hiding spot. With my luck you probably led them right back here. Baggers. What a stupid name."

The guy turned and disappeared down the hall. Clementine and Michael exchanged looks, trying very hard not to laugh before the weird little guy was out of earshot.

She turned and started examining the room. It didn't take her long to find what she was looking for.

There on the desk, weighted down by a ring, Heath's school ring to be exact. The blue stone looked black in the darkness.

She picked up the paper and opened it.

Oct. 15

Dear Mom, Dad, and Clementine,

I don't know if you'll ever see this letter, but I pray that you're alive and well. We've been hiding out at the school for the past few weeks, and Aaron and I have decided to go someplace safer. There are attacks at night. People have been searching the dorms and killing the survivors. Most of the students on my floor are already dead. I've been lucky.

We're going to head north to Vancouver, Canada. We heard some people transmitting on the CB radio. They said it's supposed to be safe there. No monsters. The university is taking thousands of refugees from America. I don't believe it, but Aaron wants to try. Safety in numbers, right?

I hope you're well, and if you find this, I wish I could offer more. I wish I could head east, but I don't believe I'd make it alive. And the others won't come with me. I already asked. Please don't think I'm a coward, but I can't make that trip alone. So I'll head north with them.

Clementine, stay safe. Stay well. Sometimes I feel like you're here with me, whispering in my ear. Call me crazy, but I think some of Mom's intuition is rubbing off on me. I'll keep that faith that you're alive and well deep inside my heart.

Love, Heath

The tears were so bad she almost couldn't finish reading the letter. When it was over, she handed it to Michael and picked up Heath's sweatshirt again to dry her face. It wouldn't do her any good to cry. According to the date, Heath had written the letter a little more than a week ago. He'd survived the earthquakes and the initial attack. He might still be alive. She didn't have to mourn him yet.

She just had to find him.

Michael handed back the letter, and she read it again before folding it and putting it in her pocket. Picking up Heath's ring, she placed it on her middle finger. It was a little too big, but she didn't think it would fall off.

Then she pulled on Heath's shirt. Go Goblins!

"I'm going to Vancouver," she said.

"I thought you might say that." Michael smiled.

"You don't have to come."

"I have this far. Do you really think I'd leave you now? I'd probably get lost trying to find my way back home. You're stuck with me."

NOTHING

We all die alone.

No matter how many friends we think we have. No matter how many toys we own. No matter how many lies we tell each other.

We all fall down.

We've all been silenced. There are no more stories to tell, no people to listen. I could send this message in a bottle in the hopes that one day someone might find it, though. I wouldn't even have to write a story; all I need is six numbers.

There are six different types of killers in the world.

1. Those who kill quickly. Efficiently.
2. Those who enjoy making each murderous moment last forever.
3. Those who kill the soul and leave their victims alive.
4. Those who kill accidentally or in self-defense.
5. Those who hunt to feed.
6. Those who hunt for the game.

The Baggers fall into all categories. I'd like to believe I'm a one or a four, but I'm really more of a six. It all depends on the day.

Game begins.

Game ends.

So quick.

Would you like to play a game of hearts?

The evil that infects us has always been around. Since the dawn of time, before names could be named, before words were written down—they have always existed. There are no records because they leave behind no trace. How do you chronicle something you cannot see?

Once upon a time an ancient civilization grew. It prospered. The people were happy and intelligent. They created cities and erected great monuments. But something always happened. They grew greedy, perhaps, or maybe they took more than the earth was willing to offer.

And that's when their downfall began. The darkness that lies beneath started to stir.

It always notices. They always come.

They kill.

There are ruins all over the world, testaments of the atrocities, and burial chambers of the lost souls. But the facts are always misinterpreted. History is inaccurate.

Things are different today. We are all connected in one form or another. We build things in China and pay for them in America. When our computers break, we talk to people halfway around the world to get them running again. On one continent millions of people go hungry while on another they grow fat.

Because of these connections, now they will destroy us all.

We are all together in this game.

I'm talking in riddles again. I'm sorry. It happens sometimes. My brain is broken and I don't know how to fix it.

When it's time for me to die, promise you'll be the one to stop me. No mercy. Let me die alone.

ARIES

She was wrong. She'd figured it out before she got halfway back to the apartment block. She never should have allowed Daniel to talk her into leaving. But even though she knew she was wrong, she didn't turn around.

Instead she went for reinforcements. But that turned out to be more difficult than she imagined.

"We have to go back."

She stood in the middle of the room; surrounded by all the people she'd risked her life protecting. They had followed her from the very beginning, but this time around they wanted to stay put.

"Think about what you're saying," Jack remonstrated. "They're in the store and you want us to go there? That's like asking to die. We're not fighters, Aries, we can't take them on."

Joy nodded. "They'll kill us."

"I don't want to die," Eve said. Nathan put his arm around her and pulled her close.

"But it's the right thing to do," Aries said. "And we have weapons now. We've got all those baseball bats. I'd do it if it were one of you."

"That's the problem," Jack said. He paused for a few moments, as if trying to figure out the right words. "Daniel's not one of us. We don't know him."

Aries stared out at the faces of her friends. "He still helped me," she pointed out. "I'd be dead without him."

They all avoided her gaze except Colin, and he was smirking.

"Fine," she said. "Then I'll go myself."

Turning, she fled the room, trying very hard to control her temper. How could they do this to her? To Daniel? Just let someone die like that, it wasn't right. Sure, it wouldn't be easy, but her father used to say that no good job comes easy.

The problem was that she knew they were right. It would be a death trap going back to the store. They'd managed to stay alive this long because they avoided conflict. They hid in the shadows and did their best to remain invisible. Not a single one of them actually knew how to fight.

Including her.

She was fooling herself. Even with a weapon at her disposal she didn't think she could use it. The biggest thing she'd ever killed before was a horsefly, and that was after it took a big chunk out of her leg. And yet they had to start fighting back, didn't they? Otherwise the monsters would win.

In the kitchen she grabbed a package of chocolate chip cookies, then silently snuck up to the third floor where she could be alone. No one ever went into the far corner room, because they considered it too dangerous. Closing the door behind her, she turned and inched her way along the side of the room toward the section where the building had caved in. Sitting down, she dangled her feet over the edge and leaned against the wall. She liked sitting here. If she closed her eyes and only allowed herself to feel the breeze against her skin, she could pretend she was sitting on the edge of a mountaintop with nothing but valleys of trees and raging rivers below.

Ten minutes later Jack came and found her. He inched along the wall until he was close enough to sit down. It was a big move for him; Aries knew he didn't like heights and it was making him nervous sitting at the edge.

"I guess you think we're all a bunch of monsters," he said.

Aries handed him the bag of cookies and he took one. "As opposed to what? All the other monsters?"

Jack made a face. "Okay, we deserve that. But we're scared. I'm terrified. It's one thing to go out looking for supplies. But to go straight into the lion's den is another story."

They sat together on the edge of the building, eating cookies. Outside, the sky was cloudy. It was threatening to rain again. Good, because there were still a few fires downtown that could use a little extinguishing.

"I'm not disagreeing with you," she said after a while. "I'm fully aware that it's suicidal. Why do you think I'm still here?"

"Something finally got through that thick head of yours?"

She laughed through a mouthful of cookie.

"I'll tell you what," Jack said. "Let's get up at dawn and go take a peek. We'll scope out the building from a distance. If it's safe, we'll go in and check up on your Daniel. Besides, the shirt you picked out for me is too tight. I can't trust a gal to do my shopping. What's this world coming to?"

She laughed again and offered up the bag of cookies a second time. But Jack wasn't paying any attention. Peering out into the darkness, his eyes narrowed in concern.

"What do you see?" She tried to follow his gaze. The road below was nothing but shadows.

One of the shadows moved.

And then another.

A third farther down the street—a shadowy person stepped from a doorway and moved behind a parked car.

Aries turned her head slightly and checked in the other direction. She could see more of them moving, sticking close to the edge of buildings, trying to maintain secrecy. But she saw them.

And a whole lot of them were coming.

"We need to get back inside," Jack whispered in her ear.

She nodded. As quietly as possible, they moved away from the crumbled edge and back toward the hallway.

They found us, she thought. *We all knew something like this would eventually happen. We couldn't stay hidden forever. It was only a matter of time.*

They raced along the hall and down to the apartment they'd been using, where they found the rest of the group in the kitchen.

"Change of plans," Jack said. "There's a whole lot of them outside. They know we're here."

Everyone started talking at once.

"They can't get in, right?" Eve said. "They can't break through the door. It's solid metal."

"How many?" Joy asked.

"Where?" Nathan immediately got up and went to the window.

Colin didn't say a word. He backed into the wall behind him, his face instantly pale.

The time to not panic was ten minutes ago. All eyes turned toward Aries. Why her? Why not Jack? He was much better at this sort of thing. Why did they expect her to have all the answers?

"At least twenty," Aries said. "Maybe more. And no, I don't think they can break down the door. And unless they have a ladder they can't reach the windows."

"That's the least of our problems," Jack said, joining Nathan at the window. "One of them is carrying gasoline. I saw a jerrican."

"What does that mean?" Eve asked. Her voice grew higher and more breathy with each word.

"They're going to burn us out," Joy cried, just as a flaming bottle crashed through the window, sending glass, gasoline, and fire across the room. Eve screamed. Nathan bolted into action, jumping straight into the flames and stomping on them with his boots. Aries grabbed a blanket and joined him.

Another bottle sailed through the air, hitting the wall this time. Glass and fire rained down onto a couch. More flames instantly sprang to life.

The sounds of bottles breaking came from other rooms in the building. They were attacking from all sides. The room grew thick with smoke as the fire spread too quickly for them to control. Aries's eyes watered, and she couldn't see more than a few feet in front of her face.

"We've got to get out of here," Jack screamed as he beat at the flames with an old pillow.

"Downstairs," Aries said. "Come on. Let's go! Stay away from the windows."

She waited at the door until everyone ran past. Jack was the last; he grabbed her arm and pulled her along.

"Ready to try out our emergency plan?" he asked.

She nodded.

It was time to leave. They'd planned for this, knew where to meet one another in case they got separated. But in all their careful preparation, neither of them ever thought it would be this sudden. She never expected they'd be driven out with such force.

"They'll kill us," she said, coughing harshly. "The second

we open the door. They're waiting to peg us off one by one."

"Then we'll have to outsmart them," Jack rasped.

"If we run at once, they might not be able to catch us all."

"Not much of a plan," he said.

"Do we have a choice?"

He shook his head. "It's not like we can distract them with ice cream and cookies. We're flat out!"

She gave him a sad smile. It was typical of Jack, always trying to lighten the moment with humor.

They regrouped in the hallway. Even in the dark she could make out the terrified expressions on their faces. The smoke wasn't as bad there, but already they could hear the crackle of flames getting closer. If they didn't move quickly, the entire building could collapse down on them.

"We're gonna make a run for it," she said. "We don't have a choice. If we stay here we'll die. If we go outside, there's a good chance that we'll make it. Nathan, Jack, and I will go first. We'll try and create a diversion. We've got four radios between us. If we work together we should be able to stay in contact. We'll meet at Second Beach like we planned."

"I want my own radio," Colin said.

"Fine," Aries said. She wasn't going to disagree with him. Not when there was so much at stake and such little time. "Everyone grab a baseball bat and nothing else. No need to weigh ourselves down."

"I should be going first, too," Joy said. "I may be the shortest, but I can run the fastest. If I can get them chasing me, it might work."

"I'll stick with Eve and we'll follow after," Nathan said. "We'll share a radio."

"I'm with team Jack," Aries said. "Colin and Joy can each have their own radio, then. Everyone okay with that?"

They all nodded.

"Let's get going, then." She turned and ran down the hallway to the second floor apartment where they were storing the radios and the rest of the supplies. Jack and Nathan followed.

She tried hard not to think about what would happen next. There were at least twenty monsters outside, quite possibly more. The odds of all of them getting out alive were slim. When she looked over at Nathan and Jack, she knew they were thinking the exact same thing.

How was she going to bear it if one of them died? They were her new family, even Colin with all his faults.

The answer, she realized, was already there. She would just live. The same way she'd been surviving all this time. Although she'd kept hope alive, she knew deep inside that her parents were most likely dead, along with almost everybody she'd ever known. Sara was dead, and she'd loved her more than anyone else on earth. So were Ms. Darcy, Becka, and Amanda.

And she'd coped. She'd survived.

No matter how much of a leader she didn't think she was, she'd get them through this. Leaders had to make tough decisions. She was making one now. She'd deal with the consequences later.

In the apartment, she gathered the radios and handed them over to Nathan, keeping one for her and Jack. From outside the window, she could hear the crowd of human monsters. They were getting excited.

No more than five minutes had passed since they set the building on fire. Funny, it already felt like hours.

"You're not going to believe this," Jack said suddenly. He was over by the window, looking down at the street. "Some guy just ran straight into the group. He's fighting them. Stupid nut's gonna get himself killed."

Aries's heart jumped into her throat.

Daniel?

MASON

Mason found the motorcycle on the side of the road just outside of Chilliwack. He was so close now to Vancouver and his promise to Chickadee. For the next few hours he drove the bike at top speed, twisting in and out of stalled traffic, rarely using the brakes, and even jumping into the ditch in some places. Several times the bike wobbled beneath him, threatening to spin out.

It was a miracle he didn't crash. No, that wasn't the right word. It was a curse.

Vancouver was a ghost town.

The bike ran out of gas right in the middle of the intersection at Main and Hastings. He got off it, letting it drop to the ground, and staggered down the street in the direction that felt right.

Everyone he cared about was dead and he felt cheated. He should have died in the school explosion along with his friends, his body under tons of concrete. The only reason he lived was because his mother got into that stupid car accident.

He didn't deserve to live. His mother's sacrifice was all in vain.

The guy back in Hope was right about him. He was a monster. A good person would have done a better job. He would have made the doctors help his mom in the hospital. He would have noticed that Chickadee needed medication, maybe even as early as Banff when she first checked the pharmacy. He never should have accused her of doing drugs. Why hadn't he picked up on it and done whatever it took to get her the medication she needed? Instead he'd ignored the signs, even when he knew something was wrong.

He should have figured out that Paul was acting weird when he told the story back in the hotel. If he'd convinced Paul to stay behind, Chickadee wouldn't have felt so betrayed. She might have been more honest with him and told him sooner. But instead she had been afraid he'd leave her too. He should have done something to make her understand that he never would have gone. That he'd be with her to the very end. He kept his promise, didn't he? He'd come to Vancouver.

He could have saved her.

Several blocks in the distance he could see the beginning of downtown Vancouver. Huge buildings graced the skyline, many of them still standing, although most of the windows had been shattered. He knew Stanley Park was on the other side. There wasn't much farther to go now.

East Hastings was a mess of looted buildings and trashed cars. Garbage was heaped in doorways, and the streets were scattered with bottles and useless retail goods. The whole place smelled like urine and desperation. He deserved to be there.

The smoke reached his nose before he saw the flames. A block later, he came across the ambush. A group of monsters disguised as humans circled around a building, carrying Molotov cocktails. They were tossing the bottles through the windows one by one.

How many people were trapped inside?

Now the group of crazies gathered by the back doors, obviously waiting for the moment when the trapped people tried to make a run for it. Some of them brandished baseball bats and one or two were holding knives.

These monsters didn't deserve to live. Trapping people like mice. It was a mob mentality, cowardly at best.

He didn't deserve to live either. The one good person who truly deserved to walk the earth was buried back in a shallow grave in a town falsely named Hope.

At least he'd be able to take a few of them down with him.

And he'd never see the ocean. Or feel it. It bothered him slightly that he'd be breaking his promise. Hopefully Chickadee would understand this was the only way he could truly punish himself for his wrongdoings.

He didn't think. Instead he ran straight at the crowd.

ARIES

Aries didn't stop to think. Grabbing one of the baseball bats, she took the stairs two at a time, her sneakers barely touching the concrete. Behind her she could hear Jack and Nathan struggling to keep up. At the bottom, she unlatched the lock, shoved open the metal door, and stepped out onto the street.

When she saw his face, she knew the stranger wasn't Daniel. But who was he? And why was he doing something so bloody suicidal? Stopping just beyond the door, she watched the stranger attack. He was in the middle of the monsters, lashing out as the crowd swarmed him. Punching blindly, he still managed to hit targets—she saw someone's nose connect with his fist, blood spurting onto the street. Another one took a kick to the side, collapsing, only to get trampled as the others closed in on the hunt.

"Come on," she heard Jack say from behind. "Get out of here while they're distracted."

It was the opportunity of all opportunities. Silently, her friends poured out of the building and split in different directions. Nathan grabbed Eve and they disappeared into the alley. Colin and Joy headed off behind the building toward Crab

Park. The monsters were so distracted by the stranger, they didn't even notice. She turned to Jack, surprised to realize that he was the only one left. The others had vanished into the night.

"We have to help him," she said.

"We owe him that much," Jack agreed.

But what could they do?

From out of nowhere, another figure slammed his way into the group. This time it *was* Daniel. She recognized his black hair and slender frame. He obviously had a weapon of some sort in his hand, and two of the monsters crumpled to the ground. One of the mob members got behind him, raising a baseball bat in the air.

She didn't think about it. She charged the group, aiming for the guy with the bat, and using her own weapon to slam him hard in the side. Someone tried to grab her by the hair and knocked the bat out of her hands, so she twisted her body around, tightened her fingers into a fist, and planted a punch right into his jaw. Her knuckles popped and cracked, and pain flared up her hand, but it was one of the most fantastic feelings she'd ever experienced in her life. She'd never punched someone before. Who knew it could be so amazing? A female got right in her face—black-veined eyes wide, teeth bared—and practically bit her nose off. Aries pulled her arm back again, felt the crazy woman's nose break under her knuckles. Only this time it hurt a lot more.

Professional fighters and movies made it look easy.

She turned around to see hands coming straight for her throat, but Jack stepped in front of her, tackling the body to the ground. They were all involved now, a fight to the finish.

The crowd started to go crazy. They were too close together. The stranger ducked a blow, forcing a monster to punch another. Soon a bunch of them were fighting among themselves, a full-blown mob of crazies, and no one seemed to know what was happening anymore.

Daniel reached for her through the mob, grabbed her by the elbow, and pulled her back. "Are you nuts?" he shouted. "What the hell are you doing? You're gonna get yourself killed. Get out of here. Go join your friends."

"I'm not leaving you," she said. "And I'm not leaving that other guy, either. He just saved everyone's lives."

Daniel pulled her farther back from the crowd and pushed her behind a parked car. "Stay there. I'll get him."

MASON

A sharp punch to the stomach and all the air was sucked out of his body. As he tripped over someone's head, Mason's knees went in opposite directions, bending in ways nature never intended. Hitting the ground hard, he felt someone kicked him twice in the side, and he instinctively curled up into the fetal position to try and withstand the blows. A boot pressed down on his fingers and he felt them snap, and his teeth clenched down tightly to keep him from screaming.

All he needed now was a good strong kick to the head and it would be over. He would not close his eyes. He'd face death head-on.

A hand reached out through the cluster of bodies. A face appeared along with it. A guy around the same age as him grabbed hold of his arm and yanked him forward.

"Come on," the guy said. "What the hell do you think you're doing? Trying to kill yourself? There are better ways to die, my friend."

"Get lost," Mason wheezed. He breathed deeply, the air beginning to return to his lungs.

"This isn't an option," the guy said. He dodged a blow and

kicked out, sending the assailant flying through the crowd. "Whatever you think you did, well, get over it. You don't deserve to die."

"What do you know." It wasn't a question.

The guy pulled Mason closer until their noses were practically touching. "I happen to know a hell of a lot. Now get your ass up off this ground and follow me. I've got a girl over there and she's gonna be pretty pissed if you don't come back with me."

Something in his eyes made Mason believe it was true. This wasn't the time or place to be dying. He allowed the stranger to help him to his feet. Together they fought their way out of the crowd and over to where a girl and guy were waiting.

"Come on," the girl said. "We don't have much time. They're gonna notice they're just fighting each other soon." She turned to the guy beside him. "You're coming too, Daniel, don't you dare think you're gonna just run off right now."

The stranger named Daniel gave a coy smile. "I wouldn't dream of it," he answered.

He's lying.

But the girl bought into it and the four of them headed off around the corner of the building. They ran for a few blocks without stopping.

Mason tried to keep up, but he'd been hit too many times. His throat and lungs burned and a stitch in his side threatened to tear his entire body into strips. After the fourth block, he stumbled and fell to his knees. He hadn't eaten the entire day and it was a good thing. If there had been food in his stomach it would now be leaving his throat and hitting the sidewalk. He stayed there a few moments, his palms flat on the pavement, his head hovering close to the ground while he coughed his lungs out.

"Go on without me," he said. "I'm seriously screwed."

"That'll teach you to take them on by yourself," the girl panted. "Whatever possessed you to try and be a hero, anyway?"

"I'm no hero."

"You saved our lives," she said.

Mason looked up at her, and for the first time noticed how big and green her eyes were. The expression on her face was concern, and for a moment he actually believed that she cared, even if she didn't know a single thing about him.

"I'm Aries," she said. She nodded to the guy beside her. "He's Jack. And the guy over there is Daniel."

"And are you?"

"Huh?"

"Are you—an Aries?"

She laughed. "No, I'm a Gemini." She held out her hand to him and he took it, allowing her to carefully help him to his feet and into the shadows of a darkened doorway. Once he was standing, the pain in his lungs started to disappear, and soon his breathing returned to normal.

"I'm Mason."

The three of them stood squashed awkwardly for a few moments while Daniel continued to watch down the street. Finally he turned around and faced the group.

"I hate to break up this happy get-together, but they've noticed we're gone. I think it's time to start moving."

Mason could hear shouting in the distance. Sure enough, shadowy figures were moving in their direction from a few blocks away.

"Can you run again?" Aries asked him.

"I'll manage," he said. "Where are we going?"

"The ocean," she said. "That's where we're meeting the others. But we'd better lose this crowd first."

He didn't believe in fate or destiny or any of that crap they talked about in the movies. But when Aries mentioned the ocean, he couldn't help but wonder if Chickadee had somehow found a way to bring him to this girl.

CLEMENTINE

She heard the pounding footsteps but didn't actually expect the guy to run right into her. She and Michael had rounded the corner, about to check out the four-leveled parking lot to see if they could find a way to get inside the Bay department store. It was late and they were looking for a place to crash for the night.

The moment her feet stepped around the building, a guy with disheveled black hair ran straight into her. Knocking her head against his chin, she fell backward into Michael, who just managed to catch her.

She saw stars, but before she had time to count them, the guy grabbed hold of her hand.

"I'd follow if I were you," he said. "They're right behind us."

"Baggers," Michael said.

Clementine looked over the stranger's shoulder, and sure enough, off in the distance, at least twenty or thirty of them were closing the gap.

"We need to hide," a girl with long auburn hair said, joining them. Beside her were two other guys, both of whom looked extremely winded. One of them was pretty battered, too. He was holding his mangled hand against his chest.

"We were heading to the parking lot," Michael said. "Just right there. Thought maybe we could get inside the Bay."

The girl and short-haired guy exchanged looks.

"We'll be trapped," she said.

"It's a good hiding spot," he said. "We can't outrun them forever."

"But how do we know they're cool?" the battered guy said as he eyed Michael warily.

"How do we know *you're* cool?" Clementine snapped.

"We are running away from them, in case you didn't notice."

"We don't have time for this," the black-haired guy said. "We'll just have to take our chances."

The girl turned to Clementine. "Let's do it."

They ran straight across the street and into the lot. Beside the ticket booth was a tiny concrete stairwell that led straight up. Above their heads was a skywalk. If they could reach it, they might be able to gain access to the store.

The skywalk was three flights up, and by the time they reached the top, everyone was breathing heavily. The girl introduced herself as Aries in a whispered, breathy voice. She then gave out everyone else's names.

"I'm Clementine," she whispered back. "And that's Michael."

"Are we done with introductions?" Daniel asked. "I'm getting really tired of all these new faces. How many others am I going to have to endure tonight?"

"Don't worry," Aries shot back. "As soon as we're safe you can go find another hole to crawl into."

Michael and Clementine exchanged glances. What sort of fight had they literally crashed into?

Down in the street below they could hear shouting as the

Baggers spread out to search. It was only a matter of time before they found the stairwell.

"We're boned."

Clementine didn't know what Daniel meant until she glanced over at the skywalk. It was in shambles, the windows broken, the floorboards uprooted and cracked. In the middle was a hole big enough to fall through. The structure seemed to be barely holding on by a thread.

"That's not gonna take our weight," Jack said. "That wouldn't even hold a baby."

"Maybe if we go one at a time?" Aries suggested.

"It was such a good idea," Clementine said. "I forgot about the earthquake."

"You couldn't tell it was damaged from below?" Daniel said. "Why didn't you just look up then?"

"Hey, don't snap at her," Michael said. "It's not her fault."

"I think we can do it," Mason said. He didn't even hesitate. Clementine held her breath as she watched him walk briskly straight out onto the skywalk, keeping to the middle where the supports might be the strongest. When he reached the hole, he simply stepped over it as if it was a pothole in the road instead of a three-story drop to the street below. Once safely across, he waved at the others to join him.

"Show-off," Daniel muttered.

Jack went next, then Aries, followed by Daniel. Jack had the most difficulty, freezing by the hole for a good thirty seconds before his legs started working again.

"Your turn," Michael said.

She stepped out onto the skywalk, immediately feeling the breeze through the broken windows against her face. The platform seemed to move beneath her, but she tried to convince herself that it was all in her head. The metal creaked under her weight, but it held. When she saw the hole, her legs began to quiver.

Dear Heath, I think I'm going to throw up.

The thought almost brought her to hysterics. But it also gave her strength. When she found her brother, they'd look back on this and he'd be proud of her for having the guts to pull off such a dangerous stunt.

She cleared the skywalk, and Michael followed without incident.

"Store's open," Mason said.

"There could be more of them in there," Jack said.

"We'll have to take our chances," Clementine said. "They're on the stairs. I can hear them."

They ran along the hallway, past the flower shop, and into the store.

The Bay was full of light.

"What the . . ." Clementine paused, her hand on her flashlight. Fluorescent lights glowed above her head, the entire store laid out in front of them like a brilliant shopping paradise.

"Generator," Aries said. "It has to be. The power's been out for weeks. But who did this? The crazies?"

"Maybe," Daniel said. "Hard to tell. The only windows are on the first floor. You could stare at the store all day and not see anything. Could be others hiding."

"But why here?" Jack said. "Why the Bay? There's no food here? Kinda pointless. Are they planning on getting their Christmas shopping done early?"

"And it's not even Halloween yet," Michael said.

"This isn't good," Daniel said. "I've got a bad feeling. Let's find the Granville Street entrance. I think we should have left ten minutes ago."

"Agreed," Aries said. "This is too creepy."

They headed for the middle of the floor, where the escalators were. As they ran past the activewear, Clementine knocked over a bunch of mannequins, sending hat-covered heads and tank tops flying. A badminton racket sailed through the air and a plastic arm bounced down the escalator steps.

"I'll say this much," Jack said as they raced downward. "I'm never gonna look at another mannequin the same way. Those things are spooky. Even the ones dressed in bras."

They made it only to the second floor before they were spotted. At the bottom of the escalator, someone screamed, a female Bagger wearing a bloodstained sundress.

"Change of plans," Michael yelled.

"Follow me," Aries said. "We'll take the stairs."

They ran off toward the women's purses. It wasn't until they reached the hosiery department that everyone stopped dead in their tracks. Jack raised his baseball bat up in the air.

"What the hell?" Mason said it best.

The area had been completely cleaned out. Hundreds of sleeping bags lined the floor, pressed tightly together like sardines. Empty cans, packaged food, and discarded bloody clothing covered the space. In the corner, piles of uneaten groceries and survival goods were stockpiled. Without thinking, Clementine reached down and picked up a discarded rag doll. Dried blood was smeared across its rosy cheeks.

"That is one big slumber party," Michael muttered. He kicked at a pile of discarded laundry.

"That explains the generator," Mason said. "They're living here. And we just walked right into their nest."

From behind them, back at the escalators, the scuttling noise of several people running echoed across the store.

"The Baggers are in the building," Clementine muttered.

"I'd ask you why you call them that, but I don't think we

have time for a chat," Jack said. "I think the proper thing to do in this situation is run."

There were no disagreements.

They headed toward a glowing exit sign and found the stairs. There was only one more flight to go before they reached the main floor. Then they raced toward the makeup and perfume counters. Clementine had always avoided these areas in the past. She had allergies to perfume and hated the way all the scents mixed together. Even now, weeks since the store saw its last real customer, the heavy smells assaulted her nose. Suppressing an intense urge to sneeze, she ran straight for the doors, pressing hard against the latch to try and get it open. It didn't budge.

"Door's locked," she said.

"Same here," Michael said, pressing both his hands against the glass in frustration. "We need something big to break it."

"I think we need another exit," Daniel said. "Look."

She hadn't seen it at first because it was dark outside and still in the light. But looking out onto Granville Street, she saw that the pavement was lined with Baggers. Dozens of them, maybe even a hundred. They stood quietly, waiting, watching the store.

"That's it," Mason said quietly. "Game over."

"No," Clementine said. "There has to be another way out." She turned to look back at the perfume counters, but the Baggers were already there. Walking down the rows, at least twenty of them were spreading out across the floor, grinning.

"We're surrounded," Aries said.

"It's been a good fight," Michael said.

"It's not over," Clementine snapped. "There's gotta be another way." She looked back over her shoulder to see that more Baggers were appearing in the street.

Michael reached out and took her hand.

"No!" she screamed. "I'm not dying this way."

One of the Baggers leaped toward her, fingers reaching for her face. She felt Michael's hand tugging her back, but he wasn't fast enough. Just as the monster reached for her, Mason shoved her out of the way and tackled the Bagger head-on, knocking him to the ground.

It was the sign the monsters were waiting for. They began to surge forward toward the group. Behind her, Clementine could hear the sounds of them banging against the doors. Glass shattered and a burst of cold wind hit her neck.

MASON

He'd seen the guy coming and managed to get Clementine out of the way before he took the hit. The pain in his wounded hand was horrible, but he clenched his teeth tightly and fought back the nausea welling up inside his stomach. The Bagger dropped to the floor, smashing its head and knocking itself unconscious. Not that it mattered. One down, several hundred more to go.

Behind them, the glass shattered. Before he had a chance to turn, one of them slammed into his back, knocking him straight onto his knees. Someone grabbed him by the hair, jerking his neck back at an awkward angle before Jack stepped in, punching the Bagger hard enough that it let go.

He nodded at Jack; there was no time for more thanks as the Baggers swarmed the store through the broken doors.

Mason started throwing punches with his good hand. He saw Clementine and Michael picking up perfume bottles and hurling them at the monsters. Daniel went down in a sea of crazies, clothing and skin blurring as they toppled over one another to get close enough for the kill. Jack and Aries stood together, the baseball bat high above his head, as the crowd closed in.

This was it.

A female Bagger circled Mason from behind, and a brief flash of metal appeared in the corner of his eye as she raised a knife toward his face. She screamed like a banshee, filthy hair whipping around her shoulders. Mason dodged her, kicking at her legs and bringing her to the ground. With his good hand, he punched another attacker in the nose, working his way through the crowd to where Aries and Jack battled their own group of monsters.

He got to them too late; saw the baseball bat driving down into the back of Jack's skull. The sound of aluminum meeting bone, and Aries screamed. Jack's knees trembled, his entire body collapsing against a display of beauty products.

Mason dived down and managed to catch Jack before he hit the ground. As he held Jack tightly, Aries was beside him in an instant, pushing his arms away so she could take the wounded guy in her arms.

Jack's eyes were closed.

"Oh, God," she whispered. "Oh, God. Jack. No."

The same Bagger grabbed Mason's hair, yanking him backward. He fought his way free, picking up a discarded perfume bottle and smashing it over the Bagger's head. He stumbled back to Aries. Jack was motionless in her arms, blood matting his hair and slowly staining her shirt a dark red.

There was no way to sugarcoat the words that came next.

"Put him down," Mason said. "We need you. Care for him when we're done."

Aries ignored him, her eyes filled with tears. Mason reached out, touching her cheek, forcing her to look at him.

"He's not dead," Mason said. "He's breathing. Don't be stupid and give up now. He's going to die if you don't fight to save him."

Aries blinked several times as the words reached her ears. Finally she nodded and carefully placed Jack's head gently on the ground. She picked up his bloody baseball bat as she stood and immediately swung it, hitting a Bagger in the shoulder.

"You're right," she said, swinging it again. "He's not going to die. I won't let him."

Mason gave her a crooked grin. The girl had guts.

Then suddenly the store groaned, rebar stretched, more windows shattered, and the floor heaved upward as if the ground had opened its mouth and taken one gigantic burp.

"Earthquake!"

The building started shaking, makeup and perfume bottles were knocked off counters, and the sickening smell of a thousand different scents filled the air.

The Baggers stopped fighting. Many of them dropped to the ground, rolling around on the floor and muttering words no one understood. Some of them screamed in unison, a creepy, high-pitched noise coming from deep within their throats. Above them, pieces of the ceiling broke apart, plaster dropping down onto the group.

"It's gonna collapse," Michael screamed. "Everyone, outside!"

Aries and Michael grabbed Jack, pulling the unconscious kid into their arms, and carried him through the broken window.

Mason ran toward the doors, jumping over the fallen Baggers and pushing through the broken glass and onto the sidewalk. Granville Street was heaving: concrete cracked and split apart while large holes opened up to swallow street lamps and abandoned cars. A fire hydrant exploded, sending a fountain of water straight up into the air.

They staggered toward the intersection of Georgia Street, while the Bay department store gave one final shudder before collapsing into itself.

The sky opened up and rain started to fall, a few quick drops that quickly changed into a heavy shower.

There were still several Baggers on the street, but the majority of them had been trapped inside the store. Those that were outside were mostly on the ground, still writhing around, doing their strange chicken dance.

As quick as it started, it ended. The earth stopped moving. In the distance, car alarms sounded and Mason could hear a dog barking. The rain continued to hit the pavement; his hair and clothing were already soaked.

"They're moving," Clementine said. Sure enough, several of the Baggers climbed to their feet, bewildered expressions on their dirt-covered faces.

"We should split up," Aries said. "We're supposed to meet the others at Second Beach in Stanley Park. You know where that is, right?"

He could feel the picture in his back pocket the second she spoke the words. *Mom and Mason—enjoying the sun*. It took willpower to keep from yanking it out and babbling about destiny.

"I've heard about it," he finally said. "I know it's somewhere in the downtown core. We must be close. But I'm not sure where to go."

"Us neither," Clementine said.

"Then I guess we stay together."

"I've got a better idea," Daniel said. "There's no way we can outrun all of them, even with their numbers down. Aries, take your friends and head for Second Beach. Tourist Boy and I are gonna stay behind and create a diversion."

"No," Aries said. "You're not leaving me again."

Tourist Boy? Mason disliked this guy more and more by the minute. But still, the creep had a point. A diversion was exactly what they needed, and he could give it to them.

"I'm in," he said.

"Then it's settled," Daniel said. Moving toward Aries, he put his hand up to her chin. "I gave you my word, and I will keep it this time. I'll meet you on the beach."

She started to protest, but Jack weakly called out her name. Clementine and Michael were holding on to him, trying to keep him on his feet. Aries leaned in toward him, and he whispered a few words in her ear. It must have worked; she nodded, crossing her arms over her chest.

"You'd better be there," she said. She tried to hand over her baseball bat, but Daniel wouldn't take it.

"Keep that, you're going to need it."

Aries went back to the others. Michael was in charge of Jack now; he'd picked him up piggyback-style. His face was flushed under the extra weight, but he looked strong enough to carry him for a good ways. Jack was semiconscious and clinging weakly to Michael's shoulders. There was no way he'd be able to walk two feet on his own.

He hoped they'd be able to make it.

Mason watched them as they headed off down Granville Street. He knew this was the right thing to do, so why did he feel so apprehensive?

Daniel turned toward him, holding out a roll of black electrical tape. "Give me your hand."

Mason held out his broken fingers. Daniel examined them briefly.

"This is gonna hurt," he warned. Pulling gently, he straightened the bone.

Mason clenched his teeth, trying hard to ignore the pain. A wave of nausea filled his stomach.

"Let's get one thing straight," Daniel said as he began to tape two of Mason's fingers together. "I picked you for a reason. The Baggers, or whatever you want to call them, are coming. They're not going to play nice. There's only one way to deal with them."

"Yeah, I get it," Mason said. "No need to be an ass about it."

Daniel finished with the tape and tossed it on the ground. "That should hold for now." He pulled something out of his pocket. The metal gleamed against the moonlight. He held the knife out to Mason.

"I'm not a kil—" But he was, wasn't he?

"I know you can do it. That's why I picked you. You're stronger than the rest of them. You've felt the darkness."

Mason took the knife in his hands. The blade was heavier than he expected.

"Feels good, doesn't it?"

"No."

"Liar."

Mason's face grew hot. "Just what are you implying? You say a lot of stuff, but none of it makes much sense. I'm not like those monsters. I'm not into killing. I don't give a damn what you think." It took him a moment to realize he was trying to convince himself as much as Daniel.

Daniel smiled. "You're right. You're not one of them. But you've got potential. I can see it inside of you. You're walking a thin line right now; it's just a matter of time till something tilts you over to either side. You need to decide, Mason, who you want to be. You can fight here for a good cause and go join your new friends and start a life that's gonna keep you clean, or you can give in to those voices that whisper about all the bad things you've done. Make your choice. I suggest you get over it. Suck it up. Whatever you did, it's not nearly as bad as you think."

Mason stepped backward, his body pressing up against the wall behind him. "Who are you? How the hell do you know these things?"

"I'm just a guy who sees a lot, and you're like an open book, my friend." Daniel pulled a second knife from his pocket. "Now, are you a warrior or are you just some monstrosity? Follow your own road."

The words hung in the air between them.

"I'm in."

ARIES

The roaring waves washed against the shore. She stood a few feet away, staring out into the darkened water. The sound was loud but strangely soothing. Her eyes grew heavy and her heartbeat relaxed to the most normal pace she'd encountered all evening. It was impossible to stare out at the ocean and not feel peaceful.

Behind her in the east, the sun was beginning to peek through the trees. Soon it would be light and they'd have to go. It wasn't safe wandering around in the day. They all knew this.

All that energy spent on running and hiding. So much had happened in the past month. She'd almost forgotten what it used to be like before all this started. Wasted days hanging at the mall with Sara, hundreds of hours spent giggling over silly things. Wouldn't it be nice if she could turn back the clock?

Time was precious. There never was enough of it to spare.

Were her parents still out there? Would she ever get the chance to go home and see for herself?

They'd made it to the beach, where they'd found the others waiting for them. Joy, Nathan, Eve, and even Colin—she was overjoyed to see them all alive. Now that Michael and Clementine had joined them, they were growing stronger.

Jack was still alive, but he couldn't see. Something had happened to his brain when the Bagger hit him. His eyes perceived nothing but blackness.

"This is bad," he'd said earlier when she helped him down onto the sand.

"We'll get through it."

"I'm only going to hold you back," he said. "This complicates things."

"You're never going to complicate anything," she said. "You're the one person who helps make all this easier. I can't do it without you, Jack."

She smiled and it hurt her to know he didn't realize just how much she cared.

But he was alive. She didn't know if his blindness was permanent, but they'd deal with it.

They would be a family and she would keep them together.

She'd keep them alive.

They just had to wait for Mason and Daniel to show, and they could head out to find a new home. She believed him when he said he'd come. There had been something different in his voice. Something truthful.

She went back over to Jack, putting her arm around him carefully as a good friend would do. She curled up against him, feeling the warmth of his body. Michael had torn up his shirt to make a bandage. Jack's head looked like he was wearing a flattened plaid hat.

"How do you feel?" she asked.

"I've got a splitting headache," he said. "And I'm blind, did I mention that? Aside from that, not bad."

She choked back a laugh.

"We have to go soon," he said.

"I know. But we can wait a few more minutes."

"Any idea where we're gonna go?"

"Wouldn't it be nice if we could stay here?" she said. "We could become beachcombers and just spend our days digging clams out of the sand."

"Sounds heavenly," he said. "But I'm allergic to shellfish."

She giggled.

"Eve suggested Shaughnessy," she said. "Over by the university. We could get one of those big mansions with a pool. That would rock."

"I'm in," Jack said. "I always knew I was destined to live somewhere rich."

In the distance a heron dove straight for the water, catching a fish in its beak. Seagulls floated lazily, completely oblivious to the shattered world around them.

"We need to start searching for other survivors," she said. "Get organized."

"Maybe we can find my brother." Clementine had come over and joined them. "He was supposed to be in Seattle, but he came here. Left me a message. Said there were survivors at the University of British Columbia."

"It's possible," Jack said. "It's just across the water. Over there to your right. At least I think it's your right. Can't tell for sure. Look for all the trees. That's Jericho Beach. UBC isn't far from there. We were just talking about finding a new hideout in Shaughnessy."

The girls looked out across the water. On the other side of English Bay, the shoreline was visible.

"Hey!" Eve's voice carried toward them. "They're here."

Aries turned around. Mason and Daniel were climbing down the stairs to the beach. She grabbed Jack's hand and gave it a squeeze. "I'll be right back." She followed Clementine over to join the group.

Everyone was happy. She realized this was the first time in weeks she'd seen people smiling and laughing all at once. It was a nice feeling. If only it would last.

There would be more hard times ahead of them. She had no reservations about it. But they would deal. They had each other and they would find a way to get through it all.

They were a group.

She reached Daniel and Mason first. Their clothes were covered in dark stains and the smell of rust overpowered the scent of salt water.

"Don't ask," Daniel said. "Because I'm not telling."

"I'm glad you're here," she said. She meant it for both of them.

"We should get going, then," Nathan said. "If we're heading to rich man's land, we've got a lot of ground to cover. Maybe we should find a shop to hole up in for the day and set out again once it gets dark. I'll carry Jack. I don't mind."

"Oooh, there's a Blenz not too far from here," Eve said. "Maybe we can figure out a way to get some coffee. I'd kill for an espresso."

"Yeah, and I'm sure we can all spend the day munching on month-old vegan brownies," Nathan said. "Seriously, wouldn't a Seven-Eleven make more sense?"

"What about Safeway?" Mason said. "We passed two on the way here."

The group continued to discuss their plans. Aries couldn't help but listen with a grin on her face. But then Daniel pressed his hand against her arm and beckoned her away.

She walked with him up the beach a ways. He was silent. She knew what was coming.

"Don't tell me." She sat down on a huge log, her feet barely touching the ground. "You're leaving."

"You know me too well." Daniel sat down beside her, their knees touching as they leaned into each other.

"Will I see you again?"

"I think so, yes."

"Good."

He smiled. "You're not going to protest?"

She glanced out over the water where the heron was still enjoying its early breakfast. "You're not going to change. I'm accepting it."

"You're going to do well, Aries," he said. "People will remember you."

"I hope so," she said. "I'm trying. We all want to make our mark in life, right? It doesn't have to be big. Sometimes we just want people to remember we were here."

"You could write your name in the sand."

She laughed. "That's not even a dent."

He reached out, his fingers pressing against her cheek. "You'll move mountains."

She stopped breathing. His eyes found hers, and he looked straight into her soul as if searching for something he'd lost. Her skin tingled as he moved his hand slightly, tilting her head to the side. The entire world slowly vanished until there was nothing to look at except him.

Lips pressed against hers. She closed her eyes, but it ended too quickly. When she opened them, he was staring back at her. She wanted to smile at him but her face was frozen. How could someone's eyes be both bright and dark at the same time?

He slid off the log and pulled a knife out of his pocket. "Then let's make a dent." Kneeling down in front of the log, he used the knife to carve her name into the wood. Then he carved his own name. By the time he finished, the others had joined them. Even Jack, who was being supported by Michael and Clementine.

They didn't even ask. Instead they lined up and each took a turn carving their names into the wood.

ARIES

DANIEL

JACK

CLEMENTINE

COLIN

JOY

NATHAN

EVE

MICHAEL

MASON

When it was over, they all stepped back to admire their work.

"It's official," Daniel said. "We exist."

Something caught Aries's eye. From across the bay, she could see tiny figures moving between the trees of Jericho Park.

She stood up and moved closer to the shore. "What is that?"

"Here." Clementine reached into her pocket and pulled

out pocket binoculars. "They're cracked, but they work. Michael gave them to me."

Aries took the binoculars and brought them up to her eyes. It took a second before her eyes got adjusted and she managed to focus on the park across the bay. From the tree line, several people were coming out onto the beach. Men and women—there were even some children.

"It's a group of people," she said.

"Baggers?"

"No, I don't think so." She watched as one of them used their own set of binoculars, staring back at her. The strangers on the beach crowded around him as he waved at her.

Aries laughed and waved back. "They see us too."

"They're still a million miles away," Michael said.

"But close enough that we can find them," she said. "And others. There will be others."

"Let me look?" Clementine asked, and Aries passed over the binoculars.

"He's not there," she said after a few minutes. "But I'm going to find him."

"I'll help you," Michael assured her.

"We'll all help you," Aries said.

They watched until the people retreated back into the woods. It didn't matter that they left. Aries knew they were there. They'd find them.

"We should go," Nathan finally said.

She nodded. Turning back to her friends, she noticed immediately that Daniel was gone. It wasn't a surprise. It was just a matter of time before he'd return, though. She was certain of that, too.

MASON

He sat down in the sand and took off his shoes and socks. Tried rolling his jeans up but couldn't get them past his calves. Not that it really mattered.

The others were still back at the log, talking among themselves, when he slipped over to the shoreline. Just as well, he kinda wanted to do this on his own. He stood up, and the sand was cool and squishy between his toes.

The ocean was before him. So gigantic. In the distance he could see an island and a few tanker boats. He wondered if anyone was on them.

The wind whipped at his hair and roared in his ears. The tangy smell of salt water and seaweed filled his nose. Bits of sand stuck to his skin, cool and wonderful.

He didn't even bother to test the water with his toe. He walked right in, the icy cold assaulting his tired feet and closing in around his ankles. Breathing rapidly, he moved farther until his jeans began to soak up the water and his knees submerged.

Closing his eyes, he felt the ocean.

NOTHING

We carved our names in the fallen tree. Our tiny mark. Our proof that we still desired life. We would not go gently into that great night.

We were leaders, followers, warriors, even cowards. Some of us were betrayers.

There are no winners in this game.

But there is tomorrow.

JEYN ROBERTS's first story was published in a middle-grade anthology called *Let Me Tell You* when she was sixteen. She graduated from the University of British Columbia with a degree in writing and psychology, and received her MA from the prestigious creative writing graduate course at Bath Spa University in England. Jeyn is a former singer, songwriter, actress, bicycle courier, and tree planter. Most recently, Jeyn taught high school in South Korea. She lives in Vancouver, Canada.

S0-CAY-449

Praise for

The Knife of Never Letting Go

Winner of the Guardian Children's Fiction Prize

"Furiously paced, terrifying, exhilarating and heartbreaking, it's a book that haunts your imagination."

Sunday Telegraph

"Original, powerful and steeped in literary richness."

The Times

"Powerful and provocative..."

Daily Mail

"Darkly imagined and brilliantly created, the painful dystopian setting of a world full of Noise, in which all thoughts can be heard as if spoken, is the background to this tense coming-of-age story."

Guardian

"Imagine a world where the thoughts of men and boys are broadcast for all to hear, good and bad. Ness's novel is at once a breakneck thriller and a fable about fear, love and redemption."

Independent on Sunday

"Ness moves things along at a breakneck pace, and Todd's world is filled with memorable characters and foul villains."

Financial Times

"A sophisticated, complex novel…"

Sunday Times

"Genuinely original vision."

Independent

"Powerful… A highly original contribution to dystopian fiction."

Irish Times

"Impressive."

The New Yorker

"This enthralling novel grips the reader throughout, presenting them with tough questions about identity, ethics and the nature of truth."

BookTrust

"A book like no other. It's one of the most gripping, fantastical reads around."

Sunday Express

"Impressive… In Prentisstown, the Noise virus has left men with the ability to hear each other's thoughts, those of animals too. When Todd finds a lone girl in the marshes he realizes they have to escape, which isn't easy when your hunters can hear your every thought. Brimming over with ideas about adolescence, faith and free will, this is intelligent, immersive storytelling."

The Scotsman

ALSO IN THE CHAOS WALKING TRILOGY

The Ask and the Answer

Monsters of Men

ALSO BY PATRICK NESS

Release

The Rest of Us Just Live Here

More Than This

The Crane Wife

A Monster Calls

Topics About Which I Know Nothing

The Crash of Hennington

PATRICK NESS

CHAOS WALKING:
BOOK ONE

WALKER
BOOKS

This is a work of fiction. Names, characters, places and incidents are either the product of the author's imagination or, if real, are used fictitiously. All statements, activities, stunts, descriptions, information and material of any other kind contained herein are included for entertainment purposes only and should not be relied on for accuracy or replicated as they may result in injury.

First published 2008 by Walker Books Ltd
87 Vauxhall Walk, London SE11 5HJ

This edition published 2018

2 4 6 8 10 9 7 5 3 1

This book has been typeset in Fairfield and ITC Tiepolo

Printed and bound by CPI Group (UK) Ltd, Croydon CR0 4YY

British Library Cataloguing in Publication Data:
a catalogue record for this book is available from the British Library

ISBN 978-1-4063-8412-3

www.walker.co.uk

patrickness.com

For Michelle Kass

IF WE HAD A KEEN VISION and feeling of all ordinary human life, it would be like hearing the grass grow and the squirrel's heart beat, and we should die of that roar which lies on the other side of silence.

George Eliot, *Middlemarch*

PART I

1

THE HOLE IN THE NOISE

THE FIRST THING you find out when yer dog learns to talk is that dogs don't got nothing much to say. About anything.

"Need a poo, Todd."

"Shut up, Manchee."

"Poo. Poo, Todd."

"I said *shut it*."

We're walking across the wild fields south-east of town, those ones that slope down to the river and head on towards the swamp. Ben's sent me to pick him some swamp apples and he's made me take Manchee with me, even tho we all know Cillian only bought him to stay on Mayor Prentiss's good side and so suddenly here's this brand new dog as a present for my birthday last year when I never said I *wanted* any dog, that what I *said* I wanted was for Cillian to finally fix the fissionbike so I wouldn't have to walk every forsaken place in this stupid town, but oh, no, happy birthday, Todd, here's a brand new puppy, Todd, and even tho you don't want him, even tho you never asked for him, guess who has to feed him and train him and wash him and take him for walks and listen to him jabber now he's got old enough for the talking germ to set his mouth moving? Guess who?

"Poo," Manchee barks quietly to himself. "Poo, poo, poo."

"Just *have* yer stupid poo and quit yapping about it."

I take a switch of grass from beside the trail and I swat after him with it. I don't reach him, I don't *mean* to reach him, but he just laughs his little barking laugh and carries on down the trail. I follow after him, switching the switch against the grass on either side, squinting from the sun, trying not to think about nothing at all.

We don't need apples from the swamp, truth to tell. Ben can buy them at Mr Phelps's store if he really wants them. Also true: going to the swamp to pick a few apples is not a job for a man cuz men are never allowed to be so idle. Now, I won't *officially* become a man for thirty more days. I've lived twelve years of thirteen long months each and another twelve months besides, all of which living means I'm still one month away from the big birthday. The plans are being planned, the preparayshuns prepared, it will be a party, I guess, tho I'm starting to get some strange pictures about it, all dark and too bright at the same time, but nevertheless I will become a man and picking apples in the swamp is not a job for a man or even an almost-man.

But Ben knows he can ask me to go and he knows I'll say yes to going because the swamp is the only place anywhere near Prentisstown where you can have half a break from all the Noise that men spill outta theirselves, all their clamour and clatter that never lets up, even when they sleep, men and the thoughts they don't know they think even when everyone can hear. Men and their Noise. I don't know how they do it, how they stand each other.

Men are Noisy creachers.

"Squirrel!" Manchee shouts and off he goes, jumping off the trail, no matter how loud I yell after him, and off I have to go, too, across the (I look round to make sure I'm alone) *goddam* fields cuz Cillian'll have a fit if Manchee falls down some *goddam* snake hole and of course it'll be my own *goddam* fault even tho I never wanted the *goddam* dog in the *goddam* first place.

"Manchee! Get back here!"

"Squirrel!"

I have to kick my way thru the grass, getting grublets stuck to my shoes. One smashes as I kick it off, leaving a green smear across my trainers, which I know from experience ain't coming out. *"Manchee!"* I rage.

"Squirrel! Squirrel! Squirrel!"

He's barking round the tree and the squirrel's skittering back and forth on the tree trunk, taunting him. **Come on, Whirler dog,** says its Noise. **Come on, come get, come on, come get. Whirler Whirler Whirler.**

"Squirrel, Todd! Squirrel!"

Goddam, animals are stupid.

I grab Manchee by the collar and hit him hard across his back leg. "Ow, Todd? Ow?" I hit him again. And again. "Ow? Todd?"

"Come *on*," I say, my own Noise raging so loud I can barely hear myself think, which is something I'm about to regret, you watch.

Whirler boy, Whirler boy, thinks the squirrel at me. **Come get, Whirler boy.**

"You can eff off, too," I say, except I don't say "eff", I say what "eff" stands for.

And I really, really shoulda looked round again.

Cuz here's Aaron, right here, rising outta the grass from nowhere, rising up and smacking me cross the face, scratching my lip with his big ring, then bringing his hand back the other way, closed as a fist, catching my cheekbone but at least missing my nose because I'm falling into the grass, trying to fall away from his punch, and I let go of Manchee's collar and off he runs back to the squirrel, barking his head off, the traitor, and I hit the grass with my knees and my hands, getting grublet stains all over everything.

And I stay there, on the ground, breathing.

Aaron stands over me, his Noise coming at me in fragments of scripture and of his next sermon and **Language, young Todd** and **the finding of a sacrifice** and **the saint chooses his path** and **God hears** and the wash of pictures that's in everyone's Noise, of things familiar and glancing flashes of–

What? What the forsaken–?

But up flies a loud bit of his sermon to block it out and I look up into his eyes and suddenly I don't wanna know. I can already taste the blood where his ring cut my lip and I don't wanna know. He *never* comes out here, men *never do*, they have their reasons, men do, and it's just me and my dog only ever but here he is and I don't don't don't wanna know.

He smiles down at me, thru that beard of his, smiles down at me in the grass.

A smiling fist.

"Language, young Todd," he says, "binds us like prisoners on a chain. Haven't you learned anything from yer church, boy?" And then he says his most familiar preaching. "If one of us falls, we all fall."

Yes, Aaron, I think.

"With yer mouth, Todd."

"Yes, Aaron," I say.

"And the effs?" he says. "And the geedees? Because don't think I didn't hear them as well. Your Noise reveals you. Reveals us all."

Not all, I think, but at the same time I say, "Sorry, Aaron."

He leans down to me, his lips close to my face, and I can smell the breath that comes outta his mouth, smell the weight of it, like fingers grabbing for me. "God hears," he whispers. "God *hears*."

And he raises a hand again and I flinch and he laughs and then he's gone, like that, heading back towards the town, taking his Noise with him.

I'm shaking from the charge to my blood at being hit, shaking from being so fired up and so surprised and so angry and so much hating this town and the men in it that it takes me a while till I can get up and go get my dog again. *What was he effing doing out here anyway?* I think and I'm so hacked off, still so raging with anger and hate (and fear, yes, fear, shut up) that I don't even look round to see if Aaron heard my Noise. I don't look round. I don't look round.

And then I do look round and I go and get my dog.

"Aaron, Todd? Aaron?"

"Don't say that name again, Manchee."

"Bleeding, Todd. Todd? Todd? Todd? Bleeding?"

"I know. Shut up."

"Whirler," he says, as if it don't mean nothing, his head as empty as the sky.

I smack his rump. "Don't say that neither."

"Ow? Todd?"

We keep on walking, staying clear of the river on our left. It runs down thru a series of gulches at the east of town, starting way up to the north past our farm and coming down the side of the town till it flattens out into a marshy part that eventually becomes the swamp. You have to avoid the river and especially that marshy part before the swamp trees start cuz that's where the crocs live, easily big enough to kill an almost-man and his dog. The sails on their backs look just like a row of rushes and if you get too close, *WHOOM!* – outta the water they come, flying at you with their claws grasping and their mouths snapping and you pretty much ain't got no chance at all then.

We get ourselves down past the marshy part and I try to take in the swamp quiet as it approaches. There's nothing to see down here no more, really, which is why men don't come. And the smell, too, I don't pretend it don't smell, but it don't smell nearly so bad as men make out. They're smelling their memories, they are, they're not smelling what's really here, they're smelling it like it was then. All the dead things. Spacks and men had different ideas for burial. Spacks just used the swamp, threw their dead right into the water, let 'em sink, which was fine cuz they were suited for swamp burial, I guess. That's what Ben says. Water and muck and Spackle skin worked fine together, didn't poison nothing, just made the swamp richer, like men do to soil.

Then suddenly, of course, there were a whole lot more spacks to bury than normal, too many for even a swamp this big to swallow, and it's a ruddy big swamp, too. And then there were no live spacks at all, were there? Just spack bodies in heaps, piling up in the swamp and rotting and stinking and it took a long time for the swamp to become swamp again and not just a mess of flies and smells and who knows what extra germs they'd kept saved up for us.

I was born into all that, all that mess, the over-crowded swamp and the over-crowded sematary and the not-crowded-enough town, so I don't remember nothing, don't remember a world without Noise. My pa died of sickness before I was born and then my ma died, of course, no surprises there. Ben and Cillian took me in, raised me. Ben says my ma was the last of the women but everyone says that about everyone's ma. Ben may not be lying, *he* believes it's true, but who knows?

I am the youngest of the whole town, tho. I used to come out and throw rocks at field crows with Reg Oliver (seven months and 8 days older) and Liam Smith (four months and 29 days older) and Seb Mundy who was next youngest to me, three months and a day older, but even he don't talk to me no more now that he's a man.

No boys do once they turn thirteen.

Which is how it goes in Prentisstown. Boys become men and they go to their men-only meetings to talk about who knows what and boys most definitely ain't allowed and if yer the last boy in town, you just have to wait, all by yerself.

Well, you and a dog you don't want.

But never mind, here's the swamp and in we go, sticking to the paths that take us round and over the worst of the water, weaving our way round the big, bulby trees that grow up and outta the bog to the needly roof, metres and metres up. The air's thick and it's dark and it's heavy, but it's not a frightening kind of thick and dark and heavy. There's lots of life here, loads of it, just ignoring the town as you please, birds and green snakes and frogs and kivits and both kinds of squirrel and (I promise you) a cassor or two and sure there's red snakes to watch out for but even tho it's dark, there's slashes of light that come down from holes in the roof and if you ask me, which you may not be, I grant you that, to me the swamp's like one big, comfy, not very Noisy room. Dark but living, living but friendly, friendly but not grasping.

Manchee lifts his leg on practically everything till he must be running outta pee and then he heads off under a bush, burbling to himself, finding a place to do his other business, I guess.

But the swamp don't mind. How could it? It's all just life, going over itself, returning and cycling and eating itself to grow. I mean, it's not that it's not Noisy here. Sure it is, there's no escaping Noise, not nowhere at all, but it's quieter than the town. The loud is a different kind of loud, because swamp loud is just curiosity, creachers figuring out who you are and if yer a threat. Whereas the town knows all about you already and wants to know more and wants to beat you with what it knows till how can you have any of yerself left at all?

Swamp Noise, tho, swamp Noise is just the birds all thinking their worrisome little birdie thoughts. **Where's food? Where's home? Where's my safety?** And the waxy squirrels, which are all little punks, teasing you if they see you, teasing themselves if they don't, and the rusty squirrels, which are like dumb little kids, and sometimes there's swamp foxes out in the leaves who you can hear faking their Noise to sound like the squirrels they eat and even less often there are mavens singing their weird maven songs and once I swear I saw a cassor running away on two long legs but Ben says I didn't, says the cassors are long gone from the swamp.

I don't know. I believe me.

Manchee comes outta the bushes and sits down next to me cuz I've stopped right there in the middle of a trail. He looks around to see what I might be seeing and then he says, "Good poo, Todd."

"I'm sure it was, Manchee."

I'd better not get another ruddy dog when my birthday comes. What I want this year is a hunting knife like the one Ben carries on the back of his belt. Now *that's* a present for a man.

"Poo," Manchee says quietly.

On we walk. The main bunch of apple trees are a little ways into the swamp, down a few paths and over a fallen log that Manchee always needs help over. When we get there, I pick him up around his stomach and lift him to the top. Even tho he knows what I'm doing, he still kicks his legs all over the place like a falling spider, making a fuss for no reason at all.

"Hold still, you gonk!"

"Down, down, down!" he yelps, scrabbling away at the air.

"Idiot dog."

I plop him on top the log and climb up myself. We both jump down to the other side, Manchee barking "Jump!" as he lands and keeping on barking "Jump!" as he runs off.

The leap over the log is where the dark of the swamp really starts and the first thing you see are the old Spackle buildings, leaning out towards you from shadow, looking like melting blobs of tan-coloured ice cream except hut-sized. No one knows or can remember what they were ever sposed to be but best guess by Ben, who's a best guess kinda guy, is that they had something to do with burying their dead. Maybe even some kind of church, even tho the spacks didn't have no kind of religion anyone from Prentisstown could reckernize.

I keep a wide distance from them and go into the little grove of wild apple trees. The apples are ripe, nearly black, almost edible, as Cillian would say. I pick one off the trunk and take a bite, the juice dribbling down my chin.

"Todd?"

"What, Manchee?" I take out the plastic bag I've got folded in my back pocket and start filling it with apples.

"Todd?" he barks again and this time I notice how he's barking it and I turn and he's pointed at the Spackle buildings and his fur's all ridged up on his back and his ears are flicking all over the place.

I stand up straight. "What is it, boy?"

He's growling now, his lips pulled back over his teeth.

I feel the charge in my blood again. "Is it a croc?" I say.

"Quiet, Todd," Manchee growls.

"But what is it?"

"*Is* quiet, Todd." He lets out a little bark and it's a real bark, a real dog bark that means nothing but "Bark!" and my body electricity goes up a bit, like charges are going to start leaping outta my skin. "Listen," he growls.

And so I listen.

And I listen.

And I turn my head a little and I listen some more.

There's a hole in the Noise.

Which can't be.

It's *weird*, it is, out there, hiding somewhere, in the trees or somewhere outta sight, a spot where your ears and your mind are telling you there's no Noise. It's like a shape you can't see except by how everything else around it is touching it. Like water in the shape of a cup, but with no cup. It's a hole and everything that falls into it stops being Noise, stops being *anything*, just stops altogether. It's not like the quiet of the swamp, which is never *quiet* obviously, just less Noisy. But this, this is a shape, a shape of *nothing*, a hole where all Noise stops.

Which is impossible.

There ain't nothing but Noise in this world, nothing but the constant thoughts of men and things coming at you and at you and at you, ever since the spacks released the Noise germ during the war, the germ that killed half the men and every single woman, my ma not excepted, the germ that drove the rest of the men mad, the germ that spelled the end for all Spackle once men's madness picked up a gun.

"Todd?" Manchee's spooked, I can hear it. "What, Todd? What's it, Todd?"

"Can you smell anything?"

"Just smell quiet, Todd," he barks, then he starts barking louder, "Quiet! Quiet!"

And then, somewhere around the spack buildings, the quiet *moves*.

My blood-charge leaps so hard it about knocks me over. Manchee yelps in a circle around me, barking and barking, making me double-spooked, and so I smack him on the rump again ("Ow, Todd?") to make myself calm down.

"There's no such thing as holes," I say. "No such thing as nothing. So it's gotta be a something, don't it?"

"Something, Todd," Manchee barks.

"Can you hear where it went?"

"It's quiet, Todd."

"You know what I mean."

Manchee sniffs the air and takes one step, two, then more towards the Spackle buildings. I guess we're looking for it, then. I start walking all slow-like up to the biggest of the melty ice cream scoops. I stay outta the way of anything that might be looking out the little bendy triangle doorway. Manchee's sniffing at the door frame but he's not growling so I take a deep breath and I look inside.

It's dead empty. The ceiling rises up to a point about another length of me above my head. Floor's dirt, swamp plants growing in it now, vines and suchlike, but nothing else. Which is to say no *real* nothing, no hole, and no telling what mighta been here before.

It's stupid but I gotta say it.

I'm wondering if the Spackle are back.

But that's impossible.

But a hole in the Noise is impossible.

So something impossible has to be true.

I can hear Manchee snuffling around again outside so I creep out and I go to the second scoop. There's writing on the outside of this one, the only written words anyone's ever seen in the spack language. The only words they ever saw fit to write down, I guess. The letters are spack letters, but Ben says they make the sound es'Paqili or suchlike, es'Paqili, the Spackle, "spacks" if you wanna spit it, which since what happened happened is what everyone does. Means "The People".

There's nothing in the second scoop neither. I step back out into the swamp and I listen again. I put my head down and I listen and I reach with the hearing parts of my brain and I listen there, too, and I listen and listen.

I listen.

"Quiet! Quiet!" Manchee barks, twice real fast and peels off running again, towards the last scoop. I take off after him, running myself, my blood charging, cuz that's where it is, that's where the hole in the Noise is.

I can hear it.

Well, I can't *hear* it, that's the whole point, but when I run towards it the emptiness of it is touching my chest and the stillness of it pulls at me and there's so much quiet in it, no, not quiet, *silence*, so much unbelievable silence that I start to feel really torn up, like I'm about to lose the most valuable thing ever, like there it is, a death, and I'm running and my eyes are watering and my chest is just crushing and there's no one to see but I still mind and my eyes start crying, they start crying, they start *effing crying*, and I stop for a minute and I bend over and Jesus H Dammit, you can just shut up right now, but I waste a whole stupid minute, just a whole stinking, stupid minute bent over there, by which time, of course, the hole is moving away, it's moved away, it's gone.

Manchee's torn twixt racing after it and coming back to me but he finally comes back to me.

"Crying, Todd?"

"Shut up," I say and aim a kick at him. It misses on purpose.

2

PRENTISSTOWN

WE GET OURSELVES outta the swamp and head back towards town and the world feels all black and grey no matter what the sun is saying. Even Manchee barely says nothing as we make our way back up thru the fields. My Noise churns and bubbles like a stew on the boil till finally I have to stop for a minute to calm myself down a little.

There's just no such thing as silence. Not here, not nowhere. Not when yer asleep, not when yer by yerself, never.

I am Todd Hewitt, I think to myself with my eyes closed. *I am twelve years and twelve months old. I live in Prentisstown on New World. I will be a man in one month's time exactly.*

It's a trick Ben taught me to help settle my Noise. You close yer eyes and as clearly and calmly as you can you tell yerself who you are, cuz that's what gets lost in all that Noise.

I am Todd Hewitt.

"Todd Hewitt," Manchee murmurs to himself beside me.

I take a deep breath and open my eyes.

That's who I am. I'm Todd Hewitt.

We walk on up away from the swamp and the river, up the slope of the wild fields to the small ridge at the south of town where the school used to be for the brief and useless time it existed. Before I was born, boys were taught by their ma at home and then when there were only boys and men left, we just got sat down in front of vids and learning modules till Mayor Prentiss outlawed such things as "detrimental to the discipline of our minds".

Mayor Prentiss, see, has a Point of View.

And so for almost half a stupid year, all the boys were gathered up by sad-faced Mr Royal and plonked out here in an out-building away from the main Noise of the town. Not that it helped. It's nearly impossible to teach anything in a classroom full of boys' Noise and *completely* impossible to give out any sort of test. You cheat even if you don't mean to and *everybody* means to.

And then one day Mayor Prentiss decided to burn all the books, every single one of them, even the ones in men's homes, cuz apparently books were detrimental as well and Mr Royal, a soft man who made himself a hard man by drinking whisky in the classroom, gave up and took a gun and put an end to himself and that was it for my classroom teaching.

Ben taught me the rest at home. Mechanics and food prep and clothes repair and farming basics and things like that. Also a lot of survival stuff like hunting and which fruits you can eat and how to follow the moons for direkshuns and how to use a knife and a gun and snakebite remedies and how to calm yer Noise as best you can.

He tried to teach me reading and writing, too, but Mayor Prentiss caught wind of it in my Noise one morning and locked Ben up for a week and that was the end of my book-learning and what with all that other stuff to learn and all the working on the farm that still has to be done every day and all the just plain surviving, I never ended up reading too good.

Don't matter. Ain't nobody in Prentisstown ever gonna write a book.

Manchee and me get past the school building and up on the little ridge and look north and there's the town in question. Not that there's all that much left of it no more. One shop, used to be two. One pub, used to be two. One clinic, one jail, one non-working petrol stayshun, one big house for the Mayor, one police stayshun. The Church. One short bit of road running thru the centre, paved back in the day, never upkept since, goes to gravel right quick. All the houses and such are out and about, outskirts like, farms, *meant* to be farms, some still are, some stand empty, some stand worse than empty.

And that's all there is of Prentisstown. Populayshun 147 and falling, falling, falling. 146 men and one almost-man.

Ben says there used to be other settlements scattered around New World, that all the ships landed about the same time, ten years or so before I was born, but that when the war started with the spacks, when the spacks released the germs and all the other settlements were wiped out, that Prentisstown was nearly wiped out, too, that it only survived cuz of Mayor Prentiss's army skills and that even tho Mayor Prentiss is a nightmare coming and going, we at least owe him that, that cuz of him we survive alone on a whole big empty womanless world that ain't got nothing good to say for itself, in a town of 146 men that dies a little more with every day that passes.

Cuz some men can't take it, can they? They off themselves like Mr Royal or some of them just plain disappear, like Mr Gault, our old neighbour who used to do the other sheep farm, or Mr Michael, our second best carpenter, or Mr Van Wijk, who vanished the same day his son became a man. It's not so uncommon. If yer whole world is one Noisy town with no future, sometimes you just have to leave even if there ain't nowhere else to go.

Cuz as me the almost-man looks up into that town, I can hear the 146 men who remain. I can hear every ruddy last one of them. Their Noise washes down the hill like a flood let loose right at me, like a fire, like a monster the size of the sky come to get you cuz there's nowhere to run.

Here's what it's like. Here's what every minute of every day of my stupid, stinking life in this stupid, stinking town is like. Never mind plugging yer ears, it don't help at all:

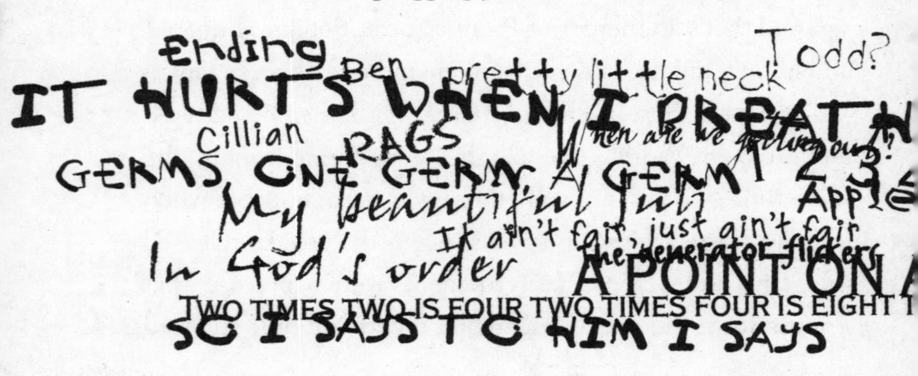

a shoulda seen the pair A Ending
Please help Tomas, God used to know a Man A germ from the spack
You, boy, you there apples
A disease ONE MONTH'S TIME
Ending
A Rags
Apples APPLES A SINGLE CIRCULAR BREATH
Take you by the back of yer neck Quiet, Todd?
Oh my Lilly Oh my Karen Oh my precious pearl OH M
Oh my Julie
YOU EVEN UP THERE? TODD?
There's only enough for my family, not a whit more
Effing spacks and their effing germs
That small, small, that precious and tasty
No More Spackle left to kill
TS AND BRUISES AND CUTS AND BRU
the barrel but keep the oil free from the stock They'll be men
What I wouldn't give for a real beefburger
What if he asks about the sheeps!
I AM AND ALL IS IN GOD'S ORDER
E YER HANDS TOGETHER WITH SOME ROPE
ease don't let the fever take my Justin Apples
my Esther my Esther oh my beautiful girl
ONE MONTH
Prentiss'll have the first go
How are we ever getting outta here!
ow are we ever getting outta here?
HAT HAVE WE DONE, OH, MY LORD?
Todd?
A disease, a germ from the spacks
l kill him, I will, for that
w are we ever getting outta here? Ending
AM A POINT AND THE POINT IS ME I'll just have the one more and go
Cillian
One hundred nineteen days without rain
Ten rows Apples
LOOK AT THE TINY HANDS Course not, Doc
r a liar, sir 4 3 2 1 OH MY NORMA
When a... you to yer face
'VE FORGOTTEN HER FACE
OLD YER THOUGHTS IN A LINE, A LINE, A LINE Just a germ, remember that
ONE MONTH'S TIME
NOTHING BUT BEASTS
eep the boy from their hands somehow, God
THE WOOD IN MY HANDS rags
the holiness of the silence The day
nd found again Oh my Kelly
OH MY JADE
CIRCLE ON A POINT ON A CIRCLE
ES EIGHT IS SIXTEEN
CUTS AND BRUISES AND CUT
THAT HEWITT BOY Todd?
THE ANTS GO MARCHING TWO
The way she used to

1 2 3 4 4 3 2 1
ILLET BEFORE WINTER
SE GOD,
DISCIPLINE, MEN!
A holy sacrament, found and unfound
SAS
Oh my Carla
TEN STRIKES THE HOUR, THE HOUR PLUS TEN
I told you
Two times sixteen is thirty-two two times thirty-two is
four
NO PAINKILLERS LEFT WE'LL RU
hold you down, hold you
AND I TOLD YOU THERE
the neck, yer neck
FATH
approaches
SHUT IT UP

And them's just the words, the voices talking and moaning and singing and crying. There's pictures, too, pictures that come to yer mind in a rush, no matter how much you don't want 'em, pictures of memories and fantasies and secrets and plans and lies, lies, lies. Cuz you can lie in the Noise, even when everyone knows what yer thinking, you can bury stuff under other stuff, you can hide it in plain sight, you just don't think it clearly or you convince yerself that the opposite of what yer hiding is true and then who's going to be able to pick out from the flood what's real water and what's not going to get you wet?

Men lie, and they lie to theirselves worst of all.

In a for instance, I've never seen a woman nor a Spackle in the flesh, obviously. I've seen 'em both in vids, of course, before they were outlawed, and I see them *all the time* in the Noise of men cuz what else do men think about except sex and enemies? But the spacks are bigger and meaner looking in the Noise than in the vids, ain't they? And Noise women have lighter hair and bigger chests and wear less clothes and are a lot freer with their affecshuns than in the vids, too. So the thing to remember, the thing that's most important of all that I might say in this here telling of things is that Noise ain't truth, Noise is what men *want* to be true, and there's a difference twixt those two things so big that it could ruddy well kill you if you don't watch out.

"Home, Todd?" Manchee barks a bit louder down by my leg cuz that's how you gotta talk in the Noise.

"Yeah, we're going," I say. We live on the other side, to the north-east, and we're going to have to go thru the town to get there so here it comes, as fast as I can get thru it.

First up is Mr Phelps's store. It's dying, the store is, like the rest of the town and Mr Phelps spends all his time despairing. Even when yer buying stuff from him and he's polite as can be, the despair of him seeps at you like pus from a cut. Ending, says his Noise, Ending, it's all ending and Rags and rags and rags and My Julie, my dear, dear Julie who was his wife and who don't wear no clothes at all in Mr Phelps's Noise.

"Hiya, Todd," he calls as Manchee and I hurry by.

"Hiya, Mr Phelps."

"Beautiful day, ain't she?"

"She sure is that, Mr Phelps."

"Beaut!" barks Manchee and Mr Phelps laughs but his Noise just keeps saying Ending and Julie and rags and pictures of what he misses about his wife and what she used to do as if it's sposed to be unique or something.

I don't think anything particular in my Noise for Mr Phelps, just my usual stuff you can't help. Tho I must admit I find myself thinking it all a little bit louder to cover up thoughts about the hole I found in the swamp, to block it out behind louder Noise.

Don't know why I should do this, don't know why I should hide it.

But I'm hiding it.

Manchee and me carry on walking pretty fast cuz next is the petrol stayshun and Mr Hammar. The petrol stayshun don't work no more cuz the fission generator that made the petrol went kerflooey last year and just sits there beside the petrol stayshun like a hulking ugly hurt toe and no one'd live next to it except Mr Hammar and Mr Hammar's *much* worse than Mr Phelps cuz he'll aim his Noise right at you.

And it's *ugly* Noise, *angry* Noise, pictures of yerself in ways that you don't want pictures of yerself, violent pictures and bloody pictures and all you can do is make yer own Noise as loud as you can and try to sweep up Mr Phelps's Noise in it, too, and send it right back to Mr Hammar. **Apples** and **Ending** and **fist over hand** and **Ben** and **Julie** and **Beaut, Todd?** and **the generator is flickering** and **rags** and **shut up, just shut up** and **Look at me, boy**.

And I turn my head anyway even tho I don't want to but sometimes you get caught off guard and so I turn my head and there's Mr Hammar in his window, looking right at me and **One month**, he thinks, and there's a picture from his Noise and it involves me standing on my own but somehow even more alone than that and I don't know what it means or if it's real or if it's a purposeful lie and so I think about a hammer going into Mr Hammar's head over and over and he just smiles from his window.

The road curves round the petrol stayshun past the clinic, which is Dr Baldwin and all the crying and moaning men do to doctors when nothing's really wrong with 'em. Today it's Mr Fox complaining about how he can't breathe which would be a pitiable thing if he didn't smoke so much. And then, as you pass the clinic, God Almighty, you get the bloody bloody pub which even at this hour of the day is just a howl of Noise because what they do there is turn the music up so loud it's meant to drown out Noise but that only works partway and so you get loud music and loud Noise and worse, *drunk* Noise, which comes at you like a mallet. Shouts and howls and weeping from men whose faces never change and just horrorpilashuns of the past and all the women that used to be. A whole *lot* about the women that used to be but nothing that makes any sense, cuz drunk Noise is like a drunk man: blurry and boring and dangerous.

It gets hard to walk around the centre of town, hard to think about the next step cuz so much Noise is weighing on yer shoulders. I honestly don't know how men do it, I don't know how *I'm* going to do it when I become a man 'less something changes on the day that I don't know about.

The road bears up past the pub and to the right, going by the police stayshun and the jail, all one place and in use more than you might think for a town so small. The sheriff is Mr Prentiss Jr who's barely two years older than me and only been a man for a short while but who took to his job right well and quick and in his cell is whoever Mayor Prentiss has told Mr Prentiss Jr to make an example of this week. Right now it's Mr Turner who didn't hand over enough of his corn yield to "the good use of the whole town", which just means he didn't give no free corn to Mr Prentiss and his men.

So you've gone thru the town with yer dog and you got all this Noise behind you, Mr Phelps and Mr Hammar and Dr Baldwin and Mr Fox and the extra extra Noise from the pub and Mr Prentiss Jr's Noise and Mr Turner's moaning Noise and yer still not done with the Noise of the town cuz here comes the Church.

The Church is why we're all here on New World in the first place, of course, and pretty much every Sunday you can hear Aaron preaching about why we left behind the corrupshun and sin of Old World and about how we'd aimed to start a new life of purity and brotherhood in a whole new Eden.

That worked out well, huh?

People still go to church tho, mainly cuz they have to, even tho the Mayor hisself hardly ever bothers, leaving the rest of us to listen to Aaron preach about how we're the only thing each of us have out here, us men together, and how all of us have gotta bind ourselves in a single community.

How if one of us falls, we all fall.

He says that one a lot.

Manchee and me are quiet as possible going past the front door of the Church. Praying Noise comes from inside, it's got a special feel to it, a special purply sick feel like men are bleeding it out, even tho it's always the same stuff but the purply blood just keeps on coming. **Help us, save us, forgive us, help us, save us, forgive us, get us outta here, please, God, please, God,**

please, God, tho as far as I know no one's never heard no Noise back from this God fella.

Aaron's in there, too, back from his walk and preaching over the prayers. I can hear his voice, not just his Noise, and it's all **sacrifice** this and **scripture** that and **blessings** here and **sainthood** there and he's going on at such a rattle his Noise is like grey fire behind him and you can't pick out anything in it and he might be up to something, mightn't he? The sermon might be covering for something and I'm beginning to wonder if I know what that something is.

And then I hear **Young Todd?** in his Noise and I say, "Hurry up, Manchee," and we scoot our way along right quick.

The last thing you pass as you crest the hill of Prentisstown is the Mayor's House which is the weirdest and hardest Noise of all cuz Mayor Prentiss–

Well, Mayor Prentiss is different.

His Noise is awful clear and I mean awful in the awful way. He believes, see, that order can be brought to Noise. He believes that Noise can be sorted out, that if you could harness it somehow, you could put it to use. And when you walk by the Mayor's House, you can hear him, hear him and the men closest to him, his deputies and things, and they're always doing these thought exercises, these counting things and imagining perfect shapes and saying orderly chants like **I AM THE CIRCLE AND THE CIRCLE IS ME** whatever that's sposed to mean and it's like he's moulding a little army into shape, like he's preparing himself for something, like he's forging some kind of Noise weapon.

It feels like a threat. It feels like the world changing and leaving you behind.

1 2 3 4 4 3 2 1 I AM THE CIRCLE AND THE CIRCLE IS ME 1 2 3 4 4 3 2 1 IF ONE OF US FALLS WE ALL FALL

I will be a man soon and men do not run in fear but I give Manchee a little push and we walk even a little faster than before, giving the Mayor's House as wide a curve as possible till we're past it and on the gravel path that heads on towards our house.

After a while, the town disappears behind us and the Noise starts to get a little bit quieter (tho it never never stops) and we can both breathe a bit easier.

Manchee barks, "Noise, Todd."

"Yesiree," I say.

"Quiet in the swamp, Todd," Manchee says. "Quiet, quiet, quiet."

"Yes," I say and then I think and I hurry and say, "Shut up, Manchee," and I smack him on his rump and he says, "Ow, Todd?" but I'm looking back towards the town but there's no stopping Noise once it's out, is there? And if it was something you could see, moving thru the air, I wonder if you could see the hole in the Noise floating right outta me, right outta my thoughts from where I was protecting it and it's such a small bit of Noise and it'd be easy to miss in the great roar of everything else but there it goes, there it goes, there it goes, heading right back towards the world of men.

3

BEN AND CILLIAN

"AND JUST WHERE do you think you've been?" Cillian says as soon as Manchee and I come into view off the path. He's lying down on the ground, deep into our little fission generator, the one outside the front of the house, fixing whatever's gone wrong with it this month. His arms are covered in grease and his face is covered in annoyance and his Noise is buzzy like mad bees and I can already feel myself getting angry and I haven't even properly got home yet.

"I was in the swamp getting apples for Ben," I say.

"There's work to be done and boys are off playing." He looks back into the generator. Something makes a clunk inside and he says, "Dammit!"

"I said I wasn't playing, if you'd ever listen!" I say but it's more like a shout. "Ben wanted apples so I was getting him some ruddy apples!"

"Uh-huh," Cillian says, looking back at me. "And where might these apples be then?"

And of course I'm not holding any apples, am I? I don't even remember dropping the bag I'd started to fill but of course I must have when–

"When what?" Cillian says.

"Quit listening so close," I say.

He sighs his Cillian sigh and here we go: "It's not like we ask you to do so much around here, Todd" – which is a lie – "but we can't keep this farm running by ourselves" – which is true – "and even if you ever finish all yer chores, which you don't" – another lie, they work me like a slave – "we'd still be playing a catch-up to nothing, now wouldn't we?" – and this is true, too. The town can't grow no more, it can only shrink, and help ain't coming.

"Pay attenshun when I talk to you," Cillian says.

"Tenshun!" Manchee barks.

"Shut up," I say.

"Don't talk to yer dog that way," Cillian says.

I wasn't talking to my dog, I think, loud and clear enough to hear.

Cillian glares at me and I glare back and this is how it always is, our Noise throbbing with red and hassle and irritashun. It's never been so good with Cillian, not never, Ben's always been the kind one, Cillian's always been the other one, but it's got worse as the day approaches when I'll finally be a man and won't have to listen to any more of his crap.

Cillian closes his eyes and breathes loudly once thru his nose. "Todd–" he starts, his voice a bit lower.

"Where's Ben?" I say.

His face hardens a little more. "Lambing starts in a week, Todd."

All I do to this is say again, "Where's Ben?"

"You get the sheep fed and into their paddocks and then I want you to fix the gate to the east field once and for all, Todd Hewitt. I have asked you at least twice before now."

I lean back on my heels. "'Well, how was your trip to the swamp, Todd?'" I say, making my voice go all sarcastic. "'Well, it was fine and dandy there, Cillian, thank you for asking.' 'Didja see anything interesting out there in the swamp, Todd?' 'Well, funny you should ask, Cillian, cuz I sure did see something interesting which might explain this here cut on my lip that you ain't asked about but I guess it'll have to just wait till the sheep are fed and I fix the *goddam fence*!'"

"Watch yer mouth," Cillian says. "I don't have time for yer games. Go do the sheep."

I clench up my fists and make a sound that sounds like "awwghgh" which tells Cillian that I just can't put up with his non-reason not for one second longer.

"Come on, Manchee," I say.

"The sheep, Todd," Cillian calls as I start walking away. "The sheep first."

"Yeah, I'll do the ruddy sheep," I mutter to myself. I'm walking away faster now, my blood jumping and Manchee's getting excited from the roar of my Noise. "Sheep!" he barks. "Sheep, sheep, Todd! Sheep, sheep, quiet, Todd! Quiet, quiet in swamp, Todd!"

"Shut up, Manchee," I say.

"What was that?" Cillian says and there's something in his voice that makes us both turn around. He's sitting up by the generator now, his full attenshun on us, his Noise coming right at us like a laser.

"Quiet, Cillian," Manchee barks.

"What does he mean 'quiet'?" Cillian's eyes and Noise are searching me all over.

"What do you care?" I turn again. "I got ruddy sheep to feed."

"Todd, wait," he calls after us but then something starts beeping on the generator and he says "Dammit!" again and has to go back to it tho I can feel all kinds of asking marks in his Noise following me, getting fainter as I head out to our fields.

Blast him, blast him and all, I think, in more or less those words and worse as I stomp across our farm. We live about a kilometre north-east of town and we do sheep on one half of the farm and wheat on the other. Wheat's harder, so Ben and Cillian do most of that. Since I was old enough to be taller than the sheep, that's who I've taken care of. Me, that is, not me and Manchee, tho another one of the false lying excuses why he was given to me was that I could teach him up as a sheep dog which for obvious reasons – by which I mean his complete stupidity – hasn't worked out to plan.

Feeding and watering and shearing and lambing and even castrating and even butchering, I do all these things. We're one of three meat and wool providers for the town, used to be one of five, soon be one of two because Mr Marjoribanks oughta be dying from his drink problem any day now. We'll fold his flock into ours. I should say *I'll* fold his flock into ours, like I did when Mr Gault disappeared two winters ago, and they'll be new ones to butcher, new ones to castrate, new ones to shear, new ones to put in pens with ewes at the right times, and will I get a thank you? No, I will not.

I am Todd Hewitt, I think, the day just keeping on not making my Noise any quieter. *I am almost a man.*

"Sheep!" say the sheep when I pass their field without stopping. "Sheep!" they say, watching me go. "Sheep! Sheep!"

"Sheep!" barks Manchee.

"Sheep!" say the sheep back.

Sheep got even less to say than dogs do.

I've been listening out for Ben's Noise over the farm and I've tracked him down to one corner of one of the wheat fields. Planting's done, harvest is months away, so there's not so much to do with the wheat at the minute, just make sure all the generators and the fission tractor and the electric threshers are ready to start working. You'd think this would mean I'd get a little help with the sheep but you would be wrong.

Ben's Noise is humming a little tune out near one of the irrigashun spouts so I take a turn and head across the field towards him. His Noise ain't nothing like Cillian's. It's calmer and clearer and tho you can't see Noise, if Cillian's always seems reddish, then Ben's seems blue or sometimes green. They're different men from each other, different as fire and water, Ben and Cillian, my more or less parents.

Story is, my ma was friends with Ben before they left for New World, that they were both members of the Church when the offer of leaving and starting up a settlement was made. Ma convinced Pa and Ben convinced Cillian and when the ships landed and the settlement started, it was my ma and pa who raised sheep on the next farm over from Ben and Cillian growing wheat and it was all friendly and nice and the sun never set and men and women sang songs together and lived and loved and never got sick and never never died.

That's the story from the Noise anyway so who knows what it was actually like before? Cuz then of course I was born and everything changed. The spacks released their woman-killing germ and that was it for my ma and then the war started and was won and that was it for pretty much the rest of New World. And there's me, just a baby, not knowing nothing bout nothing, and of course I'm not the only baby, there're loads of us, and suddenly only half a town of men to take care of all us babies and boys. So a lot of us died and I was counted among the lucky cuz it was only natural for Ben and Cillian to take me in and feed me and raise me and teach me and generally make it possible for me to go on being alive.

And so I'm kinda like their son. Well, more than "kinda like" but less than actually being so. Ben says Cillian only fights with me all the time cuz he cares about me so much but if that's true I say it's a funny way to show it, a way that don't seem much like caring at all, if you ask me.

But Ben's a different kind of man than Cillian, a *kind* kind of man that makes him not normal in Prentisstown. 145 of the men in this town, even the newly made ones just past their birthdays, even Cillian tho to a lesser degree, they see me at best as something to ignore and at worst as something to hit and so I spend most of my days figuring out ways to be ignored so as I won't get hit.

'Cept for Ben, who I can't describe much further without seeming soft and stupid and like a boy, so I won't, just to say that I never knew my pa, but if you woke up one day and had a choice of picking one from a selecshun, if someone said, here, then, boy, pick who you want, then Ben wouldn't be the worst choice you could make that morning.

He's whistling as we approach and tho I can't see him yet and he can't see me, he changes the tune as he senses me coming to a song I reckernize, **Early one mo-o-rning, just as the sun was ri-i-sing,** which he says was a favourite of my ma's but which I think is really just a favourite of his since he's whistled and sang it for me since I can remember. My blood is still storming away from Cillian but I immediately start to feel a little calmer.

Even tho it *is* a song for babies, I know, shut up.

"Ben!" Manchee barks and goes running around the irrigashun set-up.

"Hello, Manchee," I hear as I round the corner and see Ben scratching Manchee twixt the ears. Manchee's eyes are closed and his leg is thumping on the ground with pleasure and tho Ben can certainly tell from my Noise that I've been fighting with Cillian again, he don't say nothing but, "Hello, Todd."

"Hi, Ben." I look at the ground, kicking a stone.

And Ben's Noise is saying **Apples** and **Cillian** and **Yer getting so big** and **Cillian** again and **itch in the crack of my arm** and **apples** and **dinner** and **Gosh, it's warm out** and it's all so smooth and non-grasping it's like laying down in a brook on a hot day.

"You calming down there, Todd?" he finally says. "Reminding yerself who you are?"

"Yeah," I say, "just, why does he have to come at me like that? Why can't he just say hello? Not even a greeting, it's all 'I know you done something wrong and I'm gonna keep at you till I find out what it is.'"

"That's just his way, Todd. You know that."

"So you keep saying." I pick a blade of young wheat and stick the end in my mouth, not quite looking at him.

"Left the apples at the house, didja?"

I look at him. I chew on the wheat. He knows I didn't. He can tell.

"And there's a reason," he says, still scratching Manchee. "There's a reason which ain't coming clear." He's trying to read my Noise, see what truth he can sift from it, which most men think is a good enough excuse for starting a fight, but I don't mind with Ben. He cocks his head and stops scratching Manchee. "Aaron?"

"Yeah, I saw Aaron."

"He did that to yer lip?"

"Yeah."

"That sunuvahoor." He frowns and steps forward. "I just might have to have words with that man."

"Don't," I say. "Don't. It'll just be more trouble and it don't hurt that much."

He takes my chin into his fingers and lifts my head so he can see the cut. "That sunuvahoor," he says again, quietly. He touches the cut with his fingers and I flinch away.

"It's nothing," I say.

"You stay away from that man, Todd Hewitt."

"Oh, like I went running to the swamp *hoping* to run into him?"

"He ain't right."

"Well, holy crap, thanks for that bit of info, Ben," I say and then I catch a bit of his Noise that says One month and it's a new thing, a whole new bit of something that he quickly covers up with other Noise.

"What's going on, Ben?" I say. "What's going on with my birthday?"

He smiles and for a second it's not an entirely true smile, for a second it's a worried smile, but after that it's a smile true enough. "It's a surprise," he says, "so don't go looking."

Even tho I'm nearly a man and even tho I'm nearly getting on up to his height now, he still bends down a little so his face is level with mine, not too close to be uncomfortable, just close enough so that it's safe and I look away a little bit. And even tho it's Ben, even tho I trust Ben more than anyone else in this crappy little town, even tho it's Ben who saved my life and who I know would do it again, I still find myself reluctant to open up my Noise about what happened in the swamp, mainly cuz I can start to feel it pressing on my chest again whenever the thought gets near.

"Todd?" Ben says, looking at me closely.

"Quiet," Manchee barks softly. "Quiet in swamp."

Ben looks at Manchee, then back at me, his eyes going all soft and asking and full of concern. "What's he talking about, Todd?"

I sigh. "We saw something," I say. "Out there in the swamp. Well, we *didn't* see it, it hid, but it was like a rip in the Noise, like a tear–"

I stop talking cuz he's stopped listening to my voice. I've opened up my Noise for him and am remembering it as truthfully as I can and he's looking at me something fierce and from way behind me I can hear Cillian coming and he's calling "Ben?" and "Todd?" and there's concern in his voice and in his Noise and Ben's is starting to buzz a little, too, and I just keep thinking as truthfully as I can about the hole we found in the Noise but quietly, too, quietly, quietly, so as to keep the town from hearing if I can and here comes Cillian still and Ben's just looking at me and looking at me till finally I have to ask.

"Is it spacks?" I say. "Is it the Spackle? Are they back?"

"Ben?" Cillian's yelling it now as he's coming across the fields.

"Are we in danger?" I ask Ben. "Will there be another war?"

But all Ben says is, "Oh, my God," real quiet like, and then he says it again, "Oh, my God," and then, without even moving or looking away, he says, "We have to get you outta here. We have to get you outta here *right now*."

4

DON'T THINK IT

CILLIAN COMES RUNNING UP but before he says anything to us, Ben cuts him off and says, "Don't think it!"

Ben turns to me. "Don't you think it neither. You cover it up with yer Noise. You hide it. You hide it as best you can." And he's grabbing my shoulders as he's saying it and squeezing tight enough to make my blood jump even more than it already is.

"What's going on?" I say.

"Did you walk home thru town?" Cillian asks.

"*Course* I walked home thru town," I snap. "What other effing way is there to get home?"

Cillian's face tightens up but it's not with being pissed off at me snapping, it's tightening up with fear, fear I can hear loud as a shout in his Noise. They don't yell at me for "effing" neither, which makes it all somehow worse. Manchee's barking his head off by this point, "Cillian!

Quiet! Effing! Todd!" but nobody's bothering to tell him to shut up.

Cillian looks at Ben. "We're gonna have to do it now."

"I know," Ben says.

"What's going on?" I say again, all loud like. "Do *what* now?" I twist away from Ben and stand looking at them both.

Ben and Cillian take another look at each other and then back at me. "You have to leave Prentisstown," Ben says.

My eyeballs go back and forth twixt theirs but they're not letting nothing go in their Noise 'cept general worry. "What do you mean I have to leave Prentisstown?" I say. "There ain't nowhere else on New World *but* Prentisstown."

They take yet *another* look at each other.

"Stop doing that!" I say.

"Come on," Cillian says. "We've already got yer bag packed."

"How can you already have my bag packed?"

Cillian says to Ben, "We probably don't have much time."

And Ben says to Cillian, "He can go down by the river."

And Cillian says to Ben, "You know what this means."

And Ben says to Cillian, "It doesn't change the plan."

"WHAT THE EFF IS GOING ON?" I roar, but I don't say "eff", now do I? Cuz it seems the situashun calls for something a little stronger. "WHAT EFFING PLAN?"

But they're still not getting mad.

Ben lowers his voice and I can see him try to get his Noise into some kinda order and he says to me, "It's very, very important you keep what happened in the swamp outta yer Noise as best you can."

"Why? Are the spacks coming back to kill us?"

"Don't think about it!" Cillian snaps. "Cover it up, keep it deep and quiet, till yer so far outta town no one can hear you. Now, come on!"

And he takes off back towards the house, running, actually *running*.

"Come on, Todd," Ben says.

"Not till someone explains something."

"You'll get an explanashun," Ben says, taking me by the arm and pulling me along. "You'll get more than you ever wanted." And there's so much sadness to him when he says it that I don't say nothing more, just follow along running back to the house, Manchee barking his head off behind us.

By the time we make it back to the house, I'm expecting–

I don't know what I'm expecting. An army of Spackle coming outta the woods. A line-up of Mayor Prentiss's men with guns at the ready. The whole house burning down. I don't know. Ben and Cillian's Noise ain't making much sense, my own thoughts are boiling over like a volcano, and Manchee won't stop barking, so who can tell anything in all this racket?

But there's no one there. The house, *our* house, is just as it was, quiet and farm-like. Cillian busts in the back door, goes into the prayer room which we never use, and starts pulling boards up from the floor. Ben goes to the pantry and starts throwing dried foods and fruit into a cloth sack, then he goes to the toilet and takes out a small medipak and throws that in, too.

I just stand there like a doofus wondering just what in the effing blazes is going on.

I know what yer thinking: how can I *not* know if all day, every day I'm hearing every thought of the two men who run my house? That's the thing, tho. Noise is *noise*. It's crash and clatter and it usually adds up to one big mash of sound and thought and picture and half the time it's impossible to make any sense of it at all. Men's minds are messy places and Noise is like the active, breathing face of that mess. It's what's true and what's believed and what's imagined and what's fantasized and it says one thing and a completely opposite thing at the same time and even tho the truth is definitely in there, how can you tell what's true and what's not when yer getting *everything*?

The Noise is a man unfiltered, and without a filter, a man is just chaos walking.

"I ain't leaving," I say, as they keep doing their stuff. They don't pay me no mind. "I ain't leaving," I say again, as Ben steps past me into the prayer room to help Cillian lift up boards. They find what they're looking for and Cillian lifts out a rucksack, an old one I thought I'd lost. Ben opens the top and takes a quick peek thru and I can see some clothes of mine and something that looks like–

"Is that a book?" I say. "You were sposed to burn those ages ago."

But they're ignoring me and the air has just stopped right there as Ben takes it outta the rucksack and he and Cillian look at it and I see that it's not quite a book, more a journal type thing with a nice leather cover and when Ben thumbs thru it, the pages are cream-coloured and filled with handwriting.

Ben closes it like it's an important thing and he wraps it inside a plastic bag to protect it and puts it in the rucksack.

They both turn to me.

"I ain't going nowhere," I say.

And there's a knock on the front door.

For a second, nobody says nothing, everyone just freezes. Manchee's got so many things he wants to bark that nothing comes out for a minute till he finally barks "Door!" but Cillian grabs him by the collar with one hand and by the maul with the other, shutting him up. We all look up at each other, wondering what to do next.

There's another knock and then a voice comes thru the walls, "I know yer in there."

"Damn and blast," Ben says.

"Davy bloody Prentiss," Cillian says.

That's Mr Prentiss Jr. The man of the law.

"Do you not think I can hear yer Noise?" Mr Prentiss Jr says thru the door. "Benison Moore. Cillian Boyd." The voice makes a little pause. "Todd Hewitt."

"Well, so much for hiding," I say, crossing my arms, still a little annoyed at it all.

Cillian and Ben look at each other again, then Cillian lets go of Manchee, says "Stay here" to both of us and heads for the door. Ben shoves the sack of food into the rucksack and ties it shut. He hands it to me. "Put this on," he whispers.

I don't take it at first but he gestures with a serious look so I take it and put it on. It weighs a ton.

We hear Cillian open the front door. "What do you want, Davy?"

"That's Sheriff Prentiss to you, Cillian."

"We're in the middle of lunch, Davy," Cillian says. "Come back later."

"I don't think I will. I think I need to have a word with young Todd."

Ben looks at me, worry in his Noise.

"Todd's got farmwork," Cillian says. "He's just leaving out the back. I can hear him go."

And these are instructions for me and Ben, ain't they? But I ruddy well want to hear what's going on and I ignore Ben's hand on my shoulder trying to pull me towards the back door.

"You take me for a fool, Cillian?" Mr Prentiss Jr says.

"Do you really want an answer to that, Davy?"

"I can hear his Noise not twenty feet behind you. Ben's, too." We hear a shift in the mood. "I just want to talk to him. He ain't in no trouble."

"Why you got a rifle then, Davy?" Cillian asks and Ben squeezes my shoulder, probably without even thinking.

Mr Prentiss Jr's voice and Noise both change again. "Bring him out, Cillian. You know why I'm here. Seems like a funny little word floated outta yer boy into town all innocent-like and we just want to see what it's all about, that's all."

"'We'?" Cillian says.

"His Honour the Mayor would like a word with young Todd." Mr Prentiss Jr raises his voice. "Y'all come out now, you hear? Ain't no trouble going on. Just a friendly chat."

Ben nods his head at the back door all firm like and there ain't no arguing with him this time. We start stepping towards it slowly, but Manchee's kept his trap shut for just about as long as he can bear and barks, "Todd?"

"Y'all ain't thinking about sneaking out the back way, are ya?" Mr Prentiss Jr calls. "Outta my way, Cillian."

"Get off my property, Davy," Cillian says.

"I ain't telling you twice."

"I believe you've already told me about three times, Davy, so if yer threatening, it ain't working."

There's a pause but the Noise from them both gets louder and Ben and I know what's coming next and suddenly everything's moving fast and we hear a loud thump, followed quick by another two, and me and Ben and Manchee are running to the kitchen but when we get there, it's over. Mr Prentiss Jr is on the floor, holding his mouth, blood already coming from it. Cillian's got Mr Prentiss Jr's rifle in his hands and is pointing it at Mr Prentiss Jr.

"I said get off my property, Davy," he says.

Mr Prentiss Jr looks at him, then looks at us, still holding his bloody mouth. Like I say, he ain't barely two years older than me, barely able to even get a sentence out without his voice breaking, but he's had his birthday to be a man so there he is, our sheriff.

The blood from his mouth is getting on the little brown hairs he calls a moustache and everyone else calls nothing.

"You know this answers the asking, doncha?" He spits some blood and a tooth onto our floor. "You know this ain't the end." He looks right at my eye. "You found something, dincha, boy?"

Cillian aims the rifle at his head. "Out," he says.

"We got plans for you, boy." Mr Prentiss Jr smiles bloodily at me and gets to his feet. "The boy who's last. One more month, ain't it?"

I look to Cillian but all he does is cock the rifle loudly, getting his point across.

Mr Prentiss Jr looks back at us, spits again, and says, "Be seeing you," trying to sound tough but his voice squeaks and he takes off as fast he can back to the town.

Cillian slams the door behind him. "Todd's gotta go *now*. Back thru the swamp."

"I know," Ben says. "I was hoping–"

"Me, too," Cillian says.

"Whoa, whoa," I say, "I ain't going back to the swamp. There's Spackle there!"

"Keep yer thoughts quiet," Cillian says. "That's more important than you know."

"Well, since I don't know nothing, that ain't hard," I say. "I ain't going nowhere till someone tells me what's going on!"

"Todd–" Ben starts.

"They'll be coming back, Todd," Cillian says. "Davy Prentiss will come back and he won't be alone and we won't be able to protect you from all of them at once."

"But–"

"No arguing!" Cillian says.

"Come on, Todd," Ben says. "Manchee's gonna have to go with you."

"Oh, man, this just gets better," I say.

"Todd," Cillian says and I look at him and he's changed a little. There's something new in his Noise, a sadness, a sadness like grief. "Todd," he says again, then suddenly he grabs me and hugs me to him as hard as he can. It's too rough and I bash my cut lip on his collar and say "Ow!" and push him away.

"You may hate us for this, Todd," he says, "but try to believe it's only cuz we love you, all right?"

"No," I say, "it's not all right. It's not all right at all."

But Cillian's not listening, as usual. He stands up and says to Ben, "Go, run, I'll hold 'em off as long as possible."

"I'll come back a different way," Ben says, "see if I can throw 'em off the trail."

They clasp hands for a long minute, then Ben looks at me, says "Come on" and as he's dragging me outta the room to get to the back door, I see Cillian pick up the rifle again and he glances up at me and catches my eye and there's a look to him, a look written all over him and his Noise that this is a bigger goodbye than it even seems, that this is it, the last time he ever expects to see me and I open my mouth to say something but then the door closes on him and he's gone.

5

THE THINGS YOU KNOW

"I'LL GET YOU TO THE RIVER," Ben says as we hurry across our fields for the second time this morning. "You can follow it down to where it meets the swamp."

"There ain't no path that way, Ben," I say, "and there's crocs everywhere. You trying to get me killed?"

He looks back at me, his eyes all level, but he keeps on hurrying. "There's no other way, Todd."

"Crocs! Swamp! Quiet! Poo!" Manchee barks.

I've stopped even asking what's going on since nobody's seeing fit to tell me nothing so we just keep on moving past the sheep, still not in their paddocks and now maybe never getting there. "Sheep!" they say, watching us pass. On we go, past the main barn, down one of the big irrigashun tracks, turning right on a smaller one, heading towards where the wilderness starts, which pretty much means the beginning of the rest of this whole empty planet.

Ben don't start talking again till we get to the treeline.

"There's food in yer rucksack to last you for a bit but you should make it stretch as far as you can, eating what fruit you find and anything you can hunt."

"How long do I gotta make it last?" I ask. "How long till I can come back?"

Ben stops. We're just inside the trees. The river's thirty metres away but you can hear it cuz this is where it starts rushing downhill to get to the swamp.

Suddenly it feels like just about the loneliest place in the whole wide world.

"You ain't coming back, Todd," Ben says, quietly. "You can't."

"Why not?" I say and my voice comes out all mewing like a kitten but I can't help it. "What'd I do, Ben?"

Ben comes up to me. "You didn't do anything, Todd. You didn't do anything at all." He hugs me real hard and I can feel my chest start to press again and I'm so confused and frightened and angry. Nothing was different in the world this morning when I got outta bed and now here I am being sent away and Ben and Cillian acting like I'm dying and it ain't fair and I don't know why it ain't fair but it just ain't fair.

"I know it ain't fair," Ben says, pulling himself away and looking me hard in the face. "But there *is* an explanashun." He turns me round and opens my rucksack and I can feel him taking something out.

The book.

I look at him and look away. "You know I don't read too good, Ben," I say, embarrassed and stupid.

He crouches down a bit so we're truly face to face. His Noise ain't making me comfortable at all.

"I know," he says, gentle-like. "I always meant to try and spend more time–" He stops. He holds out the book again. "It's yer ma's," he says. "It's her journal, starting from the day you were born, Todd." He looks down at it. "Till the day she died."

My Noise opens wide.

My ma. My ma's own book.

Ben runs his hand over the cover. "We promised her we'd keep you safe," he says. "We promised her and then we had to put it outta our minds so there was nothing in our Noise, nothing that would let anyone know what we were gonna do."

"Including me," I say.

"It had to be including you. If just a little bit got into yer Noise and then into the town…"

He don't finish.

"Like the silence I found in the swamp today," I say. "Like that getting into town and causing all this havoc."

"No, that was a surprise." He looks up at the sky, like he's telling it just how completely a surprise it all was. "No one woulda guessed that happening."

"It's *dangerous*, Ben. I could feel it."

But all he does is hold out the book again.

I start shaking my head. "Ben–"

"I know, Todd," he says, "but try yer best."

"No, Ben–"

He catches my eyes again. He holds 'em with his own. "Do you trust me, Todd Hewitt?"

I scratch my side. I don't know how to answer. "Course I do," I say, "or at least I *did* before you started packing bags I didn't know about for me."

He looks at me harder, his Noise focused like a sun ray. "Do you trust me?" he asks again.

I look at him and yeah, I do, even now. "I trust you, Ben."

"Then trust me when I say that the things you know right now, Todd, those things ain't true."

"Which things?" I ask, my voice rising a little. "Why can't you just tell me?"

"Cuz knowledge is dangerous," he says, as serious as I've ever seen him and when I look into his Noise to see what he's hiding, it roars up and slaps me back. "If I told you now, it would buzz in you louder than a hive at honey-gathering time and Mayor Prentiss would find you fast as he could spit. And you *have* to get away from here. You have to, as far away as you can."

"But where?" I say. *"There ain't nowhere else!"*

Ben takes a deep breath. "There is," he says. "There's somewhere else."

I don't say nothing to that.

"Folded in the front of the book," Ben says, "there's a map. I made it myself but *don't look at it*, not till yer well outta town, okay? Just go to the swamp. You'll know what to do from there."

But I can tell from his Noise that he's not at all sure I'll know what to do from there. "Or what I'm gonna find there, do you?"

He don't say nothing to that.

And I'm thinking.

"How did you know to have a bag already packed?" I say, stepping back a little. "If this thing in the swamp is so unexpected, why are you so ready to chuck me out into the wilderness today?"

"It was the plan all along, ever since you were little." I see him swallow, I hear his sadness everywhere. "As soon as you were old enough to make it on yer own–"

"You were just gonna throw me out so the crocs could eat me." I'm stepping back further.

"No, Todd–" He moves forward, the book still in his hand. I step back again. He makes a gesture like, okay.

And he closes his eyes and opens up his Noise for me.

One month's time is the first thing it says–

And here comes my birthday–

The day I'll become a man–

And–

And–

And there it all is–

What happens–

What the other boys did who became men–

All alone–

All by themselves–

How every last bit of boyhood is killed off–

And–

And–

And what actually happened to the people who–

Holy crap–

And I don't want to say no more about it.

And I can't say at all how it makes me feel.

I look at Ben and he's a different man than he always was, he's a different man to the one I've always known.

Knowledge is dangerous.

"It's why no one tells you," he says. "To keep you from running."

"You wouldn't've protected me?" I say, mewing again (shut up).

"*This* is how we're protecting you, Todd," he says. "By getting you *out*. We had to be sure you could survive on yer own, that's why we taught you all that stuff. Now, Todd, you have to go–"

"If that's what's happening in a month, why wait this long? Why not take me away sooner?"

"We can't come with you. That's the whole problem. And we couldn't bear to send you off on yer own. To see you go. Not so young." He rubs the cover of the book with his fingers again. "And we were hoping there might be a miracle. One where we wouldn't have to–"

Lose you, says his Noise.

"But there ain't been no miracle," I say, after a second.

He shakes his head. He holds out the book. "I'm sorry," he says. "I'm so sorry it has to be this way."

And there's so much true sorrow in his Noise, so much worry and edginess, I know he's speaking true, I know he can't help what's happening and I hate it but I take the book from him and put it back in the plastic and into the rucksack. We don't say nothing more. What else is there to say? Everything and nothing. You can't say everything, so you don't say nothing.

He pulls me to him again, hitting my lip on his collar just like Cillian but this time I don't pull away. "Always remember," he says, "when yer ma died, you became our son, and I love you and Cillian loves you, always have, always will."

I start to say, "I don't wanna go," but it never comes out.

Cuz *BANG!!* goes the loudest thing I ever heard in Prentisstown, like something's blowing right up, right on up to the sky.

And it can only be coming from our farm.

Ben lets me go right quick. He ain't saying nothing but his Noise is screaming Cillian all over the place.

"I'll come back with you," I say. "I'll help you fight."

"No!" Ben shouts. "You have to get away. Promise me. Go thru the swamp and *get away*."

I don't say nothing for a second.

"*Promise me,*" Ben says again, demanding it this time.

"Promise!" Manchee barks and there's fear even in that.

"I promise," I say.

Ben reaches behind his back and unclasps something. He wriggles it for a second or two before it comes unlatched completely. He hands it to me. It's his hunting knife, the big ratchety one with the bone handle and the serrated edge that cuts practically everything in the world, the knife I was hoping to get for the birthday when I became a man. It's still in its belt, so I can wear it myself.

"Take it," he says. "Take it with you to the swamp. You may need it."

"I never fought a Spackle before, Ben."

He still holds out the knife and so I take it.

There's another *BANG* from the farm. Ben looks back towards it, then back to me. "Go. Follow the river down to the swamp and out. Run as fast as you can and you'd better damn well not turn back, Todd Hewitt." He takes my arm and grips it hard. "If I can find you, I'll find you, I swear it," he says. "But you keep going, Todd. You keep yer promise."

This is it. This is goodbye. A goodbye I wasn't even looking for.

"Ben–"

"Go!" he shouts and takes off, looking back once as he runs and then racing off back to the farm, back to whatever's happening at the end of the world.

6

THE KNIFE IN FRONT OF ME

"C'MON, MANCHEE," I say, turning to run, tho every bit of me wants to follow Ben as he's running across the fields a different way, just like he said, to confuse anyone out looking for Noise.

I stop for a second when I hear a bunch of smaller bangs from the direkshun of the house which gotta be rifle shots and I think of the rifle that Cillian took from Mr Prentiss Jr and all the rifles that Mayor Prentiss and his men have locked away in the town and how all those guns against Cillian's stolen rifle and the few others we got in the house ain't gonna be much of a fight for very long and it gets me to wondering what the bigger bangs were and I realize they were probably Cillian blowing up the generators to confuse the men and make everyone's Noise so loud they can't hear even the whisper of mine way out here.

All this for me to get away.

"C'mon, Manchee," I say again and we run the last few

metres to the river. Then we take a right and start following the river downhill, keeping away from the rushes at the water's edge.

The rushes where the crocs live.

I take the knife from its sheath and I keep it in my hand as we move along fast.

"What's on, Todd?" Manchee keeps barking, which is his version of "What's going on?"

"I don't know, Manchee. Shut up so I can think."

The rucksack's banging into my back as we run but we keep going as best we can, kicking thru river shrubs and jumping over fallen logs.

I'll come back. That's what I'll do. I'll come back. They said I'd know what to do and now I do know. I'll go to the swamp and kill the Spackle if I can and then I'll come back and help Cillian and Ben and then we can all get away to this somewhere else Ben was talking about.

Yeah, that's what I'll do.

"Promised, Todd," Manchee says, sounding worried as the ridge we're going along is getting closer and closer to the rushes.

"Shut up," I say. "I promised to keep on going but maybe keep on going means coming back first."

"Todd?" Manchee says and I don't believe it either.

We've gotten outta hearing distance from the farm and the river veers away east a little before it enters the top of the swamp so it's taking us away from the town, too, and after a minute there ain't nothing following us as we run 'cept my Noise and Manchee's Noise and the sound of the running river which is just loud enough to cover the Noise of a hunting croc. Ben says that's "evolushun" but he says not to think about it too much around Aaron.

I'm breathing heavy and Manchee's panting like he's about to keel over but we don't stop. The sun is starting to set, but it's still light as you please, light that don't feel like it's going to hide you. The ground is flattening out and we're getting down closer to river level as it all starts turning to marsh. Everything's getting muddier and it's making us slow down. There's more rushes, too, can't be helped.

"Listen for crocs," I say to Manchee. "Keep yer ears open."

Cuz the water from the river is slowing and if you can keep yer own Noise quiet enough you can start to hear them out there. The ground's got even wetter. We're barely making walking pace now, sloshing thru mud. I grip the knife harder and hold it out in front of me.

"Todd?" Manchee says.

"Do you hear them?" I whisper, trying to watch my step and watch the rushes and watch out for Manchee all at the same time.

"Crocs, Todd," Manchee says, pretty much as quiet as he can bark.

I stop and I listen hard.

And out there in the rushes, out there in more than one place, I can hear 'em. **Flesh,** they're saying.

Flesh and **feast** and **tooth**.

"Crap," I say.

"Crocs," Manchee says again.

"C'mon," I say and we start splashing along, cuz we're in muck now. My shoes start sinking with each step and water's coming up over the top of 'em and there's no way to go 'cept thru the rushes. I start swinging the knife as we go, trying to cut any rush that's in front of me.

I look ahead and I can see where we're going, up and to the right. We've made it past the town and it's the bit where the wild fields come down by the school and meet up with the swamp and if we get thru this marshy bit here we'll be on safe ground and can get onto the paths that head into the dark of the swamp.

Was it really only this morning I was here last?

"Hurry up, Manchee," I say. "Almost there."

Flesh and **feast** and **tooth** and I swear it's getting closer.

"C'mon!"

Flesh.

"Todd?"

I'm cutting my way thru rushes and pulling my feet outta mud and **flesh** and **feast** and **TOOTH**.

And then I hear **Whirler dog**–

And I know we're done for.

"Run!" I yell.

And we run and Manchee lets out a frightened yelp and leaps past me but I see a croc rear up outta the rushes in front of him and it jumps for him but Manchee's so scared he jumps even higher, higher than he really knows how, and the croc's teeth snap on empty air and it lands with a splash next to me looking mighty pissed off and I hear its Noise hiss **Whirler boy** and I'm running and it jumps for me and I'm not even thinking and I'm turning and I'm pushing my hand up and the croc comes crashing down on top of me and its mouth is open and its claws are out and I think I'm about to be dead and I'm thrashing my way back outta the muck up onto the dry bit and it's on its hind legs coming after me outta the rushes and it takes a minute of me yelling and of Manchee barking his head off before I realize that it's not actually coming after me no more, that the croc's dead, that my new knife is right thru its head, still stuck in the croc and the only reason the croc's still thrashing is cuz I'm still thrashing and I shake the croc off the knife and the croc falls to the ground and I sort of just fall over too in celebrayshun of not being dead.

And it's when I'm gasping for air from the rush of my blood and Manchee's barking and barking and we're both laughing from relief that I realize that we've been too loud ourselves to hear something important.

"Going somewhere, young Todd?"

Aaron. Standing right over me.

Before I can do nothing he punches me in the face.

I fall backwards onto the ground, the rucksack digging into my back and making me look like an upturned turtle. My cheek and my eye are just singing with pain and I haven't even moved properly before Aaron's grabbing me by my shirt front and the skin beneath and lifting me to my feet. I yell out from how much it hurts.

Manchee barks an angry "Aaron!" and goes for Aaron's legs, but Aaron doesn't even look before kicking him outta the way hard.

Aaron's holding me up to look him in the face. I can only keep the one non-painful eye open to meet his.

"Just what in the name of God's bounteous, glorified Eden are you doing down here in the swamp, Todd Hewitt?"

he says, his breath smelling like meat and his Noise the scariest kinda crazy you never wanna hear. "Yer sposed to be at yer farm right now, boy."

With his free hand, he punches me in the stomach. I try to bend over with the pain of it but he's still holding on to my shirt front and the skin below.

"You gotta go back," he says. "There's things you need to see."

I'm gasping for breath but the way he says it catches my ear and some of the flickers I'm catching in his Noise make it so I can see a little bit of the truth.

"You sent them," I say. "It wasn't me they heard. It was you."

"Smart boys make useless men," he says, twisting his gripping hand.

I cry out but I ruddy well keep talking, too. "They didn't hear the quiet in my Noise. They heard it in *yer* Noise and you sent them to me to keep them from coming after you."

"Oh, no, Todd," he says, "they heard it in yer Noise. I just *made sure* they did. I made sure they knew who was responsible for bringing danger to our town." He grits his teeth into a wild smile beneath his beard. "And who should be rewarded for his efforts."

"Yer crazy," I say and boy is it ever true and boy do I wish it wasn't.

His smile falls and his teeth clench. "It's mine, Todd," he says. "Mine."

I don't know what this means but I don't stop to think about it cuz I realize instead that both Aaron and I have forgotten one important thing.

I never let go of the knife.

A whole buncha things happen at once.

Aaron hears *knife* in my Noise and realizes his mistake. He pulls back his free fist to make another punch.

I pull back my knife hand and I wonder if I can actually stab him.

There's a breaking sound from the rushes and Manchee barks, "Croc!"

And all at the same time, we hear **Whirler man**.

Before Aaron can even turn, the croc is on him, clamping its teeth onto his shoulder and grabbing him with its claws and pulling him back towards the rushes. Aaron lets go of me and I fall to the ground again, clutching at all the bruises he's left on my chest. I look up and I see Aaron thrashing in the muck now, fighting with the croc and the sails on the backs of other crocs heading his way, too.

"Outta here!" Manchee's barking, almost shrieking.

"Too effing right," I say and I stumble to my feet, the rucksack knocking me a little off balance and my hurt eye trying to peel open but we don't stop and we run and we run and we run.

We get out of the marshes and run along the bottom of the fields to the start of the swamp path and we run into the swamp along it and when we get to the log that Manchee always needs help over he just sails right over it without even stopping and I'm right behind him and we're running our way to the Spackle buildings just like we were this morning.

And the knife is still in my hand and my Noise is thudding so loud and I'm so frightened and hurt and mad that I know beyond any shadow of a thought that I am going to find the Spackle hiding in his Noise hole and I am going to kill him dead dead dead for everything that's happened today.

"Where is it?" I ask Manchee. "Where's the quiet?"

Manchee's sniffing away like mad, running from building to building, and I'm doing my best to calm my Noise but there don't seem any chance of that.

"Hurry!" I say. "Before it runs–"

And it's barely outta my mouth before I hear it. The rip in the Noise, as big and horrible as life itself, I can hear it a little bit away, behind the Spackle buildings, behind some bushes.

It ain't getting away this time.

"Quiet!" Manchee barks, all keyed up, and he runs past the buildings and into the bushes.

And the quiet moves, too, and tho I can feel the pressure in my chest again and the terrible mournful things coming into my eyes, this time I don't stop, this time I run after my dog and I don't stop and I take in my breath and I swallow away the pressure and I wipe the water from my eyes and I grip the knife and I can hear Manchee barking and I can hear the silence and it's just around this tree just around this tree just around this tree and I'm yelling and I'm going round the tree and I'm running at the silence and my teeth are bared and I'm screaming and Manchee's barking and–

And I stop.

I stop right there in my tracks.

I don't, I do absolutely *not* put down the knife.

There it is, looking back at us, breathing heavy, crouched

at the base of a tree, cowering from Manchee, its eyes practically dying from fright but still trying to offer up a pitiful threat with its arms.

And I just stop.

I hold my knife.

"Spackle!" Manchee barks, tho he's too chicken to attack now that I've held back. "Spackle! Spackle! Spackle!"

"Shut up, Manchee," I say.

"Spackle!"

"I said *shut up*!" I shout, which stops him.

"Spackle?" Manchee says, unsure of things now.

I swallow, trying to get rid of the pressure in my throat, the unbelievable sadness that comes and comes as I look at it looking back at me. Knowledge is dangerous and men lie and the world keeps changing, whether I want it to or not.

Cuz it ain't a Spackle.

"It's a girl," I say.

It's a girl.

PART II

7

IF THERE WAS A GIRL

"IT'S A GIRL," I say again. I'm still catching my breath, still feeling the pressure on my chest, *definitely* still holding the knife way out in front of me.

A girl.

It's looking back at us like we're gonna kill it. It's hunched down in a little ball, trying to make itself as small as possible, only taking its eyes off Manchee to snatch quick glances of me.

Of me and my knife.

Manchee's huffing and puffing, his back fur all ridged, hopping around like the ground is hot, looking as charged up and confused as I am, tho completely hopeless about keeping in any way cool.

"What's girl?" he barks. "What's girl?"

By which he means, "What's a girl?"

"What's girl?" Manchee barks again and when the girl looks like it might be about to make a leap back over the large root where it's huddling, Manchee's bark turns into a fierce growl, "*Stay, stay, stay, stay, stay…*"

"Good dog," I say, tho I don't know *why* it's good what he's doing but what else can you say? This makes no sense, no sense at all, and everything feels like it's starting to slip, like the world is a table tilted on its side and everything on it is tipping over.

I am Todd Hewitt, I think to myself but who knows if *that's* even true any more?

"Who are you?" I finally say, if it can even hear me over all my raging Noise and Manchee's nervous breakdown. "Who are you?" I say, louder and clearer. "What are you doing here? Where did you come from?"

It looks at me, finally, for more than just a second, taking its eyes off Manchee. It looks at my knife, then it looks at my face above my knife.

She looks at me.

She does.

She.

I know what a girl is. Course I do. I seen 'em in the Noise of their fathers in town, mourned like their wives but not nearly so often. I seen 'em in vids, too. Girls are small and polite and smiley. They wear dresses and their hair is long and it's pulled into shapes behind their heads or on either side. They do all the inside-the-house chores, while boys do all the outside. They reach womanhood when they turn thirteen, just like boys reach manhood, and then they're women and they become wives.

That's how New World works, or at least that's how Prentisstown works. Worked. Was meant to, anyhow, but there ain't no girls. They're all dead. They died with their mothers and their grandmothers and their sisters and their aunties. They died in the months after I was born. All of them, every single one.

But here one is.

And its hair ain't long. *Her* hair. Her hair ain't long. And she ain't wearing no dress, she's wearing clothes that look like way newer versions of mine, so new they're almost like a uniform, even tho they're torn and muddy, and she ain't that small, she's my size, just, by the looks of her, and she's sure as all that's unholy not smiley.

No, not smiley at all.

"Spackle?" Manchee barks quietly.

"Would you effing well *shut up*?" I say.

So how do I know? How do I know it's a girl?

Well, for one, she ain't no Spackle. Spackle looked like men with everything a bit swelled up, everything a bit longer and weirder than on a man, their mouths a bit higher than they should be and their ears and eyes way, *way* different. And spacks grew their clothes right on their bodies, like lichens you could trim away to whatever shape you needed. Product of swamp-dwelling, according to another Ben-best-guess and she don't look like that and her clothes are normal and so there ain't no way she's a Spackle.

And for two, I just know. I just do. I can't tell you but I look and I see and I just know. She don't look like the girls I seen in vids or in Noise and I never seen no girl in the flesh but there she is, she's a girl and that's that. Don't ask me. Something about her shape, something about her smell, something I don't know but it's there and she's a girl.

If there was a girl, that's what she'd be.

And she ain't another boy. She just ain't. She ain't me. She ain't nothing like me at all. She's something completely other else altogether and I don't know how I know it but I know who I am, I am Todd Hewitt, and I know what I am not and I am not her.

She's looking at me. She's looking at my face, in my eyes. Looking and looking.

And I'm not hearing *nothing*.

Oh, man. My chest. It's like falling.

"Who are you?" I say again but my voice actually *catches*, like it breaks up cuz I'm so sad (shut up). I grit my teeth and I get a little madder and I say it yet again. "Who are you?" and I hold out the knife a little farther. With my other arm, I have to wipe my eyes real fast.

Something's gotta happen. Someone's gotta move. Someone's gotta do *something*.

And there ain't no someone but me, still, whatever the world's doing.

"Can you talk?" I say.

She just looks back at me.

"Quiet," Manchee barks.

"Shut it, Manchee," I say, "I need to think."

And she's still just looking back at me. With no Noise at all.

What do I do? It ain't fair. Ben told me I'd get to the swamp and I'd know what to do but I *don't* know what to do. They didn't say nothing about a girl, they didn't say nothing about why the quiet makes me ache so much I can barely stop from ruddy *weeping*, like I'm missing something so bad

I can't even think straight, like the emptiness ain't in her, it's in *me* and there ain't nothing that's ever gonna fix it.

What do I do?

What do I do?

She seems like maybe she's calming down. She's not shaking as much as she was, her arms aren't up so high, and she's not looking like she's about to run off at the first opportunity, tho how can you know for sure when a person's got no Noise? How can they *be* a person if they ain't got no Noise?

And can she hear me? *Can* she? Can a person with no Noise hear it at all?

I look at her and I think, as loud and clear as I can, *Can you hear me? Can you?*

But she don't change her face, she don't change her look.

"Okay," I say, and I take a step back. "Okay. You just stay there, okay? You just stay right there."

I take a few more steps back but I keep my eyes on her and she keeps her eyes on me. I bring my knife arm down and I slide it outta one strap of the rucksack, then I lean over and drop the rucksack to the ground. I keep the knife in one hand and with the other I open up the rucksack and fish out the book.

It's heavier than you think a thing made of words could be. And it smells of leather. And there's pages and pages of my ma's–

That'll have to wait.

"You watch her, Manchee," I say.

"Watch!" he barks.

I look inside the front cover and there's the paper folded in just like Ben said. I unfold it. There's a hand-drawn map on one side and then a whole buncha writing on the back but it's all a big block of letters which I ain't got the calmness of Noise to even try right now so I just look at the map.

Our house is right at the top and the town just below with the river Manchee and I came down off to one side leading into the swamp and that's where we are now. But there's more to it, ain't there? The swamp keeps going till it starts being a river again and there's arrows drawn along the riverbank so that's where Ben is wanting me and Manchee to go and I follow the arrows with my fingers and it leads right outta the swamp, it leads right to–

WHUMP!! The world goes bright for a second as something clubs me up side the head, right on the sore spot where Aaron punched me, and I fall over but as I'm falling I swing the knife up and I hear a little yelp of pain and I catch myself before I fall all the way down and I turn, sitting down on the ground hard, holding the back of my knife hand to the pain in my head but looking at where the attack came from and it's here that I learn my very first lesson: Things with no Noise can sneak right up on you. Sneak right up on you like they ain't even there.

The girl is on her butt, too, sitting on the ground away from me, holding on to one of her upper arms with her hand, blood coming from twixt her fingers. She's dropped the stick she hit me with and her face is all collapsed in on itself with what she must be feeling from that cut.

"WHAT THE HELL D'YOU DO THAT FOR?" I shout,

trying not to touch my face too hard. Man, am I sick of being hit today.

The girl just looks at me, her forehead still creased, holding her cut.

Which is kinda bleeding a lot.

"Stick, Todd!" Manchee barks.

"And where the hell were you?" I say to him.

"Poo, Todd."

I make a "Gah!" sound and kick some dirt at him. He scrabbles back, then starts sniffing at some bushes like there ain't nothing unusual going on in the world. Dogs got attenshun spans about as long as a matchstick. Idiot things.

It's starting to get dark now, the sun really setting, the already dark swamp getting even darker, and I still don't have no answer. Time keeps passing and I ain't sposed to wait here and I ain't sposed to go back and *there ain't sposed to be a girl*.

Boy, that cut really is bleeding on her.

"Hey," I say, my voice shaky from the charge running through me. *I am Todd Hewitt,* I think. *I am almost a man.* "Hey," I say again, trying to be a little calmer.

The girl looks at me.

"I ain't gonna hurt you," I say, breathing hard, just like her. "You hear me? I ain't gonna hurt you. As long as you don't try to hit me with no more sticks, all right?"

She looks at my eyes. Then she looks at the knife.

Is she understanding?

I lower the knife away from my face and bring it down near the ground. I don't let go of it, tho. With my free hand, I start looking thru the rucksack again till I find the medipak Ben threw in. I hold it up.

"Medipak," I say. She doesn't change. "Me-di-pak," I say slowly. I point to my own upper arm, to where the cut is on her. "Yer bleeding."

Nothing.

I sigh and I start to stand. She flinches and scoots back on her butt. I sigh again in an angry way. *"I ain't gonna hurt you."* I hold up the medipak. "It's medicine. It'll stop the bleeding."

Still nothing. Maybe there ain't nothing in her at all.

"Look," I say and I snap open the medipak. I fumble with one hand and take out a styptic pad, tearing away the paper cover with my teeth. I'm probably bleeding from where first Aaron hit me and then the girl, so I take the pad and rub it over my eye and eyebrow. I pull it away and yep, there's blood. I hold the pad out to the girl so she can see it. "See?" I point to my eye. "See? It stops things bleeding."

I take a step forward, just the one. She flinches back but not as much. I take another step, then another and then I'm next to her. She keeps looking at the knife.

"I ain't putting it down, so just forget it," I say. I push the pad towards her arm. "Even if it's deep, this stitches it up, okay? I'm trying to help you."

"Todd?" Manchee barks, full of asking marks.

"In a minute," I say. "Look, yer bleeding everywhere, okay? And I can fix it, all right? Just don't get any ideas about any more ruddy sticks."

She's watching. And she's watching. And she's watching. I'm trying to be as calm as I really don't feel. I don't know why I'm helping her, not after she whacked me on the head, but I don't know what to do about anything. Ben said there'd be answers in the swamp and there ain't no answers, there's just this girl who's bleeding cuz I cut her even tho she deserved it and if I can stop the bleeding then maybe that's doing something.

I don't know. I don't know what to do, so I just do this.

The girl's still watching me, still breathing heavy. But she ain't running and she ain't flinching and then so you can hardly tell at all she's turning her upper arm towards me a little bit so I can reach the cut.

"Todd?" Manchee barks again.

"Shush," I say, not wanting to scare the girl any more. Being this close to her silence is like my heart breaking all over the place. I can feel it, like it's pulling me down into a bottomless pit, like it's calling for me to just fall and fall and fall.

But I keep my nerve, I do. I keep it and I press the styptic pad on her arm, rubbing the cut, which is pretty deep, till it closes a bit and stops bleeding.

"Ya gotta be careful," I say. "That ain't a permanent heal. You gotta be careful with it till yer body heals the rest, okay?"

And all she does is look at me.

"Okay," I say, to myself as much as anyone cuz now that that's done, what's next?

"Todd?" Manchee barks. "Todd?"

"And no more sticks, all right?" I say to the girl. "No more hitting me."

"Todd?" Manchee again.

"And obviously my name's Todd."

And there, just there, just there in the fading light, is there a little beginning of a start of a smile? Is there?

"Can you…?" I say, looking as deep into her eyes as the pressure in my chest allows. "Can you understand me?"

"Todd," Manchee's barking picks up a notch.

I turn to him. *"What?"*

"Todd! TODD!!!"

And then we can all hear it. Pounding thru the bushes and branches breaking and running footsteps and Noise and Noise and oh, crap, Noise.

"Get up," I say to the girl. "Get up! Now!"

I grab my rucksack and put it on and the girl's looking terrified but in a not-helpful paralysed way and I shout "Come on!" to her again and I grab her arm, not thinking about the cut now, and I try to lift her to her feet but all of a sudden it's too late and there's a yell and a roar and a sound like whole trees falling down and me and the girl can only both turn to look and it's Aaron and he's mad and he's messed-up and he's coming right for us.

8

THE CHOICES OF A KNIFE

HE'S ON US IN THREE STEPS. Before I can even try and run, he's coming at me with his hands out, grabbing my neck, smashing me back against a tree.

"You little FILTH!" he screams and presses his thumbs into my throat. I scrabble at his arms, trying to slash at him with the knife, but my rucksack has fallen and the strap has pinned my arm back against the tree so he can pretty much go on strangling me for as long as it takes.

His face is a nightmare, a horrible thing I'm not gonna stop seeing even if I ever get outta this. The crocs took his left ear and a long strip of flesh with it going right down his left cheek. You can see his teeth through the gash and it's causing his left eye to bulge forward like his head's been caught in mid-explosion. There are other gashes on his chin and neck and his clothes are torn and there's blood practically everywhere and I can even see a croc tooth sticking out of a fleshy tear on his shoulder.

I'm choking for breath but not getting any at all and you can't believe how much it hurts and the world's gone spinning and my brain's going funny and I have this stupid little thought that Aaron didn't survive the croc attack after all, that he died but he's so pissed off at me that dying didn't stop him from coming here to kill me anyway.

"WHAT ARE YOU SMILING AT?" he screams, little bits of blood and spit and flesh spraying onto my face. He squeezes my neck harder and I can feel myself throwing up but there's nowhere for it to go and I can't breathe and all the lights and colours are flowing together and I'm dying and I'm going to die.

"AAH!" Aaron suddenly jerks back, letting me go. I drop to the ground and throw up all over everywhere and take in a huge gasping breath that makes me cough in a way like I'm never gonna stop. I look up and see Manchee's snout wrapped around Aaron's calf, biting it for all he's worth.

Good dog.

Aaron slams Manchee sideways with an arm, sending him flying into the bushes. I hear a thump and a yelp and a "Todd?"

Aaron whirls around to me again and I just can't stop looking at his face, at the gashes everywhere that no one could have survived, no one, it's not possible.

Maybe he really is dead.

"Where's the sign?" he says, his torn expression changing right quick and looking around in a sudden panic.

The sign?

The–

The girl.

I look, too. She's gone.

Aaron whirls again, this way, that, and then I see him hearing it the same time I do, hearing the rustle and snap as she runs, hearing the silence as it flows away from us, and without another look at me, he takes off after her and he's gone.

And just like that, I'm alone.

Just like that, like I have nothing to do with anything here.

What a stupid day this has been.

"Todd?" Manchee comes limping outta the bushes.

"I'm okay, buddy," I try to say and get some of it out despite the coughing, even tho it ain't true. "I'm okay."

I try to keep breathing thru the coughs, forehead on the ground, dribbling spit and barf everywhere.

I keep breathing and these thoughts start coming. They come all uninvited, don't they?

Cuz maybe that could be it, couldn't it? Maybe it could be over, simple as that. The girl's obviously what Aaron wants, whatever he means by "the sign", right? The girl's obviously what *the town* wants, what with all the ruckus over the quiet in my Noise. And so if Aaron can have her and the town can have her, then that could be the end of it, right? They could have what they want and leave me alone and I could go back and everything could be like it was before and, yeah, it would probably be no good for the girl but it might save Ben and Cillian.

It might save me.

I'm just *thinking* it, all right? The thoughts rush in, that's all.

Thoughts that this could be over as soon as it started.

"Over," Manchee murmurs.

And then I hear the terrible, terrible scream that of course is the girl getting caught and that's the choice made, ain't it?

The next scream comes a second later but I'm already on my feet without even really thinking it, slipping off my rucksack, leaning a bit, coughing still, reaching for more breath, but the knife in my hand and running.

They're easy to follow. Aaron's torn thru the bushes like a bullock and his Noise is throwing up a roar and always, always, always there's the silence of the girl, even behind her screams, which somehow makes it even harder to hear. I run the best I can after them, Manchee on my heels, and it ain't more than half a minute before we're there with genius me having no idea what to do now I've got here. Aaron's chased her into a bit of water about ankle-deep and got her back up against a tree. He's got her wrists in his hands but she's fighting him, fighting and kicking for all she's worth, but her face is a thing so scared I can barely get my words out.

"Leave her alone," my voice rasps but no one hears me. Aaron's Noise is blazing so loud I'm not sure he'd hear me even if I yelled. THE HOLY SACRAMENT and THE SIGN FROM GOD and THE PATH OF THE SAINT and pictures of the girl in a church, pictures of the girl drinking the wine and eating the host, pictures of the girl as an angel.

The girl as a sacrifice.

Aaron gets both of her wrists in one of his fists, fumbles

off the cord belt of his robe, and starts tying her hands together with it. The girl kicks him hard where Manchee bit him and he hits her across the face with the back of his hand.

"Leave her alone," I say again, trying to make my voice louder.

"Alone!" Manchee barks, still limping but still ferocious. What a ruddy good dog.

I step forward. Aaron's back's to me, like he don't even care I'm here, like he don't even think of me as a threat.

"Let her go," I try and shout but it just makes me cough some more. Still nothing, tho. Still nothing from Aaron or anyone.

I'm gonna have to do it. I'm gonna have to do it. Oh man oh man oh man I'm gonna have to do it.

I'm gonna have to kill him.

I raise the knife.

I've raised the knife.

Aaron turns, not even fast like, just turns like someone's called his name. He sees me standing there, knife in the air, not moving like the goddam coward idiot I am, and he smiles and boy I just can't say how awful a smile looks on that torn-up face.

"Yer Noise reveals you, young Todd," he says, letting go of the girl, who's so tied up and beaten now she don't even try to run. Aaron takes a step towards me.

I take a step back (shut up, please just shut up).

"The Mayor will be disappointed to hear about your untimely departure from the earthly plain, boy," Aaron says, taking another step. I take another step, too, the knife in the air like it's of no use at all.

"But God has no use for a coward," Aaron says, "does he, boy?"

Quick as a snake, his left arm knocks into my right, sending the knife flying out of my hand. He hits me in the face with the flat of his right hand, knocking me back down into the water and I feel his knees land on my chest and his hands pressing down on my throat to finish the job but this time my face is underwater so it's going to be a lot faster.

I struggle but I've lost. I've lost. I had my chance and I've lost and I deserve this and I'm fighting but I'm not nearly as strong as I was before and I can feel the end coming. I can feel me giving up.

I'm lost.

Lost.

And then, in the water, my hand finds a rock.

BOOM! I bring it up and hit him on the side of the head before I can think about it.

BOOM! I do it again.

BOOM! And again.

I feel him slide off me and I lift my head, choking on water and air, but I sit up and raise the rock again to hit him but he's laying down in the water, face half-in, half-out, his teeth smiling up at me thru the gash in his cheek. I scrabble back from him, coughing and spluttering, but he stays there, sinking a little, not moving.

I feel like my throat is broken but I throw up some water and can breathe a little better.

"Todd? Todd? Todd?" Manchee says, coming up to me, all licky and barky like a little puppy. I scratch him twixt the ears cuz I can't say nothing yet.

And then we both feel the silence and look up and there's the girl standing over us, her hands still tied.

Holding the knife in her fingers.

I sit frozen for a second and Manchee starts to growl but then I realize. I take a few more breaths and then I reach up and take the knife from her fingers and cut the cord Aaron bound her wrists with. It drops away and she rubs where it was tied, still staring at me, still not saying nothing.

She knows. She knows I couldn't do it.

Goddam you, I think to myself. *Goddam you.*

She looks at the knife. She looks over at Aaron, lying down in the water.

He's still breathing. He gurgles water with every breath, but he's still breathing.

I grip the knife. The girl looks at me, at the knife, at Aaron, at me again.

Is she telling me? Is she telling me to do it?

He's lying there, undefended, probably eventually drowning.

And I have a knife.

I get to my feet, fall down from dizziness, and get to my feet again. I step towards him. I raise my knife. Again.

The girl takes in a breath and I can feel her holding it.

Manchee says, "Todd?"

And I have my knife raised over Aaron. One more time, I've got my chance. One more time, I've got my knife raised.

I could do it. No one on New World would blame me. It'd be my right.

I could just do it.

But a knife ain't just a thing, is it? It's a choice, it's

something you *do*. A knife says yes or no, cut or not, die or don't. A knife takes a decision out of your hand and puts it in the world and it never goes back again.

Aaron's gonna die. His face is ripped, his head is bashed, he's sinking into shallow water without ever waking up. He tried to kill me, he wanted to kill the girl, he's responsible for the ruckus in town, he's gotta be the one who sent the Mayor to the farm and cuz of that he's responsible for Ben and Cillian. He deserves to die. He deserves it.

And I can't bring the knife down to finish the job.

Who am I?

I am Todd Hewitt.

I am the biggest, effing waste of nothing known to man.

I can't do it.

Goddam you, I think to myself again.

"Come on," I say to the girl. "We have to get outta here."

9

WHEN LUCK AIN'T WITH YOU

AT FIRST I don't think she's gonna come. There's no reason for her to, no reason for me to ask her, but when I say to her, "Come *on*," a second time more urgently and gesture with my hand, she follows me, follows Manchee, and that's how it is, that's what we do, who knows if it's right, but that's what we do.

Night's well and truly fallen. The swamp seems even thicker here, as black as anything. We rush on back a ways to get my rucksack and then around and a little bit further away in the dark to get some distance between us and Aaron's body (please let it be a body). We clamber round trees and over roots, getting deeper into the swamp. When we get to a small clearing where there's a bit of flat land and a break in the trees, I stop us.

I'm still holding the knife. It rests there in my hand, shining at me like blame itself, like the word *coward* flashing again and again. It catches the light of both moons and my God it's a powerful thing. A *powerful* thing, like I'd have to agree to be a part of *it* rather than it being a part of me.

I reach behind me and put it in the sheath between my back and the rucksack where at least I won't have to see it.

I take the rucksack off and fish thru it for a torch.

"Do you know how to use one of these?" I ask the girl, switching it on and off a coupla times.

She just looks at me, as ever.

"Never mind," I say.

My throat still hurts, my face still hurts, my chest still hurts, my Noise keeps pounding me with visions of bad news, of how good a fight Ben and Cillian managed to put up at the farm, of how long it'll take Mr Prentiss Jr to find out where I've gone, of how long it'll take him to be on his way after me, after *us* (not long at all, if he ain't already), so who ruddy cares if she knows how to use a torch. Of *course* she don't.

I get the book out of the rucksack, using the torch for a light. I open up to the map again and I follow Ben's arrows from our farm down the river and thru the swamp and then outta the swamp as it turns back into river.

It's not hard to find yer way outta the swamp. Out on the horizon beyond it, you can always see three mountains, one close and two farther away but next to each other. The river on Ben's map goes twixt the closer one and the two farther away ones and so all we gotta do is to keep heading towards that space in the middle and we should find the river again and follow it. Follow it to where the arrows keep going.

Keep going to another settlement.

There it is. Right there at the bottom of the page where the map ends.

A whole other place.

As if I don't have enough new stuff to think about.

I look up at the girl, still staring at me, maybe not even blinking. I shine the torch at her face. She winces and turns away.

"Where'd you come from?" I ask. "Is it here?"

I point the torch down at the map and put my finger on the other town. The girl don't move so I wave her over. She still don't move so I sigh and pick up the book and take it over to her and shine the torch on the page.

"I," I point to myself, "am from here." I point to our farm north of Prentisstown on the map. "This," I wave my arms around to show the swamp, "is here." I point at the swamp. "We need to go here," I point at the other town. Ben's written the other town's name underneath, but – well, whatever. "Is this where yer from?" I point to her, point to the other town, point to her again. "Are you from here?"

She looks at the map but other than that, nothing.

I sigh in frustrayshun and step away from her. It's uncomfortable being so close. "Well, I sure hope so," I say, glancing back at the map. "Cuz that's where we're going."

"Todd," Manchee barks. I look up. The girl's started to wander around in circles in the clearing, looking at stuff like it means something to her.

"What're you doing?" I ask.

She looks at me, at the torch in my hand and she points thru some trees.

"What?" I say. "We don't have time–"

She points thru the trees again and starts walking there.

"Hey!" I say. *"Hey!"*

I guess I have to follow.

"We gotta stick to the map!" I duck under branches to follow her, the rucksack getting caught left and right. "Hey! Wait up!"

I stumble on, Manchee behind me, the torch not much good against every ruddy little branch and root and puddle in a great big swamp. I keep having to drop my head and tear the rucksack free of stuff so I can barely look ahead enough to follow her. I see her standing by a fallen, burnt-looking tree, waiting for me, watching me come.

"What're you doing?" I say, finally catching up with her. "Where're you–"

And then I see.

The tree *is* burnt, *freshly* burnt and freshly knocked over, too, the unburnt splinters clean and white like new wood. And there are a buncha trees just like it, a whole line of 'em, in fact, on either side of a great ditch gouged outta the swamp, now filled with water but piled-up dirt and burnt plants all around it show that's it gotta be a new thing, like someone came thru here and dug it up in one fiery swoop.

"What happened?" I swing the torch along it. "What did this?"

She just looks off to the left, where the ditch disappears into darkness. I shine the torch down that way but it's not strong enough to see what's down there. Tho it feels like *something's* there.

The girl takes off into the darkness towards whatever it might be.

"Where're you going?" I ask, not expecting an answer and not getting any. Manchee gets twixt me and the girl, like he's following her now, instead of me, and off they go in the dark. I keep my distance but I follow, too. The silence still flows from her, *still* bothers me, like it's ready to swallow up the whole world and me with it.

I keep the torch flashing over every possible square inch of water. Crocs don't usually come this far into the swamp but that's only usually, plus there's red snakes that're poisonous and water weasels that bite and it just don't feel like luck is bothering with any of us today so if something can go wrong it's probably gonna.

We're getting closer and I shine the torch down to where we're heading and something starts glinting back, something that ain't tree or bush or animal or water.

Something metal. Something *big* and metal.

"What's that?" I say.

We get closer and at first I think it's just a big fissionbike and I wonder what kind of idiot would try and ride a fissionbike in a swamp cuz you can barely get 'em to work over flattened dirt roads much less water and roots.

But it ain't a fissionbike.

"Hold up."

The girl stops.

Whaddya know? The girl stops.

"So you can understand me, then?"

But nothing, as ever nothing.

"Well, hold up for a sec," I say cuz a thought's coming. We're still a bit away from it but I keep flicking the torch over the metal. And back over the straight line that the ditch makes. And over the metal again. And over all the burnt stuff on either side of the ditch. And a thought keeps coming.

The girl stops waiting and heads off towards the metal and I follow. We have to go round a big burnt log, still lazily smoking in one or two spots, to get to the thing and when we do it's much bigger than the biggest fissionbike and even then it looks like it's only part of an even bigger something than that. It's crumpled and burnt in most places and even tho I don't know what it looked like before it crumpled and burned, it's obviously mostly wreckage.

And it's obviously wreckage of a ship.

An air ship. Maybe even a *space* ship.

"Is this yers?" I ask, shining the torch at the girl. She don't say nothing, as usual, but she don't say it in a way that could be agreement. "Did you crash here?"

I shine the torch up and down her body, up and down her clothes, which are a bit different than what I'm used to, sure, but not so different that they couldn't have belonged to me once upon a time.

"Where'd you come from?" I say.

But of course she don't say nothing and just looks off to a place further into the darkness, crosses her arms and starts heading off there. I don't follow this time. I keep looking at the ship. That's what it's gotta be. I mean, *look* at it. A lot of it's smashed beyond recognishun but you can still see something that might be a hull, might be an engine, even something that might have been a window.

The first homes in Prentisstown, see, were made from the ships the original settlers landed in. Sure, wood and log homes got built after, but Ben says the first thing you do when you land is build immediate shelter and immediate shelter comes from the first supplies to hand. The church and the petrol stayshun back in town are still partly made outta metal hulls and holds and rooms and such. And tho this heap of wreckage is pretty pounded, if you look at it right, it might be an old Prentisstown house that fell right outta the sky. Right outta the sky on fire.

"Todd!" Manchee barks from somewhere outta sight. "Todd!"

I go running round to where the girl disappeared, round the wreckage to a bit that seems less smashed up. As I run past, I can even see a door that's been opened out the side of one wall of metal a little way up and there's even a light on inside.

"Todd!" Manchee barks and I shine the torch over to where he's barking, standing next to the girl. She's just standing there looking down at something and so I shine the torch and see that she's standing by two long piles of clothes.

Which are actually two bodies, ain't they?

I walk over, shining the torch down. There's a man, his clothes and body pretty much completely burnt away from the chest down. His face has burns, too, but not enough to disguise that he was a man. He has a wound on his forehead that woulda killed him even if the burns hadn't but it don't matter, does it, cuz he's dead either way. Dead and lying here in a swamp.

I flash the torch over and he's lying next to a woman, ain't he?

I hold my breath.

It's the first woman I ever seen in the flesh. And it's the same as the girl. I never seen a woman in real life before but if there was a real life woman, that's what she'd be.

And dead, too, of course, but nothing as obvious as burns and a gash, not even blood on her clothes so maybe she's busted up on the inside.

But a woman. An actual woman.

I shine the torch at the girl. She don't flinch away.

"That's yer ma and pa, ain't it?" I ask, my voice low.

The girl don't say nothing but it's gotta be true.

I shine the torch over the wreckage and think of the burnt ditch behind it and it can only mean one thing. She crashed here with her ma and pa. They died. She lived. And if she came from somewhere else on New World or if she came from somewhere else altogether, don't matter. They died, she lived, and she was here all alone.

And got found by Aaron.

When luck ain't with you, it's against you.

On the ground I see drag marks where the girl must have pulled the bodies out of the crash and brought them here. But the swamp ain't for burying anything but Spackle cuz after two inches of dirt you pretty much just get water and so here they sit. I hate to say it but they do smell, tho in the overall smell of the swamp it ain't as bad as you think, so who knows how long she's been here.

The girl looks at me again, not crying, not smiling, just blank as ever. Then she walks past me, walks back along the drag marks, walks to the door I saw open in the side of the wreckage, climbs up and disappears inside.

10

FOOD AND FIRE

"HEY!" I say, following her over to the wreckage. "We can't be hanging around–"

I get up to the door at the same time she pops out, making me jump back. She waits for me to step outta the way, then climbs down from the door and walks past me, carrying a bag in one hand and a coupla small packets in the other. I look back at the door and stand on tiptoes, trying to peek in. It all looks a wreck inside, as you'd expect, things tumbled everywhere, lots of busted everything.

"How'd you live thru that?" I ask, turning around.

But she's got herself busy. She's put down the bag and the packs and has taken out what looks like a small, flat green box. She sets it down on a dry-ish area of ground and piles some sticks on top of it.

I look at her in disbelief. "There ain't time to make a–"

She presses a button on the side the box and *whoosh* we've got ourselves a whole, full-sized, instant campfire.

I just stand there like a fool, my mouth wide open.

I want a campfire box.

She looks at me and rubs her arms a little bit and it's only then that I really realize I'm soaking wet and cold and achy all over and that a fire is just about the closest thing to a blessing I can think of.

I look back into the blackness of the swamp, as if I'd be able to see anyone coming. Nothing, of course, but no sounds neither. No one close. Not yet.

I look back at the fire. "Only for a second," I say.

I walk over to the fire and start warming up my hands, keeping on my rucksack. She rips open one of the packs and throws it to me and I stare at it again till she dips her fingers into her own pack, taking out what must be a piece of dried fruit or something and eating it.

She's giving me food. And fire.

Her face still has no kinda expression at all, just blank as a stone as she stands by the fire and eats. I start eating, too. The fruit or whatever are like little shrivelled dots but sweet and chewy and I've finished the whole pack in half a minute before I notice Manchee begging.

"Todd?" he says, licking his lips.

"Oh," I say, "sorry."

The girl looks at me, looks at Manchee, then takes out a small handful from her own pack and holds it out to Manchee. When he approaches, she jerks back a little like she can't help it and drops the fruit on the ground instead. Manchee don't mind. He gobbles it right up.

I nod at her. She don't nod back.

It's full-fledged night now, dark as anything outside our

little circle of light. You can only even see stars thru the hole in the treetops made by the crashing ship. I try to think back over the last week if I heard any distant booms from the swamp but anything this far out could've been drowned in the Noise of Prentisstown, I spose, and been missed by everyone.

I think of certain preachers.

Nearly everyone.

"We can't stay," I say. "I'm sorry about yer folks and all but there's others that'll be after us. Even if Aaron's dead."

At Aaron's name, she flinches, just a little. He must've said his name to her. Or something. Maybe.

"I'm sorry," I say, tho I don't know what for. I shift my rucksack on my back. It feels heavier than ever. "Thanks for the grub but we gotta go." I look at her. "If yer coming with?"

The girl looks at me for a second and then uses the tip of her boot to knock the burning sticks off the little green box. She reaches down, presses the button again and picks up the box without even burning herself.

Man, I *really* want one of those things.

She puts it in the bag she brought outta the wreckage with her and then brings the strap of the bag over her head, like her own rucksack. Like she was planning on coming with me even before now.

"Well," I say, when all she does is stare at me. "I guess we're ready then."

Neither of us move.

I look back to her ma and pa. She does, too, but only for a second. I wanna say something to her, something more, but whaddya say? I open my mouth anyway but she starts rummaging in her bag. I think it's gonna be something to, I don't know, remember her folks with or make some kind of gesture or something but she finds what she's looking for and it's only a torch. She flicks it on – so she *does* know how they work – and starts walking, first towards me, then past me, as if we're already on our way.

And that's it, like her ma and pa ain't just lying there dead.

I watch her go for a second before saying, "Oi!"

She turns back to me.

"Not that way." I point to our left. "That way."

I head off the right way, Manchee follows, and I look back and the girl's coming after us. I take one last quick look behind her and as bad as I want to stay and look thru that wreckage for more neat stuff, and boy do I, we gotta go, even tho it's night, even tho nobody's slept, we gotta go.

And so we do, catching sight of the horizon thru the trees when we can and heading towards the space twixt the close mountain and the two farther away mountains. Both moons are more than halfway to full and the sky is clear so there's at least a little bit of light to walk by, even under the swamp canopy, even in the dark.

"Keep yer ears open," I say to Manchee.

"For what?" Manchee barks.

"For things that could get us, idiot."

You can't really run in a dark swamp at night so we walk as fast as we can, me shining the torch in front of us, tripping our way round tree roots and trying not to tromp thru too much mud. Manchee goes ahead and comes back, sniffing round and sometimes barking, but nothing serious.

The girl keeps up, never falling behind but never getting too close neither. Which is good, cuz even tho my Noise is about the quietest it's been all day, the silence of her still presses on it whenever she comes too near.

It's weird that she didn't do nothing more about her ma and pa when we left, ain't it? Didn't cry or have one last visit or nothing? Am I wrong? I'd give anything to see Ben and even Cillian again, even if they were... Well, even if they are.

"Ben," Manchee says, down by my knees.

"I know." I scratch him twixt the ears.

We keep on.

I'd want to bury them, if that's what it came to. I'd want to do *something*, I don't know what. I stop and look back at the girl but her face is just the same, just the same as ever, and is it cuz she crashed and her parents died? Is it cuz Aaron found her? Is it cuz she's from somewhere else?

Don't she feel nothing? Is she just nothing at all on the inside?

She's looking at me, waiting for me to go on.

And so, after a second, I do.

Hours. There's hours of this silent night-time fast creeping. Hours of it. Who knows how far we're going or if we're heading the right way or what, but *hours*. Once in a while, I hear the Noise of a night-time creacher, swamp owls cooing their way to dinner, swooping down on probably short-tailed mice, whose Noise is so quiet it's barely like language at all, but mostly all I hear is the now-and-then fast-fading Noise of a night-time creacher running away from all the ruckus we must be making by tromping thru a swamp at night.

But the weird thing is there's still no sound of

nothing behind us, nothing chasing us, no Noise, no branches breaking, nothing. Maybe Ben and Cillian threw them off the trail. Maybe the reason I'm running ain't so important after all. Maybe–

The girl stops to pull her shoe outta some mud.

The girl.

No. They're coming. The only maybe is that maybe they're waiting till daybreak so they can come faster.

So on and on we go, getting more and more tired, stopping only once so that everyone can have a private pee off in the bushes. I get some of Ben's food outta my own rucksack and feed small bits to everyone, since it's my turn.

And then more walking and more walking.

And then there comes an hour just before dawn where there can't be no more.

"We gotta stop," I say, dropping the rucksack at the base of a tree. "We gotta rest."

The girl sets her own bag down by another tree without needing any more convincing and we both just sort of collapse down, leaning on our bags like pillows.

"Five minutes," I say. Manchee curls up by my legs and closes his eyes almost immediately. "Only five minutes," I call over to the girl, who's pulled a little blanket outta her bag to cover herself with. "Don't get too comfortable."

We gotta keep going, no question of that. I'll only close my eyes for a minute or two, just to get a little rest, and then we'll keep on going faster than before.

Just a little rest, that's all.

I open my eyes and the sun is up. Only a little but ruddy well up.

Crap. We've lost at least an hour, maybe two.

And then I realize it's a sound that's woken me.

It's Noise.

I panic, thinking of men finding us and I scramble to my feet–

Only to see that it ain't a man.

It's a cassor, towering over me and Manchee and the girl.

Food? says its Noise.

I *knew* they hadn't left the swamp.

I hear a little gasp from over where the girl's sleeping. Not sleeping no more. The cassor turns to look at her. And then Manchee's up and barking, "Get! Get! Get!" and the cassor's neck swings back our way.

Imagine the biggest bird you ever saw, imagine it got so big that it couldn't even fly no more, we're talking two and a half or even three metres tall, a super long bendy neck stretching up way over yer head. It's still got feathers but they look more like fur and the wings ain't good for much except stunning things they're about to eat. But it's the feet you gotta watch out for. Long legs, up to my chest, with claws at the end that can kill you with one kick if yer not careful.

"Don't worry," I call over to the girl. "They're friendly."

Cuz they are. Or they're sposed to be. They're sposed to eat rodents and only kick if you attack 'em, but if you *don't* attack 'em, Ben says they're friendly and dopey and'll let you feed 'em. And they're also good to eat, a combo which made the new settlers of Prentisstown so eager to hunt 'em for food that by the time I was born there wasn't a cassor to be seen within miles. Yet another thing I only ever saw in a vid or Noise.

The world keeps getting bigger.

"Get! Get!" Manchee barks, running in a circle round the cassor.

"Don't bite it!" I shout at him.

The cassor's neck is swinging about like a vine, following Manchee around like a cat after a bug. **Food?** its Noise keeps asking.

"Not food," I say, and the big neck swings my way.

Food?

"Not food," I say again. "Just a dog."

Dog? it thinks and starts following Manchee around again, trying to nip him with his beak. The beak ain't a scary thing at all, like being nipped by a goose, but Manchee's having none of it, leaping outta the way and barking, barking, barking.

I laugh at him. It's funny.

And then I hear a little laugh that ain't my own.

I look over. The girl is standing by her tree, watching the giant bird chase around my stupid dog, and she's laughing.

She's *smiling*.

She sees me looking and she stops.

Food? I hear and I turn to see the cassor starting to poke its beak into my rucksack.

"Hey!" I shout and start shooing it away.

Food?

"Here." I fish out a small block of cheese wrapped in a cloth that Ben packed.

The cassor sniffs it, bites it, and gobbles it down, its neck rippling in long waves at it swallows. It snaps its beak a few times like a man might smack his lips after he ate something. But then its neck starts rippling the other way and with a loud hack, up comes the block of cheese flying right back at me, covered in spit but not hardly even crushed, smacking me on the cheek and leaving a trail of slime across my face.

Food? says the cassor and starts slowly walking off into the swamp, as if we're no longer even as interesting as a leaf.

"Get! Get!" Manchee barks after it, but not following. I wipe the slime from my face with my sleeve and I can see the girl smiling at me while I do it.

"Think that's funny, do ya?" I say and she keeps pretending like she's not smiling but she *is*. She turns away and picks up her bag.

"Yeah," I say, taking charge of things again. "We slept way too long. We gotta go."

We get going on yet more walking without any more words or smiling. Pretty quick, the ground starts to get less even and a bit drier. The trees start to thin out some, letting the sun directly on us now and then. After a little bit, we get to a small clearing, almost like a little field that rises up to a short bluff, standing just over the treetops. We climb it and stop at the top. The girl holds out another pack of that fruity stuff. Breakfast. We eat, still standing.

Looking out over the trees, the way in front of us is clear. The larger mountain is on the horizon and you can see the two smaller mountains in the distance behind a little bit of haze.

"That's where we're going," I say, pointing. "Or where I think we're sposed to go, anyway."

She sets down her fruit pack and goes into her bag

again. She pulls out the sweetest little pair of binos you've ever seen. My old ones back home that broke years ago were like a breadbox in comparison. She holds them up to her eyes and looks for a bit, then hands 'em to me.

I take 'em and I look out to where we're going. Everything's so *clear*. The ground stretching out before us in a green forest, curving downhill into proper valleys and dales as it starts to become real land again and not just the mucky bowl of a swamp and you can even see where the marsh starts really turning back into a proper river, cutting deeper and deeper canyons as it gets closer to the mountains. If you listen, you can even hear it rushing. I look and I look and I don't see no settlement but who knows what's around the bends and curves? Who knows what's up ahead?

I look behind us, back the way we came, but it's still early enough for a mist to be covering most of the swamp, hiding everything, giving nothing away.

"Those're sweet," I say, handing her the binos. She puts them back in her bag and we stand there for a minute eating.

We stand arm's length apart cuz her silence still bothers me. I chew down on a piece of dried fruit and I wonder what it must be like to have no Noise, to *come* from a place with no Noise. What does it mean? What kind of place is it? Is it wonderful? Is it terrible?

Say you were standing on a hilltop with someone who had no Noise. Would it be like you were alone there? How would you share it? Would you want to? I mean, here we are, the girl and I, heading outta danger and into the unknown and there's no Noise overlapping us, nothing to tell us what the other's thinking. Is that how it's sposed to be?

I finish the fruit and crumple up the packet. She holds out her hand and shoves the rubbish back into her bag. No words, no exchange, just my Noise and a great big nothing from her.

Was this what it was like for my ma and pa when they first landed? Was New World a silent place all over before–

I look up at the girl suddenly.

Before.

Oh, no.

I'm such a fool.

I'm such a stupid goddam fool.

She has no Noise. And she came from a ship. Which means she came from a place with no Noise, obviously, *idiot*.

Which means she's landed here and hasn't caught the Noise germ yet.

Which means that when she does, it's gonna do what it did to all the other women.

It's gonna kill her.

It's gonna kill her.

And I'm looking at her and the sun is shining down on us and her eyes are getting wider and wider as I'm thinking it and it's then I realize something else stupid, something else obvious.

Just cuz I can't hear any Noise from her don't mean she can't hear every word of mine.

11

THE BOOK OF NO ANSWERS

"NO!" I say quickly. "Don't listen! I'm wrong! I'm wrong! It's a mistake! I'm wrong!"

But she's backing away from me, dropping her own empty packet of fruit things, her eyes getting wider.

"No, don't–"

I step towards her but she takes an even quicker step away, her bag dropping to the ground.

"It's–" I say but what *do* you say? "I'm wrong. I'm *wrong*. I was thinking of somebody else."

Which is the stupidest thing to say of all cuz she can hear my Noise, can't she? She can see me struggling to think of something to say and even if it's coming out a big mess, she can see herself all over it and besides, I surely know by now there's no taking back something that's been sent out into the world.

Dammit. Goddam it all to hell.

"Dammit!" Manchee barks.

"Why didn't you SAY you could hear me?" I shout, ignoring that she ain't said a word since I met her.

She steps back farther, putting a hand up to her face to cover her mouth, her eyes sending asking marks at me.

I try to think of something, *anything* to make it all right, but I ain't got nothing. Just Noise with death and despair all over it.

She turns and runs, back down the hill and away from me as fast as she can.

Crap.

"Wait!" I yell, already running after her.

She's going back the way we came, down across the little field and disappearing into the trees, but I'm right behind her, Manchee after me. "Stop!" I shout after her. "Wait!"

But why should she? What kind of reason could she possibly have to wait around?

You know, she's really amazingly fast when she wants to be.

"Manchee!" I call and he understands me and shoots off after her. Not that I could really lose her, any more than she could lose me. As loud as my Noise is chasing her, her silence is just as loud up ahead, even now, even knowing she's going to die, still as silent as a grave.

"Hold on!" I shout, tripping over a root and landing hard on my elbows, which jolts every ache I've got in my body and face, but I have to get up. I have to get up and go after her. "Dammit!"

"Todd!" I hear Manchee bark up ahead, outta sight. I stumble on a bit and get my way round a big mass of shrubs and there she is, sitting on a big flat rock jutting outta the ground, her knees up to her chest, rocking back and forth, eyes wide but blank as ever.

"Todd!" Manchee barks again when he sees me, then he hops up on the rock next to her and starts sniffing her.

"Leave her alone, Manchee," I say, but he doesn't. He sniffs close at her face, licks her once or twice, then sits down next to her, leaning into her side as she rocks.

"Look," I say to her, catching my breath and knowing I don't know what to say next. "Look," I say again, but nothing else is coming.

I just stand there panting, not saying nothing, and she sits there rocking till there don't seem nothing else to do but sit down on the rock myself, keeping a distance away outta respect and safety, I guess, and so that's what I do. She rocks and I sit and I wonder what to do.

We pass a good few minutes this way, a good few minutes when we should be moving, the swamp getting on with its day around us.

Till I finally have another thought.

"I might not be right." I say it as soon as I think it. "I could be wrong, you see?" I turn to her and I start talking fast. "I got lied to about everything and you can search my Noise if you want to be sure *that's* true." I stand, talking faster. "There wasn't sposed to be another settlement. Prentisstown was sposed to be it for the whole stupid planet. But there's the other place on the map! So maybe–"

And I'm thinking and I'm thinking and I'm thinking.

"Maybe the germ was only Prentisstown. And if you ain't been in the town, then maybe yer safe. Maybe yer fine.

Cuz I sure can't hear nothing from you anything like Noise and you don't seem sick. So maybe yer okay."

She's looking at me and still rocking and I don't know what she's thinking. *Maybe* probably ain't all that comforting a word when it's *maybe yer not dying*.

I keep on thinking, letting her see my Noise as free and clear as I can. "Maybe we all caught the germ and, and, and, yeah!" I get another thought, a good one. "Maybe we cut ourselves off so the other settlement wouldn't catch it! That must be it! And so if you stayed in the swamp, then yer safe!"

She stops rocking quite so much, still looking at me, maybe believing me?

But then like some doofus who don't know when to stop, I let that thought go on, don't I? Cuz if it's true that Prentisstown was cut off, then maybe that other settlement ain't gonna be too happy to see me strolling in, are they? Maybe it was the other settlement that did the cutting off in the first place, cuz maybe Prentisstown really *was* contagious.

And if you can catch the Noise from other people, then the girl can catch it from me, can't she?

"Oh, man," I say, leaning down and putting my hands on my knees, my whole body feeling like it's falling, even tho I'm still standing up. "Oh, man."

The girl hugs herself to herself again on the rock and we're back to even worse than where we started.

This ain't fair. I am telling you this ain't fair at all. *You'll know what to do when you get to the swamp, Todd. You'll know what to do.* Yeah, thanks very bloody much for that,

Ben, thanks for all yer help and concern cuz here I am and I ain't got the first clue what to do. It ain't fair. I get kicked outta my home, I get beaten up, the people who say they care for me have been lying all these years, I gotta follow a stupid map to a settlement I never knew about, I gotta somehow read a stupid book–

The book.

I slip off the rucksack and take out the book. He said all the answers were in here, so maybe they really are. Except–

I sigh and open it up. It's all written, all words, all in my ma's handwriting, pages and pages and pages of it and I–

Well, anyway. I go back to the map, to Ben's writing on the other side, the first chance I've had to look at it in something other than torchlight, which ain't really for reading. Ben's words are lined up at the top. *Go to* are the first ones, those are definitely the first words, and then there are a coupla longer words that I don't have time to sound out yet and then a coupla big paragraphs that I *really* don't have time for right now but at the bottom of the page Ben's underlined a group of words together.

I look at the girl, still rocking, and I turn my back to her. I put my finger under the first underlined word.

Let's see. *Yow*? *You*, it's gotta be *you*. *You*. Okay, me what? *M*. *Moo*? *Moose*? *Moosed*? *You moosed*. *You moosed*? What the hell does that mean? *Wuh*. *Wuh*. *Warr*. *Warren*? *Tuh*. *Tuhee*? *Tuheem*. *You moosed warren tuheem*? No, wait, *them*. It's *them*. Course it's *them*, idiot.

But *You moosed warren them*?

Huh?

'Member when I said Ben tried to teach me to read?

'Member when I said I wasn't too good at it? Well–

Well, whatever.

You moosed warren them.

Idiot.

I look at the book again, flip thru the pages. Dozens of them, dozens upon dozens, all with more words in every corner, all saying nothing to me at all, no answers of any kind.

Stupid effing book.

I shove the map back inside, slam the cover shut and throw the book on the ground.

You *idiot*.

"Stupid effing book!" I say, out loud this time, kicking it into some ferns. I turn back to the girl. She's still just rocking back and forth, back and forth, and I know, I know, okay, I *know*, but it starts to piss me off. Cuz if this is a dead end, I got nothing more to offer and she ain't offering nothing neither.

My Noise starts to crackle.

"I didn't ask for this, you know," I say. She don't even look. "Hey! I'm talking to you!"

But nothing. Nothing, nothing, nothing.

"I DON'T KNOW WHAT TO DO!" I yell and stand and start stomping around, shouting till my voice scratches. "I DON'T KNOW WHAT TO DO! I DON'T KNOW WHAT TO DO!" I turn back to the girl. "I'm SORRY! I'm sorry this happened to you but I don't know what to do about it AND STOP EFFING ROCKING!"

"Yelling, Todd," Manchee barks.

"Awwghh!" I shout, putting my hands over my face. I

take them away and nothing's changed. That's the thing I'm learning about being thrown out on yer own. Nobody does *nothing* for you. If you don't change it, it don't get changed.

"We gotta keep going," I say, picking up my rucksack all angry-like. "You ain't caught it yet, so maybe just keep yer distance from me and you'll be okay. I don't know but that's all there is so that's what we gotta do."

Rock, rock, rock.

"We can't go back so we gotta go forward and that's that."

Still rocking.

"I KNOW you can HEAR me!"

She don't even flinch.

And I'm suddenly tired all over again. "Fine," I sigh. "Fine, whatever, you stay here and rock. Who cares? Who ruddy cares about anything?"

I look at the book on the ground. Stupid thing. But it's what I got so I reach down, pick it up, put it in the plastic bag, back in my rucksack, and put my rucksack back on.

"C'mon, Manchee."

"Todd?!" he barks, looking twixt me and the girl. "Can't leave, Todd!"

"She can come if she wants," I say, "but–"

I don't even really know what the *but* might be. *But* if she wants to stay here and die all alone? *But* if she wants to go back and get caught by Mr Prentiss Jr? *But* if she wants to risk catching the Noise from me and dying that way?

What a stupid world.

"Hey," I say, trying to make my voice a little gentler but my Noise is so raging there's really no point. "You know where we were heading, right? To the river twixt the mountains. Just follow it till you come to a settlement, okay?"

Maybe she's hearing me, maybe she ain't.

"I'll keep an eye out for you," I say. "I understand if you don't wanna get too close but I'll keep an eye out for you."

I stand there for another minute to see if it sinks in.

"Well," I finally say. "Nice knowing ya."

I start walking away. When I get to the big stack of shrubs, I turn back, giving her one more chance. But she ain't changed, just rocking and rocking.

So that's that then. Off I go, Manchee reluctantly on my heels, looking back as much as he can, barking my name all the time. "Todd! Todd! Leaving, Todd? Todd! Can't leave, Todd!" I finally smack him on the rump. "Ow, Todd?"

"I don't know, Manchee, so quit asking."

We make our way back thru the trees to where the ground dries out, to the clearing and up the little bluff where we ate our breakfast and looked at the beautiful day and I had my brilliant deducshun about her death.

The little bluff where her bag still lies on the ground.

"Oh, god*dam* it!"

I look at it for a second and it's one thing after another, ain't it? I mean, do I take it back to her? Do I just hope she finds it? Will I put her in danger if I do? Will I put her in danger if I *don't*?

The sun's well up now and the sky as blue as fresh meat. I put my hands on my hips and take a long look round like men do when they're thinking. I look at the horizon, look back the way we came, the mist mostly burnt off by now and the whole swamp forest covered in sunlight. From the top of the bluff, you can see out over it, over where we drove our feet into oblivion by walking it all. If it were clear enough and you had powerful enough binos you could probably see all the way back to town.

Powerful binos.

I look down at her bag on the ground there.

I'm reaching for it when I think I hear something. Like a whisper. My Noise leaps and I look up to see if the girl's following me out after all. Which makes me more relieved than I want to say.

But it ain't the girl. I hear it again. A whisper. More than one whisper. Like the wind is carrying whispering on it.

"Todd?" Manchee says, sniffing the air.

I squint into the sunlight to look back over the swamp.

Is there something out there?

I grab the girl's bag and look thru it for the binos. There's all kinds of neat crap in there but I take the binos out and look thru them.

Just swamp is all I see, the tops of swamp trees, little clearings of swampy bits of water, the river eventually starting to form itself again. I take the binos away from my face and look them over. There are little buttons everywhere and I push a few and realize I can make everything look even closer. I do that a coupla times and I'm sure I can hear whispering now. I'm sure of it.

I find the gash in the swamp, the ditch, find the wreckage of her ship, but there's nothing there except what we left. I look over the top of the binos, wondering if I see movement. I look thru them again, a little nearer to us where some trees are rustling.

But that's only the wind, ain't it?

I scan back and forth, pressing buttons to get closer and farther away, but I keep coming back to those rustling trees. I keep the binos trained on a kinda open, gully-type thing twixt me and them.

I keep the binos there.

I keep the binos watching, my guts twisting as maybe I'm hearing whispering, maybe I ain't.

I keep watching.

Till the rustling reaches the clearing and I see the Mayor himself come outta the trees on horseback, leading other men, also on horses.

And they're heading right this way.

12

THE BRIDGE

THE MAYOR. Not just his son but actually the *Mayor*. With his clean hat and his clean face and his clean clothes and his shiny boots and his upright pose. We don't never actually get to see him much in Prentisstown, not no more, not if yer not in his close little circle, but when you do, he always looks like this, even thru a pair of binos. Like he knows how to take care of hisself and you don't.

I push some more buttons till I'm as close as I can get. There's five of them, no, six, the men whose Noise you hear doing those freaky exercises in the Mayor's house. **I AM THE CIRCLE AND THE CIRCLE IS ME**, that kinda thing. There's Mr Collins, Mr MacInerny, Mr O'Hare, and Mr Morgan, all on horses, too, itself a rare sight cuz horses are hard to keep alive on New World and the Mayor guards his personal herd with a whole raft of men with guns.

And there's Mr bloody Prentiss Jr, riding up next to his father, wearing a shiner from where Cillian hit him. Good.

But then I realize that means whatever happened at the farm is definitely over with. Whatever happened to Ben and Cillian is done. I put the binos down for a sec and swallow it away.

I put the binos back up. The group's stopped for a minute and are talking to each other, looking over a large piece of paper that's gotta be a way better map than mine and–

Oh, man.

Oh, man, you gotta be *kidding*.

Aaron.

Aaron comes walking outta the trees behind 'em.

Stinking, stupid, rutting, effing, bloody Aaron.

Most of his head is wrapped in bandages but he's pacing the ground a little way back from the Mayor, waving his hands in the air, looking like he's probably preaching even if no one looks like listening.

HOW? How could he have lived? Doesn't he ever ruddy *DIE*?

It's my fault. My stupid effing fault. Cuz I'm a coward. I'm a weak and stupid coward and cuz of that Aaron's alive and cuz of that he's leading the Mayor thru the ruddy swamp after us. Cuz I didn't kill him, he's coming to kill me.

I feel sick. I bend over double and hold my stomach, moaning a bit. My blood is charging so hard I hear Manchee creep a little ways away from me.

"It's my fault, Manchee," I say. "I did this."

"Your fault," he says, confused and just repeating what I said but right on the money, ain't he?

I make myself look thru the binos again and I see the

Mayor call Aaron over. Since men started being able to hear their thoughts, Aaron thinks animals are unclean and won't go near 'em so it takes the Mayor a coupla tries but eventually Aaron comes tromping over to look at the map. He listens while the Mayor asks him something.

And then he looks up.

Looks up thru the swamp trees and sky.

Looks up to this hilltop.

Looks right at me.

He can't see me. No way. Can he? Not without binos like the girl's and I don't see any on the men, never saw *anything* like 'em in Prentisstown. Gotta be. He can't see me.

But like a great pitiless thing he raises his arm and points, points it directly at me, like I'm sitting across a table from him.

I'm running before I can even think, running back down the bluff and back to the girl as fast as I can, reaching behind me and pulling out my knife, Manchee barking up a storm on my heels. I get into the trees and down and round the big mess of shrubs and she's still sitting on the rock but at least she looks up as I run to her.

"Come on!" I say, grabbing her arm. "We gotta go!"

She pulls back away from me but I don't let go.

"No!" I shout. "We have to go! NOW!"

She starts hitting out with her fists, clonking me a coupla times on the face.

But I ain't letting go.

"LISTEN!" I say and I open up my Noise for her. She hits me once more but then she's looking, looking at my Noise as it comes, seeing the pictures of what's waiting for us in the swamp. Check that, what's *not* waiting for us, what's making every effort to come get us. Aaron, who won't die, bending all his thoughts to finding us and coming this time with men on horseback. Who are a lot faster than we are.

The girl's face squishes up, like she's in the worst pain ever and she opens her mouth like she's going to yell but nothing comes out. Still nothing. Still no Noise, no sound, no nothing at all coming from her.

I just don't get it.

"I don't know what's ahead," I say. "I don't know nothing about nothing but whatever it is, it's gotta be better than what's behind. It's *gotta* be."

And as she hears me, her face changes. It clears up to almost blankness again and she presses her lips together.

"Go! Go! Go!" Manchee barks.

She holds out her hand for her bag. I hand it to her. She stands, shoves the binos in, loops it over her shoulder and looks me in the eye.

"Okay, then," I say.

And so that's how I set off running full out towards a river for the second time in two days, Manchee with me again and this time a girl on my heels.

Well, *past* my heels most of the time, she's ruddy fast, she is.

We go back up the hill and down the other side, the last of the swamp really starting to disappear around us and turning into regular woods. The ground gets way firmer and easier to run on and it's sloping more downhill than it is up, which may be the first piece of luck we've had. We start catching the proper river in brief glances off to our left side as we go. My rucksack's bashing me in the back as I run and I'm gasping for breath.

But I'm holding my knife.

I swear. I swear right now before God or whatever. If Aaron ever comes in my reach again, I will kill him. I ain't hesitating again. No way. No how. I ain't. I swear to you.

I will kill him.

I'll ruddy well kill him.

You just watch me.

The ground we're running on is getting a bit steeper side to side, taking us thru leafier, lighter trees and first closer to the river and then away from it again and again as we run. Manchee's tongue is hanging out of his mouth in a big pant, bouncing along as we go. My heart's thumping a million beats and my legs are about to fall off my body but still we run.

We veer close to the water again and I call out, "Wait." The girl, who's got pretty far in front of me, stops. I run to the river's edge, take a swift look round for crocs, then lean down and scoop up a few handfuls of water into my mouth. Tastes sweeter than it really should. Who knows what's in it, coming outta the swamp, but you gotta drink. I feel the girl's silence lean down next to me as she drinks, too. I scoot a little ways away. Manchee laps up his share and you can hear us all taking in great raking breaths between slurps.

I look up to where we're going, wiping my mouth. Next to the river is starting to become too rocky and steep to run on and I can see a path cutting its way up from the riverbank, going along the top of the canyon.

I blink, as I realize.

I can see a path. Someone's cut a *path*.

The girl turns and looks. The path carries up and along as the river drops below it, getting deeper and faster and turning into rapids. Someone *made* that path.

"It's gotta be the way to the other settlement," I say. "Gotta be."

And then, in the distance, we hear hoofbeats. Faint, but on their way.

I don't say another word cuz we're already on our feet and running up the path. The river falls farther and farther away beneath us and the larger mountain rears up on the other side of the river. On our side there's a thick forest starting to stretch back from the clifftops. The path's clearly been cut so men would have a place to travel down the river.

It's more than wide enough for horses. More than wide enough for five or six, in fact.

It ain't a path at all, I realize. It's a *road*.

We fly along it as it bends and turns, the girl ahead, then me, then Manchee, running along.

Till I nearly bump into her and knock her off the trail.

"What're you doing?!" I shout, grabbing onto her arms to keep us both from falling off the cliff, trying to keep the knife from accidentally killing her.

And then I see what she's seeing.

A bridge, way on up ahead of us. It goes from one cliff edge to the other, crossing the river what's gotta be thirty, forty metres above it. The road or path or whatever stops on our side at the bridge and becomes rock and dense forest beyond. There's nowhere to go but the bridge.

The first shades of an idea start to form.

The hoofbeats are louder now. I look back and see clouds of dust rising from where the Mayor is following.

"Come on!" I say, running past her, making for the bridge as fast as I can. We pound down the clifftop path, kicking up our own dust, Manchee's ears flattened back, running fast. We get there and it's way more than just a footbridge, two metres wide at least. It looks like mostly rope tied into wooden stakes driven into the rock at either end, with tight wooden planks running all the way to the other side.

I test it with my foot but it's so sturdy it don't even bounce. More than enough to take me and the girl and a dog.

More than enough to take men on horseback who wanted to cross it, in fact.

Whoever built it, meant it to last.

I look back again down the river at where we've run. More dust, louder hoofbeats, and the whispers of men's Noise on its way. I think I hear young Todd but I'm only imagining it cuz Aaron'll be way behind on foot.

But I do see what I wanna see: this bridge is the only place where you can cross the river, from back where we've run to miles on farther ahead as you look.

Maybe another piece of luck is coming our way.

"Let's go," I say. We run across and it's so well-made you can't even see twixt the gaps in the planks of wood. We might as well still be on the path. We get to the other side and the girl stops and turns to me, no doubt seeing my idea in my Noise, already waiting for me to act.

The knife is still in my hand. Power at the end of my arm.

Maybe at last I can do some good with it.

I look over where this end of the bridge is tied to the stakes in the rock. The knife has a fearsome serrated edge on part of the blade, so I choose the likeliest looking knot and start sawing on it.

I saw and saw.

The hoofbeats get louder, echoing down the canyon.

But if there suddenly *ain't* no bridge–

I saw some more.

And some more.

And some more.

And I'm just not making no progress at all.

"What the hell?" I say, looking at where I been cutting. There's hardly a scratch there. I touch the serration on the knife with my finger and it pricks and bleeds almost immediately. I look closer at the rope. It looks like it's coated in some kind of thin resin.

Some kind of ruddy tough, steel-like resin that ain't for cutting.

"I don't believe this," I say, looking up at the girl.

She's got her binos to her eyes, looking back the way we came down the river.

"Can you see 'em?"

I look down the river but you don't need binos at all. You can see 'em coming with yer own two eyes. Small but growing larger and not slowing down, thundering their hooves like there's no tomorrow.

We got three minutes. Maybe four.

Crap.

I start sawing again, fast and strong as I can, forcing my arm back and forth hard as I can make it, sweat popping out all over the place and new aches forming to keep all the old ones company. I saw and saw and saw, dripping water down my nose onto the knife.

"C'mon, c'mon," I say thru my teeth.

I lift the knife. I've managed to get thru one tiny little bit of resin on one tiny little knot on one huge effing bridge.

"Goddam it!" I spit.

I saw some more and more and more. And more and more than that, sweat running into my eyes and starting to sting.

"Todd!" Manchee barks, his alarm spilling out all over the place.

I saw more. And more.

But the only thing that happens is that the knife catches and I smash my knuckles into the stake, bloodying them.

"GODDAM IT!" I scream, throwing the knife down. It bounces along, stopping just at the girl's feet. "GODDAM IT ALL!"

Cuz that's it, ain't it?

That's the end of everything.

Our one stupid chance that wasn't a chance at all.

We can't outrun the horses and we can't cut down a stupid mega-road bridge and we're going to be caught and Ben and Cillian are dead and we're going to be killed ourselves and the world is going to end and that's it.

A redness comes over my Noise, like nothing I ever felt before, sudden and raw, like a red-hot brand pressing into my own self, a burning bright redness of everything that's made me hurt and keeps on hurting, a roaring rage of the unfairness and the injustice and the lies.

Of everything coming back to *one* thing.

I raise my eyes up to the girl's and she steps back from the force of it.

"*You*," I say and there ain't gonna be no stopping me. "This is all *you*! If you hadn't shown up in that ruddy swamp, none of this woulda happened! I'd be home RIGHT NOW! I'd be tending my effing sheep and living in my effing house and sleeping in my own EFFING BED!"

Except I don't say "effing".

"But oh NO," I shout, getting louder. "Here's YOU! Here's YOU and yer SILENCE! And the whole world gets SCREWED!"

I don't realize I'm walking towards her till I see her stepping back. But she just looks back at me.

And I don't hear a goddam thing.

"You're NOTHING!" I scream, stepping forward some more. "NOTHING! You're nothing but EMPTINESS! There's nothing in you! You're EMPTY and NOTHING and we're gonna die FOR NOTHING!"

I have my fists clenched so hard my nails are cutting into my palms. I'm so furious, my Noise raging so loud, so *red*, that I have to raise my fists to her, I have to hit her, I have to beat her, I have to make her ruddy silence STOP before it SWALLOWS ME AND THE WHOLE EFFING WORLD!

I take my fist and punch myself hard in the face.

I do it again, hitting where my eye is swollen from Aaron.

And a third time, splitting open the cut on my lip from where Aaron hit me yesterday morning.

You *fool*, you *worthless, effing fool*.

I do it again, hard enough to knock me off balance. I fall and catch myself on my hands and spit out some blood onto the path.

I look up at the girl, breathing hard.

Nothing. Just looking back at me and nothing.

We both turn to look across the river. They've got to the bit where they can see the bridge clearly. See *us* clearly on the other side. We can see the faces of the men as they ride. Hear the chatter of their Noise as it flies up the river at us. Mr MacInerny, the Mayor's best horseman, is in the lead, the Mayor riding behind, looking as calm as if it was nothing more than a Sunday ride.

We got maybe a minute, probably less.

I turn back to the girl, trying to stand, but I'm so tired. So, so tired. "We might as well run," I say, spitting out more blood. "We might as well try."

And I see her face change.

Her mouth opens wide, her eyes, too, and suddenly she yanks her bag out in front of her and shoves her hand in it.

"What're you doing?" I say.

She takes out the campfire box, looking all around her till I see her see a good sized rock. She sets the box down and raises up the rock.

"No, wait, we could use–"

She brings down the rock and the box cracks. She picks it up and twists it hard, making it crack some more. It starts to leak some kind of fluid. She moves to the bridge and starts flinging fluid all over the knots on the closest stake, shaking out the last drops into a puddle at the base.

The riders are coming up to the bridge, coming up, coming up, coming up–

"Hurry!" I say.

The girl turns to me, telling me with her hands to get back. I scrabble back a little ways, grabbing Manchee by his scruff and taking him with me. She steps back as far as she can, holding out the remains of the box at arm's length and pressing a button on it. I hear a clicking sound. She tosses the box in the air and jumps back towards me.

The horses reach the bridge–

The girl lands almost on top of me and we watch as the campfire box falls–

Falls–

Falls–

Towards the little puddle of liquid, clicking as it goes–

Mr MacInerny's horse puts a hoof on the bridge to cross it–

The campfire box lands in the puddle–

Clicks one more time–

Then–

WHOOOOMP!!!!

The air is sucked outta my lungs as a fireball WAY bigger than what you'd think for that little amount of fluid makes the world quiet for a second and then–

BOOM!!!!!

It blasts away the ropes and the stake, spraying fiery splinters all over us and obliterating all thought, Noise and sound.

When we can look up again, the bridge is already so much on fire it's starting to lean to one side and we see Mr MacInerny's horse rear up and stumble, trying to back up into four or five more oncoming horses.

The flames roar a weird bright green and the sudden heat's incredible, like the worst sunburn ever and I think we're gonna catch fire ourselves when this end of the bridge just falls right away, taking Mr MacInerny and his horse with it. We sit up and watch them fall and fall and fall into the river below, way too far to ever live thru it. The bridge is still attached at their end and it slaps the facing cliff but it's burning so fierce it won't be no time at all before the whole thing is just ash. The Mayor and Mr Prentiss Jr and the others all have to back their horses away from it.

The girl crawls away from me and we lay there a second, just breathing and coughing, trying to stop being dazed.

Holy crap.

"Y'all right?" I say to Manchee, still held by my hand.

"Fire, Todd!" he barks.

"Yeah," I cough. "Big fire. *You* all right?" I say to the girl, who's still crouching, still coughing. "Man, what was in that thing?"

But of course she don't say nothing.

"TODD HEWITT!" I hear from across the canyon.

I look up. It's the Mayor, shouting his first words ever to me in person, thru sheets of smoke and heat that make him look all wavy.

"We're not finished, young Todd," he calls, over the crackle of the burning bridge and the roar of the water below. "Not by a long way."

And he's calm and still ruddy clean and looking like there's no way he's not gonna get what he wants.

I stand up, hold out my arm and give him two fingers but he's already disappearing behind big clouds of smoke.

I cough and spit blood again. "We gotta keep moving," I say, coughing some more. "Maybe they'll turn back, maybe there's no other way across, but we shouldn't wait to find out."

I see the knife in the dust. Shame comes right quick, like a new pain all its own. The things I said. I reach down and pick it up and put it back in its sheath.

The girl's still got her head down, coughing to herself. I pick up her bag for her and hold it out for her to take.

"Come on," I say. "We can at least get away from the smoke."

She looks up at me.

I look back at her.

My face burns and not from the heat.

"I'm sorry." I look away from her, from her eyes and face, blank and quiet as ever.

I turn back up the path.

"Viola," I hear.

I spin around, look at her.

"What?" I say.

She's looking back at me.

She's opening her mouth.

She's talking.

"My name," she says. "It's Viola."

PART III

13

VIOLA

I DON'T SAY NOTHING to this for a minute. Neither does she. The fire burns, the smoke rises, Manchee's tongue hangs out in a stunned pant, till finally I say, "Viola."

She nods.

"Viola," I say again.

She don't nod this time.

"I'm Todd," I say.

"I know," she says.

She's not quite meeting my eye.

"So you can talk then?" I say, but all she does is look at me again quickly and then away. I turn to the still burning bridge, to the smoke turning into a fogbank twixt us and the other side of the river, which I don't know if it makes me feel safer or not, if not seeing the Mayor and his men is better than seeing them. "That was–" I start to say, but she's getting up and holding out her hand for her bag.

I realize I'm still holding it. I hand it to her and she takes it.

"We should go on," she says. "Away from here."

Her accent's funny, different from mine, different from anyone in Prentisstown's. Her lips make different kinds of outlines for the letters, like they're swooping down on them from above, pushing them into shape, telling them what to say. In Prentisstown, everyone talks like they're sneaking up on their words, ready to club them from behind.

Manchee's just in awe of her. "Away," he says lowly, staring up at her like she's made of food.

There's this moment now where it feels like I could start asking her stuff, like now she's talking, I could just hit her with every asking I can think of about who she is, where she's from, what happened, and them askings are all over my Noise, flying at her like pellets, but there's so much stuff wanting to come outta my mouth that nothing is and so my mouth don't move and she's holding her bag over her shoulder and looking at the ground and then she's walking past me, past Manchee, on up the trail.

"Hey," I say.

She stops and turns back.

"Wait for me," I say.

I pick up my rucksack, hooking it back over my shoulders. I press my hand against the knife in its sheath against my lower back. I make the rucksack comfortable with a shrug, say "C'mon, Manchee", and off we go up the trail, following the girl.

On this side of the river the path makes a slow turn away from the cliffside, heading into what looks like a landscape of scrub and brush, making its way around and away from the larger mountain, looming up at us on the left.

At the place where the trail turns, we both stop and look back without saying that we're gonna. The bridge is still burning like you wouldn't believe, hanging on the opposite cliff like a waterfall on fire, flames having leapt up the entire length of it, angry and greenish yellow. The smoke's so thick, it's still impossible to tell what the Mayor and his men are doing, have done, if they're gone or waiting or what. There could be a whisper of Noise coming thru but there could also *not* be a whisper of Noise, what with the fire blazing and the wood popping and the whitewater below. As we watch, the fire finishes its business on the stakes on the other side of the river and with a great *snap*, the burning bridge falls, falls, falls, clattering against the cliffside, splashing into the river, sending up more clouds of smoke and steam, making everything even foggier.

"What was in that box?" I say to the girl.

She looks at me, opens her mouth, but then closes it again, turning away.

"It's okay," I say. "I'm not gonna hurt ya."

She looks at me again and my Noise is full of just a few minutes ago when I *was* just about to hurt her, when I was just about to–

Anyway.

We don't say no more. She turns back onto the path and me and Manchee follow her into the scrub.

Knowing she can speak don't help with the silence none. Knowing she's got words in her head don't mean nothing if you can only hear 'em when she talks. Looking at the back of her head as she's walking, I still feel my heart pull towards her silence, still feel like I've lost something terrible, something so sad I want to weep.

"Weep," Manchee barks.

The back of her head just keeps on walking.

The path is still pretty wide, wide enough for horses, but the terrain around us is getting rockier, the path twistier. We can hear the river down below us to our right now but it feels like we're tending away from it a bit, getting ourselves deep into an area that feels almost walled, rockface sometimes coming up on both sides, like we're walking at the bottom of a box. Little prickly firs grow out of every crevice and yellow vines with thorns wrapping themselves around the firs' trunks and you can see and hear yellow razor lizards hissing at us as we pass. **Bite!** they say, as a threat. **Bite! Bite!**

Anything you might want to touch here would cut you.

After maybe twenty, thirty minutes the path gets to a bit where it widens out, where a few real trees start growing again, where the forest looks like it might be about to restart, where there's grass and stones low enough for sitting on. Which is what we do. Sit.

I take some dried mutton outta my rucksack and use the knife to cut strips for me, for Manchee, and for the girl. She takes them without saying anything and we sit quietly apart and eat for a minute.

I am Todd Hewitt, I think, closing my eyes and chewing, embarrassed for my Noise now, now that I know she can hear it, now that I know she can think about it.

Think about it in secret.

I am Todd Hewitt.

I will be a man in twenty-nine days' time.

Which is true, I realize, opening my eyes. Time goes on, even when yer not looking.

I take another bite. "I ain't never heard the name Viola before," I say after a while, looking only at the ground, only at my strip of mutton. She don't say nothing so I glance up in spite of myself.

To find her looking back at me.

"What?" I say.

"Your face," she says.

I frown. "What about my face?"

She makes both of her hands into fists and mimes punching herself with them.

I feel myself redden. "Yeah, well."

"And from before," she says. "From–" She stops.

"Aaron," I say.

"Aaron," Manchee barks and the girl flinches a little.

"That was his name," she says. "Wasn't it?"

I nod, chewing on my mutton. "Yep," I say. "That's his name."

"He never said it out loud. But I knew what it was."

"Welcome to New World." I take another bite, having to tear an extra-chewy bit off with my teeth, which catches one sore spot among many in my mouth. "Ow." I spit out the bit of mutton and a whole lot of extra blood.

The girl watches me spit and then sets down her food. She picks up her bag, opens it, and finds a little blue box, slightly larger than the green campfire one. She presses a button on the front to open it and takes out what looks like a white plastic cloth and a little metal scalpel. She gets up from her rock and walks over to me with them.

I'm still sitting but I lean back when she brings her hands to my face.

"Bandages," she says.

"I've got my own."

"These are better."

I lean back farther. "Yer…" I say, blowing out air thru my nose. "Yer quiet kinda…" I shake my head a little.

"Bothers you?"

"Yes."

"I know," she says. "Hold still."

She looks closer at the area around my swollen eye and then cuts off a piece of bandage with the little scalpel. She's about to put it over my eye but I can't help it and I move back from her touch. She don't say nothing, just keeps her hands up, like she's waiting. I take a deep breath, close my eyes and offer up my face.

I feel the bandage touch the swollen area and immediately it gets cooler, immediately the pain starts to edge back, like it's all being swept away by feathers. She puts another one on a cut I have at my hairline and her fingers brush my face as she puts another one just below my lower lip. It all feels so good I haven't even opened my eyes yet.

"I don't have anything for your teeth," she says.

"'S okay," I say, almost whispering it. "Man, these *are* better than mine."

"They're partially alive," she says. "Synthetic human tissue. When you're healed, they die."

"Uh-huh," I say, acting like I might know what that means.

There's a longer silence, long enough to make me open my eyes again. She's stepped back, back to a rock she can sit down on, watching me, watching my face.

We wait. Cuz it seems like we should.

And we should cuz after a little bit of waiting, she begins to talk.

"We crashed," she starts quietly, looking away. Then she clears her throat and says it again. "We crashed. There was a fire and we were flying low and we thought we'd be okay but something went wrong with the safety flumes and–" She holds open her hands to explain what follows the *and*. "We crashed."

She stops.

"Was that yer ma and pa?" I ask, after a bit.

But she just looks up into the sky, blue and spare, with clouds that look like bones. "And when the sun came up," she says, "that man came."

"Aaron."

"And it was so weird. He would shout and he would scream and then he'd *leave*. And I'd try to run away." She folds her arms. "I *kept* trying so he wouldn't find me, but I was going in circles and wherever I hid, there he'd be, I don't know how, until I found these sort of hut things."

"The Spackle buildings," I say but she ain't really listening.

She looks at me. "Then you came." She looks at Manchee. "You and your dog that talks."

"Manchee!" Manchee barks.

Her face is pale and when she meets my eyes again, her own have gone wet. "What is this place?" she asks, her voice kinda thick. "Why do the animals talk? Why do I hear your voice when your mouth isn't moving? Why do I hear your voice a whole bunch over, piled on top of each other like there's nine million of you talking at once? Why do I see pictures of other things when I look at you? Why could I see what that man..."

She fades off. She draws her knees up to her chest and hugs them. I feel like I better start talking right quick or she's gonna start rocking again.

"We're settlers," I say. She looks up at this, still hugging her knees but at least not rocking. "We *were* settlers," I continue. "Landed here to found New World about twenty years ago or so. But there were aliens here. The Spackle. And they ... didn't want us." I'm telling her what every boy in Prentisstown knows, the history even the dumbest farm boy like yours truly knows by heart. "Men tried for years to make peace but the Spackle weren't having it. And so war started."

She looks down again at the word *war*. I keep talking.

"And the way the Spackle fought, see, was with germs, with diseases. That was their weapons. They released germs that did things. One of them we think was meant to kill all our livestock but instead it just made every animal able to talk." I look at Manchee. "Which ain't as much fun as it sounds." I look back at the girl. "And another was the Noise."

I wait. She don't say nothing. But we both sorta know what's coming cuz we been here before, ain't we?

I take a deep breath. "And that one killed half the men and all the women, including my ma, and it made the thoughts of the men who survived no longer secret to the rest of the world."

She hides her chin behind her knees. "Sometimes I can hear it clearly," she says. "Sometimes I can tell exactly what you're thinking. But only sometimes. Most of the time it's just–"

"Noise," I say.

She nods. "And the aliens?"

"There ain't no more aliens."

She nods again. We sit for a minute, ignoring the obvious till it can't be ignored no longer.

"Am I going to die?" she asks quietly. "Is it going to kill me?"

The words sound different in her accent but they mean the same damn thing and my Noise can only say *probably* but I make it so my mouth says, "I don't know."

She watches me for more.

"I really *don't* know," I say, kinda meaning it. "If you'd asked me last week, I'd have been sure, but today–" I look down at my rucksack, at the book hiding inside. "I don't know." I look back at her. "I hope not."

But probably, says my Noise. *Probably yer gonna die,* and tho I try to cover it up with other Noise it's such an unfair thing it's hard not to have it right at the front.

"I'm sorry," I say.

She don't say nothing.

"But maybe if we get to the next settlement–" I say, but I don't finish cuz I don't know the answer. "You ain't sick yet. That's something."

"You must warn them," she says, down into her knees.

I look up sharply. "What?"

"Earlier, when you were trying to read that book–"

"I wasn't *trying*," I say, my voice a little bit louder all of a sudden.

"I could see the words in your whatever," she says, "and it's 'You must warn them'."

"I know that! I know what it says."

Of course it's bloody *You must warn them*. Course it is. Idiot.

The girl says, "It seemed like you were–"

"I know how to read."

She holds up her hands. "Okay."

"I do!"

"I'm just saying–"

"Well, *stop* just saying," I frown, my Noise roiling enough to get Manchee on his feet. I get to my feet as well. I pick up the rucksack and put it back on. "We should get moving."

"Warn who?" asks the girl, still sitting. "About what?"

I don't get to answer (even tho I don't *know* the answer) cuz there's a loud click above us, a loud clang-y click that in Prentisstown would mean one thing.

A rifle being cocked.

And standing on a rock above us, there's someone with a freshly-cocked rifle in both hands, looking down the sight, pointing it right at us.

"What's foremost in my mind at this partickalar juncture," says a voice rising from behind the gun, "is what do two little pups think they're doing a-burning down my bridge?"

14

THE WRONG END OF A GUN

"GUN! GUN! GUN!" Manchee starts barking, hopping back and forth in the dust.

"I'd quieten down yer beastie there," says the rifle, his face obscured by looking down the sight straight at us. "Wouldn't want anything to happen to it, now wouldja?"

"Quiet, Manchee!" I say.

He turns to me. "Gun, Todd?" he barks. "Bang, bang!"

"I know. Shut up."

He stops barking and it's quiet.

Aside from my Noise, it's *quiet*.

"I do believe I sent out an asking to a partickalar pair of pups," says the voice, "and I am a-waiting on my answer."

I look back at the girl. She shrugs her shoulders, tho I notice we both have our hands up. "What?" I say back up to the rifle.

The rifle gives an angry grunt. "I'm asking," it says, "what exactly gives ye permisshun to go a-burning down other people's bridges?"

I don't say nothing. Neither does the girl.

"D'ye think this is a *stick* I'm a-pointing at ye?" The rifle bobs up and down once.

"We were being chased," I say, for lack of nothing else.

"Chased, were ye?" says the rifle. "Who was a-chasing ye?"

And I don't know how to answer this. Would the truth be more dangerous than a lie? Is the rifle on the side of the Mayor? Would we be bounty? Or would rifle man have even *heard* of Prentisstown?

The world's a dangerous place when you don't know enough.

Like why is it so quiet?

"Oh, I heard of Prentisstown, all right," says the rifle, reading my Noise with unnerving clarity and cocking the gun again, making it ready to shoot. "And if that's where yer from–"

Then the girl speaks up and says that thing that suddenly makes me think of her as *Viola* and not *the girl* any more.

"He saved my life."

I saved her life.

Says Viola.

Funny how that works.

"Did he now?" says the rifle. "And how do you know he don't aim to just be a-saving it for himself?"

The girl, Viola, looks at me, her forehead creased. It's my turn to shrug.

"But no." The rifle's voice changes. "No, huh-uh, no, I'm not a-seeing that in ye, am I, boy? Cuz yer just a boy pup still, ain't ye?"

I swallow. "I'll be a man in 29 days."

"Not something to be proud of, pup. Not where *yer* from."

And then he lowers the gun away from his face.

And that's why it's so quiet.

He's a woman.

He's a grown woman.

He's an *old* woman.

"I'll thank ye kindly to call me *she*," the woman says, still pointing the rifle at us from chest level. "And not so old I won't still shoot ye."

She's looking at us more closely now, reading me up and down, seeing right into my Noise with a skill I've only ever felt in Ben. Her face is making all kindsa shapes, like she's considering me, like Cillian's face does when he tries to read me to see if I'm lying. Tho this woman ain't got no Noise at all so she might be singing a song in there for all I know.

She turns to Viola and pauses for another long look.

"As pups go," she says, looking back at me, "ye are as easy to read as a newborn, m'boy." She turns her face to Viola. "But ye, wee girl, yer story's not a usual one, is it?"

"I'd be happy to tell you all about it if you'd stop pointing a gun at us," Viola says.

This is so surprising even Manchee looks up. I turn to Viola with my mouth open.

We hear a chuckle from up on the rock. The old woman

is laughing to herself. Her clothes seem a real dusty leather, worn and creased for years and years with a rimmed hat and boots for ignoring mud. Like she ain't nothing more than a farmer, really.

She's still pointing the gun at us, tho.

"Ye were a-running from Prentisstown, were ye?" she asks, looking into my Noise again. There's no point in hiding it so I go ahead and put forward what we were running from, what happened at the bridge, who was chasing us. She sees all of it, I know she does, but all I see her do is wrinkle up her lips and squint her eyes a bit.

"Well, now," she says, crooking the rifle in her arm and starting to make her way down from the rocks to where we're standing. "I can't rightly say that I'm not peeved bout ye blowing up my bridge. Heard the boom all the way back at the farm, oh, yeah." She steps off the last rock and stands a little ways away from us, the force of her grown-up quiet so large I feel myself stepping back without even knowing I decided to do it. "But the only place it led to ain't been worth a-going to for a decade nor more. Only left it up outta hope." She looks us over again. "Who's to say I weren't right?"

We still have our hands in the air cuz she ain't making much sense, is she?

"I'll ask ye this once," the woman says, lifting the rifle again. "Am I gonna need this?"

I exchange a glance with Viola.

"No," I say.

"No, mam," Viola says.

Mam? I think.

"It's like *sir*, bonny boy." The woman slings the rifle over her shoulder by its strap. "For if yer a-talking to a lady." She squats down to Manchee's level. "And who might ye be, pup?"

"Manchee!" he barks.

"Oh, yeah, that's definitely who ye be, innit?" says the woman, giving him a vigorous rubbing. "And ye two pups?" she asks, not looking up. "What might yer good mothers have dubbed ye?"

Me and Viola exchange another glance. It seems like a price, giving up our names, but maybe it's a fair exchange for the gun being lowered.

"I'm Todd. That's Viola."

"As surely true as the sun a-coming up," says the woman, having succeeded in getting Manchee on his back for a tummy rub.

"Is there another way over that river?" I ask. "Another bridge? Cuz those men–"

"I'm Mathilde," the old woman interrupts, "but people who call me that don't know me, so you can call me Hildy and one day ye may even earn the right to shake my hand."

I look at Viola again. How can you tell if someone with no Noise is crazy?

The old woman cackles. "Yer a funny one there, boy." She stands up from Manchee who rolls back over and stares at her, already a worshipper. "And to answer yer asking, there's shallow crossings a couple days' travelling upstream but there ain't no bridges for a good distance more either way."

She turns her gaze back to me, steady and clear, a small

smile on her lips. She's gotta be reading my Noise again but I can't feel no prodding like I do when men try it.

And the way she keeps on looking I start to realize a few things, put a few things together. It must be right that Prentisstown was quarantined cuz of the Noise germ, huh? Cuz here's a grown-up woman who ain't dead from it, who's looking at me friendly but keeping her distance, a woman ready to greet strangers from my direkshun with a rifle.

And if I'm contagious that means Viola's probably definitely caught it by now, could be dying as we speak, and that I'm probably definitely not gonna be welcome in the settlement, probably definitely gonna be told to keep way way out and that that's probably the end of that, ain't it? My journey ended before I even found anywhere to go.

"Oh, ye won't be welcome in the settlement," the woman says. "No probably about it. But," she winks at me, actually winks, "what ye don't know won't kill ye."

"Wanna bet?" I say.

She turns back and steps up the rocks the way she came. We just watch her go till she gets to the top and turns around again.

"Ye all a-coming?" she says, as if she's invited us along and we're keeping her waiting.

I look at Viola. She calls up to the woman, "We're meant to be heading for the settlement." Viola looks at me again. "Welcome or not."

"Oh, ye'll get there," says the woman, "but what ye two pups need first is a good sleeping and a good feeding. Any blind man could see that."

The idea of sleep and hot food is so tempting, I forget

for a second that she ever pointed a gun at us. But only for a second. Cuz there's other things to think about. I make the decision for us. "We should keep on the road," I say to Viola quietly.

"I don't even know where we're going," she says, also quietly. "Do you? Honestly?"

"Ben said–"

"Ye two pups come to my farm, get some good eatings in ye, sleep on a bed – tho it ain't soft, I grant ye that – and in the morning, we'll go to the *settlement*." And that's how she says it, opening her eyes wide on it, like a word to make fun of us for calling it that.

We still don't move.

"Look at it thusly," the old woman says. "I got me a gun." She waves it. "But I'm *asking* ye to come."

"Why don't we go with her?" Viola whispers. "Just to see."

My Noise rises a little in surprise. "See what?"

"I could use a bath," she says. "I could use some sleep."

"So could I," I say, "but there's men who're after us who probably ain't gonna let one fallen bridge stop them. And besides, we don't know nothing about her. She could be a killer for all we know."

"She seems okay." Viola glances up at the woman. "A little crazy, but she doesn't seem *dangerous* crazy."

"She don't *seem* anything." I feel a little vexed, if I'm honest. "People without Noise don't seem like nothing at all."

Viola looks at me, her brows suddenly creased and her jaw set a little.

"Well, not *you*, obviously," I say.

"Every time..." she starts to say but then she just shakes her head.

"Every time what?" I whisper, but Viola just scrunches her eyes and turns to the woman.

"Hold on," she says, her voice sounding annoyed. "Let me get my stuff."

"Hey!" I say. What happened to her remembering I saved her life? "Wait a minute. We gotta follow the road. We gotta get to the settlement."

"Roads is never the fastest way to get nowhere," the woman says. "Don't ye know that?"

Viola don't say nothing, just picks up her bag, frowning all over the place. She's ready to go, ready to head off with the first quiet person she sees, ready to leave me behind at the first sweet beckoning.

And she's missing the thing I don't wanna say.

"I *can't* go, Viola," I say, low, thru clenched teeth, hating myself a little as I say it, my face turning hot, which weirdly makes a bandage fall off. "I carry the germ. I'm dangerous."

She turns to me and there's a sting in her voice. "Then maybe you shouldn't come."

My jaw drops open. "You'd do that? You'd just *leave*?"

Viola looks away from my eyes but before she can answer, the old woman speaks. "Boy pup," she says, "if it's being infeckshus yer worried about, then yer girl mate can come a-walking up ahead with ol' Hildy while ye stay back a little ways with the puppup to guard ye."

"Manchee!" Manchee barks.

"Whatever," Viola says, turning and starting to climb the rocks to where the old woman stands.

"And I told ye," the woman says, "it's *Hildy*, not *old woman*."

Viola reaches her and they walk off outta sight without another word. Just like that.

"Hildy," Manchee says to me.

"Shut up," I say.

And I don't got no choice but to climb the rocks after them, do I?

So that's how we make our way, along a much narrower path thru rocks and scrub, Viola and old Hildy keeping close together when they can, me and Manchee miles back, tripping our way towards who knows what further danger and the whole time I'm looking back over my shoulder, expecting to see the Mayor and Mr Prentiss Jr and Aaron all coming after us.

I don't know. How can you know? How can Ben and Cillian have expected me to be prepared for this? Sure, the idea of a bed and hot food sounds like something worth getting shot for but maybe it's a trick and we're being so stupid we deserve to get caught.

And there's people after us and we should be running.

But maybe there really ain't another way over that river.

And Hildy could have forced us and she didn't. And Viola said she seems okay and maybe one Noise-less person can read another.

You see? How can you know?

And who cares what Viola says?

"Look at 'em up there," I say to Manchee. "They fell together right quick. Like they're long-lost family or something."

"Hildy," Manchee says again. I swat after his rump but he runs on ahead.

Viola and Hildy are talking together but I can only hear the murmurings of words here and there. I don't know what they're saying at all. If they were normal Noisy people, it wouldn't matter how far back on the trail I was, we could all talk together and nobody'd have no automatic secrets. Everybody'd be jabbering, whether they wanted to or not.

And nobody'd be left out. Nobody'd be left on his own at the first chance you had.

We all walk on.

And I'm starting to think some more.

And I'm starting to let them get a little farther ahead, too.

And I'm thinking more.

Cuz as time passes, it's all starting to sink in.

Cuz maybe now we found Hildy, maybe she *can* take care of Viola. They're clearly peas in a pod, ain't they? Different from me, anyway. And so maybe Hildy could help her back to wherever she's from cuz obviously I can't. Obviously I ain't got nowhere I can be except Prentisstown, do I? Cuz I'm carrying a germ that'll kill her, may kill her still, may kill everybody else I meet, a germ that'll forever keep me outta that settlement, that'll probably even leave me sleeping in Hildy's barn with the sheep and the russets.

"That's it, ain't it, Manchee?" I stop walking, my chest starting to feel heavy. "There ain't no Noise out here, less I'm the one who brings it." I rub some sweat off my forehead. "We got nowhere to go. We can't go forward. We can't go back."

I sit down on a rock, realizing the truth of it all.

"We got nowhere," I say. "We got nothing."

"Got Todd," Manchee says, wagging his tail.

It ain't fair.

It just ain't fair.

The only place you belong is the place you can never go back.

And so yer always alone, forever and always.

Why'd you do it, Ben? What did I do that was so bad?

I wipe my eyes with my arm.

I wish Aaron and the Mayor *would* come and get me.

I wish it would just be over already.

"Todd?" Manchee barks, coming up to my face and trying to sniff it.

"Leave me alone," I say, pushing him away.

Hildy and Viola are getting still farther away and if I don't get up, I'll lose the trail.

I don't get up.

I can still hear them talking, tho it gets steadily quieter, no one looking back to see if I'm still following.

Hildy, I hear, and **girl pup** and **blasted leaky pipe** and **Hildy** again and **burning bridge**.

And I lift my head.

Cuz it's a new voice.

And I ain't hearing it. Not with my ears.

Hildy and Viola are getting farther away, but there's someone coming towards them, someone raising a hand in greeting.

Someone whose Noise is saying **Hello**.

15

BROTHERS IN SUFFERING

IT'S AN OLD MAN, also carrying a rifle but way down at his side, pointing to the ground. His Noise rises as he approaches Hildy, it stays risen as he puts an arm around her and kisses her in greeting, it buzzes as he turns and is introduced to Viola who stands back a little at being greeted so friendly.

Hildy is married to a man with Noise.

A full grown man, walking around Noisy as you please.

But how–?

"Hey, boy pup!" Hildy shouts back at me. "Ye going to sit there all day picking yer nose or are ye going to join us for supper?"

"Supper, Todd!" Manchee barks and takes off running towards them.

I don't think nothing. I don't know *what* to think.

"Another Noisy fella!" shouts the old man, stepping past Viola and Hildy and coming towards me. He's got Noise pouring outta him like a bright parade, all full of unwelcome welcome and pushy good feeling. **Boy pup** and **bridges falling** and **leaky pipe** and **brother in suffering** and **Hildy, my Hildy**. He's still carrying his rifle but as he reaches me, his hand's out for me to shake.

I'm so stunned that I actually shake it.

"Tam's my name!" the old man more or less shouts. "And who might ye be, pup?"

"Todd," I say.

"Pleasedtameetya, Todd!" He puts an arm around my shoulders and pretty much drags me forward up the path. I stumble along, barely keeping my balance as he pulls us to Hildy and Viola, talking all the way. "We haven't had guests for dinner in many a moon, so ye'll have to be a-scusing our humble shack. Ain't been no travellers thisaway for nigh on ten years nor more but yer welcome! Yer all welcome!"

We get to the others and I still don't know what to say and I look from Hildy to Viola to Tam and back again.

I just want the world to make sense now and then, is that so wrong?

"Not wrong at all, Todd pup," Hildy says kindly.

"How can you not have caught the Noise?" I ask, words finally making their way outta my head via my mouth. Then my heart suddenly rises, rises so high I can feel my eyes popping open and my throat start to clench, my own Noise coming all high hopeful white.

"Do you have a cure?" I say, my voice almost breaking. "Is there a cure?"

"Now if there were a cure," Tam says, still pretty much shouting, "d'ye honestly think I'd be subjecting ye to all this here rubbish a-floating outta my brain?"

"Heaven help ye if ye did," Hildy says, smiling.

"And heaven help *ye* if ye couldn't tell me what I was meant to be thinking." Tam smiles back, love fuzzing all over his Noise. "Nope, boy pup," he says to me. "No cure that I know of."

"Well, now," Hildy says, "Haven's meant to be a-working on one. So people say."

"Which people?" Tam asks, sceptical.

"Talia," Hildy says. "Susan F. My sister."

Tam makes a *pssht* sound with his lips. "I rest my case. Rumours of rumours of rumours. Can't trust yer sister to get her own name right much less any useful info."

"But–" I say, looking back and forth again and again, not wanting to let it go. "But how can you be alive then?" I say to Hildy. "The Noise kills women. *All* women."

Hildy and Tam exchange a look and I hear, no, I *feel* Tam squash something in his Noise.

"No, it don't, Todd pup," Hildy says, a little too gently. "Like I been telling yer girl mate Viola here. She's safe."

"Safe? How can she be safe?"

"Women are immune," Tam says. "Lucky buggers."

"No, they're not!" I say, my voice getting louder. "No, they're *not*! Every woman in Prentisstown caught the Noise and every single one of them *died* from it! My *ma* died from it! Maybe the version the Spackle released on us was stronger than yers but–"

"Todd pup." Tam puts a hand on my shoulder to stop me.

I shake him off but I don't know what to say next. Viola's not said a word in all of this so I look at her. She don't look at me. "I know what I know," I say, even tho that's been half the trouble, ain't it?

How can this be true?

How can this be *true*?

Tam and Hildy exchange another glance. I look into Tam's Noise but he's as expert as anyone I've met at hiding stuff away when someone starts poking. What I see, tho, is all kind.

"Prentisstown's got a sad history, pup," he says. "A whole number of things went sour there."

"Yer wrong," I say, but even my voice says I ain't sure what I'm saying he's wrong about.

"This ain't the place for it, Todd," Hildy says, rubbing Viola on the shoulder, a rub that Viola don't resist. "Ye need to get some food in ye, some sleep in ye. Vi here says ye ain't slept hardly at all in many miles of travelling. Everything will be a-looking better when yer fed and rested."

"But she's safe from me?" I ask, making a point of not looking at "Vi".

"Well, she's definitely safe from catching yer Noise," Hildy says, a smile breaking out. "What other safety she can get from ye is all down to a-knowing ye better."

I want her to be right but I also want to say she's wrong and so I don't say nothing at all.

"C'mon," Tam says, breaking the pause, "let's get to some feasting."

"No!" I say, remembering it all over again. "We ain't got time for *feasting*." I look at Viola. "There's men after us, in case you forgot. Men who ain't interested in our well-beings." I look up at Hildy. "Now, I'm sure yer feastings would be fine and all–"

"Todd pup–" Hildy starts.

"I ain't a pup!" I shout.

Hildy purses her lips and smiles with her eyebrows. "Todd pup," she says again, a little lower this time. "No man from any point beyond that river would ever set foot across it, do ye understand?"

"Yep," says Tam. "That's right."

I look from one to the other. "But–"

"I been guardian here of that bridge for ten plus years, pup," Hildy says, "and keeper of it for years before that. It's part of who I am to watch what comes." She looks over to Viola. "No one's coming. Ye all are safe."

"Yep," Tam says again, rocking back and forth on his heels.

"But–" I say again but Hildy don't let me finish.

"Time for feasting."

And that's that, it seems. Viola still don't look at me, still has her arms crossed and is now under the arm of Hildy as they walk on again. I'm stuck back with Tam who's waiting for me to start. I can't say as I feel much like walking any more but everyone else goes so I go, too. We carry on up Tam and Hildy's private little path, Tam chattering away, making enough Noise for a whole town.

"Hildy says ye blew up our bridge," he says.

"*My* bridge," Hildy says from in front of us.

"She did build it," Tam says to me. "Not that anyone's used it in forever."

"No one?" I say, thinking for a second of all those men who disappeared outta Prentisstown, all the ones who vanished while I was growing up. Not one of them got this far.

"Nice bit of engineering, that bridge was," Tam's going on, like he didn't hear me and maybe he didn't, what with how loud he's talking. "Sad to hear it's gone."

"We had no choice," I say.

"Oh, there's always choices, pup, but from what I hear, ye made the right one."

We walk on quietly for a bit. "Yer sure we're safe?" I ask.

"Well, ye can't never be sure," he says. "But Hildy's right." He grins, a little sadly, I think. "There's more than bridges being out that'll keep men that side of the river."

I try and read his Noise to see if he's telling the truth but it's almost all shiny and clean, a bright, warm place where anything you want could be true.

Nothing at all like a Prentisstown man.

"I don't understand this," I say, still gnawing on it. "It's gotta be a different kinda Noise germ."

"My Noise sound different from yers?" Tam asks, seeming genuinely curious.

I look at him and just listen for a second. Hildy and Prentisstown and russets and sheep and settlers and leaky pipe and Hildy.

"You sure think about yer wife a lot."

"She's my shining star, pup. Woulda lost myself in Noise if she hadn't put a hand out to rescue me."

"How so?" I ask, wondering what he's talking about. "Did you fight in the war?"

This stops him. His Noise goes as grey and featureless as a cloudy day and I can't read a thing off him.

"I fought, young pup," he says. "But war's not something ye talk about in the open air when the sun is shining."

"Why not?"

"I pray to all my gods ye never find out." He puts a hand on my shoulder. I don't shake it off this time.

"How do you do that?" I ask.

"Do what?"

"Make yer Noise so flat I can't read it."

He smiles. "Years of practise a-hiding things from the old woman."

"It's why I can read so good," Hildy calls back to us. "He gets better at hiding, I get better at *finding*."

They laugh together yet again. I find myself trying to send an eyeroll Viola's way about these two but Viola ain't looking at me and I stop myself from trying again.

We all come outta the rocky bit of the path and round a low rise and suddenly there's a farm ahead of us, rolling up and down little hills but you can see fields of wheat, fields of cabbage, a field of grass with a few sheep on it.

"Hello, sheep!" Tam shouts.

"Sheep!" say the sheep.

First on the path is a big wooden barn, built as water-tight and solid as the bridge, like it could last there forever if anyone asked it.

"Unless ye go a-blowing it up," Hildy says, laughing still.

"Like to see ye try," Tam laughs back.

I'm getting a little tired of them laughing about every damn thing.

Then we come round to the farmhouse, which is a totally different thing altogether. Metal, by the looks of it, like the petrol stayshun and the church back home but not nearly so banged up. Half of it shines and rolls on up to the sky like a sail and there's a chimney that curves up and out, folding down to a point, smoke coughing from its end. The other half of the house is wood built onto the metal, solid as the barn but cut and folded like–

"Wings," I say.

"Wings is right," Tam says. "And what kinda wings are they?"

I look again. The whole farmhouse looks like some kinda bird with the chimney as its head and neck and a shiny front and wooden wings stretching out behind, like a bird resting on the water or something.

"It's a swan, Todd pup," Tam says.

"A what?"

"A swan."

"What's a swan?" I say, still looking at the house.

His Noise is puzzled for a second, then I get a little pulse of sadness so I look at him. "What?"

"Nothing, pup," he says. "Memories of long ago."

Viola and Hildy are up ahead still, Viola's eyes wide and her mouth gulping like a fish.

"What did I tell ye?" Hildy asks.

Viola rushes up to the fence in front of it. She stares at the house, looking all over the metal bit, up and down, side to side. I come up by her and look, too. It's hard for a minute to think of anything to say (shut up).

"Sposed to be a swan," I finally say. "Whatever that is."

She ignores me and turns to Hildy. "Is it an Expansion Three 500?"

"What?"

"Older than that, Vi pup," Hildy says. "X Three 200."

"We got up to X Sevens," Viola says.

"Not surprised," says Hildy.

"What the ruddy hell are you talking about?" I say. "Expanshun *whatsits*?"

"Sheep!" we hear Manchee bark in the distance.

"Our settler ship," Hildy says, sounding surprised that I don't know. "An Expanshun Class Three, Series 200."

I look from face to face. Tam's Noise has a spaceship flying in it, one with a front hull that matches the upturned farmhouse.

"Oh, yeah," I say, remembering, trying to say it like I knew all along. "You build yer houses with the first tools at hand."

"Quite so, pup," Tam says. "Or ye make them works of art if yer so inclined."

"If yer wife is an engineer who can get yer damn fool sculptures to stay standing up," Hildy says.

"How do you know about all this?" I say to Viola.

She looks at the ground, away from my eyes.

"You don't mean–" I start to say but I stop.

I'm getting it.

Of *course* I'm getting it.

Way too late, like everything else, but I'm getting it.

"Yer a settler," I say. "Yer a new settler."

She looks away from me but shrugs her shoulders.

"But that ship you crashed in," I say, "that's way too tiny to be a settler ship."

"That was only a scout. My home ship is an Expansion Class Seven."

She looks at Hildy and Tam, who ain't saying nothing.

Tam's Noise is bright and curious. I can't read nothing from Hildy. I get the feeling somehow, tho, that she knew and I didn't, that Viola told her and not me, and even if it's cuz I never asked, it's still as sour a feeling as it sounds.

I look up at the sky.

"It's up there, ain't it?" I say. "Yer Expanshun Class Seven."

Viola nods.

"Yer bringing more settlers in. More settlers are coming to New World."

"Everything was broken when we crashed," Viola says. "I don't have any way to contact them. Any way to warn them not to come." She looks up with a little gasp. *"You must warn them."*

"That can't be what he meant," I say, fast. "No way."

Viola scrunches her face and eyebrows. "Why not?"

"What who meant?" Tam asks.

"How many?" I ask, still looking at Viola, feeling the world changing still and ever. "How many settlers are coming?"

Viola takes a deep breath before she answers and I'll bet you she's not even told Hildy this part.

"Thousands," she says. "There's thousands."

16

THE NIGHT OF NO APOLOGIES

"THEY WON'T be a-getting here for months," Hildy says, passing me another serving of mashed russets. Viola and I are stuffing our faces so much it's been Hildy and Tam doing all the talking.

All the *a*-talking.

"Space travel ain't like ye see it in vids," Tam says, a stream of mutton gravy tracking down his beard. "Takes years and years and years to get anywhere at all. Sixty-four to get from Old World to New World alone."

"Sixty-four years?" I say, spraying a few mashed blobs off my lips.

Tam nods. "Yer frozen for most of it, time passing you right on by, tho that's only if ye don't die on the way."

I turn to Viola. "Yer sixty-four years old?"

"Sixty-four Old World years," Tam says, tapping his fingers like he's adding something up. "Which'd be … what? Bout fifty-eight, fifty-nine New World–"

But Viola's shaking her head. "I was born on board. Never was asleep."

"So either yer ma or yer pa musta been a caretaker," Hildy says, snapping off a bite of a turnipy thing then giving me an explanashun. "One of the ones who stays awake and keeps track of the ship."

"Both of them were," Viola says. "And my dad's mother before him and granddad before that."

"Wait a minute," I say to her, two steps behind as ever. "So if we've been on New World twenty-odd years–"

"Twenty-three," says Tam. "Feels like longer."

"Then you left before we even *got* here," I say. "Or your pa or grandpa or whatever."

I look around to see if anyone's wondering what I'm wondering. "Why?" I say. "Why would you come without even knowing what's out here?"

"Why did the *first* settlers come?" Hildy asks me. "Why does anyone look for a new place to live?"

"Cuz the place yer a-leaving ain't worth staying for," Tam says. "Cuz the place yer a-leaving is so bad ye gotta leave."

"Old World's mucky, violent and crowded," Hildy says, wiping her face with a napkin, "a-splitting right into bits with people a-hating each other and a-killing each other, no one happy till everyone's miserable. Least it was all those years ago."

"I wouldn't know," Viola says, "I've never seen it. My mother and father..." She drifts off.

But I'm still thinking about being born on a spaceship, an honest to badness *spaceship*. Growing up while flying along the stars, able to go wherever you wanted, not stuck on some hateful planet which clearly don't want you. You could go anywhere. If one place didn't suit, you'd find another. Full freedom in all directions. Could there possibly be anything cooler in the whole world than that?

I don't notice there's a silence fallen at the table. Hildy's rubbing Viola's back again and I see that Viola's eyes are wet and leaking and she's started to rock a little back and forth.

"What?" I say. "What's wrong now?"

Viola's forehead just creases at me.

"*What?*" I say.

"I think maybe we talked enough about Vi's ma and pa for now," Hildy says softly. "I think maybe it's time for boy and girl pups to get some shut-eye."

"But it's hardly late at all." I look out a window. The sun ain't even hardly set. "We need to be getting to the settlement–"

"The settlement is called Farbranch," Hildy says, "and we'll get ye there first thing in the morning."

"But those men–"

"I been a-keeping the peace here since before you were born, pup," Hildy says, kindly but firmly. "I can handle whatever is or ain't a-coming."

I don't say nothing to this and Hildy ignores my Noise on the subject.

"Can I ask what yer business in Farbranch might be?" Tam says, picking at his corncob, making his asking sound less curious than his Noise says it is.

"We just need to get there," I say.

"Both of ye?"

I look at Viola. She's stopped crying but her face is still

puffy. I don't answer Tam's asking.

"Well there's plenty of work going," Hildy says, standing and taking up her plate. "If that's what yer after. They can always use more hands in the orchards."

Tam stands and they clear the table, taking the dishes into their kitchen and leaving me and Viola sitting there by ourselves. We can hear them chatting in there, lightly enough and Noise-blocked enough for us not to be able to make it out.

"Do you really think we oughta stay the whole night?" I say, keeping my voice low.

But she answers in a violent whisper, like I didn't even ask an asking. "Just because my thoughts and feelings don't spill out into the world in a shout that never stops doesn't mean I don't have them."

I turn to her, surprised. *"Huh?"*

She keeps whispering something fierce. "Every time you think, *Oh, she's just emptiness,* or, *There's nothing going on inside her,* or, *Maybe I can dump her with these two*, I hear it, okay? I hear every stupid thing you think, all right? And I understand *way* more than I want to."

"Oh, yeah?" I whisper back, tho my Noise ain't a whisper at all. "Every time *you* think something or feel something or have some stupid thought, I *don't* hear it, so how am I sposed to know any effing thing about you, huh? How am I sposed to know what's going on if you keep it secret?"

"I'm *not* keeping it secret." She's clenching her teeth now. "I'm being *normal*."

"Not normal for here, *Vi*."

"And how would you know? I can hear you being

surprised by just about everything they say. Didn't they have a school where you're from? Didn't you learn *anything*?"

"History ain't so important when yer just trying to survive," I say, spitting it out under my breath.

"That's actually when it's *most* important," Hildy says, standing at the end of the table. "And if this silly argument twixt ye two ain't enough to prove yer tired, then yer tired beyond all sense. C'mon."

Viola and I glare at each other but we get up and follow Hildy into a large common room.

"Todd!" Manchee barks from a corner, not getting up from the mutton bone Tam gave him earlier.

"We've long since took over our guest rooms for other purposes," Hildy says. "Ye'll have to make do on the settees."

We help her make up some sheets and beds, Viola still scowling, my Noise a buzzy red.

"Now," Hildy says when we're all done. "Apologize to each other."

"What?" Viola says. "*Why?*"

"I don't see how this is any of yer business," I say.

"Never go to sleep on an argument," Hildy says, hands on hips, looking like she ain't never gonna budge and would be pleased to see someone try and make her. "Not if ye want to stay friends."

Viola and I don't say nothing.

"He saved yer life?" Hildy says to Viola.

Viola looks down before finally saying, "Yeah."

"That's right, I did," I say.

"And she saved yers at the bridge, didn't she?" Hildy says.

Oh.

"Yes," Hildy says. "*Oh*. Don't ye both think that counts for something?"

We still don't say nothing.

Hildy sighs. "Fine. Any two pups so close to adulthood could maybe be left to their own apologies, I reckon." She makes her way out without even saying good night.

I turn my back on Viola and she turns her back on me. I take off my shoes and get myself under the sheet on one of Hildy's "settees" which seems to be just a fancy word for couch. Viola does the same. Manchee leaps up on my settee and curls himself by my feet.

There's no sound except my Noise and a few crackles from a fire it's too hot for. It can't be much later than dusk but the softness of the cushions and the softness of the sheet and the too-warm of the fire and I'm already pretty much closing my eyes.

"Todd?" Viola says from her settee across the room.

I swim up from sinking down to sleep. "What?"

She don't say nothing for a second and I guess she must be thinking of her apology.

But no.

"What does your book say you're supposed to do when you get to Farbranch?"

My Noise gets a bit redder. "Never you mind what my book says," I say. "That's my property, meant for me."

"You know when you showed me the map back in the woods?" she says. "And you said we had to get to this settlement? You remember what was written underneath?"

"Course I do."

"What was it?"

There ain't no poking in her voice, not that I can hear, but that's gotta be what it is, ain't it? Poking?

"Just go to sleep, will ya?" I say.

"It was *Farbranch*," she says. "The name of the place we're meant to be heading."

"Shut up." My Noise is getting buzzy again.

"There's no shame in not being able to–"

"I said, *shut up*!"

"I could help you–"

I get up suddenly, dumping Manchee off the settee with a thump. I grab my sheets and blanket under my arm and I stomp off to the room where we ate. I throw them on the floor and lay down, a room away from Viola and all her meaningless, evil quiet.

Manchee stays in there with her. Typical.

I close my eyes but I don't sleep for ages and ages.

Till I finally do, I guess.

Cuz I'm on a path and it's the swamp but it's also the town and it's also my farm and Ben's there and Cillian's there and Viola's there and they're all saying, "What're you doing here, Todd?" and Manchee's barking "Todd! Todd!" and Ben's grabbing me by the arm to drag me out the door and Cillian's got his arm round my shoulders pushing me up the path and Viola's setting the campfire box by the front door of our farmhouse and the Mayor's horse rides right thru our front door and smashes her flat and a croc with the face of Aaron is rearing up behind Ben's shoulders and I'm yelling "No!" and–

And I'm sitting up and I'm sweating everywhere and my heart's racing like a horse and I'm expecting to see the

Mayor and Aaron standing right over me.

But it's only Hildy and she's saying, "What the devil are ye a-doing in here?" She's standing in the doorway, morning sun flooding in behind her so bright I have to raise my hand to block it out.

"More comfortable," I mumble but my chest is thumping.

"I'll bet," she says, reading my just-waking Noise. "Breakfast is on."

The smell of the mutton-strip bacon frying wakes Viola and Manchee. I let Manchee out for his morning poo but Viola and I don't say nothing to each other. Tam comes in as we eat, having I guess been out feeding the sheep. That's what I'd be doing if I were home.

Home, I think.

Anyway.

"Buck up, pup," Tam says, plonking a cup of coffee down in front of me. I keep my face way down as I drink it.

"Anybody out there?" I say into my cup.

"Not a whisper," Tam says. "And it's a beautiful day."

I glance up at Viola but she ain't looking at me. In fact, we get all the way thru the food, thru washing our faces, thru changing our clothes and re-packing our bags, all without saying nothing to each other.

"Good luck to ye both," Tam says, as we're about to leave with Hildy towards Farbranch. "It's always nice when two people who don't got no one else find each other as friends."

And we really don't say nothing to that.

"C'mon, pups," Hildy says. "Time's a-wasting."

We get back on the path, which before too long reconnects with the same road that musta gone across the bridge.

"Used to be the main road from Farbranch to Prentisstown," Hildy says, hoisting her own small pack. "Or New Elizabeth, as it was then."

"As what was then?" I ask.

"Prentisstown," she says. "Used to be called New Elizabeth."

"It never did," I say, raising up my eyebrows.

Hildy looks at me, her own eyebrows mocking mine. "Was it never? I must be mistaken then."

"Must be," I say, watching her.

Viola makes a scoffing sound with her lips. I send her a look of death.

"Will there be somewhere we can stay?" she asks Hildy, ignoring me.

"I'll take ye to my sister," Hildy says. "Deputy Mayor this year, don't ye know?"

"What'll we do then?" I say, kicking at the dirt as we walk on.

"Reckon that's up to ye two," Hildy says. "Ye've gotta be the ones in charge of yer own destinies, don't ye?"

"Not so far," I hear Viola say under her breath and it's so exactly the words I have in my Noise that we both look up and catch each other's eyes.

We almost smile. But we don't.

And that's when we start hearing the Noise.

"Ah," Hildy says, hearing it too. "Farbranch."

The road comes out on the top of a little vale.

And there it is.

The other settlement. The other settlement that wasn't spozed to be.

Where Ben wanted us to go.

Where we might be safe.

The first thing I see is where the valley road winds down thru orchards, orderly rows of well-tended trees with paths and irrigashun systems, all carrying on down a hill towards buildings and a creek at the bottom, flat and easy and snaking its way back to meet the bigger river no doubt.

And all thru-out are men and women.

Most are scattered working in the orchard, wearing heavy work aprons, all the men in long sleeves, the women in long skirts, cutting down pine-like fruits with machetes or carrying away baskets or working on the irrigashun pipes and so on.

Men and women, women and men.

A coupla dozen men, maybe, is my general impression, less than Prentisstown.

Who knows how many women.

Living in a whole other place.

The Noise (and silence) of them all floats up like a light fog.

Two, please and **The way I see it is** and **Weedy waste** and **She might say yes, she might not** and **If service ends at one, then I can always** and so on and so on, never ending, amen.

I just stop in the road and gape for a second, not ready to walk down into it yet.

Cuz it's weird.

It's more than weird, truth to tell.

It's all so, I don't know, *calm*. Like normal chatter you'd have with yer mates. Nothing accidental nor abusive.

And nobody's hardly longing for nothing.

No awful, awful, despairing longing nowhere I can hear or feel.

"We sure as ruddy heck ain't in Prentisstown no more," I say to Manchee under my breath.

Not a second later, I hear Prentisstown? float in from a field right next to us.

And then I hear it in a coupla different places. Prentisstown? and Prentisstown? and then I notice that the men in the orchards nearby ain't picking fruit or whatever any more. They're standing up. They're looking at us.

"Come on," Hildy says. "Keep on a-walking. It's just curiosity."

The word Prentisstown multiplies along the fields like a crackling fire. Manchee brings hisself in closer to my legs. We're being stared at on all sides as we carry on. Even Viola steps in a bit so we're a tighter group.

"Not to worry," Hildy says. "There'll just be a lot of people who'll want to meet–"

She stops mid-sentence.

A man has stepped onto the path in front of us.

His face don't look at all like he wants to meet us.

"Prentisstown?" he says, his Noise getting uncomfortably red, uncomfortably fast.

"Morning, Matthew," Hildy says, "I was just a-bringing–"

"Prentisstown," the man says again, no longer an asking, and he's not looking at Hildy.

He's looking straight at me.

"Yer not welcome here," he says. "Not welcome at all."

And he's got the biggest machete in his hand you ever seen.

17

ENCOUNTER IN AN ORCHARD

MY HAND GOES right behind my rucksack to my own knife.

"Leave it, Todd pup," Hildy says, keeping her eyes on the man. "That's not how this is gonna go."

"What do ye think yer a-bringing into our village, Hildy?" the man says, hefting his machete in his hand, still looking at me and there's real surprise in his asking and–

And is that *hurt*?

"I'm a-bringing in a boy pup and a girl pup what's lost their way," Hildy says. "Stand aside, Matthew."

"I don't see a boy pup nowhere," Matthew says, his eyes starting to burn. He's massively tall, shoulders like an ox and a thickened brow with lots of bafflement but not much tenderness. He looks like a walking, talking thunderstorm. "I see me a Prentisstown man. I see me a Prentisstown man with Prentisstown filth all over his Prentisstown Noise."

"That's not what yer a-seeing," Hildy says. "Look close."

Matthew's Noise is already lurching on me like hands pressing in, forcing its way into my own thinking, trying to ransack the room. It's angry and asking and Noisy as a fire, so uneven I can't make hide nor hair of it.

"Ye know the law, Hildy," he says.

The law?

"The law is for men," Hildy says, her voice staying calm, like we were standing there talking bout the weather. Can't she see how red this man's Noise is getting? Red ain't yer colour if you wanna have a chat. "This here pup ain't a man yet."

"I've still got twenty-eight days," I say, without thinking.

"Yer numbers don't mean nothing here, boy," Matthew spits. "I don't care how many days away ye are."

"Calm yerself, Matthew," Hildy says, sterner than I'd want her to. But to my surprise, Matthew looks at her all sore and steps back a step. "He's a-fleeing Prentisstown, pup," she says, a little softer. "He's a-running away."

Matthew looks at her suspiciously and back to me but he's lowering the machete. A little.

"Just like ye did yerself once," Hildy says to him.

What?

"Yer from Prentisstown?" I blurt out.

Up comes the machete and Matthew steps forward again, threatening enough to start Manchee barking, "Back! Back! Back!"

"I was from *New Elizabeth*," Matthew growls, twixt clenched teeth. "I'm *never* from Prentisstown, boy, not never, and don't ye forget it."

I see clearer flashes in his Noise now. Of impossible

things, of crazy things, coming in a rush, like he can't help it, things worse than the worst of the illegal vids Mr Hammar used to let out on the sly to the oldest and rowdiest of the boys in town, the kind where people seemed to die for real but there was no way of ever knowing for sure. Images and words and blood and screaming and–

"Stop that right this second!" Hildy shouts. "Control yerself, Matthew Lyle. Control yerself *right now*."

Matthew's Noise subsides, sudden-like but still roiling, without quite so much control as Tam but still more than any man in Prentisstown.

But as soon as I think it, his machete raises again. "Ye'll not say that word in our town, boy," he says. "Not if ye know what's good for ye."

"There'll be no threats to guests of mine as long as I'm alive," Hildy says, her voice strong and clear. "Is that understood?"

Matthew looks at her, he don't nod, he don't say yes, but we all understand that he understands. He ain't happy bout it, tho. His Noise still pokes and presses at me, slapping me if it could. He finally looks over to Viola.

"And who might this be then?" he says, pointing the machete at her.

And it happens before I even know I'm doing it, I swear.

One minute I'm standing there behind everyone and the next thing I know, I'm between Matthew and Viola, I have my knife out pointing at him, my own Noise falling like an avalanche and my mouth saying, "You best take two steps away from her and you best be taking 'em right quick."

"Todd!" Hildy shouts.

And "Todd!" Manchee barks.

And "Todd!" Viola shouts.

But there I am, knife out, my heart thumping fast like it's finally figured out what I'm doing.

But there ain't no stepping back.

Now how do you suppose *that* happened?

"Give me a reason, Prentissboy," Matthew says, hoisting the machete. "Just give me one good reason."

"Enough!" Hildy says.

And her voice has got something in it this time, like the word of rule, so much so that Matthew flinches a little. He's still holding up his machete, still glaring at me, glaring at Hildy, his Noise throbbing like a wound.

And then his face twists a little.

And he begins, of all things, to cry.

Angrily, furiously trying not to, but standing there, big as a bullock, machete in hand, crying.

Which ain't what I was expecting.

Hildy's voice pulls back a bit. "Put the knife away, Todd pup."

Matthew drops his machete to the ground and puts an arm across his eyes as he snuffles and yowls and moans. I look over at Viola. She's just staring at Matthew, probably as confused as I am.

I drop the knife to my side but I don't let it go. Not yet.

Matthew's taking deep breaths, pain Noise and grief Noise dripping everywhere, and fury, too, at losing control so publicly. "It's meant to be over," he coughs. "Long over."

"I know," Hildy says, going forward and putting a hand on his arm.

"What's going on?" I say.

"Never you mind, Todd pup," Hildy says. "Prentisstown has a sad history."

"That's what Tam said," I say. "As if I don't know."

Matthew looks up. "Ye don't know the first bit of it, boy," he says, teeth clenched again.

"That's enough now," Hildy says. "This boy ain't yer enemy." She looks at me, eyes a bit wide. "And he's putting away his knife for that very reason."

I twist the knife in my hand a time or two but then I reach behind my rucksack and put it away. Matthew's glaring at me again but he's starting to back off for real now and I'm wondering who Hildy is that he's obeying her.

"They're both innocent as lambs, Matthew pup," Hildy says.

"Ain't nobody innocent," Matthew says bitterly, sniffing away his last bits of weepy snot and hefting up his machete again. "Nobody at all."

He turns his back and strides into the orchard, not looking back.

Everyone else is still staring at us.

"The day only ages," Hildy says to them, turning round in a circle. "There'll be time enough for a-meeting and a-greeting later on."

Me and Viola watch as the workers start returning to their trees and their baskets and their whatevers, some eyes still on us but most people getting back to work.

"Are you in charge here or something?" I ask.

"Or something, Todd pup. C'mon, ye haven't even seen the town yet."

"What law was he talking about?"

"Long story, pup," she says. "I'll tell ye later."

The path, still wide enough for men and vehicles and horses, tho I only see men, curves its way down thru more orchards on the hillsides of the little vale.

"What kind of fruit is that?" Viola asks, as two women cross the road in front of us with full baskets, the women watching us as they go.

"Crested pine," Hildy says. "Sweet as sugar, loaded with vitamins."

"Never heard of it," I say.

"No," Hildy says. "Ye wouldn't have."

I look at way too many trees for a settlement that can't have more than fifty people in it. "Is that all you eat here?"

"Course not," Hildy says. "We trade with the other settlements down the road."

The surprise is so clear in my Noise that even Viola laughs a little.

"Ye didn't think it was just two settlements on all of New World, did ye?" Hildy asks.

"No," I say, feeling my face turn red, "but all the other settlements were wiped out in the war."

"Mmm," Hildy says, biting her bottom lip, nodding but not saying nothing more.

"Is that Haven?" Viola says quietly.

"Is what Haven?" I ask.

"The other settlement," Viola says, not quite looking at me. "You said there was a cure for Noise in Haven."

"Ach," Hildy psshts. "That's just rumours and speckalashuns."

"Is Haven a real place?" I ask.

"It's the biggest and first of the settlements," Hildy says. "Closest New World's got to a big city. Miles away. Not for peasants like us."

"I've never heard of it," I say again.

No one says nothing to this and I get the feeling they're being polite. Viola's not really looked at me since the weirdness back there with me and Matthew and the knife. To be honest, I don't know what to make of it neither.

So everyone just keeps walking.

There's maybe seven buildings total in Farbranch, smaller than Prentisstown and just buildings after all but somehow so different, too, it feels like I've wandered right off New World into some whole other place altogether.

The first building we pass is a tiny stone church, fresh and clean and open, not at all like the darkness Aaron preached in. Farther on is a general store with a mechanic's garage by it, tho I don't see much by way of heavy machinery around. Haven't even seen a fissionbike, not even a dead one. There's a building that looks like a meeting hall, another with a doctor's snakes carved into the front, and two barn-like buidings that look like storage.

"Not much," Hildy says. "But it's home."

"Not yer home," I say. "You live way outside."

"So do most people," Hildy says. "Even when yer used to it, it's nice to only have the Noise of yer most beloved a-hanging round yer house. Town gets a bit rackety."

I listen out for rackety but it still ain't *nothing* like Prentisstown. Sure there's Noise in Farbranch, men doing their usual boring daily business, chattering their thoughts that don't mean nothing, Chop, chop, chop and I'll only give seven for the dozen and Listen to her sing there, just listen and That coop needs fixing tonight and He's gonna fall right off of that and on and on and on, so heedless and safe-sounding to me it feels like taking a bath in comparison to the black Noise I'm used to.

"Oh, it gets black, Todd pup," Hildy says. "Men still have their tempers. Women, too."

"Some people would call it impolite to always be listening to a man's Noise," I say, looking round me.

"Too true, pup." She grins. "But ye aren't a man yet. Ye said so yerself."

We cross the central strip of the town. A few men and women walk to and fro, some tipping their hats to Hildy, most just staring at us.

I stare back.

If you listen close, you can hear where the women are in town almost as clear as the men. They're like rocks that the Noise washes over and once yer used to it you can feel where their silences are, dotted all about, Viola and Hildy ten times over and I'll bet if I stopped and stood here I could tell exactly how many women are in each building.

And mixed in with the sound of so many men, you know what?

The silence don't feel half so lonesome.

And then I see some teeny, tiny people, watching us from behind a bush.

Kids.

Kids smaller than me, *younger* than me.

The first I ever seen.

A woman carrying a basket spies them and makes a shooing movement with her hands. She frowns and smiles at the same time and the kids all run off giggling round the back of the church.

I watch 'em go. I feel my chest pull a little.

"Ye coming?" Hildy calls after me.

"Yeah," I say, still watching where the kids went. I turn and keep on following, my head still twisted back.

Kids. Real kids. *Safe* enough for kids and I find myself wondering if Viola would be able to feel at home here with all these nice-seeming men, all these women and children. I find myself wondering if she'd be safe, even if I'm obviously not.

I'll bet she would.

I look at Viola and catch her looking away.

Hildy's led us to the house farthest along the buildings of Farbranch. It's got steps that go up the front and a little flag flying from a pole out front.

I stop.

"This is a mayor's house," I say. "Ain't it?"

"Deputy Mayor," Hildy says, walking up the steps, clomping her boots loud against the wood. "My sister."

"And *my* sister," says a woman opening the door, a plumper, younger, frownier version of Hildy.

"Francia," Hildy says.

"Hildy," Francia says.

They nod at each other, not hug or shake hands, just nod.

"What trouble d'ye think yer bringing into my town?" Francia says, eyeing us up.

"Yer town, is it now?" Hildy says, smiling, eyebrows up. She turns to us. "Like I told Matthew Lyle, it's just two pups a-fleeing for safety, seeking their refuge." She turns back to her sister. "And if Farbranch ain't a refuge, sister, then what is it?"

"It's not them I'm a-talking about," Francia says, looking at us, arms crossed. "It's the army that's a-following them."

18

FARBRANCH

"ARMY?" I say, my stomach knotting right up. Viola says it at the same time I do but there's nothing funny bout it this time.

"What army?" Hildy frowns.

"Rumours a-floating down from the far fields of an army a-gathering on the other side of the river," Francia says. "Men on horseback. Prentisstown men."

Hildy purses her lips. "*Five* men on horseback," she says. "Not an army. Those were just the posse sent after our young pups here."

Francia don't look too convinced. I never seen arms so crossed.

"And the river gorge crossing is down anyhow," Hildy continues, "so there ain't gonna be anyone a-coming into Farbranch any time soon." She looks back at us. "An *army*," she says, shaking her head. "Honestly."

"If there's a threat, sister," Francia says, "it's my duty–"

Hildy rolls her eyes. "Don't be a-talking to me about yer duty, sister," she says, stepping past Francia and opening the front door to the house. "I *invented* yer duty. C'mon, pups, let's get ye inside."

Viola and I don't move. Francia don't invite us to neither.

"Todd?" Manchee barks by my feet.

I take a deep breath and go up the front steps. "Howdy, mim," I say.

"*Mam,*" Viola whispers behind me.

"Howdy, mam," I say, trying not to miss a beat. "I'm Todd. That's Viola." Francia's arms are still crossed, like there's a prize for it. "There really were only five men," I say, tho the word *army* is echoing round my Noise.

"And I should just trust ye?" Francia says. "A boy who's a-being chased?" She looks down to Viola, still waiting on the bottom step. "I can just imagine why *ye* were running."

"Oh, stuff it, Francia," Hildy says, still holding the door open for us.

Francia turns and shooshes Hildy outta the way. "I'll be in charge of entry into my own house, thank ye very much," Francia says, then to us, "Well, c'mon if yer coming."

And that's how we first see the hospitality of Farbranch. We go inside. Francia and Hildy bickering twixt themselves about whether Francia's got a place to put us in for however long we might wanna stay. Hildy wins the bickering and Francia shows me and Viola to separate small rooms next to each other one floor up.

"Yer dog has to sleep outside," Francia says.

"But he's–"

"That wasn't a question," Francia says, leaving the room.

I follow her out to the landing. She don't turn back as she goes downstairs. In less than a minute, I can hear her and Hildy arguing again, trying to keep their voices down. Viola comes outta her room to listen, too. We stand there for a second, wondering.

"Whaddya think?" I say.

She don't look at me. Then it's like she decides to look at me and does.

"I don't know," she says. "What do *you* think?"

I shrug my shoulders. "She don't seem too happy to see us," I say, "but it's still safer than I've felt in a while. Behind walls and such." I shrug again. "And Ben wanted us to get here and all."

Which is true but I still ain't sure if it feels right.

Viola's clutching her arms to herself, just like Francia but not like Francia at all. "I know what you mean."

"So I guess it'll do for now."

"Yes," Viola says. "For now."

We listen to a bit more arguing.

"What you did back there–" Viola says.

"It was stupid," I say, real fast. "I don't wanna talk about it."

My face is starting to burn so I step back in my little room. I stand there and chew my lip. The room looks like it used to belong to an old person. Kinda smells that way, too, but at least it's a real bed. I go to my rucksack and I open it.

I look round to make sure no one's followed me in and I pull out the book. I open it to the map, to the arrows that point down thru the swamp, to the river on the other side. No bridge on the map but there's the settlement. With a word underneath it.

"Fayre," I say, to myself. "Fayre braw nk."

Which I guess is Farbranch.

I breathe loud thru my nose as I look at the page of writing on the back of the map. *You must warn them* (of course, of *course*, shut up) still underlined at the bottom. Like Viola said, tho, warn who? Warn Farbranch? Warn Hildy?

"About what?" I say. I thumb thru the book and there's pages of stuff, pages and pages of it, words on words on words on words, like Noise shoved down onto paper till you can't make no sense from it. How can I warn anybody about all *this*?

"Aw, Ben," I say under my breath. "What were you thinking?"

"Todd?" Hildy calls from downstairs. "Vi?"

I close the book and look at its cover.

Later. I'll ask about it later.

I *will*.

Later.

I put it away and I go downstairs. Viola's already waiting there. Hildy and Francia, arms crossed again, waiting, too.

"I've got to get back to my farm, pups," Hildy says. "Work to do for the good of all but Francia's agreed to look after ye for today and I'll come back tonight to see how yer a-getting on."

Viola and I look at each other, suddenly not wanting Hildy to leave.

"Thank ye for that," Francia says, frowning. "Despite what my sister may have told ye two about me, I'm hardly an ogre."

"She didn't say–" I start to say before I stop myself, even tho my Noise finishes it up for me. *Anything about you.*

"Yeah, well, that's typical," Francia says, glaring at Hildy but not seeming too put out. "Ye can stay here for the time being. Pa and Auntie are long dead and there's not too much call for their rooms these days."

I was right. Old person's room.

"But we're a working town here in Farbranch." Francia looks from me to Viola and back again. "And ye'll be expected to earn yer keep, even if it's just for a day or two while ye make whatever plans yer going to make."

"We're still not sure," Viola says.

"Hmmph," Francia hmmphs. "And if ye two stay on past this first cresting of the orchards, there'll be a-schooling for ye to do."

"School?" I say.

"School and church," Hildy says. "That's if ye stay long enough." I'm guessing she's reading my Noise again. "Are ye going to stay long enough?"

I don't say nothing and Viola don't say nothing and Franica hmmphs again.

"Please, Mrs Francia?" Viola says as Francia turns to talk to Hildy.

"Just Francia, child," Francia says, looking surprised. "What is it?"

"Is there somewhere I can send a message back to my ship?"

"Yer ship," Francia says. "This a-being that settler ship way out in the dark black yonder?" Her mouth draws thin. "With all them people on it?"

Viola nods. "We were supposed to report back. Let them know what we found."

Viola's voice is so quiet and her face so looking and hopeful, so open and wide and ready for disappointment that I feel that familiar tug of sadness again, pulling all Noise into it like grief, like being lost. I put a hand on the back of a settee to steady myself.

"Ah, girl pup," Hildy says, her voice getting suspiciously gentle again. "I'm guessing ye tried to contact us folks down here on New World when ye were a-scouting the planet?"

"Yeah," Viola says. "No one answered."

Hildy and Francia exchange nods. "Yer a-forgetting we were church settlers," Francia says, "getting away from worldly things to set up our own little utopia, so we let that kinda machinery go to rack and ruin as we got on with the business of surviving."

Viola's eyes get a little wider. "You have no way of communicating with anyone?"

"We don't have communicators for other *settlements*," Francia says, "much less the beyond."

"We're farmers, pup," Hildy says. "Simple farmers, looking for a simpler way of life. That was the whole point we were a-trying for in flying all this ridiculous way to get here. Setting down the things that caused such strife for people of old." She taps her fingers on a table-top. "Didn't quite work out that way, tho."

"We weren't really expecting no others," Francia says. "Not the way Old World was when we left."

"So I'm stuck here?" Viola says, her voice a little shaky.

"Until yer ship arrives," Hildy says. "I'm afraid so."

"How far out are they?" Francia asks.

"System entry in 24 weeks," Viola says quietly.

"Perihelion four weeks later. Orbital transfer two weeks after that."

"I'm sorry, child," Francia says. "Looks like yer ours for seven months."

Viola turns away from all of us, obviously taking this news in.

A lot can happen in seven months.

"Well, now," Hildy says, making her voice bright, "I hear tell they got all kindsa things in Haven. Fissioncars and city streets and more stores than ye can shake a stick at. Ye might try there before ye really start a-worrying, yes?"

Hildy makes an eye towards Francia and Francia says, "Todd pup? Why don't we get you a-working in the barn? Yer a farm boy, ain't ye?"

"But–" I start to say.

"All kinds of work to be done on a farm," Francia says, "as I'm sure ye know all too well–"

Chattering away like this, Francia gets me out the back door. Looking over my shoulder, I can see Hildy comforting Viola in soft words, unhearable words, things being said that I don't know yet again.

Francia closes the door behind us and leads me and Manchee across the main road to one of the big storage houses I saw when we were walking in. I can see men pulling handcarts up to the main front door and another man unloading the baskets of orchard fruit.

"This is east barn," Francia says, "where we store things ready to be traded. Wait here."

I wait and she walks up to the man unloading the baskets from the cart. They talk for a minute and I can hear

Prentisstown? clear as day in his Noise and the sudden surge of feeling behind it. It's a slightly different feeling than before but it fades before I can read it and Francia comes back.

"Ivan says ye can work in the back a-sweeping up."

"*Sweeping up?*" I say, kinda appalled. "I know how farms work, mim, and I–"

"I'm sure ye do but ye may have noticed that Prentisstown ain't our most popular neighbour. Best to keep ye away from everyone till we've all had a chance to get used to ye. Fair enough?"

She's still stern, still arms crossed, but actually, yeah, this seems sensible and tho her face ain't kind exactly maybe it sorta is.

"Okay," I say.

Francia nods and takes me over to Ivan, who looks about Ben's age, but short, dark-haired and arms like effing tree trunks.

"Ivan, this is Todd," Francia says.

I hold out my hand to shake. Ivan doesn't take it. He just eyeballs me something fierce.

"You'll work in back," he says. "And you'll keep yerself and yer dog outta my way."

Francia leaves us and Ivan takes me inside, points out a broom, and I get to work. And that's how I start my first day in Farbranch: inside a dark barn, sweeping dust from one corner to another, seeing one single stitch of blue sky out a door at the far end.

Oh, the joy.

"Poo, Todd," Manchee says.

"Not in here, you don't."

It's a pretty big barn, seventy-five to eighty metres from end to end, maybe, and about half full of baskets of crested pine. There's a section with big rolls of silage, too, packed up to the ceiling with thin rope, and another section with huge sheaves of wheat ready to be ground into flour.

"You sell this stuff on to other settlements?" I call out to Ivan.

"Time for chatter later," he calls back from the front.

I don't say nothing to this but something kinda rude shows up in my Noise before I can stop it. I hurry and get back to sweeping.

The morning waxes on. I think about Ben and Cillian. I think about Viola. I think about Aaron and the Mayor. I think about the word *army* and how it's making my stomach clench.

I don't know.

It don't feel right to be stopped. Not after all that running.

Everyone's acting like it's safe here but I don't know.

Manchee wanders in and out the back doors as I sweep, sometimes chasing the pink moths I stir from faint corners. Ivan keeps his distance, I keep mine, but I can see all the people who come to his door and drop off goods taking a deep, long look to the back of the barn, sometimes squinting into the darkness to see if they can find me there, the Prentisstown boy.

So they hate Prentisstown, I got that. *I* hate Prentisstown but I got more cause for grief than any of them.

I start noticing things, too, as the morning gets older. Like that tho men and women both do the heavy labour, women give more orders that more men follow. And with Francia being Deputy Mayor and Hildy being whoever she is in Farbranch, I'm beginning to think it's a town run by women. I can often hear their silences as they walk by outside and I can hear men's Noise responding to it, too, sometimes with chafing but usually in a way that just gets on with things.

Men's Noise here, too, is a *lot* more controlled than what I'm used to. With so many women around and from what I know of the Noise of Prentisstown, you'd think the sky would be full of Noisy women with no clothes doing the most remarkable things you could think of. And sure you hear that sometimes here, men are men after all, but more of the time it's songs or it's prayers or it's directed to the work at hand.

They're calm here in Farbranch but they're a little spooky.

Once in a while, I see if I can hear (not hear) Viola.

But no.

At lunchtime, Francia comes to the back of the barn with a sandwich and a jug of water.

"Where's Viola?" I ask.

"Yer welcome," Francia says.

"For what?"

Francia sighs and says, "Viola's in the orchards, gathering dropped fruits."

I want to ask how she is but I don't and Francia refuses to read it in my Noise.

"How ye getting on?" she asks.

"I know how to do a lot more than ruddy sweep."

"Mind yer language, pup. There'll be time enough to get ye to real work."

She don't stay, walking back towards the front, having another word with Ivan and then she's off to do whatever Deputy Mayors fill their days with.

Can I say? It makes no sense but I sorta like her. Probably cuz she reminds me of Cillian and all the things that used to drive me crazy about him. Memory is stupid, ain't it?

I dig into my sandwich and I'm chewing my first bite when I hear Ivan's Noise approaching.

"I'll sweep up my crumbs," I say.

To my surprise, he laughs, kinda roughly. "I'm sure ye will." He takes a bite of his own sandwich. "Francia says there's a village meeting tonight," he says after a minute.

"Bout me?" I ask.

"Bout ye both. Ye and the girl. Ye and the girl what escaped Prentisstown."

His Noise is strange. It's cautious but strong, like he's checking me out. I don't read no hostility, not towards me, anyway, but *something's* percolating in it.

"We gonna meet everyone?" I say.

"Ye might. We'll all be a-talking bout ye first."

"If there's a vote," I say, chomping on the sandwich, "I think I lose."

"Ye've got Hildy a-speaking for yer side," he says. "That counts for more than aught in Farbranch." He swallows his own bite. "And the people here are kind people and good. We've taken in Prentisstown folk before. Not for a while but from way back in the bad times."

"The war?" I say.

He looks at me, his Noise sizing me up, what I know. "Yeah," he says, "the war." He turns his head round the barn, casual-like, but I get the feeling he's looking to see if we're alone. He turns back and fixes his eye on me. An eye that's really looking for something. "And then, too," he says, "not all of us feel the same."

"Bout what?" I say, not liking his look, not liking his buzz.

"Bout history." He's talking low, his eyes still poring into me, leaning a little closer.

I lean back a little. "I don't know what you mean."

"Prentisstown's still got allies," he whispers, "hidden away in surprising places."

His Noise gets pictures in it, small ones, like Noise speaking just to me and I'm starting to see them clearer and clearer, bright things, wet things, fast things, the sun shining down on red–

"Puppies! Puppies!" Manchee barks in the corner. I jump and even Ivan startles and his Noise pictures fade right quick. Manchee keeps barking and I hear a whole raft of giggling that ain't him at all. I look.

A group of kids is kneeling down, peeking in thru a torn-away board, smiling, laughing with daring, pushing each other closer to the hole.

Pointing at me.

And all so small.

So small.

I mean, *look* at 'em.

"Get outta here, ye rats!" Ivan calls but there's humour

in his voice and Noise, all trace of what was before hidden again. There's squeals of laughter outside the hole in the wall as the kids scatter.

And that's it, they're gone.

Like I mighta made 'em up.

"Puppies, Todd!" Manchee barks. "Puppies!"

"I know," I say, scratching his head when he comes over. "I know."

Ivan claps his hands together. "That's lunch then. Back to work." He gives me one more important look before he heads back to the front of the barn.

"What was that all about?" I say to Manchee.

"Puppies," he murmurs, digging his face into my hand.

And so there follows an afternoon pretty much exactly like my morning. Sweeping, folks stopping by, a break for water where Ivan don't say nothing to me, more sweeping.

I spend some time trying to think about what we might do next. If it's even *we* who's doing it. Farbranch'll have its meeting about us and they'll definitely keep Viola till her ship arrives, anyone can see that, but will they want me?

And if they do, do I stay?

And do I warn them?

I get a burning in my stomach every time I think about the book so I keep changing the subject.

After what seems like forever, the sun starts to set. There's no more damn sweeping I can do. I've already covered the whole barn more than once, counted the baskets, re-counted them, made an attempt to fix the loose board in the wall even tho no one asked me to. There's only so much you can ruddy well do if no one lets you leave a barn.

"Ain't that the truth?" Hildy says, standing there suddenly.

"You shoudn't sneak up on people like that," I say. "All you quiet folk."

"There's some food over at Francia's house for ye and for Viola. Why don't ye go on there, get something to eat?"

"While you all have yer meeting?"

"While we all have our meeting, yes, pup," Hildy says. "Viola's already in the house, no doubt eating all yer dinner."

"Hungry, Todd!" Manchee barks.

"There's food for ye, too, puppup," Hildy says, leaning down to pet him. He flops right over on his back for her, no dignity whatsoever.

"What's this meeting really about?" I ask.

"Oh, the new settlers that are a-coming. That's big news." She looks up from Manchee to me. "And introducing ye around, of course. Getting the town used to the idea of a-welcoming ye."

"And are they gonna *a-welcome* us?"

"People are scared of what they don't know, Todd pup," she says, standing. "Once they know ye, the problem goes away."

"Will we be able to stay?"

"I reckon so," she says. "If ye want to."

I don't say nothing to that.

"Ye get on up to the house," she says. "I'll come collect ye both when the time is right."

I only nod in response and she gives a little wave and leaves, walking back across a barn that's growing ever darker. I take the broom back to where it was hanging, my steps echoing. I can hear the Noise of men and the silence of women gathering across the town in the meeting hall. The word Prentisstown filters in most heavily and my name and Viola's name and Hildy's name.

And I gotta say, tho there's fear and suspishun in it, I don't get a feeling of overwhelming non-welcome. There's more askings than there is anger of the Matthew Lyle sort.

Which, you know, maybe. Maybe that ain't so bad after all.

"C'mon, Manchee," I say, "let's go get some food."

"Food, Todd!" he barks along at my heels.

"I wonder how Viola's day was," I say.

And as I step towards the entrance to the barn I realize one bit of Noise is separating itself from the general murmuring outside.

One bit of Noise lifting from the stream.

And heading for the barn.

Coming up right outside it.

I stop, deep in the dark of the barn.

A shadow steps into the far doorway.

Matthew Lyle.

And his Noise is saying, Ye ain't going nowhere, boy.

19

FURTHER CHOICES OF A KNIFE

"BACK! BACK! BACK!" Manchee immediately starts barking.

The moons glint off Matthew Lyle's machete.

I reach behind me. I'd hidden the sheath under my shirt while I worked but the knife is definitely still there. Definitely. I take it and hold it out at my side.

"No old mama to protect ye this time," Matthew says, swinging his machete back and forth, like he's trying to cut the air into slices. "No skirts to hide ye from what ye did."

"I didn't do nothing," I say, taking a step backwards, trying to keep my Noise from showing the back door behind me.

"Don't matter," Matthew says, walking forward as I step back. "We got a law here in this town."

"I don't have no quarrel with you," I say.

"But I've got one with *ye*, boy," he says, his Noise starting to rear up and there's anger in it, sure, but that weird grief's in it, too, that raging hurt you can almost taste on yer tongue.

There's also nervousness swirling about him, edgy as you please, much as he's trying to cover it.

I step back again, farther in the dark.

"I ain't a bad man, you know," he says, suddenly and kinda confusingly but swinging the machete. "I have a wife. I have a daughter."

"They wouldn't be wanting you to hurt no innocent boy, I'm sure–"

"Quiet!" he shouts and I can hear him swallow.

He ain't sure of this. He ain't sure of what he's about to do.

What's going on here?

"I don't know why yer angry," I say, "but I'm sorry. Whatever it is–"

"What I want you to know before you pay," he says over me, like he's forcing himself not to listen to me. "What you *need* to know, boy, is that my mother's name was Jessica."

I stop stepping back. "Beg pardon?"

"My mother's name," he growls, "was Jessica."

This don't make no sense at all.

"What?" I say. "I don't know what yer–"

"Listen, boy!" he yells. "Just listen."

And then his Noise is wide open.

And I see–

And I see–

And I see–

I see what he's showing.

"That's a lie," I whisper. "That's a ruddy lie."

Which is the wrong thing to say.

With a yell, Matthew leaps forward, running towards

me the length of the barn.

"Run!" I shout to Manchee, turning and making a break for the back doors. (Shut up, you honestly think a knife is a match for a machete?) I hear Matthew still yelling, his Noise exploding after me, and I reach the back door and fling it open before I realize.

Manchee's not with me.

I turn round. When I said "run", Manchee'd run the other way, flinging himself with all his unconvincing viciousness towards the charging Matthew.

"Manchee!" I yell.

It's ruddy dark in the barn now and I can hear grunts and barks and clanks and then I hear Matthew cry out in pain at what must surely be a bite.

Good dog, I think, *Good effing dog*.

And I can't leave him, can I?

I run back into the darkness, towards where I can see Matthew hopping around and the form of Manchee dancing twixt his legs and swipes of the machete, barking his little head off.

"Todd! Todd! Todd!" he's barking.

I'm five steps away and still running when Matthew makes a two-handed strike down at the ground, embedding the tip of the machete into the wooden floor. I hear a squeal from Manchee that don't have no words, just pain, and off he flies into a dark corner.

I let out a yell and crash right into Matthew. We both go flying, toppling to the floor in a tumble of elbows and kneecaps. It hurts but mostly I'm landing on Matthew so that's okay.

We roll apart and I hear him call out in pain. I get right back up to my feet, knife in hand, a few metres away from him, far from the back door now and with Matthew blocking the front. I hear Manchee whimpering in the dark.

I also hear some Noise rising from across the village road in the direkshun of the meeting hall but there ain't time to think about that now.

"I'm not afraid to kill you," I say, tho I totally am but I'm hoping my Noise and his Noise are now so rackety and revved up that he won't be able to make any sense from it.

"That makes two of us then," he says, lunging for his machete. It don't come out first tug, or the second. I take the chance to jump back into the dark, looking for Manchee.

"Manchee?" I say, frantically looking behind the sheaves and the piles of fruit baskets. I can still hear Matthew grunting to get his machete outta the floor and the ruckus from the town is growing louder.

"Todd?" I hear from deep in the darkness.

It's coming from beside the silage rolls, down a little nook that opens up next to them back to the wall. "Manchee?" I call, sticking my head down it.

I look back real quick.

With a heave, Matthew gets his machete outta the floor.

"Todd?" Manchee says, confused and scared. "Todd?"

And here comes Matthew, coming on in slow steps, like he no longer has to hurry, his Noise reaching forward in a wave that don't brook no argument.

I have no choice. I wedge myself back into the nook and hold out my knife.

"I'll leave," I say, my voice rising. "Just let me get my dog and we'll leave."

"Too late for that," Matthew says, getting closer.

"You don't wanna do this. I can tell."

"Shut yer mouth."

"Please," I say, waving the knife. "I don't wanna hurt you."

"Do I look concerned, boy?"

Closer, closer, step by step.

There's a bang outside somewhere, off in the distance. People really are running and shouting now but neither of us look.

I press myself back into the little nook but it's really not wide enough for me. I glance round, seeing where escape might lie.

I don't find nothing much.

My knife's gonna have to do it. It's gonna have to act, even if it is against a machete.

"Todd?" I hear behind me.

"Don't worry, Manchee," I say. "It's gonna be all right."

And who knows what a dog believes?

Matthew's almost on us now.

I grip my knife.

Matthew stops a metre from me, so close I can see his eyes glinting in the dark.

"Jessica," he says.

He raises his machete above his head.

I flinch back, knife up, steeling myself–

But he pauses–

He pauses–

In a way I reckernize–

And that's enough–

With a quick prayer that it ain't the same stuff from the bridge, I swing my knife in an arc to my side, slicing right thru (thank you thank you) the ropes holding up the silage rolls, cutting the first lot clean away. The other ropes snap right quick from the sudden shift in weight and I cover my head and press myself away as the silage rolls start to tumble.

I hear thumps and clumps and an "oof" from Matthew and I look up and he's buried in silage rolls, his arm out to one side, the machete dropped. I step forward and kick it away, then turn to find Manchee.

He's back in a dark corner behind the now-fallen rolls. I race over to him.

"Todd?" he says when I get close. "Tail, Todd?"

"Manchee?" It's dark so I have to squat down next to him to see. His tail's two thirds shorter than it used to be, blood everywhere, but God bless him, still trying to wag.

"Ow, Todd?"

"It's okay, Manchee," I say, my voice and Noise near crying from relief that it's just his tail. "We'll get you fixed right up."

"Okay, Todd?"

"I'm okay," I say, rubbing his head. He nips my hand but I know he can't help it cuz he's in pain. He licks me in apology then nips me again. "Ow, Todd," he says.

"Todd Hewitt!" I hear shouted from the front of the barn.

Francia.

"I'm here!" I call, standing up. "I'm all right. Matthew went crazy–"

But I stop cuz she ain't listening to me.

"Ye gotta get yerself indoors, Todd pup," Francia says in a rush. "Ye gotta–"

She stops when she sees Matthew under the silage.

"What happened?" she says, already starting to tug away the rolls, getting the one off his face and leaning down to see if he's still breathing.

I point to the machete. "*That* happened."

Francia looks at it, then a long look up at me, her face saying something I can't read nor even begin to figure out. I don't know if Matthew's alive nor dead and I ain't never gonna find out.

"We're under attack, pup," she says, standing.

"Yer *what*?"

"Men," she says, rising. "Prentisstown men. That posse that's after ye. They're attacking the whole town."

My stomach falls right outta my shoes.

"Oh, no," I say. And then I say it again, "Oh, no."

Francia's still looking at me, her brain thinking who knows what.

"Don't give us to them," I say, backing away again. "They'll kill us."

Francia frowns at this. "What kinda woman do ye think I am?"

"I don't know," I say, "that's the whole problem."

"I'm not gonna *give* ye to them. Honestly, now. Nor Viola. In fact the feeling of the town meeting, as far along as it got, was how we were a-deciding to protect ye both from what was almost certainly a-coming." She looks down at Matthew. "Tho maybe that's a promise we couldn't keep."

"Where's Viola?"

"Back at my house," Francia says, suddenly all active again. "C'mon. We gotta get ye inside."

"Wait." I squeeze back behind the silage rolls and find Manchee still in his corner, licking his tail. He looks up at me and barks, just a little bark that's not even a word. "I'm gonna pick you up now," I say to him. "Try not to bite me too hard, okay?"

"Okay, Todd," he whimpers, yelping each time he wags his stumpy tail.

I reach down, put my arms under his tummy and hoist him up to my chest. He yelps and bites hard at my wrist, then licks it.

"It's okay, buddy," I say, holding him as best I can.

Francia's waiting for me at the doors to the barn and I follow her out into the main road.

There are people running about everywhere. I see men and women with rifles running up towards the orchards and other men and women scooting kids (there they are again) into houses and such. In the distance I can hear bangs and shouts and yelling.

"Where's Hildy?" I yell.

Francia don't say nothing. We reach her front steps.

"What about Hildy?" I ask again as we climb up.

"She went off to fight," Francia says, not looking at me, opening the door. "They would have reached her farm first. Tam was still there."

"Oh, no," I say again stupidly, like my "oh nos" will do any good.

Viola comes flying down from the upper floor as we enter.

"What took you so long?" she says, her voice kinda loud, and I don't know which one of us she's talking to. She gasps when she sees Manchee.

"Bandages," I say. "Some of those fancy ones."

She nods and races back up the stairs.

"Ye two stay here," Francia says to me. "Don't come out, whatever ye hear."

"But we need to run!" I say, not understanding this at all. "We need to get outta here!"

"No, Todd pup," she says. "If Prentisstown wants ye, then that's reason enough for us to keep ye from them."

"But they've got guns–"

"So do we," Francia says. "No posse of Prentisstown men is going to take *this* town."

Viola's back down the stairs now, digging thru her bag for bandages.

"Francia–" I say.

"Stay right here," she says. "We'll protect ye. Both of ye."

She looks at both of us, hard, like seeing if we agree, then she turns and is out the door to protect her town, I guess.

We stare at the closed door for a second, then Manchee whimpers again and I have to set him down. Viola gets out a square bandage and her little scalpel.

"I don't know if these'll work on dogs," she says.

"Better than nothing," I say.

She cuts off a little strip and I have to hold Manchee's head down while she loops it around the mess of his tail. He growls and apologizes and growls and apologizes until Viola's covered the whole wound up tight. He immediately sets to licking it when I let him go.

"Stop that," I say.

"Itches," Manchee says.

"Stupid dog." I scratch his ears. "Stupid ruddy dog."

Viola pets him, too, trying to keep him from licking off the bandage.

"Do you think we're safe?" she asks quietly, after a long minute.

"I don't know."

There's more bangs out in the distance. We both jump. More people shouting. More Noise.

"No sign of Hildy since this started," Viola says.

"I know."

Another bit of silence as we over-pet Manchee. More ruckus from up in the orchards above town.

It all seems so far away, as if it's not even happening.

"Francia told me that you can find Haven if you keep following the main river," Viola says.

I look at her. I wonder if I know what this means.

I think I do.

"You wanna leave," I say.

"They'll keep coming," she says. "We're putting the people around us in danger. Don't you think they'll keep coming if they've already come this far?"

I do. I do think this. I don't say it but I do.

"But they said they could protect us," I say.

"Do you believe that?"

I don't say nothing to this neither. I think of Matthew Lyle.

"I don't think we're safe here any more," she says.

"I don't think we're safe *anywhere*," I say. "Not on this whole planet."

"I need to contact my ship, Todd," she says, almost pleading. "They're waiting to hear from me."

"And you wanna run off into the unknown to do it?"

"You do, too," she says. "I can tell." She looks away. "If we went together..."

I look up at her at this, trying to see, trying to *know*, to know real and true.

All she does is look back.

Which is enough.

"Let's go," I say.

We pack without any more words, and fast. I get my rucksack on, she gets her bag round her shoulders, Manchee's on his feet again and walking, and out the back door we go. As simple as that, we're going. Safer for Farbranch, definitely, safer for us, who knows? Who knows if this is the right thing to do? After what Hildy and Francia seemed to promise, it's hard leaving.

But we're leaving. And that's what we're doing.

Cuz at least it's *us* who decided it. I'd rather not have no one else tell me what they'll do for me, even when they mean well.

It's full dark night outside now, tho both moons are shining bright. Everyone in town's attenshun is behind us so there's no one to stop us from running. There's a little bridge that crosses the creek that runs thru town. "How far is this Haven?" I ask, whispering as we cross.

"Kinda far," Viola whispers back.

"How far is kinda far?"

She don't say nothing for a second.

"How *far*?" I say again.

"Coupla weeks' walk," she says, not looking back.

"Coupla *weeks*!"

"Where else do we have?" she says.

And I don't have an answer so we keep on walking.

Across the creek, the road heads up the far hill of the valley. We decide to take it as the fastest way outta town then find our way back south to the river and follow that. Ben's map ends at Farbranch so the river's all we got for direkshuns from here on out.

There's so many askings that come with us as we run outta Farbranch, askings that we'll never know the answers to: Why would the Mayor and a few men go miles outta their way to attack a whole ruddy town on their own? Why are they still after us? Why are we so important? And what happened to Hildy?

And did I kill Matthew Lyle?

And was what he showed me in his Noise right there at the end a true thing?

Was that the real history of Prentisstown?

"Was what the real history?" Viola asks as we hurry on up the path.

"Nothing," I say. "And quit reading me."

We get to the top of the far hill of the valley just as another rattle of gunfire echoes across it. We stop and look.

And then we see.

Boy, do we see.

"Oh, my God," Viola says.

Under the light of the two moons, the whole valley

kinda shines, across the Farbranch buildings and back up into the hills where the orchards are.

We can see the men and women of Farbranch running back down that hill.

In retreat.

And marching over the top, are five, ten, fifteen men on horseback.

Followed by rows of men five across, carrying guns, marching in a line behind what has to be the Mayor's horses in front.

Not a posse. Not a posse at all.

It's Prentisstown. I feel like the world's crumbling at my feet. It's every ruddy man in Prentisstown.

They have three times as many people as even live in Farbranch.

Three times as many guns.

We hear gunshots and we see the men and women of Farbranch fall as they run back to their houses.

They'll take the town easily. They'll take it before the hour is thru.

Cuz the rumours were true, the rumours that Francia heard.

The word was true.

It's an army.

A whole army.

There's a whole army coming after me and Viola.

PART IV

20

ARMY OF MEN

WE DUCK BEHIND SOME BUSHES, even tho it's dark, even tho the army is across the valley, even tho they don't know we're up here and there's no way they could hear my Noise amidst all the ruckus going on down there, we duck anyway.

"Can yer binos see in the dark?" I whisper.

By way of answer Viola digs them outta her bag and holds them up to her own eyes. "What's happening?" she says, looking thru them, pressing more buttons. "Who are all those men?"

"It's Prentisstown," I say, holding out my hand. "It looks like every man in the whole effing town."

"How can it be the whole town?" She looks for a second or two more then hands the binos to me. "What kind of sense does that make?"

"You got me." The night setting on the binos turns the valley and all that's in it a bright green. I see horses galloping down the hill into the main part of town, shooting their rifles on the way, I see the people of Farbranch shooting back but mostly running, mostly falling, mostly dying. The Prentisstown army don't seem interested in taking prisoners.

"We have to get out of here, Todd," Viola says.

"Yeah," I say, but I'm still looking thru the binos.

With everything green, it's hard to make out faces. I press a few more buttons on the binos till I find the ones that take me in closer.

The first person I see for sure is Mr Prentiss Jr, in the lead, firing his rifle into the air when he don't have nothing else to shoot at. Then there's Mr Morgan and Mr Collins chasing some Farbranch men into the storage barns, firing their rifles after them. Mr O'Hare's there, too, and more of the Mayor's usual suspects on horseback, Mr Edwin, Mr Henratty, Mr Sullivan. And there's Mr Hammar, the smile on his face showing up green and evil even from this distance as he fires his rifle into the backs of fleeing women hustling away small children and I have to look away or throw up the nothing I had for dinner.

The men on foot march their way into town. The first one I reckernize is, of all people, Mr Phelps the storekeeper. Which is weird cuz he never seemed army-like at all. And there's Dr Baldwin. And Mr Fox. And Mr Cardiff who was our best milker. And Mr Tate who had the most books to burn when the Mayor outlawed them. And Mr Kearney who milled the town's wheat and who always spoke softly and who made wooden toys for each Prentisstown boy's birthday.

What are these men doing in an army?

"Todd," Viola says, pulling at my arm.

The men marching don't look none too happy, I spose. Grim and cold and scary in a different way from Mr Hammar, like they're lacking all feeling.

But they're still marching. They're still shooting. They're still kicking down doors.

"That's Mr Gillooly," I say, binos pressed to my eyes. "He can't even butcher his own meat."

"Todd," Viola says and I feel her backing away from the bushes. "Let's *go*."

What's going on? Sure, Prentisstown was as awful a place as you could ever not wanna paint it but how can it suddenly be an army? There's plenty of Prentisstown men who're bad thru and thru but not all of them. Not *all*. And Mr Gillooly with a rifle is a sight so wrong it almost hurts my eyes just to look at it.

And then of course I see the answer.

Mayor Prentiss, not even holding a gun, just one hand on his horse's reins, the other at his side, riding into town like he's out for an evening canter. He's watching the rout of Farbranch as if it was a vid and not a very interesting one at that, letting everyone else do the work but so obviously in charge no one would even think of asking him to break a sweat.

How can he make so many men do what he wants?

And is he bulletproof that he can ride so fearlessly?

"Todd," Viola says behind me. "I swear, I'll leave without you."

"No, you won't," I say. "One more second."

Cuz I'm looking from face to face now, ain't I? I'm going from Prentisstown man to Prentisstown man cuz even if they're marching into town and are gonna find out soon enough that neither me nor Viola are there and are gonna have to come this way after us, I gotta know.

I gotta know.

Face to face to face as they march and shoot and burn. Mr Wallace, Mr Asbjornsen, Mr St James, Mr Belgraves, Mr Smith the Older, Mr Smith the Younger, Mr Smith With Nine Fingers, even Mr Marjoribanks, wobbling and teetering but marching marching marching. Prentisstown man after Prentisstown man after Prentisstown man, my heart clenching and burning at each one I can identify.

"They ain't there," I say, almost to myself.

"Who isn't?" Viola says.

"Ain't!" Manchee barks, licking at his tail.

They ain't there.

Ben and Cillian ain't there.

Which, of course, is grand, ain't it? Of course they ain't part of an army of killers. Of *course* they ain't, even when every other Prentisstown man is. They wouldn't be. Not never, not no how, no matter what.

Good men, *great* men, both, even Cillian.

But if that's true, then that means the other is true, too, don't it?

If they ain't there, then that means once and for all.

And there's yer lesson.

There ain't nothing good that don't got real bad waiting to follow it.

I hope they put up the best fight ever.

I take the binos from my face and I look down and I wipe my eyes with my sleeve and I turn and I hand Viola back the binos and I say, "Let's go."

She takes them from me, squirming a little like she's itching to leave, but then she says, "I'm sorry," so she musta seen it in my Noise.

"Nothing that ain't already happened," I say, talking to the ground and readjusting the rucksack. "C'mon, before I put us in danger any worse."

I take off up the path towards the top of the hill, keeping my head down, motoring fast, Viola after me, Manchee trying to keep himself from biting at his tail as we run.

Viola matches my speed before we get far at all. "Did you see … him?" she says, between breaths.

"Aaron?"

She nods.

"No," I say. "Come to think of it, no, I didn't. And you'd think he'd be out in front."

We're quiet for a minute as we hurry on our way and wonder what that means.

The road on this side of the valley is wider and we're doing our best to keep to the darker side of it as it twists and turns up the hill. Our only lights are the moons but they're bright enough to cast our shadows running along the road which is too bright when yer running away. I never seen no night vision binos in Prentisstown but I didn't see no army neither so we're both crouching as we run without either of us saying that we will. Manchee's running on ahead of us, his nose to the ground, barking, "This way! This way!" as if he knows any better than us where we're going.

Then at the top of the hill, the road forks.

Which just figures.

"You gotta be kidding," I say.

One part of the road goes left, the other goes right.

(Well, it's a *fork*, ain't it?)

"The creek in Farbranch was flowing to the right," Viola says, "and the main river was always to our right once we crossed the bridge, so it's got to be the right fork if we want to get back there."

"But the left looks more travelled," I say. And it does. The left fork looks smoother, flatter, like the kinda thing you should be rolling carts over. The right fork is narrower with higher bushes on each side and even tho it's night you can just tell it's dusty. "Did Francia say anything about a fork?" I look back over my shoulder at the valley still erupting behind us.

"No," Viola says, also looking back. "She just said Haven was the first settlement and new settlements sprang up down the river as people moved west. Prentisstown was the farthest out. Farbranch was second farthest."

"That one probably goes to the river," I say, pointing right, then left, "that one probably goes to Haven in a straight line."

"Which one will they think we took?"

"We need to decide," I say. "Quickly now."

"To the right," she says, then turns it into an asking. "To the right?"

We hear a *BOOM* that makes us jump. A mushroom of smoke is rising in the air over Farbranch. The barn where I worked all day is on fire.

Maybe our story will turn out differently if we take the left fork, maybe the bad things that are waiting to happen to us won't happen, maybe there's happiness at the end of the left fork and warm places with the people who love us and no Noise but no silence neither and there's plenty of food and no one dies and no one dies and no one never never dies.

Maybe.

But I doubt it.

I ain't what you call a lucky person.

"Right," I decide. "Might as well be right."

We run down the right fork, Manchee at our heels, the night and a dusty road stretching out in front of us, an army and a disaster behind us, me and Viola, running side by side.

We run till we can't run and then we walk fast till we can run again. The sounds of Farbranch disappear behind us right quick and all we can hear are our footsteps beating on the path and my Noise and Manchee's barking. If there are night creachers out there, we're scaring 'em away.

Which is probably good.

"What's the next settlement?" I gasp after a good half hour's run-walking. "Did Francia say?"

"Shining Beacon," Viola says, gasping herself. "Or Shining Light." She scrunches her face. "*Blazing* Light. Blazing Beacon?"

"That's helpful."

"Wait." She stops in the path, bending at the waist to catch her breath. I stop, too. "I need water."

I hold up my hands in a way that says *And?* "So do I," I say. "You got some?"

She looks at me, her eyebrows up. "Oh."

"There was always a river."

"I guess we'd better find it then."

"I guess so." I take a deep breath to start running again.

"Todd," she says, stopping me. "I've been thinking?"

"Yeah?" I say.

"Blazing Lights or whatever?"

"Yeah?"

"If you look at it one way," she lowers her voice to a sad and uncomfortable sound and says it again, "if you look at it one way, we led an army into Farbranch."

I lick the dryness of my lips. I taste dust. And I know what she's saying.

"You must warn them," she says quietly, into the dark. "I'm sorry, but–"

"We can't go into any other settlements," I say.

"I don't think we can."

"Not till Haven."

"Not until Haven," she says, "which we have to hope is big enough to handle an army."

So, that's that then. In case we needed any further reminding, we're really on our own. Really and truly. Me and Viola and Manchee and the darkness for company. No one on the road to help us till the end, if even there, which knowing our luck so far–

I close my eyes.

I am Todd Hewitt, I think. *When it goes midnight I will be a man in twenty-seven days. I am the son of my ma and pa, may they rest in peace. I am the son of Ben and Cillian, may they–*

I am Todd Hewitt.

"I'm Viola Eade," Viola says.

I open my eyes. She has her hand out, palm down, held towards me.

"That's my surname," she says. "Eade. E-A-D-E."

I look at her for a second and then down at her outstretched hand and I reach out and I take it and press it inside my own and a second later I let go.

I shrug my shoulders to reset my rucksack. I put my hand behind my back to feel the knife and make sure it's still there. I give poor, panting, half-tail Manchee a look and then match eyes with Viola.

"Viola Eade," I say, and she nods.

And off we run into further night.

21

THE WIDER WORLD

"HOW CAN IT BE THIS FAR?" Viola asks. "It doesn't make any logical sense."

"Is there another kind of sense it does make?"

She frowns. So do I. We're tired and getting tireder and trying not to think of what we saw at Farbranch and we've walked and run what feels like half the night and still no river. I'm starting to get afraid we've taken a seriously wrong turning which we can't do nothing about cuz there ain't no turning back.

"*Isn't any* turning back," I hear Viola say behind me, under her breath.

I turn to her, eyes wide. "That's wrong on two counts," I say. "Number one, constantly reading people's Noise ain't gonna get you much welcome here."

She crosses her arms and sets her shoulders. "And the second?"

"The second is I talk how I please."

"Yes," Viola says. "That you do."

My Noise starts to rise a bit and I take a deep breath but then she says, "Shhh," and her eyes glint in the moonlight as she looks beyond me.

The sound of running water.

"River!" Manchee barks.

We take off down the road and round a corner and down a slope and round another corner and there's the river, wider, flatter and slower than when we saw it last but just as wet. We don't say nothing, just drop to our knees on the rocks at water's edge and drink, Manchee wading in up to his belly to start lapping.

Viola's next to me and as I slurp away, there's her silence again. It's a two-way thing, this is. However clear she can hear my Noise, well, out here alone, away from the chatter of others or the Noise of a settlement, there's her silence, loud as a roar, pulling at me like the greatest sadness ever, like I want to take it and press myself into it and just disappear forever down into nothing.

What a relief that would feel like right now. What a blessed relief.

"I can't avoid hearing you, you know," she says, standing up and opening her bag. "When it's quiet and just the two of us."

"And I can't avoid not hearing you," I say. "No matter what it's like." I whistle for Manchee. "Outta the water. There might be snakes."

He's ducking his rump under the current, swishing back and forth until the bandage comes off and floats away. Then he leaps out and immediately sets to licking his tail.

"Let me see," I say. He barks "Todd!" in agreement but when I come near he curls his tail as far under his belly as the new length will go. I uncurl it gently, Manchee murmuring "Tail, tail" to himself all the while.

"Whaddyaknow?" I say. "Those bandages work on dogs."

Viola's fished out two discs from her bag. She presses her thumbs inside them and they expand right up into water bottles. She kneels by the river, fills both, and tosses one to me.

"Thanks," I say, not really looking at her.

She wipes some water from her bottle. We stand on the riverbank for a second and she's putting her water bottle back into her bag and she's quiet in a way that I'm learning means she's trying to say something difficult.

"I don't mean any offence by it," she says, looking up to me, "but I think maybe it's time I read the note on the map."

I can feel myself redden, even in the dark, and I can also feel myself get ready to argue.

But then I just sigh. I'm tired and it's late and we're running *again* and she's right, ain't she? There's nothing but spitefulness that'll argue she's wrong.

I drop my rucksack and take out the book, unfolding the map from inside the front cover. I hand it to her without looking at her. She takes out her torch and shines it on the paper, turning it over to Ben's message. To my surprise, she starts reading it out loud and all of sudden, even with her own voice, it's like Ben's is ringing down the river, echoing from Prentisstown and hitting my chest like a punch.

"Go to the settlement down the river and across the

bridge," she reads. *"It's called Farbranch and the people there should welcome you."*

"And they did," I say. "Some of them."

Viola continues, *"There are things you don't know about our history, Todd, and I'm sorry for that but if you knew them you would be in great danger. The only chance you have of a welcome is yer innocence."*

I feel myself redden even more but fortunately it's too dark to see.

"Yer ma's book will tell you more but in the meantime, the wider world has to be warned, Todd. Prentisstown is on the move. The plan has been in the works for years, only waiting for the last boy in Prentisstown to become a man." She looks up. "Is that you?"

"That's me," I say, "I was the youngest boy. I turn thirteen in twenty-seven days and officially become a man according to Prentisstown law."

And I can't help but think for a minute about what Ben showed me–

About how a boy becomes–

I cover it up and say quickly, "But I got no idea what he means about them waiting for me."

"The Mayor plans to take Farbranch and who knows what else beyond. Sillian and I–"

"Cillian," I correct her. "With a K sound."

"Cillian and I will try to delay it as long as we can but we won't be able to stop it. Farbranch will be in danger and you have to warn them. Always, always, always remember that we love you like our own son and sending you away is the hardest thing we'll ever have to do. If it's at all possible, we'll see you

again, but first you must get to Farbranch as fast as you can and when you get there, you must warn them. Ben." Viola looks up. "That last part's underlined."

"I know."

And then we don't say nothing for a minute. There's blame in the air but maybe it's all coming from me.

Who can tell with a silent girl?

"My fault," I say. "It's all my fault."

Viola rereads the note to herself. "They should have *told* you," she says. "Not expected you to read it if you can't–"

"If they'd told me, Prentisstown would've heard it in my Noise and known that I knew. We wouldn't've even got the head start we had." I glance at her eyes and look away. "I shoulda given it to someone to read and that's all there is to it. Ben's a good man." I lower my voice. "Was."

She refolds the map and hands it back to me. It's useless to us now but I put it back carefully inside the front cover of the book.

"I could read that for you," Viola says. "Your mother's book. If you wanted."

I keep my back to her and put the book in my rucksack. "We need to go," I say. "We've wasted too much time here."

"Todd–"

"There's an army after us," I say. "No more time for reading."

So we set off again and do our best to run for as much and as long as we can but as the sun rises, all slow and lazy and cold, we've had no sleep and that's no sleep after a full day's work and so even with that army on our tails, we're barely able to even keep up a fast walk.

But we do, thru that next morning. The road keeps following the river as we hoped and the land starts to flatten out around us, great natural plains of grass stretching out to low hills and to higher hills beyond and, to the north at least, mountains beyond that.

It's all wild, tho. No fences, no fields of crops, and no signs of any kind of settlement or people except for the dusty road itself. Which is good in one way but weird in another.

If New World isn't sposed to have been wiped out, where is everybody?

"You think this is right?" I say, as we come round yet another dusty corner of the road with nothing beyond it but more dusty corners. "You think we're going the right way?"

Viola blows out thoughtful air. "My dad used to say, *There's only forward, Vi, only outward and up.*"

"There's only forward," I repeat.

"Outward and up," she says.

"What was he like?" I ask. "Yer pa?"

She looks down at the road and from the side I can see half a smile on her face. "He smelled like fresh bread," she says and then she moves on ahead and don't say nothing more.

Morning turns to afternoon with more of the same. We hurry when we can, walk fast when we can't hurry, and only rest when we can't help it. The river remains flat and steady, like the brown and green land around it. I can see bluehawks way up high, hovering and scouting for prey, but that's about it for signs of life.

"This is one empty planet," Viola says as we stop for a quick lunch, leaning on some rocks overlooking a natural weir.

"Oh, it's full enough," I say, munching on some cheese. "Believe me."

"I do believe you. I just meant I can see why people would want to settle here. Lots of fertile farmland, lots of potential for people to make new lives."

I chew. "People would be mistaken."

She rubs her neck and looks at Manchee, sniffing round the edges of the weir, probably smelling the wood weavers who made it living underneath.

"Why do you become a man here at thirteen?" she asks.

I look over at her, surprised. "What?"

"That note," she says. "The town waiting for the last boy to become a man." She looks at me. "Why wait?"

"That's how New World's always done it. It's sposed to be scriptural. Aaron always went on about it symbolizing the day you eat from the Tree of Knowledge and go from innocence into sin."

She gives me a funny look. "That sounds pretty heavy."

I shrug. "Ben said that the real reason was cuz a small group of people on an isolated planet need all the adults they can get so thirteen is the day you start getting real responsibilities." I throw a stray stone into the river. "Don't ask me. All I know is it's thirteen years. Thirteen cycles of thirteen months."

"*Thirteen* months?" she asks, her eyebrows up.

I nod.

"There are only twelve months in a year," she says.

"No, there ain't. There's thirteen."

"Maybe not here," she says, "but where I come from there's twelve."

I blink. "Thirteen months in a New World year," I say, feeling dumb for some reason.

She looks up like she's figuring something out. "I mean, depending on how long a day or a month is on this planet, you might be … fourteen years old already."

"That's not how it works here," I say, kinda stern, not really liking this much. "I turn thirteen in twenty-seven days."

"Fourteen and a *month*, actually," she says, still figuring it out. "Which makes you wonder how you tell how old anybody–"

"It's twenty-seven days till my birthday," I say firmly. I stand and put the rucksack back on. "Come on. We've wasted too much time talking."

It ain't till the sun's finally started to dip below the tops of the trees that we see our first sign of civilizayshun: an abandoned water mill at the river's edge, its roof burnt off who knows how many years ago. We've been walking so long we don't even talk, don't even look around much for danger, just go inside, throw our bags down against the walls and flop to the ground like it's the softest bed ever. Manchee, who don't seem to ever get tired, is busy running around, lifting his leg on all the plants that have grown up thru the cracked floorboards.

"My feet," I say, peeling off my shoes, counting five, no, *six* different blisters.

Viola lets out a weary sigh from the opposite wall. "We have to sleep," she says. "Even if."

"I know."

She looks at me. "You'll hear them coming," she says, "if they come?"

"Oh, I'll hear them," I say. "I'll definitely hear them."

We decide to take turns sleeping. I say I'll wait up first and Viola can barely say good night before she's out. I watch her sleep as the light fades. The little bit of clean we got at Hildy's house is already long gone. She looks like I must do, face smudged with dust, dark circles under her eyes, dirt under her nails.

And I start to think.

I've only known her for three days, you know? Three effing days outta my whole entire life but it's like nothing that happened before really happened, like that was all a big lie just waiting for me to find out. No, not *like*, it *was* a big lie waiting for me to find out and this is the real life now, running without safety or answer, only moving, only ever moving.

I take a sip of water and I listen to the crickets chirping **sex sex sex** and I wonder what *her* life was like before these last three days. Like, what's it like growing up on a spaceship? A place where there's never any new people, a place you can never get beyond the borders of.

A place like Prentisstown, come to think of it, where if you disappeared, you ain't never coming back.

I look back over to her. But she did get out, didn't she? She got seven *months* out with her ma and her pa on the little ship that crashed.

How's that work, I wonder?

"You need to send scout ships out ahead to make local field surveys and find the best landing sites," she says, without sitting up or even moving her head. "How does anyone ever sleep in a world with Noise?"

"You get used to it," I say. "But why so long? Why seven months?"

"That's how long it takes to set up first camp." She covers her eyes with her hand in an exhausted way. "Me and my mother and father were supposed to find the best place for the ships to land and build the first encampment and then we'd start building the first things that would be needed for settlers just landing. A control tower, a food store, a clinic." She looks at me twixt her fingers. "It's standard procedure."

"I never seen no control tower on New World," I say.

This makes her sit up. "I *know*. I can't believe you guys don't even have communicators between settlements."

"So yer not church settlers then," I say, sounding wise.

"What does that have to do with anything?" she says. "Why would any reasonable church want to be cut off from itself?"

"Ben said that they came to this world for the simpler life, said that there was even a fight in the early days whether to destroy the fission generators."

Viola looks horrified. "You would have all died."

"That's why they weren't destroyed," I shrug. "Not even after Mayor Prentiss decided to get rid of most everything else."

Viola rubs her shins and looks up into the stars coming out thru the hole in the roof. "My mother and father were so excited," she says. "A whole new world, a whole new beginning, all these plans of peace and happiness." She stops.

"I'm sorry it ain't that way," I say.

She looks down at her feet. "Would you mind waiting outside for a little while until I fall asleep?"

"Yeah," I say, "no problem."

I take my rucksack and go out the opening where the front door used to be. Manchee gets up from where he's curled and follows me. When I sit down, he recurls by my legs and falls asleep, farting happily and giving a doggy sigh. Simple to be a dog.

I watch the moons rise, the stars following 'em, the same moons and the same stars as were in Prentisstown, still out here past the end of the world. I take out the book again, the oil in the cover shining from the moonlight. I flip thru the pages.

I wonder if my ma was excited to land here, if her head was full of peace and good hope and joy everlasting.

I wonder if she found any before she died.

This makes my chest heavy so I put the book back in the rucksack and lean my head against the boards of the mill. I listen to the river flow past and the leaves shushing to themselves in the few trees around us and I look at the shadows of far distant hills on the horizon and the rustling forests on them.

I'll wait for a few minutes, then go back inside and make sure Viola's okay.

The next thing I know she's waking me up and it's hours later and my head is completely confused till I hear her saying, "Noise, Todd, I can hear Noise."

I'm on my feet before I'm fully awake, quieting Viola and a groggy Manchee barking his complaints. They get quiet and I put my ear into the night.

Whisper whisper whisper there, like a breeze whisper whisper whisper no words and far away but hovering, a storm cloud behind a mountain whisper whisper whisper.

"We gotta go," I say, already reaching for my rucksack.

"Is it the army?" Viola calls, running thru the door of the mill as she grabs her own bag.

"Army!" Manchee barks.

"Don't know," I say. "Probably."

"Could it be the next settlement?" Viola comes back, bag round her shoulders. "We can't be too far from it."

"Then why didn't we hear it when we got here?"

She bites her lip. "Damn."

"Yeah," I say. "Damn."

And so the second night after Farbranch passes like the first, running in darkness, using torches when we need them, trying not to think. Just before the sun comes up, the river moves outta the flats and into another small valley like the one by Farbranch and sure enough, there's Blazing Beacons or whatever so maybe there really are people living out this way.

They've got orchards, too, and fields of wheat, tho nothing looks near as well tended as Farbranch. Lucky for us, the main bit of town is on top of the hill with what looks like a bigger road going thru it, the left fork, maybe, and five or six buildings, most of which could use a lick of paint. Down on our dirt road by the river there are just boats and wormy-looking docks and dockhouses and whatever else you build on a flowing river.

We can't ask anyone for help. Even if we got it, the army's coming, ain't it? We should warn them but what if they're Matthew Lyles rather than Hildys? And what if by warning them we draw the army right *to* them cuz then we're in everyone's Noise? And what if the settlement knows we're the reason the army's coming and they decide to turn us over to them?

But they deserve to be warned, don't they?

But what if that endangers *us*?

You see? What's the right answer?

And so we sneak thru the settlement like thieves, running from dockhouse to dockhouse, hiding from sight of the town up the hill, waiting as quiet as we can when we see a skinny woman taking a basket into a hen house up by some trees. It's small enough that we get thru it before the sun even fully rises and we're out the other side and back on the road like it never existed, like it never happened, even to us.

"So that's that settlement then," Viola whispers as we take a look behind us and watch it disappear behind a bend. "We'll never even know what it was properly called."

"And now we *really* don't know what's ahead of us," I whisper back.

"We keep going until we get to Haven."

"And then what?"

She don't say nothing to that.

"That's a lotta faith we're putting in a word," I say.

"There's got to be something, Todd," she says, her face kinda grim. "There has to be *something* there."

I don't say nothing for a second and then I say, "I guess we'll see."

And so starts another morning. Twice on the road we see men with horse-drawn carts. Both times we hie off into the woods, Viola with her hand round Manchee's snout and me trying to keep my Noise as Prentisstown-free as possible till they pass.

Nothing much changes as the hours go by. We don't hear no more whispers from the army, if that's what it even was, but there ain't no point in finding out for sure, is there? Morning's turned into afternoon again when we see a settlement high up on a far hill. We're coming up a little hill ourselves, the river dropping down a bit, tho we can see it spreading out in the distance, what looks like the start of a plain we're gonna have to cross.

Viola points her binos at the settlement for a minute, then hands them to me. It's ten or fifteen buildings this time but even from a distance it looks scrubby and run down.

"I don't get it," Viola says. "Going by a regular schedule of settlement, subsistence farming should be years over by now. And there's obviously trade, so why is there still this much struggle?"

"You don't really know nothing about settler's lives, do you?" I say, chafing just a little.

She purses her lips. "It was required in school. I've been learning about how to set up a successful colony since I was five."

"Schooling ain't life."

"*Ain't* it?" she says, her eyebrows raising in a mock.

"*What did I say before?*" I snap back. "Some of us were busy surviving and couldn't learn about subdivided farming."

"*Subsistence.*"

"Don't care." I get myself moving again on the road.

Viola stomps after me. "We're going to be teaching you lot a thing or two when my ship arrives," she says. "You can be sure of that."

"Well, won't we dumb hicks be queuing up to kiss yer behinds in thankfulness?" I say, my Noise buzzing and not saying "behinds".

"Yes, you *will* be." She's raising her voice. "Trying to turn back the clock to the dark ages has really worked out for you, hasn't it? When we get here, you'll see how people are *supposed* to settle."

"That's *seven months* from now," I seethe at her. "You'll have plenty of time to see how the other half live."

"Todd!" Manchee barks, making us jump again, and suddenly he takes off down the road ahead of us.

"Manchee!" I yell after him. "Get back here!"

And then we both hear it.

22

WILF AND THE SEA OF THINGS

IT'S WEIRD, Noise, but almost wordless, cresting the hill in front of us and rolling down, single-minded but talking in legions, like a thousand voices singing the same thing.

Yeah.

Singing.

"What is it?" Viola asks, spooked as I am. "It's not the army, is it? How could they be in front of us?"

"Todd!" Manchee barks from the top of the small hill. "Cows, Todd! Giant cows!"

Viola's mouth twists. "Giant cows?"

"No idea," I say and I'm already heading up the little hill.

Cuz the sound–

How can I describe it?

Like how stars might sound. Or moons. But not mountains. Too floaty for mountains. It's a sound like one planet singing to another, high and stretched and full of different voices starting at different notes and sloping down to other different notes but all weaving together in a rope of sound that's sad but not sad and slow but not slow and all singing one word.

One word.

We reach the top of the hill and another plain unrolls below us, the river tumbling down to meet it and then running thru it like a vein of silver thru a rock and all over the plain, walking their way from one side of the river to the other, are creachers.

Creachers I never seen the like of in my life.

Massive, they are, four metres tall if they're an inch, covered in a shaggy, silvery fur with a thick, fluffed tail at one end and a pair of curved white horns at the other reaching right outta their brows and long necks that stretch down from wide shoulders to the grass of the plain below and these wide lips that mow it up as they trudge on dry ground and drink water as they cross the river and there's *thousands* of 'em, thousands stretching from the horizon on our right to the horizon on our left and the Noise of them all is singing one word, at different times in different notes, but one word binding 'em all together, knitting 'em as a group as they cross the plain.

"*Here,*" Viola says from somewhere off to my side. "They're singing *here*."

They're singing **Here**. Calling it from one to another in their Noise.

Here I am.

Here we are.

Here we go.

Here is all that matters.

Here.

It's–

Can I say?

It's like the song of a family where everything's always all right, it's a song of belonging that makes you belong just by hearing it, it's a song that'll always take care of you and never leave you. If you have a heart, it breaks, if you have a heart that's broken, it fixes.

It's–

Wow.

I look at Viola and she has her hand over her mouth and her eyes are wet but I can see a smile thru her fingers and I open my mouth to speak.

"Ya won't get ver far on foot," says a completely other voice to our left.

We spin round to look, my hand going right to my knife. A man driving an empty cart pulled by a pair of oxes regards us from a little side path, his mouth left hanging open like he forgot to close it.

There's a shotgun on the seat next to him, like he just put it there.

From a distance, Manchee barks "Cow!"

"They's all go round carts," says the man, "but not safe on foot, no. They's squish ya right up."

And again leaves his mouth open. His Noise, buried under all the **Here**s from the herd, seems to pretty much be saying exactly what his mouth is. I'm trying so hard not to think of certain words I'm already getting a headache.

"Ah kin give y'all a ride thrus," he says. "If ya want."

He raises an arm and points down the road, which

disappears under the feet of the herd crossing it. I hadn't even thought about how the creachers'd be blocking our way but you can see how you wouldn't wanna try walking thru them.

I turn and I start to say something, *anything*, that'll be the fastest way to get away.

But instead the most amazing thing happens.

Viola looks at the man and says, "Ah'm Hildy." She points at me. "At's Ben."

"What?" I say, barking it almost like Manchee.

"Wilf," says the man to Viola and it takes a second to realize he's saying his name.

"Hiya, Wilf," Viola says and her voice ain't her own, ain't her own at all, there's a whole new voice coming outta her mouth, stretching and shortening itself, twisting and unravelling and the more she talks the more different she sounds.

The more she sounds like Wilf.

"We're all fra Farbranch. Where yoo from?"

Wilf hangs his thumb back over his shoulder. "Bar Vista," he says. "I'm gone Brockley Falls, pick up s'plies."

"Well, at's lucky," Viola says. "We're gone Brockley Falls, too."

This is making my headache worse. I put my hands up to my temples, like I'm trying to keep my Noise inside, trying to keep all the wrong things from spilling out into the world. Luckily, the song of **Here** has made it like we're already swimming in sound.

"Hop on," Wilf says with a shrug.

"C'mon, Ben," Viola says, walking to the back of the cart and hoisting her bag on top. "Wilf's gone give us a ride."

She jumps on the cart and Wilf snaps the reins on his

oxes. They take off slowly and Wilf don't even look at me as he passes. I'm still standing there in amazement when Viola goes by, waving her hand frantically to me to get on beside her. I don't got no choice, do I? I catch up and pull myself up with my arms.

I sit down next to her and stare at her with my jaw down around my ankles. "*What are you doing?*" I finally hiss in what's sposed to be a whisper.

"*Shh!*" she shushes, looking back over her shoulder at Wilf, but he could've already forgotten he picked us up for all that's going on in his Noise. "I don't know," she whispers by my ear, "just play along."

"Play along with what?"

"If we can get to the other side of the herd, then it's between us and the army, isn't it?"

I hadn't thought about that. "But what are you doing? What do Ben and Hildy gotta do with it?"

"He has a gun," she whispers, checking on Wilf again. "And you said yourself how people might react about you being from a certain place. So, it just sort of popped out."

"But you were talking in his *voice*."

"Not very well."

"Good enough!" I say, my voice going a little loud with amazement.

"*Shh,*" she says a second time but with the combo of the herd of creachers getting closer by the second and Wilf's obvious not-too-brightness, we might as well be having a normal conversayshun.

"How do you do it?" I say, still pouring surprise out all over her.

"It's just lying, Todd," she says, trying to shush me again with her hands. "Don't you have lying here?"

Well of course we have lying here. New World and the town where I'm from (avoiding saying the name, avoiding *thinking* the name) seem to be nothing *but* lies. But that's different. I said it before, men lie all the time, to theirselves, to other men, to the world at large, but who can tell when it's a strand in all the other lies and truths floating round outta yer head? Everyone knows yer lying but everyone else is lying, too, so how can it matter? What does it change? It's just part of the river of a man, part of his Noise, and sometimes you can pick it out, sometimes you can't.

But he never stops being himself when he does it.

Cuz all I know about Viola is what she says. The only truth I got is what comes outta her mouth and so for a second back there, when she said she was Hildy and I was Ben and we were from Farbranch and she spoke just like Wilf (even tho he ain't from Farbranch) it was like all those things *became* true, just for an instant the world changed, just for a second it became made of Viola's voice and it wasn't describing a thing, it was *making* a thing, it was making us different just by saying it.

Oh, my head.

"Todd! Todd!" Manchee barks, popping up at the end of the cart, looking up thru our feet. "Todd!"

"Crap," Viola says.

I hop off the cart and sweep him up in my arms, putting one hand round his muzzle and using the other to get back on the cart. "Td?" he puffs thru closed lips.

"Quiet, Manchee," I say.

"I'm not even sure it matters," Viola says, her voice stretching out.

I look up.

"Cw," Manchee says.

A creacher is walking right past us.

We've entered the herd.

Entered the song.

And for a little while, I forget all about any kinda lies.

I've never seen the sea, only in vids. No lakes where I grew up neither, just the river and the swamp. There may have been boats once but not in my lifetime.

But if I had to imagine being on the sea, this is what I'd imagine. The herd surrounds us and takes up everything, leaving just the sky and us. It cuts around us like a current, sometimes noticing us but more usually noticing only itself and the song of **Here**, which in the midst of it is so loud it's like it's taken over the running of yer body for a while, providing the energy to make yer heart beat and yer lungs breathe.

After a while, I find myself forgetting all about Wilf and the – the other things I could think about and I'm just lying back on the cart, watching it all go by, individual creachers snuffling around, feeding, bumping each other now and again with their horns, and there's baby ones, too, and old bulls and taller ones and shorter ones and some with scars and some with scruffier fur.

Viola's laying down next to me and Manchee's little doggie brain is overwhelmed by it all and he's just watching the herd go by with his tongue hanging out and for a while, for a little while, as Wilf drives us over the plain, this is all there is in the world.

This is all there is.

I look over at Viola and she looks back at me and just smiles and shakes her head and wipes away the wet from her eyes.

Here.

Here.

We're **Here** and nowhere else.

Cuz there's nowhere else but **Here**.

"So this ... Aaron," Viola says after a while in a low voice and I know exactly why it's now that she brings him up.

It's so safe inside the **Here** we can talk about any dangers we like.

"Yeah?" I say, also keeping my voice low, watching a little family of creachers waltz by the end of the cart, the ma creacher nuzzling forward a curious baby creacher who's staring at us.

Viola turns to me from where she's lying down. "Aaron was your holy man?"

I nod. "Our one and only."

"What kind of things did he preach?"

"The usual," I say. "Hellfire. Damnayshun. Judgement."

She eyes me up. "I'm not sure that's the usual, Todd."

I shrug. "He believed we were living thru the end of the world," I say. "Who's to say he was wrong?"

She shakes her head. "That's not what the preacher we had on the ship was like. Pastor Marc. He was kind and friendly and made everything seem like it was going to be okay."

I snort. "No, that don't sound like Aaron at all. He was always saying, 'God hears' and 'If one of us falls, we all fall'.

Like he was looking forward to it."

"I heard him say that, too." She crosses her arms over herself.

The **Here** wraps us still, flowing everywhere.

I turn to her. "Did he… Did he hurt you? Back in the swamp?"

She shakes her head again and lets out a sigh. "He ranted and raved at me, and I guess it might have been preaching, but if I ran, he'd run after me and rant some more and I'd cry and ask him for help but he'd ignore me and preach some more and I'd see pictures of myself in his Noise when I didn't even know what Noise was. I've never been so scared in my life, not even when our ship was crashing."

We both look up into the sun.

"*If one of us falls, we all fall*," she says. "What does that even mean?"

Which, when I really think about it, I realize I don't know and so I don't say nothing and we just sink back into the **Here** and let it take us a little farther.

Here we are.

Not nowhere else.

After an hour or a week or a second, the creachers start thinning and we come out the other side of the herd. Manchee jumps down off the cart. We're going slow enough that there's no danger of him getting left behind so I let him. We're not thru lying there on the cart just yet.

"That was amazing," Viola says quietly, cuz the song is already starting to disappear. "I forgot all about how much my feet hurt."

"Yeah," I say.

"What *were* those?"

"'Em big thangs," Wilf says, not turning round. "Jus thangs, thass all."

Viola and I look at each other, like we forgot he was even there.

How much have we given away?

"'Em thangs got a name?" Viola asks, sitting up, acting her lie again.

"Oh, sure," Wilf says, giving the oxes freer rein now that we're outta the herd. "Packy Vines or Field Baysts or Anta Fants." We see him shrug from behind. "I just call 'em thangs, thass all."

"Thangs," Viola says.

"Things," I try.

Wilf looks back over his shoulder at us. "Say what, y'all from Farbranch?" he asks.

"Yessir," Viola says with a look at me.

Wilf nods at her. "Y'all bin seen that there army?"

My Noise spikes real loud before I can quiet it but again Wilf don't seem to notice. Viola looks at me, worry on her forehead.

"And what army's that, Wilf?" she says, the voice missing a little.

"That there army from cursed town," he says, still driving along like we're talking about vegetables. "That there army come outta swamp, come takin settlements, growin as it comes? Y'all bin seen that?"

"Where'd yoo hear bout an army, Wilf?"

"Stories," Wilf says. "Stories a-come chatterin down the

river. People talkin. Ya know. Stories. Y'all bin seen that?"

I shake my head at Viola but she says, "Yeah, we seen it."

Wilf looks back over his shoulder again. "Zit big?"

"Very big," Viola says, looking at him seriously. "Ya gotta prepare yerself, Wilf. There's danger comin. Yoo need to warn Brockley Hills."

"Brockley Falls," Wilf corrects her.

"Ya gotta warn 'em, Wilf."

We hear Wilf grunt and then we realize it's a laugh. "Ain't nobody lissnen to Wilf, I tell ya what," he says, almost to himself, then strikes the reins on the oxes again.

It takes most of the rest of the afternoon to get to the other side of the plain. Thru Viola's binos we can see the herd of things still crossing in the distance, from south to north, like they're never gonna run out. Wilf don't say nothing more about the army. Viola and I keep our talking to a bare minimum so we don't give any more away. Plus, it's so hard to keep my Noise clear it's taking mosta my concentrayshun. Manchee follows along on the road, doing his business and sniffing every flower.

When the sun is low in the sky, the cart finally creaks to a halt.

"Brockley Falls," Wilf says, nodding his head to where we can see in the distance the river tumbling off a low cliff. There's fifteen or twenty buildings gathered round the pond at the bottom of the falls before the river starts up again. A smaller road turns off from this one and leads down to it.

"We're getting off here," Viola says and we hop down, taking our bags from the cart.

"Thought ya mite," Wilf says, looking back over his shoulder at us again.

"Thank ya, Wilf," she says.

"Welcome," he says, staring off into the distance. "Best take shelter 'fore too long. Gone rain."

Both Viola and me automatically look straight up. There ain't a cloud in the sky.

"Mmm," Wilf says. "No one lissnen to Wilf."

Viola looks back at him, her voice returning to itself, trying to get the point to him clearly. "You have to warn them, Wilf. Please. If you're hearing that an army's coming, then you're right and people have to be ready."

All Wilf says is "Mmm" again before snapping the reins and turning the oxes down the split road towards Brockley Falls. He don't even look back once.

We watch him go for a while and then turn back to our own road.

"Ow," Viola says, stretching out her legs as she steps forward.

"I know," I say. "Mine too."

"You think he was right?" Viola says.

"Bout what?"

"About the army getting bigger as it marches." She imitates his voice again. "Growin as it comes."

"How do you *do* that?" I ask. "Yer not even from here."

She shrugs. "A game I used to play with my mother," she says. "Telling a story, using different voices for every character."

"Can you do my voice?" I ask, kinda tentative.

She grins. "*So you can have a conversayshun with yerself?*"

I frown. "That don't sound nothing like me."

We head back down the road, Brockley Falls disappearing behind us. The time on the cart was nice but it weren't sleep. We try to go as fast as we can but most times that ain't much more than a walk. Plus maybe the army really is caught far behind, really will have to wait behind the creachers.

Maybe. Maybe not. But within the half hour, you know what?

It's raining.

"People should listen to Wilf," Viola says, looking up.

The road's found its way back down near the river and we find a reasonably sheltered spot twixt the two. We'll eat our dinner, see if the rain stops. If it don't we got no choice but to walk in it anyway. I haven't even checked to see if Ben packed me a mac.

"What's a mac?" Viola asks as we sit down against different trees.

"A raincoat," I say, looking thru my rucksack. Nope, no mac. Great. "And what did I say bout listening too close?"

I still feel a little calm, if you wanna know the truth, tho I probably shouldn't. The song of **Here** still feels like it's being sung, even if I can't hear it, even if it's miles away back on the plain. I find myself humming it, even tho it don't have a tune, trying to get that feeling of connectedness, of *belonging*, of having someone there to say that you're **Here**.

I look over at Viola, eating outta one of her packets of fruit.

I think about my ma's book, still in my rucksack.

Stories in voices, I think.

Could I stand to hear my ma's voice spoken?

Viola crinkles the fruit packet she's just finished. "That's the last of them."

"I got some of this cheese left," I say, "and some dried mutton, but we're gonna have to start finding some of our own on the way."

"You mean like stealing?" she asks, her eyebrows up.

"I mean like hunting," I say. "But maybe stealing, too, if we have to. And there's wild fruit and I know some roots we can eat if you boil 'em first."

"Mmm." Viola frowns. "There's not much call for hunting on a spaceship."

"I could show you."

"Okay," she says, trying to sound cheerful. "Don't you need a gun?"

"Not if yer a good hunter. Rabbits are easy with snares. Fish with lines. You can catch squirrels with yer knife but there ain't much meat."

"Horse, Todd," Manchee barks, quietly.

I laugh, for the first time in what seems like forever. Viola laughs, too. "We ain't hunting *horses*, Manchee." I reach out to pet him. "Stupid dog."

"Horse," he barks again, standing up and looking down the road from the direkshun we just came.

We stop laughing.

23

A KNIFE IS ONLY AS GOOD AS THE ONE WHO WIELDS IT

THERE'S HOOFBEATS ON THE ROAD, distant but approaching at full gallop.

"Someone from Brockley Hills?" Viola says, hope and doubt both in her voice.

"Brockley *Falls*," I say, standing. "We need to hide."

We repack our bags in a hurry. It's a narrow strip of trees we've managed to get ourselves stuck in twixt the road and the river. We daren't cross the road and with the river at our backs, a fallen log is the best we're gonna get. We gather the last of our things and crouch down behind it, Manchee held twixt my knees, rain splashing everywhere.

I take out my knife.

The hoofbeats keep coming, louder and louder.

"Only one horse," Viola whispers. "It's not the army."

"Yeah," I say, "but listen how fast he's riding."

Thump budda-thump budda-thump we hear. Thru the trees we can see the dot of him approaching. He's coming full out down the road, even tho it's raining and night's falling. No one'd ride like that with good news, would they?

Viola looks behind us at the river. "Can you swim?"

"Yeah."

"Good," she says. "Because I can't."

Thump budda-thump budda-thump.

I can hear the buzz of the rider's Noise starting but for a time the galloping is louder and I can't hear it clearly.

"Horse," Manchee says from down below.

It's there. Static twixt the hoofbeats. Flashes of it. Parts of words caught. Rid– and Pa– and Dark– and Stup– and more and more.

I clench the knife harder. Viola's not saying nothing now.

Thump budda-thump budda-thump budda–

Faster and Nightfall and Shot and Whatever it–

And he's coming down the road, round a little curve we took just a hundred metres back, leaning forward–

Thump budda–

The knife turns in my hand cuz–

Shot 'em all and She was tasty and Dark here–

Thump BUDDA–

I think I reckernize–

THUMP BUDDA-THUMP BUDDA–

And he's nearer and nearer till he's almost–

And then Todd Hewitt? rings out as clear as day thru the rain and the galloping and the river.

Viola gasps.

And I can see who it is.

"Junior," Manchee barks.

It's Mr Prentiss Jr.

We try to duck down farther below the log but it ain't no use cuz we already see him pulling back hard on the reins to stop his horse, causing it to rear up and nearly throw him.

But only nearly.

And not enough to make him drop the rifle he's got under one arm.

TODD BLOODY HEWITT! screams his Noise.

"Oh, shit," I hear Viola say and I know what she means.

"Well, HOOO-EEE!" Mr Prentiss Jr yells and we're close enough to see the smile on his face and hear amazement in his voice. "Yer taking the *ROAD*?! You ain't even going *OFF TRAIL?!*"

My eyes meet Viola's. What choice did we have?

"I been hearing yer Noise for almost yer whole stupid life, boy!" He turns his horse this way and that, trying to find where exactly we are in our little strip of woods. "You think I'm not gonna hear it if ya just *HIDE*?"

There's joy in his Noise. Real joy, like he can't believe his luck.

"And wait a minute," he says and we can hear him edging his horse off the road and into the woods. "Wait just a minute. What's that beside you? That empty space of *nothing*."

He says it so nasty Viola flinches. I got the knife in my hand but he's on horseback and we know he's got a gun.

"Too effing right I've got a gun, Todd boy," he calls, no longer searching round but coming straight for us, getting his horse to step over bushes and round trees. "And I got another gun, too, another one special, just for yer little lady there, Todd."

I look at Viola. I know she sees what he's thinking, what's in his Noise, the pictures that ooze out of it. I know she does cuz I can see her face closing right up. I bump her arm and I flash my eyes over to our right, just about the only possibility we have for an escape.

"Oh, *please* run, boy," Mr Prentiss Jr calls. "Please give me a reason to hurt you."

The horse is so close we can hear its Noise, too, jittery and crazy.

There's no farther down we can crouch.

He's nearly on top of us.

I grip the knife and squeeze Viola's hand once, hard, for luck.

It's now or never.

And–

"NOW!" I yell.

We jump up and a gun blast rings out, splintering the branches over our heads, but we run anyway.

"GET!" Mr Prentiss Jr shouts to his horse and here they come.

In two bounds, his horse turns and jumps back to the road, following along it as we run. The strip twixt the road and the river ain't getting any thicker and we can see each other as we go. Branches snap and puddles splash and feet slip and he pounds along the road matching our every step.

We ain't gonna get away from him. We just ain't.

But we try, each of us taking a twisty path up and over logs and thru bushes and Manchee's panting and barking at our heels and the rain's splashing down on us and the road's getting closer and then it suddenly veers sharply towards the river and we got no choice but to cross it in front of him to get to the deeper woods on the other side and I can see Viola leaping over the boundary and onto the road with her arms pumping and Mr Prentiss Jr rounding the bend and he's twirling something in his hand and we make a dash for the other side but the horse is roaring down on us and suddenly I feel something grab my legs, binding 'em so fast and so tight I fall right off my feet.

"Aaagh!" I yell and I hit my face into muck and fallen leaves and the rucksack goes over my head and nearly rips my arms off as it flies off my back and Viola sees me fall and she's nearly cross the road but I see mud curling up from where her feet are digging in to stop herself and I shout, "NO! RUN! RUN!" and she locks my eyes and I see something change on her face but who knows what it means and as the horse bears down she turns and disappears into the woods and Manchee runs back to me and barks "Todd! Todd!" and I'm caught I'm caught I'm caught.

Cuz Mr Prentiss Jr is standing over me, breathing hard, high on his white horse, rifle cocked and pointed. I know what's happened. He's thrown a rope with weights at either end right at my legs and they've twisted round and caught me, expert, just like a hunter after swamp deer. I'm stuck down here in the mud on my belly, caught like an animal.

"My pa sure is gonna be glad to see you," he says, his horse nervy and stepping side to side. **Rain**, I can hear it thinking, and **Is it a snake?**

"I was just sposed to see if there were rumours of you on

the road ahead," Mr Prentiss Jr sneers, "but here you are, in the real honest-to-God flesh."

"Eff you," I say and do you think I say eff?

I've still got the knife in my hand.

"And it sure is making me quake with fear," he says, moving the rifle so I'm looking right down the barrel. "Drop it."

I hold my arm out away from me and drop the knife. It splashes in the mud and I'm still on my belly.

"Yer little lady sure didn't show you no loyalty, now did she?" he says, hopping off his horse, calming it with his free hand. Manchee growls at him but Mr Prentiss Jr just laughs. "What happened to its tail?"

Manchee jumps, his teeth bared, but Mr Prentiss Jr is faster, kicking him away with a vicious boot to the face. Manchee yelps and cowers into the bushes.

"Friends abandoning you right and left, Todd." He walks over to me. "But that's the lesson you learn, eh? Dogs is dogs and women turn out to be dogs, too."

"You *shut* up," I say, clenching my teeth.

His Noise goes all fake sympathy and triumph. "Poor, poor Toddy. All this time travelling with a woman and I'm guessing you never figured out what to do with one."

"You stop talking bout her," I spit. I'm still on my belly and my legs are still tied.

But I find I can bend my knees.

His Noise gets uglier, louder, but his face is all blank like a terror from a dream. "What you do, Todd," he says, squatting down to get closer to me, "is you keep the ones that're whores and you shoot the ones that're not."

He leans even closer. I can see the pathetic hairs on his upper lip, not even made darker by the rain coming down. He's only two years older than me. Only two years bigger.

Snake? thinks the horse.

I put my hands slowly down on the ground.

I push a little into the mud.

"After I tie you up," he says, turning it into a whispering taunt, "I'll go find yer little lady and let you know which kind she is."

Which is when I jump.

I push up with my hands and kick forward hard with my legs, launching myself right at his face. The top of my head hits his nose with a crunch and he falls backwards, me coming down right on top of him. I hit him hard in the face with each fist while he's still too surprised to react and then ram my knee into the man's place twixt his legs.

He curls up like a bug and lets out a low, angry moan and I roll off him back over to my knife, picking it up and getting to my feet and I kick the gun away and I jump in front of the horse screaming "Snake! Snake!" and waving my arms which does the trick instantly and it turns and runs back down the road with a terrified whinny, riderless into the rain.

I look round and *BAM!* Mr Prentiss Jr hits me across the bridge of the nose with his fist but I don't fall and he yells "You piece of–" and I swing my arm out with the knife in it and I make him jump back and I swing it again, water pouring outta my eyes from both the punch and the rain and he steps away from me, looking for his gun and limping a little and he sees it in the mud and he turns his body to fetch it and I'm not thinking at all and I jump on him, knocking him back down and he hits me with his elbow but I don't fall off and my Noise is screaming and his Noise is screaming.

And I don't even know how but I've got him on his back and the point of my knife held up under his chin.

We both stop struggling.

"Why are you after us?!" I shout into his face. "Why are you chasing us?!"

And him and his stupid pathetic non-moustache *smile*.

I knee him again twixt his legs.

He groans again and spits at me but I've still got the knife which has now made a little cut.

"My father wants you," he finally says.

"Why?" I say. "Why does he want us?"

"*Us?*" His eyes go wide. "There's no effing *us*. He wants you, Todd. Just you."

I can't believe this. "What?" I say. "*Why?*"

But he's not answering. He's looking into my Noise. He's looking and searching.

"Hey!" I say, slapping him cross the face with the back of my hand. "Hey! I'm asking you an asking!"

But the smile's back. I can't effing believe it but the smile's back.

"You know what my father always says, Todd Hewitt?" he leers up at me. "He says a knife is only as good as the one who wields it."

"Shut up," I say.

"Yer a fighter, I'll give you that." Still smiling, still bleeding a little below his chin. "But you ain't no killer."

"Shut *up*!" I yell but I know he can see in my Noise that I heard those exact words from Aaron.

"Oh, yeah?" he says. "Whaddya gonna do about it? *Kill* me?"

"I WILL," I shout. "I'll *KILL* you!"

He just licks some rain from his lips and laughs. I have him pinned to the ground with a knife up under his chin and he's *laughing*.

"STOP IT!" I scream at him and I raise the knife.

He keeps on laughing and then he looks at me and he says–

He says–

He says *this*–

"You wanna hear how Ben and Cillian screamed for mercy before I shot 'em twixt the eyes?"

And my Noise buzzes red.

And I clench the knife to strike at him.

And I'm going to kill him.

I'm going to *kill* him.

And–

And–

And–

And right at the top of my swing–

Right at the moment when I start to bring it down–

Right at the moment when the power is mine to command and do with as I please–

I hesitate–

Again–

I hesitate–

Only for a second–

But goddam me–

Goddam me forever and forever–

Cuz in that second he kicks up his legs, throws me off him and elbows me in the throat. I lean over choking and I can only feel his hand wrench the knife away from my own.

As easy as candy from a baby.

"Now, Todd," he says, standing over me, "let me show you a thing or two about wielding."

24

THE DEATH OF THE WORTHLESS COWARD

I DESERVE IT. I've done everything wrong. I deserve it. If I had the knife back I'd kill myself with it. Except I'd probably be too much of a coward to do that, too.

"Yer some piece of work, Todd Hewitt," Mr Prentiss Jr says, examining my knife.

I'm kneeling now, knees in the mud, hand at my throat, still trying to get my breath.

"You had this fight won and then you went and just threw it away." He runs a finger up the blade. "Stupid as well as yella."

"Just finish it," I mumble into the mud.

"What was that?" Mr Prentiss Jr says, the smile back, his Noise bright.

"Just FINISH IT!" I shout up to him.

"Oh, I'm not gonna kill you," he says, his eyes flashing. "My pa wouldn't be too happy with that, now would he?"

He steps up to me and holds the knife near my face.

He puts the tip of it into my nose so I have to hold my head back farther and farther.

"But there's lots of things you can do with a knife," he says, "without killing a man."

I'm not even looking round no more for ways to get away.

I'm looking right into his eyes which are awake and alive and about to win, his Noise the same, pictures of him in Farbranch, pictures from back at my farm, pictures of me kneeling in front of him.

There ain't nothing in my Noise but a pit full of my stupidity and worthlessness and hate.

I'm sorry, Ben.

I'm so, so sorry.

"But then again," he says, "you *ain't* a man, are ya?" He lowers his voice. "And you never will be."

He moves the knife in his hand, turning the blade towards my cheek.

I close my eyes.

And I feel a wash of silence flow over me from behind.

My eyes snap open.

"Well, looky here," Mr Prentiss Jr says, glancing up over the top of my head. My back is to the deeper woods opposite the river and I can feel the quiet of Viola standing there as clearly as if I could see her.

"Run!" I yell, without turning round. "Get away from here."

She ignores me. "Step back," I hear her say to Mr Prentiss Jr. "I'm warning you."

"Yer warning *me*?" he says, pointing to himself with the knife, the smile back on his face.

Then he jumps a little as something smacks him in the chest and sticks there. It looks like a bunch of little wires with a plastic bulb on the end. Mr Prentiss Jr puts the knife underneath it and tries to flick it off but it stays stuck. He looks up at Viola, smirking. "Whatever this is sposed to be, sister," he says, "it didn't work."

And *SMACKFLASH!!*

There's a huge clap of light and I feel a hand on the back of my collar yank me back to the point of choking. I fall back and away as Mr Prentiss Jr's body jerks into a spasm, flinging the knife out to one side, sparks and little flashes of lightning flying out of the wires and into his body. Smoke and steam comes from everywhere, his sleeves, his collar, his pantlegs. Viola's still pulling me back outta the way by my neck when he falls to the ground, face first in the muck, right on top of his rifle.

She lets go and we tumble together on a little bank by the side of the road. I grab my neck again and we lay there breathing heavily for a second. The sparks and flashes stop and Mr Prentiss Jr twitches in the mud.

"I was afraid –" Viola says twixt deep breaths "– all this water around –" breath "– that I might take you and me with him –" breath "– but he was about to cut–"

I stand without saying nothing, my Noise focused, my eyes on the knife. I go right to it.

"Todd–" Viola says.

I pick it up and stand over him. "Is he dead?" I ask without looking at Viola.

"Shouldn't be," she says. "It was just the voltage from a–"

I raise the knife.

"Todd, no!"

"Give me one good reason," I say, knife still hovering, eyes still on him.

"You're not a killer, Todd," she says.

I spin round to her, my Noise roaring up like a beast. "Don't SAY THAT!! Don't you EVER SAY THAT!!"

"Todd," she says, her hand out, her voice calming.

"I'M why we're in this mess! They're not looking for YOU! They're looking for *ME!*" I turn back to Mr Prentiss Jr. "And if I could kill one of them, then maybe we–"

"Todd, no, listen to me," she says, coming closer. "Listen to me!" I look at her. My Noise is so ugly and my face so twisted she hesitates a little but then she takes another step forward. "Listen to me while I tell you something."

And then out pour more words from her than I ever heard before.

"When you found me, back there in the swamp, I had been running from that man, from Aaron, for four days, and you were only the second person I'd ever seen on this planet and you came at me with that same knife and for all I knew you were exactly like him."

Her hands are still up, like I'm Mr Prentiss Jr's long-gone horse in need of calming.

"But before I even understood what was going on with the Noise and with Prentisstown and with whatever your story was, I could tell about you. People can tell, Todd. We can see that you won't hurt us. That that's not you."

"You hit me in the face with a branch," I say.

She puts her hands on her hips. "Well, what did you expect? You came at me with a knife. But I didn't hit you hard enough to hurt you badly, did I?"

I don't say nothing.

"And I was right," she says. "You bandaged my arm. You rescued me from Aaron when you didn't have to. You took me out of the swamp where I would have been killed. You stood up for me to that man in the orchard. You came with me when we needed to leave Farbranch."

"No," I say, my voice low, "no, yer not reading the story right. We're only having to run cuz I couldn't–"

"I think I'm finally *understanding* the story, Todd," she says. "Why are they coming after you so fiercely? Why is a whole army chasing you across towns and rivers and plains and the whole stupid planet?" She points to Mr Prentiss Jr. "I heard what he said. Don't you wonder why they want you so badly?"

The pit in me is just getting blacker and darker. "Cuz I'm the one who don't fit."

"Exactly!"

My eyes go wide. "Why is that good news? I have an army who wants to kill me cuz I'm not a killer."

"Wrong," she says. "You have an army who wants to *make* you a killer."

I blink. "Huh?"

She takes another step forward. "If they can turn you into the kind of man they want–"

"Boy," I say. "Not a man yet."

She waves this away. "If they can snuff out that part of you that's good, the part of you that won't kill, then they win, don't you see? If they can do it to you, they can do it to anyone. And they win. They *win*!"

She's near me now and she reaches out her hand and puts it on my arm, the one still holding the knife.

"We beat them," she says, "*you* beat them by not becoming what they want."

I clench my teeth. "He killed Ben and Cillian."

She shakes her head. "No, he *said* he did. And you believed him."

We look down at him. He's not twitching no more and the steam is starting to lessen.

"I know this kind of boy," she says. "We have this kind of boy even on spaceships. He's a liar."

"He's a man."

"How can you keep *saying that*?" she asks, her voice finally snappy. "How can you keep saying that he's a man and you're not? Just because of some stupid *birthday*? If you were where I came from you'd already be fourteen and a month!"

"I'm not where yer from!" I shout. "I'm from *here* and that's how it works here!"

"Well, how it works here is *wrong*." She lets go of my arm and kneels down by Mr Prentiss Jr. "We'll tie him up. We'll tie him up good and tight and we'll get the heck out of here, all right?"

I don't let go of the knife.

I will never let go of this knife, no matter what she says, no matter how she says it.

She looks up and around. "Where's Manchee?"

Oh, no.

We find him in the bushes. He growls at us without words, just animal growls. He's holding his left eye shut and there's blood around his mouth. It takes a bunch of tries but I finally catch him while Viola takes out her medipak-of-wonders. I hold him down as she forces him to swallow a pill that makes him go floppy and then she cleans out his broken teeth and puts a cream in his eye. She tapes a bandage to it and he looks so small and beaten that when he says "Thawd?" thru one-eyed grogginess I just hug him to me and sit for a bit, under the bushes, outta the rain, while Viola repacks everything and gets my rucksack outta the mud.

"Your clothes are all wet," she says after a while. "And the food is smashed. But the book's still in the plastic. The book's all right."

And the thought of my ma knowing what a coward her son would be one day makes me want to throw the book in the river.

But I don't.

We go to tie up Mr Prentiss Jr with his own rope and find that the electric shock has blown the wooden stock right off of his rifle. Which is a shame cuz it coulda come in handy.

"What was that you shocked him with?" I ask, huffing and puffing as we drag him to the side of the road. Knocked out people are *heavy*.

"A device for telling the ship in space where I am on the planet," she says. "It took forever to pull apart."

I stand up. "How will yer ship know where you are now?"

She shrugs. "We just have to hope that Haven'll have something."

I watch her go to her own bag and pick it up. I sure hope Haven has half what she's expecting.

We leave. Mr Prentiss Jr was right about the stupidity of staying on the road, so we keep twenty or thirty metres away from it on the non-river side, trying to keep it in sight as best we can. We take turns carrying Manchee as the night passes.

We don't talk much neither.

Cuz she might have a point, right? Yeah, okay, maybe that's what the army's after, maybe if they can make me join, they can make anyone join. Maybe I'm their test, who knows, the whole town's crazy enough to believe something like that.

If one of us falls, we all fall.

But for one that don't explain why Aaron's after us and for two I've heard her lie now, ain't I? Her words sound good but who's to know if she's making truth up rather than just saying it?

Cuz I'm *never* going to join the army and Mayor Prentiss must know that, not after what they did to Ben and Cillian, the truth of Mr Prentiss Jr's Noise or not, so that's where she's dead wrong. Whatever they want, whatever the weakness is in me that I can't kill a man even when he deserves it, it's got to change for me to be a man. It's *got* to or how can I hold my head up?

Midnight passes and I'm twenty-five days and a million years from becoming a man.

Cuz if I'd killed Aaron, he couldn't've told Mayor Prentiss where he'd seen me last.

If I coulda killed Mr Prentiss Jr back at the farm,

he wouldn't've led the Mayor's men to Ben and Cillian and wouldn't've lived to harm Manchee so.

If I'd been any kinda killer, I coulda stayed and helped Ben and Cillian defend themselves.

Maybe if I was a killer, they wouldn't be dead.

And that's a trade I'd make any day.

I'll be a killer, if that's what it takes.

Watch me.

The terrain's getting rougher and steeper as the river starts making canyons again. We rest for a while under a rocky outcropping and eat the last of the food that didn't get ruined by the fight with Mr Prentiss Jr.

I lay Manchee across my lap. "What was in that pill?"

"It was just a little crumb of a human painkiller," she says. "I hope it's not too much."

I run my hand over his fur. He's warm and asleep so at least still living.

"Todd–" she says, but I stop her.

"I wanna keep moving as long as we can," I say. "I know we should sleep but let's go till we can't go no more."

She waits a minute and then she says, "Okay", and we don't say nothing more, just finish the last of the food.

The rain keeps up all night as we go and there's no racket like rainfall in the woods, a billion drops pattering down a billion leaves, the river swelling and roaring, the squish of the mud under our feet. I hear Noise now and again in the distance, probably from woodland creachers but always outta sight, always gone when we get near.

"Is there anything out here that could harm us?" Viola asks me, having to raise her voice over the rain.

"Too many to count," I say. I gesture to Manchee in her arms. "He awake yet?"

"Not yet," she says, worry in her voice. "I hope I–"

And that's how unprepared we are when we step round another rocky outcropping and into the campsite.

We both stop immediately and take in what's in front of our eyes, all in a flash.

A fire burning.

Freshly caught fish hanging from a spit over it.

A man leaning over a stone, scraping scales from another fish.

That man looking up as we step into his campsite.

In an *instant*, like knowing Viola was a girl even tho I'd never seen one, I know in the second it takes me to reach for my knife, I know that he's not a man at all.

He's a Spackle.

25

KILLER

THE WORLD STOPS SPINNING.

The rain stops falling, the fire stops burning, my heart stops beating.

A Spackle.

There ain't no more Spackle.

They all died in the wars.

There ain't no more Spackle.

And here's one standing right in front of me.

He's tall and thin like in the vids I remember, white skin, long fingers and arms, the mouth mid-face where it ain't sposed to be, the ear flaps down by the jaw, eyes blacker than swamp stones, lichen and moss growing where clothes should be.

Alien. As alien as you can be.

Holy crap.

You might as well just crumple up the world I know and throw it away.

"Todd?" Viola says.

"Don't move," I say.

Cuz thru the sound of the rain I can hear the Spackle's *Noise*.

No words come out clear, just pictures, skewed up strange and with all the wrong colours, but pictures of me and Viola standing in front of him, looking shocked.

Pictures of the knife now outstretched in my hand.

"Todd," Viola says, a small warning in her voice.

Cuz his Noise has more in it. It's got feelings, washing up in a buzz.

Feelings of fear.

I feel his fear.

Good.

My Noise turns red.

"Todd," Viola says again.

"Quit saying my name," I say.

The Spackle pulls himself slowly upright from where he's skinning the fish. He's made his camp underneath another rocky outcropping down the slope of a small hill. A good part of it's dry and I see bags and a roll of moss that might be a bed.

There's also something shiny and long resting against the rock.

I can see the Spackle picture it in his Noise.

It's the spear he's been using to catch fish in the river.

"*Don't*," I say to him.

I think for a second, but *only* for a second, how clear I understand all this, how clear I can see him standing in the river, how easy he is to read, even tho it's all pictures.

But the second passes in a flash.

Cuz I see him thinking about making a leap for the spear.

"Todd?" she says. "Put the knife down."

And he makes his leap.

I leap at the same time.

(Watch me.)

"No!" I hear Viola scream but my Noise is roaring way too loud for me to hear it as more than a whisper.

Cuz all I'm thinking as I take running steps across the campsite, knife up and ready, bearing down on the Spackle, all skinny knees and elbows as he stumbles heading for his spear, all I'm thinking and sending forward to him in my red, red Noise are images and words and feelings, of all I know, all that's happened to me, all the times I failed to use the knife, every bit of me screaming–

I'll show you who's a killer.

I get to him before he gets to the spear, barrelling into him with my shoulder. We fall to the less muddy dirt with a thud and his arms and legs are all over me, long, like wrestling with a spider, and he's striking me about the head but they're little more than slaps really and I realize and I realize and I realize–

I realize he's weaker than me.

"Todd, stop it!" I hear Viola call.

He scrabbles away from me and I thump him on the side of his head with a fist and he's so light it topples him over onto a pile of rocks and he looks back up at me and his mouth is making a hissing sound and there's terror and panic flying outta his Noise.

"STOP IT!" Viola screams. "Can't you see how scared he is?"

"And well he should be!" I yell back.

Cuz there ain't no stopping my Noise now.

I step towards him and he tries to crawl away but I grab him by his long white ankle and drag him off the rocks back onto the ground and he's making this horrible *keening* sound and I ready my knife.

And Viola must've put Manchee down somewhere cuz she grabs my arm and she pulls it back to stop me cutting down the spack and I push into her with my body to shake her off but she won't let go and we go stumbling away from the Spackle who cowers down by a rock, his hands in front of his face.

"Let go of me!" I yell.

"Please, Todd!" she yells back, pulling and twisting my arm. "Stop this, please!"

I twist my arm around and use my free one to push her away and when I turn the Spackle's skittered along the ground–

Heading for his spear–

Has his fingers on the end–

And all my hate erupts into me like a volcano at full bright red–

And I fall on him–

And I punch the knife into his chest.

It crunches as it goes in, turning to the side as it hits a bone and the Spackle screams the most terrible, terrible sound and dark red blood (red, it's red, they bleed *red*) sprays outta the wound and he brings a long arm up and scratches across my face and I pull back my arm and I stab him again and a long screeching breath comes outta his mouth with a loud gurgle and his arms and legs still scramble around him and he looks at me with his black, black eyes and his Noise filled with pain and bafflement and fear–

And I twist the knife–

And he won't die and he won't die and he won't die–

And in a moan and a shudder he dies.

And his Noise stops altogether.

I gag in my throat and I yank out the knife and paddle my way back along the mud.

I look at my hands, at the knife. There's blood all over everything. The knife is covered with it, even all over the handle, and both my hands and arms and the front of my clothes and a splash on my face that I wipe away mingling with my own blood from the scratch.

Even with the rain coming down on me now there's more of it than seems possible.

The Spackle lays where I–

Where I killed him.

I hear Viola make a choking and gasping sound and I look up to her and when I do she flinches back from me.

"You don't know!" I shout at her. "You don't know anything! They started the war. They killed my ma! All of it, everything that's happened, is their fault!"

And then I throw up.

And I keep throwing up.

And when my Noise starts to calm I throw up all over again.

I keep my head to the ground.

The world has stopped.

The world is still stopped.

I don't hear nothing from Viola but her silence. I feel my rucksack digging into the back of my neck as I lean forward. I don't look over at the Spackle.

"He woulda killed us," I finally say, talking into the ground.

Viola don't say nothing.

"He woulda killed us," I say again.

"He was *terrified*!" Viola cries, her voice breaking. "Even I could see how scared he was."

"He went for his spear," I say, lifting my head.

"Because you came after him with a knife!" I can see her now. Her eyes are wide and growing more blank, like they did when she closed up on herself and started rocking.

"They killed everyone on New World," I say.

She shakes her head, fiercely. "You idiot! You stupid fucking IDIOT!"

She don't say effing.

"How many times have you found out that what you've been told isn't true?" she says, backing away from me even further, her face twisting. "How many times?"

"Viola–"

"Weren't all the Spackle killed in the war?" she says and my God how I hate how frightened her voice sounds. "Huh? *Weren't they*?"

And the last of my anger drops outta my Noise as I

realize how I've been the fool again–

And I turn round to the Spackle–

And I see the campsite–

And I see the fish on the lines–

And (no no no no no) I see the fear that was coming from his Noise–

(No no no, please no.)

And there's nothing left for me to throw up but I heave anyway–

And I'm a killer–

I'm a killer–

I'm a killer–

(Oh, please no) I'm a killer.

I start to shake. I start to shake so bad I can't stand up. I find I'm saying "No" over and over again and the fear in his Noise keeps echoing around mine and there's nowhere to run from it, it's just there and there and there and I'm shaking so bad I can't even stay on my hands and knees and I fall into the mud and I can still see the blood everywhere and the rain's not washing it off.

I squeeze my eyes shut tight.

And there's only blackness.

Only blackness and nothing.

One more time, I've ruined everything. One more time, I've done everything wrong.

From a long way away I can hear Viola saying my name.

But it's so far away.

And I'm alone. Here and always, alone.

I hear my name again.

From a far, far distance I feel a pull on my arm.

It's only when I hear a squib of Noise not my own that I open my eyes.

"I think there's more of them out there," Viola whispers down near my ear.

I raise my head. My own Noise is so filled with junk and horror that it's hard to hear clearly and the rain is still falling, heavy as ever, and I take a stupid moment to wonder if we'll ever get dry again and then I hear it, murmuring and indistinct in the trees, impossible to pin down but definitely out there.

"If they didn't want to kill us before," Viola says, "they'll sure want to do it now."

"We need to go." I try to get to my feet. I'm still shaking and it takes a try or two, but I do.

I'm still holding the knife. It's sticky with blood.

I throw it to the ground.

Viola's face is a terrible thing, grieved and scared and horrified, all at me, all at me, but as ever we ain't got no choice so I just say again, "We need to go," and I go to pick up Manchee from where she'd set him down in the dry lee of the Spackle's outcropping.

He's still sleeping and shivering from the cold when I pick him up and I bury my face in his fur and breathe in his familiar doggy stink.

"*Hurry*," Viola says.

And I turn back to her to see her looking all around, the Noise still whispering all around thru the woods and the rain, the fear still on her face.

She returns her gaze to me and I find it impossible to hold and so I look away.

But as I'm looking away, I see movement behind her.

I see the bushes part behind where she's standing.

And I see her see my face changing.

And she turns in time to see Aaron coming outta the woods behind her.

And he's grabbing her by the neck with one hand and smashing a cloth over her nose and mouth with the other and as I call out and take a step forward I hear her scream from beneath it and she tries to fight with her hands but Aaron's holding her tight and by the time I've taken my second and third steps she's already swooning from whatever's on the cloth and on my fourth and fifth steps he's dropping her to the ground and Manchee is still in my arms and on my sixth step he's reaching behind his back and I don't have my knife and I have Manchee with me and I can only run towards him and on my seventh step I see him bring around a wooden staff that's been strapped to his back and it swings thru the air and strikes me full on the side of my head with a

CRACK

and I fall and Manchee tumbles from my arms and I crash into the ground on my belly and my head is ringing so hard I can't even catch myself and the world goes wobbly and grey and full of only pain and I'm on the ground and everything is tilting and sliding and my arms and legs weigh too much to lift and my face is half in the mud but half turned up and I can see Aaron watching me on the ground and I see his Noise and Viola in it and I see him see my knife shining red in the mud and he picks it up and I try to crawl away but the weight of my body sticks me to the spot and I can only watch as he stands over me.

"I have no further use for you, boy," he says and he raises the knife over his head and the last thing I see is him bringing it down with the full force of his arm.

PART V

26

THE END OF ALL THINGS

FALLING NO FALLING no please *help me Falling* The Knife *The Knife* Spackle spacks are dead, all spacks dead *VIOLA* sorry, please, sorry *he's got a spear* FALLING Please please *Aaron, behind you! He's coming!* no further use to me, boy *Viola falling*, Viola Eade spackle *the screaming and the blood and no* WATCH ME watch me no *please* watch me he woulda killed us *Ben* please I'm sorry *Aaron! Run!* E-A-D-E More of them *we have to get outta here* FALLING falling dark blood *The Knife* dead run *I'm a killer please no* SPACKLE *Viola Viola Viola*–

"Viola!" I try and scream but it's blackness, it's blackness with no sound, blackness and I've fallen and I have no voice–

"Viola," I try again and there's water in my lungs and an ache in my gut and pain, pain in my–

"Aaron," I whisper to myself and no one. "Run, it's Aaron."

And then I fall again and it's blackness…

…

…

"Todd?"

…

"Todd?"

Manchee.

"Todd?"

I can feel a dog's tongue on my face which means I can feel my face which means I can tell where it is and with a rush of air clanging into me, I open my eyes.

Manchee's standing right by my head, shifting from foot to foot, licking his lips and nose nervously, the bandage still over his eye, but he's all blurry and it's hard to–

"Todd?"

I try to say his name to calm him but all I do is cough and a sharp pain soars thru my back. I'm still down on my belly in the muck, where I fell when Aaron–

Aaron.

When Aaron hit me in the head with his staff. I try to raise my head and a blinding ache stretches over the right side of my skull all the way down to my jaw and I have to lie there gritting my teeth for a minute just letting it hurt and blaze before I can even try speaking again.

"Todd?" Manchee whimpers.

"I'm here, Manchee," I finally mutter but it comes up outta my chest like a growl held back by goo and it sets off more coughing–

Which I have to cut short cuz of the sharp pain in my back.

My back.

I stifle another cough and a horror feeling spreads out from my gut into the rest of me.

The last thing I saw before–

No.

Oh, no.

I cough a little in my throat, trying not to move any muscle at all, failing at it and surviving the pain till it ebbs as far as it's gonna and then I work on making my mouth move without killing me.

"Is there a knife in me, Manchee?" I rasp.

"Knife, Todd," he barks and there's worry all over him. "Back, Todd."

He comes forward to lick my face again, the dog way of trying to make it better. All I do is breathe and not move for a minute. I close my eyes and pull air inside, despite how my lungs are complaining and already seem full.

I am Todd Hewitt, I think, which is a mistake, cuz here comes all of it back, falling on me, dragging me down and the Spackle's blood and Viola's face frightened of me and Aaron coming outta the woods and taking her–

I start to weep but the pain from the grip of the weep is so bad that for a minute I feel paralysed and a living fire burns thru my arms and back and there's nothing to do but suffer it till it goes.

Slowly, slowly, slowly, I start to uncurl one arm from beneath me. My head and back hurt so bad I think I pass out for a minute but I wake again and slowly, slowly, slowly reach my hand up and behind me, crawling my fingers up my wet filthy shirt and up the wet filthy rucksack which unbelievably I'm still wearing and up and back till there it is under my fingertips.

The handle of the knife. Sticking outta my back.

But I'd be dead.

I'd be *dead*.

Am I dead?

"Not dead, Todd," Manchee barks. "Sack! Sack!"

The knife is sticking in me, up high twixt my shoulder blades, the pain's telling me all about it very specifically, but the knife's gone thru the rucksack first, something in the rucksack's stopped the knife from going all the way in–

The book.

My ma's book.

I feel with my fingers again, slowly as I can, but yes, Aaron raised his arm and brought it down thru the book in the rucksack and it's stopped it from going all the way thru my body.

(Like it did thru the Spackle.)

I close my eyes again and try to take as deep a breath as possible which ain't too deep and then I hold it till I can get my fingers round the knife and then I have to breathe and wait till the pain passes and then I try to pull but it's the heaviest thing in the world and I have to wait and breathe and try again and I pull and the pain in my back increases like a gun firing and I scream out uncontrollably as I feel the knife come outta my back.

I gasp and pant for a minute and try to stop from weeping again, all the while holding the knife away from me, still stuck thru the book and the rucksack.

Manchee licks my face once more.

"Good boy," I say, tho I don't know why.

It takes what feels like a lifetime to get the rucksack straps off my arms and finally be able to cast the knife and the whole mess aside. Even then, I can't come near standing up and I must pass out again cuz Manchee's licking my face and I'm having to open my eyes and cough in my breath all over again.

As I lay there, still in the muck, I wish to myself more than anything in the whole world that Aaron's knife had gone thru me, that I was as dead as the Spackle, that I could finish falling down that pit, down down down till there's only blackness, down into the nowhere where there's no more Todd to blame or screw things up or fail Ben or fail Viola, and I could fall away forever into nothingness and never have to worry no more.

But here's Manchee, licking away.

"Get off." I reach up an arm to push him away.

Aaron coulda killed me, coulda killed me so easy.

The knife thru my neck, the knife in my eye, the knife across my throat. I was his for the killing and he didn't kill me. He musta known what he was doing. He *musta*.

Was he leaving me for the Mayor to find? But why was he so far ahead of the army? How could he have come all this way without a horse like Mr Prentiss Jr? How long had he been following us?

How long before he stepped outta the bushes and took Viola away?

I let out a little moan.

That's why he left me alive. So I could live knowing that he took Viola. That's how he wins, ain't it? That's how he makes me suffer. Living and having the sight of him taking her forever in my Noise.

A new kinda energy runs thru me and I make myself sit up, ignoring the pain and bringing myself forward and breathing till I can think about standing. The rattle in my lungs and the pain in my back make me cough more but I grit my teeth and get thru it.

Cuz I have to find her.

"Viola," Manchee barks.

"Viola," I say and I grit my teeth even harder and try to get to my feet.

But it's too much, the pain takes my legs from me and I topple back in the mud and I just lay there pulled tight from it all and struggling to breathe and my mind goes all woozy and hot and in my Noise I'm running and I'm running and I'm running towards nothing and I'm hot all over and I'm sweating and I'm running in my Noise and I can hear Ben from behind the trees and I'm running towards him and he's singing the song, he's singing the song from my bedtimes, the song that's for boys and not men but when I hear it my heart stretches and it's *early one morning just as the sun was rising*.

I come back to myself. The song comes with me.

Cuz the song goes:

Early one morning just as the sun was rising,

I heard a maiden call from the valley below.

"Oh don't deceive me, oh never leave me."

I open my eyes.

Don't deceive me. Never leave me.

I have to find her.

I have to find her.

I look up. The sun is in the sky but I have no idea how much time has passed since Aaron took Viola. That was just before dawn. It's cloudy but bright now and so it could be late morning or early afternoon. It might not even be the same day, a thought I try to push away. I close my eyes and I try to listen. The rain's stopped so there's none of that clatter but the only Noise I can hear belongs to me and to Manchee and the distant wordless chatter of woodland creachers getting on with their lives that ain't got nothing to do with mine.

No sound of Aaron. No space of silence for Viola.

I open my eyes and I see her bag.

Dropped in the struggle with Aaron, of no use or interest to him and just left on the ground like it don't belong to no one, like it don't matter that it's Viola's.

That bag so full of stupid and useful things.

My chest clenches and I cough painfully.

I can't seem to stand so I crawl forward, gasping at the pain in my back and head but still crawling, Manchee barking, worried, "Todd, Todd," all the time, and it takes forever, it takes *too effing long* but I get to the bag and I have to lean hunched with the pain for a minute before I can do anything with it. When I can breathe again I open it and fish around till I find the box with the bandages. There's only one left but it'll have to do. Then I start on the process of taking off my shirt which requires more stopping, more breathing, inch by inch, but finally it's off my burning back and over my burning head and I can see blood and mud everywhere on it.

I find the scalpel in her medipak and cut the bandage in two. I put one part on my head, holding it till it sticks, and reach around slowly and put the other on my back. For a minute it hurts even more as the bandage material, the human cell whatever the hell she talked about, crawls into the wounds and makes a bind. I clench my teeth thru it but then the medicine starts to work and a flush of cool flows into my bloodstream. I wait for it to work enough till I can stand up. I'm wobbly when I first get to my feet but I can manage to just stand for a minute.

After another I can take a step. And then another.

But where do I go?

I've no idea where he took her. I've no idea how much time has passed. He could already be all the way back to the army by now.

"Viola?" Manchee barks, whimpering.

"I don't know, fella," I say. "Let me think."

Even with the bandages doing their thing I can't stand up straight all the way but I do my best and look around. The Spackle's body is on the edge of my vision but I turn myself so I can't see it.

Oh don't deceive me. Oh never leave me.

I sigh and I know what I have to do.

"There ain't nothing for it," I say to Manchee. "We have to go back to the army."

"Todd?" he whines.

"There ain't nothing for it," I say again and I put everything outta my head but moving.

First things first I need a new shirt.

I keep the Spackle to my back and turn to the rucksack.

The knife is still thru the cloth of the rucksack and the book inside. I don't really wanna touch it and even in my haze I don't wanna see what's become of the book but I have to get the knife out so I brace the sack with my foot and pull hard. It takes a few tugs but it comes out and I drop it to the ground.

I look at it on the wet moss. There's blood all over it still. Spackle blood mostly but my blood brighter red at the tip. I wonder if that means that Spackle blood got into my blood when Aaron stabbed me. I wonder if there are extra special viruses you can catch directly from Spackle.

But there's no time for further wondering.

I open the rucksack and take out the book.

There's a knife-shaped hole all the way thru and out the other side. The knife is so sharp and Aaron must be so strong that it's hardly ruined the book at all. The pages have a slit running thru them all the way thru the book, my blood and Spackle blood staining the edges just a little, but it's still readable.

I could still read it, still have it read.

If I ever deserve to.

I push that thought away too and take out a clean shirt. I cough as I do and even with the bandages it hurts so I have to wait till I stop. My lungs feel filled with water, like I'm carrying a pile of river stones in my chest, but I put the shirt on, I gather what useable things I can still get from my rucksack, some clothes, my own medipak, what ain't been ruined by Mr Prentiss Jr or the rain and I take them and my ma's book over to Viola's bag and put them inside cuz there's no way I can carry a rucksack on my back no more.

And then there's still the asking, ain't there?

Where do I go?

I follow the road back to the army, that's where I go.

I go to the army and somehow I save her, even if it's changing my place for hers.

And for that I can't go unarmed, can I?

No, I can't.

I look at the knife again, sitting there on the moss like a thing without properties, a thing made of metal as separate from a boy as can be, a thing which casts all blame from itself to the boy who uses it.

I don't wanna touch it. Not at all. Not never again. But I have to go over and I have to clean off the blood as best I can on some wet leaves and I have to sheath it behind me in the belt that's still around my waist.

I have to do these things. There ain't no choice.

The Spackle hovers on the edge of my vision but I do not look at it as I handle the knife.

"C'mon, Manchee." I loop Viola's bag as gingerly as I can over one shoulder.

Don't deceive me. Never leave me.

Time to go.

"We're gonna find her," I say.

I keep the campsite behind me and head off in the direkshun of the road. Best to just get on it and walk back to 'em as fast as I can. I'll hear 'em coming and can get outta the way and then I guess I'll see if there's any way I can save her.

Which might mean meeting them head on.

I push my way thru a row of bushes when I hear Manchee bark, "Todd?"

I turn, trying to keep from seeing the campsite. "C'mon, boy."

"Todd!"

"I said, c'mon, now. I mean it."

"This way, Todd," he barks and wags his half-tail.

I turn more fully to him. "What'd you say?"

He's pointing his nose in another direkshun altogether from the one I'm going. "This way," he barks. He rubs at the bandage over his eye with a paw, knocking it off and squinting at me with the injured eye.

"What do you mean 'This way'?" I ask, a feeling in my chest.

He's nodding his head and pushing his front feet in a direkshun not only away from the road but in the opposite direkshun from the army. "Viola," he barks, turning round in a circle and then facing that way again.

"You can smell her?" I ask, my chest rising.

He barks a bark of yes.

"You can *smell* her?"

"This way, Todd!"

"Not back to the road?" I say. "Not back to the army?"

"Todd!" he barks, feeling the rise in my Noise and getting excited himself.

"Yer sure?" I say. "You gotta be sure, Manchee. You gotta be."

"This way!" and off he runs, thru the bushes and off on a track parallel to the river, away from the army.

And towards Haven.

Who knows why and who cares cuz in the moment I'm running after him as best as my injuries will let me, in the moment I see him bounding away and ahead, I think to myself, *Good dog, good bloody dog*.

27

ON WE GO

"THIS WAY, TODD," Manchee barks, taking us round another outcropping.

Ever since we left the Spackle campsite, the terrain's been getting more and more rugged. The woods have been rising up into hills for an hour or two now and we rush up 'em and down 'em and up 'em again and sometimes it's more like hiking than running. When we get up to the top of one, I see more and more rolling away in front of me, hills under trees, a few so steep you have to go around rather than over. The road and the river twist thru 'em on snaky paths off to my right and sometimes it's all I can do to keep them in sight.

Even with the bandages doing their best to hold me together, every step I take jars my back and my head and every once in a while I can't help but stop and sometimes throw up my empty stomach.

But on we go.

Faster, I think to myself. *Go faster, Todd Hewitt*.

They've got at least half a day's march on us, maybe even a *day* and a half, and I don't know where they're going or what Aaron plans on doing when he gets there and so on we go.

"Yer sure?" I keep asking Manchee.

"This way," he keeps barking.

The thing that makes no sense is that we're pretty much on the path that Viola and I would have taken anyway, following the river, keeping back from the road, and heading east towards Haven. I don't know why Aaron's going there, I don't know why he'd head away from the army, but that's where Manchee's smelling their scents and so that's the way we go.

We keep on thru the middle of the day, up hills, down hills, and onwards, thru trees that turn from the broad leaves of the trees on the plains to more needly kinds, taller and more arrow-like. The trees even smell different, sending a sharp tang in the air I can taste on my tongue. Manchee and I hop over all manner of streams and creeks that feed the river and I stop now and then to refill the water bottles and on we go.

I try not to think at all. I try to keep my mind pointed ahead, pointed towards Viola and finding her. I try not to think about how she looked after I killed the Spackle. I try not to think about how afraid she was of me or how she backed away like I might hurt her. I try not to think about how scared she musta been when Aaron came after her and I was no use.

And I try not to think about the Spackle's Noise and the

fear that was in it or how surprised he musta been being killed for nothing more than being a fisherman or how the crunch felt up my arm when the knife went in him or how dark red his blood was flowing out onto me or the bafflement pouring outta him and into my Noise as he died as he died as he died as he–

I don't think about it.

On we go, on we go.

Afternoon passes into early evening, the forest and the hills seem never-ending, and there comes another problem.

"Food, Todd?"

"There ain't none left," I say, dirt giving way under my feet as we make our way down a slope. "I don't got nothing for myself neither."

"Food?"

I don't know how long it is since I ate last, don't know how long since I really slept, for that matter, since passing out ain't sleeping.

And I've lost track of how many days till I become a man but I can tell you it's never felt farther away.

"Squirrel!" Manchee suddenly barks and tears around the trunk of a needly tree and into a mess of ferns beyond. I didn't even see the squirrel but I can hear **Whirler dog** and "Squirrel!" and **Whirler-whirler-whirler-** and then it stops short.

Manchee jumps out with a waxy squirrel drooping in his maul, bigger and browner than the ones from the swamp. He drops it on the ground in front of me, a gristly, bloody plop, and I ain't so hungry no more.

"Food?" he barks.

"That's all right, boy." I look anywhere but the mess. "You can have it."

I'm sweating more than normal and I take big drinks of water as Manchee finishes his meal. Little gnats cloud round us in near-invisible swarms and I keep having to bat 'em away. I cough again, ignoring the pain in my back, the pain in my head, and when he's done and ready to go, I wobble just a little but on we go again.

Keep moving, Todd Hewitt. Keep going.

I don't dare sleep. Aaron may not so I can't. On and on, the clouds passing sometimes without me noticing, the moons rising, stars peeping. I come down to the bottom of a low hill and scare my way thru a whole herd of what look like deer but their horns are all different than the deer I know from Prentisstown and anyway they're off flying thru the trees away from me and a barking Manchee before I hardly register they're even there.

On we go still thru midnight (twenty-four days left? Twenty-three?). We've come the whole day without hearing no more sounds of Noise or other settlements, not that I could see anyway, even when I was close enough to see brief snatches of the river and the road. But as we reach the top of another wooded hill and the moons are directly overhead, I finally hear the Noise of men, clear as a crash.

We stop, crouching down even tho it's night.

I look out from our hilltop. The moons are high and I can see two long huts in two separate clearings on hillsides across the way. From one I can hear the murmuring ruckus of sleeping men's Noise. Julia? and on horseback and tell him it ain't so and up the river past morning and lots of things that make no sense cuz dreaming Noise is the weirdest of all. From the other hut, there's silence, the aching silence of women, I can feel it even from here, men in one hut, women in another, which I guess is one way of solving the problem of sleeping, and the touch of the silence from the women's side makes me think of Viola and I have to keep my balance against a tree trunk for a minute.

But where there's people, there's food.

"Can you find yer way back to the trail if we leave it?" I whisper to my dog, stifling a cough.

"Find trail," Manchee barks, seriously.

"Yer sure?"

"Todd smell," he barks. "Manchee smell."

"Keep quiet as we go then." We start creeping our way down the hill, moving softly as we can thru the trees and brush till we get to the bottom of a little dale with the huts above us, sleeping on hillsides.

I can hear my own Noise spreading out into the world, hot and fusty, like the sweat that keeps pouring down my sides, and I try to keep it quiet and grey and flat, like Tam did, Tam who controlled his Noise better than any man in Prentisstown–

And there's yer proof.

Prentisstown? I hear from the men's hut almost immediately.

We stop dead. My shoulders slump. It's still dream Noise I'm hearing but the word repeats thru the sleeping men like echoes down a valley. Prentisstown? and Prentisstown? and Prentisstown? like they don't know what the word means yet.

But they will when they wake.

Idiot.

"Let's go," I say, turning and scurrying back the way we came, back to our trail.

"Food?" Manchee barks.

"Come *on*."

And so, still, no food for me but on we go, thru the night, rushing the best we can.

Faster, Todd. Get yer bloody self moving.

On we go, on we go, up hills, grabbing onto plants sometimes to pull myself up, and down hills, holding on to rocks to keep my balance now and then, the scent keeping well clear of anywhere easy it might be to walk, like the flatter parts down by the road or riverbank, and I'm coughing and sometimes stumbling and as the sun starts to show itself there comes a time when I can't, when I just can't, when my legs crumple beneath me and I have to sit down.

I just have to.

(I'm sorry.)

My back is aching and my head is aching and I'm sweating so stinking much and I'm so hungry and I just have to sit down at the base of a tree, just for a minute, I just have to and I'm sorry, I'm sorry, I'm sorry.

"Todd?" Manchee mumbles, coming up to me.

"I'm fine, boy."

"Hot, Todd," he says, meaning me.

I cough, my lungs rattling like rocks falling down a hill.

Get up, Todd Hewitt. Get off yer goddam butt and get going.

My mind drifts, I can't help it, I try to hold on to Viola

but there my mind goes and I'm little and I'm sick in bed and I'm *real* sick and Ben's staying in my room with me cuz the fever is making me see things, horrible things, shimmering walls, people who ain't there, Ben growing fangs and extra arms, all kindsa stuff and I'm screaming and pulling away but Ben is there with me and he's singing the song and he's giving me cool water and he's taking out tabs of medicine–

Medicine.

Ben giving me medicine.

I come back to myself.

I lift my head and go thru Viola's bag, taking out her medipak again. It's got all kindsa pills in it, too many. There's writing on the little packets but the words make no sense to me and I can't risk taking the tranquilizer that knocked out Manchee. I open my own medipak, nowhere near as good as hers, but there's white tabs in it that I know are at least pain relievers, however cruddy and homemade. I chew up two and then two more.

Get up, you worthless piece of crap.

I sit and breathe for a while and fight fight fight against falling asleep, waiting for the pills to work and as the sun starts to peek up over the top of a far hill I reckon I'm feeling a little better.

Don't know if I actually am but there ain't no choice.

Get up, Todd Hewitt. Get an effing MOVE ON!

"Okay," I say, breathing heavy and rubbing my knees with my hands. "Which way, Manchee?"

On we go.

The scent carries like it did before, avoiding the road,

avoiding any buildings we might see at a distance, but always onward, always towards Haven, only Aaron knows why. Mid-morning we find another small creek heading down to the river. I check for crocs, tho it's really too small a place, and refill the water bottles. Manchee wades in, lapping it up, snapping unsuccessfully at these little brass-coloured fishes that swim by, nibbling at his fur.

I sit on my knees and wash some of the sweat from my face. The water is cold as a slap and it wakes me up a little. I wish I knew if we were even gaining on 'em. I wish I knew how far they were ahead.

And I wish he'd never found us.

And I wish he'd never found Viola in the first place.

And I wish Ben and Cillian hadn't lied to me.

And I wish Ben was here right now.

And I wish I was back in Prentisstown.

I rest back on my heels, looking up into the sun.

No. No, I don't. I don't wish I was back in Prentisstown. Not no more, I don't.

And if Aaron hadn't found her then *I* might not have found her and that's no good neither.

"C'mon, Manchee," I say, turning round to pick up the bag again.

Which is when I see the turtle, sunning itself on a rock.

I freeze.

I never seen this kinda turtle before. Its shell is craggy and sharp, with a dark red streak going down either side. The turtle's got its shell all the way open to catch as much warmth as possible, its soft back fully exposed.

You can eat a turtle.

Its Noise ain't nothing but a long **ahhhhhh** sound, exhaling under sunlight. It don't seem too concerned about us, probably thinking it can snap its shell shut and dive underwater faster than we could get to it. And even if we did get to it, we wouldn't be able to get the shell back open to eat it.

Unless you had a knife to kill it with.

"Turtle!" Manchee barks, seeing it. He keeps back cuz the swamp turtles we know have more than enough snap to get after a dog. The turtle just sits there, not taking us seriously.

I reach behind my back for the knife.

I'm halfway there when I feel the pain twixt my shoulder blades.

I stop. I swallow.

(Spackle and pain and bafflement.)

I glance down into the water, seeing myself, my hair a bird's nest, bandage across half my head, dirtier than an old ewe.

One hand reaching for my knife.

(Red blood and fear and fear and fear.)

I stop reaching.

I take my hand away.

I stand. "C'mon, Manchee," I say. I don't look at the turtle, don't even listen for its Noise. Manchee barks at it a few more times but I'm already crossing the creek and on we go, on we go, on we go.

So I can't hunt.

And I can't get near settlements.

And so if I don't find Viola and Aaron soon I'll starve to death if this coughing don't kill me first.

"Great," I say to myself and there's nothing to do but keep going as fast as I can.

Not fast enough, Todd. Move yer effing feet, you gonk.

Morning turns to another midday, midday turns to another afternoon. I take more tabs, we keep on going, no food, no rest, just forward, forward, forward. The path is starting to tend downhill again, so at least that's a blessing. Aaron's scent moves closer to the road but I'm feeling so poor I don't even look up when I hear distant Noise now and then.

It ain't his and there's no silence that's hers so why bother?

Afternoon turns into another evening and it's when we're coming down a steep hillside that I fall.

My legs slip out from under me and I'm not quick enough to catch myself and I fall down and keep falling, sliding down the hill, bumping into bushes, picking up speed, feeling a tearing in my back, and I reach out to stop myself but my hands are too slow to catch anything and I judder judder judder along the leaves and grass and then I hit a bump and skip up into the air, tumbling over onto my shoulders, pain searing thru them, and I call out loud and I don't stop falling till I come to a thicket of brambles at the bottom of the hill and ram into 'em with a thump.

"Todd! Todd! Todd!" I hear Manchee, running down after me, but all I can do is try and withstand the pain again and the tired again and the gunk in my lungs and the hunger gnawing in my belly and bramble scratches all over me and I think I'd be crying if I had any energy left at all.

"Todd?" Manchee barks, circling round me, trying to find a way into the brambles.

"Gimme a minute," I say and push myself up a little. Then I lean forward and fall right over on my face.

Get up, I think. *Get up, you piece of filth, GET UP!*

"Hungry, Todd," Manchee says, meaning me that's hungry. "Eat. Eat, Todd."

I push with hands on the ground, coughing as I come up, spitting up handfuls of gunk from my lungs. I get to my knees at least.

"Food, Todd."

"I know," I say. "I know."

I feel so dizzy I have to put my head back down on the ground. "Just gimme a sec," I say, whispering it into the leaves on the ground. "Just a quick sec."

And I fall again into blackness.

I don't know how long I'm out but I wake to Manchee barking. "People!" he's barking. "People! Todd, Todd, Todd! People!"

I open my eyes. "What people?" I say.

"This way," he barks. "People. Food, Todd. Food!"

I take shallow breaths, coughing all the way, my body weighing ninety million pounds, and I push my way out the other side of the bramble. I look up and over.

I'm in a ditch right by the road.

I can see carts up ahead on the left, a whole string of 'em, pulled by oxes and by horses, disappearing round a bend.

"Help," I say, but my voice comes out like a gasp with not near enough volume.

Get up.

"Help," I call again, but it's only to myself.

Get up.

It's over. I can't stand no more. I can't move no more. It's over.

Get up.

But it's over.

The last cart disappears round the bend and it's over.

... *give up.*

I put my head down, right down, on the roadside, grit and pebbles digging into my cheek. A shiver shakes me and I roll to my side and pull myself to myself, curling my legs to my chest, and I close my eyes and I've failed and I've failed and please won't the darkness just take me please please please–

"That you, Ben?"

I open my eyes.

It's Wilf.

28

THE SMELL OF ROOTS

"Y'ALL RIGHT, BEN?" he asks, putting a hand under my armpit to help me up but even with that I can't barely stand nor even raise my head much and so I feel his other hand under my other armpit. That don't work neither so he goes even further than that and lifts me over his shoulder. I stare down at the back of his legs as he carries me to his cart.

"Hoo is it, Wilf?" I hear a woman's voice ask.

"'s Ben," Wilf says. "Lookin poorly."

Next thing I know he's setting me down on the back of his cart. It's piled rag-tag with parcels and boxes covered in leather skins, bits of furniture and large baskets, all tumbled together, almost overflowing with itself.

"It's too late," I say. "It's over."

The woman's walked over the back of the cart from the seat and hops down to face me. She's broad with a worn dress and flyaway hair and lines at the corners of her eyes and her voice is quick, like a mouse. "What's over, young'un?"

"She's gone." I feel my chin crumpling and my throat pulling. "I lost her."

I feel a cool hand on my forehead and it feels so good I press into it. She takes it away and says, "Fever," to Wilf.

"Yup," Wilf says.

"Best make a poultice," the woman says and I think she heads off into the ditch but that don't make no sense.

"Where's Hildy, Ben?" Wilf says, trying to get his eyes to meet mine. Mine are so watery it's hard to even see him.

"Her name ain't Hildy," I say.

"Ah know," Wilf says, "but at's whatcha call her."

"She's gone," I say, my eyes filling. My head falls forward again. I feel Wilf put a hand on my shoulder and he squeezes it.

"Todd?" I hear Manchee bark, unsure, a ways off the road.

"I ain't called Ben," I say to Wilf, still not looking up.

"Ah know," Wilf says again. "But at's what we're callin ya."

I look up to him. His face and his Noise are as blank as I remember but the lesson of forever and ever is that knowing a man's mind ain't knowing the man.

Wilf don't say nothing more and goes back to the front of the cart. The woman comes back with a seriously foul-smelling rag in her hands. It stinks of roots and mud and ugly herbs but I'm so tired I let her tie it round my forehead, right over the bandage that's still stuck on the side of my head.

"At should work onna fever," she says, hopping back up. We both lurch forward a little bit as Wilf snaps the rein on his oxes. The woman's eyes are wide open, looking into mine like searching for exciting news. "Yoo runnin from the army, too?"

Her quiet next to me reminds me so much of Viola it's all I can do not to just lean against her. "Kinda," I say.

"Yoo's what told Wilf about it, huh?" she says. "Yoo's and a girl told Wilf bout the army, told him to tell people, tell people they had to gettaway, dincha?"

I look up at her, smelly brown root water dripping down my face, and I turn back to look at Wilf, up there driving his cart. He hears me looking. "They lissened to Wilf," he says.

I look up and past him to the road ahead. As we go round a bend, I can hear not only the rush of the river to my right again, like an old friend, an old foe, I can see a line of carts stretching on up ahead of us on the road at least as far as the next bend, carts packed with belongings just like Wilf's and all kindsa people straggled along the tops, holding on to anything that won't knock 'em off.

It's a caravan. Wilf is taking the rear of a long caravan. Men and women and I think even children, too, if I can see clearly thru the stink of the thing tied round my head, their Noise and silence floating up and back like a great, clattery thing all its own.

Army I hear a lot. Army and army and army.

And cursed town.

"Brockley Falls?" I ask.

"Bar Vista, too," the woman says, nodding her head fast. "And others. Rumour's been flyin up the river and road. Army from cursed town comin and comin, growin as it comes, with men pickin up arms to join in."

Growing as it comes, I think.

"Thousands strong, they say," says the woman.

Wilf makes a scoffing sound. "Ain't no thousand people 'tween here and cursed town."

The woman twists her lips. "Ah'm only sayin what people are sayin."

I look back at the empty road behind us, Manchee panting along a little distance away, and I remember Ivan, the man in the barn at Farbranch, who told me that not everyone felt the same about history, that Pren– that my town had allies still. Maybe not thousands, but still maybe growing. Getting bigger and bigger as it marches on till it's so big how can anyone stand against it?

"We're going to Haven," the woman says. "They'll pruhtekt us there."

"Haven," I mumble to myself.

"Say they even got a cure for Noise in them there parts," the woman says. "Now there's a thing Ah'd like to see." She laughs out loud at herself. "Or *hear*, Ah guess." She slaps her thigh.

"They got Spackle there?" I ask.

The woman turns to me surprised. "Spackle don't come near people," she says. "Not no more, not since the war. They's keep to theirselves and we's keep to ourselves and such is the peace kept." It sounds like she's reciting the last part. "Tain't hardly none left anyway."

"I gotta go." I put my hands down and try to lift myself up. "I gotta find her."

All that happens is that I lose my balance and fall off the end of the cart. The woman calls to Wilf to stop and they both lift me back up on it, the woman getting Manchee up top, too. She clears a few boxes away to lay me down and Wilf gets the cart going again. He snaps the oxes a bit harder this time and I can feel us moving along faster – faster than I could walk at least.

"Eat," the woman says, holding up some bread to my face. "Yoo can't go nowhere till yoo eat."

I take the bread from her and eat a bite, then tear into the rest so hungrily I forget to give some to Manchee. The woman just takes out some more and gives some to both of us, watching wide-eyed at every move I make.

"Thanks," I say.

"Ah'm Jane," she says. Her eyes are still way open, like she's just bursting to say stuff. "Didja see the army?" she asks. "With yer own eyes?"

"I did," I say. "In Farbranch."

She sucks in her breath. "So it's true." Not an asking, just saying it.

"*Told* yoo it were true," Wilf says from up front.

"Ah hear they're cuttin off people's heads and boilin their eyes," Jane says.

"Jane!" Wilf snaps.

"Ah'm just *sayin*."

"They're killing folk," I say, low. "Killing's enough."

Jane's eyes dart all over my face and Noise but all she says after a bit is, "Wilf told me all bout yoo," and I can't figure out at all what her smile means.

A drip from the rag makes it to my mouth and I gag and spit and cough some more. "What *is* this?" I say, pressing the rag with my fingers and wincing from the smell.

"Poultice," Jane says. "For fevers and ague."

"It *stinks*."

"Evil smell draws out evil fever," she says, as if telling me a lesson everyone knows.

"Evil?" I say. "Fever ain't evil. It's *fever*."

"Yeah, and this poultice treats fever."

I stare at her. Her eyes never leave me and the wide open part of them is starting to make me uncomfortable. It's how Aaron looks when he's pinning you down, how he looks when he's imparting a sermon with his fists, when he's preaching you into a hole you might never come out of.

It's a mad look, I realize.

I try to check the thought but Jane don't give no sign she heard.

"I gotta go," I say again. "Thank you kindly for the food and the poultry but I gotta go."

"Yoo can't go off in these woods here, nosirree," she says, still staring, still not blinking. "Them's dangerous woods, them is."

"What do you mean, dangerous?" I push myself away from her a little.

"Settlements up the way," she says, her eyes even wider and a smile now, like she can't wait to tell me. "Crazy as anything. Noise sent 'em wild. Hear tell of one where everyone wears masks so's no one kin see their faces. There's another where no one don't do nothing but sing all day long they gone so crazy. And one where everyone's walls are made a glass and no one wears no clothes cuz no one's got secrets in Noise, do they?"

She's closer to me now. I can smell her breath, which is worse than the rag, and I feel the silence behind all these words. How can that be so? How can silence contain so much racket?

"People can keep secrets in Noise," I say. "People can keep all kindsa secrets."

"Leave a boy alone," Wilf says from his seat.

Jane's face goes slack. "Sorry," she says, a little grudgingly.

I raise up a little, feeling the benefit of food in my belly whatever the stinking rag may or may not be doing.

We've pulled closer to the rest of the caravan, close enough for me to see the backs of a few heads and hear more closely the Noise of men chattering up and down and the silence of women twixt them, like stones in a creek.

Every now and then one of them, usually a man, glances back at us, and I feel like they're seeking me out, seeing what I'm made of.

"I need to find her," I say.

"Yer girl?" Jane asks.

"Yeah," I say. "Thank you, but I need to go."

"But yer fever! And the other settlements!"

"I'll take my chances." I untie the dirty rag. "C'mon, Manchee."

"Yoo can't go," Jane says, eyes wider than ever, worry on her face. "The army–"

"I'll worry about the army." I pull myself up, readying to jump down off the cart. I'm still pretty unsteady so I have to take a cloudy breath or two before I do anything.

"But they'll get yoo!" Jane says, her voice rising. "Yer from Prentisstown–"

I look up, sharp.

Jane slaps a hand over her mouth.

"*Wife!*" Wilf yells, turning his head round from the front of the cart.

"Ah didn't mean it," she whispers to me.

But it's too late. Already the word is bouncing up and down the caravan in a way that's become too familiar, not just the word, but what pins it to me, what everyone knows or thinks they know about me, already faces turning about to look deeper at the last cart in the caravan, oxes and horses drawing to a stop as people turn more fully to examine us.

Faces and Noise aimed right back down the road at us.

"Who yoo got back there, Wilf?" a man's voice says from just one cart up.

"Feverish boy," Wilf shouts back. "Crazy with sickness. Don't know what he's sayin."

"Yoo entirely sure about that?"

"Yessir," Wilf says. "Sick boy."

"Bring him out," a woman's voice calls. "Let's see him."

"What if he's a spy?" another woman's voice calls, rising in pitch. "Leadin the army right to us?"

"We don't want no spies!" cries a different man.

"He's Ben," Wilf says. "He's from Farbranch. Got nightmares of cursed town army killin what he loves. I vouch for him."

No one shouts nothing for a minute but the Noise of the men buzzes in the air like a swarm. Everyone's face is still on us. I try to make my own look more feverish and put the invasion of Farbranch first and foremost. It ain't hard and it makes my heart sick.

And there's a long moment where nobody says nothing and it's as loud as a screaming crowd.

And then it's enough.

Slowly but slowly the oxes and horses start moving forward again, pulling away from us, people still looking back but at least getting farther away. Wilf snaps the reins on his oxes but keeps them slower than the rest, letting a distance open between us and everyone else.

"Ah'm *sorry*," Jane says again, breathless. "Wilf told me not to say. He told me but–"

"That's okay," I say, just wanting her to stop talking already.

"Ah'm so so sorry."

There's a lurch and Wilf's stopped the cart. He waits till the caravan's off a good distance then hops down and comes back.

"No one lissens to Wilf," he says, maybe with a small smile. "But when they do, they believe him."

"I need to go," I say.

"Yup," he says. "T'ain't safe."

"Ah'm sorry," Jane keeps saying.

I jump off the cart, Manchee following me. Wilf reaches for Viola's bag and holds it open. He looks at Jane, who understands him. She takes an armful of fruits and breads and puts them in the bag, then another armful of dried meats.

"Thanks," I say.

"Hope yoo find her," Wilf says as I close the bag.

"I hope so, too."

With a nod, Wilf goes and reseats himself on the cart and snaps the reins on his oxes.

"Be careful," Jane calls after me, in the loudest whisper you ever heard. "Watch out for the crazies."

I stand for a minute and watch 'em pull away, coughing still, feverish still, but feeling better for the food if not the smell of roots and I'm hoping Manchee can find the trail again and I'm also wondering just exactly what kinda welcome I'm gonna get if I ever do get to Haven.

29

AARON IN A THOUSAND WAYS

IT TAKES A LITTLE WHILE, a horrible little while, for Manchee to find the scent again once we're back in the woods but then he barks, "This way," and we're off again.

He's a good bloody dog, have I said that?

Night's fully fallen by now and I'm still sweating and I'm still coughing enough to win a contest and my feet ain't made of nothing but blisters and my head's still buzzy with feverish Noise but I've got food in my belly and more in the bag to see me thru a coupla days and so all that matters is still ahead of us.

"Can you smell her, Manchee?" I ask, as we balance on a log across a stream. "Is she still alive?"

"Smell Viola," he barks, jumping off the other side. "Viola fear."

Which hits me a little and I quicken my step. Another midnight (twenty-two days? Twenty-one?) and my torch battery gives out. I take out Viola's but it's the last we got. More hills and steeper, too, as we go on thru the night, harder to climb up, dangerous to climb down but we go and go and go, Manchee sniffing away, eating Wilf's dried meat as we stumble forward, me coughing away, taking the shortest rests possible, usually bent double against trees, and the sun starts coming up over a hill so it's like we're walking up into the sunrise.

And it's when light hits us full that I see the world start to shimmer.

I stop, hanging on to a fern to keep my balance against the steepness of the hill. Everything's woozy for a second and I close my eyes but it don't help as there's just a wash of colours and sparkles behind my eyelids and my body is jelly-like and waving in the breeze I can feel coming off the hilltop and when it passes, it don't really pass altogether, the world keeping its weird brightness, like I've woke up in a dream.

"Todd?" Manchee barks, worry there, no doubt from seeing who knows what in my Noise.

"The fever," I say, coughing again. "I shouldn't've thrown away that filthy rag."

Ain't nothing for it.

I take the last of the pain tabs from my medipak and we gotta keep going.

We get to the top of the hill and for a minute all the other hills in front of us and the river and the road down below rumble up and down like they're on a blanket someone's shaking and I do my best to blink it away till it calms down enough to keep walking. Manchee whines by my feet.

I nearly tip over when I try and scratch him so instead I focus on getting down the hill without falling.

I think again of the knife at my back, of the blood that was on it when it went into my body and my blood mixed with the Spackle's and who knows what now spinning round my insides since Aaron stabbed me.

"I wonder if he knew," I say, to Manchee, to myself, to no one, as we get to the bottom of the hill and I lean against a tree to make the world stop moving. "I wonder if he killed me slow."

"*Course I did,*" Aaron says, leaning out from behind the tree.

I yell out and fall back away from him and fling my arms in front of me trying to slap him away and I hit the ground on my butt and start scampering back before I look up–

And he's gone.

Manchee's got his head cocked at me. "Todd?"

"Aaron," I say, my heart thundering, my breath catching and turning into meatier and meatier coughs.

Manchee sniffs the air again, sniffs the ground around him. "Trail this way," he barks, shifting from foot to foot.

I look around me, coughing away, the world spotty and wavy.

No sign of him, no Noise other than mine, no silence of Viola. I close my eyes again.

I am Todd Hewitt, I think against the swirling. *I am Todd Hewitt.*

Keeping my eyes shut, I feel for the water bottle and take a swig and I tear a piece from Wilf's bread and chew it down. Only then do I open my eyes again.

Nothing.

Nothing but woods and another hill to climb.

And sunlight that shimmers.

The morning passes and at the bottom of yet another hill there's yet another creek. I refill the water bottles and take a few drinks from the cold water with my hands.

I feel *bad*, ain't no two ways about it, my skin's tingling and sometimes I'm shivering and sometimes I'm sweating and sometimes my head weighs a million pounds. I lean into the creek and splash myself with the cold.

I sit up and Aaron is reflected in the water.

"*Killer*," he says, a smile across his torn-up face.

I jump back, scrabbling away for my knife (and feeling the pain shoot thru my shoulders again) but when I look up he ain't there and Manchee's made no sign of stopping his fish-chasing.

"I'm coming to find you," I say to the air, air that's started to move more and more with the wind.

Manchee's head pops up from the water. "Todd?"

"I'll find you if it's the last thing I do."

"*Killer*," I hear again, whispered along the wind.

I lay for a second, breathing heavy, coughing but keeping my eyes peeled. I go back to the creek and I splash so much cold water on myself it makes my chest hurt.

I pick myself up and we carry on.

The cold water does the trick for a little while and we manage a few more hills as the sun gets to midday in the sky with minimal shimmer. When things do start to wobble again I stop us and we eat.

"*Killer*," I hear from the bushes around us and then

again from another part of the forest. "*Killer.*" And again from somewhere else. "*Killer.*"

I don't look up, just eat my food.

It's just the Spackle blood, I tell myself. Just the fever and the sickness and that's all.

"*Is that all?*" Aaron says from across the clearing. "*If that's all I am, why you chasing me so bad?*"

He's wearing his Sunday robes and his face is all healed up like he's back in Prentisstown, his hands clasped in front of him like he's ready to lead us in prayer and he's glowing in the sun and he's smiling down at me.

The smiling fist I remember so well.

"*The Noise binds us all, young Todd,*" he says, his voice slithering and shiny like a snake. "*If one of us falls, we all fall.*"

"You ain't here," I say, clenching my teeth.

"Here, Todd," Manchee barks.

"*Ain't I?*" Aaron says and disappears in a shimmer.

My brain knows this Aaron ain't real but my heart don't care and it's beating in my chest like a race. It's hard to catch my breath and I waste more time waiting just to be able to stand up and move on into the afternoon.

The food's helping, God bless Wilf and his crazy wife, but sometimes we can't go much faster than a stumble. I start to see Aaron outta the corner of my eye pretty much all the time, hiding behind trees, leaning against rocks, standing on top of woodfall, but I just turn my head away and keep stumbling.

And then, from a hilltop, I see the road cross the river again down below. The landscape's moving in a way that turns my stomach but I can definitely see a bridge down there, taking the road to the other side so there's nothing now twixt me and the river.

I wonder for a minute about that other fork we never took back in Farbranch. I wonder where *that* road is in the middle of all this wilderness. I look from the hilltop to my left but there's just woods as far as I can see and more hills that move like hills shouldn't. I have to close my eyes for a minute.

We make our way down, too slow, too *slow*, the scent taking us close to the road and towards the bridge, a high rickety one with rails. Water's gathered where the road turns into it, filling it with puddles and muck.

"Did he cross the river, Manchee?" I put my hands on my knees to catch my breath and cough.

Manchee sniffs the ground like a maniac, crossing the road, re-crossing it, going to the bridge and back to where we stand. "Wilf smell," he barks. "Cart smell."

"I can see the tracks," I say, rubbing my face with my hands. "What about Viola?"

"Viola!" Manchee barks. "This way."

He heads away from the road, keeping to this side of the river and following it. "Good dog," I say twixt raggedy breaths. "Good dog."

I follow him thru branches and bushes, the river rushing closer to my right than it's been in days.

And I step right into a settlement.

I stand up straight and cough in surprise.

It's been destroyed.

The buildings, eight or ten of them, are charcoal and ash and there ain't a whisper of Noise nowhere.

For a second I think the army's been here but then I see plants growing up in the burnt-out buildings and no smoke is rising from any fire and the wind just blows thru it like only the dead live here. I look round and there's a few decrepit docks on the river, just down from the bridge, one lonely old boat knocking against it in the current and a few more half-sunk boats piled halfway up the riverbank along from what may have been a mill before it became a pile of burnt wood.

It's cold and it's long dead and here's another place on New World that never made it to subdivided farming.

And I turn back round and in the centre of it stands Aaron.

His face is back to how it was when the crocs tore it open, peeled half away, his tongue lolling out the side of the gash in his cheek.

And he's still smiling.

"Join us, young Todd," he says. *"The church is always open."*

"I'll kill you," I say, the wind stealing my words but I know he can hear me cuz I can hear every last thing he's saying.

"You won't," he says, stepping forward, his fists clenched by his sides. *"Cuz I says you ain't a real killer, Todd Hewitt."*

"Try me," I say, my voice sounding strange and metallic.

He smiles again, his teeth poking out the side of his face, and in a wash of shimmer he's right in front of me. He puts his cut up hands to the opening of his robe and pulls it apart enough to show his bare chest.

"Here's yer chance, Todd Hewitt, to eat from the Tree of Knowledge." His voice is deep in my head. *"Kill me."*

The wind's making me shiver but I feel hot and sweaty at the same time and I can't get no more than a third of a breath down my lungs and my head is starting to ache in a way that food ain't helping and whenever I look anywhere fast everything I see has to slide into place to catch up.

I clench my teeth.

I'm probably dying.

But he's going first.

I reach behind me, ignoring the pain twixt my shoulders, and I grab the knife outta the sheath. I hold it in front of me. It's shiny with fresh blood and glinting in sunlight even tho I'm standing in shadow.

Aaron pulls his smile wider than his face can really go and he pushes his chest out to me.

I raise the knife.

"Todd?" Manchee barks. "Knife, Todd?"

"*Go ahead, Todd,*" Aaron says and I swear I smell the dankness of him. "*Cross over from innocence to sin. If you can.*"

"I've done it," I say. "I've already killed."

"*Killing a Spackle ain't killing a man,*" he says, grinning away at how stupid I am. "*Spackles are devils put here to test us. Killing one's like killing a turtle.*" He widens his eyes. "'*Cept you can't do that neither now, can ya?*"

I grip the knife hard and I make a snarling sound and the world wavers.

But the knife still ain't falling.

There's a bubbling sound and gooey blood pours outta the gash in Aaron's face and I realize he's laughing.

"*It took a long, long time for her to die,*" he whispers.

And I call out from the pain–

And I raise the knife higher–

And I aim it at his heart–

And he's still smiling–

And I bring the knife down–

And stab it right into Viola's chest.

"No!" I say, in the second that it's too late.

She looks up from the knife and right at me. Her face is filled with pain and confused Noise spills from her just like the Spackle that I–

(That I killed.)

And she looks at me with tears in her eyes and she opens her mouth and she says, "*Killer*".

And as I reach out for her, she's gone in a shimmer.

And the knife, clean of all blood, is still in my hand.

I fall onto my knees and then pitch forward and lie on the ground in the burnt-out settlement, breathing and coughing and weeping and wailing as the world melts around me so bad I don't feel like it's even solid no more.

I can't kill him.

I want to. I want to *so bad*. But I can't.

Cuz it ain't me and cuz I lose her.

I can't. I can't I can't I can't.

I give in to the shimmering and I disappear for a while.

It's good old Manchee, the friend who's proved truest, who wakes me up with licks to my face and a worried murmured word coming thru his Noise and his whines.

"Aaron," he's yelping, quiet and tense. "Aaron."

"Leave off, Manchee."

"Aaron," he whimpers, licking away.

"He ain't really there," I say, trying to sit up. "It's just something–"

It's just something Manchee can't see.

"Where is he?" I say, getting up too fast, causing everything to swirl bright pink and orange. I reel back from what's waiting for me.

There are a hundred Aarons at a hundred different places, all standing round me. There are Violas, too, frightened and looking to me for help, and Spackles with my knife sticking outta their chests and there're all talking at once, all talking to me in a roar of voices.

"Coward," they're saying. All of 'em. "Coward" over and over again.

But I wouldn't be a Prentisstown boy if I couldn't ignore Noise.

Coward Coward Coward
Coward
Coward
COWARD Coward Coward
Coward Coward

"Where, Manchee?" I say, getting to my feet, trying not to see how everything's pitching and sliding.

Coward Coward Coward
COWARD COWARD
Coward Coward
Coward Coward Coward
Coward COWARD
Coward Coward Coward

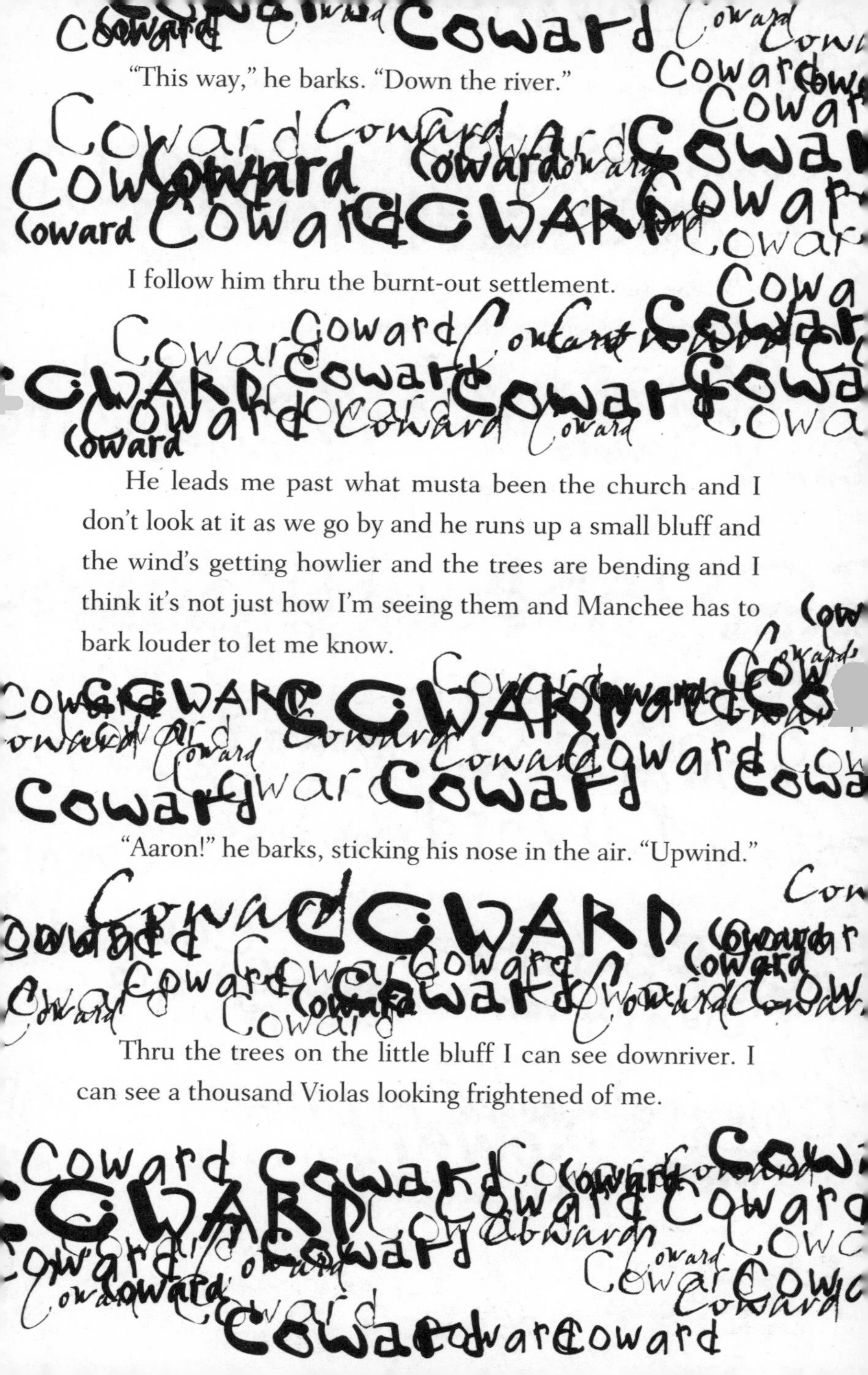

"This way," he barks. "Down the river."

I follow him thru the burnt-out settlement.

He leads me past what musta been the church and I don't look at it as we go by and he runs up a small bluff and the wind's getting howlier and the trees are bending and I think it's not just how I'm seeing them and Manchee has to bark louder to let me know.

"Aaron!" he barks, sticking his nose in the air. "Upwind."

Thru the trees on the little bluff I can see downriver. I can see a thousand Violas looking frightened of me.

I can see a thousand Spackle with my knife killing them.

I can see a thousand Aarons looking back at me and calling me "Coward" with the worst smile you ever seen.

And beyond them, in a camp by the side of the river, I see an Aaron who ain't looking back at me at all.

I see an Aaron kneeling down in prayer.

And I see Viola on the ground in front of him.

"Aaron," Manchee barks.

"Aaron," I say.

Coward.

30

A BOY CALLED TODD

"*WHAT ARE WE GONNA DO?*" says the boy, creeping up to my shoulder.

I raise my head from the cold river water and let it splash down my back. I stumbled back down from the bluff, elbowing my way thru crowds all calling me coward, and I got to the riverbank and I plunged my head straight in and now the cold is making me shake violently but it's also calming the world down. I know it won't last, I know the fever and spack blood infection will win in the end, but for now, I'm gonna need to see as clearly as possible.

"*How are we gonna get to them?*" the boy asks, moving round to my other side. "*He'll hear our Noise.*"

The shivering makes me cough, *everything* makes me cough, and I spit out handfuls of green goo from my lungs, but then I hold my breath and plunge in my head again.

The cold of the water feels like a vice but I hold it there, hearing the bubbling of the water rushing by and the wordless barks of a worried Manchee hopping around my feet. I can feel the bandage on my head detach and wash away in the current. I think of Manchee wriggling the bandage off his tail in a different part of the river and I forget and I laugh underwater.

I lift my head up, choking and gasping and coughing more.

I open my eyes. The world shines like it shouldn't and there are all kindsa stars out even tho the sun is still up but at least the ground has stopped floating and all the excess Aarons and Violas and Spackles are gone.

"*Can we really do it alone?*" asks the boy.

"Ain't no choice," I say to myself.

And I turn to look at him.

He's got a brown shirt like mine, no scars on his head, a rucksack on his back, a book in one hand and a knife in the other. I'm shaking from the cold still and it's all I can do to stand but I breathe and cough and shake and look at him.

"C'mon, Manchee," I say and I head back across the burnt-out settlement, back to the bluff. Just walking is tough, like the ground could cave away at any minute, cuz I weigh more than a mountain but less than a feather, but I'm walking, I'm keeping walking, I'm keeping the bluff in sight, I'm reaching it, I'm taking the first steps up it, I'm taking the next steps, I'm grabbing on to branches to pull myself along, I'm reaching the top, I'm leaning against a tree at the top, and I'm looking out.

"*Is it really him?*" says the boy behind my ear.

I squint out across the trees, tracing my eye down the river.

And there's still a campsite, still at the river's edge, so

far away they're just specks against other specks. I still have Viola's bag around my shoulders and I reach for her binos, holding 'em up to my eyes but shaking so much it's hard to get a clear image. They're far enough away that the wind's covering up his Noise but I'm sure I feel her silence out there.

I'm sure of it.

"Aaron," Manchee says. "Viola."

So I know it's not a shimmer and in the shakiness I can just about catch him still kneeling, praying some prayer, and Viola laid out on the ground in front of him.

I don't know what's happening. I don't know what he's doing.

But it's really them.

All this walking and stumbling and coughing and dying and it's really really them, by God it's really them.

I may not be too late and it's only how my chest rises and my throat grips that I realize all along I've thought I *was* too late.

But I'm not.

I lean down again and (shut up) I cry, I cry, I'm *crying* but it has to pass cuz I have to figure it out, I have to figure it out, it's down to me, there's only me, I have to find a way, I have to save her, I have to save–

"*What are we gonna do?*" the boy asks again, standing a little way away, book still in one hand, knife in the other.

I put my palms into my eyes and rub hard, trying to think straight, trying to concentrate, trying not to listen–

"*What if this is the sacrifice?*" says the boy.

I look up. "What sacrifice?"

"The sacrifice you saw in his Noise," he says. *"The sacrifice of–"*

"Why would he do it here?" I say. "Why would he come all this way and stop in the middle of a stupid forest and do it here?"

The boy's expression doesn't change. *"Maybe he has to,"* he says, *"before she dies."*

I step forward and have to catch my balance. "Dies of what?" I say, my voice snappy, my head aching and buzzy again.

"Fear," says the boy, taking a step backwards. *"Disappointment."*

I turn away. "I ain't listening to this."

"Listening, Todd?" Manchee barks. "Viola, Todd. This way."

I lean back again against the tree. I've got to think. I've got to ruddy *think*.

"We can't approach," I say, my voice thick. "He'll hear us coming."

"He'll kill her if he hears us," says the boy.

"Ain't talking to you." I cough up more gunk, which makes my head spin, which makes me cough more. "Talking to my dog," I finally choke out.

"Manchee," Manchee says, licking my hand.

"And I can't kill him," I say.

"You can't kill him," says the boy.

"Even if I want to."

"Even if he deserves it."

"And so there has to be another way."

"If she's not too scared to see you."

I look at him again. Still there, still book and knife and rucksack.

"You need to leave," I say. "You need to go away from me and never come back."

"Yer probably too late to save her."

"Yer of no use to me at all," I say, raising my voice.

"But I'm a killer," he says and the knife has blood on it.

I close my eyes and grit my teeth. "You stay behind," I say. "You stay *behind*."

"Manchee?" Manchee barks.

I open my eyes. The boy isn't there. "Not you, Manchee," I say, reaching out and rubbing his ears.

Then I regard him, Manchee. "Not you," I say again.

And I'm thinking. In the clouds and the swirls and the shimmers and the lights and the ache and the buzz and the shaking and the coughing, I'm thinking.

And I'm thinking.

I rub the ears of my dog, my stupid goddam ruddy *great* dog that I never wanted but who hung around anyway and who followed me thru the swamp and who bit Aaron when he was trying to choke me and who found Viola when she was lost and who's licking my hand with his little pink tongue and whose eye is still mostly squinted shut from where Mr Prentiss Jr kicked him and whose tail is way way shorter from when Matthew Lyle cut it off when my dog – *my dog* – went after a man with a machete to save me and who's right there when I need pulling back from the darkness I fall into and who tells me who I am whenever I forget.

"Todd," he murmurs, rubbing his face into my hand and

thumping his back leg against the ground.

"I got an idea," I say.

"*What if it don't work?*" says the boy from behind the tree.

I ignore him and I pick up the binos again. Shaking still, I find Aaron's campsite one more time and look at the area around it. They're near the river's edge and there's a forked tree just this side of them along the riverbank, bleached and leafless, like it maybe once got struck by lightning.

It'll do.

I put down the binos and take Manchee's head in both hands. "We're gonna save her," I say, right to my dog. "Both of us."

"Save her, Todd," he barks, wagging his little stump.

"*It won't work*," says the boy, still outta sight.

"Then you should stay behind," I say to the air, riding thru a cough while I send pictures of Noise to my dog to tell him what he needs to do. "It's simple, Manchee. Run and run."

"Run and run!" he barks.

"Good boy." I rub his ears again. "Good boy."

I pull myself to my feet and half-walk, half-slide, half-stumble my way back down the little bluff into the burnt-out settlement. There's a thump in my head now, like I can hear my poisoned blood pumping, and everything in the world throbs with it. If I squeeze my eyes nearly shut, the swirling lights ain't so bad and everything sort of stays in its place.

The first thing I need is a stick. Manchee and I tear thru the burnt-out buildings, looking for one the right size.

Pretty much everything is black and crumbly but that suits me fine.

"Thith one, Thawd?" Manchee says, using his mouth to pull one about half the length of himself out from under what looks like a burnt-up pile of stacked chairs. What happened in this place?

"Perfect." I take it from him.

"This won't work," the boy says, hiding in a dark corner. I can see the glint of the knife in one of his hands. *"You won't save her."*

"I will." I break off some larger splinters from the stick. Only one end is blackened charcoal but that's exactly what I want. "Can you carry this?" I say to Manchee, holding it out.

He takes it in his mouth, tosses it a little to get it comfortable, but then it rests just fine. "Yeth!" he barks.

"Great." I stand up straight and nearly fall over. "Now we need a fire."

"You can't make a fire," the boy says, already outside waiting for us. *"Her fire-making box is broken."*

"You don't know nothing," I say, not looking at him. "Ben taught me."

"Ben's dead," says the boy.

"Early one mor-r-ning," I sing, loud and clear, making the whirly shapes of the world go spangly and weird, but I keep on singing. "Just as the sun was ri-i-sing."

"Yer not strong enough to make a fire."

"I heard a maiden call from the val-l-ley below." I find a long, flat piece of wood and use the knife to carve a little hollow in it. "Oh, don't dece-e-ive me." I carve a rounded end to another smaller stick. "Oh, never le-e-ave me."

"*How could you use a poor maiden so?*" the boy finishes.

I ignore him. I put the rounded end of the stick into the little hollow and start spinning it twixt my hands, pressing hard into the wood. The rhythm of it matches the thumping in my head and I start to see me in the woods with Ben, him and me racing to see who could get the first smoke. He always won and half the time I could never get any sorta fire at all. But those were times.

Those were times.

"C'mon," I say to myself. I'm sweating and coughing and woozy but I'm making my hands keep on spinning. Manchee's barking at the wood to try and help it along.

And then a little finger of smoke rises from the hollow.

"Ha!" I cry out. I protect it from the wind with my hand and blow on it to make it catch. I use some dried moss as kindling and when the first little flame shoots out it's as near as I've come to joy since I don't know when. I throw some small sticks on it, wait for them to catch, too, then some larger ones, and pretty soon there's a real fire burning in front of me. A real one.

I leave it to burn for a minute. I'm counting on us being downwind to keep the smoke from Aaron.

And I'm counting on that wind for other reasons, too.

I lurch my way towards the riverbank, using tree trunks to keep me upright, till I make it to the dock. "C'mon, c'mon," I say under my breath as I steady myself to walk down it. It creaks under my feet and once I nearly pitch over into the river but I do finally make it to the boat still tied there.

"*It'll sink,*" says the boy, standing knee-high in the river.

I hop in the little boat and after a lot of wobbling and coughing, I stand up in it. It's rickety and narrow and warping.

But it floats.

"You don't know how to steer a boat."

I get out and cross the dock and make my way back to the settlement and search round till I find a flat enough piece of wood to use as an oar.

And that's all I need.

We're ready.

The boy's standing there, holding the things of mine in each hand, rucksack on his back, no real nothing on his face, no Noise that I can hear.

I stare him down. He don't say nothing.

"Manchee?" I call but he's already at my feet.

"Here, Todd!"

"Good boy." We go to the fire. I take the stick he found and put the already burnt end into it. After a minute, the end is red hot and smoky, with flames catching on the new wood. "You sure you can hold this?" I say.

He takes the non-burning end into his maul and there he is, best ruddy dog in the universe, ready to carry fire to the enemy.

"Ready, friend?" I say.

"Weddy, Thawd!" he says, mouth full, tail wagging so fast I see it as a blur.

"He'll kill Manchee," the boy says.

I stand, world spinning and shining, my body barely my own, my lungs coughing up bits of themselves, my head thumping, my legs shaking, my blood boiling, but I stand.

I ruddy well stand.

"I am Todd Hewitt," I say to the boy. "And I am leaving you here."

"You can't never do that," he says, but I'm already turning to Manchee and saying "Go on, boy," and he takes off back up the bluff and down the other side, burning stick in his mouth, and I count to a hundred, loud, so's I can't hear no one say nothing and then I make myself count to a hundred again and that's enough and I lurch as fast as I can back to the dock and the boat and I get myself in and I take the oar onto my lap and I use the knife to cut away the last of the raggedy rope tying the little boat in place.

"You can't never leave me behind," the boy says, standing on the dock, book in one hand, knife in the other.

"Watch me," I say and he gets smaller and smaller in the shimmering and fading light as the boat pulls away from the dock and starts making its way downstream.

Towards Aaron.

Towards Viola.

Towards whatever waits for me down the river.

31

THE WICKED ARE PUNISHED

THERE'S BOATS IN PRENTISSTOWN but no one's used 'em since I can remember. We got the river, sure, this same one that's sloshing me back and forth, but our stretch is rocky and fast and when it does slow down and spread out, the only peaceful area is a marsh full of crocs. After that, it's all wooded swamp. So I ain't never been on a boat and even tho it looks like it should be easy to steer one down a river, it ain't.

The one bit of luck I got is that the river here is pretty calm, despite some splashing from the wind. The boat drifts out into the current and is taken and moves its way downriver whether I do anything or not so I can put all my coughing energy into trying to keep the boat from spinning around as it goes.

It takes a minute or two before I'm successful.

"Dammit," I say under my breath. "Effing thing."

But after some splashing with the oar (and one or two

full spins, shut up) I'm figuring out how to keep it more or less pointed the right way and when I look up, I realize I'm probably already halfway there.

I swallow and shake and cough.

This is the plan. It's probably not a very good one but it's all that my shimmering, flickering brain's gonna let me have.

Manchee'll take the burning stick upwind of Aaron and drop it somewhere to catch fire and make Aaron think I've lit up my own campsite. Then Manchee'll run back to *Aaron's* campsite, barking up a storm, pretending he's trying to tell me he's found Aaron. This is simple since all he has to do is bark my name, which is what he does all the time anyway.

Aaron'll chase him. Aaron'll try to kill him. Manchee'll be faster (Run and run, Manchee, run and run). Aaron'll see the smoke. Aaron, who fears me not one tiny little bit, will go off into the woods towards the smoke to finish me off once and for all.

I'll float downstream, come upon his campsite from the riverside while he's out in the woods looking for me, and I'll rescue Viola. I'll pick up Manchee there, too, when he circles back round ahead of a chasing Aaron (run and run).

Yeah, okay, that's the plan.

I know.

I *know*, but if it don't work, then I'll have to kill him.

And if it comes to that, it can't matter what I become and it can't matter what Viola thinks.

It can't.

It'll have to be done and so I'll have to do it.

I take out the knife.

The blade still has dried blood smeared on it here and there, my blood, Spackle blood, but the rest of it still shines, shimmering and flickering, flickering and shimmering. The tip of it juts out and up like an ugly thumb and the serras-huns along one side spring up like gnashing teeth and the blade edge pulses like a vein full of blood.

The knife is alive.

As long as I hold it, as long as I use it, the knife lives, lives in order to take life, but it has to be commanded, it has to have me to tell it to kill, and it wants to, it wants to plunge and thrust and cut and stab and gouge, but I have to want it to as well, my will has to join with its will.

I'm the one who allows it and I'm the one responsible.

But the knife wanting it makes it easier.

If it comes to it, will I fail?

"*No*," whispers the knife.

"*Yes*," whispers the wind down the river.

A drop of sweat from my forehead splashes on the blade and the knife is just a knife again, just a tool, just a piece of metal in my hand.

Just a knife.

I lay it on the floor of the boat.

I'm shaking again, still. I cough up more goo. I look up and around me, ignoring the waviness of the world and letting the wind cool me down. The river's starting to bend and I keep on floating down it.

Here it comes, I think. Ain't no stopping it.

I look up and over the trees to my left.

My teeth are chattering.

I don't see no smoke yet.

C'mon, boy, it's the next thing that has to happen.

And no smoke.

And no smoke.

And the river's bending more.

C'mon, Manchee.

And no smoke.

And *chatter chatter chatter* go my teeth. I huddle my arms to myself–

And *smoke*! The first small puffs of it, coming up like cotton balls farther down the river.

Good dog, I think, holding my teeth together. *Good dog*.

The boat's tending a bit mid-river so I row as best I can and guide it back to the river's edge.

I'm shaking so bad I can barely hang on to the oar.

The river's bending more.

And there's the forked tree, the tree struck by lightning, coming up on my left.

The sign that I'm almost there.

Aaron'll be just beyond it.

Here it comes.

I cough and sweat and tremble but I'm not letting go of the oar. I row some more, closer to the edge. If Viola can't run for any reason, I'm gonna have to beach it to go get her.

I keep my Noise as blank as I can but the world's closing up in folds of light and shimmer so there's no chance of that. I'll just have to hope the wind's loud enough and that Manchee–

"Todd! Todd! Todd!" I hear from a distance. My dog, barking my name to lure Aaron away. "Todd! Todd! Todd!"

The wind's keeping me from hearing Aaron's Noise so I don't even know if this is working but I'm moving past the forked tree so there's nothing for it now–

"Todd! Todd!"

C'mon, *c'mon*–

The forked tree passing by–

I crouch down in the boat–

"Todd! Todd!" getting fainter, moving back–

Snappings of branches–

And then I hear "TODD HEWITT!!" roared loud as a lion–

As a lion *moving away*–

"C'mon," I whisper to myself, "c'mon, c'mon, c'mon–"

My clenched fists trembling around the oar and–

Round the bend and–

Past the tree and–

The campsite comes and–

There she is.

There she is.

Aaron's gone and there she is.

Lying on the ground in the middle of his campsite.

Not moving.

My heart ratchets up and I cough without even noticing and I say, "Please, please, please," under my breath and I paddle the board furiously and get the boat closer and closer to the river's edge and I stand and leap out into the water and I fall on my rump but I still catch the front of the boat in my hands and "please, please, please" and I get up and I drag the boat far enough up the riverbank and I let go and I run and stumble and run to Viola Viola Viola–

"Please," I say as I run, my chest clenching and coughing and hurting, "*Please*."

I get to her and there she is. Her eyes are closed and her mouth is open a little and I put my head to her chest, shutting out the buzz of my Noise and the shouting of the wind and the barking and yelling versions of my name coming outta the woods around me.

"Please," I whisper.

And *thump, thump*.

She's alive.

"Viola," I whisper fiercely. I'm starting to see little flashing spots before my eyes but I ignore them. "Viola!"

I shake her shoulders and take her face in my hand and shake that, too.

"Wake up," I whisper. "Wake up, wake up, wake up!"

I can't carry her. I'm too shaking and lopsided and weak.

But I'll ruddy well carry her if I have to.

"Todd! Todd! Todd!" I hear Manchee barking from deep in the woods.

"Todd Hewitt!" I hear Aaron yell as he chases my dog.

And then, from below me, I hear, "Todd?"

"Viola?" I say and my throat is clenching and my eyes are blurring.

But she's looking back at me.

"You don't look too good," she says, her voice slurring and her eyes sleepy. I notice some bruising underneath her eyes and my stomach clenches in anger.

"Ya gotta get up," I whisper.

"He drugged..." she says, closing her eyes.

"Viola?" I say, shaking her again. "He's coming back,

Viola. We gotta get outta here."

I can't hear no more barking.

"We gotta go," I say. "Now!"

"I weigh too much," she says, her words melting together.

"Please, Viola," I say and I'm practically *weeping* it. "*Please*."

She blinks open her eyes.

She looks into mine.

"You came for me," she says.

"I did," I say, coughing.

"You came for me," she says again, her face crumpling a little.

Which is when Manchee comes flying outta the bushes, barking my name like his life depended on it.

"TODD! TODD! TODD!" he yelps, running towards us and past. "Aaron! Coming! Aaron!"

Viola lets out a little cry and with a push that nearly knocks me over she gets to her feet and catches me as I fall and we steady ourselves against each other and I manage to point to the boat.

"There!" I say, trying hard to catch my breath.

And we run for it–

Across the campsite–

Towards the boat and the river–

Manchee bounding on ahead and clearing the front of the boat with a leap–

Viola's stumbling ahead of me–

And we're five–

Four–

Three steps away–

And Aaron comes pounding outta the woods behind us–

His Noise so loud I don't even need to look–

"TODD HEWITT!!"

And Viola's reached the front of the boat and is falling in–

And two steps–

And one–

And I reach it and push with all my strength to get it back into the river–

And "TODD HEWITT!!"

And he's closer–

And the boat don't move–

"I WILL PUNISH THE WICKED!"

And closer still–

And the boat don't move–

And his Noise is hitting me as hard as a punch–

And the boat *moves*–

Step and step and my feet are in the water and the boat's moving–

And I'm falling–

And I don't have the strength to get in the boat–

And I'm falling into the water as the boat moves away–

And Viola grabs my shirt and yanks me up till my head and shoulders are over the front–

"NO, YOU DON'T!" Aaron roars–

And Viola calls out as she pulls me again and my front's in the boat–

And Aaron's in the water–

And he's grabbing my feet–

"No!" Viola screams and grips me harder, pulling with all her strength–

And I'm lifted in the air–

And the boat stops–

And Viola's face is twisted in the effort–

But it's a tug of war which only Aaron's ever gonna win–

And then I hear "TODD!" barked in a voice so ferocious I wonder for a minute if a croc's raised outta the water–

But it's Manchee–

It's Manchee–

It's my dog my dog my dog and he's leaping past Viola and I feel his feet hit my back and leave it again as he launches himself at Aaron with a snarl and a howl and a "TODD!" and Aaron calls out in anger–

And he lets go of my feet.

Viola lurches back but she don't let go and I go tumbling into the boat on top of her.

The lurch pushes us farther out into the river.

The boat is starting to pull away.

My head tips and whirls as I spin round and I have to stay on my hands and knees for balance but I'm up as much I can and leaning out the boat and I'm calling, "Manchee!"

Aaron's fallen back into the soft sand at the river's edge, his robe getting tangled up in his legs. Manchee's going for his face, all teeth and claws, growls and roars. Aaron tries to shake him off but Manchee gets a bite either side of Aaron's nose and gives his head a twist.

He rips Aaron's nose clean away from his face.

Aaron yells out in pain, blood shooting everywhere.

"Manchee!" I scream. "Hurry, Manchee!"

"Manchee!" Viola yells.

"C'mon, boy!"

And Manchee looks up from Aaron to see me calling him–

And that's where Aaron takes his chance.

"*No!*" I scream.

He grabs Manchee violently by his scruff, lifting him off the ground and up in one motion.

"Manchee!"

I hear splashing and I'm dimly aware that Viola's got the oar and is trying to stop us going any farther into the river and the world is shimmering and throbbing and–

And Aaron has my dog.

"GET BACK HERE!" Aaron yells, holding Manchee out at arm's length. He's too heavy to be picked up by his scruff and he's yelping from the pain but he can't quite get his head round to bite Aaron's arm.

"Let him go!" I yell.

Aaron lowers his face–

There's blood pouring outta the hole where his nose used to be and tho the gash in his cheek is healed you can still see his teeth and it's this mess that repeats, almost calmly this time, burbling thru the blood and gore, "Come back to me, Todd Hewitt."

"Todd?" Manchee yelps.

Viola's rowing furiously to keep us outta the current but she's weak from the drugs and we're getting farther and farther away. "No," I can hear her saying. "No."

"Let him go!" I scream.

"The girl or the dog, Todd," Aaron calls, still with the

calm that's so much scarier than when he was shouting. "The choice is yers."

I reach for the knife and I hold it out in front of me but my head spins too much and I fall off my hands and smack my teeth on the boat seat.

"Todd?" Viola says, still rowing against the current, the boat twisting and turning.

I sit up tasting blood and the world waves so much it nearly knocks me over again.

"I'll kill you," I say, but so quietly I might as well be talking to myself.

"Last chance, Todd," Aaron says, no longer sounding so calm.

"Todd?" Manchee's still yelping. "Todd?"

And no–

"I'll kill you," but my voice is a whisper–

And no–

And there ain't no choice–

And the boat's out in the current–

And I look at Viola, still rowing against it, tears dripping off her chin–

She looks back at me–

And there ain't no choice–

"No," she says, her voice choking. "Oh, no, Todd–"

And I put my hand on her arm to stop her rowing.

Aaron's Noise roars up in red and black.

The current takes us.

"I'm sorry!" I cry as the river takes us away, my words ragged things torn from me, my chest pulled so tight I can't barely breathe. "I'm sorry, Manchee!"

"Todd?" he barks, confused and scared and watching me leave him behind. *"Todd?"*

"Manchee!" I scream.

Aaron brings his free hand towards my dog.

"MANCHEE!"

"Todd?"

And Aaron wrenches his arms and there's a *CRACK* and a scream and a cut-off yelp that tears my heart in two forever and forever.

And the pain is too much it's too much it's too much and my hands are on my head and I'm rearing back and my mouth is open in a never-ending wordless wail of all the blackness that's inside me.

And I fall back into it.

And I know nothing more as the river takes us away and away and away.

PART VI

32

DOWNRIVER

THE SOUND OF WATER.

And bird noise.

Where's my safety? they sing. *Where's my safety?*

Behind it, there's music.

I swear there's music.

Layers of it, flutey and strange and familiar–

And there's light against the darkness, sheets of it, white and yellow.

And warmth.

And softness on my skin.

And a silence there next to me, pulling against me as strong as it ever did.

I open my eyes.

I'm in a bed, under a cover, in a small square room with white walls and sunlight pouring in at least two open windows with the sound of the river rushing by outside and birds flitting in the trees (and music, is that music?) and for a minute it's not just that I don't know where I am, I also don't know *who* I am or what's happened or why there's an ache in my–

I see Viola, curled up asleep on a chair next to the bed, breathing thru her mouth, her hands pressed twixt her thighs.

I'm still too groggy to make my own mouth move and say her name just yet but my Noise must say it loud enough cuz her eyes flutter open and catch mine and she's outta her seat in a flash with her arms wrapped around me and squishing my nose against her collarbone.

"Oh, Jesus, *Todd*," she says, holding so tight it kinda hurts.

I put one hand on her back and I inhale her scent.

Flowers.

"I thought you were never coming back," she says, squeezing tight. "I thought you were dead."

"Wasn't I?" I croak, trying to remember.

"You were sick," Viola says, sitting back, knees still on my bed. "*Really* sick. Doctor Snow wasn't sure you'd ever wake up and when a doctor admits *that* much–"

"Who's Doctor Snow?" I ask, looking round the little room. "Where are we? Are we in Haven? And what's that music?"

"We're in a settlement called Carbonel Downs," she says. "We floated down the river and–"

She stops cuz she sees me looking at the foot of the bed.

At the space where Manchee ain't.

I remember.

My chest closes up. My throat clenches shut. I can hear him barking in my Noise. *"Todd?"* he's saying, wondering why I'm leaving him behind. *"Todd?"* with an asking mark, just like that, forever asking where I'm going without him.

"He's gone," I say, like I'm saying it to myself.

Viola seems like she's about to say something but when I glance up at her, her eyes are shiny and all she does is nod, which is the right thing, the thing I'd want.

He's gone.

He's gone.

And I don't know what to say about that.

"Is that Noise I hear?" says a loud voice, preceded by its own Noise thru a door opening itself at the foot of the bed. A man enters, a *big* man, tall and broad with glasses that make his eyes bug out and a flip in his hair and a crooked smile and Noise coming at me so filled with relief and joy it's all I can do not to crawl out the window behind me.

"Doctor Snow," Viola says to me, scooting off the bed to make way.

"Pleased to finally meet you, Todd," Doctor Snow says, smiling big and sitting down on the bed and taking a device outta his front shirt pocket. He sticks two ends of it into his ears and places the other end on my chest without asking. "Could you take a deep breath for me?"

I don't do nothing, just look at him.

"I'm checking if your lungs are clear," he says and I realize what it is I'm noticing. His accent's the closest to Viola's I ever heard on New World. "Not exactly the same," he says, "but close."

"He's the one who made you well," Viola says.

I don't say nothing but I take a deep breath.

"Good," Doctor Snow says, placing the end of the device on another part of my chest. "Once more." I breathe in and out. I find that I *can* breathe in and out, all the way down to the bottom of my lungs.

"You were a very sick boy," he says. "I wasn't sure we were going to be able to beat it. You weren't even giving off Noise until yesterday." He looks me in the eye. "Haven't seen that sort of sickness for a long time."

"Yeah, well," I say.

"Haven't heard of a Spackle attack for a *very* long time," he says. I don't say nothing to this, just breathe deep. "That's great, Todd," the doctor says. "Could you take off your shirt, please?"

I look at him, then over to Viola.

"I'll wait outside," she says and out she goes.

I reach behind me to pull my shirt over my head and as I do I realize there's no pain twixt my shoulderblades.

"Took some stitches, that one," Doctor Snow says, moving around behind me. He puts the device against my back.

I flinch away. "That's cold."

"She wouldn't leave your side," he says, ignoring me and checking different places for my breath. "Not even to sleep."

"How long I been here?"

"This is the fifth morning."

"*Five days?*" I say and he barely has a chance to say yes before I'm pulling back the covers and getting outta the bed. "We gotta get outta here," I say, a little unsteady on my feet but standing nonetheless.

Viola leans back in the doorway. "I've been trying to tell them that."

"You're safe here," Doctor Snow says.

"We've heard that before," I say. I look to Viola for support but all she does is stifle a smile and I realize I'm standing there in just a pair of holey and seriously worn-out underpants that ain't covering as much as they should. "Hey!" I say, moving my hands down to the important bits.

"You're safe as you're going to be anywhere," Doctor Snow says behind me, handing me a pair of my trousers from a neatly washed pile by the bed. "We were one of the main fronts in the war. We know how to defend ourselves."

"That was Spackle." I turn my back to Viola and shove my legs in the trousers. "This is men. A *thousand* men."

"So the rumours say," Doctor Snow says. "Even though it's not actually numerically possible."

"I don't know nothing from numerickly," I say, "but they got guns."

"*We* have guns."

"And horses."

"We've got horses."

"Do you have men who'll join them?" I say, challenging him.

He don't say nothing to that, which is satisfying. Then again, it ain't satisfying at all. I button up my trousers. "We need to go."

"You need to rest," the doctor says.

"We ain't staying and waiting for the army to show up." I turn to include Viola, turn without thinking to the space where my dog'd be waiting for me to include him too.

There's a quiet moment when my Noise fills the room with Manchee, just fills it with him, side to side, barking and barking and needing a poo and barking some more.

And dying.

I don't know what to say about that neither.

(He's gone, he's gone.)

I feel empty. All over empty.

"No one's going to make you do anything you don't want to, Todd," Doctor Snow says gently. "But the elder-men of the village would like to talk to you before you leave us."

I tighten my mouth. "Bout what?"

"About anything that might help."

"How can I *help?*" I say, grabbing a washed shirt to put on. "The army will come and kill everyone here who don't join it. That's it."

"This is our home, Todd," he says. "We're going to defend it. We have no choice."

"Then count me out–" I start to say.

"Daddy?" we hear.

There's a little boy standing in the doorway next to Viola.

An actual boy.

He's looking up at me, eyes wide open, his Noise a funny, bright, roomy thing and I can hear myself described as skinny and scar and sleeping boy and at the same time there are all kindsa warm thoughts towards his pa with just the word daddy repeated over and over again, meaning everything you'd want it to: askings about me, identifying his daddy, telling him he loves him, all in one word, repeated forever.

"Hey, fella," Doctor Snow says. "Jacob, this is Todd. All woke up."

Jacob looks at me solemnly, a finger in his mouth, and gives a little nod. "Goat's not milking," he says quietly.

"Is she not?" Doctor Snow says, standing up. "Well, we'd better go see if we can talk her into it, hadn't we?"

Daddy daddy daddy says Jacob's Noise.

"I'll see to the goat," Doctor Snow is saying to me, "and then I'll go round up the rest of the eldermen."

I can't stop staring at Jacob. Who can't stop staring at me.

He's so much closer than the kids I saw at Farbranch.

And he's so *small*.

Was I that small?

Doctor Snow's still talking. "I'll bring the eldermen back here, see if you can't help us." He leans down till I'm looking at him. "And if we can't help you."

His Noise is sincere, truthful. I believe he means what he says. I also believe he's mistaken.

"Maybe," he says, with a smile. "Maybe not. You haven't even seen the place yet. Come on, Jake." He takes his son's hand. "There's food in the kitchen. I'll bet you're starved. Be back within the hour."

I go to the door to watch them leave. Jacob, finger still in his mouth, looks back at me till he and his pa disappear outta the house.

"How old is that?" I ask Viola, still looking down the hallway. "I don't even know how old that is."

"He's four," she says. "He's told me about 800 times. Which seems kind of young to be milking goats."

"Not on New World, it ain't," I say. I turn back to her and her hands are on her hips and she's giving me a serious look.

"Come and eat," she says. "We need to talk."

33

CARBONEL DOWNS

SHE LEADS ME TO A KITCHEN as clean and bright as the bedroom. River still rushing by outside, birds still Noisy, music still–

"What *is* that music?" I say, going to the window to look out. Sometimes it seems like I reckernize it but when I listen close, it's voices changing over voices, running around itself.

"It's from loudspeakers up in the main settlement," Viola says, taking a plate of cold meat outta the fridge.

I sit down at the table. "Is there some kinda festival going on?"

"No," she says, in a way that means *just wait*. "Not a festival." She gets out bread and some orange fruit I ain't never seen before and then some red-coloured drink that tastes of berries and sugar.

I dig into the food. "Tell me."

"Doctor Snow is a good man," she says, like I need to

know this first. "Everything about him is good and kind and he worked so hard to save you, Todd, I mean it."

"Okay. So what's up?"

"That music plays all day and all night," she says, watching me eat. "It's faint here at the house, but in the settlement, you can't hear yourself think."

I pause at a mouthful of bread. "Like the pub."

"What pub?"

"The pub in Prent–" I stop. "Where do they think we're from?"

"Farbranch."

I sigh. "I'll do my best." I take a bite of the fruit. "The pub where I come from played music all the time to try and drown out the Noise."

She nods. "I asked Doctor Snow why they did it here, and he said, 'To keep men's thoughts private'."

I shrug. "It makes an awful racket, but it kinda makes sense, don't it? One way to deal with the Noise."

"*Men's* thoughts, Todd," she says. "*Men*. And you notice he said he was going to ask the elder*men* to come seek out your advice?"

I get a horrible thought. "Did the women all die here, too?"

"Oh, there's women," she says, fiddling with a butter knife. "They clean and they cook and they make babies and they all live in a big dormitory outside of town where they can't interfere in men's business."

I put down a forkful of meat. "I saw a place like that when I was coming to find you. Men sleeping in one place, women in another."

"Todd," she says, looking at me. "They wouldn't listen to me. Not one thing. Not a word I said about the army. They kept calling me *little girl* and practically patting me on the bloody head." She crosses her arms. "The only reason they want to talk to you about it now is because caravans of refugees started showing up on the river road."

"Wilf," I say.

Her eyes scan over me, reading my Noise. "Oh," she says. "No, I haven't seen him."

"Wait a minute." I swallow some more drink. It feels like I haven't drunk anything for years. "How did we get so far ahead of the army? How come if I've been here five days we ain't been overrun yet?"

"We were in that boat for a day and a half," she says, running her nail at something stuck on the table.

"A day and a half," I repeat, thinking about this. "We musta come miles."

"Miles and miles," she says. "I just let us float and float and float. I was too afraid to stop at the places I passed. You wouldn't believe some of the things..." She drifts off, shaking her head.

I remember Jane's warnings. "Naked people and glass houses?" I ask.

Viola looks at me strange. "No," she says, curling her lip. "Just poverty. Just horrible, horrible poverty. Some of those places looked like they would have eaten us so I just kept on and on and you got sicker and sicker and then on the second morning I saw Doctor Snow and Jacob out fishing and I could see in his Noise he was a doctor and as weird as this place is about women, it's at least clean."

I look around the clean, clean kitchen. "We can't stay," I say.

"No, we can't." She puts her head in her hands. "I was so worried about you." There's feeling in her voice. "I was so worried about the army coming and nobody *listening* to me." She smacks the table in frustration. "And I was feeling so bad about–"

She stops. Her face creases and she looks away.

"Manchee," I say, out loud, for the first time since–

"I'm so sorry, Todd," she says, her eyes watery.

"Ain't yer fault." I stand up fast, scooting my chair back.

"He would have killed you," she says, "and then he would have killed Manchee just because he could."

"Stop talking about it, please," I say, leaving the kitchen and going back to the bedroom. Viola follows me. "I'll talk to these elder folks," I say, picking up Viola's bag from the floor and stuffing the rest of the washed clothes in it. "And then we'll go. How far are we from Haven, do you know?"

Viola makes a tiny smile. "Two days."

I stand up straight. "We came that far downriver?"

"We came that far."

I whistle quietly to myself. Two days. Just two days. Till whatever there is in Haven.

"Todd?"

"Yeah?" I say, putting her bag round my shoulders.

"Thank you," she says.

"For what?"

"For coming after me."

Everything's gone still.

"Ain't nothing," I say, feeling my face get hot and looking

away. She don't say nothing more. "You all right?" I ask, still not looking at her. "From when he took you?"

"I don't really–" she starts to say but we hear a door close and a sing-song daddy daddy daddy floating down the hall towards us. Jacob hugs the door frame of the room rather than come on in.

"Daddy sent me to fetch you," he says.

"Oh?" I raise my eyebrows. "I'm meant to come to *them* now, am I?"

Jacob nods, very serious.

"Well, in that case, we're coming," I rearrange the sack and looking at Viola. "And then we're going."

"Too right," Viola says and the way she says it makes me glad. We head out into the hallway after Jacob but he stops us at the door.

"Just you," he says, looking at me.

"Just me what?"

Viola crosses her arms. "He means just you to talk to the eldermen."

Jacob nods, again very serious. I look at Viola and back to Jacob. "Well now," I say, squatting down to his level. "Why don't you just go tell yer daddy that both me and Viola will be along in a minute. Okay?"

Jacob opens his mouth. "But he said–"

"I don't really care what he said," I say gently. "Go."

He gives a little gasp and runs out the door.

"I think I'm maybe thru of men telling me what to do," I say and I'm surprised at the weariness in my voice and suddenly I feel like I wanna get back in that bed and sleep for another five days.

"You going to be all right to walk to Haven?" Viola says.

"Try and stop me," I say and she smiles again.

I head on out the front door.

And for a third time I'm expecting Manchee to come bounding out with us.

His absence is so big it's like he's there and all the air goes outta my lungs again and I have to wait and breathe deep and swallow.

"Oh, man," I say to myself.

His last *Todd?* hangs in my Noise like a wound.

That's another thing about Noise. Everything that's ever happened to you just keeps right on talking, for ever and ever.

I see the last of Jacob's dust as he runs on up the trail thru some trees towards the rest of the settlement. I look round. Doctor Snow's house ain't too big but it stretches out to a deck overlooking the river. There's a small dock and a really low bridge connecting the wide path that comes from the centre of Carbonel Downs to the river road that carries along on the other side. The road across the river, the one we spent so much time coming down, is almost hidden behind a row of trees as it carries on past the settlement on the final two days towards Haven.

"God," I say. "It's like paradise compared to the rest of New World."

"There's more to paradise than nice buildings," Viola says.

I look round some more. Doctor Snow's got a well-kept front garden on the path to the settlement. Looking up the path, I can see more buildings thru the trees and hear that music playing.

That weird music. Constantly changing to keep you from getting used to it, I guess. It's nothing I reckernize but it's louder out here and I guess on one level you ain't *sposed* to reckernize it but I swear I heard something in it when I was waking up–

"It's almost unbearable in the middle of the settlement," Viola says. "Most of the women don't even bother coming in from the dormitory." She frowns. "Which I guess is the whole point."

"Wilf's wife told me bout a settlement where everyone–"

I stop cuz the music changes.

Except it don't change.

The music from the settlement stays the same, messy and wordy and bending around itself like a monkey.

But there's more.

There's more music than just it.

And it's getting louder.

"Do you hear that?" I say.

I turn.

And turn again. Viola, too.

Trying to figure out what we're hearing.

"Maybe someone's set up another loudspeaker across the river," she says. "Just in case the women were getting any uppity ideas about leaving."

But I ain't listening to her.

"No," I whisper. "No, it can't be."

"What?" Viola says, her voice changing.

"Shh." I listen close again, trying to calm my Noise so I can hear it.

"It's coming from the river," she whispers.

"Shh," I say again, cuz my chest is starting to rise, my Noise starting to buzz too loud to be of any use at all.

Out there, against the rush of the water and the Noise of the birdsong, there's–

"A song," Viola says, real quiet. "Someone's singing."

Someone's singing.

And what they're singing is:

Early one mor-r-ning, just as the sun was ri-i-sing...

And my Noise surges louder as I say it.

"Ben."

34

OH NEVER LEAVE ME

I RUN DOWN TO THE RIVER'S EDGE and stop and listen again.

Oh don't deceive me.

"Ben?" I say, trying to shout and whisper at the same time.

Viola comes thumping up behind me. "Not *your* Ben?" she says. "Is it your Ben?"

I shush her with my hand and listen and try to pick away the river and the birds and my own Noise and there, just there under it all–

Oh never leave me.

"Other side of the river," Viola says and takes off across the bridge, feet smacking against the wood. I'm right behind her, passing her, listening and looking and listening and looking and there and there and there–

There in the leafy shrubs on the other side of the water–

It's Ben.

It really is Ben.

He's crouched down behind leafy greenery, hand against a tree trunk, watching me come to him, watching me run across the bridge, and as I near him, his face relaxes and his Noise opens up as wide as his arms and I'm flying into 'em both, leaping off the bridge and into the bushes and nearly knocking him over and my heart is busting open and my Noise is as bright as the whole blue sky and–

And everything's gonna be all right.

Everything's gonna be all right.

Everything's gonna be all right.

It's Ben.

And he's gripping me tight and he's saying, "Todd," and Viola's standing back a ways, letting me greet him, and I'm hugging him and hugging him and it's Ben, oh Christ Almighty, it's Ben Ben Ben.

"It's me," he says, laughing a little cuz I'm crushing the air outta his lungs. "Oh, it's good to see ya, Todd."

"Ben," I say, leaning back from him and I don't know what to do with my hands so I just grab his shirt front in my fists and shake him in a way that's gotta mean love. "Ben," I say again.

He nods and smiles.

But there's creases round his eyes and already I can see the beginnings of it, so soon it's gotta be right up front in his Noise, and I have to ask, "Cillian?"

He don't say nothing but he shows it to me, Ben running back to a farmhouse already in flames, already burning down, with some of the Mayor's men inside but with Cillian, too, and Ben grieving, grieving still.

"Aw, no," I say, my stomach sinking, tho I'd long guessed it to be true.

But guessing a thing ain't knowing a thing.

Ben nods again, slow and sad, and I notice now that he's dirty and there's blood clotted on his nose and he looks like he ain't eaten for a week but it's still Ben and he can still read me like no other cuz his Noise is already asking me bout Manchee and I'm already showing him and here at last my eyes properly fill and rush over and he takes me in his arms again and I cry for real over the loss of my dog and of Cillian and of the life that was.

"I left him," I say and keep saying, snot-filled and coughing. "I left him."

"I know," he says and I can tell it's true cuz I hear the same words in his Noise. I left him, he thinks.

But after only a minute I feel him gently pushing me back and he says, "Listen, Todd, there ain't much time."

"Ain't much time for what?" I sniffle but I see he's looking over at Viola.

"Hi," she says, eyes all alert.

"Hi," Ben says. "You must be her."

"I must be," she says.

"You been taking care of Todd?"

"We've been taking care of each other."

"Good," Ben says, and his Noise goes warm and sad. "Good."

"C'mon," I say, taking his arm and trying to pull him back towards the footbridge. "We can get you something to eat. And there's a doctor–"

But Ben ain't moving. "Can you keep an eye out for us?"

he asks Viola. "Let us know if you see anything, anything at all. Either from the settlement or the road."

Viola nods and catches my eye as she steps outta the green and back to the path.

"Things have escalated," Ben says to me, low, serious as a heart attack. "You gotta get to a place called Haven. Fast as you can."

"I *know* that, Ben," I say, "why do you–?"

"There's an army after you."

"I know that, *too*. *And* Aaron. But now that yer here we can–"

"I can't come with you," he says.

My mouth hangs open. "What? *Course* you can–"

But he's shaking his head. "You know I can't."

"We can find a way," I say, but already my Noise is whirling, thinking, remembering.

"Prentisstown men ain't welcome anywhere on New World," he says.

I nod. "They ain't too happy bout Prentisstown *boys*, neither."

He takes my arm again. "Has anyone hurt you?"

I look at him quietly. "Lots of people," I say.

He bites his lip and his Noise gets even sadder.

"I looked for you," he says. "Day and night, following the army, getting round it, ahead of it, listening for rumours of a boy and a girl travelling alone. And here you are and yer okay and I knew you would be. I knew it." He sighs and there's so much love and sadness in it I know he's about to say the truth. "But I'm a danger to you in New World." He gestures at the bush we're hiding in, hiding in like thieves.

"Yer gonna have to make it the rest of the way alone."

"I ain't alone," I say, without thinking.

He smiles, but it's still sad. "No," he says. "No, yer not, are ya?" He looks around us again, peering thru the leaves and over the river to Doctor Snow's house. "Were you sick?" he asks. "I heard yer Noise yesterday morning coming down the river but it was feverish and sleeping. I been waiting here ever since. I was worried something was really wrong."

"I was sick," I say and shame starts to cloud my Noise like a slow fog.

Ben looks at me close again. "What happened, Todd?" he says, gently reading into my Noise like he always could. "What's happened?"

I open up my Noise for him, all of it from the beginning, the crocs that attacked Aaron, the race thru the swamp, Viola's ship, being chased by the Mayor on horseback, the bridge, Hildy and Tam, Farbranch and what happened there, the fork in the road, Wilf and the things that sang *Here*, Mr Prentiss Jr and Viola saving me.

And the Spackle.

And what I did.

I can't look at Ben.

"Todd," he says.

I'm still looking at the ground.

"Todd," he says again. "Look at me."

I look up at him. His eyes, blue as ever, catching mine and holding them. "We've all made mistakes, Todd. All of us."

"I killed it," I say. I swallow. "I killed *him*. It was a him."

"You were acting on what you knew. You were acting on what you thought best."

"And that *excuses* it?"

But there's something in his Noise. Something off and telling.

"What is it, Ben?"

He lets out a breath. "It's time you knew, Todd," he says. "Time you knew the truth."

There's a snap of branches as Viola comes rushing back to us.

"Horse on the road," she says, outta breath.

We listen. Hoofbeats, down the river road, coming fast. Ben slinks back a little farther into the bushes. We go with him but the horseman is coming so quick he ain't interested in us at all. We hear him thunder by on the road and turn up the bridge that heads straight into Carbonel Downs, hooves clattering on boards and then on dirt till they're swallowed up by the loudspeaker sounds.

"That can't be good news," Viola says.

"It'll be the army," Ben says. "By now they're probably not more than a few hours from here."

"What!?" I say, rearing back. Viola jumps, too.

"I told you we don't have much time," Ben says.

"Then we gotta *go*!" I say. "You gotta come with us. We'll tell people–"

"No," he says. "No. You get yerselves to Haven. That's all there is to it. It's yer best chance."

We pelt him with sudden askings.

"Is Haven safe then?" Viola asks. "From an army?"

"Is it true they have a cure for the Noise?" I ask.

"Will they have communicators? Will I be able to contact my ship?"

"Are you sure it's safe? Are you *sure*?"

Ben raises his hands to stop us. "I don't know," he says. "I haven't been there in twenty years."

Viola stands up straight.

"Twenty years?" she says. "Twenty *years*?" Her voice is rising. "Then how can we know what we'll find when we get there? How do we know it's even still *there*?"

I rub my hand across my face and I think it's the emptiness where Manchee used to be that makes me realize, realize what we never wanted to know.

"We don't," I say, only saying the truth. "We never did."

Viola lets out a little sound and her shoulders slump down. "No," she says. "I guess we didn't."

"But there's always hope," Ben says. "You always have to hope."

We both look at him and there must be a word for how we're doing it but I don't know what it is. We're looking at him like he's speaking a foreign language, like he just said he was moving to one of the moons, like he's telling us it's all just been a bad dream and there's candy for everybody.

"There ain't a whole lotta hope out here, Ben," I say.

He shakes his head. "What d'you think's been driving you on? What d'you think's got you this far?"

"Fear," Viola says.

"Desperayshun," I say.

"No," he says, taking us both in. "No, no, no. You've come farther than most people on this planet will do in their lifetimes. You've overcome obstacles and dangers and things that should've killed you. You've outrun an army and a madman and deadly illness and seen things most people will never see. How do you think you could have possibly come this far if you didn't have hope?"

Viola and I exchange a glance.

"I see what yer trying to say, Ben–" I start.

"Hope," he says, squeezing my arm on the word. "It's hope. I am looking into yer eyes right now and I am telling you that there's hope for you, hope for you both." He looks up at Viola and back at me. "There's hope waiting for you at the end of the road."

"You don't know that," Viola says and my Noise, as much as I don't want it to, agrees with her.

"No," Ben says, "but I believe it. I believe it for you. And that's why it's hope."

"Ben–"

"Even if you don't believe it," he says, "believe that I do."

"I'd believe it more if you were coming with us," I say.

"He ain't coming?" Viola says, surprised, then corrects herself. "*Isn't* coming?"

Ben looks at her, opens his mouth and closes it again.

"What's the truth, Ben?" I ask. "What's the truth we need to know?"

Ben takes a long slow breath thru his nose. "Okay," he says.

But then a loud and clear "Todd?" comes calling from across the river.

And that's when we notice the music of Carbonel Downs is competing with the Noise of men now crossing the bridge.

Many men.

That's the other purpose of the music, I guess. So you can't hear men coming.

"Viola?" Doctor Snow is calling. "What are you two doing over there?"

I stand up straight and look over. Doctor Snow is crossing the bridge, little Jacob's hand in his, leading a group of men who look like less friendly versions of himself and they're eyeing us up and they're seeing Ben and seeing me and Viola talking to him.

And their Noise is starting to turn different colours as what they're seeing starts making sense to them.

And I see that some of 'em have rifles.

"Ben?" I say quietly.

"You need to run," he says, under his breath. "You need to run *now*."

"I ain't leaving you. Not again."

"Todd–"

"Too late," Viola says.

Cuz they're on us now, past the end of the bridge and heading towards the bushes where we're not really hiding no more.

Doctor Snow reaches us first. He looks Ben up and down. "And who might this be then?"

And the sound of his Noise ain't happy at all.

35

THE LAW

"THIS IS BEN," I say, trying to raise my Noise to block all the askings coming from the men.

"And who's Ben when he's at home?" Doctor Snow asks, his eyes alert and looking.

"Ben's my pa," I say. Cuz it's true, ain't it? In all that's important. "My father."

"Todd," I hear Ben say behind me, all kindsa feelings in his Noise, but warning most of all.

"Your father?" says a bearded man behind Doctor Snow, his fingers flexing along the stock of his rifle, tho not lifting it.

Not yet.

"You might want to be careful who you start claiming as a parent, Todd," Doctor Snow says slowly, pulling Jacob closer to him.

"You said the boy was from Farbranch," says a third man with a purple birthmark under his eye.

"That's what the girl told us." Doctor Snow looks at Viola. "Didn't you, Vi?"

Viola holds his look but don't say nothing.

"Can't trust the word of a woman," says the beard. "This is a Prentisstown man if I ever saw one."

"Leading the army right to us," says the birthmark.

"The boy is innocent," says Ben and when I turn I can see his hands are in the air. "I'm the one you want."

"Correction," says the beard, his voice angry and getting angrier. "You're the one we *don't* want."

"Hold on a minute, Fergal," Doctor Snow says. "Something's not right here."

"You know the law," says the birthmark.

The law.

Farbranch talked about the law, too.

"I also know these aren't normal circumstances," Doctor Snow says, then turns back to us. "We should at least give them a chance to explain themselves."

I hear Ben take a breath. "Well, I–"

"Not you," the beard interrupts.

"What's the story, Todd?" Doctor Snow says. "And it's become really important you tell us the truth."

I look from Viola to Ben and back again.

Which side of the truth do I tell?

I hear the cock of a rifle. The beard's raised his gun. And so have one or two of the men behind him.

"The longer you wait," the beard says, "the more you look like spies."

"We ain't spies," I say in a hurry.

"The army your girl's been talking about has been spotted

marching down the river road," Doctor Snow says. "One of our scouts just reported them as less than an hour away."

"Oh, no," I hear Viola whisper.

"She ain't my girl," I say, low.

"What?" Doctor Snow says.

"What?" Viola says.

"She's her own girl," I say. "She don't belong to anyone."

And does Viola ever *look* at me.

"Whichever," the birthmark says. "We've got a Prentisstown army marching on us and a Prentisstown man hiding in our bushes and a Prentisstown boy who's been in our midst for the last week. Looks mighty fishy if you ask me."

"He was sick," Doctor Snow says. "He was out cold."

"So you say," says the birthmark.

Doctor Snow turns to him real slow. "Are you calling me a liar now, Duncan? Remember, please, that you're talking to the head of the council of eldermen."

"You telling me you're not seeing a plot here, Jackson?" says the birthmark, not backing down and raising his own rifle. "We're sitting ducks. Who knows what they've told their army?" He aims his rifle at Ben. "But we'll be putting an end to that right now."

"We ain't *spies*," I say again. "We're running from the army just as hard as you should be."

And the men look at each other.

In their Noise, I can hear just these thoughts about the army, about running from it instead of defending the town. I can also see anger bubbling, anger at having to make this choice, anger at not knowing the best way to protect their families. And I can see the anger focussing itself, not on the army, not on themselves for being unprepared despite Viola warning 'em for days, not at the world for the state it's in.

They're focussing their anger on Ben.

They're focussing their anger on Prentisstown in the form of one man.

Doctor Snow kneels down to get to Jacob's level. "Hey, fella," he says to his son. "Why don't you run on back to the house now, okay?"

Daddy daddy daddy I hear in Jacob's Noise. "Why, Daddy?" he says, staring at me.

"Well, I'll betcha the goat's getting lonely," Doctor Snow says. "And who wants a lonely goat, huh?"

Jacob looks at his father, back at me and Ben, then to the men around him. "Why is everyone so upset?" he says.

"Oh," Doctor Snow says, "we're just figuring some things out, is all. It'll all be right soon enough. You just run on back home, make sure the goat's okay."

Jacob thinks about this for a second, then says, "Okay, Daddy."

Doctor Snow kisses him on the top of the head and ruffles his hair. Jacob goes running back over the bridge towards Doctor Snow's house. When Doctor Snow turns back to us, a whole raft of pointed guns accompany him.

"You can see how this doesn't look good, Todd," he says, and there's real sadness in his voice.

"He doesn't know," Ben says.

"Shut your hole, murderer!" says the beard, gesturing with his rifle.

Murderer?

"Tell me true," Doctor Snow says to me. "Are you from Prentisstown?"

"He *saved* me from Prentisstown," Viola speaks up. "If it hadn't been for him–"

"Shut up, girl," says the beard.

"Now's not really the time for women to be talking, Vi," Doctor Snow says.

"But–" Viola says, her face getting red.

"Please," Doctor Snow says. Then he looks at Ben. "What have you told your army? How many men we have? What our fortifications are like–"

"I've been *running* from the army," Ben says, hands still in the air. "Look at me. Do I look like a well-tended soldier? I haven't told them anything. I've been on the run, looking for my..." He pauses and I know the reason. "For my son," he says.

"You did this knowing the law?" Doctor Snow asks.

"I know the law," Ben says. "How could I possibly not know the law?"

"What ruddy LAW?" I yell. "What the hell is everyone talking about?"

"Todd is innocent," Ben says. "You can search his Noise for as long as you like and you won't find anything to say I'm lying."

"You can't trust them," says the beard, still looking down his gun. "You know you can't."

"We don't know anything," Doctor Snow says. "Not for ten years or more."

"We know they've raised themselves into an army," says the birthmark.

"Yes, but I don't see any crime in this boy," Doctor Snow says. "Do you?"

A dozen different Noises come poking at me like sticks.

He turns to Viola. "And all the girl is guilty of is a lie that saved her friend's life."

Viola looks away from me, face still red with anger.

"And we've got bigger problems," Doctor Snow continues. "An army coming that may or may not know all about how we're preparing to meet them."

"We ain't SPIES!" I shout.

But Doctor Snow is turning to the other men. "Take the boy and the girl back into town. The girl can go with the women and the boy is well enough to fight alongside us."

"Wait a minute!" I yell.

Doctor Snow turns to Ben. "And though I do believe you're just a man out looking for his son, the law's the law."

"Is that your final ruling?" the beard says.

"If the eldermen agree," Doctor Snow says. There's a general but reluctant nodding of heads, all serious and curt. Doctor Snow looks at me. "I'm sorry, Todd."

"Hold on!" I say, but the birthmark's is already stepping forward and grabbing my arm. "Let go of me!"

Another man's grabbing on to Viola and she's resisting just as much as I am.

"Ben!" I call, looking back at him. "*Ben!*"

"Go, Todd," he says.

"No, Ben!"

"Remember I love you."

"What're they gonna do?" I say, still pulling away from

the birthmark's hand. I turn to Doctor Snow. "What're you gonna do?"

He don't say nothing but I can see it in his Noise.

What the law demands.

"The HELL you are!" I yell and with my free arm I'm already reaching for my knife and bringing it round towards the birthmark's hand, slicing it across the top. He yelps and lets go.

"Run!" I say to Ben. "Run, already!"

I see Viola biting the hand of the man who's grabbing her. He calls out and she stumbles back.

"You, too!" I say to her. "Get outta here!"

"I wouldn't," says the beard and there are rifles cocking all over the place.

The birthmark is cursing and he raises his arm to strike but I've got my knife out in front of me. "Try it," I say thru my teeth. "*Come on!*"

"ENOUGH!" Doctor Snow yells.

And in the sudden silence that follows, we hear the hoofbeats.

Thump budda-thump budda-thump.

Horses. Five of 'em. Ten. Maybe even fifteen.

Roaring down the road like the devil hisself is on their tail.

"Scouts?" I say to Ben tho I know they ain't.

He shakes his head. "Advance party."

"They'll be armed," I say to Doctor Snow and the men, thinking fast. "They'll have as many guns as you."

Doctor Snow's thinking, too. I can see his Noise whirring, see him thinking how much time they've got before the horses get here, how much trouble me and Ben and Viola are going to cause, how much time we'll waste.

I see him decide.

"Let them go."

"What?" says the beard, his Noise itching to shoot *something*. "He's a traitor and a murderer."

"And we've got a town to protect," Doctor Snow says firmly. "I've got a son to keep safe. So do you, Fergal."

The beard frowns but says nothing more.

Thump budda-thump budda-thump comes the sound from the road.

Doctor Snow turns to us. "Go," he says. "I can only hope you haven't sealed our fate."

"We haven't," I say, "and that's the truth."

Doctor Snow purses his lips. "I'd like to believe you." He turns to the men. "Come on!" he shouts. "Get to your posts! Hurry!"

The group of men breaks up, scurrying back to Carbonel Downs, the beard and the birthmark still seething at us as they go, looking for a reason to use their guns, but we don't give 'em one. We just watch 'em go.

I find I'm shaking a little.

"Holy crap," Viola says, bending at the waist.

"We gotta get outta here," I say. "The army's gonna be more interested in us than it is in them."

I still have Viola's bag with me, tho all it's got in it any more are a few clothes, the water bottles, the binos and my ma's book, still in its plastic bag.

All the things we got in the world.

Which means we're ready to go.

"This is only gonna keep happening," Ben says. "I can't come with you."

"Yes, you can," I say. "You can leave later but we're going now and yer coming with us. We ain't leaving you to be caught by no army." I look over to Viola. "Right?"

She puts her shoulders back and looks decisive. "Right," she says.

"That's settled then," I say.

Ben looks back and forth twixt the two of us. He furrows his brow. "Only till I know yer safe."

"Too much talking," I say. "Not enough running."

36

ANSWERS TO ASKINGS

WE STAY OFF THE RIVER ROAD for obvious reasons and tear thru the trees, heading, as always, towards Haven, snapping thru twigs and branches, getting away from Carbonel Downs as fast as our legs can carry us.

It's not ten minutes before we hear the first gunshots.

We don't look back. We don't look back.

We run and the sounds fade.

We keep running.

Me and Viola are both faster than Ben and sometimes we have to slow down to let him catch up.

We run past one, then two small, empty settlements, places that obviously heeded the rumours about the army better than Carbonel Downs did. We keep to the woods twixt the river and the road but we don't even see any caravans. They must be high-tailing it to Haven.

On we run.

Night falls and we keep on running.

"You all right?" I ask Ben, when we stop by the river to refill the bottles.

"Keep on going," he says, gasping. "Keep on going."

Viola sends me a worried look.

"I'm sorry we don't got food," I say, but he just shakes his head and says, "Keep going."

So we keep going.

Midnight comes and we run thru that, too.

(Who knows how many days? Who cares any more?)

Till finally, Ben says, "Wait," and stops, hands on his knees, breathing hard in a real unhealthy way.

I look around us by the light of the moons. Viola's looking, too. She points. "There."

"Up there, Ben," I say, pointing up the small hill Viola's seen. "We'll be able to get a view."

Ben don't say nothing, just gasps and nods his head and follows us. There's trees all the way up the side but a well-tended path and a wide clearing at the top.

When we get there, we see why.

"A sematary," I say.

"A what?" Viola says, looking round at all the square stones marking out their graves. Must be a hundred, maybe two, in orderly rows and well-kept grass. Settler life is hard and it's short and lotsa New World people have lost the battle.

"It's a place for burying dead folk," I say.

Her eyes widen. "A place for doing *what*?"

"Don't people die in space?" I ask.

"Yeah," she says. "But we burn them. We don't put them in *holes*." She crosses her arms around herself, mouth and forehead frowning, peering around at the graves. "How can this be sanitary?"

Ben still hasn't said anything, just flopped down by a gravestone and leant against it, catching his breath. I take a swig from a water bottle and then hand it to Ben. I look out and around us. You can see down the road for a piece and there's a view of the river, too, rushing by us on the left now. It's a clear sky, the stars out, the moons starting to crescent in the sky above us.

"Ben?" I say, looking up into the night.

"Yeah?" he says, drinking down his water.

"You all right?"

"Yeah." His breath's getting back to normal. "I'm built for farm labour. Not sprinting."

I look at the moons one more time, the smaller one chasing the larger one, two brightnesses up there, still light enough to cast shadows, ignorant of the troubles of men.

I look into myself. I look deep into my Noise.

And I realize I'm ready.

This is the last chance.

And I'm ready.

"I think it's time," I say. I look back at him. "I think now's the time, if it's ever gonna be."

He licks his lips and swallows his water. He puts the cap back on the bottle. "I know," he says.

"Time for what?" Viola asks.

"Where should I start?" Ben asks.

I shrug. "Anywhere," I say, "as long as it's true."

I can hear Ben's Noise gathering, gathering up the whole story, taking one stream out of the river, finally, the one that tells what really happened, the one hidden for so long and so deep I didn't even know it was there for my whole up-growing life.

Viola's silence has gone more silent than usual, as still as the night, waiting to hear what he might say.

Ben takes a deep breath.

"The Noise germ wasn't Spackle warfare," he says. "That's the first thing. The germ was here when we landed. A naturally occurring phenomenon, in the air, always had been, always will be. We got outta our ships and within a day everyone could hear everyone's thoughts. Imagine our surprise."

He pauses, remembering.

"Except it *wasn't* everyone," Viola says.

"It was just the men," I say.

Ben nods. "No one knows why. Still don't. Our scientists were mainly agriculturalists and the doctors couldn't find a reason and so for a while, there was chaos. Just ... *chaos*, like you wouldn't believe. Chaos and confusion and Noise Noise Noise." He scratches underneath his chin. "A lotta men scattered theirselves into far communities, getting away from Haven as fast as roads could be cut. But soon folk realized there was nothing to be done about it so for a while we all tried to live with it the best we could, found different ways to deal with it, different communities taking their own paths. Same as we did when we realized all our livestock were talking, too, and pets and local creachers."

He looks up into the sky and to the sematary around us and the river and road below.

"Everything on this planet talks to each other," he says.

"Everything. That's what New World is. Informayshun, all the time, never stopping, whether you want it or not. The Spackle knew it, evolved to live with it, but we weren't equipped for it. Not even close. And too much informayshun can drive a man mad. Too much informayshun becomes just Noise. And it never, never stops."

He pauses and the Noise is there, of course, like it always is, his and mine and Viola's silence only making it louder.

"As the years went by," he goes on, "times were hard all over New World and getting harder. Crops failing and sickness and no prosperity and no Eden. Definitely no Eden. And a preaching started spreading in the land, a poisonous preaching, a preaching that started to blame."

"They blamed the aliens," Viola says.

"The Spackle," I say and the shame returns.

"They blamed the Spackle," Ben confirms. "And somehow preaching became a movement and a movement became a war." He shakes his head. "They didn't stand a chance. We had guns, they didn't, and that was the end of the Spackle."

"Not all," I say.

"No," he says. "Not all. But they learned better than to come too near men again, I tell you that."

A brief wind blows across the hilltop. When it stops, it's like we're the only three people left on New World. Us and the sematary ghosts.

"But the war's not the end of the story," Viola says quietly.

"No," Ben says. "The story ain't finished, ain't even *half* finished."

And I know it ain't. And I know where it's heading.

And I changed my mind. I don't want it to finish.

But I do, too.

I look into Ben's eyes, into his Noise.

"The war didn't stop with the Spackle," I say. "Not in Prentisstown."

Ben licks his lips and I can feel unsteadiness in his Noise and hunger and grief at what he's already imagining is our next parting.

"War is a monster," he says, almost to himself. "War is the devil. It starts and it consumes and it grows and grows and grows." He's looking at me now. "And otherwise normal men become monsters, too."

"They couldn't stand the silence," Viola says, her voice still. "They couldn't stand women knowing everything about them and them knowing nothing about women."

"*Some* men thought that," Ben says. "Not all. Not me, not Cillian. There were good men in Prentisstown."

"But enough thought it," I say.

"Yes," he nods.

There's another pause as the truth starts to show itself.

Finally. And forever.

Viola is shaking her head. "Are you saying…?" she says. "Are you really saying…?"

And here it is.

Here's the thing that's the centre of it all.

Here's the thing that's been growing in my head since I left the swamp, seen in flashes of men along the way, most clearly in Matthew Lyle's but also in the reakshuns of everyone who even hears the word Prentisstown.

Here it is.

The truth.

And I don't want it.

But I say it anyway.

"After they killed the Spackle," I say, "the men of Prentisstown killed the women of Prentisstown."

Viola gasps even tho she's got to have guessed it, too.

"Not *all* the men," Ben says. "But many. Allowing themselves to be swayed by Mayor Prentiss and the preachings of Aaron, who used to say that what was hidden must be evil. They killed all the women and all the men who tried to protect them."

"My ma," I say.

Ben just nods in confirmayshun.

I feel a sickness in my stomach.

My ma dying, being killed by men I probably saw every day.

I have to sit down on a gravestone.

I have to think of something else, I just do. I have to put something else in my Noise so I can stand it.

"Who was Jessica?" I say, remembering Matthew Lyle's Noise back in Farbranch, remembering the violence in it, the Noise that now makes sense even tho it don't make no sense at all.

"Some people could see what was coming," Ben says. "Jessica Elizabeth was our Mayor and she could see the way the wind was blowing."

Jessica Elizabeth, I think. New Elizabeth.

"She organized some of the girls and younger boys to flee across the swamp," Ben continues. "But before she could go herself with the women and the men who hadn't lost their minds, the Mayor's men attacked."

"And that was that," I say, feeling numb all over. "New Elizabeth becomes Prentisstown."

"Yer ma never thought it would happen," Ben says, smiling sadly to himself at some memory. "So full of love that woman, so full of hope in the goodness of others." He stops smiling. "And then there came a moment when it was too late to flee and you were way too young to be sent away and so she gave you to us, told us to keep you safe, no matter what."

I look up. "How was staying in Prentisstown keeping me safe?"

Ben's staring right at me, sadness everywhere around him, his Noise so weighted with it, it's a wonder he can stay upright.

"Why didn't you leave?" I ask.

He rubs his face. "Cuz we didn't think the attack would really happen either. Or *I* didn't, anyway, and we had put the farm together and I thought it would blow over before anything really bad happened. I thought it was just rumours and paranoia, including on the part of yer ma, right up to the last." He frowns. "I was wrong. I was stupid." He looks away. "I was wilfully blind."

I remember his words comforting me about the Spackle.

We've all made mistakes, Todd. All of us.

"And then it was too late," Ben says. "The deed was done and word of what Prentisstown had done spread like wildfire, starting with the few who'd managed to escape it. All men from Prentisstown were declared criminals. We couldn't leave."

Viola's arms are still crossed. "Why didn't someone come and get you? Why didn't the rest of New World come after you?"

"And do what?" Ben says, sounding tired. "Fight another war but this time with heavily armed men? Lock us up in a giant prison? They laid down the law that if any man from Prentisstown crossed the swamp, he'd be executed. And then they left us to it."

"But they must have..." Viola says, holding her palms to the air. "Something. I don't know."

"If it ain't happening on yer doorstep," Ben says, "it's easier to think, *Why go out and* find *trouble*? We had the whole of the swamp twixt us and New World. The Mayor sent word that Prentisstown would be a town in exile. Doomed, of course, to a slow death. We'd agree never to leave and if we ever did, he'd hunt us down and kill us himself."

"Didn't people try?" Viola says. "Didn't they try and get away?"

"They *tried*," Ben says, full of meaning. "It wasn't uncommon for people to disappear."

"But if you and Cillian were innocent–" I start.

"We *weren't* innocent," Ben says strongly, and suddenly his Noise tastes bitter. He sighs. "We weren't."

"What do you mean?" I ask, raising my head. The sickness in my stomach ain't leaving. "What do you mean you weren't innocent?"

"You let it happen," Viola says. "You didn't die with the other men who were protecting the women."

"We didn't fight," he says, "and we didn't die." He shakes his head. "Not innocent at all."

"Why didn't you fight?" I ask.

"Cillian wanted to," Ben says quickly. "I want you to know that. He wanted to do whatever he could to stop them. He would have given his life." He looks away once more. "But I wouldn't let him."

"Why not?"

"I get it," Viola whispers.

I look at her, cuz I sure don't. "Get what?"

Viola keeps looking at Ben. "They either die fighting for what's right and leave you an unprotected baby," she says, "or they become complicit with what's wrong and keep you alive."

I don't know what complicit means but I can guess.

They did it for me. All that horror. They did it for me.

Ben and Cillian. Cillian and Ben.

They did it so I could live.

I don't know how I feel about any of this.

Doing what's right should be easy.

It shouldn't be just another big mess like everything else.

"So we waited," Ben says. "In a town-sized prison. Full of the ugliest Noise you ever heard before men started denying their own pasts, before the Mayor came up with his grand plans. And so we waited for the day you were old enough to get away on yer own, innocent as we could keep you." He rubs a hand over his head. "But the Mayor was waiting, too."

"For me?" I ask, tho I know it's true.

"For the last boy to become a man," Ben says. "When boys became men, they were told the truth. Or a version of it, anyway. And then they were made complicit themselves."

I remember his Noise from back on the farm, about my birthday, about how a boy becomes a man.

About what complicity really means and how it can be passed on.

How it was waiting to be passed on to me.

And about the men who–

I put it outta my head.

"That don't make no sense," I say.

"You were the last," Ben says. "If he could make every single boy in Prentisstown a man by his own meaning, then he's God, ain't he? He's created all of us and is in complete control."

"*If one of us falls*," I say.

"*We all fall*," Ben finishes. "That's why he wants you. Yer a symbol. Yer the last innocent boy of Prentisstown. If he can make you fall, then his army is complete and of his own perfect making."

"And if not?" I say, tho I'm wondering if I've already fallen.

"If not," Ben says, "he'll kill you."

"So Mayor Prentiss is as mad as Aaron, then," Viola says.

"Not quite," Ben says. "Aaron is mad. But the Mayor knows enough to use madness to achieve his ends."

"Which are what?" Viola says.

"This world," Ben says calmly. "He wants all of it."

I open my mouth to ask more stuff I don't wanna know but then, as if there was never gonna be anything else that could ever happen, we hear it.

Thump budda-thump budda-thump. Coming down the road, relentless, like a joke that ain't ever gonna be funny.

"You've *got* to be kidding," Viola says.

Ben's already back on his feet, listening. "It sounds like just one horse."

We all look down the road, shining a little in the moonlight.

"Binos," Viola says, now right by my side. I fish 'em out without another word, click on the night setting and look, searching out the sound as it rings thru the night air.

Budda-thump budda-thump.

I search down the road farther and farther back till–

There it is.

There *he* is.

Who else?

Mr Prentiss Jr, alive and well and untied and back on his horse.

"Damn," I hear from Viola, reading my Noise as I hand her the binos.

"*Davy Prentiss?*" Ben says, also reading my Noise.

"The one and only." I put the water bottles back in Viola's bag. "We gotta go."

Viola hands the binos to Ben and he looks for himself. He takes them away from his eyes and gives the binos a quick once over. "Nifty," he says.

"We need to go," Viola says. "As always."

Ben turns to us, binos still in his hand. He's looking from one of us to the other and I see what's forming in his Noise.

"Ben–" I start.

"No," he says. "This is where I leave you."

"*Ben–*"

"I can handle Davy bloody Prentiss."

"He has a gun," I say. "You don't."

Ben comes up to me. "Todd," he says.

"No, Ben," I say, my voice getting louder. "I ain't listening."

He looks me in the eye and I notice he don't seem to be having to bend down any more to do it.

"Todd," he says again. "I atone for the wrong I've done by keeping you safe."

"You can't leave me, Ben," I say, my voice getting wet (shut up). "Not again."

He's shaking his head. "I can't come to Haven with you. You know I can't. I'm the enemy."

"We can *explain* what happened."

But he's still shaking his head.

"The horse is getting closer," Viola says.

Thump budda-thump budda-thump.

"The only thing that makes me a man," Ben says, his voice steady as a rock, "is seeing you safely into becoming a man yerself."

"I ain't a man yet, Ben," I say, my throat catching (shut *up*). "I don't even know how many days I got left."

And then he smiles and it's the smile that tells me it's over.

"Sixteen," he says. "Sixteen days till yer birthday." He takes my chin and lifts it. "But you've been a man for a good while now. Don't let *no one* tell you otherwise."

"Ben–"

"Go," he says and he comes up to me and hands Viola the binos behind my back and takes me in his arms. "No father could be prouder," I hear him say by my ear.

"No," I say, my words slurring. "It ain't fair."

"It ain't." He pulls himself away. "But there's hope at the end of the road. You remember that."

"Don't go," I say.

"I have to. Danger's coming."

"Closer and closer," Viola says, binos to her eyes.

Budda-thump budda-THUMP.

"I'll stop him. I'll buy you time." Ben looks at Viola. "You take care of Todd," he says. "I have yer word?"

"You have my word," Viola says.

"Ben, please," I whisper. "Please."

He grips my shoulders for a last time. "Remember," he says. *"Hope."*

And he don't say nothing more and he turns and runs down the hill from the sematary to the road. When he gets to the bottom, he looks back and sees us still watching him.

"What are you waiting for?" he shouts. "Run!"

37

WHAT'S THE POINT?

I WON'T SAY WHAT I FEEL when we run down the other side of the hill and away from Ben, for ever this time cuz how is there any life after this?

Life equals running and when we stop running maybe that's how we'll know life is finally finished.

"Come on, Todd," Viola calls, looking back over her shoulder. "Please, hurry."

I don't say nothing.

I run.

We get down the hill and back by the river. Again. With the road on our other side. *Again*.

Always the same.

The river's louder than it was, rushing by with some force, but who cares? What does it matter?

Life ain't fair.

It ain't.

Not never.

It's pointless and stupid and there's only suffering and pain and people who want to hurt you. You can't love nothing or no one cuz it'll all be taken away or ruined and you'll be left alone and constantly having to fight, constantly having to run just to stay alive.

There's nothing good in this life. Not nothing good nowhere.

What's the effing point?

"The point is," Viola says, stopping halfway thru a dense patch of scrub to hit me *really hard* on the shoulder, "he cared enough about you to maybe sacrifice himself and if you just GIVE UP" – she shouts that part – "then you're saying that the sacrifice is worth *nothing*!"

"Ow," I say, rubbing my shoulder. "But why should he have to sacrifice himself? Why should I have to lose him *again*?"

She steps up close to me. "Do you think you're the only person who's lost someone?" she says in a dangerous whisper. "Do you forget that my parents are dead, too?"

I did.

I did forget.

I don't say nothing.

"All I've got now is you," she says, her voice still angry. "And all you've got now is *me*. And I'm mad he left, too, and I'm mad my parents died and I'm mad we ever thought of coming to this planet in the first place but that's how it is and it's crap that it's just us but we can't do anything about it."

I still don't say nothing.

But there she is and I look at her, *really* look at her, for probably the first time since I saw her cowering next to a log back in the swamp when I thought she was a Spackle.

A lifetime ago.

She's still kinda cleaned up from the days in Carbonel Downs (only yesterday, only just yesterday) but there's dirt on her cheeks and she's skinnier than she used to be and there are dark patches under her eyes and her hair is messy and tangled and her hands are covered in sooty blackness and her shirt has a green stain of grass across the front from when she once fell and there's a cut on her lip from when a branch smacked her when we were running with Ben (and no bandages left to stitch it up) and she's looking at me.

And she's telling me she's all I've got.

And that I'm all *she's* got.

And I feel a little bit how that feels.

The colours in my Noise go different.

Her voice softens but only a little. "Ben's gone and Manchee's gone and my mother and father are gone," she says. "And I hate all of that. I *hate* it. But we're almost at the end of the road. We're almost there. And if you don't give up, I don't give up."

"Do you believe there's hope at the end?" I ask.

"No," she says simply, looking away. "No, I don't, but I'm still going." She eyes me. "You coming with?"

I don't have to answer.

We carry on running.

But.

"We should just take the road," I say, holding back yet another branch.

"But the army," she says. "And the horses."

"They know where we're going. We know where they're going. We all seem to have taken the same route to get to Haven."

"And we'll hear them coming," she agrees. "And the road's fastest.

"The road's fastest."

And she says, "Then let's just take the effing road and get ourselves to Haven."

I smile, a little. "You said *effing*," I say. "You actually said the word *effing*."

So we take the effing road, as fast as our tiredness will let us. It's still the same dusty, twisty, sometimes muddy river road that it was all those miles and miles ago and the same leafy, tree-filled New World all around us.

If you were just landing here and didn't know nothing about nothing you really might think it was Eden after all.

A wide valley is opening up around us, flat at the bottom where the river is but distant hills beginning to climb up on either side. The hills are lit only by moonlight, no sign of distant settlements or anyway of ones with lights still burning.

No sign of Haven ahead neither but we're at the flattest point of the valley and can't see much past the twists in the road either before us or back. Forest still covers both sides of the river and you'd be tempted to think that all of New World had closed up and everyone left, leaving just this road behind 'em.

We go on.

And on.

Not till the first stripes of dawn start appearing down

the valley in front of us do we stop to take on more water.

We drink. There's only my Noise and the river rushing by.

No hoofbeats. No other Noise.

"You know this means he succeeded," Viola says, not meeting my eye. "Whatever he did, he stopped the man on the horse."

I just *mm* and nod.

"And we never heard gunshots."

I *mm* and nod again.

"I'm sorry for shouting at you before," she says. "I just wanted you to keep going. I didn't want you to stop."

"I know."

We're leaning against a pair of trees by the riverbank. The road is to our backs and across the river is just trees and the far side of the valley rises up and then only the sky above, getting lighter and more blue and bigger and emptier till even the stars start leaving it.

"When we left on the scout ship," Viola says, looking up across the river with me, "I was really upset leaving my friends behind. Just a few kids from the other caretaker families, but still. I thought I'd be the only one my age on this planet for seven whole months."

I drink some water. "I didn't have friends back in Prentisstown."

She turns to me. "What do you mean, no friends? You had to have friends."

"I had a few for a while, boys a coupla months older than me. But when boys become men they stop talking to boys," I shrug. "I was the last boy. In the end there was just me and Manchee."

She gazes up into the fading stars. "It's a stupid rule."

"It is."

We don't say nothing more, just me and Viola by the riverside, resting ourselves as another dawn comes.

Just me and her.

We stir after a minute, get ourselves ready to go again.

"We could reach Haven by tomorrow," I say. "If we keep on going."

"Tomorrow," Viola nods. "I hope there's food."

It's her turn to carry the bag so I hand it to her and the sun is peeking up over the end of the valley where it looks like the river's running right into it and as the light hits the hills across the river from us, something catches my eye.

Viola turns immediately at the spark in my Noise. "What?"

I shield my eyes from the new sun. There's a little trail of dust rising from the top of the far hills.

And it's moving.

"What is that?" I say.

Viola fishes out the binos and looks thru 'em. "I can't see properly," she says. "Trees in the way."

"Someone travelling?"

"Maybe that's the other road. The fork we didn't take."

We watch for a minute or two as the dust trail keeps rising, heading towards Haven at the slow speed of a distant cloud. It's weird seeing it without any sound.

"I wish I knew where the army was," I say. "How far they were behind us."

"Maybe Carbonel Downs put up too good a fight." Viola points the binos upriver to see the way we came but it's too flat, too twisty. All there is to be seen is trees. Trees and sky and quiet and a silent trail of dust making its way along the far hilltops.

"We should go," I say. "I'm starting to feel a little spooked."

"Let's go then," Viola says, quiet-like.

Back on the road.

Back to the life of running.

We have no food with us so breakfast is a yellow fruit that Viola spies on some trees we pass that she swears she ate in Carbonel Downs. They become lunch, too, but it's better than nothing.

I think again of the knife at my back.

Could I hunt, if there was time?

But there ain't no time.

We run past midday and into afternoon. The world is still abandoned and spooky. Just me and Viola running along the valley bottom, no settlements to be seen, no caravans or carts, no other sound loud enough to be heard over the rushing of the river, getting bigger by the hour, to the point where it's hard even to hear my Noise, where even if we want to talk, we have to raise our voices.

But we're too hungry to talk. And too tired to talk. And running too much to talk.

And so on we go.

And I find myself watching Viola.

The trail of dust on the far hilltop follows us as we run, pulling ahead slowly as the day gets older and finally disappearing in the distance and I watch her checking it as we hurry on. I watch her run next to me, flinching at the aches in her legs. I watch her rub them when we rest and watch her when she drinks from the water bottles.

Now that I've seen her, I can't stop seeing her.

She catches me. "What?"

"Nothing," I say and look away cuz I don't know either.

The river and the road have straightened out as the valley gets steeper and closer on both sides. We can see a little bit back the way we came. No army yet, no horsemen neither. The quiet is almost scarier than if there was Noise everywhere.

Dusk comes, the sun setting itself in the valley behind us, setting over wherever the army might be and whatever's left of New World back there, whatever's happened to the men who fought against the army and the men who joined.

Whatever's happened to the women.

Viola runs in front of me.

I watch her run.

Just after nightfall we finally come to another settlement, another one with docks on the river, another one abandoned. There are only five houses in total along a little strip of the road, one with what looks like a small general store tacked onto the front.

"Hold on," Viola says, stopping.

"Dinner?" I say, catching my breath.

She nods.

It takes about six kicks to open the door of the general store and tho there clearly ain't no one here at all, I still look round expecting to be punished. Inside, it's mostly cans but we find a dry loaf of bread, some bruised fruit and a few strips of dried meat.

"These aren't more than a day or two old," Viola says, twixt mouthfuls. "They must have fled to Haven yesterday or the day before."

"Rumours of an army are a powerful thing," I say, not chewing my dried meat well enough before I swallow and coughing up a little bit of it.

We fill our bellies as best we can and I shove the rest of the food into Viola's bag, now hanging round my shoulders. I see the book when I do. Still there, still wrapped in its plastic bag, still with the knife-shaped slash all the way thru it.

I reach in thru the plastic bag, rubbing my fingers across the cover. It's soft to the touch and the binding still gives off a faint whiff of leather.

The book. My ma's book. It's come all the way with us. Survived its own injury. Just like us.

I look up at Viola.

She catches me again.

"*What?*" she says.

"Nothing." I put the book back in the bag with the food. "Let's go."

Back on the road, back down the river, back towards Haven.

"This should be our last night, you know," Viola says. "If Doctor Snow was right, we'll be there tomorrow."

"Yeah," I say, "and the world will change."

"Again."

"Again," I agree.

We go on a few more paces.

"You starting to feel hope?" Viola asks, her voice curious.

"No," I say, fuddling my Noise. "You?"

Her eyebrows are up but she shakes her head. "No, no."

"But we're going anyway."

"Oh, yeah," Viola says. "Hell or high water."

"It'll probably be both," I say.

The sun sets, the moons rise again, smaller crescents than the night before. The sky is still clear, the stars still up, the world still quiet, just the rush of the river, getting steadily louder.

Midnight comes.

Fifteen days.

Fifteen days till–

Till what?

We carry on thru the night, the sky falling slowly past us, our words stopping a little as dinner wears off and tiredness takes hold again. Just before dawn we find two overturned carts in the road, grains of wheat spilled everywhere and a few empty baskets rolled on their sides across the road.

"They didn't even take the time to save everything," Viola says. "They left half of it on the ground."

"Good a place as any for breakfast." I flip over one of the baskets, drag it over to where the road overlooks the river and sit down on it.

Viola picks up another basket, brings it over right next to me and sits down. There are glimmers of light in the sky as the sun gets set to rise, the road pointing right towards it, the river, too, rushing towards the dawn. I open up the bag and take out the general store food, handing some to Viola and eating what I've got. We drink from the water bottles.

The bag is open on my lap. There are our remaining clothes and there are the binos.

And there's the book again.

I feel her silence next to me, feel the pull of it on me and the hollows in my chest and stomach and head and I remember the ache I used to feel when she got too close, how it felt like grief, how it felt like a loss, like I was falling, falling into nothing, how it clenched me up and made me want to weep, made me actually *weep*.

But now–

Now, not so much.

I look over to her.

She's gotta know what's in my Noise. I'm the only one around and she's got better and better at reading it despite how loud the river's getting.

But she sits there, quietly eating, waiting for me to say.

Waiting for me to ask.

Cuz this is what I'm thinking.

When the sun comes up, it'll be the day we get to Haven, the day we get to a place filled with more people than I've ever seen together in my life, a place filled with so much Noise you can't never be alone, unless they found a cure, in which case I'll be the only Noisy one which would actually be worse.

We get to Haven, we'll be part of a city.

It won't just be Todd and Viola, sitting by a river as the sun comes up, eating our breakfast, the only two people on the face of the planet.

It'll be everyone, all together.

This might be our last chance.

I look away from her to speak. "You know that thing with voices that you do?"

"Yeah," she says, quiet.

I take out the book.

"D'you think you could do a Prentisstown voice?"

38

I HEARD A MAIDEN CALL

"*My Dearest Todd*," Viola reads, copying Ben's accent as best she can. Which is pretty ruddy good. "*My dearest son*."

My ma's voice. My ma speaking.

I cross my arms and look down into the wheat spilled across the ground.

"*I begin this journal on the day of yer birth, the day I first held you in my arms rather than in my belly. You kick just as much outside as in! And yer the most beautiful thing that's ever happened in the whole entire universe. Yer easily the most beautiful thing on New World and there's no contest in New Elizabeth, that's for sure*."

I feel my face getting red but the sun's still not high enough for anyone to see.

"*I wish yer pa were here to see you, Todd, but New World and the Lord above saw fit to take him with the sickness five months ago and we'll both just have to wait to see him in the next world.*

"You look like him. Well, babies don't look much like anything but babies but I'm telling you you look like him. Yer going to be tall, Todd, cuz yer pa was tall. Yer going to be strong, cuz yer pa was strong. And yer going to be handsome, oh, are you ever going to be handsome. The ladies of New World won't know what hit them."

Viola turns a page and I don't look at her. I sense she's not looking at me neither and I wouldn't wanna see a smile on her face right about now.

Cuz that weird thing's happening too.

Her words are not her words and they're coming outta her mouth sounding like a lie but making a new truth, creating a different world where my ma is talking directly to me, Viola speaking with a voice not her own and the world, for a little while at least, the world is all for me, the world's being made just for me.

"Let me tell you bout the place you've been born into, son. It's called New World and it's a whole planet made entirely of hope–"

Viola stops, just for a second, then carries on.

"We landed here almost exactly ten years ago looking for a new way of life, one clean and simple and honest and good, one different from Old World in all respects, where people could live in safety and peace with God as our guide and with love for our fellow man.

"There've been struggles. I won't begin this story to you with a lie, Todd. It ain't been easy here–

"Oooh, listen to me, writing down 'ain't' when addressing my son. That's settler life for you, I spose, not much time for niceties and it's easy to sink to the level of people who revel

in squandering their manners. But there's not much harm in 'ain't', surely? Okay, that's decided then. My first bad choice as a mother. Say 'ain't' all you like, Todd. I promise not to correct you."

Viola purses her lips but I don't say nothing so she continues.

"So there's been hardship and sickness on New World and in New Elizabeth. There's something called the Noise here on this planet that men have been struggling with since we landed but the strange thing is you'll be one of the boys in the settlement who won't know any different and so it'll be hard to explain to you what life was like before and why it's so difficult now but we're managing the best we can.

"A man called David Prentiss, who's got a son just a bit older than you, Todd, and who's one of our better organizers – I believe he was a caretaker on the ship over, if memory serves me correct–"

Viola pauses at this, too, but this time it's me who waits for her to say something. She don't.

"He convinced Jessica Elizabeth, our Mayor, to found this little settlement on the far side of an enormous swamp so that the Noise of the rest of New World can't never reach us unless we allow it to. It's still Noisy as anything here in New Elizabeth but at least it's people we know, at least it's people we trust. For the most part.

"My role here is that I farm several fields of wheat up north of the settlement. Since yer pa passed, our close friends Ben and Cillian have been helping me out since theirs is the next farm over. I can't wait for you to meet them. Well wait, you already have! They've already held you and said hello so look

at that, one day in the world and you've already made two friends. It's a good way to start, son.

"In fact, I'm sure you'll do fine cuz you came out two weeks early. Clearly you'd decided you'd had enough and wanted to see what this world had to offer you. I can't blame you. The sky is so big and blue and the trees so green and this is a world where the animals talk to you, really talk, and you can even talk back and there's so much wonder to be had, so much just waiting for you, Todd, that I almost can't stand that it's not happening for you right now, *that yer going to have to wait to see all that's possible, all the things you might do."*

Viola takes a breath and says, "There's a break in the page here and a little space and then it says *Later* like she got interrupted." She looks up at me. "You okay?"

"Yeah, yeah," I nod real fast, my arms still crossed. "Carry on."

It's getting lighter, the sun truly coming up. I turn away from her a little.

She reads.

"*Later.*

"*Sorry, son, had to stop for a minute for a visit from our holy man, Aaron.*"

Another pause, another lick of the lips.

"*We've been lucky to have him, tho I must admit of late he's not been saying things I exactly agree with about the natives of New World. Which are called the Spackle, by the way, and which were a BIG surprise, since they were so shy at first neither the original planners back on Old World or our first scout ships even knew they were here!*

"They're very sweet creachers. Different and maybe primitive and no spoken or written language that we can really find but I don't agree with some of the thinking of the people here that the Spackle are animals rather than intelligent beings. And Aaron's been preaching lately about how God has made a dividing line twixt us and them and–

"Well that's not really something to discuss on yer first day, is it? Aaron believes what he believes devoutly, has been a pillar of faith for all of us these long years and should anyone find this journal and read it, let me say here for the record that it was a privilege to have him come by and bless you on yer first day of life. Okay?

"But I will say also on yer first day that the attractiveness of power is something you should learn about before you get too much older, it's the thing that separates men from boys, tho not in the way most men think.

"And that's all I'll say. Prying eyes and all that.

"Oh, son, there's so much wonder in the world. Don't let no one tell you otherwise. Yes, life has been hard here on New World and I'll even admit to you here, cuz if I'm going to start out at all it has to be an honest start, I'll tell you that I was nearly given to despair. Things in the settlement are maybe more complicated than I can quite explain right now and there's things you'll learn for yerself before too long whether I like it or not and there've been difficulties with food and with sickness and it was hard enough even before I lost yer pa and I nearly gave up.

"But I didn't give up. I didn't give up cuz of you, my beautiful, beautiful boy, my wondrous son who might make something better of this world, who I promise to raise only

with love and hope and who I swear will see this world come good. I swear it.

"Cuz when I held you for the first time this morning and fed you from my own body, I felt so much love for you it was almost like pain, almost like I couldn't stand it one second longer.

"But only almost.

"And I sang to you a song that my mother sang to me and her mother sang to her and it goes,"

And here, amazingly, Viola sings.

Actually *sings*.

My skin goes gooseflesh, my chest crushes. She musta heard the whole tune in my Noise and of course Ben singing it cuz here it comes, rolling outta her mouth like the peal of a bell.

The voice of Viola making the world into the voice of my ma, singing the song.

"Early one morning, just as the sun was rising,

I heard a maiden call from the valley below,

'Oh don't deceive me, oh never leave me,

How could you use a poor maiden so?'"

I can't look at her.

I can't look at her.

I put my hands to my head.

"And it's a sad song, Todd, but it's also a promise. I'll never deceive you and I'll never leave you and I promise you this so you can one day promise it to others and know that it's true.

"Oh, ha, Todd! That's you crying. That's you crying from yer cot, waking up from yer first sleep on yer first day, waking up and asking the world to come to you.

"And so for today I have to put this aside.

"Yer calling for me, son, and I will answer."

Viola stops and there's only the river and my Noise.

"There's more," Viola says after a while when I don't raise my head, flipping thru the pages. "There's a lot more." She looks at me. "Do you want me to read more?" She looks back at the book. "Do you want me to read the end?"

The end.

Read the last thing my ma wrote in the last days before—

"No," I say quickly.

Yer calling for me, son, and I will answer.

In my Noise forever.

"No," I say again. "Let's leave it there for now."

I glance over at Viola and I see that her face is pulled as sad as my Noise feels. Her eyes are wet and her chin shakes, just barely, just a tremble in the dawn sunlight. She sees me watching, feels my Noise watching her, and she turns away to face the river.

And there, in that morning, in that new sunrise, I realize something.

I realize something important.

So important that as it dawns fully I have to stand up.

I know what she's thinking.

I *know* what she's thinking.

Even looking at her back, I know what she's thinking and feeling and what's going on inside her.

The way she's turned her body, the way she's holding her head and her hands and the book in her lap, the way she's stiffening a little in her back as she hears all this in my Noise.

I can read it.

I can read *her*.

Cuz she's thinking about how her own parents also came here with hope like my ma. She's wondering if the hope at the end of our road is just as false as the one that was at the end of my ma's. And she's taking the words of my ma and putting them into the mouths of her own ma and pa and hearing them say that they love her and they miss her and they wish her the world. And she's taking the song of my ma and she's weaving it into everything else till it becomes a sad thing all her own.

And it hurts her, but it's an okay hurt, but it hurts still, but it's good, but it hurts.

She hurts.

I know all this.

I *know* it's true.

Cuz I can read her.

I can read her Noise even tho she ain't got none.

I know who she is.

I know Viola Eade.

I raise my hands to the side of my head to hold it all in.

"Viola," I whisper, my voice shaking.

"I know," she says quietly, pulling her arms tight around her, still facing away from me.

And I look at her sitting there and she looks across the river and we wait as the dawn fully arrives, each of us knowing.

Each of us knowing the other.

39

THE FALLS

THE SUN CREEPS UP into the sky and the river is loud as we look across it and we can now see it rushing fast down towards the valley's end, throwing up whitewater and rapids.

It's Viola who breaks the spell that's fallen twixt us. "You know what it has to be, don't you?" she says. She takes out the binos and looks downriver. The sun is rising at the end of the valley. She has to shield the lenses with her hand.

"What is it?" I say.

She presses a button or two and looks again.

"What do you see?" I ask.

She hands the binos to me.

I look downriver, following the rapids, the foam, right to–

Right to the end.

A few kilometres away, the river ends in mid-air.

"Another falls," I say.

"Looks way bigger than the one we saw with Wilf," she says.

"The road'll find a way past it," I say. "Shouldn't bother us."

"That's not what I mean."

"What then?"

"I mean," she says, frowning a bit at my denseness, "that falls that big're bound to have a city at the bottom of them. That if you had to choose a place anywhere on a planet for first settlement, then a valley at the base of a waterfall with rich farmland and ready water might just look perfect from space."

My Noise rises a little but only a little.

Cuz who would dare to think?

"Haven," I say.

"I'll bet you anything we've found it," she says. "I'll bet you when we get to that waterfall we'll be able to see it below us."

"If we run," I say, "we could be there in an hour. Less than."

She looks me in the eye for the first time since my ma's book.

And she says, "*If* we run?"

And then she smiles.

A genuine smile.

And I know what that means, too.

We grab up our few things and go.

Faster than before.

My feet are tired and sore. Hers must be, too. I've got blisters and aches and my heart hurts from all I miss and all that's gone. And hers does, too.

But we run.

Boy, do we run.

Cuz maybe (shut up)–

Just maybe (don't think it)–

Maybe there really *is* hope at the end of the road.

The river grows wider and straighter as we rush on and the walls of the valley move in closer and closer, the one on our side getting so close the edge of the road starts to slope up. Spray from the rapids is floating in the air. Our clothes get wet, our faces, too, and hands. The roar becomes thunderous, filling up the world with itself, almost like a physical thing, but not in a bad way. Like it's washing you, like it's washing the Noise away.

And I think, *Please let Haven be at the bottom of the falls. Please.*

Cuz I see Viola looking back to me as we run and there's brightness on her face and she keeps urging me on with tilts of her head and smiles and I think how hope may be the thing that pulls you forward, may be the thing that keeps you going, but that it's dangerous, too, that it's painful and risky, that it's making a dare to the world and when has the world ever let us win a dare?

Please let Haven be there.

Oh please oh please oh please.

The road finally starts rising a bit, pulling up above the river slightly as the water starts really crashing thru rocky rapids. There ain't no more wooded bits twixt us and it now at all, just a hill climbing up steeper and steeper on our right side as the valley closes in and then nothing but river and the falls ahead.

"Almost there," Viola calls from ahead of me, running, her hair bouncing off the back of her neck, the sun shining down on everything.

And then.

And then, at the edge of the cliff, the road comes to a lip and takes a sudden angle down and to the right.

And that's where we stop.

The falls are huge, half a kilometre across easy. The water roars over the cliff in a violent white foam, sending spray hundreds of metres out into the sheer drop and above and all around, soaking us in our clothes and throwing rainbows all over the place as the rising sun lights it.

"Todd," Viola says, so faintly I can barely hear it.

But I don't need to.

I know what she means.

As soon as the falls start falling, the valley opens up again, wide as the sky itself, taking the river that starts again at the base of the falls, which crashes forward with whitewater before it pools and calms down and becomes a river again.

And flows into Haven.

Haven.

Gotta be.

Spread out below us like a table full of food.

"There it is," Viola says.

And I feel her fingers wrap around my own.

The falls to our left, spray and rainbows in the sky, the sun rising ahead of us, the valley below.

And Haven, sitting waiting.

It's three, maybe four kilometres away down the farther valley.

But there it is.

There it ruddy well is.

I look round us, round to where the road has taken a sharp turn at our feet, sloping down and cutting into the valley wall to our right but then zig-zagging its way steeply down in a twisty pattern so even it's like a zipper running down the hillside to where it picks up the river again.

And follows it right into Haven.

"I want to see it," Viola says, letting go of my hand and taking out the binos. She looks thru them, wipes spray off the lenses, and looks some more. "It's beautiful," she says and that's all she says and she just looks and wipes off more spray.

After a minute and without saying nothing more, she hands me the binos and I get my first look at Haven.

The spray is so thick, even wiping it down you can't see details like people or anything but there are all kindsa different buildings, mostly surrounding what looks like a big church at the centre, but other big buildings, too, and proper roads curling outta the middle thru trees to more groups of buildings.

There's gotta be at least fifty buildings in all.

Maybe a *hundred*.

It's the biggest thing I've ever seen in my entire life.

"I've got to say," Viola shouts, "it's kind of smaller than I expected."

But I don't really hear her.

With the binos, I follow the river road back from it and I see what's probably a roadblock with what might be a fortified fence running away from it and to either side.

"They're getting ready," I say. "They're getting ready to fight."

Viola looks at me, worried. "You think it's big enough? You think we're safe?"

"Depends on if the rumours of the army are true or not."

I look behind us, by instinct, as if the army was just waiting there for us to move on. I look up the valley hill next to us. Could be a good view.

"Let's find out," I say.

We run back down the road a piece, looking for a good climbing spot, find one and make our way up. My legs feel light as I climb, my Noise clearer than it's been in days. I'm sad for Ben, I'm sad for Cillian, I'm sad for Manchee, I'm sad for what's happened to me and Viola.

But Ben was right.

There's hope at the bottom of the biggest waterfall.

And maybe it don't hurt so much after all.

We climb up thru the trees. The hill is steep above the river and we have to pull on vines and hang on to rocks to make our way up high enough to look back down the road, till the valley is stretching out beneath us.

I still have the binos and I look downriver and down the road and over the treetops. I keep having to wipe spray away.

I look.

"Can you see them?" Viola asks.

I look, the river getting smaller into the far distance, back and back and back.

"No," I say.

I look.

And again.

And–

There.

Down in the deepest curve of the road in the deepest part of the valley, in farthest shadow against the rising sun, there they are.

A mass that's gotta be the army, marching its way forward, so far away I can only tell it's them at all cuz it looks like dark water flowing into a dry riverbed. It's hard to get detail at this distance but I can't see individual men and I don't think I can see horses.

Just a mass, a mass pouring itself down the road.

"How big is it?" she asks. "How big has it grown?"

"I don't know," I say. "Three hundred? Four? I don't know. We're too far to really–"

I stop.

"We're too far to really tell." I crack another smile. "Miles and miles."

"We beat them," Viola says, a smile coming, too. "We ran and they chased us and we beat them."

"We'll get to Haven and we'll warn whoever's in charge," I say, talking faster, my Noise rising with excitement. "But they've got battle lines and the approach is real narrow and the army's at *least* the rest of the day away, maybe even tonight, too, and I swear that can't be a thousand men."

I swear it.

(But.)

Viola's smiling the tiredest, happiest smile I ever saw. She takes my hand again. "We beat them."

But then the risks of hope rise again and my Noise greys

a little. "Well, we ain't there yet and we don't know if Haven can–"

But she's shaking her head. "Nuh-uh," she says. "We beat them. You listen to me and you be happy, Todd Hewitt. We've spent all this time outrunning an army and guess what? We outran them."

She looks at me, smiling, expecting something from me.

My Noise is buzzing and happy and warm and tired and relieved and a little bit worried still but I'm thinking that maybe she's right, maybe we did win and maybe I should put my arms round her if it didn't feel weird and I find that in the middle of it all I do actually agree with her.

"We beat them," I say.

And then she does stick her arms round me and pulls tight, like we might fall down, and we just stand there on the wet hillside and breathe for a little bit.

She smells a little less like flowers but it's okay.

And I look out and the falls are below us, charging away, and Haven glitters thru the sunlit spray and the sun is shining down the length of the river above the falls, lighting it up like a snake made of metal.

And I let my Noise bubble with little sparks of happy and my gaze flow back along the length of the river and–

No.

Every muscle in my body jolts.

"What?" Viola says, jumping back.

She whips her head round to where I'm looking.

"*What?*" she says again.

And then she sees.

"No," she says. "No, it can't be."

Coming down the river is a boat.

Close enough to see without binos.

Close enough to see the rifle and the robe.

Close enough to see the scars and the righteous anger.

Rowing his way furiously towards us, coming like judgement itself.

Aaron.

40

THE SACRIFICE

"HAS HE SEEN US?" Viola asks, her voice pulled taut.

I point the binos. Aaron rears up in them, huge and terrifying. I press a few buttons to push him back. He's not looking at us, just rowing like an engine to get the boat to the side of the river and the road.

His face is torn and horrible, clotted and bloody, the hole in his cheek, the new hole where his nose used to be, and still, underneath all that, a look feroshus and devouring, a look without mercy, a look that won't stop, that won't never, never stop.

War makes monsters of men, I hear Ben saying.

There's a monster coming towards us.

"I don't think he's seen us," I say. "Not yet."

"Can we outrun him?"

"He's got a gun," I say, "and you can see all the way down that road to Haven."

"Off the road then. Through the trees."

"There ain't that many twixt us and the road down. We'll have to be fast."

"I can be fast," she says.

And we jump on down the hill, skidding down leaves and wet vines, using rocks as handholds best we can. The tree cover is light and we can still see down the river, see Aaron as he rows.

Which means he can see us if he looks in the right place.

"Hurry!" Viola says.

Down–

And down–

And sliding to the road–

And squelching in the mud at the roadside–

And as we get to the road he's outta sight again, still up the river–

But only for a second–

Cuz there he is–

The current bringing him fast–

Coming down the river–

In full view–

Looking right at us.

The roar of the falls is loud enough to eat you, but I still hear it.

I'd hear it if I was on the other side of the planet.

"TODD HEWITT!"

And he's reaching for his rifle.

"Go!" I shout.

Viola's feet hit the ground running and I'm right behind

her, heading for the lip of the road that goes down to the zigzags.

It's fifteen steps, maybe twenty till we can disappear over the edge–

We run like we've spent the last two weeks resting–

Pound pound pound against the road–

I check back over my shoulder–

To see Aaron try to take the rifle in one hand–

Try to balance it while keeping the boat steady–

It's bouncing in the rapids, knocking him back and forth–

"He won't be able to," I yell to Viola. "He can't row and fire at the same–"

CRACK!

A pop of mud flies up outta the road next to Viola's feet ahead of me–

I cry out and Viola cries out and we both instinctively flinch down–

Running faster and faster–

Pound pound pound–

Run run run run run my Noise chugs like a rocket–

Not looking back–

Five steps–

Run run–

Three–

CRACK!

And Viola falls–

"NO!" I shout–

And she's falling over the lip of the road, tripping down the other side and crashing down in a roll–

"NO!" I shout again and leap after her–

Stumbling down the steep incline–

Pounding down to where she's rolling–

No–

Not this–

Not now–

Not when we're–

Please no–

And she tumbles to some low shrubs at the side of the road and keeps going into them–

And stops face down.

And I'm racing towards her and I'm barely in control of my own standing up and I'm kneeling down already in the brush and I'm grabbing her and rolling her over and I'm looking for the blood and the shot and I'm saying, "*No no no no no–*"

And I'm almost blinded by rage and despair and the false promise of hope and no no no–

And she opens her eyes–

She's opening her eyes and she's grabbing me and she's saying, "I'm not hit, I'm not hit."

"Yer not?" I say, shaking her a little. "Yer sure?"

"I just fell," she says. "I swear I felt the bullet fly right by my eyes and I fell. I'm not hurt."

And I'm breathing heavy and heavy and heavy.

"Thank God," I say. "Thank God."

And the world spins and my Noise whirls.

And she's already getting to her feet and I'm up after her standing in the scrub and looking at the road around and below us.

The falls are crashing over the cliff to our left and the twisting road is both behind us and in front of us as it starts doubling back on itself and making the steep zipper down to the bottom of the falls.

It's a clear shot all the way.

No trees, just low scrub.

"He'll pick us off," Viola says, looking back up to the top of the road, to where we can't see Aaron no doubt making his way to the river's edge, stomping thru roaring water, *walking* on it for all I know.

"TODD HEWITT!" we hear again, faint over the roar of the water but loud as the whole entire universe.

"There's nowhere to hide," Viola says, looking around us and down. "Not till we get to the bottom."

I'm looking round, too. The hillsides are too steep, the road too open, the areas between the road's double-backs too shallow with shrubs.

Nowhere to hide.

"TODD HEWITT!"

Viola points up. "We could get up to those trees on top of the hill."

But it's so steep, I can already hear the hope failing in her voice.

And I spin round, looking still–

And then I see.

A little faint trail, skinny as anything, hardly even there, leading away from the first turn of the road and towards the falls. It disappears after a few metres but I follow it to where it might have gone.

Right to the cliffside.

Right down sharp to a place almost below the falls.

Right to a ledge that's almost hidden.

A ledge underneath the waterfall itself.

I take a few steps outta the scrub and back onto the road. The little trail disappears.

So does the ledge.

"What is it?" Viola asks.

I go back into the scrub again.

"There," I say, pointing. "Can you see it?"

She squints where I'm pointing. The fall is casting a little shadow on the ledge, darkening where the little trail ends.

"You can see it from here," I say, "but you can't see it from the road." I look at her. "We'll hide."

"He'll hear you," she says. "He'll come after us."

"Not over this roar, not if I don't shout in my Noise."

Her forehead creases and she looks down at the road to Haven and up to where Aaron's gotta be coming any second.

"We're so close," she says.

I take her arm and start pulling on it. "Come on. Just till he passes. Just till dark. With luck he'll think we doubled back into the trees above."

"If he finds us, we're trapped."

"And if we run for the city, he shoots us." I look in her eyes. "It's a chance. It gives us a *chance*."

"Todd–"

"Come with me," I say, looking right into her as hard as I can, pouring out as much hope as I can muster. *Oh never leave me*. "I promise I'll get you to Haven tonight." I squeeze her arm. *Oh don't deceive me*. "I promise you."

She looks right back at me, listening to it all, and then gives a single, sharp nod and we run to the little trail and down to where it ends and jump over the scrub to where it should continue and–

"TODD HEWITT!"

He's almost to the falls–

And we scrabble down a steep embankment next to the edge of the water, the steepness of the hill rearing above us–

And slide down and over to the edge of the cliff–

The falls straight ahead–

And I get to the edge and I suddenly have to lean back into Viola cuz the drop goes straight down–

She grabs onto my shirt and holds me up–

And the water is smashing down right in front of us to the rocks below–

And the ledge leading under it all is just there–

Needing a jump over emptiness to get to it–

"I didn't see this part," I say, Viola grabbing at my waist to keep us from tumbling over.

"TODD HEWITT!"

He's close, he's so close–

"Now or never, Todd," she says in my ear–

And she lets go of me–

And I jump across–

And I'm in the air–

And the edge of the falls is shooting over my head–

And I land–

And I turn–

And she's jumping after me–

And I grab her and we fall backwards onto the ledge together–

And we lay there breathing–

And listening–

And all we hear for a second is the roar of the water over us now–

And then, faint, against it all–

"TODD HEWITT!"

And he suddenly sounds miles away.

And Viola's on top of me and I'm breathing heavy into her face and she's breathing heavy into mine.

And we're looking in each other's eyes.

And it's too loud to hear my Noise.

After a second, she puts her hands on either side of me and pushes herself away. She looks up as she does and her eyes go wide.

I can just hear her say, "Wow."

I roll away and look up.

Wow.

The ledge is more than just a little ledge. It carries on till it's back, *way* back under the waterfall. We're standing at the beginning of a tunnel with one wall made of rock and another made of pure falling water, roaring past white and clean and so fast it looks almost solid.

"Come on," I say and head on down the ledge, my shoes slipping and sliding under me. It's rocky and wet and slimy and we lean as close as we can to the rock side, away from the thundering water.

The noise is just tremendous. All-consuming, like a real thing you could taste and touch.

So loud, Noise is obliterated.

So loud, it's the quietest I've ever felt.

We scramble on down the ledge, under the falls, making our way over rocky bumps and little pools with green goop growing in them. There are roots, too, hanging down from the rocks above, belonging to who knows what kinda plant.

"Do these look like steps to you?" Viola shouts, her voice small in the roar.

"TODD HEWITT!!" we hear from what sounds like a million miles away.

"Is he finding us?" Viola asks.

"I don't know," I say. "I don't think so."

The cliff face isn't even and the ledge curves round it as it stretches forward. We're both soaking wet and the water is cold and it's not easy grabbing onto the roots to keep our balance.

Then the ledge suddenly drops down and widens out, carved steps becoming more obvious. It's almost a stairway down.

Someone's been here before.

We descend, the water thundering inches away from us.

We get to the bottom.

"Whoa," Viola says behind me and I just know she's looking up.

The tunnel opens up abruptly and the ledge widens at the same time to become a cavern made of water, the rocks stretching up way over our heads, the falls slamming down past them in a wall curving way out like a moving, living sail, enclosing the wall and the shelf under our feet.

But that's not the whoa.

"It's a church," I say.

It's a church. Someone has moved or carved rocks into four rows of simple pews with an aisle down the middle, all facing a taller rock, a pulpit, a pulpit with a flat surface which a preacher could stand on and preach with a blazing white wall of water crashing down behind him, the morning sun lighting it up like a sheet of stars, filling the room with shimmering sparkles on every shiny wet surface, all the way back to a carved circle in the stone with two smaller carved circles orbiting it to one side, New World and its moons, the settler's new home of hope and God's promise somehow painted a waterproof white and practically *glowing* on the rock wall, looking down and lighting up the church.

The church underneath a waterfall.

"It's beautiful," Viola says.

"It's abandoned," I say, cuz after the first shock of finding a church I see where a few of the pews have been knocked from their places and not replaced and there's writing all over the walls, some of it carved in with tools, some of it written in the same waterproof paint as the New World carving, most of it nonsense. *P.M.+M.A.* and *Willz & Chillz 4Ever* and *Abandon All Hope Ye Who* something something.

"It's kids," Viola says. "Sneaking in here, making it their own place."

"Yeah? Do kids do that?"

"Back on the ship we had an unused venting duct that we snuck into," she says, looking around. "Marked it up worse than this."

We wander in, looking round us, mouths open. The point of the roof where the water leaves the cliff must be a good ten metres above us and the ledge five metres wide easy.

"It musta been a natural cavern," I say. "They musta found it and thought it was some kinda miracle."

Viola crosses her arms against herself. "And then they found it wasn't very practical as a church."

"Too wet," I say. "Too cold."

"I'll bet it was when they first landed," she says, looking up at the white New World. "I'll bet it was in the first year. Everything hopeful and new." She turns round, taking it all in. "Before reality set in."

I turn slowly, too. I can see exactly what they were thinking. The way the sun hits the falls, turning everything bright white, and it's so loud and so silent at the same time that even without the pulpit and the pews it would have felt like we'd somehow walked into a church anyway, like it'd be holy even if no man had ever seen it.

And then I notice that at the end of the pews, there's nothing beyond. It stops and it's a fifty-metre drop to the rocks below.

So this is where we're gonna have to wait.

This is where we're gonna have to hope.

In the church under water.

"Todd Hewitt!" barely drifts in down the tunnel to us.

Viola visibly shivers. "What do we do now?"

"We wait till nightfall," I say. "Sneak out and hope he don't see us."

I sit down on one of the stone benches. Viola sits down next to me. She lifts the bag over her head and sets it on the stone floor.

"What if he finds the trail?" she asks.

"We hope he don't."

"But what if he does?"

I reach behind me and take out the knife.

The knife.

Both of us look at it, the white water reflecting off of it, droplets of spray already catching and pooling on its blade, making it shine like a little torch.

The knife.

We don't say nothing about it, just watch it gleam in the middle of the church.

"Todd Hewitt!"

Viola looks up to the entrance and puts her hands to her face and I can see her clench her teeth. "What does he even *want*?" she suddenly rages. "If the army's all about you, what does he want with me? Why was he shooting at me? I don't understand it."

"Crazy people don't need an explanayshun for nothing," I say.

But my Noise is remembering the sacrifice that I saw him making of her way back in the swamp.

The sign, he called her.

A gift from God.

I don't know if Viola hears this or if she remembers it herself cuz she says, "I don't think I'm the sacrifice."

"What?"

She turns to me, her face perplexed. "I don't think it's me," she says. "He kept me asleep almost the entire time I was with him and when I did wake up, I kept seeing confusing things in his Noise, things that didn't make sense."

"He's mad," I say. "Madder than most."

She don't say nothing more, just looks out into the waterfall.

And reaches over and takes my hand.

"TODD HEWITT!"

I feel her hand jump right as my heart leaps.

"That's closer," she says. "He's getting closer."

"He won't find us."

"He will."

"Then we'll deal with it."

We both look at the knife.

"TODD HEWITT!"

"He's found it," she says, grabbing my arm and squeezing into me.

"Not yet."

"We were almost there," she says, her voice high and breaking a little. "Almost there."

"We'll get there."

"TODD HEWITT!"

And it's definitely louder.

He's found the tunnel.

I grip my knife and I look over to Viola, her face looking straight back up the tunnel, so much fear on it my chest begins to hurt.

I grip the knife harder.

If he *touches* her–

And my Noise reels back to the start of our journey, to Viola before she said anything, to Viola when she told me her name, to Viola when she talked to Hildy and Tam, to when she took on Wilf's accent, to when Aaron grabbed her and stole her away, to waking up to her in Doctor Snow's house, to her promise to Ben, to when she took on my ma's voice and made the whole world change, just for a little while.

All the things we've been thru.

How she cried when we left Manchee behind.

Telling me I was all she had.

When I found out I could read her, silence or not.

When I thought Aaron had shot her on the road.

How I felt in those few terrible seconds.

How it would feel to lose her.

The pain and the unfairness and the injustice.

The rage.

And how I wished it was me.

I look at the knife in my hand.

And I realize she's right.

I realize what's been right all along, as insane as it is.

She's not the sacrifice.

She's not.

If one of us falls, we all fall.

"I know what he wants," I say, standing up.

"What?" Viola says.

"TODD HEWITT!"

Definitely coming down the tunnel now.

Nowhere to run.

He's coming.

She stands, too, and I move myself twixt her and the tunnel.

"Get down behind one of the pews," I say. "Hide."

"Todd–"

I move away from her, my hand staying on her arm till I'm too far away.

"Where are you going?" she says, her voice tightening.

I look back the way we came, up the tunnel of water.

He'll be here any second.

"TODD HEWITT!"

"He'll *see* you!" she says.

I hold up the knife in front of me.

The knife that's caused so much trouble.

The knife that holds so much power.

"Todd!" Viola says. "What are you *doing*?"

I turn to her. "He won't hurt you," I say. "Not when he knows I know what he wants."

"What does he want?"

I search her out, standing among the pews, the white planet and moons glowing down on her, the water shining watery light over her, I search out her face and the language of her body as she stands there watching me, and I find I still know who she is, that she's still Viola Eade, that silent don't mean empty, that it *never* meant empty.

I look right into her eyes.

"I'm gonna greet him like a man," I say.

And even tho it's too loud for her to hear my Noise, even tho she can't read my thoughts, she looks back at me.

And I see her understand.

She pulls herself up a little taller.

"I'm not hiding," she says. "If you're not, I'm not."

And that's all I need.

I nod.

"Ready?" I ask.

She looks at me.

She nods once, firmly.

I turn back to the tunnel.

I close my eyes.

I take a deep breath.

And with every bit of air in my lungs and every last note of Noise in my head, I rear up–

And I shout, as loud as I can–

"AARON!!!!!!"

And I open my eyes and I wait for him to come.

41

IF ONE OF US FALLS

I SEE HIS FEET FIRST, slipping down the steps some but not hurrying, taking his time now that he knows we're here.

I hold the knife in my right hand, my left hand out and ready, too. I stand in the aisle of the little pews, as much in the centre of the church as I can get. Viola's back behind me a bit, down one of the rows.

I'm ready.

I realize I *am* ready.

Everything that's happened has brought me here, to this place, with this knife in my hand, and something worth saving.

Someone.

And if it's a choice twixt her and him, there is no choice, and the army can go sod itself.

And so I'm ready.

As I'll ever be.

Cuz I know what he wants.

"Come on," I say, under my breath.

Aaron's legs appear, then his arms, one carrying the rifle, the other holding his balance against the wall.

And then his face.

His terrible, terrible face.

Half torn away, the gash in his cheek showing his teeth, the hole where his nose used to be open and gaping, making him look barely human.

And he's smiling.

Which is when I feel all the fear.

"Todd Hewitt," he says, almost as a greeting.

I raise my voice over the water, willing it not to shake. "You can put the rifle down, Aaron."

"Oh, can I, now?" he says, eyes widening, taking in Viola behind me. I don't look back at her but I know she's facing Aaron, I know she's giving him all the bravery she's got.

And that makes me stronger.

"I know what you want," I say. "I figured it out."

"Have you, young Todd?" Aaron says and I see he can't help himself, he looks into my Noise, the little he can hear over the roar.

"She's not the sacrifice," I say.

He says nothing, just takes the first steps into the church, eyes glancing up at the cross and the pews and the pulpit.

"And I'm not the sacrifice neither," I say.

His evil smile draws wider. A new tear opens up at the edge of his gash, blood waving down it in the spray. "A clever mind is a friend of the devil," he says, which I think is his way of saying I'm right.

I steady my feet and turn with him as he steps round towards the pulpit half of the church, the half nearer the edge.

"It's you," I say. "The sacrifice is you."

And I open my Noise as loud as it'll go so that both he and Viola can see I'm telling the truth.

Cuz the thing Ben showed me back when I left our farm, the way that a boy in Prentisstown becomes a man, the reason that boys who've become men don't talk to boys who are still boys, the reason that boys who've become men are *complicit* in the crimes of Prentisstown is–

It's–

And I make myself say it–

It's by killing another man.

All by theirselves.

All those men who disappeared, who *tried* to disappear.

They didn't disappear after all.

Mr Royal, my old schoolteacher, who took to whisky and shot himself, *didn't* shoot himself. He was shot by Seb Mundy on his thirteenth birthday, made to stand alone and pull the trigger as the rest of the men of Prentisstown watched. Mr Gault, whose sheep flock we took over when he disappeared two winters ago, only *tried* to disappear. He was found by Mayor Prentiss running away thru the swamp and Mayor Prentiss was true to his agreement with the law of New World and executed him, only he did it by waiting till Mr Prentiss Jr's thirteenth birthday and having his son torture Mr Gault to death without the help of no one else.

And so on and so on. Men I knew killed by boys I knew to become men theirselves. If the Mayor's men had a captured escapee hidden away for a boy's thirteenth, then fine. If not, they'd just take someone from Prentisstown who they didn't like and *say* he disappeared.

One man's life was given over to a boy to end, all on his own.

A man dies, a man is born.

Everyone complicit. Everyone guilty.

Except me.

"Oh my God," I hear Viola say.

"But I was gonna be different, wasn't I?" I say.

"You were the last, Todd Hewitt," Aaron says. "The final soldier in God's perfect army."

"I don't think God's got nothing to do with yer army," I say. "Put down the rifle. I know what I have to do."

"But are you a messenger, Todd?" he asks, cocking his head, pulling his impossible smile wider. "Or are you a deceiver?"

"Read me," I say. "Read me if you don't believe I can do it."

He's at the pulpit now, facing me down the centre aisle, reaching out his Noise over the sound of the falls, pushing it towards me, grabbing at what he can, and the sacrifice and God's perfect work and the martyrdom of the saint I hear.

"Perhaps, young Todd," he says.

And he sets the rifle down on the pulpit.

I swallow and grip the knife harder.

But he looks over at Viola and laughs a little laugh. "No," he says. "Little girls will try to take advantage, won't they?"

And, almost casually, he tosses the rifle off the ledge into the waterfall.

It goes so fast, we don't even see it disappear.

But it's gone.

And so there's just me and Aaron.

And the knife.

He opens his arms and I realize he's assuming his preacher's pose, the one from his own pulpit, back in Prentisstown. He leans against the pulpit stone here and holds his palms up and raises his eyes to the white shining roof of water above us.

His lips move silently.

He's *praying*.

"Yer mad," I say.

He looks at me. "I'm blessed."

"You want me to kill you."

"Wrong, Todd Hewitt," he says, taking a step forward down the aisle towards me. "Hate is the key. Hate is the driver. Hate is the fire that purifies the soldier. The soldier must *hate*."

He takes another step.

"I don't want you to kill me," he says. "I want you to *murder* me."

I take a step back.

The smile flickers. "Perhaps the boy promises bigger than he can deliver."

"Why?" I say, stepping back some more. Viola moves back, too, behind and around me, underneath the carving of New World. "Why are you doing this? What possible sense does this make?"

"God has told me my path," he says.

"I been here for almost thirteen years," I say, "and the only thing I ever heard was *men*."

"God works thru men," Aaron says.

"So does evil," Viola says.

"Ah," Aaron says. "It speaks. Words of temptayshun to lull–"

"Shut up," I say. "Don't you talk to her."

I'm past the back row of pews now. I move to my right, Aaron follows till we're moving in a slow circle, Aaron's hands still out, my knife still up, Viola keeping behind me, the spray covering everything. The room slowly turns around us, the ledge still slippery, the wall of water shining white with the sun.

And the roar, the constant roar.

"You were the final test," Aaron says. "The last boy. The one that completes us. With you in the army, there's no weak link. We would be truly blessed. If one of us falls, we all fall, Todd. And all of us have to fall." He clenches his fists and looks up again. "So we can be reborn! So we can take this cursed world and remake it in–"

"I wouldn't've done it," I say and he scowls at the interrupshun. "I wouldn't've killed anyone."

"Ah, yes, Todd Hewitt," Aaron says. "And that's why yer so very very special, ain't ya? The boy who can't kill."

I sneak a glance back to Viola, off to my side a little. We're still going round in the little circle.

And Viola and I are reaching the side with the tunnel in it.

"But God demands a sacrifice," Aaron's saying. "God

demands a martyr. And who better for the special boy to kill than God's very own mouthpiece?"

"I don't think God tells you anything," I say. "Tho I can believe he wants you dead."

Aaron's eyes go so crazy and empty I get a chill. "I'll be a saint," he says, a small fire burning in his voice. "It is my destiny."

He's reached the end of the aisle and is following us past the last row of benches.

Viola and I are backing up still.

Almost to the tunnel.

"But how to motivate the boy?" Aaron continues, eyes like holes. "How to bring him into manhood?"

And his Noise opens up to me, loud as thunder.

My eyes widen.

My stomach sinks to my feet.

My shoulders hunch down as I feel weakness on me.

I can see it. It's a fantasy, a lie, but the lies of men are as vivid as their truths and I can see every bit of it.

He was going to murder Ben.

That's how he was going to force me to kill him. That's how they woulda done it. To perfect their army and make me a killer, they were going to murder Ben.

And make me watch.

Make me hate enough to kill Aaron.

My Noise starts to rumble, loud enough to hear. "*You effing piece of–*"

"But then God sent a sign," Aaron says, looking at Viola, his eyes even wider now, the blood pouring from the gash, the hole where his nose used to be stretching taut. "The girl," he says. "A gift from the heavens."

"Don't you look at her!" I yell. "Don't you even *look at her!*"

Aaron turns back to me, the smile still there. "Yes, Todd, yes," he says. "That's yer path, that's the path you'll take. The boy with the soft heart, the boy who couldn't kill. What would he kill for? Who would he protect?"

Another step back, another step nearer the tunnel.

"And when her cursed, evil silence polluted our swamp, I thought God had sent me a sacrifice to make myself, one last example of the evil that hides itself which I could destroy and purify." He cocks his head. "But then her true purpose was revealed." He looks at her and back at me. "Todd Hewitt would protect the helpless."

"She ain't helpless," I say.

"And then you *ran*." Aaron's eyes widen, as if in false amazement. "You ran rather than fulfil yer destiny." He lifts his eyes to the church again. "Thereby making victory over you all the sweeter."

"You ain't won yet," I say.

"Haven't I?" He smiles again. "Come, Todd. Come to me with hate in yer heart."

"I *will*," I say. "I'll do it."

But another step back.

"You've been near before, young Todd," Aaron says. "In the swamp, the knife raised, me killing the girl, but no. You hesitate. You injure but you do not kill. And then I steal her from you and you hunt her down, as I knew you would, suffering from the wound I gave you, but again, not enough. You sacrifice yer beloved dog rather than see her come to harm, you let me break his very body rather than serve yer proper purpose."

"You shut up!" I say.

He holds his palms up to me.

"Here I am, Todd," he says. "Fulfil yer purpose. Become a man." He lowers his head till his eyes are looking up at me. "*Fall.*"

I curl my lip.

I stand up straighter.

"I already *am* a man," I say.

And my Noise says it, too.

He stares at me. As if staring thru me.

And then he *sighs*.

Like he's *disappointed*.

"Not yet a man," he says, his face changing. "Perhaps not ever."

I don't step back.

"Pity," he says.

And he leaps at me–

"Todd!" Viola yells–

"Run!" I scream–

But I'm not stepping back–

I'm moving forward–

And the fight is on.

I'm charging at him and he's throwing himself at me and I'm holding the knife but at the last second, I leap to the side, letting him slam hard into the wall–

He whirls around, face in a snarl, swinging an arm round to hit me and I duck and slash at it with the knife, cutting across his forearm, and it don't even slow him down–

And he's swinging at me with his other arm and he's catching me just under the jaw–

Knocking me back–

"Todd!" Viola calls again–

I tumble backwards onto the last pew, falling hard–

But I'm looking up–

Aaron's turning to Viola–

She's at the bottom of the stairs–

"Go!" I yell–

But she's got a big flat stone in her hands and launches it at Aaron with a grimace and an angry grunt and he ducks and tries to deflect it with one hand but it catches him cross the forehead, causing him to stumble away from both her and me, towards the ledge, towards the front of the church–

"Come on!" Viola yells to me–

I scramble to my feet–

But Aaron's turned, too–

Blood running down his face–

His mouth open in a yell–

He jumps forward like a spider, grabbing Viola's right arm–

She punches fiercely with her left hand, bloodying it on his face–

But he don't let go–

I'm yelling as I fly at them–

Knife out–

But again I turn it at the last minute–

And I just knock into him–

We land on the upslope of the stairs, Viola falling back, me on top of Aaron, his arms boxing my head and he reaches forward with his horrible face and *takes a bite* out of an exposed area of my neck–

I yell and jerk back, punching him with a backhand as I go–

Scooting away from him back into the church, holding my neck–

He comes at me again, his fist flying forward–

Catching me on the eye–

My head jerks back–

I stumble thru the rows of pews, back to the centre of the church–

Another punch–

I raise my knife hand to block it–

But keep the knife edge sideways–

And he hits me again–

I scrabble away from him on the wet stone–

Up the aisle towards the pulpit–

And a third time his fist reaches my face–

And I feel two teeth tear outta their roots–

And I nearly fall–

And then I do fall–

My back and head hitting the pulpit stone–

And I drop the knife.

It clatters away towards the edge.

Useless as ever.

"*Yer Noise reveals you!*" Aaron screams. "*Yer Noise reveals you!*" He's stepping forward to me now, standing over me. "*From the moment I stepped into this sacred place, I knew it would be thus!*" He stops at my feet, staring down at me, his fists clenched and bloody with my blood, his face bloody with his own. "You will *never* be a man, Todd Hewitt! *Never!*"

I see Viola outta the corner of my eye frantically looking for more rocks–

"I'm already a man," I say, but I've fallen, I've dropped the knife, my voice is faltering, my hand over the bleeding from my neck.

"*You rob me of my sacrifice!*" His eyes have turned to burning diamonds, his Noise blazing a red so fierce it's practically steaming the water away from him. "I will kill you." He bows his head to me. "And you will die knowing that I killed her slowly."

I clench my teeth together.

I start to pull myself to my ruddy feet.

"Come on if yer coming," I growl.

Aaron yells out and takes a step towards me–

Hands reaching out for me–

My face rising to meet him–

And Viola *CLUMPS* him on the side of the head with a rock she can barely lift–

He stumbles–

Leaning towards the pews and catching himself–

And he stumbles again–

But he doesn't fall.

He *doesn't ruddy fall.*

He staggers but he stands, twixt me and Viola, uncurling himself, his back to Viola but towering over her, a whole rivulet of blood spouting from the side of his head now, but he's effing well tall as a nightmare–

He really is a monster.

"You ain't human," I say.

"I have told you, young Todd," he says, his voice low and monstrous, his Noise glowering at me with a fury so pure it nearly knocks me back. "I am a saint."

He lashes his arm out in Viola's direkshun without even looking her way, catching her square on the eye, knocking her back as she calls out and falls falls falls, tripping over a pew, hitting her head hard on the rocks–

And not rising.

"Viola!" I yell–

And I leap past him–

He lets me go–

I reach her–

Her legs are up on the stone bench–

Her head's on the stone floor–

A little stream of blood running from it–

"Viola!" I say and I lift her–

And her head falls back–

"VIOLA!" I yell–

And I hear a low rumble from behind me–

Laughter.

He's laughing.

"You were always going to betray her," he says. "It was foreseen."

"You SHUT UP!"

"And do you know *why*?"

"I'll KILL YOU!"

He lowers his voice to a whisper–

But a whisper I can feel shiver thru my entire body–

"You've already fallen."

And my Noise blazes red.

Redder than it's ever been.

Murderous red.

"Yes, Todd," Aaron hisses. "Yes, that's the way."

I lay Viola gently down and I stand and face him.

And my hate is so big, it fills the cavern.

"Come on, boy," he says. "Purify yerself."

I look at the knife–

Resting in a puddle of water–

Near the ledge by the pulpit behind Aaron–

Where I dropped it–

And I hear it calling to me–

Take me, it says–

Take me and use me, it says–

Aaron holds open his arms.

"Murder me," he says. "Become a man."

Never let me go, says the knife–

"I'm sorry," I whisper under my breath tho I don't know who to or what for–

I'm sorry–

And I leap–

Aaron doesn't move, arms open as if to embrace me–

I barrel into him with my shoulder–

He doesn't resist–

My Noise screams red–

We fall past the pulpit to the ledge–

I'm on top of him–

He still doesn't resist–

I punch his face–

Over–
And over–
And over–
Breaking it further–
Breaking it into bloody messy pieces–
Hate pouring outta me thru my fists–
And still I pound him–
Still I hit–
Thru the breaking of bone–
And the snapping of gristle–
And an eye crushed under my knuckles–
Till I can no longer feel my hands–
And still I hit–
And his blood spills on me and over–
And the red of it matches the red of my Noise–
And then I lean back, still on him, covered in his blood–
And he's laughing, he's laughing *still*–
And he's gurgling "Yes" thru broken teeth, "Yes–"
And the red rises in me–
And I can't hold it back–
And the hate–
And I look over–
At the knife–
Just a metre away–
On the ledge–
By the pulpit–
Calling for me–
Calling–
And this time I know–
This time I know–

I'm going to use it.

And I jump for it–
My hand outstretched–
My Noise so red I can barely see–
Yes, says the knife–

Yes.

Take me.
Take the power in yer hand–

But another hand is there first–

Viola.

And as I fall towards it there's a rush in me–
A rush in my Noise–
A rush from seeing her there–
From seeing her alive–
A rush that rises higher than the red–
And "Viola," I say–
Just "Viola".

And she picks up the knife.

My momentum is tumbling me towards the edge and I'm turning to try and catch myself and I can see her lifting the knife and I can see her stepping forward and I'm falling into the ledge and my fingers are slipping on wet stone and I can see Aaron sitting up and he's only got one eye now and it's staring at Viola as she's raising the knife and she's bringing it forward and I can't stop her and Aaron is trying to rise and Viola's moving towards him and I'm hitting the ledge with my shoulder and stopping just short of falling over and I'm watching and what's left of Aaron's Noise is radiating anger and fear and it's saying *No–*

It's saying *Not you–*

And Viola's raising her arm–

Raising the knife–

And bringing it down–

And down–

And down–

And plunging it straight into the side of Aaron's neck–

So hard the point comes out the other side–

And there's a crunch, a crunch I remember–

Aaron falls over from the force of it–

And Viola lets go of the knife–

She steps back.

Her face is white.

I can hear her breathing over the roar.

I lift myself with my hands–

And we watch.

Aaron's pushing himself up.

He's pushing himself up, one hand clawing at the knife, but it stays in his neck. His remaining eye is wide open, his tongue lolling outta his mouth.

He gets to his knees.

And then to his feet.

Viola cries out a little and steps back.

Steps back till she's next to me.

We can hear him trying to swallow.

Trying to breathe.

He steps forward but stumbles against the pulpit.

He looks our way.

His tongue swells and writhes.

He's trying to say something.

He's trying to say something to me.

He's trying to make a word.

But he can't.

He can't.

His Noise is just wild colours and pictures and things I won't ever be able to say.

He catches my eye.

And his Noise stops.

Completely stops.

At last.

And gravity takes his body and he slumps sideways.

Away from the pulpit.

And over the edge.

And disappears under the wall of water.

Taking the knife with him.

42

LAST ROAD TO HAVEN

VIOLA SITS DOWN NEXT TO ME so hard and fast it's like she fell there.

She's breathing heavy and staring into the space where Aaron was. The sunlight thru the falls casts waves of watery light over her face but that's the only thing on it that moves.

"Viola?" I say, leaping up into a squat next to her.

"He's gone," she says.

"Yeah," I say. "He's gone."

And she just breathes.

My Noise is rattling like a crashing spaceship full of reds and whites and things so different it's like my head is being pulled apart.

I woulda done it.

I woulda done it for her.

But instead–

"I woulda done it," I say. "I was ready to do it."

She looks at me, her eyes wide. "Todd?"

"I woulda killed him myself." I find my voice raising a little. "I was ready to do it!"

And then her chin starts shaking, not as if she's going to cry, but actually *shaking* and then her shoulders, too, and her eyes are getting wider and she's shaking harder and nothing leaves my Noise and it's all still there but something else enters it and it's for her and I grab her and hold her to me and we rock back and forth for a while so she can just shake all she wants to.

She don't speak for a long time, just makes little moaning sounds in her throat, and I remember just after I killed the Spackle, how I could feel the crunch running down my arm, how I could keep seeing his blood, how I saw him die again and again.

How I do still.

(But I woulda.)

(I was ready.)

(But the knife is gone.)

"Killing someone ain't nothing like it is in stories," I say into the top of her head. "Ain't nothing at all."

(But I woulda.)

She's still shaking and we're still right next to a raging, roaring waterfall and the sun's higher in the sky and there's less light in the church and we're wet and bloody and bloody and wet.

And cold and shaking.

"Come on," I say, making to stand. "First thing we need to do is get dry, okay?"

I get her to her feet. I go get the bag, still on the floor twixt two pews and go back to her and hold out my hand.

"The sun is up," I say. "It'll be warm outside."

She looks at my hand for a minute before taking it.

But she takes it.

We make our way round the pulpit, unable to keep from looking where Aaron was, his blood already washed away by the spray.

(I woulda done it.)

(But the knife.)

I can feel my hand shaking in hers and I don't know which one of us it is.

We get to the steps and it's halfway up that she first speaks.

"I feel sick," she says.

"I know," I say.

And we stop and she leans closer to the waterfall and is sick.

A lot.

I guess this it what happens when you kill someone in real life.

She leans forward, her hair wet and tangled down. She spits.

But she don't look up.

"I couldn't let you," she says. "He would have won."

"I woulda done it," I say.

"I know," she says, into her hair, into the falls. "That's why I did it."

I let out a breath. "You shoulda let me."

"No." She looks up from being crouched over. "I *couldn't* let you." She wipes her mouth and coughs again. "But it's not just that."

"What then?" I say.

She looks into my eyes. Her own are wide and they're bloodshot from the barfing.

And they're older than they used to be.

"I *wanted* to, Todd," she says, her forehead creasing. "I *wanted* to do it. I *wanted* to kill him." She puts her hands to her face. "Oh my God," she breathes. "Oh my God, oh my God, oh my God."

"Stop it," I say, taking her arms and pulling her hands away. "Stop it. He was evil. He was *crazy* evil–"

"I know!" she shouts. "But I keep seeing him. I keep seeing the knife going into his–"

"Yeah, okay, you wanted to," I stop her before she gets worse. "So what? So did *I*. But he *made* you want to. He made it so it was him or us. That's why he was evil. Not what you did or what I did, what *he* did, okay?"

She looks up at me. "He did just what he promised," she says, her voice a little quieter. "He made me fall."

She moans again and clamps her hands over her mouth, her eyes welling up.

"No," I say strongly. "No, see, here's the thing, here's what I think, okay?"

I look up to the water and the tunnel and I don't know what I think but she's there and I can see it and I don't know what she's thinking but *I know what she's thinking* and I can see her and she's teetering on the edge and she's looking at me and she's asking me to save her.

Save her like she saved me.

"Here's what I think," I say and my voice is stronger and thoughts are coming, thoughts that trickle into my Noise like whispers of the truth. "I think maybe *everybody* falls," I say. "I think maybe we all do. And I don't think that's the asking."

I pull on her arms gently to make sure she's listening.

"I think the asking is whether we get back up again."

And the water's rushing by and we're shaking from the cold and everything else and she stares at me and I wait and I hope.

And I see her step back from the edge.

I see her come back to me.

"Todd," she says and it ain't an asking.

It's just my name.

It's who I am.

"Come on," I say. "Haven's waiting."

I take her hand again and we make our way up the rest of the steps and back to the flatter part of the ledge, following the curves out from the centre, steadying ourselves again on the slippery stones. The jump back to the embankment is harder this time cuz we're so wet and weak but I take a running go at it and then catch Viola as she comes tumbling after me.

And we're in sunlight.

We breathe it in for a good long while, getting the wettest of the wet off of us before we gather up and climb the little embankment, pushing ourselves thru the scrub to the trail and back to the road.

We look down the hill, down the zigzag trail.

It's still there. Haven's still there.

"Last bit," I say.

Viola rubs her arms to dry herself a little more. She

squints at me, looking close. "You get hit in the face a lot, you know that?"

I bring my fingers up. My eye is starting to swell some and I notice a gap on the side of my mouth where I lost a few teeth.

"Thanks," I say. "It wasn't hurting till you said that."

"Sorry." She smiles a little and puts her hand up to the back of her own head and winces.

"How's yers?" I ask.

"Sore," she says, "but I'll live."

"Yer indestructible, you," I say.

She smiles again.

And then there's a weird *zipSNICK* sound in the air and Viola lets out a little gasp, a little *oh* sound.

We look each other in the eyes for a second, in the sunshine, both of us surprised but not sure why.

And then I follow her glance down her front.

There's blood on her shirt.

Her own blood.

New blood.

Pouring out a little hole just to the right of her belly button.

She touches the blood and holds up her fingers.

"Todd?" she says.

And then she falls forward.

I catch her, stumbling back a bit from the weight.

And I look up behind her.

Up to the clifftop, right where the road begins.

Mr Prentiss Jr.

On horseback.

Hand outstretched.

Holding a pistol.

"Todd?" Viola says against my chest. "I think someone *shot* me, Todd."

There are no words.

No words in my head or my Noise.

Mr Prentiss Jr kicks his horse and edges him down the road towards us.

Pistol still pointed.

There's nowhere to run.

And I don't got my knife.

The world unfolds as clear and as slow as the worst pain, Viola starting to pant heavy against me, Mr Prentiss Jr riding down the road, and my Noise rising with the knowledge that we're finished, that there's no way out this time, that if the world wants you, it's gonna keep on coming till it gets you.

And who am I that can fix it? Who am I that can change this if the world wants it so badly? Who am I to stop the end of the world if it keeps on coming?

"I think she wants you *bad*, Todd," Mr Prentiss Jr sneers.

I clench my teeth.

My Noise rises red and purple.

I'm Todd bloody Hewitt.

That's who I effing well am.

I look him right in the eye, sending my Noise straight for him, and I spit out in a rasp, "I'll thank you to call me *Mr Hewitt.*"

Mr Prentiss Jr flinches, actually *flinches* a little and pulls his reins involuntarily, making his horse rear up for a second.

"Come on, now," he says, his voice slightly less sure.

And he knows we both can hear it.

"Hands up," he says. "I'm taking you to my father."

And I do the most amazing thing.

The most amazing thing I ever did.

I ignore him.

I kneel Viola down to the dirt road.

"It burns, Todd," she says, her voice low.

I set her down and drop the bag and slip my shirt off my back, crumpling it up and holding it against the bullet hole. "You hold that tight, you hear me?" I say, my anger rising like lava. "This won't take a second."

I look up at *Davy* Prentiss.

"Get up," he says, his horse still jumpy and edgy from the heat coming off me. "I ain't telling you twice, Todd."

I stand.

I step forward.

"I said put yer hands up," Davy says, his horse whinnying and bluffing and clopping from foot to foot.

I march towards him.

Faster.

Till I'm running.

"I'll shoot you!" Davy shouts, waving the gun, trying to control his horse which is sending **Charge! Charge!** all over the place in its Noise.

"No, you won't!" I yell, running right up to the horse's head and sending a crash of Noise right at it.

SNAKE!

The horse rears up on its back legs.

"Goddammit, Todd!" Davy yells, wheeling and whirling,

trying to control his horse with the one hand that's not holding the pistol.

I jump in, slap the horse's front quarters and jump back. The horse whinnies and rears up again.

"Yer a dead man!" Davy shouts, going in a full circle with the horse jumping and rearing.

"Yer *half* right," I say.

And I'm seeing my chance–

The horse neighs loudly and shakes its head back and forth–

I wait–

Davy pulls on the reins–

I dodge–

I wait–

"*Effing horse!*" Davy shouts–

He tries to jerk the reins again–

The horse is twisting round one more time–

I wait–

The horse brings Davy round to me, careening him low in the saddle–

And there's my chance–

My fist is back and waiting–

BOOM!

I catch him cross the face like a hammer falling–

I swear I feel his nose break under my fist–

He calls out in pain and falls from the saddle–

Dropping the pistol in the dust–

I jump back–

Davy's foot catches in the stirrup–

The horse rears round again–

I smack its hindquarters as hard as I can–

And the horse has had enough.

It charges back up the hill, back up the road, Davy's foot still caught, making him bounce hard against rocks and dirt as he's dragged, fast, up the incline–

The pistol's in the dust–

I move for it–

"Todd?" I hear.

And there's no time.

There's no time at all.

Without hardly thinking, I leave the pistol and I run back down to Viola at the edge of the scrub.

"I think I'm dying, Todd," she says.

"Yer not dying," I say, getting an arm under her shoulders and another under her knees.

"I'm cold."

"Yer *not effing dying!*" I say. "Not today!"

And I stand, with her in my arms, and I'm at the top of the zigzag that goes down into Haven.

And that's not going to be fast enough.

I plunge straight down. Straight down thru the scrub.

"Come on!" I say out loud as my Noise forgets itself and all there is in the universe is my legs moving.

Come on!

I run.

Thru scrub–

And across road–

Thru more scrub–

Across road again as it doubles back–

Down and down–

Kicking up clods of earth and jumping over bushes–

Stumbling over roots–

Come on.

"Hang on," I say to Viola. "You hang on, you hear me?"

Viola grunts every time we land hard–

But that means she's still breathing.

Down–

And down–

Come on.

Please.

I skid on some bracken–

But I do not fall–

Road and scrub–

My legs aching at the steepness–

Scrub and road–

Down–

Please–

"Todd?"

"Hang on!"

I reach the bottom of the hill and I hit it running.

She's so light in my arms.

So light.

I run to where the road rejoins the river, the road into Haven, trees springing up again all around us, the river rushing on.

"Hang on!" I say again, running down the road, fast as my feet will carry me.

Come on.

Please.

Round curves and corners–

Under trees and by the riverbank–

Up ahead I see the battlement I spotted with the binos from the hill above, huge wooden Xs piled up in a long row out to either side with an opening across the road.

"HELP!" I'm shouting as we come to it. "HELP US!"

I run.

Come on.

"I don't think I can–" Viola says, her voice breathless.

"Yes you CAN!" I shout. "Don't you DARE give up!"

I run.

The battlement's coming–

But there's no one.

There's no one there.

I run thru the opening on the road and to the other side.

I stop long enough to take a turn round.

There's *no one.*

"Todd?"

"We're almost there," I say.

"I'm losing it, Todd–"

And her head rolls back.

"No, yer NOT!" I shout at her face. "You WAKE UP, Viola Eade! You keep yer ruddy eyes open."

And she tries. I see her try.

And her eyes open, only a little, but open.

And I run again as fast as I can.

And I'm shouting "HELP!" as I go.

"HELP!"

Please.

"HELP!"

And her breath is starting to gasp.

"HELP US!"

Please no.

And I'm not seeing NO ONE.

The houses I pass are shut up and empty. The road turns from dirt to paved and still no one out and about.

"HELP!"

My feet slam against the pavement–

The road is leading to the big church up ahead, a clearing of the trees, the steeple shining down onto a town square in front of it.

And no one's there neither.

No.

"HELP!"

I race on to the square, crossing it, looking all around, listening out–

No.

No.

It's empty.

Viola's breathing heavy in my arms.

And Haven is empty.

I reach the middle of the square.

I don't see nor hear a soul.

I spin around again.

"HELP!" I cry.

But there's no one.

Haven is completely empty.

There ain't no hope here at all.

Viola slips a little from my grasp and I have to kneel to catch her. My shirt has dropped from her wound and I use one hand to hold it in place.

There ain't nothing left. The bag, the binos, my ma's book, I'm realizing it's all left up on the hillside.

Me and Viola are all we got, everything we have in the world.

And she's bleeding *so much*–

"Todd?" she says, her voice low and slurring.

"Please," I say, my eyes welling, my voice cracking. "Please."

Please please please please please–

"Well, since you asked so nicely," comes a voice across the square, hardly even raising itself to a shout.

I look up.

Coming round the side of the church is a single horse.

With a single rider.

"No," I whisper.

No.

No.

"Yes, Todd," says Mayor Prentiss. "I'm afraid so."

He rides his horse almost lazily across the square towards me. He looks as cool and unruffled as ever, no sweat marking his clothes, even wearing riding gloves, even clean boots.

This ain't possible.

This ain't possible at all.

"How can you be here?" I say, my voice rising. "How–?"

"Even a simpleton knows there's two roads to Haven," he says, his voice calm and silky, almost smirking but not quite.

The dust we saw. The dust we saw moving towards Haven yesterday.

"But *how*?" I say, so stunned I can barely get the words out. "The army's a day away at least–"

"Sometimes the rumour of an army is just as effective as the army itself, my boy," he says. "The terms of surrender were most favourable. One of which was clearing the streets so I could welcome you here myself." He looks back up towards the falls. "Tho I was of course expecting my son to bring you."

I look around the square and now I can see faces, faces peering outta windows, outta doors.

I can see four more men on horseback coming round the church.

I look back at Mayor Prentiss.

"Oh, it's *President* Prentiss now," he says. "You'll do well to remember that."

And then I realize.

I can't hear his Noise.

I can't hear *anyone's*.

"No," he says. "I imagine you can't, tho that's an interesting story and not what you might–"

Viola slips a little more from my hands, the shift of it making her give a pained gasp. "Please!" I say. "Save her! I'll do anything you say! I'll join the army! I'll–"

"All good things to those who wait," the Mayor says, finally looking a little annoyed.

He dismounts in one easy movement and starts taking off his gloves one finger at a time.

And I know we've lost.

Everything is lost.

Everything is over.

"As the newly appointed President of this fair planet of ours," the Mayor says, holding out his hand as if to show me the world for the first time, "let me be the very first to welcome you to its new capital city."

"Todd?" Viola whispers, her eyes closed.

I hold her tightly to me.

"I'm sorry," I whisper to her. "I'm so sorry."

We've run right into a trap.

We've run right off the end of the world.

"Welcome," says the Mayor, "to New Prentisstown."

END OF BOOK ONE

Praise for Book Two

The Ask and the Answer

Winner of the Costa Children's Book Award

"Original and suspenseful."

The Times

"A faster-paced, more action-packed novel would be hard to find."

Financial Times

"A twisting, action-packed plot explores themes of loyalty, manipulation, moral ambiguity and violence with an underlying search for redemption and love."

Daily Mail

"Ness is both accessible and sophisticated, handling big subjects – terrorism, feminism, genocide, love – in prose that is simple and heart-stopping."

Sunday Times

"Mesmerizing, terrifying and tense."

Independent

"Gripping… A stunningly clear depiction of the moral wreckage of civil war: power-lust, shifting loyalties, betrayals and seductive competing justifications for violence."

Wall Street Journal

"A must-read."

Sunday Express

"No one who read Patrick Ness's brilliant *The Knife of Never Letting Go*, with its thrilling imagination and maddening cliff-hanger ending, will need any prompting to devour its sequel ... it is every bit as ambitious as the first book but the ambition is easily matched by the execution, with powerful prose and tight plotting that pull the reader on at a terrifying speed."

Independent on Sunday

"Grapples with the problems of colonization and genocide... Ness neatly paves the way for what looks to be a thunderous conclusion."

Daily Telegraph

"A dazzlingly imagined, morally complex, compulsively plotted tale."

Costa Book Awards Judges

"A harrowing read but I could not put it down."

The Bookseller

"Exciting."

Irish Independent

"Beautifully written ... presents a provocative examination of the nature of evil and humanity."

Publishers Weekly

"Thrilling."

Time Out

"A masterly exercise in the art of storytelling."

Irish Times

Praise for Book Three

Monsters of Men

Winner of the Carnegie Medal

"Chaos Walking is remarkable, and its conclusion, *Monsters of Men*, a triumph. This is an intensely moral, thoughtful work."

The Times

"Extraordinary."

Guardian

"Gripping, thrilling, hurtling… The most perfect conclusion to any big series I've read… A stunning climax – pulse-racing, tear-jerking, mind-boggling…"

Independent on Sunday

"A dramatic and powerful finale… War is the subject but, as ever, in Ness's challenging and uncomfortable narrative it is the moral choices and the consequences of those choices that underpin the action… The ending is superbly well handled and Ness brings this original series to a close with the high-level tension and ambiguity he has maintained throughout."

Daily Mail

"Left me drained and gasping … a fitting end to a brilliant and challenging series."

Literary Review

"A novel that triumphantly concludes what will almost certainly come to be seen as one of the outstanding literary achievements of the present century."

Irish Times

"Lives up to all expectations... An electrifying ending to a brilliant series."

Daily Express

"As addictive as its predecessors... It maintains a breakneck pace and ratchets up the suspense to almost unbearable levels."

Books Quarterly

"As in his preceding books, Ness offers incisive appraisals of violence, power, and human nature..."

Publishers Weekly

"This is science fiction at its best, and is a singular fusion of brutality and idealism that is, at last, perfectly human."

Booklist

"An explosive quality pervades *Monsters of Men*, the concluding instalment of the Chaos Walking trilogy. The breathtaking novel sees Todd and Viola ensnared in the ravages of war. It contains an enduring message regarding individual connections and communications and the danger of their failure. With the feel of prophetic epic, this is innovative, intense writing at its incendiary best."

The Bookseller

ALSO BY PATRICK NESS

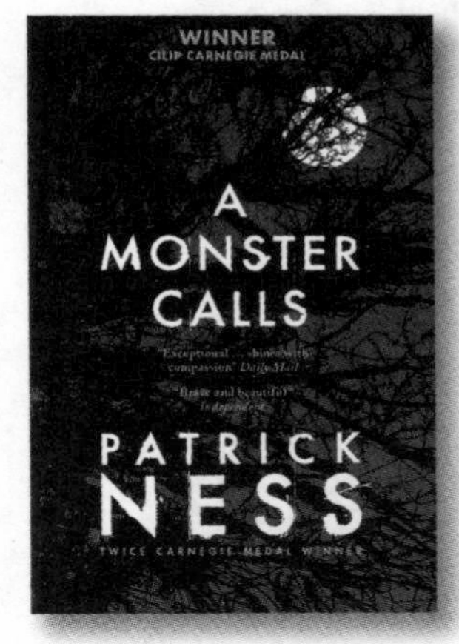

"Patrick Ness is an insanely beautiful writer."
JOHN GREEN

"Genuinely original vision."
INDEPENDENT

Photo © Helen Giles 2013

Patrick Ness is the award-winning and bestselling author of *A Monster Calls*, *More Than This*, *The Rest of Us Just Live Here* and *Release*. He has won every major prize in children's fiction, including the Carnegie Medal twice. He has written the screenplay for the film of *A Monster Calls* and *Class*, the BBC Dr Who spin-off. The first Chaos Walking film is slated for release in 2019. He lives in London.

@Patrick_Ness @WalkerBooksUK
@WalkerBooksYA #ChaosWalking